# Madame Bovary

Bilingual Edition: English–French

Gustave Flaubert

Sleeping Cat Press

**MADAME BOVARY, BILINGUAL EDITION: ENGLISH–FRENCH**

Sleeping Cat Press (an imprint of Sleeping Cat Books)
http://sleepingcatpress.com
http://sleepingcatbooks.com



Cover design: Sarah E. Holroyd
Interior design: Sarah E. Holroyd

ISBN-13: 978-0-9864006-5-0

The original French novel was published by Michel Lévy Frères in Paris in 1857.

The original English translation was made by Eleanor Marx Aveling (16 January 1855–31 March 1898), published by Vizetelly & Co. in London in 1886.

The cover image is a portion of *Young Lady in a Boat* painted in 1870 by James Tissot (1836–1902).

# Also available from Sleeping Cat Press

Bilingual Editions

*The Picture of Dorian Gray, Bilingual Edition: English–French*

*Selected Works of Edgar Allan Poe, Bilingual Edition: English–French*

*Fables of Jean de La Fontaine, Bilingual Edition: English–French*

*Candide, Bilingual Edition: English–French*

*Shakespeare's Sonnets, Bilingual Edition: English–French*

*New Fairy Tales for Small Children, Bilingual Edition: English–French*

*The Tales of Mother Goose, Bilingual Edition: English–French*

*The Count of Monte Cristo, Unabridged Bilingual Edition: English–French, Vols. 1–4*

*The Last of the Mohicans, Bilingual Edition: English–French*

*ABC Short Stories, Bilingual Edition: English–French*

*A Christmas Carol, Illustrated Bilingual Edition: English–French*

Other Works

*A Dickens Christmas: A Christmas Carol and Other Stories*

*The Storm is Coming: An Anthology*

*Trip of a Lifetime: An Anthology*

*Lords of the Housetops: Thirteen Illustrated Cat Tales*

# TABLE OF CONTENTS

# Introduction

Gustave Flaubert was born on December 12, 1821 in Rouen in northern France, the son of the director and senior surgeon of the major hospital in the city. In 1840 he moved to Paris to study law, but an attack of epilepsy in 1846 prompted him to abandon law and return to Rouen, where he spent the rest of his life, when he wasn't travelling. He never married, but had a long-time affair with the poet Louise Colet. Flaubert was open about his involvement with prostitutes during his travels, as evidenced in the letters he wrote to friends while abroad. Because of this open lifestyle, he contracted syphilis, and suffered from other venereal diseases for most of his life. He died on May 8, 1880 of a cerebral hemorrhage at the age of 58 and was buried in his family's vault in Rouen.

Flaubert was never a prolific writer, compared to his contemporaries. He was painstaking in his writing, often spending a week on completing a single page. He was never satisfied with his work and always pursued "le mot juste," the perfect word.

He began writing his first published novel, Madame Bovary, in 1850, spending the next five years on it. It was published in 1856 in serial form in La Revue de Paris between October 1 and December 15, and caused an uproar among public prosecutors for obscenity. Flaubert was taken to court in January of 1857 and acquitted on February 7. The publicity fairly guaranteed that the novel would be widely read, and when it was published in April of that year as a single volume, it was extremely popular.

Flaubert is currently regarded as one of the most influential French novelists, and perhaps the leading proponent of literary realism in France at the time. As the British critic James Wood noted, "Novelists should thank Flaubert the way poets thank spring; it all begins again with him...Flaubert decisively established what most readers and writers think of as modern realist narration."[1]

1 James Wood, *How Fiction Works* (New York: Farrar, Straus and Giroux, 2008), 29.

Madame Bovary has been made into an opera and several films, as well as being a strong influence on the plot lines of several others. It has been adapted many times as a television miniseries and made-for-TV movie. The themes of despair, unhappiness, and the inability to communicate with those around you are just as identifiable to readers today as they were in the mid-nineteenth century, which is why Madame Bovary continues to find new readers.

Learning a foreign language can be difficult. A common method of practicing sentence structure and increasing vocabulary is to read fiction or poetry in the foreign language. But pausing to consult a dictionary or grammar reference can break your concentration and disrupt the flow of the story. With a bilingual text, the native language text that corresponds to the foreign language is on the facing page, making it a much simpler matter to glance across the spine and consult the familiar wording.

Sleeping Cat Press is proud to present this series of bilingual English–French books. Given the nature of foreign language translations and the differences in grammar conventions between English and French, the same paragraph in each language is rarely made up of the same number of words. At times this leads to inelegant paragraph spacing. Some paragraphs in this volume are condensed, while others are widely spaced, and there are some spaces between paragraphs. But it is essential for each paragraph to begin on the same line in both language versions, so these spacing inconsistencies could not be helped. In addition, in a few instances the English translation had paragraph breaks where the original French text did not, or had one paragraph where the French had two. Such instances have been changed to align the English paragraph structure with the French.

We hope you find this volume useful as you expand your understanding of the new language.

Sarah E. Holroyd

# Part 1

# Première Partie

# Chapter 1

We were in class when the head-master came in, followed by a "new fellow," not wearing the school uniform, and a school servant carrying a large desk. Those who had been asleep woke up, and every one rose as if just surprised at his work.

The head-master made a sign to us to sit down. Then, turning to the class-master, he said to him in a low voice—

"Monsieur Roger, here is a pupil whom I recommend to your care; he'll be in the second. If his work and conduct are satisfactory, he will go into one of the upper classes, as becomes his age."

The "new fellow," standing in the corner behind the door so that he could hardly be seen, was a country lad of about fifteen, and taller than any of us. His hair was cut square on his forehead like a village chorister's; he looked reliable, but very ill at ease. Although he was not broad-shouldered, his short school jacket of green cloth with black buttons must have been tight about the arm-holes, and showed at the opening of the cuffs red wrists accustomed to being bare. His legs, in blue stockings, looked out from beneath yellow trousers, drawn tight by braces, He wore stout, ill-cleaned, hob-nailed boots.

We began repeating the lesson. He listened with all his ears, as attentive as if at a sermon, not daring even to cross his legs or lean on his elbow; and when at two o'clock the bell rang, the master was obliged to tell him to fall into line with the rest of us.

When we came back to work, we were in the habit of throwing our caps on the ground so as to have our hands more free; we used from the door to toss them under the form, so that they hit against the wall and made a lot of dust: it was "the thing."

But, whether he had not noticed the trick, or did not dare to attempt it, the "new fellow," was still holding his cap on his knees even after prayers were over. It was one of those head-gears of composite order,

# Chapitre 1

Nous étions à l'Étude, quand le Proviseur entra, suivi d'un nouveau habillé en bourgeois et d'un garçon de classe qui portait un grand pupitre. Ceux qui dormaient se réveillèrent, et chacun se leva comme surpris dans son travail.

Le Proviseur nous fit signe de nous rasseoir; puis, se tournant vers le maître d'études:

— Monsieur Roger, lui dit-il à demi-voix, voici un élève que je vous recommande, il entre en cinquième. Si son travail et sa conduite sont méritoires, il passera dans les grands, où l'appelle son âge.

Resté dans l'angle, derrière la porte, si bien qu'on l'apercevait à peine, le nouveau était un gars de la campagne, d'une quinzaine d'années environ, et plus haut de taille qu'aucun de nous tous. Il avait les cheveux coupés droit sur le front, comme un chantre de village, l'air raisonnable et fort embarrassé. Quoiqu'il ne fût pas large des épaules, son habit-veste de drap vert à boutons noirs devait le gêner aux entournures et laissait voir, par la fente des parements, des poignets rouges habitués à être nus. Ses jambes, en bas bleus, sortaient d'un pantalon jaunâtre très tiré par les bretelles. Il était chaussé de souliers forts, mal cirés, garnis de clous.

On commença la récitation des leçons. Il les écouta de toutes ses oreilles, attentif comme au sermon, n'osant même croiser les cuisses, ni s'appuyer sur le coude, et, à deux heures, quand la cloche sonna, le maître d'études fut obligé de l'avertir, pour qu'il se mît avec nous dans les rangs.

Nous avions l'habitude, en entrant en classe, de jeter nos casquettes par terre, afin d'avoir ensuite nos mains plus libres; il fallait, dès le seuil de la porte, les lancer sous le banc, de façon à frapper contre la muraille en faisant beaucoup de poussière; c'était là le genre.

Mais, soit qu'il n'eût pas remarqué cette manoeuvre ou qu'il n'eut osé s'y soumettre, la prière était finie que le nouveau tenait encore sa casquette sur ses deux genoux. C'était une de ces coiffures d'ordre compos-

in which we can find traces of the bearskin, shako, billycock hat, sealskin cap, and cotton night-cap; one of those poor things, in fine, whose dumb ugliness has depths of expression, like an imbecile's face. Oval, stiffened with whalebone, it began with three round knobs; then came in succession lozenges of velvet and rabbit-skin separated by a red band; after that a sort of bag that ended in a cardboard polygon covered with complicated braiding, from which hung, at the end of a long thin cord, small twisted gold threads in the manner of a tassel. The cap was new; its peak shone.

"Rise," said the master.

He stood up; his cap fell. The whole class began to laugh.

He stooped to pick it up. A neighbor knocked it down again with his elbow; he picked it up once more.

"Get rid of your helmet," said the master, who was a bit of a wag.

There was a burst of laughter from the boys, which so thoroughly put the poor lad out of countenance that he did not know whether to keep his cap in his hand, leave it on the ground, or put it on his head. He sat down again and placed it on his knee.

"Rise," repeated the master, "and tell me your name."

The new boy articulated in a stammering voice an unintelligible name.

"Again!"

The same sputtering of syllables was heard, drowned by the tittering of the class.

"Louder!" cried the master; "louder!"

The "new fellow" then took a supreme resolution, opened an inordinately large mouth, and shouted at the top of his voice as if calling someone in the word "Charbovari."

A hubbub broke out, rose in crescendo with bursts of shrill voices (they yelled, barked, stamped, repeated "Charbovari! Charbovari"), then died away into single notes, growing quieter only with great difficulty, and now and again suddenly recommencing along the line of a form whence rose here and there, like a damp cracker going off, a stifled laugh.

ite, où l'on retrouve les éléments du bonnet à poil, du chapska, du chapeau rond, de la casquette de loutre et du bonnet de coton, une de ces pauvres choses, enfin, dont la laideur muette a des profondeurs d'expression comme le visage d'un imbécile. Ovoïde et renflée de baleines, elle commençait par trois boudins circulaires; puis s'alternaient, séparés par une bande rouge, des losanges de velours et de poils de lapin; venait ensuite une façon de sac qui se terminait par un polygone cartonné, couvert d'une broderie en soutache compliquée, et d'où pendait, au bout d'un long cordon trop mince, un petit croisillon de fils d'or, en manière de gland. Elle était neuve; la visière brillait.

— Levez-vous, dit le professeur.

Il se leva; sa casquette tomba. Toute la classe se mit à rire.

Il se baissa pour la reprendre. Un voisin la fit tomber d'un coup de coude, il la ramassa encore une fois.

— Débarrassez-vous donc de votre casque, dit le professeur, qui était un homme d'esprit.

Il y eut un rire éclatant des écoliers qui décontenança le pauvre garçon, si bien qu'il ne savait s'il fallait garder sa casquette à la main, la laisser par terre ou la mettre sur sa tête. Il se rassit et la posa sur ses genoux.

— Levez-vous, reprit le professeur, et dites-moi votre nom.

Le nouveau articula, d'une voix bredouillante, un nom inintelligible.

— Répétez!

Le même bredouillement de syllabes se fit entendre, couvert par les huées de la classe.

— Plus haut! cria le maître, plus haut!

Le nouveau, prenant alors une résolution extrême, ouvrit une bouche démesurée et lança à pleins poumons, comme pour appeler quelqu'un, ce mot: Charbovari.

Ce fut un vacarme qui s'élança d'un bond, monta en crescendo, avec des éclats de voix aigus (on hurlait, on aboyait, on trépignait, on répétait: Charbovari! Charbovari!), puis qui roula en notes isolées, se calmant à grand-peine, et parfois qui reprenait tout à coup sur la ligne d'un banc où saillissait encore çà et là, comme un pétard mal éteint, quelque rire étouffé.

However, amid a rain of impositions, order was gradually re-established in the class; and the master having succeeded in catching the name of "Charles Bovary," having had it dictated to him, spelt out, and re-read, at once ordered the poor devil to go and sit down on the punishment form at the foot of the master's desk. He got up, but before going hesitated.

"What are you looking for?" asked the master.

"My c-a-p," timidly said the "new fellow," casting troubled looks round him.

"Five hundred lines for all the class!" shouted in a furious voice stopped, like the *Quos ego*, a fresh outburst. "Silence!" continued the master indignantly, wiping his brow with his handkerchief, which he had just taken from his cap. "As to you, 'new boy,' you will conjugate '*ridiculus sum*' twenty times."

Then, in a gentler tone:

"Come, you'll find your cap again; it hasn't been stolen."

Quiet was restored. Heads bent over desks, and the "new fellow" remained for two hours in an exemplary attitude, although from time to time some paper pellet flipped from the tip of a pen came bang in his face. But he wiped his face with one hand and continued motionless, his eyes lowered.

In the evening, at preparation, he pulled out his pens from his desk, arranged his small belongings, and carefully ruled his paper. We saw him working conscientiously, looking up every word in the dictionary, and taking the greatest pains. Thanks, no doubt, to the willingness he showed, he had not to go down to the class below. But though he knew his rules passably, he had little finish in composition. It was the cure of his village who had taught him his first Latin; his parents, from motives of economy, having sent him to school as late as possible.

His father, Monsieur Charles Denis Bartolome Bovary, retired assistant-surgeon-major, compromised about 1812 in certain conscription scandals, and forced at this time to leave the service, had taken advantage of his fine figure to get hold of a dowry of sixty thousand francs

Cependant, sous la pluie des pensums, l'ordre peu à peu se rétablit dans la classe, et le professeur, parvenu à saisir le nom de Charles Bovary, se l'étant fait dicter, épeler et relire, commanda tout de suite au pauvre diable d'aller s'asseoir sur le banc de paresse, au pied de la chaire. Il se mit en mouvement, mais, avant de partir, hésita.

— Que cherchez-vous? demanda le professeur.

— Ma cas… fit timidement le nouveau, promenant autour de lui des regards inquiets.

— Cinq cents vers à toute la classe! exclamé d'une voix furieuse, arrêta, comme le *Quos ego*, une bourrasque nouvelle. — Restez donc tranquilles! continuait le professeur indigné, et s'essuyant le front avec son mouchoir qu'il venait de prendre dans sa toque: Quant à vous, le nouveau, vous me copierez vingt fois le verbe *ridiculus sum*.

Puis, d'une voix plus douce:

— Eh! vous la retrouverez, votre casquette; on ne vous l'a pas volée!

Tout reprit son calme. Les têtes se courbèrent sur les cartons, et le nouveau resta pendant deux heures dans une tenue exemplaire, quoiqu'il y eût bien, de temps à autre, quelque boulette de papier lancée d'un bec de plume qui vînt s'éclabousser sur sa figure. Mais il s'essuyait avec la main, et demeurait immobile, les yeux baissés.

Le soir, à l'Étude, il tira ses bouts de manches de son pupitre, mit en ordre ses petites affaires, régla soigneusement son papier. Nous le vîmes qui travaillait en conscience, cherchant tous les mots dans le dictionnaire et se donnant beaucoup de mal. Grâce, sans doute, à cette bonne volonté dont il fit preuve, il dut de ne pas descendre dans la classe inférieure; car, s'il savait passablement ses règles, il n'avait guère d'élégance dans les tournures. C'était le curé de son village qui lui avait commencé le latin, ses parents, par économie, ne l'ayant envoyé au collège que le plus tard possible.

Son père, M. Charles-Denis-Bartholomé Bovary, ancien aide-chirurgien-major, compromis, vers 1812, dans des affaires de conscription, et forcé, vers cette époque, de quitter le service, avait alors profité de ses avantages personnels pour saisir au passage une dot de soixante

that offered in the person of a hosier's daughter who had fallen in love with his good looks. A fine man, a great talker, making his spurs ring as he walked, wearing whiskers that ran into his moustache, his fingers always garnished with rings and dressed in loud colours, he had the dash of a military man with the easy go of a commercial traveller. Once married, he lived for three or four years on his wife's fortune, dining well, rising late, smoking long porcelain pipes, not coming in at night till after the theatre, and haunting cafes. The father-in-law died, leaving little; he was indignant at this, "went in for the business," lost some money in it, then retired to the country, where he thought he would make money. But, as he knew no more about farming than calico, as he rode his horses instead of sending them to plough, drank his cider in bottle instead of selling it in cask, ate the finest poultry in his farmyard, and greased his hunting-boots with the fat of his pigs, he was not long in finding out that he would do better to give up all speculation.

For two hundred francs a year he managed to live on the border of the provinces of Caux and Picardy, in a kind of place half farm, half private house; and here, soured, eaten up with regrets, cursing his luck, jealous of everyone, he shut himself up at the age of forty-five, sick of men, he said, and determined to live at peace.

His wife had adored him once on a time; she had bored him with a thousand servilities that had only estranged him the more. Lively once, expansive and affectionate, in growing older she had become (after the fashion of wine that, exposed to air, turns to vinegar) ill-tempered, grumbling, irritable. She had suffered so much without complaint at first, until she had seem him going after all the village drabs, and until a score of bad houses sent him back to her at night, weary, stinking drunk. Then her pride revolted. After that she was silent, burying her anger in a dumb stoicism that she maintained till her death. She was constantly going about looking after business matters. She called on the lawyers, the president, remembered when bills fell due, got them renewed, and at home ironed, sewed, washed, looked after the workmen, paid the accounts, while he, troubling himself about nothing,

mille francs, qui s'offrait en la fille d'un marchand bonnetier, devenue amoureuse de sa tournure. Bel homme, hâbleur, faisant sonner haut ses éperons, portant des favoris rejoints aux moustaches, les doigts toujours garnis de bagues et habillé de couleurs voyantes, il avait l'aspect d'un brave, avec l'entrain facile d'un commis voyageur. Une fois marié, il vécut deux ou trois ans sur la fortune de sa femme, dînant bien, se levant tard, fumant dans de grandes pipes en porcelaine, ne rentrant le soir qu'après le spectacle et fréquentant les cafés. Le beau-père mourut et laissa peu de chose; il en fut indigné, se lança dans la fabrique, y perdit quelque argent, puis se retira dans la campagne, où il voulut faire valoir. Mais, comme il ne s'entendait guère plus en culture qu'en indiennes, qu'il montait ses chevaux au lieu de les envoyer au labour, buvait son cidre en bouteilles au lieu de le vendre en barriques, mangeait les plus belles volailles de sa cour et graissait ses souliers de chasse avec le lard de ses cochons, il ne tarda point à s'apercevoir qu'il valait mieux planter là toute spéculation.

Moyennant deux cents francs par an, il trouva donc à louer dans un village, sur les confins du pays de Caux et de la Picardie, une sorte de logis moitié ferme, moitié maison de maître; et, chagrin, rongé de regrets, accusant le ciel, jaloux contre tout le monde, il s'enferma dès l'âge de quarante-cinq ans, dégoûté des hommes, disait-il, et décidé à vivre en paix.

Sa femme avait été folle de lui autrefois; elle l'avait aimé avec mille servilités qui l'avaient détaché d'elle encore davantage. Enjouée jadis, expansive et tout aimante, elle était, en vieillissant, devenue (à la façon du vin éventé qui se tourne en vinaigre) d'humeur difficile, piaillarde, nerveuse. Elle avait tant souffert, sans se plaindre, d'abord, quand elle le voyait courir après toutes les gotons de village et que vingt mauvais lieux le lui renvoyaient le soir, blasé et puant l'ivresse! Puis l'orgueil s'était révolté. Alors elle s'était tue, avalant sa rage dans un stoïcisme muet, qu'elle garda jusqu'à sa mort. Elle était sans cesse en courses, en affaires. Elle allait chez les avoués, chez le président, se rappelait l'échéance des billets, obtenait des retards; et, à la maison, repassait, cousait, blanchissait, surveillait les ouvriers, soldait les mémoires, tandis que, sans s'inquiéter de rien, Monsieur, continuellement engourdi

eternally besotted in sleepy sulkiness, whence he only roused himself to say disagreeable things to her, sat smoking by the fire and spitting into the cinders.

When she had a child, it had to be sent out to nurse. When he came home, the lad was spoilt as if he were a prince. His mother stuffed him with jam; his father let him run about barefoot, and, playing the philosopher, even said he might as well go about quite naked like the young of animals. As opposed to the maternal ideas, he had a certain virile idea of childhood on which he sought to mould his son, wishing him to be brought up hardily, like a Spartan, to give him a strong constitution. He sent him to bed without any fire, taught him to drink off large draughts of rum and to jeer at religious processions. But, peaceable by nature, the lad answered only poorly to his notions. His mother always kept him near her; she cut out cardboard for him, told him tales, entertained him with endless monologues full of melancholy gaiety and charming nonsense. In her life's isolation she centered on the child's head all her shattered, broken little vanities. She dreamed of high station; she already saw him, tall, handsome, clever, settled as an engineer or in the law. She taught him to read, and even, on an old piano, she had taught him two or three little songs. But to all this Monsieur Bovary, caring little for letters, said, "It was not worth while. Would they ever have the means to send him to a public school, to buy him a practice, or start him in business? Besides, with cheek a man always gets on in the world." Madame Bovary bit her lips, and the child knocked about the village.

He went after the labourers, drove away with clods of earth the ravens that were flying about. He ate blackberries along the hedges, minded the geese with a long switch, went haymaking during harvest, ran about in the woods, played hop-scotch under the church porch on rainy days, and at great fetes begged the beadle to let him toll the bells, that he might hang all his weight on the long rope and feel himself borne upward by it in its swing.

Meanwhile he grew like an oak; he was strong on hand, fresh of colour.

dans une somnolence boudeuse dont il ne se réveillait que pour lui dire des choses désobligeantes, restait à fumer au coin du feu, en crachant dans les cendres.

Quand elle eut un enfant, il le fallut mettre en nourrice. Rentré chez eux, le marmot fut gâté comme un prince. Sa mère le nourrissait de confitures; son père le laissait courir sans souliers, et, pour faire le philosophe, disait même qu'il pouvait bien aller tout nu, comme les enfants des bêtes. À l'encontre des tendances maternelles, il avait en tête un certain idéal viril de l'enfance, d'après lequel il tâchait de former son fils, voulant qu'on l'élevât durement, à la spartiate, pour lui faire une bonne constitution. Il l'envoyait se coucher sans feu, lui apprenait à boire de grands coups de rhum et à insulter les processions. Mais, naturellement paisible, le petit répondait mal à ses efforts. Sa mère le traînait toujours après elle; elle lui découpait des cartons, lui racontait des histoires, s'entretenait avec lui dans des monologues sans fin, pleins de gaietés mélancoliques et de chatteries babillardes. Dans l'isolement de sa vie, elle reporta sur cette tête d'enfant toutes ses vanités éparses, brisées. Elle rêvait de hautes positions, elle le voyait déjà grand, beau, spirituel, établi, dans les ponts et chaussées ou dans la magistrature. Elle lui apprit à lire, et même lui enseigna, sur un vieux piano qu'elle avait, à chanter deux ou trois petites romances. Mais, à tout cela, M. Bovary, peu soucieux des lettres, disait que ce n'était pas la peine! Auraient-ils jamais de quoi l'entretenir dans les écoles du gouvernement, lui acheter une charge ou un fonds de commerce? D'ailleurs, avec du toupet, un homme réussit toujours dans le monde. Madame Bovary se mordait les lèvres, et l'enfant vagabondait dans le village.

Il suivait les laboureurs, et chassait, à coups de motte de terre, les corbeaux qui s'envolaient. Il mangeait des mûres le long des fossés, gardait les dindons avec une gaule, fanait à la moisson, courait dans le bois, jouait à la marelle sous le porche de l'église les jours de pluie, et, aux grandes fêtes, suppliait le bedeau de lui laisser sonner les cloches, pour se pendre de tout son corps à la grande corde et se sentir emporter par elle dans sa volée.

Aussi poussa-t-il comme un chêne. Il acquit de fortes mains, de belles couleurs.

When he was twelve years old his mother had her own way; he began lessons. The cure took him in hand; but the lessons were so short and irregular that they could not be of much use. They were given at spare moments in the sacristy, standing up, hurriedly, between a baptism and a burial; or else the cure, if he had not to go out, sent for his pupil after the Angelus. They went up to his room and settled down; the flies and moths fluttered round the candle. It was close, the child fell asleep, and the good man, beginning to doze with his hands on his stomach, was soon snoring with his mouth wide open. On other occasions, when Monsieur le Cure, on his way back after administering the viaticum to some sick person in the neighbourhood, caught sight of Charles playing about the fields, he called him, lectured him for a quarter of an hour and took advantage of the occasion to make him conjugate his verb at the foot of a tree. The rain interrupted them or an acquaintance passed. All the same he was always pleased with him, and even said the "young man" had a very good memory.

Charles could not go on like this. Madame Bovary took strong steps. Ashamed, or rather tired out, Monsieur Bovary gave in without a struggle, and they waited one year longer, so that the lad should take his first communion.

Six months more passed, and the year after Charles was finally sent to school at Rouen, where his father took him towards the end of October, at the time of the St. Romain fair.

It would now be impossible for any of us to remember anything about him. He was a youth of even temperament, who played in playtime, worked in school-hours, was attentive in class, slept well in the dormitory, and ate well in the refectory. He had in loco parentis a wholesale ironmonger in the Rue Ganterie, who took him out once a month on Sundays after his shop was shut, sent him for a walk on the quay to look at the boats, and then brought him back to college at seven o'clock before supper. Every Thursday evening he wrote a long letter to his mother with red ink and three wafers; then he went over his history note-books, or read an old volume of "Anarchasis" that was knocking about the study. When he went for walks he talked to the servant, who, like himself, came from the country.

À douze ans, sa mère obtint que l'on commençât ses études. On en chargea le curé. Mais les leçons étaient si courtes et si mal suivies, qu'elles ne pouvaient servir à grand-chose. C'était aux moments perdus qu'elles se donnaient, dans la sacristie, debout, à la hâte, entre un baptême et un enterrement; ou bien le curé envoyait chercher son élève après l'Angélus, quand il n'avait pas à sortir. On montait dans sa chambre, on s'installait: les moucherons et les papillons de nuit tournoyaient autour de la chandelle. Il faisait chaud, l'enfant s'endormait; et le bonhomme, s'assoupissant les mains sur son ventre, ne tardait pas à ronfler, la bouche ouverte. D'autres fois, quand M. le curé, revenant de porter le viatique à quelque malade des environs, apercevait Charles qui polissonnait dans la campagne, il l'appelait, le sermonnait un quart d'heure et profitait de l'occasion pour lui faire conjuguer son verbe au pied d'un arbre. La pluie venait les interrompre, ou une connaissance qui passait. Du reste, il était toujours content de lui, disait même que le jeune homme avait beaucoup de mémoire.

Charles ne pouvait en rester là. Madame fut énergique. Honteux, ou fatigué plutôt, Monsieur céda sans résistance, et l'on attendit encore un an que le gamin eût fait sa première communion.

Six mois se passèrent encore; et, l'année d'après, Charles fut définitivement envoyé au collège de Rouen, où son père l'amena lui-même, vers la fin d'octobre, à l'époque de la foire Saint- Romain.

Il serait maintenant impossible à aucun de nous de se rien rappeler de lui. C'était un garçon de tempérament modéré, qui jouait aux récréations, travaillait à l'étude, écoutant en classe, dormant bien au dortoir, mangeant bien au réfectoire. Il avait pour correspondant un quincaillier en gros de la rue Ganterie, qui le faisait sortir une fois par mois, le dimanche, après que sa boutique était fermée, l'envoyait se promener sur le port à regarder les bateaux, puis le ramenait au collège dès sept heures, avant le souper. Le soir de chaque jeudi, il écrivait une longue lettre à sa mère, avec de l'encre rouge et trois pains à cacheter; puis il repassait ses cahiers d'histoire, ou bien lisait un vieux volume d'Anacharsis qui traînait dans l'étude. En promenade, il causait avec le domestique, qui était de la campagne comme lui.

By dint of hard work he kept always about the middle of the class; once even he got a certificate in natural history. But at the end of his third year his parents withdrew him from the school to make him study medicine, convinced that he could even take his degree by himself.

His mother chose a room for him on the fourth floor of a dyer's she knew, overlooking the Eau-de-Robec. She made arrangements for his board, got him furniture, table and two chairs, sent home for an old cherry-tree bedstead, and bought besides a small cast-iron stove with the supply of wood that was to warm the poor child. Then at the end of a week she departed, after a thousand injunctions to be good now that he was going to be left to himself.

The syllabus that he read on the notice-board stunned him; lectures on anatomy, lectures on pathology, lectures on physiology, lectures on pharmacy, lectures on botany and clinical medicine, and therapeutics, without counting hygiene and materia medica—all names of whose etymologies he was ignorant, and that were to him as so many doors to sanctuaries filled with magnificent darkness.

He understood nothing of it all; it was all very well to listen—he did not follow. Still he worked; he had bound note-books, he attended all the courses, never missed a single lecture. He did his little daily task like a mill-horse, who goes round and round with his eyes bandaged, not knowing what work he is doing.

To spare him expense his mother sent him every week by the carrier a piece of veal baked in the oven, with which he lunched when he came back from the hospital, while he sat kicking his feet against the wall. After this he had to run off to lectures, to the operation-room, to the hospital, and return to his home at the other end of the town. In the evening, after the poor dinner of his landlord, he went back to his room and set to work again in his wet clothes, which smoked as he sat in front of the hot stove.

On the fine summer evenings, at the time when the close streets are empty, when the servants are playing shuttle-cock at the doors, he opened his window and leaned out. The river, that makes of this quar-

À force de s'appliquer, il se maintint toujours vers le milieu de la classe; une fois même, il gagna un premier accessit d'histoire naturelle. Mais à la fin de sa troisième, ses parents le retirèrent du collège pour lui faire étudier la médecine, persuadés qu'il pourrait se pousser seul jusqu'au baccalauréat.

Sa mère lui choisit une chambre, au quatrième, sur l'Eau-de-Robec, chez un teinturier de sa connaissance: Elle conclut les arrangements pour sa pension, se procura des meubles, une table et deux chaises, fit venir de chez elle un vieux lit en merisier, et acheta de plus un petit poêle en fonte, avec la provision de bois qui devait chauffer son pauvre enfant. Puis elle partit au bout de la semaine, après mille recommandations de se bien conduire, maintenant qu'il allait être abandonné à lui-même.

Le programme des cours, qu'il lut sur l'affiche, lui fit un effet d'étourdissement: cours d'anatomie, cours de pathologie, cours de physiologie, cours de pharmacie, cours de chimie, et de botanique, et de clinique, et de thérapeutique, sans compter l'hygiène ni la matière médicale, tous noms dont il ignorait les étymologies et qui étaient comme autant de portes de sanctuaires pleins d'augustes ténèbres.

Il n'y comprit rien; il avait beau écouter, il ne saisissait pas. Il travaillait pourtant, il avait des cahiers reliés, il suivait tous les cours; il ne perdait pas une seule visite. Il accomplissait sa petite tâche quotidienne à la manière du cheval de manège, qui tourne en place les yeux bandés, ignorant de la besogne qu'il broie.

Pour lui épargner de la dépense, sa mère lui envoyait chaque semaine, par le messager, un morceau de veau cuit au four, avec quoi il déjeunait le matin; quand il était rentré de l'hôpital, tout en battant la semelle contre le mur. Ensuite il fallait courir aux leçons, à l'amphithéâtre, à l'hospice, et revenir chez lui, à travers toutes les rues. Le soir, après le maigre dîner de son propriétaire, il remontait à sa chambre et se remettait au travail, dans ses habits mouillés qui fumaient sur son corps, devant le poêle rougi.

Dans les beaux soirs d'été; à l'heure où les rues tièdes sont vides, quand les servantes, jouent au volant sur le seuil des portes, il ouvrait sa fenêtre et s'accoudait. La rivière, qui fait de ce quartier de Rouen

ter of Rouen a wretched little Venice, flowed beneath him, between the bridges and the railings, yellow, violet, or blue. Working men, kneeling on the banks, washed their bare arms in the water. On poles projecting from the attics, skeins of cotton were drying in the air. Opposite, beyond the roots spread the pure heaven with the red sun setting. How pleasant it must be at home! How fresh under the beech-tree! And he expanded his nostrils to breathe in the sweet odours of the country which did not reach him.

He grew thin, his figure became taller, his face took a saddened look that made it nearly interesting.

Naturally, through indifference, he abandoned all the resolutions he had made. Once he missed a lecture; the next day all the lectures; and, enjoying his idleness, little by little, he gave up work altogether.

He got into the habit of going to the public-house, and had a passion for dominoes. To shut himself up every evening in the dirty public room, to push about on marble tables the small sheep bones with black dots, seemed to him a fine proof of his freedom, which raised him in his own esteem. It was beginning to see life, the sweetness of stolen pleasures; and when he entered, he put his hand on the door-handle with a joy almost sensual. Then many things hidden within him came out; he learnt couplets by heart and sang them to his boon companions, became enthusiastic about Beranger, learnt how to make punch, and, finally, how to make love.

Thanks to these preparatory labours, he failed completely in his examination for an ordinary degree. He was expected home the same night to celebrate his success.

He started on foot, stopped at the beginning of the village, sent for his mother, and told her all. She excused him, threw the blame of his failure on the injustice of the examiners, encouraged him a little, and took upon herself to set matters straight. It was only five years later that Monsieur Bovary knew the truth; it was old then, and he accepted it. Moreover, he could not believe that a man born of him could be a fool.

So Charles set to work again and crammed for his examination, ceaselessly learning all the old questions by heart. He passed pretty well.

comme une ignoble petite Venise, coulait en bas, sous lui, jaune, violette ou bleue, entre ses ponts et ses grilles. Des ouvriers, accroupis au bord, lavaient leurs bras dans l'eau. Sur des perches partant du haut des greniers, des écheveaux de coton séchaient à l'air. En face, au-delà des toits, le grand ciel pur s'étendait, avec le soleil rouge se couchant. Qu'il devait faire bon là-bas! Quelle fraîcheur sous la hêtraie! Et il ouvrait les narines pour aspirer les bonnes odeurs de la campagne, qui ne venaient pas jusqu'à lui.

Il maigrit, sa taille s'allongea, et sa figure prit une sorte d'expression dolente qui la rendit presque intéressante.

Naturellement, par nonchalance; il en vint à se délier de toutes les résolutions qu'il s'était faites. Une fois, il manqua la visite, le lendemain son cours, et, savourant la paresse, peu à peu, n'y retourna plus.

Il prit l'habitude du cabaret, avec la passion des dominos. S'enfermer chaque soir dans un sale appartement public, pour y taper sur des tables de marbre de petits os de mouton marqués de points noirs, lui semblait un acte précieux de sa liberté, qui le rehaussait d'estime vis-à-vis de lui-même. C'était comme l'initiation au monde, l'accès des plaisirs défendus; et, en entrant, il posait la main sur le bouton de la porte avec une joie presque sensuelle. Alors, beaucoup de choses comprimées en lui, se dilatèrent; il apprit par coeur des couplets qu'il chantait aux bienvenues, s'enthousiasma pour Béranger, sut faire du punch et connut enfin l'amour.

Grâce à ces travaux préparatoires, il échoua complètement à son examen d'officier de santé. On l'attendait le soir même à la maison pour fêter son succès.

Il partit à pied et s'arrêta vers l'entrée du village, où il fit demander sa mère, lui conta tout. Elle l'excusa, rejetant l'échec sur l'injustice des examinateurs, et le raffermit un peu, se chargeant d'arranger les choses. Cinq ans plus tard seulement, M. Bovary connut la vérité; elle était vieille, il l'accepta, ne pouvant d'ailleurs supposer qu'un homme issu de lui fût un sot.

Charles se remit donc au travail et prépara sans discontinuer les matières de son examen, dont il apprit d'avance toutes les questions par

What a happy day for his mother! They gave a grand dinner.

Where should he go to practice? To Tostes, where there was only one old doctor. For a long time Madame Bovary had been on the look-out for his death, and the old fellow had barely been packed off when Charles was installed, opposite his place, as his successor.

But it was not everything to have brought up a son, to have had him taught medicine, and discovered Tostes, where he could practice it; he must have a wife. She found him one—the widow of a bailiff at Dieppe—who was forty-five and had an income of twelve hundred francs.

Though she was ugly, as dry as a bone, her face with as many pimples as the spring has buds, Madame Dubuc had no lack of suitors. To attain her ends Madame Bovary had to oust them all, and she even succeeded in very cleverly baffling the intrigues of a port-butcher backed up by the priests.

Charles had seen in marriage the advent of an easier life, thinking he would be more free to do as he liked with himself and his money. But his wife was master; he had to say this and not say that in company, to fast every Friday, dress as she liked, harass at her bidding those patients who did not pay. She opened his letter, watched his comings and goings, and listened at the partition-wall when women came to consult him in his surgery.

She must have her chocolate every morning, attentions without end. She constantly complained of her nerves, her chest, her liver. The noise of footsteps made her ill; when people left her, solitude became odious to her; if they came back, it was doubtless to see her die. When Charles returned in the evening, she stretched forth two long thin arms from beneath the sheets, put them round his neck, and having made him sit down on the edge of the bed, began to talk to him of her troubles: he was neglecting her, he loved another. She had been warned she would be unhappy; and she ended by asking him for a dose of medicine and a little more love.

coeur. Il fut reçu avec une assez bonne note. Quel beau jour pour sa mère! On donna un grand dîner.

Où irait-il exercer son art? À Tostes. Il n'y avait là qu'un vieux médecin. Depuis longtemps madame Bovary guettait sa mort, et le bonhomme n'avait point encore plié bagage, que Charles était installé en face, comme son successeur.

Mais ce n'était pas tout que d'avoir élevé son fils, de lui avoir fait apprendre la médecine et découvert Tostes pour l'exercer: il lui fallait une femme. Elle lui en trouva une: la veuve d'un huissier de Dieppe, qui avait quarante-cinq ans et douze cents livres de rente.

Quoiqu'elle fût laide, sèche comme un cotret, et bourgeonnée comme un printemps, certes madame Dubuc ne manquait pas de partis à choisir. Pour arriver à ses fins, la mère Bovary fut obligée de les évincer tous, et elle déjoua même fort habilement les intrigues d'un charcutier qui était soutenu par les prêtres.

Charles avait entrevu dans le mariage l'avènement d'une condition meilleure, imaginant qu'il serait plus libre et pourrait disposer de sa personne et de son argent. Mais sa femme fut le maître; il devait devant le monde dire ceci, ne pas dire cela, faire maigre tous les vendredis, s'habiller comme elle l'entendait, harceler par son ordre les clients qui ne payaient pas. Elle décachetait ses lettres, épiait ses démarches, et l'écoutait, à travers la cloison, donner ses consultations dans son cabinet, quand il y avait des femmes.

Il lui fallait son chocolat tous les matins, des égards à n'en plus finir. Elle se plaignait sans cesse de ses nerfs, de sa poitrine, de ses humeurs. Le bruit des pas lui faisait mal; on s'en allait, la solitude lui devenait odieuse; revenait-on près d'elle, c'était pour la voir mourir, sans doute. Le soir, quand Charles rentrait, elle sortait de dessous ses draps ses longs bras maigres, les lui passait autour du cou, et, l'ayant fait asseoir au bord du lit, se mettait à lui parler de ses chagrins: il l'oubliait, il en aimait une autre! On lui avait bien dit qu'elle serait malheureuse; et elle finissait en lui demandant quelque sirop pour sa santé et un peu plus d'amour.

# Chapter 2

One night towards eleven o'clock they were awakened by the noise of a horse pulling up outside their door. The servant opened the garret-window and parleyed for some time with a man in the street below. He came for the doctor, had a letter for him. Natasie came downstairs shivering and undid the bars and bolts one after the other. The man left his horse, and, following the servant, suddenly came in behind her. He pulled out from his wool cap with grey top-knots a letter wrapped up in a rag and presented it gingerly to Charles, who rested on his elbow on the pillow to read it. Natasie, standing near the bed, held the light. Madame in modesty had turned to the wall and showed only her back.

This letter, sealed with a small seal in blue wax, begged Monsieur Bovary to come immediately to the farm of the Bertaux to set a broken leg. Now from Tostes to the Bertaux was a good eighteen miles across country by way of Longueville and Saint-Victor. It was a dark night; Madame Bovary junior was afraid of accidents for her husband. So it was decided the stable-boy should go on first; Charles would start three hours later when the moon rose. A boy was to be sent to meet him, and show him the way to the farm, and open the gates for him.

Towards four o'clock in the morning, Charles, well wrapped up in his cloak, set out for the Bertaux. Still sleepy from the warmth of his bed, he let himself be lulled by the quiet trot of his horse. When it stopped of its own accord in front of those holes surrounded with thorns that are dug on the margin of furrows, Charles awoke with a start, suddenly remembered the broken leg, and tried to call to mind all the fractures he knew. The rain had stopped, day was breaking, and on the branches of the leafless trees birds roosted motionless, their little feathers bristling in the cold morning wind. The flat country

# Chapitre 2

Une nuit, vers onze heures, ils furent réveillés par le bruit d'un cheval qui s'arrêta juste à la porte. La bonne ouvrit la lucarne du grenier et parlementa quelque temps avec un homme resté en bas, dans la rue. Il venait chercher le médecin; il avait une lettre. Nastasie descendit les marches en grelottant, et alla ouvrir la serrure et les verrous, l'un après l'autre. L'homme laissa son cheval, et, suivant la bonne, entra tout à coup derrière elle. Il tira de dedans son bonnet de laine à houppes grises, une lettre enveloppée dans un chiffon, et la présenta délicatement à Charles, qui s'accouda sur l'oreiller pour la lire. Nastasie, près du lit, tenait la lumière. Madame, par pudeur, restait tournée vers la ruelle et montrait le dos.

Cette lettre, cachetée d'un petit cachet de cire bleue, suppliait M. Bovary de se rendre immédiatement à la ferme des Bertaux, pour remettre une jambe cassée. Or il y a, de Tostes aux Bertaux, six bonnes lieues de traverse, en passant par Longueville et Saint- Victor. La nuit était noire. Madame Bovary jeune redoutait les accidents pour son mari. Donc il fut décidé que le valet d'écurie prendrait les devants. Charles partirait trois heures plus tard, au lever de la lune. On enverrait un gamin à sa rencontre, afin de lui montrer le chemin de la ferme et d'ouvrir les clôtures devant lui.

Vers quatre heures du matin, Charles, bien enveloppé dans son manteau, se mit en route pour les Bertaux. Encore endormi par la chaleur du sommeil, il se laissait bercer au trot pacifique de sa bête. Quand elle s'arrêtait d'elle-même devant ces trous entourés d'épines que l'on creuse au bord des sillons, Charles se réveillant en sursaut, se rappelait vite la jambe cassée, et il tâchait de se remettre en mémoire toutes les fractures qu'il savait. La pluie ne tombait plus; le jour commençait à venir, et, sur les branches des pommiers sans feuilles, des oiseaux se tenaient immobiles, hérissant leurs petites plumes au vent froid du matin. La plate

stretched as far as eye could see, and the tufts of trees round the farms at long intervals seemed like dark violet stains on the cast grey surface, that on the horizon faded into the gloom of the sky. Charles from time to time opened his eyes, his mind grew weary, and, sleep coming upon him, he soon fell into a doze wherein, his recent sensations blending with memories, he became conscious of a double self, at once student and married man, lying in his bed as but now, and crossing the operation theatre as of old. The warm smell of poultices mingled in his brain with the fresh odour of dew; he heard the iron rings rattling along the curtain-rods of the bed and saw his wife sleeping. As he passed Vassonville he came upon a boy sitting on the grass at the edge of a ditch.

"Are you the doctor?" asked the child.

And on Charles's answer he took his wooden shoes in his hands and ran on in front of him.

The general practitioner, riding along, gathered from his guide's talk that Monsieur Rouault must be one of the well-to-do farmers. He had broken his leg the evening before on his way home from a Twelfth-night feast at a neighbour's. His wife had been dead for two years. There was with him only his daughter, who helped him to keep house.

The ruts were becoming deeper; they were approaching the Bertaux. The little lad, slipping through a hole in the hedge, disappeared; then he came back to the end of a courtyard to open the gate. The horse slipped on the wet grass; Charles had to stoop to pass under the branches. The watchdogs in their kennels barked, dragging at their chains. As he entered the Bertaux, the horse took fright and stumbled.

It was a substantial-looking farm. In the stables, over the top of the open doors, one could see great cart-horses quietly feeding from new racks. Right along the outbuildings extended a large dunghill, from which manure liquid oozed, while amidst fowls and turkeys, five or six peacocks, a luxury in Chauchois farmyards, were foraging on the top of it. The sheepfold was long, the barn high, with walls smooth as your hand. Under the cart-shed were two large carts and four ploughs, with their whips, shafts and harnesses complete, whose fleeces of blue

campagne s'étalait à perte de vue, et les bouquets d'arbres autour des fermes faisaient, à intervalles éloignés, des taches d'un violet noir sur cette grande surface grise, qui se perdait à l'horizon dans le ton morne du ciel. Charles, de temps à autre, ouvrait les yeux; puis, son esprit se fatiguant et le sommeil revenant de soi-même, bientôt il entrait dans une sorte d'assoupissement où, ses sensations récentes se confondant avec des souvenirs, lui-même se percevait double, à la fois étudiant et marié, couché dans son lit comme tout à l'heure, traversant une salle d'opérés comme autrefois. L'odeur chaude des cataplasmes se mêlait dans sa tête à la verte odeur de la rosée; il entendait rouler sur leur tringle les anneaux de fer des lits et sa femme dormir… Comme il passait par Vassonville, il aperçut, au bord d'un fossé, un jeune garçon assis sur l'herbe.

— Êtes-vous le médecin? demanda l'enfant.

Et, sur la réponse de Charles, il prit ses sabots à ses mains et se mit à courir devant lui.

L'officier de santé, chemin faisant, comprit aux discours de son guide que M. Rouault devait être un cultivateur des plus aisés. Il s'était cassé la jambe, la veille au soir, en revenant de faire les Rois, chez un voisin. Sa femme était morte depuis deux ans. Il n'avait avec lui que sa demoiselle, qui l'aidait à tenir la maison.

Les ornières devinrent plus profondes. On approchait des Bertaux. Le petit gars, se coulant alors par un trou de haie, disparut, puis, il revint au bout d'une cour en ouvrir la barrière. Le cheval glissait sur l'herbe mouillée; Charles se baissait pour passer sous les branches. Les chiens de garde à la niche aboyaient en tirant sur leur chaîne. Quand il entra dans les Bertaux, son cheval eut peur et fit un grand écart.

C'était une ferme de bonne apparence. On voyait dans les écuries, par le dessus des portes ouvertes, de gros chevaux de labour qui mangeaient tranquillement dans des râteliers neufs. Le long des bâtiments s'étendait un large fumier, de la buée s'en élevait, et, parmi les poules et les dindons, picoraient dessus cinq ou six paons, luxe des basses-cours cauchoises. La bergerie était longue, la grange était haute, à murs lisses comme la main. Il y avait sous le hangar deux grandes charrettes et quatre charrues, avec leurs fouets, leurs colliers, leurs équipages com-

wool were getting soiled by the fine dust that fell from the granaries. The courtyard sloped upwards, planted with trees set out symmetrically, and the chattering noise of a flock of geese was heard near the pond.

A young woman in a blue merino dress with three flounces came to the threshold of the door to receive Monsieur Bovary, whom she led to the kitchen, where a large fire was blazing. The servant's breakfast was boiling beside it in small pots of all sizes. Some damp clothes were drying inside the chimney-corner. The shovel, tongs, and the nozzle of the bellows, all of colossal size, shone like polished steel, while along the walls hung many pots and pans in which the clear flame of the hearth, mingling with the first rays of the sun coming in through the window, was mirrored fitfully.

Charles went up the first floor to see the patient. He found him in his bed, sweating under his bed-clothes, having thrown his cotton nightcap right away from him. He was a fat little man of fifty, with white skin and blue eyes, the forepart of his head bald, and he wore earrings. By his side on a chair stood a large decanter of brandy, whence he poured himself a little from time to time to keep up his spirits; but as soon as he caught sight of the doctor his elation subsided, and instead of swearing, as he had been doing for the last twelve hours, began to groan freely.

The fracture was a simple one, without any kind of complication. Charles could not have hoped for an easier case. Then calling to mind the devices of his masters at the bedsides of patients, he comforted the sufferer with all sorts of kindly remarks, those caresses of the surgeon that are like the oil they put on bistouries. In order to make some splints a bundle of laths was brought up from the cart-house. Charles selected one, cut it into two pieces and planed it with a fragment of windowpane, while the servant tore up sheets to make bandages, and Mademoiselle Emma tried to sew some pads. As she was a long time before she found her work-case, her father grew impatient; she did not answer, but as she sewed she pricked her fingers, which she then put to her mouth to suck them.

Charles was surprised at the whiteness of her nails. They were shiny, delicate at the tips, more polished than the ivory of Dieppe, and almond-

plets, dont les toisons de laine bleue se salissaient à la poussière fine qui tombait des greniers. La cour allait en montant; plantée d'arbres symétriquement espacés, et le bruit gai d'un troupeau d'oies retentissait près de la mare.

Une jeune femme, en robe de mérinos bleu garnie de trois volants, vint sur le seuil de la maison pour recevoir M. Bovary, qu'elle fit entrer dans la cuisine, où flambait un grand feu. Le déjeuner des gens bouillonnait alentour, dans des petits pots de taille inégale. Des vêtements humides séchaient dans l'intérieur de la cheminée. La pelle, les pincettes et le bec du soufflet, tous de proportion colossale, brillaient comme de l'acier poli, tandis que le long des murs s'étendait une abondante batterie de cuisine, où miroitait inégalement la flamme claire du foyer, jointe aux premières lueurs du soleil arrivant par les carreaux.

Charles monta, au premier, voir le malade. Il le trouva dans son lit, suant sous ses couvertures et ayant rejeté bien loin son bonnet de coton. C'était un gros petit homme de cinquante ans, à la peau blanche, à l'oeil bleu, chauve sur le devant de la tête, et qui portait des boucles d'oreilles. Il avait à ses côtés, sur une chaise, une grande carafe d'eau-de-vie, dont il se versait de temps à autre pour se donner du coeur au ventre; mais, dès qu'il vit le médecin, son exaltation tomba, et, au lieu de sacrer comme il faisait depuis douze heures, il se prit à geindre faiblement.

La fracture était simple, sans complication d'aucune espèce. Charles n'eût osé en souhaiter de plus facile. Alors, se rappelant les allures de ses maîtres auprès du lit des blessés, il réconforta le patient avec toutes sortes de bons mots; caresses chirurgicales qui sont comme l'huile dont on graisse les bistouris. Afin d'avoir des attelles, on alla chercher, sous la charreterie, un paquet de lattes. Charles en choisit une, la coupa en morceaux et la polit avec un éclat de vitre, tandis que la servante déchirait des draps pour faire des bandes, et que mademoiselle Emma tâchait à coudre des coussinets. Comme elle fut longtemps avant de trouver son étui, son père s'impatienta; elle ne répondit rien; mais, tout en cousant, elle se piquait les doigts, qu'elle portait ensuite à sa bouche pour les sucer.

Charles fut surpris de la blancheur de ses ongles. Ils étaient brillants, fins du bout, plus nettoyés que les ivoires de Dieppe, et taillés en

shaped. Yet her hand was not beautiful, perhaps not white enough, and a little hard at the knuckles; besides, it was too long, with no soft inflections in the outlines. Her real beauty was in her eyes. Although brown, they seemed black because of the lashes, and her look came at you frankly, with a candid boldness.

The bandaging over, the doctor was invited by Monsieur Rouault himself to "pick a bit" before he left.

Charles went down into the room on the ground floor. Knives and forks and silver goblets were laid for two on a little table at the foot of a huge bed that had a canopy of printed cotton with figures representing Turks. There was an odour of iris-root and damp sheets that escaped from a large oak chest opposite the window. On the floor in corners were sacks of flour stuck upright in rows. These were the overflow from the neighbouring granary, to which three stone steps led. By way of decoration for the apartment, hanging to a nail in the middle of the wall, whose green paint scaled off from the effects of the saltpetre, was a crayon head of Minerva in gold frame, underneath which was written in Gothic letters "To dear Papa."

First they spoke of the patient, then of the weather, of the great cold, of the wolves that infested the fields at night. Mademoiselle Rouault did not at all like the country, especially now that she had to look after the farm almost alone. As the room was chilly, she shivered as she ate. This showed something of her full lips, that she had a habit of biting when silent.

Her neck stood out from a white turned-down collar. Her hair, whose two black folds seemed each of a single piece, so smooth were they, was parted in the middle by a delicate line that curved slightly with the curve of the head; and, just showing the tip of the ear, it was joined behind in a thick chignon, with a wavy movement at the temples that the country doctor saw now for the first time in his life. The upper part of her cheek was rose-coloured. She had, like a man, thrust in between two buttons of her bodice a tortoise-shell eyeglass.

amande. Sa main pourtant n'était pas belle, point assez pâle peut-être, et un peu sèche aux phalanges; elle était trop longue aussi, et sans molles inflexions de lignes sur les contours. Ce qu'elle avait de beau, c'étaient les yeux; quoiqu'ils fussent bruns, ils semblaient noirs à cause des cils, et son regard arrivait franchement à vous avec une hardiesse candide.

Une fois le pansement fait, le médecin fut invité, par M. Rouault lui-même, à prendre un morceau avant de partir.

Charles descendit dans la salle, au rez-de-chaussée. Deux couverts, avec des timbales d'argent, y étaient mis sur une petite table, au pied d'un grand lit à baldaquin revêtu d'une indienne à personnages représentant des Turcs. On sentait une odeur d'iris et de draps humides, qui s'échappait de la haute armoire en bois de chêne, faisant face à la fenêtre. Par terre, dans les angles, étaient rangés, debout, des sacs de blé. C'était le trop-plein du grenier proche, où l'on montait par trois marches de pierre. Il y avait, pour décorer l'appartement, accrochée à un clou, au milieu du mur dont la peinture verte s'écaillait sous le salpêtre, une tête de Minerve au crayon noir, encadrée de dorure, et qui portait au bas, écrit en lettres gothiques: «À mon cher papa.»

On parla d'abord du malade, puis du temps qu'il faisait, des grands froids, des loups qui couraient les champs, la nuit. Mademoiselle Rouault ne s'amusait guère à la campagne, maintenant surtout qu'elle était chargée presque à elle seule des soins de la ferme. Comme la salle était fraîche, elle grelottait tout en mangeant, ce qui découvrait un peu ses lèvres charnues, qu'elle avait coutume de mordillonner à ses moments de silence.

Son cou sortait d'un col blanc, rabattu. Ses cheveux, dont les deux bandeaux noirs semblaient chacun d'un seul morceau, tant ils étaient lisses, étaient séparés sur le milieu de la tête par une raie fine, qui s'enfonçait légèrement selon la courbe du crâne; et, laissant voir à peine le bout de l'oreille, ils allaient se confondre par derrière en un chignon abondant, avec un mouvement ondé vers les tempes, que le médecin de campagne remarqua là pour la première fois de sa vie. Ses pommettes étaient roses. Elle portait, comme un homme, passé entre deux boutons de son corsage, un lorgnon d'écaille.

When Charles, after bidding farewell to old Rouault, returned to the room before leaving, he found her standing, her forehead against the window, looking into the garden, where the bean props had been knocked down by the wind. She turned round.

"Are you looking for anything?" she asked.

"My whip, if you please," he answered.

He began rummaging on the bed, behind the doors, under the chairs. It had fallen to the floor, between the sacks and the wall. Mademoiselle Emma saw it, and bent over the flour sacks. Charles out of politeness made a dash also, and as he stretched out his arm, at the same moment felt his breast brush against the back of the young girl bending beneath him. She drew herself up, scarlet, and looked at him over her shoulder as she handed him his whip.

Instead of returning to the Bertaux in three days as he had promised, he went back the very next day, then regularly twice a week, without counting the visits he paid now and then as if by accident.

Everything, moreover, went well; the patient progressed favourably; and when, at the end of forty-six days, old Rouault was seen trying to walk alone in his "den," Monsieur Bovary began to be looked upon as a man of great capacity. Old Rouault said that he could not have been cured better by the first doctor of Yvetot, or even of Rouen.

As to Charles, he did not stop to ask himself why it was a pleasure to him to go to the Bertaux. Had he done so, he would, no doubt, have attributed his zeal to the importance of the case, or perhaps to the money he hoped to make by it. Was it for this, however, that his visits to the farm formed a delightful exception to the meagre occupations of his life? On these days he rose early, set off at a gallop, urging on his horse, then got down to wipe his boots in the grass and put on black gloves before entering. He liked going into the courtyard, and noticing the gate turn against his shoulder, the cock crow on the wall, the lads run to meet him. He liked the granary and the stables; he liked old Rouault, who pressed his hand and called him his saviour; he liked the small wooden shoes of Mademoiselle Emma on the scoured flags of the

Quand Charles, après être monté dire adieu au père Rouault, rentra dans la salle avant de partir, il la trouva debout, le front contre la fenêtre, et qui regardait dans le jardin, où les échalas des haricots avaient été renversés par le vent. Elle se retourna.

— Cherchez-vous quelque chose? demanda-t-elle.

— Ma cravache, s'il vous plaît, répondit-il.

Et il se mit à fureter sur le lit, derrière les portes, sous les chaises; elle était tombée à terre, entre les sacs et la muraille. Mademoiselle Emma l'aperçut; elle se pencha sur les sacs de blé. Charles, par galanterie, se précipita et, comme il allongeait aussi son bras dans le même mouvement, il sentit sa poitrine effleurer le dos de la jeune fille, courbée sous lui. Elle se redressa toute rouge et le regarda par-dessus l'épaule, en lui tendant son nerf de boeuf.

Au lieu de revenir aux Bertaux trois jours après, comme il l'avait promis, c'est le lendemain même qu'il y retourna, puis deux fois la semaine régulièrement, sans compter les visites inattendues qu'il faisait de temps à autre, comme par mégarde.

Tout, du reste, alla bien; la guérison s'établit selon les règles, et quand, au bout de quarante-six jours, on vit le père Rouault qui s'essayait à marcher seul dans sa masure, on commença à considérer M. Bovary comme un homme de grande capacité. Le père Rouault disait qu'il n'aurait pas été mieux guéri par les premiers médecins d'Yvetot ou même de Rouen.

Quant à Charles, il ne chercha point à se demander pourquoi il venait aux Bertaux avec plaisir. Y eût-il songé, qu'il aurait sans doute attribué son zèle à la gravité du cas, ou peut-être au profit qu'il en espérait. Était-ce pour cela, cependant, que ses visites à la ferme faisaient, parmi les pauvres occupations de sa vie, une exception charmante? Ces jours-là il se levait de bonne heure, partait au galop, poussait sa bête, puis il descendait pour s'essuyer les pieds sur l'herbe, et passait ses gants noirs avant d'entrer. Il aimait à se voir arriver dans la cour, à sentir contre son épaule la barrière qui tournait, et le coq qui chantait sur le mur, les garçons qui venaient à sa rencontre. Il aimait la grange et les écuries; il aimait le père Rouault; qui lui tapait dans la main en l'appelant son sauveur; il aimait les petits sabots de mademoiselle Emma sur les dalles

kitchen—her high heels made her a little taller; and when she walked in front of him, the wooden soles springing up quickly struck with a sharp sound against the leather of her boots.

She always accompanied him to the first step of the stairs. When his horse had not yet been brought round she stayed there. They had said "Good-bye"; there was no more talking. The open air wrapped her round, playing with the soft down on the back of her neck, or blew to and fro on her hips the apron-strings, that fluttered like streamers. Once, during a thaw the bark of the trees in the yard was oozing, the snow on the roofs of the outbuildings was melting; she stood on the threshold, and went to fetch her sunshade and opened it. The sunshade of silk of the colour of pigeons' breasts, through which the sun shone, lighted up with shifting hues the white skin of her face. She smiled under the tender warmth, and drops of water could be heard falling one by one on the stretched silk.

During the first period of Charles's visits to the Bertaux, Madame Bovary junior never failed to inquire after the invalid, and she had even chosen in the book that she kept on a system of double entry a clean blank page for Monsieur Rouault. But when she heard he had a daughter, she began to make inquiries, and she learnt the Mademoiselle Rouault, brought up at the Ursuline Convent, had received what is called "a good education"; and so knew dancing, geography, drawing, how to embroider and play the piano. That was the last straw.

"So it is for this," she said to herself, "that his face beams when he goes to see her, and that he puts on his new waistcoat at the risk of spoiling it with the rain. Ah! that woman! That woman!"

And she detested her instinctively. At first she solaced herself by allusions that Charles did not understand, then by casual observations that he let pass for fear of a storm, finally by open apostrophes to which he knew not what to answer.

"Why did he go back to the Bertaux now that Monsieur Rouault was cured and that these folks hadn't paid yet? Ah! it was because a young lady was there, some one who know how to talk, to embroider, to be witty. That was what he cared about; he wanted town misses." And she went on—

lavées de la cuisine; ses talons hauts la grandissaient un peu, et, quand elle marchait devant lui, les semelles de bois, se relevant vite, claquaient avec un bruit sec contre le cuir de la bottine.

Elle le reconduisait toujours jusqu'à la première marche du perron. Lorsqu'on n'avait pas encore amené son cheval, elle restait là. On s'était dit adieu, on ne parlait plus; le grand air l'entourait, levant pêle-mêle les petits cheveux follets de sa nuque, ou secouant sur sa hanche les cordons de son tablier, qui se tortillaient comme des banderoles. Une fois, par un temps de dégel, l'écorce des arbres suintait dans la cour, la neige sur les couvertures des bâtiments se fondait. Elle était sur le seuil; elle alla chercher son ombrelle, elle l'ouvrit. L'ombrelle, de soie gorge de pigeon, que traversait le soleil, éclairait de reflets mobiles la peau blanche de sa figure. Elle souriait là- dessous à la chaleur tiède; et on entendait les gouttes d'eau, une à une, tomber sur la moire tendue.

Dans les premiers temps que Charles fréquentait les Bertaux, madame Bovary jeune ne manquait pas de s'informer du malade, et même sur le livre qu'elle tenait en partie double, elle avait choisi pour M. Rouault une belle page blanche. Mais quand elle sut qu'il avait une fille, elle alla aux informations; et elle apprit que mademoiselle Rouault, élevée au couvent, chez les Ursulines, avait reçu, comme on dit, une belle éducation, qu'elle savait, en conséquence, la danse, la géographie, le dessin, faire de la tapisserie et toucher du piano. Ce fut le comble!

— C'est donc pour cela, se disait-elle, qu'il a la figure si épanouie quand il va la voir, et qu'il met son gilet neuf, au risque de l'abîmer à la pluie? Ah! cette femme! cette femme!...

Et elle la détesta, d'instinct. D'abord, elle se soulagea par des allusions, Charles ne les comprit pas; ensuite, par des réflexions incidentes qu'il laissait passer de peur de l'orage; enfin, par des apostrophes à brûle-pourpoint auxquelles il ne savait que répondre.

— D'où vient qu'il retournait aux Bertaux, puisque M. Rouault était guéri et que ces gens-là n'avaient pas encore payé? Ah! c'est qu'il y avait là-bas une personne, quelqu'un qui savait causer, une brodeuse, un bel esprit. C'était là ce qu'il aimait: il lui fallait des demoiselles de ville! — Et elle reprenait:

"The daughter of old Rouault a town miss! Get out! Their grandfather was a shepherd, and they have a cousin who was almost had up at the assizes for a nasty blow in a quarrel. It is not worth while making such a fuss, or showing herself at church on Sundays in a silk gown like a countess. Besides, the poor old chap, if it hadn't been for the colza last year, would have had much ado to pay up his arrears."

For very weariness Charles left off going to the Bertaux. Heloise made him swear, his hand on the prayer-book, that he would go there no more after much sobbing and many kisses, in a great outburst of love. He obeyed then, but the strength of his desire protested against the servility of his conduct; and he thought, with a kind of naive hypocrisy, that his interdict to see her gave him a sort of right to love her. And then the widow was thin; she had long teeth; wore in all weathers a little black shawl, the edge of which hung down between her shoulder-blades; her bony figure was sheathed in her clothes as if they were a scabbard; they were too short, and displayed her ankles with the laces of her large boots crossed over grey stockings.

Charles's mother came to see them from time to time, but after a few days the daughter-in-law seemed to put her own edge on her, and then, like two knives, they scarified him with their reflections and observations. It was wrong of him to eat so much. Why did he always offer a glass of something to everyone who came? What obstinacy not to wear flannels!

In the spring it came about that a notary at Ingouville, the holder of the widow Dubuc's property, one fine day went off, taking with him all the money in his office. Heloise, it is true, still possessed, besides a share in a boat valued at six thousand francs, her house in the Rue St. Francois; and yet, with all this fortune that had been so trumpeted abroad, nothing, excepting perhaps a little furniture and a few clothes, had appeared in the household. The matter had to be gone into. The house at Dieppe was found to be eaten up with mortgages to its foundations; what she had placed with the notary God only knew, and her share in the boat did not exceed one thousand crowns. She had lied, the good lady! In his exasperation, Monsieur Bovary the elder, smashing a chair on the flags,

— La fille au père Rouault, une demoiselle de ville! Allons donc! leur grand-père était berger, et ils ont un cousin qui a failli passer par les assises pour un mauvais coup, dans une dispute. Ce n'est pas la peine de faire tant de fla-fla, ni de se montrer le dimanche à l'église avec une robe de soie, comme une comtesse. Pauvre bonhomme, d'ailleurs, qui sans les colzas de l'an passé, eût été bien embarrassé de payer ses arrérages!

Par lassitude, Charles cessa de retourner aux Bertaux. Héloïse lui avait fait jurer qu'il n'irait plus, la main sur son livre de messe, après beaucoup de sanglots et de baisers, dans une grande explosion d'amour. Il obéit donc; mais la hardiesse de son désir protesta contre la servilité de sa conduite, et, par une sorte d'hypocrisie naïve, il estima que cette défense de la voir était pour lui comme un droit de l'aimer. Et puis la veuve était maigre; elle avait les dents longues; elle portait en toute saison un petit châle noir dont la pointe lui descendait entre les omoplates; sa taille dure était engainée dans des robes en façon de fourreau, trop courtes, qui découvraient ses chevilles, avec les rubans de ses souliers larges s'entrecroisant sur des bas gris.

La mère de Charles venait les voir de temps à autre; mais, au bout de quelques jours, la bru semblait l'aiguiser à son fil; et alors, comme deux couteaux, elles étaient à le scarifier par leurs réflexions et leurs observations. Il avait tort de tant manger! Pourquoi toujours offrir la goutte au premier venu? Quel entêtement que de ne pas vouloir porter de flanelle!

Il arriva qu'au commencement du printemps, un notaire d'Ingouville, détenteur de fonds de la veuve Dubuc, s'embarqua, par une belle marée, emportant avec lui tout l'argent de son étude. Héloïse, il est vrai, possédait encore, outre une part de bateau évaluée six mille francs, sa maison de la rue Saint- François; et cependant, de toute cette fortune que l'on avait fait sonner si haut, rien, si ce n'est un peu de mobilier et quelques nippes, n'avait paru dans le ménage. Il fallut tirer la chose au clair. La maison de Dieppe se trouva vermoulue d'hypothèques jusque dans ses pilotis; ce qu'elle avait mis chez le notaire, Dieu seul le savait, et la part de barque n'excéda point mille écus. Elle avait donc menti, la bonne dame! Dans son exaspération, M. Bovary père, brisant une chaise con-

accused his wife of having caused misfortune to the son by harnessing him to such a harridan, whose harness wasn't worth her hide. They came to Tostes. Explanations followed. There were scenes. Heloise in tears, throwing her arms about her husband, implored him to defend her from his parents. Charles tried to speak up for her. They grew angry and left the house.

But "the blow had struck home." A week after, as she was hanging up some washing in her yard, she was seized with a spitting of blood, and the next day, while Charles had his back turned to her drawing the window-curtain, she said, "O God!" gave a sigh and fainted. She was dead! What a surprise!

When all was over at the cemetery Charles went home. He found no one downstairs; he went up to the first floor to their room; saw her dress still hanging at the foot of the alcove; then, leaning against the writing-table, he stayed until the evening, buried in a sorrowful reverie. She had loved him after all!

tre les pavés, accusa sa femme d'avoir fait le malheur de leur fils en l'attelant à une haridelle semblable, dont les harnais ne valaient pas la peau. Ils vinrent à Tostes. On s'expliqua. Il y eut des scènes. Héloïse, en pleurs, se jetant dans les bras de son mari, le conjura de la défendre de ses parents. Charles voulut parler pour elle. Ceux-ci se fâchèrent, et ils partirent.

Mais le coup était porté. Huit jours après, comme elle étendait du linge dans sa cour, elle fut prise d'un crachement de sang, et le lendemain, tandis que Charles avait le dos tourné pour fermer le rideau de la fenêtre, elle dit: «Ah! mon Dieu!» poussa un soupir et s'évanouit. Elle était morte! Quel étonnement!

Quand tout fut fini au cimetière, Charles rentra chez lui. Il ne trouva personne en bas; il monta au premier, dans la chambre, vit sa robe encore accrochée au pied de l'alcôve; alors, s'appuyant contre le secrétaire, il resta jusqu'au soir perdu dans une rêverie douloureuse. Elle l'avait aimé, après tout.

# Chapter 3

One morning old Rouault brought Charles the money for setting his leg—seventy-five francs in forty-sou pieces, and a turkey. He had heard of his loss, and consoled him as well as he could.

"I know what it is," said he, clapping him on the shoulder; "I've been through it. When I lost my dear departed, I went into the fields to be quite alone. I fell at the foot of a tree; I cried; I called on God; I talked nonsense to Him. I wanted to be like the moles that I saw on the branches, their insides swarming with worms, dead, and an end of it. And when I thought that there were others at that very moment with their nice little wives holding them in their embrace, I struck great blows on the earth with my stick. I was pretty well mad with not eating; the very idea of going to a cafe disgusted me—you wouldn't believe it. Well, quite softly, one day following another, a spring on a winter, and an autumn after a summer, this wore away, piece by piece, crumb by crumb; it passed away, it is gone, I should say it has sunk; for something always remains at the bottom as one would say—a weight here, at one's heart. But since it is the lot of all of us, one must not give way altogether, and, because others have died, want to die too. You must pull yourself together, Monsieur Bovary. It will pass away. Come to see us; my daughter thinks of you now and again, d'ye know, and she says you are forgetting her. Spring will soon be here. We'll have some rabbit-shooting in the warrens to amuse you a bit."

Charles followed his advice. He went back to the Bertaux. He found all as he had left it, that is to say, as it was five months ago. The pear trees were already in blossom, and Farmer Rouault, on his legs again, came and went, making the farm more full of life.

Thinking it his duty to heap the greatest attention upon the doctor because of his sad position, he begged him not to take his hat off, spoke

# Chapitre 3

Un matin, le père Rouault vint apporter à Charles le payement de sa jambe remise: soixante et quinze francs en pièces de quarante sous, et une dinde. Il avait appris son malheur, et l'en consola tant qu'il put.

— Je sais ce que c'est! disait-il en lui frappant sur l'épaule; j'ai été comme vous, moi aussi! Quand j'ai eu perdu ma pauvre défunte, j'allais dans les champs pour être tout seul; je tombais au pied d'un arbre, je pleurais, j'appelais le bon Dieu, je lui disais des sottises; j'aurais voulu être comme les taupes, que je voyais aux branches, qui avaient des vers leur grouillant dans le ventre, crevé, enfin. Et quand je pensais que d'autres, à ce moment-là, étaient avec leurs bonnes petites femmes à les tenir embrassées contre eux, je tapais de grands coups par terre avec mon bâton; j'étais quasiment fou, que je ne mangeais plus; l'idée d'aller seulement au café me dégoûtait, vous ne croiriez pas. Eh bien, tout doucement, un jour chassant l'autre, un printemps sur un hiver et un automne par-dessus un été, ça a coulé brin à brin, miette à miette; ça s'en est allé, c'est parti, c'est descendu, je veux dire, car il vous reste toujours quelque chose au fond, comme qui dirait… un poids, là, sur la poitrine! Mais, puisque c'est notre sort à tous, on ne doit pas non plus se laisser dépérir, et, parce que d'autres sont morts, vouloir mourir… Il faut vous secouer, monsieur Bovary; ça se passera! Venez nous voir; ma fille pense à vous de temps à autre, savez-vous bien, et elle dit comme ça que vous l'oubliez. Voilà le printemps bientôt; nous vous ferons tirer un lapin dans la garenne, pour vous dissiper un peu.

Charles suivit son conseil. Il retourna aux Bertaux; il retrouva tout comme la veille, comme il y avait cinq mois, c'est-à-dire. Les poiriers déjà étaient en fleur, et le bonhomme Rouault, debout maintenant, allait et venait, ce qui rendait la ferme plus animée.

Croyant qu'il était de son devoir de prodiguer au médecin le plus de politesses possible, à cause de sa position douloureuse, il le pria de

to him in an undertone as if he had been ill, and even pretended to be angry because nothing rather lighter had been prepared for him than for the others, such as a little clotted cream or stewed pears. He told stories. Charles found himself laughing, but the remembrance of his wife suddenly coming back to him depressed him.

Coffee was brought in; he thought no more about her.

He thought less of her as he grew accustomed to living alone. The new delight of independence soon made his loneliness bearable. He could now change his meal-times, go in or out without explanation, and when he was very tired stretch himself at full length on his bed. So he nursed and coddled himself and accepted the consolations that were offered him. On the other hand, the death of his wife had not served him ill in his business, since for a month people had been saying, "The poor young man! what a loss!" His name had been talked about, his practice had increased; and moreover, he could go to the Bertaux just as he liked. He had an aimless hope, and was vaguely happy; he thought himself better looking as he brushed his whiskers before the looking-glass.

One day he got there about three o'clock. Everybody was in the fields. He went into the kitchen, but did not at once catch sight of Emma; the outside shutters were closed. Through the chinks of the wood the sun sent across the flooring long fine rays that were broken at the corners of the furniture and trembled along the ceiling. Some flies on the table were crawling up the glasses that had been used, and buzzing as they drowned themselves in the dregs of the cider. The daylight that came in by the chimney made velvet of the soot at the back of the fireplace, and touched with blue the cold cinders. Between the window and the hearth Emma was sewing; she wore no fichu; he could see small drops of perspiration on her bare shoulders.

After the fashion of country folks she asked him to have something to drink. He said no; she insisted, and at last laughingly offered to have a glass of liqueur with him. So she went to fetch a bottle of curacao from the cupboard, reached down two small glasses, filled one to the brim, poured scarcely anything into the other, and, after having clinked

ne point se découvrir la tête, lui parla à voix basse, comme s'il eût été malade, et même fit semblant de se mettre en colère de ce que l'on n'avait pas apprêté à son intention quelque chose d'un peu plus léger que tout le reste, tels que des petits pots de crème ou des poires cuites. Il conta des histoires. Charles se surprit à rire; mais le souvenir de sa femme, lui revenant tout à coup, l'assombrit.

On apporta le café; il n'y pensa plus.

Il y pensa moins, à mesure qu'il s'habituait à vivre seul. L'agrément nouveau de l'indépendance lui rendit bientôt la solitude plus supportable. Il pouvait changer maintenant les heures de ses repas, rentrer ou sortir sans donner de raisons, et, lorsqu'il était bien fatigué, s'étendre de ses quatre membres, tout en large, dans son lit. Donc, il se choya, se dorlota et accepta les consolations qu'on lui donnait. D'autre part, la mort de sa femme ne l'avait pas mal servi dans son métier, car on avait répété durant un mois: «Ce pauvre jeune homme! quel malheur!» Son nom s'était répandu, sa clientèle s'était accrue; et puis il allait aux Bertaux tout à son aise. Il avait un espoir sans but, un bonheur vague; il se trouvait la figure plus agréable en brossant ses favoris devant son miroir.

Il arriva un jour vers trois heures; tout le monde était aux champs; il entra dans la cuisine, mais n'aperçut point d'abord Emma; les auvents étaient fermés. Par les fentes du bois, le soleil allongeait sur les pavés de grandes raies minces, qui se brisaient à l'angle des meubles et tremblaient au plafond. Des mouches, sur la table, montaient le long des verres qui avaient servi, et bourdonnaient en se noyant au fond, dans le cidre resté. Le jour qui descendait par la cheminée, veloutant la suie de la plaque, bleuissait un peu les cendres froides. Entre la fenêtre et le foyer, Emma cousait; elle n'avait point de fichu, on voyait sur ses épaules nues de petites gouttes de sueur.

Selon la mode de la campagne, elle lui proposa de boire quelque chose. Il refusa, elle insista, et enfin lui offrit, en riant, de prendre un verre de liqueur avec elle. Elle alla donc chercher dans l'armoire une bouteille de curaçao, atteignit deux petits verres, emplit l'un jusqu'au bord, versa à peine dans l'autre, et, après avoir trinqué, le porta à sa

glasses, carried hers to her mouth. As it was almost empty she bent back to drink, her head thrown back, her lips pouting, her neck on the strain. She laughed at getting none of it, while with the tip of her tongue passing between her small teeth she licked drop by drop the bottom of her glass.

She sat down again and took up her work, a white cotton stocking she was darning. She worked with her head bent down; she did not speak, nor did Charles. The air coming in under the door blew a little dust over the flags; he watched it drift along, and heard nothing but the throbbing in his head and the faint clucking of a hen that had laid an egg in the yard. Emma from time to time cooled her cheeks with the palms of her hands, and cooled these again on the knobs of the huge fire-dogs.

She complained of suffering since the beginning of the season from giddiness; she asked if sea-baths would do her any good; she began talking of her convent, Charles of his school; words came to them. They went up into her bedroom. She showed him her old music-books, the little prizes she had won, and the oak-leaf crowns, left at the bottom of a cupboard. She spoke to him, too, of her mother, of the country, and even showed him the bed in the garden where, on the first Friday of every month, she gathered flowers to put on her mother's tomb. But the gardener they had never knew anything about it; servants are so stupid! She would have dearly liked, if only for the winter, to live in town, although the length of the fine days made the country perhaps even more wearisome in the summer. And, according to what she was saying, her voice was clear, sharp, or, on a sudden all languor, drawn out in modulations that ended almost in murmurs as she spoke to herself, now joyous, opening big naive eyes, then with her eyelids half closed, her look full of boredom, her thoughts wandering.

Going home at night, Charles went over her words one by one, trying to recall them, to fill out their sense, that he might piece out the life she had lived before he knew her. But he never saw her in his thoughts other than he had seen her the first time, or as he had just left her. Then he asked himself what would become of her—if she would be married,

bouche. Comme il était presque vide, elle se renversait pour boire; et, la tête en arrière, les lèvres avancées, le cou tendu, elle riait de ne rien sentir, tandis que le bout de sa langue, passant entre ses dents fines, léchait à petits coups le fond du verre.

Elle se rassit et elle reprit son ouvrage, qui était un bas de coton blanc où elle faisait des reprises; elle travaillait le front baissé; elle ne parlait pas, Charles non plus. L'air, passant par le dessous de la porte, poussait un peu de poussière sur les dalles; il la regardait se traîner, et il entendait seulement le battement intérieur de sa tête, avec le cri d'une poule, au loin, qui pondait dans les cours. Emma, de temps à autre, se rafraîchissait les joues en y appliquant la paume de ses mains; qu'elle refroidissait après cela sur la pomme de fer des grands chenets.

Elle se plaignit d'éprouver, depuis le commencement de la saison, des étourdissements; elle demanda si les bains de mer lui seraient utiles; elle se mit à causer du couvent, Charles de son collège, les phrases leur vinrent. Ils montèrent dans sa chambre. Elle lui fit voir ses anciens cahiers de musique, les petits livres qu'on lui avait donnés en prix et les couronnes en feuilles de chêne, abandonnées dans un bas d'armoire. Elle lui parla encore de sa mère, du cimetière, et même lui montra dans le jardin la plate- bande dont elle cueillait les fleurs, tous les premiers vendredis de chaque mois, pour les aller mettre sur sa tombe. Mais le jardinier qu'ils avaient n'y entendait rien; on était si mal servi! Elle eût bien voulu, ne fût-ce au moins que pendant l'hiver, habiter la ville, quoique la longueur des beaux jours rendît peut-être la campagne plus ennuyeuse encore durant l'été; — et, selon ce qu'elle disait, sa voix était claire, aiguë, ou se couvrant de langueur tout à coup, traînait des modulations qui finissaient presque en murmures, quand elle se parlait à elle-même, — tantôt joyeuse, ouvrant des yeux naïfs, puis les paupières à demi closes, le regard noyé d'ennui, la pensée vagabondant.

Le soir, en s'en retournant, Charles reprit une à une les phrases qu'elle avait dites, tâchant de se les rappeler, d'en compléter le sens, afin de se faire la portion d'existence qu'elle avait vécu dans le temps qu'il ne la connaissait pas encore. Mais jamais il ne put la voir en sa pensée, différemment qu'il ne l'avait vue la première fois, ou telle qu'il venait de la quitter tout à

and to whom! Alas! Old Rouault was rich, and she!—so beautiful! But Emma's face always rose before his eyes, and a monotone, like the humming of a top, sounded in his ears, "If you should marry after all! If you should marry!" At night he could not sleep; his throat was parched; he was athirst. He got up to drink from the water-bottle and opened the window. The night was covered with stars, a warm wind blowing in the distance; the dogs were barking. He turned his head towards the Bertaux.

Thinking that, after all, he should lose nothing, Charles promised himself to ask her in marriage as soon as occasion offered, but each time such occasion did offer the fear of not finding the right words sealed his lips.

Old Rouault would not have been sorry to be rid of his daughter, who was of no use to him in the house. In his heart he excused her, thinking her too clever for farming, a calling under the ban of Heaven, since one never saw a millionaire in it. Far from having made a fortune by it, the good man was losing every year; for if he was good in bargaining, in which he enjoyed the dodges of the trade, on the other hand, agriculture properly so called, and the internal management of the farm, suited him less than most people. He did not willingly take his hands out of his pockets, and did not spare expense in all that concerned himself, liking to eat well, to have good fires, and to sleep well. He liked old cider, underdone legs of mutton, glorias well beaten up. He took his meals in the kitchen alone, opposite the fire, on a little table brought to him all ready laid as on the stage.

When, therefore, he perceived that Charles's cheeks grew red if near his daughter, which meant that he would propose for her one of these days, he chewed the cud of the matter beforehand. He certainly thought him a little meagre, and not quite the son-in-law he would have liked, but he was said to be well brought-up, economical, very learned, and no doubt would not make too many difficulties about the dowry. Now, as old Rouault would soon be forced to sell twenty-two acres of "his property," as he owed a good deal to the mason, to the harness-maker, and as the shaft of the cider-press wanted renewing:

l'heure. Puis il se demanda ce qu'elle deviendrait, si elle se marierait, et à qui? hélas! le père Rouault était bien riche, et elle!... si belle! Mais la figure d'Emma revenait toujours se placer devant ses yeux, et quelque chose de monotone comme le ronflement d'une toupie bourdonnait à ses oreilles: «Si tu te mariais, pourtant! si tu te mariais!» La nuit, il ne dormit pas, sa gorge était serrée, il avait soif; il se leva pour aller boire à son pot à l'eau et il ouvrit la fenêtre; le ciel était couvert d'étoiles, un vent chaud passait, au loin des chiens aboyaient. Il tourna la tête du côté des Bertaux.

Pensant qu'après tout l'on ne risquait rien, Charles se promit de faire la demande quand l'occasion s'en offrirait; mais, chaque fois qu'elle s'offrit, la peur de ne point trouver les mots convenables lui collait les lèvres.

Le père Rouault n'eût pas été fâché qu'on le débarrassât de sa fille, qui ne lui servait guère dans sa maison. Il l'excusait intérieurement, trouvant qu'elle avait trop d'esprit pour la culture, métier maudit du ciel, puisqu'on n'y voyait jamais de millionnaire. Loin d'y avoir fait fortune, le bonhomme y perdait tous les ans; car, s'il excellait dans les marchés, où il se plaisait aux ruses du métier, en revanche la culture proprement dite, avec le gouvernement intérieur de la ferme, lui convenait moins qu'à personne. Il ne retirait pas volontiers ses mains de dedans ses poches, et n'épargnait point la dépense pour tout ce qui regardait sa vie, voulant être bien nourri, bien chauffé, bien couché. Il aimait le gros cidre, les gigots saignants, les glorias longuement battus. Il prenait ses repas dans la cuisine, seul, en face du feu, sur une petite table qu'on lui apportait toute servie, comme au théâtre.

Lorsqu'il s'aperçut donc que Charles avait les pommettes rouges près de sa fille, ce qui signifiait qu'un de ces jours on la lui demanderait en mariage, il rumina d'avance toute l'affaire. Il le trouvait bien un peu gringalet, et ce n'était pas là un gendre comme il l'eût souhaité; mais on le disait de bonne conduite, économe, fort instruit, et sans doute qu'il ne chicanerait pas trop sur la dot. Or, comme le père Rouault allait être forcé de vendre vingt-deux acres de son bien, qu'il devait beaucoup au maçon, beaucoup au bourrelier, que l'arbre du pressoir était à remettre:

"If he asks for her," he said to himself, "I'll give her to him."

At Michaelmas Charles went to spend three days at the Bertaux. The last had passed like the others in procrastinating from hour to hour. Old Rouault was seeing him off; they were walking along the road full of ruts; they were about to part. This was the time. Charles gave himself as far as to the corner of the hedge, and at last, when past it—

"Monsieur Rouault," he murmured, "I should like to say something to you."

They stopped. Charles was silent.

"Well, tell me your story. Don't I know all about it?" said old Rouault, laughing softly.

"Monsieur Rouault—Monsieur Rouault," stammered Charles.

"I ask nothing better", the farmer went on. "Although, no doubt, the little one is of my mind, still we must ask her opinion. So you get off—I'll go back home. If it is 'yes', you needn't return because of all the people about, and besides it would upset her too much. But so that you mayn't be eating your heart, I'll open wide the outer shutter of the window against the wall; you can see it from the back by leaning over the hedge."

And he went off.

Charles fastened his horse to a tree; he ran into the road and waited. Half an hour passed, then he counted nineteen minutes by his watch. Suddenly a noise was heard against the wall; the shutter had been thrown back; the hook was still swinging.

The next day by nine o'clock he was at the farm. Emma blushed as he entered, and she gave a little forced laugh to keep herself in countenance. Old Rouault embraced his future son-in-law. The discussion of money matters was put off; moreover, there was plenty of time before them, as the marriage could not decently take place till Charles was out of mourning, that is to say, about the spring of the next year.

The winter passed waiting for this. Mademoiselle Rouault was busy with her trousseau. Part of it was ordered at Rouen, and she made herself chemises and nightcaps after fashion-plates that she borrowed.

— S'il me la demande, se dit-il; je la lui donne.

À l'époque de la Saint-Michel, Charles était venu passer trois jours aux Bertaux. La dernière journée s'était écoulée comme les précédentes, à reculer de quart d'heure en quart d'heure. Le père Rouault lui fit la conduite; ils marchaient dans un chemin creux, ils s'allaient quitter; c'était le moment. Charles se donna jusqu'au coin de la haie, et enfin, quand on l'eut dépassée:

— Maître Rouault, murmura-t-il, je voudrais bien vous dire quelque chose.

Ils s'arrêtèrent. Charles se taisait.

— Mais contez-moi votre histoire! est-ce que je ne sais pas tout? dit le père Rouault, en riant doucement.

— Père Rouault…, père Rouault…, balbutia Charles.

— Moi, je ne demande pas mieux, continua le fermier. Quoique sans doute la petite soit de mon idée, il faut pourtant lui demander son avis. Allez-vous-en donc; je m'en vais retourner chez nous. Si c'est oui, entendez-moi bien, vous n'aurez pas besoin de revenir, à cause du monde, et, d'ailleurs, ça la saisirait trop. Mais pour que vous ne vous mangiez pas le sang, je pousserai tout grand l'auvent de la fenêtre contre le mur: vous pourrez le voir par derrière, en vous penchant sur la haie.

Et il s'éloigna.

Charles attacha son cheval à un arbre. Il courut se mettre dans le sentier; il attendit. Une demi-heure se passa, puis il compta dix- neuf minutes à sa montre. Tout à coup un bruit se fit contre le mur; l'auvent s'était rabattu, la cliquette tremblait encore.

Le lendemain, dès neuf heures, il était à la ferme. Emma rougit quand il entra, tout en s'efforçant de rire un peu; par contenance. Le père Rouault embrassa son futur gendre. On remit à causer des arrangements d'intérêt; on avait, d'ailleurs, du temps devant soi, puisque le mariage ne pouvait décemment avoir lieu avant la fin du deuil de Charles, c'est-à-dire vers le printemps de l'année prochaine.

L'hiver se passa dans cette attente. Mademoiselle Rouault s'occupa de son trousseau. Une partie en fut commandée à Rouen, et elle se confectionna des chemises et des bonnets de nuit, d'après des dessins de modes

When Charles visited the farmer, the preparations for the wedding were talked over; they wondered in what room they should have dinner; they dreamed of the number of dishes that would be wanted, and what should be entrees.

Emma would, on the contrary, have preferred to have a midnight wedding with torches, but old Rouault could not understand such an idea. So there was a wedding at which forty-three persons were present, at which they remained sixteen hours at table, began again the next day, and to some extent on the days following.

qu'elle emprunta. Dans les visites que Charles faisait à la ferme, on causait des préparatifs de la noce; on se demandait dans quel appartement se donnerait le dîner; on rêvait à la quantité de plats qu'il faudrait et quelles seraient les entrées.

Emma eût, au contraire, désiré se marier à minuit, aux flambeaux; mais le père Rouault ne comprit rien à cette idée. Il y eut donc une noce, où vinrent quarante-trois personnes, où l'on resta seize heures à table, qui recommença le lendemain et quelque peu les jours suivants.

# Chapter 4

The guests arrived early in carriages, in one-horse chaises, two-wheeled cars, old open gigs, waggonettes with leather hoods, and the young people from the nearer villages in carts, in which they stood up in rows, holding on to the sides so as not to fall, going at a trot and well shaken up. Some came from a distance of thirty miles, from Goderville, from Normanville, and from Cany. All the relatives of both families had been invited, quarrels between friends arranged, acquaintances long since lost sight of written to.

From time to time one heard the crack of a whip behind the hedge; then the gates opened, a chaise entered. Galloping up to the foot of the steps, it stopped short and emptied its load. They got down from all sides, rubbing knees and stretching arms. The ladies, wearing bonnets, had on dresses in the town fashion, gold watch chains, pelerines with the ends tucked into belts, or little coloured fichus fastened down behind with a pin, and that left the back of the neck bare. The lads, dressed like their papas, seemed uncomfortable in their new clothes (many that day hand-sewed their first pair of boots), and by their sides, speaking never a work, wearing the white dress of their first communion lengthened for the occasion were some big girls of fourteen or sixteen, cousins or elder sisters no doubt, rubicund, bewildered, their hair greasy with rose pomade, and very much afraid of dirtying their gloves. As there were not enough stable-boys to unharness all the carriages, the gentlemen turned up their sleeves and set about it themselves. According to their different social positions they wore tail-coats, overcoats, shooting jackets, cutaway-coats; fine tail-coats, redolent of family respectability, that only came out of the wardrobe on state occasions; overcoats with long tails flapping in the wind and round capes and pockets like sacks; shooting jackets

# Chapitre 4

Les conviés arrivèrent de bonne heure dans des voitures, carrioles à un cheval, chars à bancs à deux roues, vieux cabriolets sans capote, tapissières à rideaux de cuir, et les jeunes gens des villages les plus voisins dans des charrettes où ils se tenaient debout, en rang, les mains appuyées sur les ridelles pour ne pas tomber, allant au trot et secoués dur. Il en vint de dix lieues loin, de Goderville, de Normanville, et de Cany. On avait invité tous les parents des deux familles, on s'était raccommodé avec les amis brouillés, on avait écrit à des connaissances perdues de vue depuis longtemps.

De temps à autre, on entendait des coups de fouet derrière la haie; bientôt la barrière s'ouvrait: c'était une carriole qui entrait. Galopant jusqu'à la première marche du perron, elle s'y arrêtait court, et vidait son monde, qui sortait par tous les côtés en se frottant les genoux et en s'étirant les bras. Les dames, en bonnet, avaient des robes à la façon de la ville, des chaînes de montre en or, des pèlerines à bouts croisés dans la ceinture, ou de petits fichus de couleur attachés dans le dos avec une épingle, et qui leur découvraient le cou par derrière. Les gamins, vêtus pareillement à leurs papas, semblaient incommodés par leurs habits neufs (beaucoup même étrennèrent ce jour-là la première paire de bottes de leur existence), et l'on voyait à côté d'eux, ne soufflant mot dans la robe blanche de sa première communion rallongée pour la circonstance, quelque grande fillette de quatorze ou seize ans, leur cousine ou leur soeur aînée sans doute, rougeaude, ahurie, les cheveux gras de pommade à la rose, et ayant bien peur de salir ses gants. Comme il n'y avait point assez de valets d'écurie pour dételer toutes les voitures, les messieurs retroussaient leurs manches et s'y mettaient eux-mêmes. Suivant leur position sociale différente, ils avaient des habits, des redingotes, des vestes, des habits-vestes: — bons habits, entourés de toute la considération d'une famille, et qui ne sortaient de l'armoire que pour les solenni-

of coarse cloth, generally worn with a cap with a brass-bound peak; very short cutaway-coats with two small buttons in the back, close together like a pair of eyes, and the tails of which seemed cut out of one piece by a carpenter's hatchet. Some, too (but these, you may be sure, would sit at the bottom of the table), wore their best blouses—that is to say, with collars turned down to the shoulders, the back gathered into small plaits and the waist fastened very low down with a worked belt.

And the shirts stood out from the chests like cuirasses! Everyone had just had his hair cut; ears stood out from the heads; they had been close-shaved; a few, even, who had had to get up before daybreak, and not been able to see to shave, had diagonal gashes under their noses or cuts the size of a three-franc piece along the jaws, which the fresh air en route had enflamed, so that the great white beaming faces were mottled here and there with red dabs.

The mairie was a mile and a half from the farm, and they went thither on foot, returning in the same way after the ceremony in the church. The procession, first united like one long coloured scarf that undulated across the fields, along the narrow path winding amid the green corn, soon lengthened out, and broke up into different groups that loitered to talk. The fiddler walked in front with his violin, gay with ribbons at its pegs. Then came the married pair, the relations, the friends, all following pell-mell; the children stayed behind amusing themselves plucking the bell-flowers from oat-ears, or playing amongst themselves unseen. Emma's dress, too long, trailed a little on the ground; from time to time she stopped to pull it up, and then delicately, with her gloved hands, she picked off the coarse grass and the thistledowns, while Charles, empty handed, waited till she had finished. Old Rouault, with a new silk hat and the cuffs of his black coat covering his hands up to the nails, gave his arm to Madame Bovary senior. As to Monsieur Bovary senior, who, heartily despising all these folk, had come simply in a frock-coat of military cut with one row of

tés; redingotes à grandes basques flottant au vent, à collet cylindrique, à poches larges comme des sacs; vestes de gros drap, qui accompagnaient ordinairement quelque casquette cerclée de cuivre à sa visière; habits-vestes très courts, ayant dans le dos deux boutons rapprochés comme une paire d'yeux, et dont les pans semblaient avoir été coupés à même un seul bloc, par la hache du charpentier. Quelques-uns encore (mais ceux-là, bien sûr, devaient dîner au bas bout de la table) portaient des blouses de cérémonie, c'est-à-dire dont le col était rabattu sur les épaules, le dos froncé à petits plis et la taille attachée très bas par une ceinture cousue.

Et les chemises sur les poitrines bombaient comme des cuirasses! Tout le monde était tondu à neuf, les oreilles s'écartaient des têtes, on était rasé de près; quelques-uns même qui s'étaient levés dès avant l'aube, n'ayant pas vu clair à se faire la barbe, avaient des balafres en diagonale sous le nez, ou, le long des mâchoires, des pelures d'épiderme larges comme des écus de trois francs, et qu'avait enflammées le grand air pendant la route, ce qui marbrait un peu de plaques roses toutes ces grosses faces blanches épanouies.

La mairie se trouvant à une demi-lieue de la ferme, on s'y rendit à pied, et l'on revint de même, une fois la cérémonie faite à l'église. Le cortège, d'abord uni comme une seule écharpe de couleur, qui ondulait dans la campagne, le long de l'étroit sentier serpentant entre les blés verts, s'allongea bientôt et se coupa en groupes différents, qui s'attardaient à causer. Le ménétrier allait en tête, avec son violon empanaché de rubans à la coquille; les mariés venaient ensuite, les parents, les amis tout au hasard, et les enfants restaient derrière, s'amusant à arracher les clochettes des brins d'avoine, ou à se jouer entre eux, sans qu'on les vît. La robe d'Emma, trop longue, traînait un peu par le bas; de temps à autre, elle s'arrêtait pour la tirer, et alors délicatement, de ses doigts gantés, elle enlevait les herbes rudes avec les petits dards des chardons, pendant que Charles, les mains vides, attendait qu'elle eût fini. Le père Rouault, un chapeau de soie neuf sur la tête et les parements de son habit noir lui couvrant les mains jusqu'aux ongles, donnait le bras à madame Bovary mère. Quant à M. Bovary père, qui, méprisant au fond tout ce monde-là, était venu simplement avec une redingote à un rang de boutons d'une coupe

buttons—he was passing compliments of the bar to a fair young peasant. She bowed, blushed, and did not know what to say. The other wedding guests talked of their business or played tricks behind each other's backs, egging one another on in advance to be jolly. Those who listened could always catch the squeaking of the fiddler, who went on playing across the fields. When he saw that the rest were far behind he stopped to take breath, slowly rosined his bow, so that the strings should sound more shrilly, then set off again, by turns lowering and raising his neck, the better to mark time for himself. The noise of the instrument drove away the little birds from afar.

The table was laid under the cart-shed. On it were four sirloins, six chicken fricassees, stewed veal, three legs of mutton, and in the middle a fine roast suckling pig, flanked by four chitterlings with sorrel. At the corners were decanters of brandy. Sweet bottled-cider frothed round the corks, and all the glasses had been filled to the brim with wine beforehand. Large dishes of yellow cream, that trembled with the least shake of the table, had designed on their smooth surface the initials of the newly wedded pair in nonpareil arabesques. A confectioner of Yvetot had been intrusted with the tarts and sweets. As he had only just set up on the place, he had taken a lot of trouble, and at dessert he himself brought in a set dish that evoked loud cries of wonderment. To begin with, at its base there was a square of blue cardboard, representing a temple with porticoes, colonnades, and stucco statuettes all round, and in the niches constellations of gilt paper stars; then on the second stage was a dungeon of Savoy cake, surrounded by many fortifications in candied angelica, almonds, raisins, and quarters of oranges; and finally, on the upper platform a green field with rocks set in lakes of jam, nutshell boats, and a small Cupid balancing himself in a chocolate swing whose two uprights ended in real roses for balls at the top.

Until night they ate. When any of them were too tired of sitting, they went out for a stroll in the yard, or for a game with corks in the granary, and then returned to table. Some towards the finish went to sleep and

militaire, il débitait des galanteries d'estaminet à une jeune paysanne blonde. Elle saluait, rougissait, ne savait que répondre. Les autres gens de la noce causaient de leurs affaires ou se faisaient des niches dans le dos, s'excitant d'avance à la gaieté; et, en y prêtant l'oreille, on entendait toujours le crin-crin du ménétrier qui continuait à jouer dans la campagne. Quand il s'apercevait qu'on était loin derrière lui, il s'arrêtait à reprendre haleine, cirait longuement de colophane son archet, afin que les cordes grinçassent mieux, et puis il se remettait à marcher, abaissant et levant tour à tour le manche de son violon, pour se bien marquer la mesure à lui-même. Le bruit de l'instrument faisait partir de loin les petits oiseaux.

C'était sous le hangar de la charreterie que la table était dressée. Il y avait dessus quatre aloyaux, six fricassées de poulets, du veau à la casserole, trois gigots, et, au milieu, un joli cochon de lait rôti, flanqué de quatre andouilles à l'oseille. Aux angles, se dressait l'eau de vie dans des carafes. Le cidre doux en bouteilles poussait sa mousse épaisse autour des bouchons, et tous les verres, d'avance, avaient été remplis de vin jusqu'au bord. De grands plats de crème jaune, qui flottaient d'eux-mêmes au moindre choc de la table, présentaient, dessinés sur leur surface unie, les chiffres des nouveaux époux en arabesques de nonpareille. On avait été chercher un pâtissier à Yvetot, pour les tourtes et les nougats. Comme il débutait dans le pays, il avait soigné les choses; et il apporta, lui-même, au dessert, une pièce montée qui fit pousser des cris. À la base, d'abord, c'était un carré de carton bleu figurant un temple avec portiques, colonnades et statuettes de stuc tout autour, dans des niches constellées d'étoiles en papier doré; puis se tenait au second étage un donjon en gâteau de Savoie, entouré de menues fortifications en angélique, amandes, raisins secs, quartiers d'oranges; et enfin, sur la plate-forme supérieure, qui était une prairie verte où il y avait des rochers avec des lacs de confitures et des bateaux en écales de noisettes, on voyait un petit Amour, se balançant à une escarpolette de chocolat, dont les deux poteaux étaient terminés par deux boutons de rose naturels, en guise de boules, au sommet.

Jusqu'au soir, on mangea. Quand on était trop fatigué d'être assis, on allait se promener dans les cours ou jouer une partie de bouchon dans la grange; puis on revenait à table. Quelques-uns, vers la fin, s'y endormirent

snored. But with the coffee everyone woke up. Then they began songs, showed off tricks, raised heavy weights, performed feats with their fingers, then tried lifting carts on their shoulders, made broad jokes, kissed the women. At night when they left, the horses, stuffed up to the nostrils with oats, could hardly be got into the shafts; they kicked, reared, the harness broke, their masters laughed or swore; and all night in the light of the moon along country roads there were runaway carts at full gallop plunging into the ditches, jumping over yard after yard of stones, clambering up the hills, with women leaning out from the tilt to catch hold of the reins.

Those who stayed at the Bertaux spent the night drinking in the kitchen. The children had fallen asleep under the seats.

The bride had begged her father to be spared the usual marriage pleasantries. However, a fishmonger, one of their cousins (who had even brought a pair of soles for his wedding present), began to squirt water from his mouth through the keyhole, when old Rouault came up just in time to stop him, and explain to him that the distinguished position of his son-in-law would not allow of such liberties. The cousin all the same did not give in to these reasons readily. In his heart he accused old Rouault of being proud, and he joined four or five other guests in a corner, who having, through mere chance, been several times running served with the worst helps of meat, also were of opinion they had been badly used, and were whispering about their host, and with covered hints hoping he would ruin himself.

Madame Bovary, senior, had not opened her mouth all day. She had been consulted neither as to the dress of her daughter-in-law nor as to the arrangement of the feast; she went to bed early. Her husband, instead of following her, sent to Saint-Victor for some cigars, and smoked till daybreak, drinking kirsch-punch, a mixture unknown to the company. This added greatly to the consideration in which he was held.

Charles, who was not of a facetious turn, did not shine at the wedding. He answered feebly to the puns, doubles entendres, compliments, and chaff that it was felt a duty to let off at him as soon as the soup appeared.

et ronflèrent. Mais, au café, tout se ranima; alors on entama des chansons, on fit des tours de force, on portait des poids, on passait sous son pouce, on essayait à soulever les charrettes sur ses épaules, on disait des gaudrioles; on embrassait les dames. Le soir, pour partir, les chevaux gorgés d'avoine jusqu'aux naseaux, eurent du mal à entrer dans les brancards; ils ruaient, se cabraient, les harnais se cassaient, leurs maîtres juraient ou riaient; et toute la nuit, au clair de la lune, par les routes du pays, il y eut des carrioles emportées qui couraient au grand galop, bondissant dans les saignées, sautant par-dessus les mètres de cailloux, s'accrochant aux talus, avec des femmes qui se penchaient en dehors de la portière pour saisir les guides.

Ceux qui restèrent aux Bertaux passèrent la nuit à boire dans la cuisine. Les enfants s'étaient endormis sous les bancs.

La mariée avait supplié son père qu'on lui épargnât les plaisanteries d'usage. Cependant, un mareyeur de leurs cousins (qui même avait apporté, comme présent de noces, une paire de soles) commençait à souffler de l'eau avec sa bouche par le trou de la serrure, quand le père Rouault arriva juste à temps pour l'en empêcher, et lui expliqua que la position grave de son gendre ne permettait pas de telles inconvenances. Le cousin, toutefois, céda difficilement à ces raisons. En dedans de lui-même, il accusa le père Rouault d'être fier, et il alla se joindre dans un coin à quatre ou cinq autres des invités qui, ayant eu par hasard plusieurs fois de suite à table les bas morceaux des viandes, trouvaient aussi qu'on les avait mal reçus, chuchotaient sur le compte de leur hôte et souhaitaient sa ruine à mots couverts.

Madame Bovary mère n'avait pas desserré les dents de la journée. On ne l'avait consultée ni sur la toilette de la bru, ni sur l'ordonnance du festin; elle se retira de bonne heure. Son époux, au lieu de la suivre, envoya chercher des cigares à Saint-Victor et fuma jusqu'au jour, tout en buvant des grogs au kirsch, mélange inconnu à la compagnie, et qui fut pour lui comme la source d'une considération plus grande encore.

Charles n'était point de complexion facétieuse, il n'avait pas brillé pendant la noce. Il répondit médiocrement aux pointes, calembours, mots à double entente, compliments et gaillardises que l'on se fit un devoir de lui décocher dès le potage.

The next day, on the other hand, he seemed another man. It was he who might rather have been taken for the virgin of the evening before, whilst the bride gave no sign that revealed anything. The shrewdest did not know what to make of it, and they looked at her when she passed near them with an unbounded concentration of mind. But Charles concealed nothing. He called her "my wife", tutoyed her, asked for her of everyone, looked for her everywhere, and often he dragged her into the yards, where he could be seen from far between the trees, putting his arm around her waist, and walking half-bending over her, ruffling the chemisette of her bodice with his head.

Two days after the wedding the married pair left. Charles, on account of his patients, could not be away longer. Old Rouault had them driven back in his cart, and himself accompanied them as far as Vassonville. Here he embraced his daughter for the last time, got down, and went his way. When he had gone about a hundred paces he stopped, and as he saw the cart disappearing, its wheels turning in the dust, he gave a deep sigh. Then he remembered his wedding, the old times, the first pregnancy of his wife; he, too, had been very happy the day when he had taken her from her father to his home, and had carried her off on a pillion, trotting through the snow, for it was near Christmas-time, and the country was all white. She held him by one arm, her basket hanging from the other; the wind blew the long lace of her Cauchois headdress so that it sometimes flapped across his mouth, and when he turned his head he saw near him, on his shoulder, her little rosy face, smiling silently under the gold bands of her cap. To warm her hands she put them from time to time in his breast. How long ago it all was! Their son would have been thirty by now. Then he looked back and saw nothing on the road. He felt dreary as an empty house; and tender memories mingling with the sad thoughts in his brain, addled by the fumes of the feast, he felt inclined for a moment to take a turn towards the church. As he was afraid, however, that this sight would make him yet more sad, he went right away home.

Le lendemain, en revanche, il semblait un autre homme. C'est lui plutôt que l'on eût pris pour la vierge de la veille, tandis que la mariée ne laissait rien découvrir où l'on pût deviner quelque chose. Les plus malins ne savaient que répondre, et ils la considéraient, quand elle passait près d'eux, avec des tensions d'esprit démesurées. Mais Charles ne dissimulait rien. Il l'appelait ma femme, la tutoyait, s'informait d'elle à chacun, la cherchait partout, et souvent il l'entraînait dans les cours, où on l'apercevait de loin, entre les arbres, qui lui passait le bras sous la taille et continuait à marcher à demi penché sur elle, en lui chiffonnant avec sa tête la guimpe de son corsage.

Deux jours après la noce, les époux s'en allèrent: Charles, à cause de ses malades, ne pouvait s'absenter plus longtemps. Le père Rouault les fit reconduire dans sa carriole et les accompagna lui-même jusqu'à Vassonville. Là, il embrassa sa fille une dernière fois, mit pied à terre et reprit sa route. Lorsqu'il eut fait cent pas environ, il s'arrêta, et, comme il vit la carriole s'éloignant, dont les roues tournaient dans la poussière, il poussa un gros soupir. Puis il se rappela ses noces, son temps d'autrefois, la première grossesse de sa femme; il était bien joyeux, lui aussi, le jour qu'il l'avait emmenée de chez son père dans sa maison, quand il la portait en croupe en trottant sur la neige; car on était aux environs de Noël et la campagne était toute blanche; elle le tenait par un bras, à l'autre était accroché son panier; le vent agitait les longues dentelles de sa coiffure cauchoise, qui lui passaient quelquefois sur la bouche, et, lorsqu'il tournait la tête, il voyait près de lui, sur son épaule, sa petite mine rosée qui souriait silencieusement, sous la plaque d'or de son bonnet. Pour se réchauffer les doigts, elle les lui mettait, de temps en temps, dans la poitrine. Comme c'était vieux tout cela! Leur fils, à présent, aurait trente ans! Alors il regarda derrière lui, il n'aperçut rien sur la route. Il se sentit triste comme une maison démeublée; et, les souvenirs tendres se mêlant aux pensées noires dans sa cervelle obscurcie par les vapeurs de la bombance, il eut bien envie un moment d'aller faire un tour du côté de l'église. Comme il eut peur, cependant, que cette vue ne le rendît plus triste encore, il s'en revint tout droit chez lui.

Monsieur and Madame Charles arrived at Tostes about six o'clock. The neighbors came to the windows to see their doctor's new wife.

The old servant presented herself, curtsied to her, apologised for not having dinner ready, and suggested that madame, in the meantime, should look over her house.

M. et madame Charles arrivèrent à Tostes, vers six heures. Les voisins se mirent aux fenêtres pour voir la nouvelle femme de leur médecin.

La vieille bonne se présenta, lui fit ses salutations, s'excusa de ce que le dîner n'était pas prêt, et engagea Madame, en attendant, à prendre connaissance de sa maison.

# Chapter 5

The brick front was just in a line with the street, or rather the road. Behind the door hung a cloak with a small collar, a bridle, and a black leather cap, and on the floor, in a corner, were a pair of leggings, still covered with dry mud. On the right was the one apartment, that was both dining and sitting room. A canary yellow paper, relieved at the top by a garland of pale flowers, was puckered everywhere over the badly stretched canvas; white calico curtains with a red border hung crossways at the length of the window; and on the narrow mantelpiece a clock with a head of Hippocrates shone resplendent between two plate candlesticks under oval shades. On the other side of the passage was Charles's consulting room, a little room about six paces wide, with a table, three chairs, and an office chair. Volumes of the "Dictionary of Medical Science," uncut, but the binding rather the worse for the successive sales through which they had gone, occupied almost along the six shelves of a deal bookcase. The smell of melted butter penetrated through the walls when he saw patients, just as in the kitchen one could hear the people coughing in the consulting room and recounting their histories. Then, opening on the yard, where the stable was, came a large dilapidated room with a stove, now used as a wood-house, cellar, and pantry, full of old rubbish, of empty casks, agricultural implements past service, and a mass of dusty things whose use it was impossible to guess.

The garden, longer than wide, ran between two mud walls with espaliered apricots, to a hawthorn hedge that separated it from the field. In the middle was a slate sundial on a brick pedestal; four flower beds with eglantines surrounded symmetrically the more useful kitchen garden bed. Right at the bottom, under the spruce bushes, was a cure in plaster reading his breviary.

# Chapitre 5

La façade de briques était juste à l'alignement de la rue, ou de la route plutôt. Derrière la porte se trouvaient accrochés un manteau à petit collet, une bride, une casquette de cuir noir, et, dans un coin, à terre, une paire de houseaux encore couverts de boue sèche. À droite était la salle, c'est-à-dire l'appartement où l'on mangeait et où l'on se tenait. Un papier jaune-serin, relevé dans le haut par une guirlande de fleurs pâles, tremblait tout entier sur sa toile mal tendue; des rideaux de calicot blanc, bordés d'un galon rouge, s'entrecroisaient le long des fenêtres, et sur l'étroit chambranle de la cheminée resplendissait une pendule à tête d'Hippocrate, entre deux flambeaux d'argent plaqué, sous des globes de forme ovale. De l'autre côté du corridor était le cabinet de Charles, petite pièce de six pas de large environ, avec une table, trois chaises et un fauteuil de bureau. Les tomes du Dictionnaire des sciences médicales, non coupés, mais dont la brochure avait souffert dans toutes les ventes successives par où ils avaient passé, garnissaient presque à eux seuls, les six rayons d'une bibliothèque en bois de sapin. L'odeur des roux pénétrait à travers la muraille, pendant les consultations, de même que l'on entendait de la cuisine, les malades tousser dans le cabinet et débiter toute leur histoire. Venait ensuite, s'ouvrant immédiatement sur la cour, où se trouvait l'écurie, une grande pièce délabrée qui avait un four, et qui servait maintenant de bûcher, de cellier, de garde-magasin, pleine de vieilles ferrailles, de tonneaux vides, d'instruments de culture hors de service, avec quantité d'autres choses poussiéreuses dont il était impossible de deviner l'usage.

Le jardin, plus long que large, allait, entre deux murs de bauge couverts d'abricots en espalier, jusqu'à une haie d'épines qui le séparait des champs. Il y avait au milieu un cadran solaire en ardoise, sur un piédestal de maçonnerie; quatre plates-bandes garnies d'églantiers maigres entouraient symétriquement le carré plus utile des végétations sérieuses. Tout au fond, sous les sapinettes, un curé de plâtre lisait son bréviaire.

Emma went upstairs. The first room was not furnished, but in the second, which was their bedroom, was a mahogany bedstead in an alcove with red drapery. A shell box adorned the chest of drawers, and on the secretary near the window a bouquet of orange blossoms tied with white satin ribbons stood in a bottle. It was a bride's bouquet; it was the other one's. She looked at it. Charles noticed it; he took it and carried it up to the attic, while Emma seated in an arm-chair (they were putting her things down around her) thought of her bridal flowers packed up in a bandbox, and wondered, dreaming, what would be done with them if she were to die.

During the first days she occupied herself in thinking about changes in the house. She took the shades off the candlesticks, had new wallpaper put up, the staircase repainted, and seats made in the garden round the sundial; she even inquired how she could get a basin with a jet fountain and fishes. Finally her husband, knowing that she liked to drive out, picked up a second-hand dogcart, which, with new lamps and splashboard in striped leather, looked almost like a tilbury.

He was happy then, and without a care in the world. A meal together, a walk in the evening on the highroad, a gesture of her hands over her hair, the sight of her straw hat hanging from the window-fastener, and many another thing in which Charles had never dreamed of pleasure, now made up the endless round of his happiness. In bed, in the morning, by her side, on the pillow, he watched the sunlight sinking into the down on her fair cheek, half hidden by the lappets of her night-cap. Seen thus closely, her eyes looked to him enlarged, especially when, on waking up, she opened and shut them rapidly many times. Black in the shade, dark blue in broad daylight, they had, as it were, depths of different colours, that, darker in the centre, grew paler towards the surface of the eye. His own eyes lost themselves in these depths; he saw himself in miniature down to the shoulders, with his handkerchief round his head and the top of his shirt open. He rose. She came to the window to see him off, and stayed leaning on the sill between two pots of geranium, clad in her dressing gown hanging loosely about

Emma monta dans les chambres. La première n'était point meublée; mais la seconde, qui était la chambre conjugale, avait un lit d'acajou dans une alcôve à draperie rouge. Une boîte en coquillages décorait la commode; et, sur le secrétaire, près de la fenêtre, il y avait, dans une carafe, un bouquet de fleurs d'oranger, noué par des rubans de satin blanc. C'était un bouquet de mariée, le bouquet de l'autre! Elle le regarda. Charles s'en aperçut, il le prit et l'alla porter au grenier, tandis qu'assise dans un fauteuil (on disposait ses affaires autour d'elle), Emma songeait à son bouquet de mariage, qui était emballé dans un carton, et se demandait, en rêvant, ce qu'on en ferait; si par hasard elle venait à mourir.

Elle s'occupa, les premiers jours, à méditer des changements dans sa maison. Elle retira les globes des flambeaux, fit coller des papiers neufs, repeindre l'escalier et faire des bancs dans le jardin, tout autour du cadran solaire; elle demanda même comment s'y prendre pour avoir un bassin à jet d'eau avec des poissons. Enfin son mari, sachant qu'elle aimait à se promener en voiture, trouva un boc d'occasion, qui, ayant une fois des lanternes neuves et des gardes-crotte en cuir piqué, ressembla presque à un tilbury.

Il était donc heureux et sans souci de rien au monde. Un repas en tête-à-tête, une promenade le soir sur la grande route, un geste de sa main sur ses bandeaux, la vue de son chapeau de paille accroché à l'espagnolette d'une fenêtre, et bien d'autres choses encore où Charles n'avait jamais soupçonné de plaisir, composaient maintenant la continuité de son bonheur. Au lit, le matin, et côte à côté sur l'oreiller, il regardait la lumière du soleil passer parmi le duvet de ses joues blondes, que couvraient à demi les pattes escalopées de son bonnet. Vus de si près, ses yeux lui paraissaient agrandis, surtout quand elle ouvrait plusieurs fois de suite ses paupières en s'éveillant; noirs à l'ombre et bleu foncé au grand jour, ils avaient comme des couches de couleurs successives, et qui plus épaisses dans le fond, allaient en s'éclaircissant vers la surface de l'émail. Son oeil, à lui, se perdait dans ces profondeurs, et il s'y voyait en petit jusqu'aux épaules, avec le foulard qui le coiffait et le haut de sa chemise entrouvert. Il se levait. Elle se mettait à la fenêtre pour le voir partir; et elle restait accoudée sur le bord, entre deux pots de géraniums,

her. Charles, in the street buckled his spurs, his foot on the mounting stone, while she talked to him from above, picking with her mouth some scrap of flower or leaf that she blew out at him. Then this, eddying, floating, described semicircles in the air like a bird, and was caught before it reached the ground in the ill-groomed mane of the old white mare standing motionless at the door. Charles from horseback threw her a kiss; she answered with a nod; she shut the window, and he set off. And then along the highroad, spreading out its long ribbon of dust, along the deep lanes that the trees bent over as in arbours, along paths where the corn reached to the knees, with the sun on his back and the morning air in his nostrils, his heart full of the joys of the past night, his mind at rest, his flesh at ease, he went on, re-chewing his happiness, like those who after dinner taste again the truffles which they are digesting.

Until now what good had he had of his life? His time at school, when he remained shut up within the high walls, alone, in the midst of companions richer than he or cleverer at their work, who laughed at his accent, who jeered at his clothes, and whose mothers came to the school with cakes in their muffs? Later on, when he studied medicine, and never had his purse full enough to treat some little work-girl who would have become his mistress? Afterwards, he had lived fourteen months with the widow, whose feet in bed were cold as icicles. But now he had for life this beautiful woman whom he adored. For him the universe did not extend beyond the circumference of her petticoat, and he reproached himself with not loving her. He wanted to see her again; he turned back quickly, ran up the stairs with a beating heart. Emma, in her room, was dressing; he came up on tiptoe, kissed her back; she gave a cry.

He could not keep from constantly touching her comb, her ring, her fichu; sometimes he gave her great sounding kisses with all his mouth on her cheeks, or else little kisses in a row all along her bare arm from the tip of her fingers up to her shoulder, and she put him away half-smiling, half-vexed, as you do a child who hangs about you.

vêtue de son peignoir, qui était lâche autour d'elle. Charles, dans la rue, bouclait ses éperons sur la borne; et elle continuait à lui parler d'en haut, tout en arrachant avec sa bouche quelque bribe de fleur ou de verdure qu'elle soufflait vers lui, et qui voltigeant, se soutenant, faisant dans l'air des demi-cercles comme un oiseau, allait, avant de tomber, s'accrocher aux crins mal peignés de la vieille jument blanche, immobile à la porte. Charles, à cheval, lui envoyait un baiser; elle répondait par un signe, elle refermait la fenêtre, il partait. Et alors, sur la grande route qui étendait sans en finir son long ruban de poussière, par les chemins creux où les arbres se courbaient en berceaux, dans les sentiers dont les blés lui montaient jusqu'aux genoux, avec le soleil sur ses épaules et l'air du matin à ses narines, le coeur plein des félicités de la nuit, l'esprit tranquille, la chair contente, il s'en allait ruminant son bonheur, comme ceux qui mâchent encore, après dîner, le goût des truffes qu'ils digèrent.

Jusqu'à présent, qu'avait-il eu de bon dans l'existence? Était-ce son temps de collège, où il restait enfermé entre ces hauts murs, seul au milieu de ses camarades plus riches ou plus forts que lui dans leurs classes, qu'il faisait rire par son accent, qui se moquaient de ses habits, et dont les mères venaient au parloir avec des pâtisseries dans leur manchon? Était-ce plus tard, lorsqu'il étudiait la médecine et n'avait jamais la bourse assez ronde pour payer la contredanse à quelque petite ouvrière qui fût devenue sa maîtresse? Ensuite il avait vécu pendant quatorze mois avec la veuve, dont les pieds, dans le lit, étaient froids comme des glaçons. Mais, à présent, il possédait pour la vie cette jolie femme qu'il adorait. L'univers, pour lui, n'excédait pas le tour soyeux de son jupon; et il se reprochait de ne pas l'aimer, il avait envie de la revoir; il s'en revenait vite, montait l'escalier; le coeur battant. Emma, dans sa chambre, était à faire sa toilette; il arrivait à pas muets, il la baisait dans le dos, elle poussait un cri.

Il ne pouvait se retenir de toucher continuellement à son peigne, à ses bagues, à son fichu; quelquefois, il lui donnait sur les joues de gros baisers à pleine bouche, ou c'étaient de petits baisers à la file tout le long de son bras nu, depuis le bout des doigts jusqu'à l'épaule; et elle le repoussait, à demi souriante et ennuyée, comme on fait à un enfant qui se pend après vous.

Before marriage she thought herself in love; but the happiness that should have followed this love not having come, she must, she thought, have been mistaken. And Emma tried to find out what one meant exactly in life by the words felicity, passion, rapture, that had seemed to her so beautiful in books.

Avant qu'elle se mariât, elle avait cru avoir de l'amour; mais le bonheur qui aurait dû résulter de cet amour n'étant pas venu, il fallait qu'elle se fût trompée, songeait-elle. Et Emma cherchait à savoir ce que l'on entendait au juste dans la vie par les mots de félicité, de passion et d'ivresse, qui lui avaient paru si beaux dans les livres.

# Chapter 6

She had read "Paul and Virginia," and she had dreamed of the little bamboo-house, the nigger Domingo, the dog Fidele, but above all of the sweet friendship of some dear little brother, who seeks red fruit for you on trees taller than steeples, or who runs barefoot over the sand, bringing you a bird's nest.

When she was thirteen, her father himself took her to town to place her in the convent. They stopped at an inn in the St. Gervais quarter, where, at their supper, they used painted plates that set forth the story of Mademoiselle de la Valliere. The explanatory legends, chipped here and there by the scratching of knives, all glorified religion, the tendernesses of the heart, and the pomps of court.

Far from being bored at first at the convent, she took pleasure in the society of the good sisters, who, to amuse her, took her to the chapel, which one entered from the refectory by a long corridor. She played very little during recreation hours, knew her catechism well, and it was she who always answered Monsieur le Vicaire's difficult questions. Living thus, without ever leaving the warm atmosphere of the classrooms, and amid these pale-faced women wearing rosaries with brass crosses, she was softly lulled by the mystic languor exhaled in the perfumes of the altar, the freshness of the holy water, and the lights of the tapers. Instead of attending to mass, she looked at the pious vignettes with their azure borders in her book, and she loved the sick lamb, the sacred heart pierced with sharp arrows, or the poor Jesus sinking beneath the cross he carries. She tried, by way of mortification, to eat nothing a whole day. She puzzled her head to find some vow to fulfil.

When she went to confession, she invented little sins in order that she might stay there longer, kneeling in the shadow, her hands joined, her face against the grating beneath the whispering of the priest. The comparisons of betrothed, husband, celestial lover, and eternal mar-

# Chapitre 6

Elle avait lu Paul et Virginie et elle avait rêvé la maisonnette de bambous, le nègre Domingo, le chien Fidèle, mais surtout l'amitié douce de quelque bon petit frère, qui va chercher pour vous des fruits rouges dans des grands arbres plus hauts que des clochers, ou qui court pieds nus sur le sable, vous apportant un nid d'oiseau.

Lorsqu'elle eut treize ans, son père l'amena lui-même à la ville, pour la mettre au couvent. Ils descendirent dans une auberge du quartier Saint-Gervais, où ils eurent à leur souper des assiettes peintes qui représentaient l'histoire de mademoiselle de la Vallière. Les explications légendaires, coupées çà et là par l'égratignure des couteaux, glorifiaient toutes la religion, les délicatesses du coeur et les pompes de la Cour.

Loin de s'ennuyer au couvent les premiers temps, elle se plut dans la société des bonnes soeurs, qui, pour l'amuser, la conduisaient dans la chapelle, où l'on pénétrait du réfectoire par un long corridor. Elle jouait fort peu durant les récréations, comprenait bien le catéchisme, et c'est elle qui répondait toujours à M. le vicaire dans les questions difficiles. Vivant donc sans jamais sortir de la tiède atmosphère des classes et parmi ces femmes au teint blanc portant des chapelets à croix de cuivre, elle s'assoupit doucement à la langueur mystique qui s'exhale des parfums de l'autel, de la fraîcheur des bénitiers et du rayonnement des cierges. Au lieu de suivre la messe, elle regardait dans son livre les vignettes pieuses bordées d'azur, et elle aimait la brebis malade, le Sacré-Coeur percé de flèches aiguës, ou le pauvre Jésus, qui tombe en marchant sur sa croix. Elle essaya, par mortification, de rester tout un jour sans manger. Elle cherchait dans sa tête quelque voeu à accomplir.

Quand elle allait à confesse, elle inventait de petits péchés afin de rester là plus longtemps, à genoux dans l'ombre, les mains jointes, le visage à la grille sous le chuchotement du prêtre. Les comparaisons de fiancé, d'époux, d'amant céleste et de mariage éternel qui reviennent

riage, that recur in sermons, stirred within her soul depths of unexpected sweetness.

In the evening, before prayers, there was some religious reading in the study. On week-nights it was some abstract of sacred history or the Lectures of the Abbe Frayssinous, and on Sundays passages from the "Genie du Christianisme," as a recreation. How she listened at first to the sonorous lamentations of its romantic melancholies reechoing through the world and eternity! If her childhood had been spent in the shop-parlour of some business quarter, she might perhaps have opened her heart to those lyrical invasions of Nature, which usually come to us only through translation in books. But she knew the country too well; she knew the lowing of cattle, the milking, the ploughs. Accustomed to calm aspects of life, she turned, on the contrary, to those of excitement. She loved the sea only for the sake of its storms, and the green fields only when broken up by ruins. She wanted to get some personal profit out of things, and she rejected as useless all that did not contribute to the immediate desires of her heart, being of a temperament more sentimental than artistic, looking for emotions, not landscapes.

At the convent there was an old maid who came for a week each month to mend the linen. Patronized by the clergy, because she belonged to an ancient family of noblemen ruined by the Revolution, she dined in the refectory at the table of the good sisters, and after the meal had a bit of chat with them before going back to her work. The girls often slipped out from the study to go and see her. She knew by heart the love songs of the last century, and sang them in a low voice as she stitched away. She told stories, gave them news, went errands in the town, and on the sly lent the big girls some novel, that she always carried in the pockets of her apron, and of which the good lady herself swallowed long chapters in the intervals of her work. They were all love, lovers, sweethearts, persecuted ladies fainting in lonely pavilions, postilions killed at every stage, horses ridden to death on every page, sombre forests, heartaches, vows, sobs, tears and kisses, little skiffs by moonlight, nightingales

dans les sermons lui soulevaient au fond de l'âme des douceurs inattendues.

Le soir, avant la prière, on faisait dans l'étude une lecture religieuse. C'était, pendant la semaine, quelque résumé d'Histoire sainte ou les Conférences de l'abbé Frayssinous, et, le dimanche, des passages du Génie du christianisme, par récréation. Comme elle écouta, les premières fois, la lamentation sonore des mélancolies romantiques se répétant à tous les échos de la terre et de l'éternité! Si son enfance se fût écoulée dans l'arrière-boutique d'un quartier marchand, elle se serait peut-être ouverte alors aux envahissements lyriques de la nature, qui, d'ordinaire, ne nous arrivent que par la traduction des écrivains. Mais elle connaissait trop la campagne; elle savait le bêlement des troupeaux, les laitages, les charrues. Habituée aux aspects calmes, elle se tournait, au contraire, vers les accidentés. Elle n'aimait la mer qu'à cause de ses tempêtes, et la verdure seulement lorsqu'elle était clairsemée parmi les ruines. Il fallait qu'elle pût retirer des choses une sorte de profit personnel; et elle rejetait comme inutile tout ce qui ne contribuait pas à la consommation immédiate de son coeur, — étant de tempérament plus sentimentale qu'artiste, cherchant des émotions et non des paysages.

Il y avait au couvent une vieille fille qui venait tous les mois, pendant huit jours, travailler à la lingerie. Protégée par l'archevêché comme appartenant à une ancienne famille de gentilshommes ruinés sous la Révolution, elle mangeait au réfectoire à la table des bonnes soeurs, et faisait avec elles, après le repas, un petit bout de causette avant de remonter à son ouvrage. Souvent les pensionnaires s'échappaient de l'étude pour l'aller voir. Elle savait par coeur des chansons galantes du siècle passé, qu'elle chantait à demi-voix, tout en poussant son aiguille. Elle contait des histoires, vous apprenait des nouvelles, faisait en ville vos commissions, et prêtait aux grandes, en cachette, quelque roman qu'elle avait toujours dans les poches de son tablier, et dont la bonne demoiselle elle-même avalait de longs chapitres, dans les intervalles de sa besogne. Ce n'étaient qu'amours, amants, amantes, dames persécutées s'évanouissant dans des pavillons solitaires, postillons qu'on tue à tous les relais, chevaux qu'on crève à toutes les pages, forêts sombres, troubles du coeur, serments, sanglots, larmes et

in shady groves, "gentlemen" brave as lions, gentle as lambs, virtuous as no one ever was, always well dressed, and weeping like fountains. For six months, then, Emma, at fifteen years of age, made her hands dirty with books from old lending libraries. Through Walter Scott, later on, she fell in love with historical events, dreamed of old chests, guard-rooms and minstrels. She would have liked to live in some old manor-house, like those long-waisted chatelaines who, in the shade of pointed arches, spent their days leaning on the stone, chin in hand, watching a cavalier with white plume galloping on his black horse from the distant fields. At this time she had a cult for Mary Stuart and enthusiastic veneration for illustrious or unhappy women. Joan of Arc, Heloise, Agnes Sorel, the beautiful Ferroniere, and Clemence Isaure stood out to her like comets in the dark immensity of heaven, where also were seen, lost in shadow, and all unconnected, St. Louis with his oak, the dying Bayard, some cruelties of Louis XI, a little of St. Bartholomew's Day, the plume of the Bearnais, and always the remembrance of the plates painted in honour of Louis XIV.

In the music class, in the ballads she sang, there was nothing but little angels with golden wings, madonnas, lagunes, gondoliers;-mild compositions that allowed her to catch a glimpse athwart the obscurity of style and the weakness of the music of the attractive phantasmagoria of sentimental realities. Some of her companions brought "keepsakes" given them as new year's gifts to the convent. These had to be hidden; it was quite an undertaking; they were read in the dormitory. Delicately handling the beautiful satin bindings, Emma looked with dazzled eyes at the names of the unknown authors, who had signed their verses for the most part as counts or viscounts.

She trembled as she blew back the tissue paper over the engraving and saw it folded in two and fall gently against the page. Here behind the balustrade of a balcony was a young man in a short cloak, holding in his arms a young girl in a white dress wearing an alms-bag at her belt; or there were nameless portraits of English ladies with fair curls, who looked at you from under their round straw hats with their

baisers, nacelles au clair de lune, rossignols dans les bosquets, messieurs braves comme des lions, doux comme des agneaux, vertueux comme on ne l'est pas, toujours bien mis, et qui pleurent comme des urnes. Pendant six mois, à quinze ans, Emma se graissa donc les mains à cette poussière des vieux cabinets de lecture. Avec Walter Scott, plus tard, elle s'éprit de choses historiques, rêva bahuts, salle des gardes et ménestrels. Elle aurait voulu vivre dans quelque vieux manoir, comme ces châtelaines au long corsage, qui, sous le trèfle des ogives, passaient leurs jours, le coude sur la pierre et le menton dans la main, à regarder venir du fond de la campagne un cavalier à plume blanche qui galope sur un cheval noir. Elle eut dans ce temps-là le culte de Marie Stuart, et des vénérations enthousiastes à l'endroit des femmes illustres ou infortunées. Jeanne d'Arc, Héloïse, Agnès Sorel, la belle Ferronnière et Clémence Isaure, pour elle, se détachaient comme des comètes sur l'immensité ténébreuse de l'histoire, où saillissaient encore çà et là, mais plus perdus dans l'ombre et sans aucun rapport entre eux, saint Louis avec son chêne, Bayard mourant, quelques férocités de Louis XI, un peu de Saint-Barthélemy, le panache du Béarnais, et toujours le souvenir des assiettes peintes où Louis XIV était vanté.

À la classe de musique, dans les romances qu'elle chantait, il n'était question que de petits anges aux ailes d'or, de madones, de lagunes, de gondoliers, pacifiques compositions qui lui laissaient entrevoir, à travers la niaiserie du style et les imprudences de la note, l'attirante fantasmagorie des réalités sentimentales. Quelques-unes de ses camarades apportaient au couvent les keepsakes qu'elles avaient reçus en étrennes. Il les fallait cacher, c'était une affaire; on les lisait au dortoir. Maniant délicatement leurs belles reliures de satin, Emma fixait ses regards éblouis sur le nom des auteurs inconnus qui avaient signé, le plus souvent, comtes ou vicomtes, au bas de leurs pièces.

Elle frémissait, en soulevant de son haleine le papier de soie des gravures, qui se levait à demi plié et retombait doucement contre la page. C'était, derrière la balustrade d'un balcon, un jeune homme en court manteau qui serrait dans ses bras une jeune fille en robe blanche, portant une aumônière à sa ceinture; ou bien les portraits anonymes des ladies anglaises à boucles blondes, qui, sous leur chapeau de paille rond, vous

large clear eyes. Some there were lounging in their carriages, gliding through parks, a greyhound bounding along in front of the equipage driven at a trot by two midget postilions in white breeches. Others, dreaming on sofas with an open letter, gazed at the moon through a slightly open window half draped by a black curtain. The naive ones, a tear on their cheeks, were kissing doves through the bars of a Gothic cage, or, smiling, their heads on one side, were plucking the leaves of a marguerite with their taper fingers, that curved at the tips like peaked shoes. And you, too, were there, Sultans with long pipes reclining beneath arbours in the arms of Bayaderes; Djiaours, Turkish sabres, Greek caps; and you especially, pale landscapes of dithyrambic lands, that often show us at once palm trees and firs, tigers on the right, a lion to the left, Tartar minarets on the horizon; the whole framed by a very neat virgin forest, and with a great perpendicular sunbeam trembling in the water, where, standing out in relief like white excoriations on a steel-grey ground, swans are swimming about.

And the shade of the argand lamp fastened to the wall above Emma's head lighted up all these pictures of the world, that passed before her one by one in the silence of the dormitory, and to the distant noise of some belated carriage rolling over the Boulevards.

When her mother died she cried much the first few days. She had a funeral picture made with the hair of the deceased, and, in a letter sent to the Bertaux full of sad reflections on life, she asked to be buried later on in the same grave. The goodman thought she must be ill, and came to see her. Emma was secretly pleased that she had reached at a first attempt the rare ideal of pale lives, never attained by mediocre hearts. She let herself glide along with Lamartine meanderings, listened to harps on lakes, to all the songs of dying swans, to the falling of the leaves, the pure virgins ascending to heaven, and the voice of the Eternal discoursing down the valleys. She wearied of it, would not confess it, continued from habit, and at last was surprised to feel herself soothed, and with no more sadness at heart than wrinkles on her brow.

regardent avec leurs grands yeux clairs. On en voyait d'étalées dans des voitures, glissant au milieu des parcs, où un lévrier sautait devant l'attelage que conduisaient au trot deux petits postillons en culotte blanche. D'autres, rêvant sur des sofas près d'un billet décacheté, contemplaient la lune, par la fenêtre entrouverte, à demi drapée d'un rideau noir. Les naïves, une larme sur la joue, becquetaient une tourterelle à travers les barreaux d'une cage gothique, ou, souriant la tête sur l'épaule, effeuillaient une marguerite de leurs doigts pointus, retroussés comme des souliers à la poulaine. Et vous y étiez aussi, sultans à longues pipes, pâmés sous des tonnelles, aux bras des bayadères, djiaours, sabres turcs, bonnets grecs, et vous surtout, paysages blafards des contrées dithyrambiques, qui souvent nous montrez à la fois des palmiers, des sapins, des tigres à droite, un lion à gauche, des minarets tartares à l'horizon, au premier plan des ruines romaines, puis des chameaux accroupis; — le tout encadré d'une forêt vierge bien nettoyée, et avec un grand rayon de soleil perpendiculaire tremblotant dans l'eau, où se détachent en écorchures blanches, sur un fond d'acier gris, de loin en loin, des cygnes qui nagent.

Et l'abat-jour du quinquet, accroché dans la muraille au-dessus de la tête d'Emma, éclairait tous ces tableaux du monde, qui passaient devant elle les uns après les autres, dans le silence du dortoir et au bruit lointain de quelque fiacre attardé qui roulait encore sur les boulevards.

Quand sa mère mourut, elle pleura beaucoup les premiers jours. Elle se fit faire un tableau funèbre avec les cheveux de la défunte, et, dans une lettre qu'elle envoyait aux Bertaux, toute pleine de réflexions tristes sur la vie, elle demandait qu'on l'ensevelît plus tard dans le même tombeau. Le bonhomme la crut malade et vint la voir. Emma fut intérieurement satisfaite de se sentir arrivée du premier coup à ce rare idéal des existences pâles, où ne parviennent jamais les coeurs médiocres. Elle se laissa donc glisser dans les méandres lamartiniens, écouta les harpes sur les lacs, tous les chants de cygnes mourants, toutes les chutes de feuilles, les vierges pures qui montent au ciel, et la voix de l'Éternel discourant dans les vallons. Elle s'en ennuya, n'en voulut point convenir, continua par habitude, ensuite par vanité, et fut enfin surprise de se sentir apaisée, et sans plus de tristesse au coeur que de rides sur son front.

The good nuns, who had been so sure of her vocation, perceived with great astonishment that Mademoiselle Rouault seemed to be slipping from them. They had indeed been so lavish to her of prayers, retreats, novenas, and sermons, they had so often preached the respect due to saints and martyrs, and given so much good advice as to the modesty of the body and the salvation of her soul, that she did as tightly reined horses; she pulled up short and the bit slipped from her teeth. This nature, positive in the midst of its enthusiasms, that had loved the church for the sake of the flowers, and music for the words of the songs, and literature for its passional stimulus, rebelled against the mysteries of faith as it grew irritated by discipline, a thing antipathetic to her constitution. When her father took her from school, no one was sorry to see her go. The Lady Superior even thought that she had latterly been somewhat irreverent to the community.

Emma, at home once more, first took pleasure in looking after the servants, then grew disgusted with the country and missed her convent. When Charles came to the Bertaux for the first time, she thought herself quite disillusioned, with nothing more to learn, and nothing more to feel.

But the uneasiness of her new position, or perhaps the disturbance caused by the presence of this man, had sufficed to make her believe that she at last felt that wondrous passion which, till then, like a great bird with rose-coloured wings, hung in the splendour of the skies of poesy; and now she could not think that the calm in which she lived was the happiness she had dreamed.

Les bonnes religieuses, qui avaient si bien présumé de sa vocation, s'aperçurent avec de grands étonnements que mademoiselle Rouault semblait échapper à leur soin. Elles lui avaient, en effet, tant prodigué les offices, les retraites, les neuvaines et les sermons, si bien prêché le respect que l'on doit aux saints et aux martyrs, et donné tant de bons conseils pour la modestie du corps et le salut de son âme, qu'elle fit comme les chevaux que l'on tire par la bride: elle s'arrêta court et le mors lui sortit des dents. Cet esprit, positif au milieu de ses enthousiasmes, qui avait aimé l'église pour ses fleurs, la musique pour les paroles des romances, et la littérature pour ses excitations passionnelles, s'insurgeait devant les mystères de la foi, de même qu'elle s'irritait davantage contre la discipline, qui était quelque chose d'antipathique à sa constitution. Quand son père la retira de pension, on ne fut point fâché de la voir partir. La supérieure trouvait même qu'elle était devenue, dans les derniers temps, peu révérencieuse envers la communauté.

Emma, rentrée chez elle, se plut d'abord au commandement des domestiques, prit ensuite la campagne en dégoût et regretta son couvent. Quand Charles vint aux Bertaux pour la première fois, elle se considérait comme fort désillusionnée, n'ayant plus rien à apprendre, ne devant plus rien sentir.

Mais l'anxiété d'un état nouveau, ou peut-être l'irritation causée par la présence de cet homme, avait suffi à lui faire croire qu'elle possédait enfin cette passion merveilleuse qui jusqu'alors s'était tenue comme un grand oiseau au plumage rose planant dans la splendeur des ciels poétiques; — et elle ne pouvait s'imaginer à présent que ce calme où elle vivait fût le bonheur qu'elle avait rêvé.

# Chapter 7

She thought, sometimes, that, after all, this was the happiest time of her life—the honeymoon, as people called it. To taste the full sweetness of it, it would have been necessary doubtless to fly to those lands with sonorous names where the days after marriage are full of laziness most suave. In post chaises behind blue silken curtains to ride slowly up steep road, listening to the song of the postilion re-echoed by the mountains, along with the bells of goats and the muffled sound of a waterfall; at sunset on the shores of gulfs to breathe in the perfume of lemon trees; then in the evening on the villa-terraces above, hand in hand to look at the stars, making plans for the future. It seemed to her that certain places on earth must bring happiness, as a plant peculiar to the soil, and that cannot thrive elsewhere. Why could not she lean over balconies in Swiss chalets, or enshrine her melancholy in a Scotch cottage, with a husband dressed in a black velvet coat with long tails, and thin shoes, a pointed hat and frills?

Perhaps she would have liked to confide all these things to someone. But how tell an undefinable uneasiness, variable as the clouds, unstable as the winds? Words failed her—the opportunity, the courage.

If Charles had but wished it, if he had guessed it, if his look had but once met her thought, it seemed to her that a sudden plenty would have gone out from her heart, as the fruit falls from a tree when shaken by a hand. But as the intimacy of their life became deeper, the greater became the gulf that separated her from him.

Charles's conversation was commonplace as a street pavement, and everyone's ideas trooped through it in their everyday garb, without exciting emotion, laughter, or thought. He had never had the curiosity, he said, while he lived at Rouen, to go to the theatre to see the actors

# Chapitre 7

Elle songeait quelquefois que c'étaient là pourtant les plus beaux jours de sa vie, la lune de miel, comme on disait. Pour en goûter la douceur, il eût fallu, sans doute, s'en aller vers ces pays à noms sonores où les lendemains de mariage ont de plus suaves paresses! Dans des chaises de poste, sous des stores de soie bleue, on monte au pas des routes escarpées, écoutant la chanson du postillon, qui se répète dans la montagne avec les clochettes des chèvres et le bruit sourd de la cascade. Quand le soleil se couche, on respire au bord des golfes le parfum des citronniers; puis, le soir, sur la terrasse des villas, seuls et les doigts confondus, on regarde les étoiles en faisant des projets. Il lui semblait que certains lieux sur la terre devaient produire du bonheur, comme une plante particulière au sol et qui pousse mal tout autre part. Que ne pouvait-elle s'accouder sur le balcon des chalets suisses ou enfermer sa tristesse dans un cottage écossais, avec un mari vêtu d'un habit de velours noir à longues basques, et qui porte des bottes molles, un chapeau pointu et des manchettes!

Peut-être aurait-elle souhaité faire à quelqu'un la confidence de toutes ces choses. Mais comment dire un insaisissable malaise, qui change d'aspect comme les nuées, qui tourbillonne comme le vent? Les mots lui manquaient donc, l'occasion, la hardiesse.

Si Charles l'avait voulu cependant, s'il s'en fût douté, si son regard, une seule fois, fût venu à la rencontre de sa pensée, il lui semblait qu'une abondance subite se serait détachée de son coeur, comme tombe la récolte d'un espalier quand on y porte la main. Mais, à mesure que se serrait davantage l'intimité de leur vie; un détachement intérieur se faisait qui la déliait de lui.

La conversation de Charles était plate comme un trottoir de rue, et les idées de tout le monde y défilaient dans leur costume ordinaire, sans exciter d'émotion, de rire ou de rêverie. Il n'avait jamais été curieux, disait-il, pendant qu'il habitait Rouen, d'aller voir au théâtre les acteurs

from Paris. He could neither swim, nor fence, nor shoot, and one day he could not explain some term of horsemanship to her that she had come across in a novel.

A man, on the contrary, should he not know everything, excel in manifold activities, initiate you into the energies of passion, the refinements of life, all mysteries? But this one taught nothing, knew nothing, wished nothing. He thought her happy; and she resented this easy calm, this serene heaviness, the very happiness she gave him.

Sometimes she would draw; and it was great amusement to Charles to stand there bolt upright and watch her bend over her cardboard, with eyes half-closed the better to see her work, or rolling, between her fingers, little bread-pellets. As to the piano, the more quickly her fingers glided over it the more he wondered. She struck the notes with aplomb, and ran from top to bottom of the keyboard without a break. Thus shaken up, the old instrument, whose strings buzzed, could be heard at the other end of the village when the window was open, and often the bailiff's clerk, passing along the highroad bare-headed and in list slippers, stopped to listen, his sheet of paper in his hand.

Emma, on the other hand, knew how to look after her house. She sent the patients' accounts in well-phrased letters that had no suggestion of a bill. When they had a neighbour to dinner on Sundays, she managed to have some tasty dish—piled up pyramids of greengages on vine leaves, served up preserves turned out into plates—and even spoke of buying finger-glasses for dessert. From all this much consideration was extended to Bovary.

Charles finished by rising in his own esteem for possessing such a wife. He showed with pride in the sitting room two small pencil sketches by her that he had had framed in very large frames, and hung up against the wallpaper by long green cords. People returning from mass saw him at his door in his wool-work slippers.

He came home late—at ten o'clock, at midnight sometimes. Then he asked for something to eat, and as the servant had gone to bed, Emma

de Paris. Il ne savait ni nager, ni faire des armes, ni tirer le pistolet, et il ne put, un jour, lui expliquer un terme d'équitation qu'elle avait rencontré dans un roman.

Un homme, au contraire, ne devait-il pas, tout connaître, exceller en des activités multiples, vous initier aux énergies de la passion, aux raffinements de la vie, à tous les mystères? Mais il n'enseignait rien, celui-là, ne savait rien, ne souhaitait rien. Il la croyait heureuse; et elle lui en voulait de ce calme si bien assis, de cette pesanteur sereine, du bonheur même qu'elle lui donnait.

Elle dessinait quelquefois; et c'était pour Charles un grand amusement que de rester là, tout debout à la regarder penchée sur son carton, clignant des yeux afin de mieux voir son ouvrage, ou arrondissant, sur son pouce, des boulettes de mie de pain. Quant au piano, plus les doigts y couraient vite, plus il s'émerveillait. Elle frappait sur les touches avec aplomb, et parcourait du haut en bas tout le clavier sans s'interrompre. Ainsi secoué par elle, le vieil instrument, dont les cordes frisaient, s'entendait jusqu'au bout du village si la fenêtre était ouverte, et souvent le clerc de l'huissier qui passait sur la grande route, nu-tête et en chaussons, s'arrêtait à l'écouter, sa feuille de papier à la main.

Emma, d'autre part; savait conduire sa maison. Elle envoyait aux malades le compte des visites, dans des lettres bien tournées, qui ne sentaient pas la facture. Quand ils avaient, le dimanche, quelque voisin à dîner, elle trouvait moyen d'offrir un plat coquet, s'entendait à poser sur des feuilles de vigne les pyramides de reines-claudes, servait renversés les pots de confitures dans une assiette, et même elle parlait d'acheter des rince-bouche pour le dessert. Il rejaillissait de tout cela beaucoup de considération sur Bovary.

Charles finissait par s'estimer davantage de ce qu'il possédait une pareille femme. Il montrait avec orgueil, dans la salle, deux petits croquis d'elle, à la mine de plomb, qu'il avait fait encadrer de cadres très larges et suspendus contre le papier de la muraille à de longs cordons verts. Au sortir de la messe, on le voyait sur sa porte avec de belles pantoufles en tapisserie.

Il rentrait tard, à dix heures, minuit quelquefois. Alors il demandait à manger, et, comme la bonne était couchée, c'était Emma qui le

waited on him. He took off his coat to dine more at his ease. He told her, one after the other, the people he had met, the villages where he had been, the prescriptions he had written, and, well pleased with himself, he finished the remainder of the boiled beef and onions, picked pieces off the cheese, munched an apple, emptied his water-bottle, and then went to bed, and lay on his back and snored.

As he had been for a time accustomed to wear nightcaps, his handkerchief would not keep down over his ears, so that his hair in the morning was all tumbled pell-mell about his face and whitened with the feathers of the pillow, whose strings came untied during the night. He always wore thick boots that had two long creases over the instep running obliquely towards the ankle, while the rest of the upper continued in a straight line as if stretched on a wooden foot. He said that "was quite good enough for the country."

His mother approved of his economy, for she came to see him as formerly when there had been some violent row at her place; and yet Madame Bovary senior seemed prejudiced against her daughter-in-law. She thought "her ways too fine for their position"; the wood, the sugar, and the candles disappeared as "at a grand establishment," and the amount of firing in the kitchen would have been enough for twenty-five courses. She put her linen in order for her in the presses, and taught her to keep an eye on the butcher when he brought the meat. Emma put up with these lessons. Madame Bovary was lavish of them; and the words "daughter" and "mother" were exchanged all day long, accompanied by little quiverings of the lips, each one uttering gentle words in a voice trembling with anger.

In Madame Dubuc's time the old woman felt that she was still the favorite; but now the love of Charles for Emma seemed to her a desertion from her tenderness, an encroachment upon what was hers, and she watched her son's happiness in sad silence, as a ruined man looks through the windows at people dining in his old house. She recalled to him as remembrances her troubles and her sacrifices, and, comparing these with Emma's negligence, came to the conclusion that it was not reasonable to adore her so exclusively.

servait. Il retirait sa redingote pour dîner plus à son aise. Il disait les uns après les autres tous les gens qu'il avait rencontrés, les villages où il avait été, les ordonnances qu'il avait écrites, et satisfait de lui-même, il mangeait le reste du miroton, épluchait son fromage, croquait une pomme, vidait sa carafe, puis s'allait mettre au lit, se couchait sur le dos et ronflait.

Comme il avait eu longtemps l'habitude du bonnet de coton, son foulard ne lui tenait pas aux oreilles; aussi ses cheveux, le matin, étaient rabattus pêle-mêle sur sa figure et blanchis par le duvet de son oreiller, dont les cordons se dénouaient pendant la nuit. Il portait toujours de fortes bottes, qui avaient au cou-de- pied deux plis épais obliquant vers les chevilles, tandis que le reste de l'empeigne se continuait en ligne droite, tendu comme par un pied de bois. Il disait que c'était bien assez bon pour la campagne.

Sa mère l'approuvait en cette économie; car elle le venait voir comme autrefois, lorsqu'il y avait eu chez elle quelque bourrasque un peu violente; et cependant madame Bovary mère semblait prévenue contre sa bru. Elle lui trouvait un genre trop relevé pour leur position de fortune; le bois, le sucre et la chandelle filaient comme dans une grande maison, et la quantité de braise qui se brûlait à la cuisine aurait suffi pour vingt-cinq plats! Elle rangeait son linge dans les armoires et lui apprenait à surveiller le boucher quand il apportait la viande. Emma recevait ces leçons; madame Bovary les prodiguait; et les mots de ma fille et de ma mère s'échangeaient tout le long du jour, accompagnés d'un petit frémissement des lèvres, chacune lançant des paroles douces d'une voix tremblante de colère.

Du temps de madame Dubuc, la vieille femme se sentait encore la préférée; mais, à présent, l'amour de Charles pour Emma lui semblait une désertion de sa tendresse, un envahissement sur ce qui lui appartenait; et elle observait le bonheur de son fils avec un silence triste, comme quelqu'un de ruiné qui regarde, à travers les carreaux, des gens attablés dans son ancienne maison. Elle lui rappelait, en manière de souvenirs, ses peines et ses sacrifices, et, les comparant aux négligences d'Emma, concluait qu'il n'était point raisonnable de l'adorer d'une façon si exclusive.

Charles knew not what to answer: he respected his mother, and he loved his wife infinitely; he considered the judgment of the one infallible, and yet he thought the conduct of the other irreproachable. When Madam Bovary had gone, he tried timidly and in the same terms to hazard one or two of the more anodyne observations he had heard from his mamma. Emma proved to him with a word that he was mistaken, and sent him off to his patients.

And yet, in accord with theories she believed right, she wanted to make herself in love with him. By moonlight in the garden she recited all the passionate rhymes she knew by heart, and, sighing, sang to him many melancholy adagios; but she found herself as calm after as before, and Charles seemed no more amorous and no more moved.

When she had thus for a while struck the flint on her heart without getting a spark, incapable, moreover, of understanding what she did not experience as of believing anything that did not present itself in conventional forms, she persuaded herself without difficulty that Charles's passion was nothing very exorbitant. His outbursts became regular; he embraced her at certain fixed times. It was one habit among other habits, and, like a dessert, looked forward to after the monotony of dinner.

A gamekeeper, cured by the doctor of inflammation of the lungs, had given madame a little Italian greyhound; she took her out walking, for she went out sometimes in order to be alone for a moment, and not to see before her eyes the eternal garden and the dusty road.

She went as far as the beeches of Banneville, near the deserted pavilion which forms an angle of the wall on the side of the country. Amidst the vegetation of the ditch there are long reeds with leaves that cut you.

She began by looking round her to see if nothing had changed since last she had been there. She found again in the same places the foxgloves and wallflowers, the beds of nettles growing round the big stones, and the patches of lichen along the three windows, whose shutters, always closed, were rotting away on their rusty iron bars. Her thoughts, aimless at first, wandered at random, like her greyhound,

Charles ne savait que répondre; il respectait sa mère, et il aimait infiniment sa femme; il considérait le jugement de l'une comme infaillible, et cependant il trouvait l'autre irréprochable. Quand madame Bovary était partie, il essayait de hasarder timidement, et dans les mêmes termes, une ou deux des plus anodines observations qu'il avait entendu faire à sa maman; Emma, lui prouvant d'un mot qu'il se trompait, le renvoyait à ses malades.

Cependant, d'après des théories qu'elle croyait bonnes, elle voulut se donner de l'amour. Au clair de lune, dans le jardin, elle récitait tout ce qu'elle savait par coeur de rimes passionnées et lui chantait en soupirant des adagios mélancoliques; mais elle se trouvait ensuite aussi calme qu'auparavant, et Charles n'en paraissait ni plus amoureux ni plus remué.

Quand elle eut ainsi un peu battu le briquet sur son coeur sans en faire jaillir une étincelle, incapable, du reste, de comprendre ce qu'elle n'éprouvait pas, comme de croire à tout ce qui ne se manifestait point par des formes convenues, elle se persuada sans peine que la passion de Charles n'avait plus rien d'exorbitant. Ses expansions étaient devenues régulières; il l'embrassait à de certaines heures. C'était une habitude parmi les autres, et comme un dessert prévu d'avance, après la monotonie du dîner.

Un garde-chasse, guéri par Monsieur, d'une fluxion de poitrine, avait donné à Madame une petite levrette d'Italie; elle la prenait pour se promener, car elle sortait quelquefois, afin d'être seule un instant et de n'avoir plus sous les yeux l'éternel jardin avec la route poudreuse.

Elle allait jusqu'à la hêtraie de Banneville, près du pavillon abandonné qui fait l'angle du mur, du côté des champs. Il y a dans le saut-de-loup, parmi les herbes, de longs roseaux à feuilles coupantes.

Elle commençait par regarder tout alentour, pour voir si rien n'avait changé depuis la dernière fois qu'elle était venue. Elle retrouvait aux mêmes places les digitales et les ravenelles, les bouquets d'orties entourant les gros cailloux, et les plaques de lichen le long des trois fenêtres, dont les volets toujours clos s'égrenaient de pourriture, sur leurs barres de fer rouillées. Sa pensée, sans but d'abord, vagabondait au hasard,

who ran round and round in the fields, yelping after the yellow butterflies, chasing the shrew-mice, or nibbling the poppies on the edge of a cornfield. Then gradually her ideas took definite shape, and, sitting on the grass that she dug up with little prods of her sunshade, Emma repeated to herself:

"Good heavens! Why did I marry?"

She asked herself if by some other chance combination it would have not been possible to meet another man; and she tried to imagine what would have been these unrealised events, this different life, this unknown husband. All, surely, could not be like this one. He might have been handsome, witty, distinguished, attractive, such as, no doubt, her old companions of the convent had married. What were they doing now? In town, with the noise of the streets, the buzz of the theatres and the lights of the ballroom, they were living lives where the heart expands, the senses bourgeon out. But she—her life was cold as a garret whose dormer window looks on the north, and ennui, the silent spider, was weaving its web in the darkness in every corner of her heart. She recalled the prize days, when she mounted the platform to receive her little crowns, with her hair in long plaits. In her white frock and open prunella shoes she had a pretty way, and when she went back to her seat, the gentlemen bent over her to congratulate her; the courtyard was full of carriages; farewells were called to her through their windows; the music master with his violin case bowed in passing by. How far all of this! How far away!

She called Djali, took her between her knees, and smoothed the long delicate head, saying:

"Come, kiss mistress; you have no troubles."

Then noting the melancholy face of the graceful animal, who yawned slowly, she softened, and comparing her to herself, spoke to her aloud as to somebody in trouble whom one is consoling.

Occasionally there came gusts of winds, breezes from the sea rolling in one sweep over the whole plateau of the Caux country, which brought even to these fields a salt freshness. The rushes, close to the ground, whistled; the branches trembled in a swift rustling, while their

comme sa levrette, qui faisait des cercles dans la campagne, jappait après les papillons jaunes, donnait la chasse aux musaraignes; ou mordillait les coquelicots sur le bord d'une pièce de blé. Puis ses idées peu à peu se fixaient, et, assise sur le gazon, qu'elle fouillait à petits coups avec le bout de son ombrelle, Emma se répétait:

— Pourquoi, mon Dieu! me suis-je mariée?

Elle se demandait s'il n'y aurait pas eu moyen, par d'autres combinaisons du hasard, de rencontrer un autre homme; et elle cherchait à imaginer quels eussent été ces événements non survenus, cette vie différente, ce mari qu'elle ne connaissait pas. Tous, en effet, ne ressemblaient pas à celui-là. Il aurait pu être beau, spirituel, distingué, attirant, tels qu'ils étaient sans doute, ceux qu'avaient épousés ses anciennes camarades du couvent. Que faisaient-elles maintenant? À la ville, avec le bruit des rues, le bourdonnement des théâtres et les clartés du bal, elles avaient des existences où le coeur se dilate, où les sens s'épanouissent. Mais elle, sa vie était froide comme un grenier dont la lucarne est au nord, et l'ennui, araignée silencieuse, filait sa toile dans l'ombre à tous les coins de son coeur. Elle se rappelait les jours de distribution de prix, où elle montait sur l'estrade pour aller chercher ses petites couronnes. Avec ses cheveux en tresse, sa robe blanche et ses souliers de prunelle découverts, elle avait une façon gentille, et les messieurs, quand elle regagnait sa place, se penchaient pour lui faire des compliments; la cour était pleine de calèches, on lui disait adieu par les portières, le maître de musique passait en saluant, avec sa boîte à violon. Comme c'était loin, tout cela! comme c'était loin!

Elle appelait Djali, la prenait entre ses genoux, passait ses doigts sur sa longue tête fine et lui disait:

— Allons, baisez maîtresse, vous qui n'avez pas de chagrins.

Puis, considérant la mine mélancolique du svelte animal qui bâillait avec lenteur, elle s'attendrissait, et, le comparant à elle-même, lui parlait tout haut, comme à quelqu'un d'affligé que l'on console.

Il arrivait parfois des rafales de vent, brises de la mer qui, roulant d'un bond sur tout le plateau du pays de Caux, apportaient, jusqu'au loin dans les champs, une fraîcheur salée. Les joncs sifflaient à ras de terre, et les feuilles des hêtres bruissaient en un frisson rapide, tandis que les

summits, ceaselessly swaying, kept up a deep murmur. Emma drew her shawl round her shoulders and rose.

In the avenue a green light dimmed by the leaves lit up the short moss that crackled softly beneath her feet. The sun was setting; the sky showed red between the branches, and the trunks of the trees, uniform, and planted in a straight line, seemed a brown colonnade standing out against a background of gold. A fear took hold of her; she called Djali, and hurriedly returned to Tostes by the high road, threw herself into an armchair, and for the rest of the evening did not speak.

But towards the end of September something extraordinary fell upon her life; she was invited by the Marquis d'Andervilliers to Vaubyessard.

Secretary of State under the Restoration, the Marquis, anxious to re-enter political life, set about preparing for his candidature to the Chamber of Deputies long beforehand. In the winter he distributed a great deal of wood, and in the Conseil General always enthusiastically demanded new roads for his arrondissement. During the dog-days he had suffered from an abscess, which Charles had cured as if by miracle by giving a timely little touch with the lancet. The steward sent to Tostes to pay for the operation reported in the evening that he had seen some superb cherries in the doctor's little garden. Now cherry trees did not thrive at Vaubyessard; the Marquis asked Bovary for some slips; made it his business to thank his personally; saw Emma; thought she had a pretty figure, and that she did not bow like a peasant; so that he did not think he was going beyond the bounds of condescension, nor, on the other hand, making a mistake, in inviting the young couple.

On Wednesday at three o'clock, Monsieur and Madame Bovary, seated in their dog-cart, set out for Vaubyessard, with a great trunk strapped on behind and a bonnet-box in front of the apron. Besides these Charles held a bandbox between his knees.

They arrived at nightfall, just as the lamps in the park were being lit to show the way for the carriages.

cimes, se balançant toujours, continuaient leur grand murmure. Emma serrait son châle contre ses épaules et se levait.

Dans l'avenue, un jour vert rabattu par le feuillage éclairait la mousse rase qui craquait doucement sous ses pieds. Le soleil se couchait; le ciel était rouge entre les branches, et les troncs pareils des arbres plantés en ligne droite semblaient une colonnade brune se détachant sur un fond d'or; une peur la prenait, elle appelait Djali, s'en retournait vite à Tostes par la grande route, s'affaissait dans un fauteuil, et de toute la soirée ne parlait pas.

Mais, vers la fin de septembre, quelque chose d'extraordinaire tomba dans sa vie: elle fut invitée à la Vaubyessard, chez le marquis d'Andervilliers.

Secrétaire d'État sous la Restauration, le Marquis, cherchant à rentrer dans la vie politique, préparait de longue main sa candidature à la Chambre des députés. Il faisait, l'hiver, de nombreuses distributions de fagots, et, au Conseil général, réclamait avec exaltation toujours des routes pour son arrondissement. Il avait eu, lors des grandes chaleurs, un abcès dans la bouche, dont Charles l'avait soulagé comme par miracle, en y donnant à point un coup de lancette. L'homme d'affaires, envoyé à Tostes pour payer l'opération, conta, le soir, qu'il avait vu dans le jardinet du médecin des cerises superbes. Or, les cerisiers poussaient mal à la Vaubyessard, M. le Marquis demanda quelques boutures à Bovary, se fit un devoir de l'en remercier lui-même, aperçut Emma, trouva qu'elle avait une jolie taille et qu'elle ne saluait point en paysanne; si bien qu'on ne crut pas au château outrepasser les bornes de la condescendance, ni d'autre part commettre une maladresse, en invitant le jeune ménage.

Un mercredi, à trois heures, M. et madame Bovary, montés dans leur boc, partirent pour la Vaubyessard, avec une grande malle attachée par derrière et une boîte à chapeau qui était posée devant le tablier. Charles avait, de plus, un carton entre les jambes.

Ils arrivèrent à la nuit tombante, comme on commençait à allumer des lampions dans le parc, afin d'éclairer les voitures.

# Chapter 8

The chateau, a modern building in Italian style, with two projecting wings and three flights of steps, lay at the foot of an immense green-sward, on which some cows were grazing among groups of large trees set out at regular intervals, while large beds of arbutus, rhododendron, syringas, and guelder roses bulged out their irregular clusters of green along the curve of the gravel path. A river flowed under a bridge; through the mist one could distinguish buildings with thatched roofs scattered over the field bordered by two gently sloping, well timbered hillocks, and in the background amid the trees rose in two parallel lines the coach houses and stables, all that was left of the ruined old chateau.

Charles's dog-cart pulled up before the middle flight of steps; servants appeared; the Marquis came forward, and, offering his arm to the doctor's wife, conducted her to the vestibule.

It was paved with marble slabs, was very lofty, and the sound of footsteps and that of voices re-echoed through it as in a church. Opposite rose a straight staircase, and on the left a gallery overlooking the garden led to the billiard room, through whose door one could hear the click of the ivory balls. As she crossed it to go to the drawing room, Emma saw standing round the table men with grave faces, their chins resting on high cravats. They all wore orders, and smiled silently as they made their strokes. On the dark wainscoting of the walls large gold frames bore at the bottom names written in black letters. She read: "Jean-Antoine d'Andervilliers d'Yvervonbille, Count de la Vaubyessard and Baron de la Fresnay, killed at the battle of Coutras on the 20th of October, 1587." And on another: "Jean-Antoine-Henry-Guy d'Andervilliers de la Vaubyessard, Admiral of France and Chevalier of the Order of St. Michael, wounded at the battle of the Hougue-Saint-Vaast on the 29th of May, 1692; died at Vaubyessard on the 23rd of January 1693." One could

# Chapitre 8

Le château, de construction moderne, à l'Italienne, avec deux ailes avançant et trois perrons, se déployait au bas d'une immense pelouse où paissaient quelques vaches, entre des bouquets de grands arbres espacés, tandis que des bannettes d'arbustes, rhododendrons, seringas et boules-de-neige bombaient leurs touffes de verdure inégales sur la ligne courbe du chemin sablé. Une rivière passait sous un pont; à travers la brume, on distinguait des bâtiments à toit de chaume, éparpillés dans la prairie, que bordaient en pente douce deux coteaux couverts de bois, et par derrière, dans les massifs, se tenaient, sur deux lignes parallèles, les remises et les écuries, restes conservés de l'ancien château démoli.

Le boc de Charles s'arrêta devant le perron du milieu; des domestiques parurent; le Marquis s'avança, et, offrant son bras à la femme du médecin, l'introduisit dans le vestibule.

Il était pavé de dalles en marbre, très haut, et le bruit des pas, avec celui des voix, y retentissait comme dans une église. En face montait un escalier droit, et à gauche une galerie donnant sur le jardin conduisait à la salle de billard dont on entendait, dès la porte, caramboler les boules d'ivoire. Comme elle la traversait pour aller au salon, Emma vit autour du jeu des hommes à figure grave, le menton posé sur de hautes cravates, décorés tous, et qui souriaient silencieusement, en poussant leur queue. Sur la boiserie sombre du lambris, de grands cadres dorés portaient, au bas de leur bordure, des noms écrits en lettres noires. Elle lut: «Jean-Antoine d'Andervilliers d'Yverbonville, comte de la Vaubyessard et baron de la Fresnaye, tué à la bataille de Coutras, le 20 octobre 1587.» Et sur un autre: «Jean-Antoine-Henry-Guy d'Andervilliers de la Vaubyessard, amiral de France et chevalier de l'ordre de Saint-Michel, blessé au combat de la Hougue-Saint- Vaast, le 29 mai 1692, mort à la Vaubyessard le 23 janvier 1693.» Puis on distinguait à peine ceux qui

hardly make out those that followed, for the light of the lamps lowered over the green cloth threw a dim shadow round the room. Burnishing the horizontal pictures, it broke up against these in delicate lines where there were cracks in the varnish, and from all these great black squares framed in with gold stood out here and there some lighter portion of the painting—a pale brow, two eyes that looked at you, perukes flowing over and powdering red-coated shoulders, or the buckle of a garter above a well-rounded calf.

The Marquis opened the drawing room door; one of the ladies (the Marchioness herself) came to meet Emma. She made her sit down by her on an ottoman, and began talking to her as amicably as if she had known her a long time. She was a woman of about forty, with fine shoulders, a hook nose, a drawling voice, and on this evening she wore over her brown hair a simple guipure fichu that fell in a point at the back. A fair young woman sat in a high-backed chair in a corner; and gentlemen with flowers in their buttonholes were talking to ladies round the fire.

At seven dinner was served. The men, who were in the majority, sat down at the first table in the vestibule; the ladies at the second in the dining room with the Marquis and Marchioness.

Emma, on entering, felt herself wrapped round by the warm air, a blending of the perfume of flowers and of the fine linen, of the fumes of the viands, and the odour of the truffles. The silver dish covers reflected the lighted wax candles in the candelabra, the cut crystal covered with light steam reflected from one to the other pale rays; bouquets were placed in a row the whole length of the table; and in the large-bordered plates each napkin, arranged after the fashion of a bishop's mitre, held between its two gaping folds a small oval shaped roll. The red claws of lobsters hung over the dishes; rich fruit in open baskets was piled up on moss; there were quails in their plumage; smoke was rising; and in silk stockings, knee-breeches, white cravat, and frilled shirt, the steward, grave as a judge, offering ready carved dishes between the shoulders of the guests, with a touch of the spoon gave you the piece chosen. On the large stove of porcelain inlaid with copper baguettes

suivaient, car la lumière des lampes, rabattue sur le tapis vert du billard, laissait flotter une ombre dans l'appartement. Brunissant les toiles horizontales, elle se brisait contre elles en arêtes fines, selon les craquelures du vernis; et de tous ces grands carrés noirs bordés d'or sortaient, çà et là, quelque portion plus claire de la peinture, un front pâle, deux yeux qui vous regardaient, des perruques se déroulant sur l'épaule poudrée des habits rouges, ou bien la boucle d'une jarretière au haut d'un mollet rebondi.

Le Marquis ouvrit la porte du salon; une des dames se leva (la Marquise elle-même), vint à la rencontre d'Emma et la fit asseoir près d'elle, sur une causeuse, où elle se mit à lui parler amicalement, comme si elle la connaissait depuis longtemps. C'était une femme de la quarantaine environ, à belles épaules, à nez busqué, à la voix traînante, et portant, ce soir-là, sur ses cheveux châtains, un simple fichu de guipure qui retombait par derrière, en triangle. Une jeune personne blonde se tenait à côté, dans une chaise à dossier long; et des messieurs, qui avaient une petite fleur à la boutonnière de leur habit, causaient avec les dames, tout autour de la cheminée.

À sept heures, on servit le dîner. Les hommes, plus nombreux, s'assirent à la première table, dans le vestibule, et les dames à la seconde, dans la salle à manger, avec le Marquis et la Marquise.

Emma se sentit, en entrant, enveloppée par un air chaud, mélange du parfum des fleurs et du beau linge, du fumet des viandes et de l'odeur des truffes. Les bougies des candélabres allongeaient des flammes sur les cloches d'argent; les cristaux à facettes, couverts d'une buée mate, se renvoyaient des rayons pâles; des bouquets étaient en ligne sur toute la longueur de la table, et, dans les assiettes à large bordure, les serviettes, arrangées en manière de bonnet d'évêque, tenaient entre le bâillement de leurs deux plis chacune un petit pain de forme ovale. Les pattes rouges des homards dépassaient les plats; de gros fruits dans des corbeilles à jour s'étageaient sur la mousse; les cailles avaient leurs plumes, des fumées montaient; et, en bas de soie, en culotte courte, en cravate blanche, en jabot, grave comme un juge, le maître d'hôtel, passant entre les épaules des convives les plats tout découpés, faisait d'un coup de sa cuiller sauter pour vous le morceau qu'on choisissait. Sur le grand poêle

the statue of a woman, draped to the chin, gazed motionless on the room full of life.

Madame Bovary noticed that many ladies had not put their gloves in their glasses.

But at the upper end of the table, alone amongst all these women, bent over his full plate, and his napkin tied round his neck like a child, an old man sat eating, letting drops of gravy drip from his mouth. His eyes were bloodshot, and he wore a little queue tied with black ribbon. He was the Marquis's father-in-law, the old Duke de Laverdiere, once on a time favourite of the Count d'Artois, in the days of the Vaudreuil hunting-parties at the Marquis de Conflans', and had been, it was said, the lover of Queen Marie Antoinette, between Monsieur de Coigny and Monsieur de Lauzun. He had lived a life of noisy debauch, full of duels, bets, elopements; he had squandered his fortune and frightened all his family. A servant behind his chair named aloud to him in his ear the dishes that he pointed to stammering, and constantly Emma's eyes turned involuntarily to this old man with hanging lips, as to something extraordinary. He had lived at court and slept in the bed of queens!

Iced champagne was poured out. Emma shivered all over as she felt it cold in her mouth. She had never seen pomegranates nor tasted pineapples. The powdered sugar even seemed to her whiter and finer than elsewhere.

The ladies afterwards went to their rooms to prepare for the ball.

Emma made her toilet with the fastidious care of an actress on her debut. She did her hair according to the directions of the hairdresser, and put on the barege dress spread out upon the bed. Charles's trousers were tight across the belly.

"My trouser-straps will be rather awkward for dancing," he said.

"Dancing?" repeated Emma.

"Yes!"

"Why, you must be mad! They would make fun of you; keep your place. Besides, it is more becoming for a doctor," she added.

de porcelaine à baguette de cuivre, une statue de femme drapée jusqu'au menton regardait immobile la salle pleine de monde.

Madame Bovary remarqua que plusieurs dames n'avaient pas mis leurs gants dans leur verre.

Cependant, au haut bout de la table, seul parmi toutes ces femmes, courbé sur son assiette remplie, et la serviette nouée dans le dos comme un enfant, un vieillard mangeait, laissant tomber de sa bouche des gouttes de sauce. Il avait les yeux éraillés et portait une petite queue enroulée d'un ruban noir. C'était le beau-père du marquis, le vieux duc de Laverdière, l'ancien favori du comte d'Artois, dans le temps des parties de chasse au Vaudreuil, chez le marquis de Conflans, et qui avait été, disait-on, l'amant de la reine Marie-Antoinette entre MM. de Coigny et de Lauzun. Il avait mené une vie bruyante de débauches, pleine de duels, de paris, de femmes enlevées, avait dévoré sa fortune et effrayé toute sa famille. Un domestique, derrière sa chaise, lui nommait tout haut, dans l'oreille, les plats qu'il désignait du doigt en bégayant; et sans cesse les yeux d'Emma revenaient d'eux-mêmes sur ce vieil homme à lèvres pendantes comme sur quelque chose d'extraordinaire et d'auguste. Il avait vécu à la Cour et couché dans le lit des reines!

On versa du vin de Champagne à la glace. Emma frissonna de toute sa peau en sentant ce froid dans sa bouche. Elle n'avait jamais vu de grenades ni mangé d'ananas. Le sucre en poudre même lui parut plus blanc et plus fin qu'ailleurs.

Les dames, ensuite, montèrent dans leurs chambres s'apprêter pour le bal.

Emma fit sa toilette avec la conscience méticuleuse d'une actrice à son début. Elle disposa ses cheveux d'après les recommandations du coiffeur, et elle entra dans sa robe de barège, étalée sur le lit. Le pantalon de Charles le serrait au ventre.

— Les sous-pieds vont me gêner pour danser, dit-il.

— Danser? reprit Emma.

— Oui!

— Mais tu as perdu la tête! on se moquerait de toi, reste à ta place. D'ailleurs, c'est plus convenable pour un médecin, ajouta- t-elle.

Charles was silent. He walked up and down waiting for Emma to finish dressing.

He saw her from behind in the glass between two lights. Her black eyes seemed blacker than ever. Her hair, undulating towards the ears, shone with a blue lustre; a rose in her chignon trembled on its mobile stalk, with artificial dewdrops on the tip of the leaves. She wore a gown of pale saffron trimmed with three bouquets of pompon roses mixed with green.

Charles came and kissed her on her shoulder.

"Let me alone!" she said; "you are tumbling me."

One could hear the flourish of the violin and the notes of a horn. She went downstairs restraining herself from running.

Dancing had begun. Guests were arriving. There was some crushing. She sat down on a form near the door.

The quadrille over, the floor was occupied by groups of men standing up and talking and servants in livery bearing large trays. Along the line of seated women painted fans were fluttering, bouquets half hid smiling faces, and gold stoppered scent-bottles were turned in partly-closed hands, whose white gloves outlined the nails and tightened on the flesh at the wrists. Lace trimmings, diamond brooches, medallion bracelets trembled on bodices, gleamed on breasts, clinked on bare arms. The hair, well-smoothed over the temples and knotted at the nape, bore crowns, or bunches, or sprays of mytosotis, jasmine, pomegranate blossoms, ears of corn, and corn-flowers. Calmly seated in their places, mothers with forbidding countenances were wearing red turbans.

Emma's heart beat rather faster when, her partner holding her by the tips of the fingers, she took her place in a line with the dancers, and waited for the first note to start. But her emotion soon vanished, and, swaying to the rhythm of the orchestra, she glided forward with slight movements of the neck. A smile rose to her lips at certain delicate phrases of the violin, that sometimes played alone while the other instruments were silent; one could hear the clear clink of the louis d'or that were being thrown down upon the card tables in the next room;

Charles se tut. Il marchait de long en large, attendant qu'Emma fût habillée.

Il la voyait par derrière, dans la glace, entre deux flambeaux. Ses yeux noirs semblaient plus noirs. Ses bandeaux, doucement bombés vers les oreilles, luisaient d'un éclat bleu; une rose à son chignon tremblait sur une tige mobile, avec des gouttes d'eau factices au bout de ses feuilles. Elle avait une robe de safran pâle, relevée par trois bouquets de roses pompon mêlées de verdure.

Charles vint l'embrasser sur l'épaule.

— Laisse-moi! dit-elle, tu me chiffonnes.

On entendit une ritournelle de violon et les sons d'un cor. Elle descendit l'escalier, se retenant de courir.

Les quadrilles étaient commencés. Il arrivait du monde. On se poussait. Elle se plaça près de la porte, sur une banquette.

Quand la contredanse fut finie, le parquet resta libre pour les groupes d'hommes causant debout et les domestiques en livrée qui apportaient de grands plateaux. Sur la ligne des femmes assises, les éventails peints s'agitaient, les bouquets cachaient à demi le sourire des visages, et les flacons à bouchon d'or tournaient dans des mains entrouvertes dont les gants blancs marquaient la forme des ongles et serraient la chair au poignet. Les garnitures de dentelles, les broches de diamants, les bracelets à médaillon frissonnaient aux corsages, scintillaient aux poitrines, bruissaient sur les bras nus. Les chevelures, bien collées sur les fronts et tordues à la nuque, avaient, en couronnes, en grappes ou en rameaux, des myosotis, du jasmin, des fleurs de grenadier, des épis ou des bleuets. Pacifiques à leurs places, des mères à figure renfrognée portaient des turbans rouges.

Le coeur d'Emma lui battit un peu lorsque, son cavalier la tenant par le bout des doigts, elle vint se mettre en ligne et attendit le coup d'archet pour partir. Mais bientôt l'émotion disparut; et, se balançant au rythme de l'orchestre, elle glissait en avant, avec des mouvements légers du cou. Un sourire lui montait aux lèvres à certaines délicatesses du violon, qui jouait seul, quelquefois, quand les autres instruments se taisaient; on entendait le bruit clair des louis d'or qui se versaient à côté, sur le tapis des tables; puis tout reprenait à la fois, le cornet à pistons

then all struck again, the cornet-a-piston uttered its sonorous note, feet marked time, skirts swelled and rustled, hands touched and parted; the same eyes falling before you met yours again.

A few men (some fifteen or so), of twenty-five to forty, scattered here and there among the dancers or talking at the doorways, distinguished themselves from the crowd by a certain air of breeding, whatever their differences in age, dress, or face.

Their clothes, better made, seemed of finer cloth, and their hair, brought forward in curls towards the temples, glossy with more delicate pomades. They had the complexion of wealth—that clear complexion that is heightened by the pallor of porcelain, the shimmer of satin, the veneer of old furniture, and that an ordered regimen of exquisite nurture maintains at its best. Their necks moved easily in their low cravats, their long whiskers fell over their turned-down collars, they wiped their lips upon handkerchiefs with embroidered initials that gave forth a subtle perfume. Those who were beginning to grow old had an air of youth, while there was something mature in the faces of the young. In their unconcerned looks was the calm of passions daily satiated, and through all their gentleness of manner pierced that peculiar brutality, the result of a command of half-easy things, in which force is exercised and vanity amused—the management of thoroughbred horses and the society of loose women.

A few steps from Emma a gentleman in a blue coat was talking of Italy with a pale young woman wearing a parure of pearls. They were praising the breadth of the columns of St. Peter's, Tivoly, Vesuvius, Castellamare, and Cassines, the roses of Genoa, the Coliseum by moonlight. With her other ear Emma was listening to a conversation full of words she did not understand. A circle gathered round a very young man who the week before had beaten "Miss Arabella" and "Romolus," and won two thousand louis jumping a ditch in England. One complained that his racehorses were growing fat; another of the printers' errors that had disfigured the name of his horse.

The atmosphere of the ball was heavy; the lamps were growing dim. Guests were flocking to the billiard room. A servant got upon a chair

lançait un éclat sonore, les pieds retombaient en mesure, les jupes se bouffaient et frôlaient, les mains se donnaient, se quittaient; les mêmes yeux, s'abaissant devant vous, revenaient se fixer sur les vôtres.

Quelques hommes (une quinzaine) de vingt-cinq à quarante ans, disséminés parmi les danseurs ou causant à l'entrée des portes, se distinguaient de la foule par un air de famille, quelles que fussent leurs différences d'âge, de toilette ou de figure.

Leurs habits, mieux faits, semblaient d'un drap plus souple, et leurs cheveux, ramenés en boucles vers les tempes, lustrés par des pommades plus fines. Ils avaient le teint de la richesse, ce teint blanc que rehaussent la pâleur des porcelaines, les moires du satin, le vernis des beaux meubles, et qu'entretient dans sa santé un régime discret de nourritures exquises. Leur cou tournait à l'aise sur des cravates basses; leurs favoris longs tombaient sur des cols rabattus; ils s'essuyaient les lèvres à des mouchoirs brodés d'un large chiffre, d'où sortait une odeur suave. Ceux qui commençaient à vieillir avaient l'air jeune, tandis que quelque chose de mûr s'étendait sur le visage des jeunes. Dans leurs regards indifférents flottait la quiétude de passions journellement assouvies; et, à travers leurs manières douces, perçait cette brutalité particulière que communique la domination de choses à demi faciles, dans lesquelles la force s'exerce et où la vanité s'amuse, le maniement des chevaux de race et la société des femmes perdues.

À trois pas d'Emma, un cavalier en habit bleu causait Italie avec une jeune femme pâle, portant une parure de perles. Ils vantaient la grosseur des piliers de Saint-Pierre, Tivoli, le Vésuve, Castellamare et les Cassines, les roses de Gênes, le Colisée au clair de lune. Emma écoutait de son autre oreille une conversation pleine de mots qu'elle ne comprenait pas. On entourait un tout jeune homme qui avait battu, la semaine d'avant, Miss Arabelle et Romulus, et gagné deux mille louis à sauter un fossé, en Angleterre. L'un se plaignait de ses coureurs qui engraissaient; un autre, des fautes d'impression qui avaient dénaturé le nom de son cheval.

L'air du bal était lourd; les lampes pâlissaient. On refluait dans la salle de billard. Un domestique monta sur une chaise et cassa deux

and broke the window-panes. At the crash of the glass Madame Bovary turned her head and saw in the garden the faces of peasants pressed against the window looking in at them. Then the memory of the Bertaux came back to her. She saw the farm again, the muddy pond, her father in a blouse under the apple trees, and she saw herself again as formerly, skimming with her finger the cream off the milk-pans in the dairy. But in the refulgence of the present hour her past life, so distinct until then, faded away completely, and she almost doubted having lived it. She was there; beyond the ball was only shadow overspreading all the rest. She was just eating a maraschino ice that she held with her left hand in a silver-gilt cup, her eyes half-closed, and the spoon between her teeth.

A lady near her dropped her fan. A gentlemen was passing.

"Would you be so good," said the lady, "as to pick up my fan that has fallen behind the sofa?"

The gentleman bowed, and as he moved to stretch out his arm, Emma saw the hand of a young woman throw something white, folded in a triangle, into his hat. The gentleman, picking up the fan, offered it to the lady respectfully; she thanked him with an inclination of the head, and began smelling her bouquet.

After supper, where were plenty of Spanish and Rhine wines, soups a la bisque and au lait d'amandes, puddings a la Trafalgar, and all sorts of cold meats with jellies that trembled in the dishes, the carriages one after the other began to drive off. Raising the corners of the muslin curtain, one could see the light of their lanterns glimmering through the darkness. The seats began to empty, some card-players were still left; the musicians were cooling the tips of their fingers on their tongues. Charles was half asleep, his back propped against a door.

At three o'clock the cotillion began. Emma did not know how to waltz. Everyone was waltzing, Mademoiselle d'Andervilliers herself and the Marquis; only the guests staying at the castle were still there, about a dozen persons.

One of the waltzers, however, who was familiarly called Viscount, and whose low cut waistcoat seemed moulded to his chest, came a sec-

vitres; au bruit des éclats de verre, madame Bovary tourna la tête et aperçut dans le jardin, contre les carreaux, des faces de paysans qui regardaient. Alors le souvenir des Bertaux lui arriva. Elle revit la ferme, la mare bourbeuse, son père en blouse sous les pommiers, et elle se revit elle-même, comme autrefois, écrémant avec son doigt les terrines de lait dans la laiterie. Mais, aux fulgurations de l'heure présente, sa vie passée, si nette jusqu'alors, s'évanouissait tout entière, et elle doutait presque de l'avoir vécue. Elle était là; puis autour du bal, il n'y avait plus que de l'ombre, étalée sur tout le reste. Elle mangeait alors une glace au marasquin, qu'elle tenait de la main gauche dans une coquille de vermeil, et fermait à demi les yeux, la cuiller entre les dents.

Une dame, près d'elle, laissa tomber son éventail. Un danseur passait.

— Que vous seriez bon, monsieur, dit la dame, de vouloir bien ramasser mon éventail, qui est derrière ce canapé!

Le monsieur s'inclina, et, pendant qu'il faisait le mouvement d'étendre son bras, Emma vit la main de la jeune dame qui jetait dans son chapeau quelque chose de blanc, plié en triangle. Le monsieur, ramenant l'éventail, l'offrit à la dame, respectueusement; elle le remercia d'un signe de tête et se mit à respirer son bouquet.

Après le souper, où il y eut beaucoup de vins d'Espagne et de vins du Rhin, des potages à la bisque et au lait d'amandes, des puddings à la Trafalgar et toutes sortes de viandes froides avec des gelées alentour qui tremblaient dans les plats, les voitures, les unes après les autres, commencèrent à s'en aller. En écartant du coin le rideau de mousseline, on voyait glisser dans l'ombre la lumière de leurs lanternes. Les banquettes s'éclaircirent; quelques joueurs restaient encore; les musiciens rafraîchissaient, sur leur langue, le bout de leurs doigts; Charles dormait à demi, le dos appuyé contre une porte.

À trois heures du matin, le cotillon commença. Emma ne savait pas valser. Tout le monde valsait, mademoiselle d'Andervilliers elle- même et la marquise; il n'y avait plus que les hôtes du château, une douzaine de personnes à peu près.

Cependant, un des valseurs, qu'on appelait familièrement vicomte, et dont le gilet très ouvert semblait moulé sur la poitrine, vint une sec-

ond time to ask Madame Bovary to dance, assuring her that he would guide her, and that she would get through it very well.

They began slowly, then went more rapidly. They turned; all around them was turning—the lamps, the furniture, the wainscoting, the floor, like a disc on a pivot. On passing near the doors the bottom of Emma's dress caught against his trousers. Their legs commingled; he looked down at her; she raised her eyes to his. A torpor seized her; she stopped. They started again, and with a more rapid movement; the Viscount, dragging her along disappeared with her to the end of the gallery, where panting, she almost fell, and for a moment rested her head upon his breast. And then, still turning, but more slowly, he guided her back to her seat. She leaned back against the wall and covered her eyes with her hands.

When she opened them again, in the middle of the drawing room three waltzers were kneeling before a lady sitting on a stool. She chose the Viscount, and the violin struck up once more.

Everyone looked at them. They passed and re-passed, she with rigid body, her chin bent down, and he always in the same pose, his figure curved, his elbow rounded, his chin thrown forward. That woman knew how to waltz! They kept up a long time, and tired out all the others.

Then they talked a few moments longer, and after the goodnights, or rather good mornings, the guests of the chateau retired to bed.

Charles dragged himself up by the balusters. His "knees were going up into his body." He had spent five consecutive hours standing bolt upright at the card tables, watching them play whist, without understanding anything about it, and it was with a deep sigh of relief that he pulled off his boots.

Emma threw a shawl over her shoulders, opened the window, and leant out.

The night was dark; some drops of rain were falling. She breathed in the damp wind that refreshed her eyelids. The music of the ball was still murmuring in her ears. And she tried to keep herself awake in order to prolong the illusion of this luxurious life that she would soon have to give up.

onde fois encore inviter madame Bovary, l'assurant qu'il la guiderait et qu'elle s'en tirerait bien.

Ils commencèrent lentement, puis allèrent plus vite. Ils tournaient: tout tournait autour d'eux, les lampes, les meubles, les lambris, et le parquet, comme un disque sur un pivot. En passant auprès des portes, la robe d'Emma, par le bas, s'éraflait au pantalon; leurs jambes entraient l'une dans l'autre; il baissait ses regards vers elle, elle levait les siens vers lui; une torpeur la prenait, elle s'arrêta. Ils repartirent; et, d'un mouvement plus rapide, le vicomte, l'entraînant, disparut avec elle jusqu'au bout de la galerie, où, haletante, elle faillit tomber, et, un instant, s'appuya la tête sur sa poitrine. Et puis, tournant toujours, mais plus doucement, il la reconduisit à sa place; elle se renversa contre la muraille et mit la main devant ses yeux.

Quand elle les rouvrit, au milieu du salon, une dame assise sur un tabouret avait devant elle trois valseurs agenouillés. Elle choisit le Vicomte, et le violon recommença.

On les regardait. Ils passaient et revenaient, elle immobile du corps et le menton baissé, et lui toujours dans sa même pose, la taille cambrée, le coude arrondi, la bouche en avant. Elle savait valser, celle-là! Ils continuèrent longtemps et fatiguèrent tous les autres.

On causa quelques minutes encore, et, après les adieux ou plutôt le bonjour, les hôtes du château s'allèrent coucher.

Charles se traînait à la rampe, les genoux lui rentraient dans le corps. Il avait passé cinq heures de suite, tout debout devant les tables, à regarder jouer au whist sans y rien comprendre. Aussi poussa-t-il un grand soupir de satisfaction lorsqu'il eut retiré ses bottes.

Emma mit un châle sur ses épaules, ouvrit la fenêtre et s'accouda.

La nuit était noire. Quelques gouttes de pluie tombaient. Elle aspira le vent humide qui lui rafraîchissait les paupières. La musique du bal bourdonnait encore à ses oreilles, et elle faisait des efforts pour se tenir éveillée, afin de prolonger l'illusion de cette vie luxueuse qu'il lui faudrait tout à l'heure abandonner.

Day began to break. She looked long at the windows of the chateau, trying to guess which were the rooms of all those she had noticed the evening before. She would fain have known their lives, have penetrated, blended with them.

But she was shivering with cold. She undressed, and cowered down between the sheets against Charles, who was asleep.

There were a great many people to luncheon. The repast lasted ten minutes; no liqueurs were served, which astonished the doctor. Next, Mademoiselle d'Andervilliers collected some pieces of roll in a small basket to take them to the swans on the ornamental waters, and they went to walk in the hot-houses, where strange plants, bristling with hairs, rose in pyramids under hanging vases, whence, as from overfilled nests of serpents, fell long green cords interlacing. The orangery, which was at the other end, led by a covered way to the outhouses of the chateau. The Marquis, to amuse the young woman, took her to see the stables. Above the basket-shaped racks porcelain slabs bore the names of the horses in black letters. Each animal in its stall whisked its tail when anyone went near and said "Tchk! tchk!" The boards of the harness room shone like the flooring of a drawing room. The carriage harness was piled up in the middle against two twisted columns, and the bits, the whips, the spurs, the curbs, were ranged in a line all along the wall.

Charles, meanwhile, went to ask a groom to put his horse to. The dog-cart was brought to the foot of the steps, and, all the parcels being crammed in, the Bovarys paid their respects to the Marquis and Marchioness and set out again for Tostes.

Emma watched the turning wheels in silence. Charles, on the extreme edge of the seat, held the reins with his two arms wide apart, and the little horse ambled along in the shafts that were too big for him. The loose reins hanging over his crupper were wet with foam, and the box fastened on behind the chaise gave great regular bumps against it.

They were on the heights of Thibourville when suddenly some horsemen with cigars between their lips passed laughing. Emma thought she

Le petit jour parut. Elle regarda les fenêtres du château, longuement, tâchant de deviner quelles étaient les chambres de tous ceux qu'elle avait remarqués la veille. Elle aurait voulu savoir leurs existences, y pénétrer, s'y confondre.

Mais elle grelottait de froid. Elle se déshabilla et se blottit entre les draps, contre Charles qui dormait.

Il y eut beaucoup de monde au déjeuner. Le repas dura dix minutes; on ne servit aucune liqueur, ce qui étonna le médecin. Ensuite mademoiselle d'Andervilliers ramassa des morceaux de brioche dans une bannette, pour les porter aux cygnes sur la pièce d'eau, et on s'alla promener dans la serre chaude, où des plantes bizarres, hérissées de poils, s'étageaient en pyramides sous des vases suspendus, qui, pareils à des nids de serpents trop pleins, laissaient retomber, de leurs bords, de longs cordons verts entrelacés. L'orangerie, que l'on trouvait au bout, menait à couvert jusqu'aux communs du château. Le Marquis, pour amuser la jeune femme, la mena voir les écuries. Au-dessus des râteliers en forme de corbeille, des plaques de porcelaine portaient en noir le nom des chevaux. Chaque bête s'agitait dans sa stalle, quand on passait près d'elle, en claquant de la langue. Le plancher de la sellerie luisait à l'oeil comme le parquet d'un salon. Les harnais de voiture étaient dressés dans le milieu sur deux colonnes tournantes, et les mors, les fouets, les étriers, les gourmettes rangés en ligne tout le long de la muraille.

Charles, cependant, alla prier un domestique d'atteler son boc. On l'amena devant le perron, et, tous les paquets y étant fourrés, les époux Bovary firent leurs politesses au Marquis et à la Marquise, et repartirent pour Tostes.

Emma, silencieuse, regardait tourner les roues. Charles, posé sur le bord extrême de la banquette, conduisait les deux bras écartés, et le petit cheval trottait l'amble dans les brancards, qui étaient trop larges pour lui. Les guides molles battaient sur sa croupe en s'y trempant d'écume, et la boîte ficelée derrière le boc donnait contre la caisse de grands coups réguliers.

Ils étaient sur les hauteurs de Thibourville, lorsque devant eux, tout à coup, des cavaliers passèrent en riant, avec des cigares à la bouche.

recognized the Viscount, turned back, and caught on the horizon only the movement of the heads rising or falling with the unequal cadence of the trot or gallop.

A mile farther on they had to stop to mend with some string the traces that had broken.

But Charles, giving a last look to the harness, saw something on the ground between his horse's legs, and he picked up a cigar-case with a green silk border and beblazoned in the centre like the door of a carriage.

"There are even two cigars in it," said he; "they'll do for this evening after dinner."

"Why, do you smoke?" she asked.

"Sometimes, when I get a chance."

He put his find in his pocket and whipped up the nag.

When they reached home the dinner was not ready. Madame lost her temper. Nastasie answered rudely.

"Leave the room!" said Emma. "You are forgetting yourself. I give you warning."

For dinner there was onion soup and a piece of veal with sorrel. Charles, seated opposite Emma, rubbed his hands gleefully.

"How good it is to be at home again!"

Nastasie could be heard crying. He was rather fond of the poor girl. She had formerly, during the wearisome time of his widowhood, kept him company many an evening. She had been his first patient, his oldest acquaintance in the place.

"Have you given her warning for good?" he asked at last.

"Yes. Who is to prevent me?" she replied.

Then they warmed themselves in the kitchen while their room was being made ready. Charles began to smoke. He smoked with lips protruding, spitting every moment, recoiling at every puff.

"You'll make yourself ill," she said scornfully.

He put down his cigar and ran to swallow a glass of cold water at the pump. Emma seizing hold of the cigar case threw it quickly to the back

Emma crut reconnaître le Vicomte: elle se détourna, et n'aperçut à l'horizon que le mouvement des têtes s'abaissant et montant, selon la cadence inégale du trot ou du galop.

Un quart de lieue plus loin, il fallut s'arrêter pour raccommoder, avec de la corde, le reculement qui était rompu.

Mais Charles, donnant au harnais un dernier coup d'oeil, vit quelque chose par terre, entre les jambes de son cheval; et il ramassa un porte-cigares tout bordé de soie verte et blasonné à son milieu comme la portière d'un carrosse.

— Il y a même deux cigares dedans, dit-il; ce sera pour ce soir, après dîner.

— Tu fumes donc? demanda-t-elle.

— Quelquefois, quand l'occasion se présente.

Il mit sa trouvaille dans sa poche et fouetta le bidet.

Quand ils arrivèrent chez eux, le dîner n'était point prêt. Madame s'emporta. Nastasie répondit insolemment.

— Partez! dit Emma. C'est se moquer, je vous chasse.

Il y avait pour dîner de la soupe à l'oignon, avec un morceau de veau à l'oseille. Charles, assis devant Emma, dit en se frottant les mains d'un air heureux:

— Cela fait plaisir de se retrouver chez soi!

On entendait Nastasie qui pleurait. Il aimait un peu cette pauvre fille. Elle lui avait, autrefois, tenu société pendant bien des soirs, dans les désoeuvrements de son veuvage. C'était sa première pratique, sa plus ancienne connaissance du pays.

— Est-ce que tu l'as renvoyée pour tout de bon? dit-il enfin.

— Oui. Qui m'en empêche? répondit-elle.

Puis ils se chauffèrent dans la cuisine, pendant qu'on apprêtait leur chambre. Charles se mit à fumer. Il fumait en avançant les lèvres, crachant à toute minute, se reculant à chaque bouffée.

— Tu vas te faire mal, dit-elle dédaigneusement.

Il déposa son cigare, et courut avaler, à la pompe, un verre d'eau froide. Emma, saisissant le porte-cigares, le jeta vivement au fond de

of the cupboard.

The next day was a long one. She walked about her little garden, up and down the same walks, stopping before the beds, before the espalier, before the plaster curate, looking with amazement at all these things of once-on-a-time that she knew so well. How far off the ball seemed already! What was it that thus set so far asunder the morning of the day before yesterday and the evening of to-day? Her journey to Vaubyessard had made a hole in her life, like one of those great crevices that a storm will sometimes make in one night in mountains. Still she was resigned. She devoutly put away in her drawers her beautiful dress, down to the satin shoes whose soles were yellowed with the slippery wax of the dancing floor. Her heart was like these. In its friction against wealth something had come over it that could not be effaced.

The memory of this ball, then, became an occupation for Emma. Whenever the Wednesday came round she said to herself as she awoke, "Ah! I was there a week—a fortnight—three weeks ago." And little by little the faces grew confused in her remembrance. She forgot the tune of the quadrilles; she no longer saw the liveries and appointments so distinctly; some details escaped her, but the regret remained with her.

l'armoire.

La journée fut longue, le lendemain! Elle se promena dans son jardinet, passant et revenant par les mêmes allées, s'arrêtant devant les plates-bandes, devant l'espalier, devant le curé de plâtre, considérant avec ébahissement toutes ces choses d'autrefois qu'elle connaissait si bien. Comme le bal déjà lui semblait loin! Qui donc écartait, à tant de distance, le matin d'avant-hier et le soir d'aujourd'hui? Son voyage à la Vaubyessard avait fait un trou dans sa vie, à la manière de ces grandes crevasses qu'un orage, en une seule nuit, creuse quelquefois dans les montagnes. Elle se résigna pourtant; elle serra pieusement dans la commode sa belle toilette et jusqu'à ses souliers de satin, dont la semelle s'était jaunie à la cire glissante du parquet. Son coeur était comme eux: au frottement de la richesse, il s'était placé dessus quelque chose qui ne s'effacerait pas.

Ce fut donc une occupation pour Emma que le souvenir de ce bal. Toutes les fois que revenait le mercredi, elle se disait en s'éveillant: «Ah! il y a huit jours... il y a quinze jours..., il y a trois semaines, j'y étais!» Et peu à peu, les physionomies se confondirent dans sa mémoire, elle oublia l'air des contredanses, elle ne vit plus si nettement les livrées et les appartements; quelques détails s'en allèrent; mais le regret lui resta.

# Chapter 9

Often when Charles was out she took from the cupboard, between the folds of the linen where she had left it, the green silk cigar case.

She looked at it, opened it, and even smelt the odour of the lining—a mixture of verbena and tobacco. Whose was it? The Viscount's? Perhaps it was a present from his mistress. It had been embroidered on some rosewood frame, a pretty little thing, hidden from all eyes, that had occupied many hours, and over which had fallen the soft curls of the pensive worker. A breath of love had passed over the stitches on the canvas; each prick of the needle had fixed there a hope or a memory, and all those interwoven threads of silk were but the continuity of the same silent passion. And then one morning the Viscount had taken it away with him. Of what had they spoken when it lay upon the wide-mantelled chimneys between flower-vases and Pompadour clocks? She was at Tostes; he was at Paris now, far away! What was this Paris like? What a vague name! She repeated it in a low voice, for the mere pleasure of it; it rang in her ears like a great cathedral bell; it shone before her eyes, even on the labels of her pomade-pots.

At night, when the carriers passed under her windows in their carts singing the "Marjolaine," she awoke, and listened to the noise of the iron-bound wheels, which, as they gained the country road, was soon deadened by the soil.

"They will be there to-morrow!" she said to herself.

And she followed them in thought up and down the hills, traversing villages, gliding along the highroads by the light of the stars. At the end of some indefinite distance there was always a confused spot, into which her dream died.

She bought a plan of Paris, and with the tip of her finger on the map she walked about the capital. She went up the boulevards, stopping at

# Chapitre 9

Souvent, lorsque Charles était sorti, elle allait prendre dans l'armoire, entre les plis du linge où elle l'avait laissé, le porte-cigares en soie verte.

Elle le regardait, l'ouvrait, et même elle flairait l'odeur de sa doublure, mêlée de verveine et de tabac. À qui appartenait-il?... Au Vicomte. C'était peut-être un cadeau de sa maîtresse. On avait brodé cela sur quelque métier de palissandre, meuble mignon que l'on cachait à tous les yeux, qui avait occupé bien des heures et où s'étaient penchées les boucles molles de la travailleuse pensive. Un souffle d'amour avait passé parmi les mailles du canevas; chaque coup d'aiguille avait fixé là une espérance ou un souvenir, et tous ces fils de soie entrelacés n'étaient que la continuité de la même passion silencieuse. Et puis le Vicomte, un matin, l'avait emporté avec lui. De quoi avait-on parlé, lorsqu'il restait sur les cheminées à large chambranle, entre les vases de fleurs et les pendules Pompadour? Elle était à Tostes. Lui, il était à Paris, maintenant; là-bas! Comment était ce Paris? Quel nom démesuré! Elle se le répétait à demi-voix, pour se faire plaisir; il sonnait à ses oreilles comme un bourdon de cathédrale, il flamboyait à ses yeux jusque sur l'étiquette de ses pots de pommade.

La nuit, quand les mareyeurs, dans leurs charrettes, passaient sous ses fenêtres en chantant la Marjolaine, elle s'éveillait, et écoutant le bruit des roues ferrées, qui, à la sortie du pays, s'amortissait vite sur la terre:

— Ils y seront demain! se disait-elle.

Et elle les suivait dans sa pensée, montant et descendant les côtes, traversant les villages, filant sur la grande route à la clarté des étoiles. Au bout d'une distance indéterminée, il se trouvait toujours une place confuse où expirait son rêve.

Elle s'acheta un plan de Paris, et, du bout de son doigt, sur la carte, elle faisait des courses dans la capitale. Elle remontait les boulevards,

every turning, between the lines of the streets, in front of the white squares that represented the houses. At last she would close the lids of her weary eyes, and see in the darkness the gas jets flaring in the wind and the steps of carriages lowered with much noise before the peristyles of theatres.

She took in "La Corbeille," a lady's journal, and the "Sylphe des Salons." She devoured, without skipping a word, all the accounts of first nights, races, and soirees, took interest in the debut of a singer, in the opening of a new shop. She knew the latest fashions, the addresses of the best tailors, the days of the Bois and the Opera. In Eugene Sue she studied descriptions of furniture; she read Balzac and George Sand, seeking in them imaginary satisfaction for her own desires. Even at table she had her book by her, and turned over the pages while Charles ate and talked to her. The memory of the Viscount always returned as she read. Between him and the imaginary personages she made comparisons. But the circle of which he was the centre gradually widened round him, and the aureole that he bore, fading from his form, broadened out beyond, lighting up her other dreams.

Paris, more vague than the ocean, glimmered before Emma's eyes in an atmosphere of vermilion. The many lives that stirred amid this tumult were, however, divided into parts, classed as distinct pictures. Emma perceived only two or three that hid from her all the rest, and in themselves represented all humanity. The world of ambassadors moved over polished floors in drawing rooms lined with mirrors, round oval tables covered with velvet and gold-fringed cloths. There were dresses with trains, deep mysteries, anguish hidden beneath smiles. Then came the society of the duchesses; all were pale; all got up at four o'clock; the women, poor angels, wore English point on their petticoats; and the men, unappreciated geniuses under a frivolous outward seeming, rode horses to death at pleasure parties, spent the summer season at Baden, and towards the forties married heiresses. In the private rooms of restaurants, where one sups after midnight by the light of wax candles, laughed the motley crowd of men of let-

s'arrêtant à chaque angle, entre les lignes des rues, devant les carrés blancs qui figurent les maisons. Les yeux fatigués à la fin, elle fermait ses paupières, et elle voyait dans les ténèbres se tordre au vent des becs de gaz, avec des marche- pieds de calèches, qui se déployaient à grand fracas devant le péristyle des théâtres.

Elle s'abonna à la Corbeille, journal des femmes, et au Sylphe des salons. Elle dévorait, sans en rien passer, tous les comptes rendus de premières représentations, de courses et de soirées, s'intéressait au début d'une chanteuse, à l'ouverture d'un magasin. Elle savait les modes nouvelles, l'adresse des bons tailleurs, les jours de Bois ou d'Opéra. Elle étudia, dans Eugène Sue, des descriptions d'ameublements; elle lut Balzac et George Sand, y cherchant des assouvissements imaginaires pour ses convoitises personnelles. À table même, elle apportait son livre, et elle tournait les feuillets, pendant que Charles mangeait en lui parlant. Le souvenir du Vicomte revenait toujours dans ses lectures. Entre lui et les personnages inventés, elle établissait des rapprochements. Mais le cercle dont il était le centre peu à peu s'élargit autour de lui, et cette auréole qu'il avait, s'écartant de sa figure, s'étala plus au loin, pour illuminer d'autres rêves.

Paris, plus vague que l'Océan, miroitait donc aux yeux d'Emma dans une atmosphère vermeille. La vie nombreuse qui s'agitait en ce tumulte y était cependant divisée par parties, classée en tableaux distincts. Emma n'en apercevait que deux ou trois qui lui cachaient tous les autres, et représentaient à eux seuls l'humanité complète. Le monde des ambassadeurs marchait sur des parquets luisants, dans des salons lambrissés de miroirs, autour de tables ovales couvertes d'un tapis de velours à crépines d'or. Il y avait là des robes à queue, de grands mystères, des angoisses dissimulées sous des sourires. Venait ensuite la société des duchesses; on y était pâle; on se levait à quatre heures; les femmes, pauvres anges! portaient du point d'Angleterre au bas de leur jupon, et les hommes, capacités méconnues sous des dehors futiles, crevaient leurs chevaux par partie de plaisir, allaient passer à Bade la saison d'été, et, vers la quarantaine enfin, épousaient des héritières. Dans les cabinets de restaurant où l'on soupe après minuit riait, à la clarté des bougies, la foule bigarrée des gens

ters and actresses. They were prodigal as kings, full of ideal, ambitious, fantastic frenzy. This was an existence outside that of all others, between heaven and earth, in the midst of storms, having something of the sublime. For the rest of the world it was lost, with no particular place and as if non-existent. The nearer things were, moreover, the more her thoughts turned away from them. All her immediate surroundings, the wearisome country, the middle-class imbeciles, the mediocrity of existence, seemed to her exceptional, a peculiar chance that had caught hold of her, while beyond stretched, as far as eye could see, an immense land of joys and passions. She confused in her desire the sensualities of luxury with the delights of the heart, elegance of manners with delicacy of sentiment. Did not love, like Indian plants, need a special soil, a particular temperature? Signs by moonlight, long embraces, tears flowing over yielded hands, all the fevers of the flesh and the languors of tenderness could not be separated from the balconies of great castles full of indolence, from boudoirs with silken curtains and thick carpets, well-filled flower-stands, a bed on a raised dias, nor from the flashing of precious stones and the shoulder-knots of liveries.

The lad from the posting house who came to groom the mare every morning passed through the passage with his heavy wooden shoes; there were holes in his blouse; his feet were bare in list slippers. And this was the groom in knee-britches with whom she had to be content! His work done, he did not come back again all day, for Charles on his return put up his horse himself, unsaddled him and put on the halter, while the servant-girl brought a bundle of straw and threw it as best she could into the manger.

To replace Nastasie (who left Tostes shedding torrents of tears) Emma took into her service a young girl of fourteen, an orphan with a sweet face. She forbade her wearing cotton caps, taught her to address her in the third person, to bring a glass of water on a plate, to knock before coming into a room, to iron, starch, and to dress her—wanted to make a lady's-maid of her. The new servant obeyed without a murmur, so as not to be sent away; and as madame usu-

de lettres et des actrices. Ils étaient, ceux- là, prodigues comme des rois, pleins d'ambitions idéales et de délires fantastiques. C'était une existence au-dessus des autres, entre ciel et terre, dans les orages, quelque chose de sublime. Quant au reste du monde, il était perdu, sans place précise, et comme n'existant pas. Plus les choses, d'ailleurs, étaient voisines, plus sa pensée s'en détournait. Tout ce qui l'entourait immédiatement, campagne ennuyeuse, petits bourgeois imbéciles, médiocrité de l'existence, lui semblait une exception dans le monde, un hasard particulier où elle se trouvait prise, tandis qu'au delà s'étendait à perte de vue l'immense pays des félicités et des passions. Elle confondait, dans son désir, les sensualités du luxe avec les joies du coeur, l'élégance des habitudes et les délicatesses du sentiment. Ne fallait-il pas à l'amour, comme aux plantes indiennes, des terrains préparés, une température particulière? Les soupirs au clair de lune, les longues étreintes, les larmes qui coulent sur les mains qu'on abandonne, toutes les fièvres de la chair et les langueurs de la tendresse ne se séparaient donc pas du balcon des grands châteaux qui sont pleins de loisirs, d'un boudoir à stores de soie avec un tapis bien épais, des jardinières remplies, un lit monté sur une estrade, ni du scintillement des pierres précieuses et des aiguillettes de la livrée.

Le garçon de la poste, qui, chaque matin, venait panser la jument, traversait le corridor avec ses gros sabots; sa blouse avait des trous, ses pieds étaient nus dans des chaussons. C'était là le groom en culotte courte dont il fallait se contenter! Quand son ouvrage était fini, il ne revenait plus de la journée; car Charles, en rentrant, mettait lui-même son cheval à l'écurie, retirait la selle et passait le licou, pendant que la bonne apportait une botte de paille et la jetait, comme elle le pouvait, dans la mangeoire.

Pour remplacer Nastasie (qui enfin partit de Tostes, en versant des ruisseaux de larmes), Emma prit à son service une jeune fille de quatorze ans, orpheline et de physionomie douce. Elle lui interdit les bonnets de coton, lui apprit qu'il fallait vous parler à la troisième personne, apporter un verre d'eau dans une assiette, frapper aux portes avant d'entrer, et à repasser, à empeser, à l'habiller, voulut en faire sa femme de chambre. La nouvelle bonne obéissait sans murmure pour

ally left the key in the sideboard, Felicite every evening took a small supply of sugar that she ate alone in her bed after she had said her prayers.

Sometimes in the afternoon she went to chat with the postilions. Madame was in her room upstairs.

She wore an open dressing gown that showed between the shawl facings of her bodice a pleated chamisette with three gold buttons. Her belt was a corded girdle with great tassels, and her small garnet coloured slippers had a large knot of ribbon that fell over her instep. She had bought herself a blotting book, writing case, pen-holder, and envelopes, although she had no one to write to; she dusted her what-not, looked at herself in the glass, picked up a book, and then, dreaming between the lines, let it drop on her knees. She longed to travel or to go back to her convent. She wished at the same time to die and to live in Paris.

Charles in snow and rain trotted across country. He ate omelettes on farmhouse tables, poked his arm into damp beds, received the tepid spurt of blood-lettings in his face, listened to death-rattles, examined basins, turned over a good deal of dirty linen; but every evening he found a blazing fire, his dinner ready, easy-chairs, and a well-dressed woman, charming with an odour of freshness, though no one could say whence the perfume came, or if it were not her skin that made odorous her chemise.

She charmed him by numerous attentions; now it was some new way of arranging paper sconces for the candles, a flounce that she altered on her gown, or an extraordinary name for some very simple dish that the servant had spoilt, but that Charles swallowed with pleasure to the last mouthful. At Rouen she saw some ladies who wore a bunch of charms on the watch-chains; she bought some charms. She wanted for her mantelpiece two large blue glass vases, and some time after an ivory necessaire with a silver-gilt thimble. The less Charles understood these refinements the more they seduced him. They added something to the pleasure of the senses and to the comfort of his fireside. It was like a golden dust sanding all along the narrow path of his life.

n'être point renvoyée; et, comme Madame, d'habitude, laissait la clef au buffet, Félicité, chaque soir prenait une petite provision de sucre qu'elle mangeait toute seule, dans son lit, après avoir fait sa prière.

L'après-midi, quelquefois, elle allait causer en face avec les postillons. Madame se tenait en haut, dans son appartement.

Elle portait une robe de chambre tout ouverte, qui laissait voir, entre les revers à châle du corsage, une chemisette plissée avec trois boutons d'or. Sa ceinture était une cordelière à gros glands, et ses petites pantoufles de couleur grenat avaient une touffe de rubans larges, qui s'étalait sur le cou-de-pied. Elle s'était acheté un buvard, une papeterie, un porte-plume et des enveloppes, quoiqu'elle n'eût personne à qui écrire; elle époussetait son étagère, se regardait dans la glace, prenait un livre, puis, rêvant entre les lignes, le laissait tomber sur ses genoux. Elle avait envie de faire des voyages ou de retourner vivre à son couvent. Elle souhaitait à la fois mourir et habiter Paris.

Charles, à la neige à la pluie, chevauchait par les chemins de traverse. Il mangeait des omelettes sur la table des fermes, entrait son bras dans des lits humides, recevait au visage le jet tiède des saignées écoutait des râles, examinait des cuvettes, retroussait bien du linge sale; mais il trouvait, tous les soirs, un feu flambant, la table servie, des meubles souples, et une femme en toilette fine, charmante et sentant frais, à ne savoir même d'où venait cette odeur, ou si ce n'était pas sa peau qui parfumait sa chemise.

Elle le charmait par quantité de délicatesses: c'était tantôt une manière nouvelle de façonner pour les bougies des bobèches de papier, un volant qu'elle changeait à sa robe, ou le nom extraordinaire d'un mets bien simple, et que la bonne avait manqué, mais que Charles, jusqu'au bout, avalait avec plaisir. Elle vit à Rouen des dames qui portaient à leur montre un paquet de breloques; elle acheta des breloques. Elle voulut sur sa cheminée deux grands vases de verre bleu, et, quelque temps après, un nécessaire d'ivoire, avec un dé de vermeil. Moins Charles comprenait ces élégances, plus il en subissait la séduction. Elles ajoutaient quelque chose au plaisir de ses sens et à la douceur de son foyer. C'était comme une Poussière d'or qui sablait tout du long le petit sentier de sa vie.

He was well, looked well; his reputation was firmly established. The country-folk loved him because he was not proud. He petted the children, never went to the public house, and, moreover, his morals inspired confidence. He was specially successful with catarrhs and chest complaints. Being much afraid of killing his patients, Charles, in fact only prescribed sedatives, from time to time and emetic, a footbath, or leeches. It was not that he was afraid of surgery; he bled people copiously like horses, and for the taking out of teeth he had the "devil's own wrist."

Finally, to keep up with the times, he took in "La Ruche Medicale," a new journal whose prospectus had been sent him. He read it a little after dinner, but in about five minutes the warmth of the room added to the effect of his dinner sent him to sleep; and he sat there, his chin on his two hands and his hair spreading like a mane to the foot of the lamp. Emma looked at him and shrugged her shoulders. Why, at least, was not her husband one of those men of taciturn passions who work at their books all night, and at last, when about sixty, the age of rheumatism sets in, wear a string of orders on their ill-fitting black coat? She could have wished this name of Bovary, which was hers, had been illustrious, to see it displayed at the booksellers', repeated in the newspapers, known to all France. But Charles had no ambition. An Yvetot doctor whom he had lately met in consultation had somewhat humiliated him at the very bedside of the patient, before the assembled relatives. When, in the evening, Charles told her this anecdote, Emma inveighed loudly against his colleague. Charles was much touched. He kissed her forehead with a tear in his eyes. But she was angered with shame; she felt a wild desire to strike him; she went to open the window in the passage and breathed in the fresh air to calm herself.

"What a man! What a man!" she said in a low voice, biting her lips.

Besides, she was becoming more irritated with him. As he grew older his manner grew heavier; at dessert he cut the corks of the empty bottles; after eating he cleaned his teeth with his tongue; in taking soup he made a gurgling noise with every spoonful; and, as he was getting fatter,

Il se portait bien, il avait bonne mine; sa réputation était établie tout à fait. Les campagnards le chérissaient parce qu'il n'était pas fier. Il caressait les enfants, n'entrait jamais au cabaret, et, d'ailleurs, inspirait de la confiance par sa moralité. Il réussissait particulièrement dans les catarrhes et maladies de poitrine. Craignant beaucoup de tuer son monde, Charles, en effet, n'ordonnait guère que des potions calmantes, de temps à autre de l'émétique, un bain de pieds ou des sangsues. Ce n'est pas que la chirurgie lui fît peur; il vous saignait les gens largement, comme des chevaux, et il avait pour l'extraction des dents une poigne d'enfer.

Enfin, pour se tenir au courant, il prit un abonnement à la Ruche médicale, journal nouveau dont il avait reçu le prospectus. Il en lisait, un peu après son dîner; mais la chaleur de l'appartement, jointe à la digestion, faisait qu'au bout de cinq minutes il s'endormait; et il restait là, le menton sur ses deux mains, et les cheveux étalés comme une crinière jusqu'au pied de la lampe. Emma le regardait en haussant les épaules. Que n'avait-elle, au moins, pour mari un de ces hommes d'ardeurs taciturnes qui travaillent la nuit dans les livres, et portent enfin, à soixante ans, quand vient l'âge des rhumatismes, une brochette de croix, sur leur habit noir, mal fait. Elle aurait voulu que ce nom de Bovary, qui était le sien, fût illustre, le voir étalé chez les libraires, répété dans les journaux, connu par toute la France. Mais Charles n'avait point d'ambition! Un médecin d'Yvetot, avec qui dernièrement il s'était trouvé en consultation, l'avait humilié quelque peu, au lit même du malade, devant les parents assemblés. Quand Charles lui raconta, le soir, cette anecdote, Emma s'emporta bien haut contre le confrère. Charles en fut attendri. Il la baisa au front avec une larme. Mais elle était exaspérée de honte, elle avait envie de le battre, elle alla dans le corridor ouvrir la fenêtre et huma l'air frais pour se calmer.

— Quel pauvre homme! quel pauvre homme! disait-elle tout bas, en se mordant les lèvres.

Elle se sentait, d'ailleurs, plus irritée de lui. Il prenait, avec l'âge, des allures épaisses; il coupait, au dessert, le bouchon des bouteilles vides; il se passait, après manger, la langue sur les dents; il faisait, en avalant sa soupe, un gloussement à chaque gorgée, et, comme il commençait

the puffed-out cheeks seemed to push the eyes, always small, up to the temples.

Sometimes Emma tucked the red borders of his under-vest unto his waistcoat, rearranged his cravat, and threw away the dirty gloves he was going to put on; and this was not, as he fancied, for himself; it was for herself, by a diffusion of egotism, of nervous irritation. Sometimes, too, she told him of what she had read, such as a passage in a novel, of a new play, or an anecdote of the "upper ten" that she had seen in a feuilleton; for, after all, Charles was something, an ever-open ear, and ever-ready approbation. She confided many a thing to her greyhound. She would have done so to the logs in the fireplace or to the pendulum of the clock.

At the bottom of her heart, however, she was waiting for something to happen. Like shipwrecked sailors, she turned despairing eyes upon the solitude of her life, seeking afar off some white sail in the mists of the horizon. She did not know what this chance would be, what wind would bring it her, towards what shore it would drive her, if it would be a shallop or a three-decker, laden with anguish or full of bliss to the portholes. But each morning, as she awoke, she hoped it would come that day; she listened to every sound, sprang up with a start, wondered that it did not come; then at sunset, always more saddened, she longed for the morrow.

Spring came round. With the first warm weather, when the pear trees began to blossom, she suffered from dyspnoea.

From the beginning of July she counted how many weeks there were to October, thinking that perhaps the Marquis d'Andervilliers would give another ball at Vaubyessard. But all September passed without letters or visits.

After the ennui of this disappointment her heart once more remained empty, and then the same series of days recommenced.

So now they would thus follow one another, always the same, immovable, and bringing nothing. Other lives, however flat, had at least the chance of some event. One adventure sometimes brought with it infinite consequences and the scene changed. But nothing happened to

d'engraisser, ses yeux, déjà petits, semblaient remontés vers les tempes par la bouffissure de ses pommettes.

Emma, quelquefois, lui rentrait dans son gilet la bordure rouge de ses tricots, rajustait sa cravate, ou jetait à l'écart les gants déteints qu'il se disposait à passer; et ce n'était pas, comme il croyait, pour lui; c'était pour elle-même, par expansion d'égoïsme, agacement nerveux. Quelquefois aussi, elle lui parlait des choses qu'elles avait lues, comme d'un passage de roman, d'une pièce nouvelle, ou de l'anecdote du grand monde que l'on racontait dans le feuilleton; car, enfin, Charles était quelqu'un, une oreille toujours ouverte, une approbation toujours prête. Elle faisait bien des confidences à sa levrette! Elle en eût fait aux bûches de la cheminée et au balancier de la pendule.

Au fond de son âme, cependant, elle attendait un événement. Comme les matelots en détresse, elle promenait sur la solitude de sa vie des yeux désespérés, cherchant au loin quelque voile blanche dans les brumes de l'horizon. Elle ne savait pas quel serait ce hasard, le vent qui le pousserait jusqu'à elle, vers quel rivage il la mènerait, s'il était chaloupe ou vaisseau à trois ponts, chargé d'angoisses ou plein de félicités jusqu'aux sabords. Mais, chaque matin, à son réveil, elle l'espérait pour la journée, et elle écoutait tous les bruits, se levait en sursaut, s'étonnait qu'il ne vînt pas; puis, au coucher du soleil, toujours plus triste, désirait être au lendemain.

Le printemps reparut. Elle eut des étouffements aux premières chaleurs, quand les poiriers fleurirent.

Dès le commencement de juillet, elle compta sur ses doigts combien de semaines lui restaient pour arriver au mois d'octobre, pensant que le marquis d'Andervilliers, peut-être, donnerait encore un bal à la Vaubyessard. Mais tout septembre s'écoula sans lettres ni visites.

Après l'ennui de cette déception, son coeur de nouveau resta vide, et alors la série des mêmes journées recommença.

Elles allaient donc maintenant se suivre ainsi à la file, toujours pareilles, innombrables, et n'apportant rien! Les autres existences, si plates qu'elles fussent, avaient du moins la chance d'un événement. Une aventure amenait parfois des péripéties à l'infini, et le décor changeait.

her; God had willed it so! The future was a dark corridor, with its door at the end shut fast.

She gave up music. What was the good of playing? Who would hear her? Since she could never, in a velvet gown with short sleeves, striking with her light fingers the ivory keys of an Erard at a concert, feel the murmur of ecstasy envelop her like a breeze, it was not worth while boring herself with practicing. Her drawing cardboard and her embroidery she left in the cupboard. What was the good? What was the good? Sewing irritated her.

"I have read everything," she said to herself.

And she sat there making the tongs red-hot, or looked at the rain falling.

How sad she was on Sundays when vespers sounded! She listened with dull attention to each stroke of the cracked bell. A cat slowly walking over some roof put up his back in the pale rays of the sun. The wind on the highroad blew up clouds of dust. Afar off a dog sometimes howled; and the bell, keeping time, continued its monotonous ringing that died away over the fields.

But the people came out from church. The women in waxed clogs, the peasants in new blouses, the little bare-headed children skipping along in front of them, all were going home. And till nightfall, five or six men, always the same, stayed playing at corks in front of the large door of the inn.

The winter was severe. The windows every morning were covered with rime, and the light shining through them, dim as through ground-glass, sometimes did not change the whole day long. At four o'clock the lamp had to be lighted.

On fine days she went down into the garden. The dew had left on the cabbages a silver lace with long transparent threads spreading from one to the other. No birds were to be heard; everything seemed asleep, the espalier covered with straw, and the vine, like a great sick serpent under the coping of the wall, along which, on drawing near, one saw the many-footed woodlice crawling. Under the spruce by the hedgerow, the

Mais, pour elle, rien n'arrivait, Dieu l'avait voulu! L'avenir était un corridor tout noir, et qui avait au fond sa porte bien fermée.

Elle abandonna la musique. Pourquoi jouer? qui l'entendrait? Puisqu'elle ne pourrait jamais, en robe de velours à manches courtes, sur un piano d'Érard, dans un concert, battant de ses doigts légers les touches d'ivoire, sentir, comme une brise, circuler autour d'elle un murmure d'extase, ce n'était pas la peine de s'ennuyer à étudier. Elle laissa dans l'armoire ses cartons à dessin et la tapisserie. À quoi bon? à quoi bon? La couture l'irritait.

— J'ai tout lu, se disait-elle.

Et elle restait à faire rougir les pincettes, ou regardant la pluie tomber.

Comme elle était triste le dimanche, quand on sonnait les vêpres! Elle écoutait, dans un hébétement attentif, tinter un à un les coups fêlés de la cloche. Quelque chat sur les toits, marchant lentement, bombait son dos aux rayons pâles du soleil. Le vent, sur la grande route, soufflait des traînées de poussière. Au loin, parfois, un chien hurlait: et la cloche, à temps égaux, continuait sa sonnerie monotone qui se perdait dans la campagne.

Cependant on sortait de l'église. Les femmes en sabots cirés, les paysans en blouse neuve, les petits enfants qui sautillaient nu- tête devant eux, tout rentrait chez soi. Et, jusqu'à la nuit, cinq ou six hommes, toujours les mêmes, restaient à jouer au bouchon, devant la grande porte de l'auberge.

L'hiver fut froid. Les carreaux, chaque matin, étaient chargés de givre, et la lumière, blanchâtre à travers eux, comme par des verres dépolis, quelquefois ne variait pas de la journée. Dès quatre heures du soir, il fallait allumer la lampe.

Les jours qu'il faisait beau, elle descendait dans le jardin. La rosée avait laissé sur les choux des guipures d'argent avec de longs fils clairs qui s'étendaient de l'un à l'autre. On n'entendait pas d'oiseaux, tout semblait dormir, l'espalier couvert de paille et la vigne comme un grand serpent malade sous le chaperon du mur, où l'on voyait, en s'approchant, se traîner des cloportes à pattes nombreuses. Dans les sapinettes, près

curie in the three-cornered hat reading his breviary had lost his right foot, and the very plaster, scaling off with the frost, had left white scabs on his face.

Then she went up again, shut her door, put on coals, and fainting with the heat of the hearth, felt her boredom weigh more heavily than ever. She would have liked to go down and talk to the servant, but a sense of shame restrained her.

Every day at the same time the schoolmaster in a black skullcap opened the shutters of his house, and the rural policeman, wearing his sabre over his blouse, passed by. Night and morning the post-horses, three by three, crossed the street to water at the pond. From time to time the bell of a public house door rang, and when it was windy one could hear the little brass basins that served as signs for the hairdresser's shop creaking on their two rods. This shop had as decoration an old engraving of a fashion-plate stuck against a windowpane and the wax bust of a woman with yellow hair. He, too, the hairdresser, lamented his wasted calling, his hopeless future, and dreaming of some shop in a big town—at Rouen, for example, overlooking the harbour, near the theatre—he walked up and down all day from the mairie to the church, sombre and waiting for customers. When Madame Bovary looked up, she always saw him there, like a sentinel on duty, with his skullcap over his ears and his vest of lasting.

Sometimes in the afternoon outside the window of her room, the head of a man appeared, a swarthy head with black whiskers, smiling slowly, with a broad, gentle smile that showed his white teeth. A waltz immediately began and on the organ, in a little drawing room, dancers the size of a finger, women in pink turbans, Tyrolians in jackets, monkeys in frock coats, gentlemen in knee-breeches, turned and turned between the sofas, the consoles, multiplied in the bits of looking glass held together at their corners by a piece of gold paper. The man turned his handle, looking to the right and left, and up at the windows. Now and again, while he shot out a long squirt of brown saliva against the milestone, with his knee raised his instrument, whose hard

de la haie, le curé en tricorne qui lisait son bréviaire avait perdu le pied droit et même le plâtre, s'écaillant à la gelée, avait fait des gales blanches sur sa figure.

Puis elle remontait, fermait la porte, étalait les charbons, et, défaillant à la chaleur du foyer, sentait l'ennui plus lourd qui retombait sur elle. Elle serait bien descendue causer avec la bonne, mais une pudeur la retenait.

Tous les jours, à la même heure, le maître d'école, en bonnet de soie noire, ouvrait les auvents de sa maison, et le garde- champêtre passait, portant son sabre sur sa blouse. Soir et matin, les chevaux de la poste, trois par trois, traversaient la rue pour aller boire à la mare. De temps à autre, la porte d'un cabaret faisait tinter sa sonnette, et, quand il y avait du vent; l'on entendait grincer sur leurs deux tringles les petites cuvettes en cuivre du perruquier, qui servaient d'enseigne à sa boutique. Elle avait pour décoration une vieille gravure de modes collée contre un carreau et un buste de femme en cire, dont les cheveux étaient jaunes. Lui aussi, le perruquier, il se lamentait de sa vocation arrêtée, de son avenir perdu, et, rêvant quelque boutique dans une grande. ville, comme à Rouen par exemple, sur le port, près du théâtre, il restait toute la journée à se promener en long, depuis la mairie jusqu'à l'église, sombre, et attendant la clientèle. Lorsque madame Bovary levait les yeux, elle le voyait toujours là, comme une sentinelle en faction, avec son bonnet grec sur l'oreille et sa veste de lasting.

Dans l'après-midi, quelquefois, une tête d'homme apparaissait derrière les vitres de la salle, tête hâlée, à favoris noirs, et qui souriait lentement d'un large sourire doux à dents blanches. Une valse aussitôt commençait, et, sur l'orgue, dans un petit salon, des danseurs hauts comme le doigt, femmes en turban rose, Tyroliens en jaquette, singes en habit noir, messieurs en culotte courte, tournaient, tournaient entre les fauteuils, les canapés, les consoles, se répétant dans les morceaux de miroir que raccordait à leurs angles un filet de papier doré. L'homme faisait aller sa manivelle, regardant à droite, à gauche et vers les fenêtres. De temps à autre, tout en lançant contre la borne un long jet de salive brune, il soulevait du genou son instrument, dont la bretelle dure lui

straps tired his shoulder; and now, doleful and drawling, or gay and hurried, the music escaped from the box, droning through a curtain of pink taffeta under a brass claw in arabesque. They were airs played in other places at the theatres, sung in drawing rooms, danced to at night under lighted lustres, echoes of the world that reached even to Emma. Endless sarabands ran through her head, and, like an Indian dancing girl on the flowers of a carpet, her thoughts leapt with the notes, swung from dream to dream, from sadness to sadness. When the man had caught some coppers in his cap, he drew down an old cover of blue cloth, hitched his organ on to his back, and went off with a heavy tread. She watched him going.

But it was above all the meal-times that were unbearable to her, in this small room on the ground floor, with its smoking stove, its creaking door, the walls that sweated, the damp flags; all the bitterness in life seemed served up on her plate, and with smoke of the boiled beef there rose from her secret soul whiffs of sickliness. Charles was a slow eater; she played with a few nuts, or, leaning on her elbow, amused herself with drawing lines along the oilcloth table cover with the point of her knife.

She now let everything in her household take care of itself, and Madame Bovary senior, when she came to spend part of Lent at Tostes, was much surprised at the change. She who was formerly so careful, so dainty, now passed whole days without dressing, wore grey cotton stockings, and burnt tallow candles. She kept saying they must be economical since they were not rich, adding that she was very contented, very happy, that Tostes pleased her very much, with other speeches that closed the mouth of her mother-in-law. Besides, Emma no longer seemed inclined to follow her advice; once even, Madame Bovary having thought fit to maintain that mistresses ought to keep an eye on the religion of their servants, she had answered with so angry a look and so cold a smile that the good woman did not interfere again.

Emma was growing difficult, capricious. She ordered dishes for herself, then she did not touch them; one day drank only pure milk, the

fatiguait l'épaule; et, tantôt dolente et traînarde, ou joyeuse et précipitée, la musique de la boîte s'échappait en bourdonnant à travers un rideau de taffetas rose, sous une grille de cuivre en arabesque. C'étaient des airs que l'on jouait ailleurs sur les théâtres; que l'on chantait dans les salons, que l'on dansait le soir sous des lustres éclairés, échos du monde qui arrivaient jusqu'à Emma. Des sarabandes à n'en plus finir se déroulaient dans sa tête; et, comme une bayadère sur les fleurs d'un tapis, sa pensée bondissait avec les notes, se balançait de rêve en rêve, de tristesse en tristesse. Quand l'homme avait reçu l'aumône dans sa casquette, il rabattait une vieille couverture de laine bleue, passait son orgue sur son dos et s'éloignait d'un pas lourd. Elle le regardait partir.

Mais c'était surtout aux heures des repas qu'elle n'en pouvait plus, dans cette petite salle au rez-de-chaussée, avec le poêle qui fumait, la porte qui criait, les murs qui suintaient, les pavés humides; toute l'amertume de l'existence, lui semblait servie sur son assiette, et, à la fumée du bouilli, il montait du fond de son âme comme d'autres bouffées d'affadissement. Charles était long à manger; elle grignotait quelques noisettes, ou bien, appuyée du coude, s'amusait, avec la pointe de son couteau, à faire des raies sur la toile cirée.

Elle laissait maintenant tout aller dans son ménage, et madame Bovary mère, lorsqu'elle vint passer à Tostes une partie du carême, s'étonna fort de ce changement. Elle, en effet, si soigneuse autrefois et délicate, elle restait à présent des journées entières sans s'habiller, portait des bas de coton gris, s'éclairait à la chandelle. Elle répétait qu'il fallait économiser, puisqu'ils n'étaient pas riches, ajoutant qu'elle était très contente, très heureuse, que Tostes lui plaisait beaucoup, et autres discours nouveaux qui fermaient la bouche à la belle-mère. Du reste, Emma ne semblait plus disposée à suivre ses conseils; une fois même, madame Bovary s'étant avisée de prétendre que les maîtres devaient surveiller la religion de leurs domestiques, elle lui avait répondu d'un oeil si colère et avec un sourire tellement froid, que la bonne femme ne s'y frotta plus.

Emma devenait difficile, capricieuse. Elle se commandait des plats pour elle, n'y touchait point, un jour ne buvait que du lait pur, et, le len-

next cups of tea by the dozen. Often she persisted in not going out, then, stifling, threw open the windows and put on light dresses. After she had well scolded her servant she gave her presents or sent her out to see neighbours, just as she sometimes threw beggars all the silver in her purse, although she was by no means tender-hearted or easily accessible to the feelings of others, like most country-bred people, who always retain in their souls something of the horny hardness of the paternal hands.

Towards the end of February old Rouault, in memory of his cure, himself brought his son-in-law a superb turkey, and stayed three days at Tostes. Charles being with his patients, Emma kept him company. He smoked in the room, spat on the firedogs, talked farming, calves, cows, poultry, and municipal council, so that when he left she closed the door on him with a feeling of satisfaction that surprised even herself. Moreover she no longer concealed her contempt for anything or anybody, and at times she set herself to express singular opinions, finding fault with that which others approved, and approving things perverse and immoral, all of which made her husband open his eyes widely.

Would this misery last for ever? Would she never issue from it? Yet she was as good as all the women who were living happily. She had seen duchesses at Vaubyessard with clumsier waists and commoner ways, and she execrated the injustice of God. She leant her head against the walls to weep; she envied lives of stir; longed for masked balls, for violent pleasures, with all the wildness that she did not know, but that these must surely yield.

She grew pale and suffered from palpitations of the heart. Charles prescribed valerian and camphor baths. Everything that was tried only seemed to irritate her the more.

On certain days she chatted with feverish rapidity, and this over-excitement was suddenly followed by a state of torpor, in which she remained without speaking, without moving. What then revived her was pouring a bottle of eau-de-cologne over her arms.

As she was constantly complaining about Tostes, Charles fancied that her illness was no doubt due to some local cause, and fixing on this

demain, des tasses de thé à la douzaine. Souvent elle s'obstinait à ne pas sortir, puis elle suffoquait, ouvrait les fenêtres, s'habillait en robe légère. Lorsqu'elle avait bien rudoyé sa servante, elle lui faisait des cadeaux ou l'envoyait se promener chez les voisines, de même qu'elle jetait parfois aux pauvres toutes les pièces blanches de sa bourse, quoiqu'elle ne fût guère tendre cependant, ni facilement accessible à l'émotion d'autrui, comme la plupart des gens issus de campagnards, qui gardent toujours à l'âme quelque chose de la callosité des mains paternelles.

Vers la fin de février, le père Rouault, en souvenir de sa guérison, apporta lui-même à son gendre une dinde superbe, et il resta trois jours à Tostes. Charles étant à ses malades, Emma lui tint compagnie. Il fuma dans la chambre, cracha sur les chenets, causa culture, veaux, vaches, volailles et conseil municipal; si bien qu'elle referma la porte, quand il fut parti, avec un sentiment de satisfaction qui la surprit elle-même. D'ailleurs, elle ne cachait plus son mépris pour rien, ni pour personne; et elle se mettait quelquefois à exprimer des opinions singulières, blâmant ce que l'on approuvait, et approuvant des choses perverses ou immorales: ce qui faisait ouvrir de grands yeux à son mari.

Est-ce que cette misère durerait toujours? est-ce qu'elle n'en sortirait pas? Elle valait bien cependant toutes celles qui vivaient heureuses! Elle avait vu des duchesses à la Vaubyessard qui avaient la taille plus lourde et les façons plus communes, et elle exécrait l'injustice de Dieu; elle s'appuyait la tête aux murs pour pleurer; elle enviait les existences tumultueuses, les nuits masquées, les insolents plaisirs avec tous les éperdúments qu'elle ne connaissait pas et qu'ils devaient donner.

Elle pâlissait et avait des battements de coeur. Charles lui administra de la valériane et des bains de camphre. Tout ce que l'on essayait semblait l'irriter davantage.

En de certains jours, elle bavardait avec une abondance fébrile; à ces exaltations succédaient tout à coup des torpeurs où elle restait sans parler, sans bouger. Ce qui la ranimait alors, c'était de se répandre sur les bras un flacon d'eau de Cologne.

Comme elle se plaignait de Tostes continuellement, Charles imagina que la cause de sa maladie était sans doute dans quelque influence

idea, began to think seriously of setting up elsewhere.

From that moment she drank vinegar, contracted a sharp little cough, and completely lost her appetite.

It cost Charles much to give up Tostes after living there four years and "when he was beginning to get on there." Yet if it must be! He took her to Rouen to see his old master. It was a nervous complaint: change of air was needed.

After looking about him on this side and on that, Charles learnt that in the Neufchatel arrondissement there was a considerable market town called Yonville-l'Abbaye, whose doctor, a Polish refugee, had decamped a week before. Then he wrote to the chemist of the place to ask the number of the population, the distance from the nearest doctor, what his predecessor had made a year, and so forth; and the answer being satisfactory, he made up his mind to move towards the spring, if Emma's health did not improve.

One day when, in view of her departure, she was tidying a drawer, something pricked her finger. It was a wire of her wedding bouquet. The orange blossoms were yellow with dust and the silver bordered satin ribbons frayed at the edges. She threw it into the fire. It flared up more quickly than dry straw. Then it was, like a red bush in the cinders, slowly devoured. She watched it burn. The little pasteboard berries burst, the wire twisted, the gold lace melted; and the shriveled paper corollas, fluttering like black butterflies at the back of the stove, at lest flew up the chimney.

When they left Tostes at the month of March, Madame Bovary was pregnant.

locale, et, s'arrêtant à cette idée, il songea sérieusement à aller s'établir ailleurs.

Dès lors, elle but du vinaigre pour se faire maigrir, contracta une petite toux sèche et perdit complètement l'appétit.

Il en coûtait à Charles d'abandonner Tostes après quatre ans de séjour et au moment où il commençait à s'y poser. S'il le fallait, cependant! Il la conduisit à Rouen voir son ancien maître. C'était une maladie nerveuse: on devait la changer d'air.

Après s'être tourné de côté et d'autre, Charles apprit qu'il y avait dans l'arrondissement de Neufchâtel, un fort bourg nommé Yonville-l'Abbaye, dont le médecin, qui était un réfugié polonais, venait de décamper la semaine précédente. Alors il écrivit au pharmacien de l'endroit pour savoir quel était le chiffre de la population, la distance où se trouvait le confrère le plus voisin, combien par année gagnait son prédécesseur, etc.; et, les réponses ayant été satisfaisantes, il se résolut à déménager vers le printemps, si la santé d'Emma ne s'améliorait pas.

Un jour qu'en prévision de son départ elle faisait des rangements dans un tiroir, elle se piqua les doigts à quelque chose. C'était un fil de fer de son bouquet de mariage. Les boutons d'oranger étaient jaunes de poussière, et les rubans de satin, à liséré d'argent, s'effiloquaient par le bord. Elle le jeta dans le feu. Il s'enflamma plus vite qu'une paille sèche. Puis ce fut comme un buisson rouge sur les cendres, et qui se rongeait lentement. Elle le regarda brûler. Les petites baies de carton éclataient, les fils d'archal se tordaient, le galon se fondait; et les corolles de papier, racornies, se balançant le long de la plaque comme des papillons noirs, enfin s'envolèrent par la cheminée.

Quand on partit de Tostes, au mois de mars, madame Bovary était enceinte.

# Part 11

# Deuxième Partie

# Chapter 1

Yonville-l'Abbaye (so called from an old Capuchin abbey of which not even the ruins remain) is a market-town twenty-four miles from Rouen, between the Abbeville and Beauvais roads, at the foot of a valley watered by the Rieule, a little river that runs into the Andelle after turning three water-mills near its mouth, where there are a few trout that the lads amuse themselves by fishing for on Sundays.

We leave the highroad at La Boissiere and keep straight on to the top of the Leux hill, whence the valley is seen. The river that runs through it makes of it, as it were, two regions with distinct physiognomies—all on the left is pasture land, all of the right arable. The meadow stretches under a bulge of low hills to join at the back with the pasture land of the Bray country, while on the eastern side, the plain, gently rising, broadens out, showing as far as eye can follow its blond cornfields. The water, flowing by the grass, divides with a white line the colour of the roads and of the plains, and the country is like a great unfolded mantle with a green velvet cape bordered with a fringe of silver.

Before us, on the verge of the horizon, lie the oaks of the forest of Argueil, with the steeps of the Saint-Jean hills scarred from top to bottom with red irregular lines; they are rain tracks, and these brick-tones standing out in narrow streaks against the grey colour of the mountain are due to the quantity of iron springs that flow beyond in the neighboring country.

Here we are on the confines of Normandy, Picardy, and the Ile-de-France, a bastard land whose language is without accent and its landscape is without character. It is there that they make the worst Neufchatel cheeses of all the arrondissement; and, on the other hand, farming is costly because so much manure is needed to enrich this friable soil full of sand and flints.

# Chapitre 1

Yonville-l'Abbaye (ainsi nommé à cause d'une ancienne abbaye de Capucins dont les ruines n'existent même plus) est un bourg à huit lieues de Rouen, entre la route d'Abbeville et celle de Beauvais, au fond d'une vallée qu'arrose la Rieule, petite rivière qui se jette dans l'Andelle, après avoir fait tourner trois moulins vers son embouchure, et où il y a quelques truites, que les garçons, le dimanche, s'amusent à pêcher à la ligne.

On quitte la grande route à la Boissière et l'on continue à plat jusqu'au haut de la côte des Leux, d'où l'on découvre la vallée. La rivière qui la traverse en fait comme deux régions de physionomie distincte: tout ce qui est à gauche est en herbage, tout ce qui est à droite est en labour. La prairie s'allonge sous un bourrelet de collines basses pour se rattacher par derrière aux pâturages du pays de Bray, tandis que, du côté de l'est, la plaine, montant doucement, va s'élargissant et étale à perte de vue ses blondes pièces de blé. L'eau qui court au bord de l'herbe sépare d'une raie blanche la couleur des prés et celle des sillons, et la campagne ainsi ressemble à un grand manteau déplié qui a un collet de velours vert, bordé d'un galon d'argent.

Au bout de l'horizon, lorsqu'on arrive, on a devant soi les chênes de la forêt d'Argueil, avec les escarpements de la côte Saint- Jean, rayés du haut en bas par de longues traînées rouges, inégales; ce sont les traces des pluies, et ces tons de brique, tranchant en filets minces sur la couleur grise de la montagne, viennent de la quantité de sources ferrugineuses qui coulent au delà, dans le pays d'alentour.

On est ici sur les confins de la Normandie, de la Picardie et de l'Île-de-France, contrée bâtarde où le langage est sans accentuation, comme le paysage sans caractère. C'est là que l'on fait les pires fromages de Neufchâtel de tout l'arrondissement, et, d'autre part, la culture y est coûteuse, parce qu'il faut beaucoup de fumier pour engraisser ces terres friables pleines de sable et de cailloux.

Up to 1835 there was no practicable road for getting to Yonville, but about this time a cross-road was made which joins that of Abbeville to that of Amiens, and is occasionally used by the Rouen wagoners on their way to Flanders. Yonville-l'Abbaye has remained stationary in spite of its "new outlet." Instead of improving the soil, they persist in keeping up the pasture lands, however depreciated they may be in value, and the lazy borough, growing away from the plain, has naturally spread riverwards. It is seem from afar sprawling along the banks like a cowherd taking a siesta by the water-side.

At the foot of the hill beyond the bridge begins a roadway, planted with young aspens, that leads in a straight line to the first houses in the place. These, fenced in by hedges, are in the middle of courtyards full of straggling buildings, wine-presses, cart-sheds and distilleries scattered under thick trees, with ladders, poles, or scythes hung on to the branches. The thatched roofs, like fur caps drawn over eyes, reach down over about a third of the low windows, whose coarse convex glasses have knots in the middle like the bottoms of bottles. Against the plaster wall diagonally crossed by black joists, a meagre pear-tree sometimes leans and the ground-floors have at their door a small swing-gate to keep out the chicks that come pilfering crumbs of bread steeped in cider on the threshold. But the courtyards grow narrower, the houses closer together, and the fences disappear; a bundle of ferns swings under a window from the end of a broomstick; there is a blacksmith's forge and then a wheelwright's, with two or three new carts outside that partly block the way. Then across an open space appears a white house beyond a grass mound ornamented by a Cupid, his finger on his lips; two brass vases are at each end of a flight of steps; scutcheons blaze upon the door. It is the notary's house, and the finest in the place.

The Church is on the other side of the street, twenty paces farther down, at the entrance of the square. The little cemetery that surrounds it, closed in by a wall breast high, is so full of graves that the old stones,

Jusqu'en 1835, il n'y avait point de route praticable pour arriver à Yonville; mais on a établi vers cette époque un chemin de grande vicinalité qui relie la route d'Abbeville à celle d'Amiens, et sert quelquefois aux rouliers allant de Rouen dans les Flandres. Cependant, Yonville-l'Abbaye est demeuré stationnaire, malgré ses débouchés nouveaux. Au lieu d'améliorer les cultures, on s'y obstine encore aux herbages, quelque dépréciés qu'ils soient, et le bourg paresseux, s'écartant de la plaine, a continué naturellement à s'agrandir vers la rivière. On l'aperçoit de loin, tout couché en long sur la rive, comme un gardeur de vaches qui fait la sieste au bord de l'eau.

Au bas de la côte, après le pont, commence une chaussée plantée de jeunes trembles, qui vous mène en droite ligne jusqu'aux premières maisons du pays. Elles sont encloses de haies, au milieu de cours pleines de bâtiments épars, pressoirs, charreteries et bouilleries, disséminés sous les arbres touffus portant des échelles, des gaules ou des faux accrochées dans leur branchage. Les toits de chaume, comme des bonnets de fourrure rabattus sur des yeux, descendent jusqu'au tiers à peu près des fenêtres basses, dont les gros verres bombés sont garnis d'un noeud dans le milieu, à la façon des culs de bouteilles. Sur le mur de plâtre que traversent en diagonale des lambourdes noires, s'accroche parfois quelque maigre poirier, et les rez-de-chaussée ont à leur porte une petite barrière tournante pour les défendre des poussins, qui viennent picorer, sur le seuil, des miettes de pain bis trempé de cidre. Cependant les cours se font plus étroites, les habitations se rapprochent, les haies disparaissent; un fagot de fougères se balance sous une fenêtre au bout d'un manche à balai; il y a la forge d'un maréchal et ensuite un charron avec deux ou trois charrettes neuves, en dehors, qui empiètent sur la route. Puis, à travers une claire-voie, apparaît une maison blanche au delà d'un rond de gazon que décore un Amour, le doigt posé sur la bouche; deux vases en fonte sont à chaque bout du perron; des panonceaux brillent à la porte; c'est la maison du notaire, et la plus belle du pays.

L'église est de l'autre côté de la rue, vingt pas plus loin, à l'entrée de la place. Le petit cimetière qui l'entoure, clos d'un mur à hauteur d'appui, est si bien rempli de tombeaux, que les vieilles pierres à ras du sol font

level with the ground, form a continuous pavement, on which the grass of itself has marked out regular green squares. The church was rebuilt during the last years of the reign of Charles X. The wooden roof is beginning to rot from the top, and here and there has black hollows in its blue colour. Over the door, where the organ should be, is a loft for the men, with a spiral staircase that reverberates under their wooden shoes.

The daylight coming through the plain glass windows falls obliquely upon the pews ranged along the walls, which are adorned here and there with a straw mat bearing beneath it the words in large letters, "Mr. So-and-so's pew." Farther on, at a spot where the building narrows, the confessional forms a pendant to a statuette of the Virgin, clothed in a satin robe, coifed with a tulle veil sprinkled with silver stars, and with red cheeks, like an idol of the Sandwich Islands; and, finally, a copy of the "Holy Family, presented by the Minister of the Interior," overlooking the high altar, between four candlesticks, closes in the perspective. The choir stalls, of deal wood, have been left unpainted.

The market, that is to say, a tiled roof supported by some twenty posts, occupies of itself about half the public square of Yonville. The town hall, constructed "from the designs of a Paris architect," is a sort of Greek temple that forms the corner next to the chemist's shop. On the ground-floor are three Ionic columns and on the first floor a semicircular gallery, while the dome that crowns it is occupied by a Gallic cock, resting one foot upon the "Charte" and holding in the other the scales of Justice.

But that which most attracts the eye is opposite the Lion d'Or inn, the chemist's shop of Monsieur Homais. In the evening especially its argand lamp is lit up and the red and green jars that embellish his shop-front throw far across the street their two streams of colour; then across them as if in Bengal lights is seen the shadow of the chemist leaning over his desk. His house from top to bottom is placarded with inscriptions written in large hand, round hand, printed hand: "Vichy, Seltzer, Barege waters, blood purifiers, Raspail patent medicine, Arabian racahout, Darcet lozenges, Regnault paste, trusses, baths, hygienic chocolate," etc. And the signboard, which takes up all the breadth of the shop, bears in

un dallage continu, où l'herbe a dessiné de soi-même des carrés verts réguliers. L'église a été rebâtie à neuf dans les dernières années du règne de Charles X. La voûte en bois commence à se pourrir par le haut, et, de place en place, a des enfonçures noires dans sa couleur bleue. Au-dessus de la porte, où seraient les orgues, se tient un jubé pour les hommes, avec un escalier tournant qui retentit sous les sabots.

Le grand jour, arrivant par les vitraux tout unis, éclaire obliquement les bancs rangés en travers de la muraille, que tapisse çà et là quelque paillasson cloué, ayant au-dessous de lui ces mots en grosses lettres: «Banc de M. un tel.» Plus loin, à l'endroit où le vaisseau se rétrécit, le confessionnal fait pendant à une statuette de la Vierge, vêtue d'une robe de satin, coiffée d'un voile de tulle semé d'étoiles d'argent, et tout empourprée aux pommettes comme une idole des îles Sandwich; enfin une copie de la Sainte Famille, envoi du ministre de l'intérieur, dominant le maître-autel entre quatre chandeliers, termine au fond la perspective. Les stalles du choeur, en bois de sapin, sont restées sans être peintes.

Les halles, c'est-à-dire un toit de tuiles supporté par une vingtaine de poteaux, occupent à elles seules la moitié environ de la grande place d'Yonville. La mairie, construite sur les dessins d'un architecte de Paris, est une manière de temple grec qui fait l'angle, à côté de la maison du pharmacien. Elle a, au rez-de- chaussée, trois colonnes ioniques et, au premier étage, une galerie à plein cintre, tandis que le tympan qui la termine est rempli par un coq gaulois, appuyé d'une patte sur la Charte et tenant de l'autre les balances de la justice.

Mais ce qui attire le plus les yeux, c'est, en face de l'auberge du Lion d'or, la pharmacie de M. Homais! Le soir, principalement, quand son quinquet est allumé et que les bocaux rouges et verts qui embellissent sa devanture allongent au loin, sur le sol, leurs deux clartés de couleur; alors, à travers elles, comme dans des feux du Bengale, s'entrevoit l'ombre du pharmacien, accoudé sur son pupitre. Sa maison, du haut en bas, est placardée d'inscriptions écrites en anglaise, en ronde, en moulée: «Eaux de Vichy, de Seltz et de Barèges, robs dépuratifs, médecine Raspail, racahout des Arabes, pastilles Darcet, pâte Regnault, bandages; bains, chocolats de santé, etc.» Et l'enseigne, qui tient toute la largeur de la

gold letters, "Homais, Chemist." Then at the back of the shop, behind the great scales fixed to the counter, the word "Laboratory" appears on a scroll above a glass door, which about half-way up once more repeats "Homais" in gold letters on a black ground.

Beyond this there is nothing to see at Yonville. The street (the only one) a gunshot in length and flanked by a few shops on either side stops short at the turn of the highroad. If it is left on the right hand and the foot of the Saint-Jean hills followed the cemetery is soon reached.

At the time of the cholera, in order to enlarge this, a piece of wall was pulled down, and three acres of land by its side purchased; but all the new portion is almost tenantless; the tombs, as heretofore, continue to crowd together towards the gate. The keeper, who is at once grave-digger and church beadle (thus making a double profit out of the parish corpses), has taken advantage of the unused plot of ground to plant potatoes there. From year to year, however, his small field grows smaller, and when there is an epidemic, he does not know whether to rejoice at the deaths or regret the burials.

"You live on the dead, Lestiboudois!" the curie at last said to him one day.

This grim remark made him reflect; it checked him for some time; but to this day he carries on the cultivation of his little tubers, and even maintains stoutly that they grow naturally.

Since the events about to be narrated, nothing in fact has changed at Yonville. The tin tricolour flag still swings at the top of the church-steeple; the two chintz streamers still flutter in the wind from the linen-draper's; the chemist's fetuses, like lumps of white amadou, rot more and more in their turbid alcohol, and above the big door of the inn the old golden lion, faded by rain, still shows passers-by its poodle mane.

On the evening when the Bovarys were to arrive at Yonville, Widow Lefrancois, the landlady of this inn, was so very busy that she sweated great drops as she moved her saucepans. To-morrow was market-day. The meat had to be cut beforehand, the fowls drawn, the soup and coffee made. Moreover, she had the boarders' meal to see to,

boutique, porte en lettres d'or: Homais, pharmacien. Puis, au fond de la boutique, derrière les grandes balances scellées sur le comptoir, le mot laboratoire se déroule au-dessus d'une porte vitrée qui, à moitié de sa hauteur, répète encore une fois Homais, en lettres d'or, sur un fond noir.

Il n'y a plus ensuite rien à voir dans Yonville. La rue (la seule), longue d'une portée de fusil et bordée de quelques boutiques, s'arrête court au tournant de la route. Si on la laisse sur la droite et que l'on suive le bas de la côte Saint-Jean, bientôt on arrive au cimetière.

Lors du choléra, pour l'agrandir, on a abattu un pan de mur et acheté trois acres de terre à côté; mais toute cette portion nouvelle est presque inhabitée, les tombes, comme autrefois, continuant à s'entasser vers la porte. Le gardien, qui est en même temps fossoyeur et bedeau à l'église (tirant ainsi des cadavres de la paroisse un double bénéfice), a profité, du terrain vide pour y semer des pommes de terre. D'année en année, cependant, son petit champ se rétrécit, et, lorsqu'il survient une épidémie, il ne sait pas s'il doit se réjouir des décès ou s'affliger des sépultures.

— Vous vous nourrissez des morts, Lestiboudois! lui dit enfin un jour, M. le curé.

Cette parole sombre le fit réfléchir; elle l'arrêta pour quelque temps; mais, aujourd'hui encore, il continue la culture de ses tubercules, et même soutient avec aplomb qu'ils poussent naturellement.

Depuis les événements que l'on va raconter; rien, en effet, n'a changé à Yonville. Le drapeau tricolore de fer-blanc tourne toujours au haut du clocher de l'église; la boutique du marchand de nouveautés agite encore au vent ses deux banderoles d'indienne; les foetus du pharmacien, comme des paquets d'amadou blanc, se pourrissent de plus en plus dans leur alcool bourbeux, et, au- dessus de la grande porte de l'auberge, le vieux lion d'or, déteint par les pluies, montre toujours aux passants sa frisure de caniche.

Le soir que les époux Bovary devaient arriver à Yonville, madame veuve Lefrançois, la maîtresse de cette auberge, était si fort affairée, qu'elle suait à grosses gouttes en remuant ses casseroles. C'était le lendemain jour de marché dans le bourg. Il fallait d'avance tailler les viandes, vider les poulets, faire de la soupe et du café. Elle avait, de plus, le

and that of the doctor, his wife, and their servant; the billiard-room was echoing with bursts of laughter; three millers in a small parlour were calling for brandy; the wood was blazing, the brazen pan was hissing, and on the long kitchen table, amid the quarters of raw mutton, rose piles of plates that rattled with the shaking of the block on which spinach was being chopped. From the poultry-yard was heard the screaming of the fowls whom the servant was chasing in order to wring their necks.

A man slightly marked with small-pox, in green leather slippers, and wearing a velvet cap with a gold tassel, was warming his back at the chimney. His face expressed nothing but self-satisfaction, and he appeared to take life as calmly as the goldfinch suspended over his head in its wicker cage: this was the chemist.

"Artemise!" shouted the landlady, "chop some wood, fill the water bottles, bring some brandy, look sharp! If only I knew what dessert to offer the guests you are expecting! Good heavens! Those furniture-movers are beginning their racket in the billiard-room again; and their van has been left before the front door! The 'Hirondelle' might run into it when it draws up. Call Polyte and tell him to put it up. Only think, Monsieur Homais, that since morning they have had about fifteen games, and drunk eight jars of cider! Why, they'll tear my cloth for me," she went on, looking at them from a distance, her strainer in her hand.

"That wouldn't be much of a loss," replied Monsieur Homais. "You would buy another."

"Another billiard-table!" exclaimed the widow.

"Since that one is coming to pieces, Madame Lefrancois. I tell you again you are doing yourself harm, much harm! And besides, players now want narrow pockets and heavy cues. Hazards aren't played now; everything is changed! One must keep pace with the times! Just look at Tellier!"

The hostess reddened with vexation. The chemist went on:

"You may say what you like; his table is better than yours; and if one were to think, for example, of getting up a patriotic pool for Poland or the sufferers from the Lyons floods—"

repas de ses pensionnaires, celui du médecin, de sa femme et de leur bonne; le billard retentissait d'éclats de rire; trois meuniers, dans la petite salle, appelaient pour qu'on leur apportât de l'eau-de-vie; le bois flambait, la braise craquait, et, sur la longue table de la cuisine, parmi les quartiers de mouton cru, s'élevaient des piles d'assiettes qui tremblaient aux secousses du billot où l'on hachait des épinards. On entendait, dans la basse-cour, crier les volailles que la servante poursuivait pour leur couper le cou.

Un homme en pantoufles de peau verte, quelque peu marqué de petite vérole et coiffé d'un bonnet de velours à gland d'or, se chauffait le dos contre la cheminée. Sa figure n'exprimait rien que la satisfaction de soi-même, et il avait l'air aussi calme dans la vie que le chardonneret suspendu au-dessus de sa tête, dans une cage d'osier: c'était le pharmacien.

— Artémise! criait la maîtresse d'auberge, casse de la bourrée, emplis les carafes, apporte de l'eau-de-vie, dépêche-toi! Au moins, si je savais quel dessert offrir à la société que vous attendez! Bonté divine! les commis du déménagement recommencent leur tintamarre dans le billard! Et leur charrette qui est restée sous la grande porte! L'Hirondelle est capable de la défoncer en arrivant! Appelle Polyte pour qu'il la remise!... Dire que, depuis le matin, monsieur Homais, ils ont peut-être fait quinze parties et bu huit pots de cidre!... Mais ils vont me déchirer le tapis, continuait-elle en les regardant de loin, son écumoire à la main.

— Le mal ne serait pas grand, répondit M. Homais vous en achèteriez un autre.

— Un autre billard! exclama la veuve.

— Puisque celui-là ne tient plus, madame Lefrançois; je vous le répète, vous vous faites tort! vous vous faites grand tort! Et puis les amateurs, à présent, veulent des blouses étroites et des queues lourdes. On ne joue plus la bille; tout est changé! Il faut marcher avec son siècle! Regardez Tellier, plutôt...

L'hôtesse devint rouge de dépit. Le pharmacien ajouta:

— Son billard, vous avez beau dire, est plus mignon que le vôtre; et qu'on ait l'idée, par exemple de monter une poule patriotique pour la Pologne ou les inondés de Lyon...

"It isn't beggars like him that'll frighten us," interrupted the landlady, shrugging her fat shoulders. "Come, come, Monsieur Homais; as long as the 'Lion d'Or' exists people will come to it. We've feathered our nest; while one of these days you'll find the 'Cafe Francais' closed with a big placard on the shutters. Change my billiard-table!" she went on, speaking to herself, "the table that comes in so handy for folding the washing, and on which, in the hunting season, I have slept six visitors! But that dawdler, Hivert, doesn't come!"

"Are you waiting for him for your gentlemen's dinner?"

"Wait for him! And what about Monsieur Binet? As the clock strikes six you'll see him come in, for he hasn't his equal under the sun for punctuality. He must always have his seat in the small parlour. He'd rather die than dine anywhere else. And so squeamish as he is, and so particular about the cider! Not like Monsieur Leon; he sometimes comes at seven, or even half-past, and he doesn't so much as look at what he eats. Such a nice young man! Never speaks a rough word!"

"Well, you see, there's a great difference between an educated man and an old carabineer who is now a tax-collector."

Six o'clock struck. Binet came in.

He wore a blue frock-coat falling in a straight line round his thin body, and his leather cap, with its lappets knotted over the top of his head with string, showed under the turned-up peak a bald forehead, flattened by the constant wearing of a helmet. He wore a black cloth waistcoat, a hair collar, grey trousers, and, all the year round, well-blacked boots, that had two parallel swellings due to the sticking out of his big-toes. Not a hair stood out from the regular line of fair whiskers, which, encircling his jaws, framed, after the fashion of a garden border, his long, wan face, whose eyes were small and the nose hooked. Clever at all games of cards, a good hunter, and writing a fine hand, he had at home a lathe, and amused himself by turning napkin rings, with which he filled up his house, with the jealousy of an artist and the egotism of a bourgeois.

— Ce ne sont pas des gueux comme lui qui nous font peur! interrompit l'hôtesse, en haussant ses grosses épaules. Allez! allez! monsieur Homais, tant que le Lion d'or vivra, on y viendra. Nous avons du foin dans nos bottes, nous autres! Au lieu qu'un de ces marins vous verrez le Café français fermé, et avec une belle affiche sur les auvents!... Changer mon billard, continuait-elle en se parlant à elle-même, lui qui m'est si commode pour ranger ma lessive, et sur lequel, dans le temps de la chasse, j'ai mis coucher jusqu'à six voyageurs!... Mais ce lambin d'Hivert qui n'arrive pas!

— L'attendez-vous pour le dîner de vos messieurs? demanda le pharmacien.

— L'attendre? Et M. Binet donc! À six heures battant vous allez le voir entrer, car son pareil n'existe pas sur la terre pour l'exactitude. Il lui faut toujours sa place dans la petite salle! On le tuerait plutôt que de le faire dîner ailleurs! et dégoûté qu'il est! et si difficile pour le cidre! Ce n'est pas comme M. Léon; lui, il arrive quelquefois à sept heures, sept heures et demie même; il ne regarde seulement pas à ce qu'il mange. Quel bon jeune homme! jamais un mot plus haut que l'autre.

— C'est qu'il y a bien de la différence, voyez-vous, entre quelqu'un qui a reçu de l'éducation et un ancien carabinier qui est percepteur.

Six heures sonnèrent. Binet entra.

Il était vêtu d'une redingote bleue, tombant droit d'elle-même tout autour de son corps maigre, et sa casquette de cuir, à pattes nouées par des cordons sur le sommet de sa tête, laissait voir, sous la visière relevée, un front chauve, qu'avait déprimé l'habitude du casque. Il portait un gilet de drap noir, un col de crin, un pantalon gris, et, en toute saison, des bottes bien cirées qui avaient deux renflements parallèles, à cause de la saillie de ses orteils. Pas un poil ne dépassait la ligne de son collier blond, qui, contournant la mâchoire, encadrait comme la bordure d'une plate-bande sa longue figure terne, dont les yeux étaient petits et le nez busqué. Fort à tous les jeux de cartes, bon chasseur et possédant une belle écriture, il avait chez lui un tour, où il s'amusait à tourner des ronds de serviette dont il encombrait sa maison, avec la jalousie d'un artiste et l'égoïsme d'un bourgeois.

He went to the small parlour, but the three millers had to be got out first, and during the whole time necessary for laying the cloth, Binet remained silent in his place near the stove. Then he shut the door and took off his cap in his usual way.

"It isn't with saying civil things that he'll wear out his tongue," said the chemist, as soon as he was along with the landlady.

"He never talks more," she replied. "Last week two travelers in the cloth line were here—such clever chaps who told such jokes in the evening, that I fairly cried with laughing; and he stood there like a dab fish and never said a word."

"Yes," observed the chemist; "no imagination, no sallies, nothing that makes the society-man."

"Yet they say he has parts," objected the landlady.

"Parts!" replied Monsieur Homais; "he, parts! In his own line it is possible," he added in a calmer tone.

And he went on:

"Ah! That a merchant, who has large connections, a jurisconsult, a doctor, a chemist, should be thus absent-minded, that they should become whimsical or even peevish, I can understand; such cases are cited in history. But at least it is because they are thinking of something. Myself, for example, how often has it happened to me to look on the bureau for my pen to write a label, and to find, after all, that I had put it behind my ear!"

Madame Lefrancois just then went to the door to see if the "Hirondelle" were not coming. She started. A man dressed in black suddenly came into the kitchen. By the last gleam of the twilight one could see that his face was rubicund and his form athletic.

"What can I do for you, Monsieur le Curie?" asked the landlady, as she reached down from the chimney one of the copper candlesticks placed with their candles in a row. "Will you take something? A thimbleful of Cassis? A glass of wine?"

The priest declined very politely. He had come for his umbrella, that he had forgotten the other day at the Ernemont convent, and after ask-

Il se dirigea vers la petite salle; mais il fallut d'abord en faire sortir les trois meuniers; et, pendant tout le temps que l'on fut à mettre son couvert, Binet resta silencieux à sa place, auprès du poêle; puis il ferma la porte et retira sa casquette, comme d'usage.

— Ce ne sont pas les civilités qui lui useront la langue! dit le pharmacien, dès qu'il fut seul avec l'hôtesse.

— Jamais il ne cause davantage, répondit-elle; il est venu ici, la semaine dernière, deux voyageurs en draps, des garçons pleins d'esprit qui contaient, le soir, un tas de farces que j'en pleurais de rire; eh bien, il restait là, comme une alose, sans dire un mot.

— Oui, fit le pharmacien, pas d'imagination, pas de saillies, rien de ce qui constitue l'homme de société!

— On dit pourtant qu'il a des moyens, objecta l'hôtesse.

— Des moyens? répliqua M. Homais; lui! des moyens? Dans sa partie, c'est possible, ajouta-t-il d'un ton plus calme.

Et il reprit:

— Ah! qu'un négociant qui a des relations considérables, qu'un jurisconsulte, un médecin, un pharmacien soient tellement absorbés qu'ils en deviennent fantasques et bourrus même, je le comprends; on en cite des traits dans les histoires! Mais, au moins, c'est qu'ils pensent à quelque chose. Moi, par exemple, combien de fois m'est-il arrivé de chercher ma plume sur mon bureau pour écrire une étiquette, et de trouver, en définitive, que je l'avais placée à mon oreille!

Cependant, madame Lefrançois alla sur le seuil regarder si l'Hirondelle n'arrivait pas. Elle tressaillit. Un homme vêtu de noir entra tout à coup dans la cuisine. On distinguait, aux dernières lueurs du crépuscule, qu'il avait la figure rubiconde et le corps athlétique.

— Qu'y a-t-il pour votre service, monsieur le curé? demanda la maîtresse d'auberge, tout en atteignant sur la cheminée un des flambeaux de cuivre qui s'y trouvaient rangés en colonnade avec leurs chandelles; voulez-vous prendre quelque chose? un doigt de cassis, un verre de vin?

L'ecclésiastique refusa fort civilement. Il venait chercher son parapluie, qu'il avait oublié l'autre jour au couvent d'Ernemont, et, après

ing Madame Lefrancois to have it sent to him at the presbytery in the evening, he left for the church, from which the Angelus was ringing.

When the chemist no longer heard the noise of his boots along the square, he thought the priest's behaviour just now very unbecoming. This refusal to take any refreshment seemed to him the most odious hypocrisy; all priests tippled on the sly, and were trying to bring back the days of the tithe.

The landlady took up the defence of her curie.

"Besides, he could double up four men like you over his knee. Last year he helped our people to bring in the straw; he carried as many as six trusses at once, he is so strong."

"Bravo!" said the chemist. "Now just send your daughters to confess to fellows which such a temperament! I, if I were the Government, I'd have the priests bled once a month. Yes, Madame Lefrancois, every month—a good phlebotomy, in the interests of the police and morals."

"Be quiet, Monsieur Homais. You are an infidel; you've no religion."

The chemist answered:

"I have a religion, my religion, and I even have more than all these others with their mummeries and their juggling. I adore God, on the contrary. I believe in the Supreme Being, in a Creator, whatever he may be. I care little who has placed us here below to fulfil our duties as citizens and fathers of families; but I don't need to go to church to kiss silver plates, and fatten, out of my pocket, a lot of good-for-nothings who live better than we do. For one can know Him as well in a wood, in a field, or even contemplating the eternal vault like the ancients. My God! Mine is the God of Socrates, of Franklin, of Voltaire, and of Beranger! I am for the profession of faith of the 'Savoyard Vicar,' and the immortal principles of '89! And I can't admit of an old boy of a God who takes walks in his garden with a cane in his hand, who lodges his friends in the belly of whales, dies uttering a cry, and rises again at the end of three days; things absurd in themselves, and completely opposed, moreover, to all physical laws, which prove to us, by the way, that priests have

avoir prié madame Lefrançois de le lui faire remettre au presbytère dans la soirée, il sortit pour se rendre à l'église, où l'on sonnait l'Angelus.

Quand le pharmacien n'entendit plus sur la place le bruit de ses souliers, il trouva fort inconvenante sa conduite de tout à l'heure. Ce refus d'accepter un rafraîchissement lui semblait une hypocrisie des plus odieuses; les prêtres godaillaient tous sans qu'on les vît, et cherchaient à ramener le temps de la dîme.

L'hôtesse prit la défense de son curé:

— D'ailleurs, il en plierait quatre comme vous sur son genou. Il a, l'année dernière, aidé nos gens à rentrer la paille; il en portait jusqu'à six bottes à la fois, tant il est fort!

— Bravo! dit le pharmacien. Envoyez donc vos filles en confesse à des gaillards d'un tempérament pareil! Moi, si j'étais le gouvernement, je voudrais qu'on saignât les prêtres une fois par mois. Oui, madame Lefrançois, tous les mois, une large phlébotomie, dans l'intérêt de la police et des moeurs!

— Taisez-vous donc, monsieur Homais! vous êtes un impie! vous n'avez pas de religion!

Le pharmacien répondit:

— J'ai une religion, ma religion, et même j'en ai plus qu'eux tous, avec leurs momeries et leurs jongleries! J'adore Dieu, au contraire! je crois en l'Être suprême, à un Créateur, quel qu'il soit, peu m'importe, qui nous a placés ici-bas pour y remplir nos devoirs de citoyen et de père de famille; mais je n'ai pas besoin d'aller, dans une église, baiser des plats d'argent, et engraisser de ma poche un tas de farceurs qui se nourrissent mieux que nous! Car on peut l'honorer aussi bien dans un bois, dans un champ, ou même en contemplant la voûte éthérée, comme les anciens. Mon Dieu, à moi, c'est le Dieu de Socrate, de Franklin, de Voltaire et de Béranger! Je suis pour la Profession de foi du vicaire savoyard et les immortels principes de 89! Aussi, je n'admets pas un bonhomme de bon Dieu qui se promène dans son parterre la canne à la main, loge ses amis dans le ventre des baleines, meurt en poussant un cri et ressuscite au bout de trois jours: choses absurdes en elles-mêmes et complètement opposées, d'ailleurs, à toutes les lois de la physique; ce qui nous démon-

always wallowed in turpid ignorance, in which they would fain engulf the people with them."

He ceased, looking round for an audience, for in his bubbling over the chemist had for a moment fancied himself in the midst of the town council. But the landlady no longer heeded him; she was listening to a distant rolling. One could distinguish the noise of a carriage mingled with the clattering of loose horseshoes that beat against the ground, and at last the "Hirondelle" stopped at the door.

It was a yellow box on two large wheels, that, reaching to the tilt, prevented travelers from seeing the road and dirtied their shoulders. The small panes of the narrow windows rattled in their sashes when the coach was closed, and retained here and there patches of mud amid the old layers of dust, that not even storms of rain had altogether washed away. It was drawn by three horses, the first a leader, and when it came down-hill its bottom jolted against the ground.

Some of the inhabitants of Yonville came out into the square; they all spoke at once, asking for news, for explanations, for hampers. Hivert did not know whom to answer. It was he who did the errands of the place in town. He went to the shops and brought back rolls of leather for the shoemaker, old iron for the farrier, a barrel of herrings for his mistress, caps from the milliner's, locks from the hair-dresser's and all along the road on his return journey he distributed his parcels, which he threw, standing upright on his seat and shouting at the top of his voice, over the enclosures of the yards.

An accident had delayed him. Madame Bovary's greyhound had run across the field. They had whistled for him a quarter of an hour; Hivert had even gone back a mile and a half expecting every moment to catch sight of her; but it had been necessary to go on. Emma had wept, grown angry; she had accused Charles of this misfortune. Monsieur Lheureux, a draper, who happened to be in the coach with her, had tried to console her by a number of examples of lost dogs recognizing their masters at the end of long years. One, he said had been told of, who had come back to Paris from Constantinople. Another had gone one hundred and fifty

tre, en passant, que les prêtres ont toujours croupi dans une ignorance turpide, où ils s'efforcent d'engloutir avec eux les populations.

Il se tut, cherchant des yeux un public autour de lui, car, dans son effervescence, le pharmacien un moment s'était cru en plein conseil municipal. Mais la maîtresse d'auberge ne l'écoutait plus; elle tendait son oreille à un roulement éloigné. On distingua le bruit d'une voiture mêlé à un claquement de fers lâches qui battaient la terre, et l'Hirondelle enfin s'arrêta devant la porte.

C'était un coffre jaune porté par deux grandes roues qui, montant jusqu'à la hauteur de la bâche, empêchaient les voyageurs de voir la route et leur salissaient les épaules. Les petits carreaux de ses vasistas étroits tremblaient dans leurs châssis quand la voiture était fermée, et gardaient des taches de boue, çà et là, parmi leur vieille couche de poussière, que les pluies d'orage même ne lavaient pas tout à fait. Elle était attelée de trois chevaux, dont le premier en arbalète, et, lorsqu'on descendait les côtes, elle touchait du fond en cahotant.

Quelques bourgeois d'Yonville arrivèrent sur la place; ils parlaient tous à la fois, demandant des nouvelles, des explications et des bourriches; Hivert ne savait auquel répondre. C'était lui qui faisait à la ville les commissions du pays. Il allait dans les boutiques, rapportait des rouleaux de cuir au cordonnier, de la ferraille au maréchal, un baril de harengs pour sa maîtresse, des bonnets de chez la modiste, des toupets de chez le coiffeur; et, le long de la route, en s'en revenant, il distribuait ses paquets, qu'il jetait par-dessus les clôtures des cours, debout sur son siège, et criant à pleine poitrine, pendant que ses chevaux allaient tout seuls.

Un accident l'avait retardé: la levrette de madame Bovary s'était enfuie à travers champs. On l'avait sifflée un grand quart d'heure. Hivert même était retourné d'une demi-lieue en arrière, croyant l'apercevoir à chaque minute; mais il avait fallu continuer la route. Emma avait pleuré, s'était emportée; elle avait accusé Charles de ce malheur. M. Lheureux, marchand d'étoffes, qui se trouvait avec elle dans la voiture, avait essayé de la consoler par quantité d'exemples de chiens perdus, reconnaissant leur maître au bout de longues années. On en citait un, disait-il, qui était revenu de Constantinople à Paris. Un autre avait fait cinquante lieues

miles in a straight line, and swum four rivers; and his own father had possessed a poodle, which, after twelve years of absence, had all of a sudden jumped on his back in the street as he was going to dine in town.

en ligne droite et passé quatre rivières à la nage; et son père à lui-même avait possédé un caniche qui, après douze ans d'absence, lui avait tout à coup sauté sur le dos, un soir, dans la rue, comme il allait dîner en ville.

# Chapter 2

Emma got out first, then Felicite, Monsieur Lheureux, and a nurse, and they had to wake up Charles in his corner, where he had slept soundly since night set in.

Homais introduced himself; he offered his homages to madame and his respects to monsieur; said he was charmed to have been able to render them some slight service, and added with a cordial air that he had ventured to invite himself, his wife being away.

When Madame Bovary was in the kitchen she went up to the chimney. With the tips of her fingers she caught her dress at the knee, and having thus pulled it up to her ankle, held out her foot in its black boot to the fire above the revolving leg of mutton. The flame lit up the whole of her, penetrating with a crude light the woof of her gowns, the fine pores of her fair skin, and even her eyelids, which she blinked now and again. A great red glow passed over her with the blowing of the wind through the half-open door.

On the other side of the chimney a young man with fair hair watched her silently.

As he was a good deal bored at Yonville, where he was a clerk at the notary's, Monsieur Guillaumin, Monsieur Leon Dupuis (it was he who was the second habitue of the "Lion d'Or") frequently put back his dinner-hour in hope that some traveler might come to the inn, with whom he could chat in the evening. On the days when his work was done early, he had, for want of something else to do, to come punctually, and endure from soup to cheese a tete-a-tete with Binet. It was therefore with delight that he accepted the landlady's suggestion that he should dine in company with the newcomers, and they passed into the large parlour where Madame Lefrancois, for the purpose of showing off, had had the table laid for four.

Homais asked to be allowed to keep on his skull-cap, for fear of coryza.

# Chapitre 2

Emma descendit la première, puis Félicité, M. Lheureux, une nourrice, et l'on fut obligé de réveiller Charles dans son coin, où il s'était endormi complètement dès que la nuit était venue.

Homais se présenta; il offrit ses hommages à Madame, ses civilités à Monsieur, dit qu'il était charmé d'avoir pu leur rendre quelque service, et ajouta d'un air cordial qu'il avait osé s'inviter lui- même, sa femme d'ailleurs étant absente.

Madame Bovary, quand elle fut dans la cuisine, s'approcha de la cheminée. Du bout de ses deux doigts, elle prit sa robe à la hauteur du genou, et, l'ayant ainsi remontée jusqu'aux chevilles, elle tendit à la flamme, par-dessus le gigot qui tournait, son pied chaussé d'une bottine noire. Le feu l'éclairait en entier, pénétrant d'une lumière crue la trame de sa robe, les pores égaux de sa peau blanche et même les paupières de ses yeux qu'elle clignait de temps à autre. Une grande couleur rouge passait sur elle, selon le souffle du vent qui venait par la porte entrouverte.

De l'autre côté de la cheminée, un jeune homme à chevelure blonde la regardait silencieusement.

Comme il s'ennuyait beaucoup à Yonville, où il était clerc chez maître Guillaumin, souvent M. Léon Dupuis (c'était lui, le second habitué du Lion d'or) reculait l'instant de son repas, espérant qu'il viendrait quelque voyageur à l'auberge avec qui causer dans la soirée. Les jours que sa besogne était finie il lui fallait bien, faute de savoir que faire, arriver à l'heure exacte, et subir depuis la soupe jusqu'au fromage le tête-à-tête de Binet. Ce fut donc avec joie qu'il accepta la proposition de l'hôtesse de dîner en la compagnie des nouveaux venus, et l'on passa dans la grande salle, où madame Lefrançois, par pompe, avait fait dresser les quatre couverts.

Homais demanda la permission de garder son bonnet grec, de peur des coryzas.

Then, turning to his neighbour:

"Madame is no doubt a little fatigued; one gets jolted so abominably in our 'Hirondelle.'"

"That is true," replied Emma; "but moving about always amuses me. I like change of place."

"It is so tedious," sighed the clerk, "to be always riveted to the same places."

"If you were like me," said Charles, "constantly obliged to be in the saddle"—

"But," Leon went on, addressing himself to Madame Bovary, "nothing, it seems to me, is more pleasant—when one can," he added.

"Moreover," said the druggist, "the practice of medicine is not very hard work in our part of the world, for the state of our roads allows us the use of gigs, and generally, as the farmers are prosperous, they pay pretty well. We have, medically speaking, besides the ordinary cases of enteritis, bronchitis, bilious affections, etc., now and then a few intermittent fevers at harvest-time; but on the whole, little of a serious nature, nothing special to note, unless it be a great deal of scrofula, due, no doubt, to the deplorable hygienic conditions of our peasant dwellings. Ah! you will find many prejudices to combat, Monsieur Bovary, much obstinacy of routine, with which all the efforts of your science will daily come into collision; for people still have recourse to novenas, to relics, to the priest, rather than come straight to the doctor or the chemist. The climate, however, is not, truth to tell, bad, and we even have a few nonagenarians in our parish. The thermometer (I have made some observations) falls in winter to 4 degrees Centigrade at the outside, which gives us 24 degrees Reaumur as the maximum, or otherwise 54 degrees Fahrenheit (English scale), not more. And, as a matter of fact, we are sheltered from the north winds by the forest of Argueil on the one side, from the west winds by the St. Jean range on the other; and this heat, moreover, which, on account of the aqueous vapours given off by the river and the considerable number of cattle in the fields, which, as you know, exhale much ammonia, that is to say, nitrogen, hydrogen

Puis, se tournant vers sa voisine:

— Madame, sans doute, est un peu lasse? On est si épouvantablement cahoté dans notre Hirondelle!

— Il est vrai, répondit Emma; mais le dérangement m'amuse toujours; j'aime à changer de place.

— C'est une chose si maussade, soupira le clerc, que de vivre cloué aux mêmes endroits!

— Si vous étiez comme moi, dit Charles, sans cesse obligé d'être à cheval…

— Mais, reprit Léon. s'adressant à madame Bovary, rien n'est plus agréable, il me semble; quand on le peut, ajouta-t-il.

— Du reste, disait l'apothicaire, l'exercice de la médecine n'est pas fort pénible en nos contrées; car l'état de nos routes permet l'usage du cabriolet, et, généralement, l'on paye assez bien, les cultivateurs étant aisés. Nous avons, sous le rapport médical, à part les cas ordinaires d'entérite, bronchite, affections bilieuses, etc., de temps à autre quelques fièvres intermittentes à la moisson, mais, en somme, peu de choses graves, rien de spécial à noter, si ce n'est beaucoup d'humeurs froides, et qui tiennent sans doute aux déplorables conditions hygiéniques de nos logements de paysan. Ah! vous trouverez bien des préjugés à combattre, monsieur Bovary; bien des entêtements de la routine, où se heurteront quotidiennement tous les efforts de votre science; car on a recours encore aux neuvaines, aux reliques, au curé, plutôt que de venir naturellement chez le médecin ou chez le pharmacien. Le climat, pourtant, n'est point, à vrai dire, mauvais, et même nous comptons dans la commune quelques nonagénaires. Le thermomètre (j'en ai fait les observations) descend en hiver jusqu'à quatre degrés, et, dans la forte saison, touche vingt-cinq, trente centigrades tout au plus, ce qui nous donne vingt-quatre Réaumur au maximum, ou autrement cinquante- quatre Fahrenheit (mesure anglaise), pas davantage! — et, en effet, nous sommes abrités des vents du nord par la forêt d'Argueil d'une part, des vents d'ouest par la côte Saint-Jean de l'autre, et cette chaleur, cependant, qui à cause de la vapeur d'eau dégagée par la rivière et la présence considérable de bestiaux dans les prairies, lesquels exhalent, comme vous savez, beaucoup

and oxygen (no, nitrogen and hydrogen alone), and which sucking up into itself the humus from the ground, mixing together all those different emanations, unites them into a stack, so to say, and combining with the electricity diffused through the atmosphere, when there is any, might in the long run, as in tropical countries, engender insalubrious miasmata—this heat, I say, finds itself perfectly tempered on the side whence it comes, or rather whence it should come—that is to say, the southern side—by the south-eastern winds, which, having cooled themselves passing over the Seine, reach us sometimes all at once like breezes from Russia."

"At any rate, you have some walks in the neighbourhood?" continued Madame Bovary, speaking to the young man.

"Oh, very few," he answered. "There is a place they call La Pature, on the top of the hill, on the edge of the forest. Sometimes, on Sundays, I go and stay there with a book, watching the sunset."

"I think there is nothing so admirable as sunsets," she resumed; "but especially by the side of the sea."

"Oh, I adore the sea!" said Monsieur Leon.

"And then, does it not seem to you," continued Madame Bovary, "that the mind travels more freely on this limitless expanse, the contemplation of which elevates the soul, gives ideas of the infinite, the ideal?"

"It is the same with mountainous landscapes," continued Leon. "A cousin of mine who travelled in Switzerland last year told me that one could not picture to oneself the poetry of the lakes, the charm of the waterfalls, the gigantic effect of the glaciers. One sees pines of incredible size across torrents, cottages suspended over precipices, and, a thousand feet below one, whole valleys when the clouds open. Such spectacles must stir to enthusiasm, incline to prayer, to ecstasy; and I no longer marvel at that celebrated musician who, the better to inspire his imagination, was in the habit of playing the piano before some imposing site."

"You play?" she asked.

"No, but I am very fond of music," he replied.

d'ammoniaque, c'est-à-dire azote, hydrogène et oxygène (non, azote et hydrogène seulement), et qui, pompant à elle l'humus de la terre, confondant toutes ces émanations différentes, les réunissant en un faisceau, pour ainsi dire, et se combinant de soi-même avec l'électricité répandue dans l'atmosphère, lorsqu'il y en a, pourrait à la longue, comme dans les pays tropicaux, engendrer des miasmes insalubres; — cette chaleur, dis-je, se trouve justement tempérée du côté où elle vient, ou plutôt d'où elle viendrait, c'est-à-dire du côté sud, par les vents de sud- est, lesquels, s'étant rafraîchis d'eux-mêmes en passant sur la Seine, nous arrivent quelquefois tout d'un coup, comme des brises de Russie!

— Avez-vous du moins quelques Promenades dans les environs? continuait madame Bovary parlant au jeune homme.

— Oh! fort peu, répondit-il. Il y a un endroit que l'on nomme la Pâture, sure le haut de la côte, à la lisière de la forêt. Quelque-fois, le dimanche, je vais là, et j'y reste avec un livre, à regarder le soleil couchant.

— Je ne trouve rien d'admirable comme les soleils couchants, reprit-elle, mais au bord de la mer, surtout.

— Oh! j'adore la mer, dit M. Léon.

— Et puis ne vous semble-t-il pas, répliqua madame Bovary, que l'esprit vogue plus librement sur cette étendue sans limites, dont la contemplation vous élève l'âme et donne des idées d'infini, d'idéal?

— Il en est de même des paysages de montagnes, reprit Léon. J'ai un cousin qui a voyagé en Suisse l'année dernière, et qui me disait qu'on ne peut se figurer la poésie des lacs, le charme des cascades, l'effet gigantesque des glaciers. On voit des pins d'une grandeur incroyable, en travers des torrents, des cabanes suspendues sur des précipices, et, à mille pieds sous vous, des vallées entières, quand les nuages s'entrouvrent. Ces spectacles doivent enthousiasmer, disposer à la prière, à l'extase! Aussi je ne m'étonne plus de ce musicien célèbre qui, pour exciter mieux son imagination, avait coutume d'aller jouer du piano devant quelque site imposant.

— Vous faites de la musique? demanda-t-elle.

— Non, mais je l'aime beaucoup, répondit-il.

"Ah! don't you listen to him, Madame Bovary," interrupted Homais, bending over his plate. "That's sheer modesty. Why, my dear fellow, the other day in your room you were singing 'L'Ange Gardien' ravishingly. I heard you from the laboratory. You gave it like an actor."

Leon, in fact, lodged at the chemist's where he had a small room on the second floor, overlooking the Place. He blushed at the compliment of his landlord, who had already turned to the doctor, and was enumerating to him, one after the other, all the principal inhabitants of Yonville. He was telling anecdotes, giving information; the fortune of the notary was not known exactly, and "there was the Tuvache household," who made a good deal of show.

Emma continued:

"And what music do you prefer?"

"Oh, German music; that which makes you dream."

"Have you been to the opera?"

"Not yet; but I shall go next year, when I am living at Paris to finish reading for the bar."

"As I had the honour of putting it to your husband," said the chemist, "with regard to this poor Yanoda who has run away, you will find yourself, thanks to his extravagance, in the possession of one of the most comfortable houses of Yonville. Its greatest convenience for a doctor is a door giving on the Walk, where one can go in and out unseen. Moreover, it contains everything that is agreeable in a household—a laundry, kitchen with offices, sitting-room, fruit-room, and so on. He was a gay dog, who didn't care what he spent. At the end of the garden, by the side of the water, he had an arbour built just for the purpose of drinking beer in summer; and if madame is fond of gardening she will be able—"

"My wife doesn't care about it," said Charles; "although she has been advised to take exercise, she prefers always sitting in her room reading."

"Like me," replied Leon. "And indeed, what is better than to sit by one's fireside in the evening with a book, while the wind beats against the window and the lamp is burning?"

— Ah! ne l'écoutez pas, madame Bovary, interrompit Homais en se penchant sur son assiette, c'est modestie pure. — Comment, mon cher! Eh! l'autre jour, dans votre chambre, vous chantiez *l'Ange gardien* à ravir. Je vous entendais du laboratoire; vous détachiez cela comme un acteur.

Léon, en effet, logeait chez le pharmacien, où il avait une petite pièce au second étage, sur la place. Il rougit à ce compliment de son propriétaire, qui déjà s'était tourné vers le médecin et lui énumérait les uns après les autres les principaux habitants d'Yonville. Il racontait des anecdotes, donnait des renseignements; on ne savait pas au juste la fortune du notaire, et il y avait la maison Tuvache qui faisait beaucoup d'embarras.

Emma reprit:

— Et quelle musique préférez-vous?

— Oh! la musique allemande, celle qui porte à rêver.

— Connaissez-vous les Italiens?

— Pas encore; mais je les verrai l'année prochaine, quand j'irai habiter Paris, pour finir mon droit.

— C'est comme j'avais l'honneur, dit le pharmacien, de l'exprimer à M. votre époux, à propos de ce pauvre Yanoda qui s'est enfui; vous vous trouverez, grâce aux folies qu'il a faites, jouir d'une des maisons les plus confortables d'Yonville. Ce qu'elle a principalement de commode pour un médecin, c'est une porte sur l'Allée, qui permet d'entrer et de sortir sans être vu. D'ailleurs, elle est fournie de tout ce qui est agréable à un ménage: buanderie, cuisine avec office, salon de famille, fruitier, etc. C'était un gaillard qui n'y regardait pas! Il s'était fait construire, au bout du jardin, à côté de l'eau, une tonnelle tout exprès pour boire de la bière en été, et si Madame aime le jardinage, elle pourra…

— Ma femme ne s'en occupe guère, dit Charles; elle aime mieux, quoiqu'on lui recommande l'exercice, toujours rester dans sa chambre, à lire.

— C'est comme moi, répliqua Léon; quelle meilleure chose, en effet, que d'être le soir au coin du feu avec un livre, pendant que le vent bat les carreaux, que la lampe brûle?…

"What, indeed?" she said, fixing her large black eyes wide open upon him.

"One thinks of nothing," he continued; "the hours slip by. Motionless we traverse countries we fancy we see, and your thought, blending with the fiction, playing with the details, follows the outline of the adventures. It mingles with the characters, and it seems as if it were yourself palpitating beneath their costumes."

"That is true! That is true?" she said.

"Has it ever happened to you," Leon went on, "to come across some vague idea of one's own in a book, some dim image that comes back to you from afar, and as the completest expression of your own slightest sentiment?"

"I have experienced it," she replied.

"That is why," he said, "I especially love the poets. I think verse more tender than prose, and that it moves far more easily to tears."

"Still in the long run it is tiring," continued Emma. "Now I, on the contrary, adore stories that rush breathlessly along, that frighten one. I detest commonplace heroes and moderate sentiments, such as there are in nature."

"In fact," observed the clerk, "these works, not touching the heart, miss, it seems to me, the true end of art. It is so sweet, amid all the disenchantments of life, to be able to dwell in thought upon noble characters, pure affections, and pictures of happiness. For myself, living here far from the world, this is my one distraction; but Yonville affords so few resources."

"Like Tostes, no doubt," replied Emma; "and so I always subscribed to a lending library."

"If madame will do me the honour of making use of it", said the chemist, who had just caught the last words, "I have at her disposal a library composed of the best authors, Voltaire, Rousseau, Delille, Walter Scott, the 'Echo des Feuilletons'; and in addition I receive various periodicals, among them the 'Fanal de Rouen' daily, having the advantage to be its correspondent for the districts of Buchy, Forges, Neufchatel, Yonville, and vicinity."

— N'est-ce pas? dit-elle, en fixant sur lui ses grands yeux noirs tout ouverts.

— On ne songe à rien, continuait-il, les heures passent. On se promène immobile dans des pays que l'on croit voir, et votre pensée, s'enlaçant à la fiction, se joue dans les détails ou poursuit le contour des aventures. Elle se mêle aux personnages; il semble que c'est vous qui palpitez sous leurs costumes.

— C'est vrai! c'est vrai! disait-elle.

— Vous est-il arrivé parfois, reprit Léon, de rencontrer dans un livre une idée vague que l'on a eue, quelque image obscurcie qui revient de loin, et comme l'exposition entière de votre sentiment le plus délié?

— J'ai éprouvé cela, répondit-elle.

— C'est pourquoi, dit-il, j'aime surtout les poètes. Je trouve les vers plus tendres que la prose, et qu'ils font bien mieux pleurer.

— Cependant ils fatiguent à la longue, reprit Emma; et maintenant, au contraire, j'adore les histoires qui se suivent tout d'une haleine, où l'on a peur. Je déteste les héros communs et les sentiments tempérés, comme il y en a dans la nature.

— En effet, observa le clerc, ces ouvrages ne touchant pas le coeur, s'écartent, il me semble, du vrai but de l'Art. Il est si doux, parmi les désenchantements de la vie, de pouvoir se reporter en idée sur de nobles caractères, des affections pures et des tableaux de bonheur. Quant à moi, vivant ici, loin du monde, c'est ma seule distraction; mais Yonville offre si peu de ressources!

— Comme Tostes, sans doute, reprit Emma; aussi j'étais toujours abonnée à un cabinet de lecture.

— Si Madame veut me faire l'honneur d'en user, dit le pharmacien, qui venait d'entendre ces derniers mots, j'ai moi-même à sa disposition une bibliothèque composée des meilleurs auteurs: Voltaire, Rousseau, Delille, Walter Scott, l'Écho des feuilletons, etc., et je reçois, de plus, différentes feuilles périodiques, parmi lesquelles le Fanal de Rouen, quotidiennement, ayant l'avantage d'en être le correspondant pour les circonscriptions de Buchy, Forges, Neufchâtel, Yonville et les alentours.

For two hours and a half they had been at table; for the servant Artemis, carelessly dragging her old list slippers over the flags, brought one plate after the other, forgot everything, and constantly left the door of the billiard-room half open, so that it beat against the wall with its hooks.

Unconsciously, Leon, while talking, had placed his foot on one of the bars of the chair on which Madame Bovary was sitting. She wore a small blue silk necktie, that kept up like a ruff a gauffered cambric collar, and with the movements of her head the lower part of her face gently sunk into the linen or came out from it. Thus side by side, while Charles and the chemist chatted, they entered into one of those vague conversations where the hazard of all that is said brings you back to the fixed centre of a common sympathy. The Paris theatres, titles of novels, new quadrilles, and the world they did not know; Tostes, where she had lived, and Yonville, where they were; they examined all, talked of everything till to the end of dinner.

When coffee was served Felicite went away to get ready the room in the new house, and the guests soon raised the siege. Madame Lefrancois was asleep near the cinders, while the stable-boy, lantern in hand, was waiting to show Monsieur and Madame Bovary the way home. Bits of straw stuck in his red hair, and he limped with his left leg. When he had taken in his other hand the cure's umbrella, they started.

The town was asleep; the pillars of the market threw great shadows; the earth was all grey as on a summer's night.

But as the doctor's house was only some fifty paces from the inn, they had to say good-night almost immediately, and the company dispersed.

As soon as she entered the passage, Emma felt the cold of the plaster fall about her shoulders like damp linen. The walls were new and the wooden stairs creaked. In their bedroom, on the first floor, a whitish light passed through the curtainless windows. She could catch glimpses of tree tops, and beyond, the fields, half-drowned in the fog that lay reeking in the moonlight along the course of the river. In the middle

Depuis deux heures et demie, on était à table; car la servante Artémise, traînant nonchalamment sur les carreaux ses savates de lisière, apportait les assiettes les unes après les autres, oubliait tout, n'entendait à rien et sans cesse laissait entrebâillée la porte du billard, qui battait contre le mur du bout de sa clenche.

Sans qu'il s'en aperçût, tout en causant, Léon avait posé son pied sur un des barreaux de la chaise où madame Bovary était assise. Elle portait une petite cravate de soie bleue, qui tenait droit comme une fraise un col de batiste tuyauté; et, selon les mouvements de tête qu'elle faisait, le bas de son visage s'enfonçait dans le linge ou en sortait avec douceur. C'est ainsi, l'un près de l'autre, pendant que Charles et le pharmacien devisaient, qu'ils entrèrent dans une de ces vagues conversations où le hasard des phrases vous ramène toujours au centre fixe d'une sympathie commune. Spectacles de Paris, titres de romans, quadrilles nouveaux, et le monde qu'ils ne connaissaient pas, Tostes où elle avait vécu, Yonville où ils étaient, ils examinèrent tout, parlèrent de tout jusqu'à la fin du dîner.

Quand le café fut servi, Félicité s'en alla préparer la chambre dans la nouvelle maison, et les convives bientôt levèrent le siège. Madame Lefrançois dormait auprès des cendres, tandis que le garçon d'écurie, une lanterne à la main, attendait M. et madame Bovary pour les conduire chez eux. Sa chevelure rouge était entremêlée de brins de paille, et il boitait de la jambe gauche. Lorsqu'il eut pris de son autre main le parapluie de M. le curé, l'on se mit en marche.

Le bourg était endormi. Les piliers des halles allongeaient de grandes ombres. La terre était toute grise, comme par une nuit d'été.

Mais, la maison du médecin se trouvant à cinquante pas de l'auberge, il fallut presque aussitôt se souhaiter le bonsoir, et la compagnie se dispersa.

Emma, dès le vestibule, sentit tomber sur ses épaules, comme un linge humide, le froid du plâtre. Les murs étaient neufs, et les marches de bois craquèrent. Dans la chambre, au premier, un jour blanchâtre passait par les fenêtres sans rideaux. On entrevoyait des cimes d'arbres, et plus loin la prairie, à demi noyée dans le brouillard, qui fumait au clair de la lune, selon le cours de la rivière. Au milieu de l'appartement,

of the room, pell-mell, were scattered drawers, bottles, curtain-rods, gilt poles, with mattresses on the chairs and basins on the ground—the two men who had brought the furniture had left everything about carelessly.

This was the fourth time that she had slept in a strange place. The first was the day of her going to the convent; the second, of her arrival at Tostes; the third, at Vaubyessard; and this was the fourth. And each one had marked, as it were, the inauguration of a new phase in her life. She did not believe that things could present themselves in the same way in different places, and since the portion of her life lived had been bad, no doubt that which remained to be lived would be better.

pêle-mêle, il y avait des tiroirs de commode, des bouteilles, des tringles, des bâtons dorés avec des matelas sur des chaises et des cuvettes sur le parquet, — les deux hommes qui avaient apporté, les meubles ayant tout laissé là, négligemment.

C'était la quatrième fois qu'elle couchait dans un endroit inconnu. La première avait été le jour de son entrée au couvent, la seconde celle de son arrivée à Tostes, la troisième à la Vaubyessard, la quatrième était celle-ci; et chacune s'était trouvée faire dans sa vie comme l'inauguration d'une phase nouvelle. Elle ne croyait pas que les choses pussent se représenter les mêmes à des places différentes, et, puisque la portion vécue avait été mauvaise, sans doute ce qui restait à consommer serait meilleur.

# Chapter 3

The next day, as she was getting up, she saw the clerk on the Place. She had on a dressing-gown. He looked up and bowed. She nodded quickly and reclosed the window.

Leon waited all day for six o'clock in the evening to come, but on going to the inn, he found no one but Monsieur Binet, already at table.

The dinner of the evening before had been a considerable event for him; he had never till then talked for two hours consecutively to a "lady." How then had he been able to explain, and in such language, the number of things that he could not have said so well before? He was usually shy, and maintained that reserve which partakes at once of modesty and dissimulation. At Yonville he was considered "well-bred." He listened to the arguments of the older people, and did not seem hot about politics—a remarkable thing for a young man. Then he had some accomplishments; he painted in water-colours, could read the key of G, and readily talked literature after dinner when he did not play cards. Monsieur Homais respected him for his education; Madame Homais liked him for his good-nature, for he often took the little Homais into the garden—little brats who were always dirty, very much spoilt, and somewhat lymphatic, like their mother. Besides the servant to look after them, they had Justin, the chemist's apprentice, a second cousin of Monsieur Homais, who had been taken into the house from charity, and who was useful at the same time as a servant.

The druggist proved the best of neighbours. He gave Madame Bovary information as to the trades-people, sent expressly for his own cider merchant, tasted the drink himself, and saw that the casks were properly placed in the cellar; he explained how to set about getting in a supply of butter cheap, and made an arrangement with Lestiboudois,

# Chapitre 3

Le lendemain, à son réveil, elle aperçut le clerc sur la place. Elle était en peignoir. Il leva la tête et la salua. Elle fit une inclination rapide et referma la fenêtre.

Léon attendit pendant tout le jour que six heures du soir fussent arrivées; mais, en entrant à l'auberge, il ne trouva personne que M. Binet, attablé.

Ce dîner de la veille était pour lui un événement considérable; jamais, jusqu'alors, il n'avait causé pendant deux heures de suite avec une dame. Comment donc avoir pu lui exposer, et en un tel langage, quantité de choses qu'il n'aurait pas si bien dites auparavant? il était timide d'habitude et gardait cette réserve qui participe à la fois de la pudeur et de la dissimulation. On trouvait à Yonville qu'il avait des manières comme il faut. Il écoutait raisonner les gens mûrs, et ne paraissait point exalté en politique, chose remarquable pour un jeune homme. Puis il possédait des talents, il peignait à l'aquarelle, savait lire la clef de sol, et s'occupait volontiers de littérature après son dîner, quand il ne jouait pas aux cartes. M Homais le considérait pour son instruction; madame Homais l'affectionnait pour sa complaisance, car souvent il accompagnait au jardin les petits Homais, marmots toujours barbouillés, fort mal élevés et quelque peu lymphatiques, comme leur mère. Ils avaient pour les soigner, outre la bonne, Justin, l'élève en pharmacie, un arrière-cousin de M. Homais que l'on avait pris dans la maison par charité, et qui servait en même temps de domestique.

L'apothicaire se montra le meilleur des voisins. Il renseigna madame Bovary sur les fournisseurs, fit venir son marchand de cidre tout exprès, goûta la boisson lui-même, et veilla dans la cave à ce que la futaille fut bien placée; il indiqua encore la façon de s'y prendre pour avoir une provision de beurre à bon marché, et conclut un arrangement avec

the sacristan, who, besides his sacerdotal and funeral functions, looked after the principal gardens at Yonville by the hour or the year, according to the taste of the customers.

The need of looking after others was not the only thing that urged the chemist to such obsequious cordiality; there was a plan underneath it all.

He had infringed the law of the 19th Ventose, year xi., article I, which forbade all persons not having a diploma to practise medicine; so that, after certain anonymous denunciations, Homais had been summoned to Rouen to see the procurer of the king in his own private room; the magistrate receiving him standing up, ermine on shoulder and cap on head. It was in the morning, before the court opened. In the corridors one heard the heavy boots of the gendarmes walking past, and like a far-off noise great locks that were shut. The druggist's ears tingled as if he were about to have an apoplectic stroke; he saw the depths of dungeons, his family in tears, his shop sold, all the jars dispersed; and he was obliged to enter a cafe and take a glass of rum and seltzer to recover his spirits.

Little by little the memory of this reprimand grew fainter, and he continued, as heretofore, to give anodyne consultations in his back-parlour. But the mayor resented it, his colleagues were jealous, everything was to be feared; gaining over Monsieur Bovary by his attentions was to earn his gratitude, and prevent his speaking out later on, should he notice anything. So every morning Homais brought him "the paper," and often in the afternoon left his shop for a few moments to have a chat with the Doctor.

Charles was dull: patients did not come. He remained seated for hours without speaking, went into his consulting room to sleep, or watched his wife sewing. Then for diversion he employed himself at home as a workman; he even tried to do up the attic with some paint which had been left behind by the painters. But money matters worried him. He had spent so much for repairs at Tostes, for madame's toilette, and for the moving, that the whole dowry, over three thousand crowns, had slipped away in two years. Then how many things had been spoilt or lost during their carriage from Tostes to Yonville, without count-

Lestiboudois, le sacristain, qui, outre ses fonctions sacerdotales et mortuaires, soignait les principaux jardins d'Yonville à l'heure ou à l'année, selon le goût des personnes.

Le besoin de s'occuper d'autrui ne poussait pas seul le pharmacien à tant de cordialité obséquieuse, et il y avait là-dessous un plan.

Il avait enfreint la loi du 19 ventôse an XI, article Ier, qui défend à tout individu non porteur de diplôme l'exercice de la médecine; si bien que, sur des dénonciations ténébreuses, Homais avait été mandé à Rouen, près M le procureur du roi, en son cabinet particulier. Le magistrat l'avait reçu debout, dans sa robe, hermine à l'épaule et toque en tête. C'était le matin, avant l'audience. On entendait dans le corridor passer les fortes bottes des gendarmes, et comme un bruit lointain de grosses serrures qui se fermaient. Les oreilles du pharmacien lui tintèrent à croire qu'il allait tomber d'un coup de sang; il entrevit des culs de basse-fosse, sa famille en pleurs, la pharmacie vendue, tous les bocaux disséminés; et il fut obligé d'entrer dans un café prendre un verre de rhum avec de l'eau de Seltz, pour se remettre les esprits.

Peu à peu, le souvenir de cette admonition s'affaiblit, et il continuait, comme autrefois, à donner des consultations anodines dans son arrière-boutique. Mais le maire lui en voulait, des confrères étaient jaloux, il fallait tout craindre; en s'attachant M. Bovary par des politesses, c'était gagner sa gratitude, et empêcher qu'il ne parlât plus tard, s'il s'apercevait de quelque chose. Aussi, tous les matins, Homais lui apportait le journal, et souvent, dans l'après-midi, quittait un instant la pharmacie pour aller chez l'officier de santé faire la conversation.

Charles était triste: la clientèle n'arrivait pas. Il demeurait assis pendant de longues heures, sans parler, allait dormir dans son cabinet ou regardait coudre sa femme. Pour se distraire, il s'employa chez lui comme homme de peine, et même il essaya de peindre le grenier avec un reste de couleur que les peintres avaient laissé. Mais les affaires d'argent le préoccupaient. Il en avait tant dépensé pour les réparations de Tostes, pour les toilettes de Madame et pour le déménagement, que toute la dot, plus de trois mille écus, s'était écoulée en deux ans. Puis, que de choses endommagées ou perdues dans le transport de Tostes à

ing the plaster cure, who falling out of the coach at an over-severe jolt, had been dashed into a thousand fragments on the pavements of Quincampoix!

A pleasanter trouble came to distract him, namely, the pregnancy of his wife. As the time of her confinement approached he cherished her the more. It was another bond of the flesh establishing itself, and, as it were, a continued sentiment of a more complex union. When from afar he saw her languid walk, and her figure without stays turning softly on her hips; when opposite one another he looked at her at his ease, while she took tired poses in her armchair, then his happiness knew no bounds; he got up, embraced her, passed his hands over her face, called her little mamma, wanted to make her dance, and half-laughing, half-crying, uttered all kinds of caressing pleasantries that came into his head. The idea of having begotten a child delighted him. Now he wanted nothing. He knew human life from end to end, and he sat down to it with serenity.

Emma at first felt a great astonishment; then was anxious to be delivered that she might know what it was to be a mother. But not being able to spend as much as she would have liked, to have a swing-bassinette with rose silk curtains, and embroidered caps, in a fit of bitterness she gave up looking after the trousseau, and ordered the whole of it from a village needlewoman, without choosing or discussing anything. Thus she did not amuse herself with those preparations that stimulate the tenderness of mothers, and so her affection was from the very outset, perhaps, to some extent attenuated.

As Charles, however, spoke of the boy at every meal, she soon began to think of him more consecutively.

She hoped for a son; he would be strong and dark; she would call him George; and this idea of having a male child was like an expected revenge for all her impotence in the past. A man, at least, is free; he may travel over passions and over countries, overcome obstacles, taste of the most far-away pleasures. But a woman is always hampered. At once inert and flexible, she has against her the weakness of the flesh and legal dependence. Her will, like the veil of her bonnet, held by a string,

Yonville, sans compter le curé de plâtre, qui, tombant de la charrette à un cahot trop fort, s'était écrasé en mille morceaux sur le pavé de Quincampoix!

Un souci meilleur vint le distraire, à savoir la grossesse de sa femme. À mesure que le terme en approchait, il la chérissait davantage. C'était un autre lien de la chair s'établissant et comme le sentiment continu d'une union plus complexe. Quand il voyait de loin sa démarche paresseuse et sa taille tourner mollement sur ses hanches sans corset, quand vis-à-vis l'un de l'autre il la contemplait tout à l'aise et qu'elle prenait, assise, des poses fatiguées dans son fauteuil, alors son bonheur ne se tenait plus; il se levait, il l'embrassait, passait ses mains sur sa figure, l'appelait petite maman, voulait la faire danser, et débitait, moitié riant, moitié pleurant, toutes sortes de plaisanteries caressantes qui lui venaient à l'esprit. L'idée d'avoir engendré le délectait. Rien ne lui manquait à présent. Il connaissait l'existence humaine tout du long, et il s'y attablait sur les deux coudes avec sérénité.

Emma d'abord sentit un grand étonnement, puis eut envie d'être délivrée, pour savoir quelle chose c'était que d'être mère. Mais, ne pouvant faire les dépenses qu'elle voulait, avoir un berceau en nacelle avec des rideaux de soie rose et des béguins brodés, elle renonça au trousseau dans un accès d'amertume, et le commanda d'un seul coup à une ouvrière du village, sans rien choisir ni discuter. Elle ne s'amusa donc pas à ces préparatifs où la tendresse des mères se met en appétit, et son affection, dès l'origine, en fut peut-être atténuée de quelque chose:

Cependant, comme Charles, à tous les repas, parlait du marmot, bientôt elle y songea d'une façon plus continue.

Elle souhaitait un fils; il serait fort et brun, elle l'appellerait Georges; et cette idée d'avoir pour enfant un mâle était comme la revanche en espoir de toutes ses impuissances passées. Un homme, au moins, est libre; il peut parcourir les passions et les pays, traverser les obstacles, mordre aux bonheurs les plus lointains. Mais une femme est empêchée continuellement. Inerte et flexible à la fois, elle a contre elle les mollesses de la chair avec les dépendances de la loi. Sa volonté, comme le voile de

flutters in every wind; there is always some desire that draws her, some conventionality that restrains.

She was confined on a Sunday at about six o'clock, as the sun was rising.

"It is a girl!" said Charles.

She turned her head away and fainted.

Madame Homais, as well as Madame Lefrancois of the Lion d'Or, almost immediately came running in to embrace her. The chemist, as man of discretion, only offered a few provincial felicitations through the half-opened door. He wished to see the child and thought it well made.

Whilst she was getting well she occupied herself much in seeking a name for her daughter. First she went over all those that have Italian endings, such as Clara, Louisa, Amanda, Atala; she liked Galsuinde pretty well, and Yseult or Leocadie still better. Charles wanted the child to be called after her mother; Emma opposed this. They ran over the calendar from end to end, and then consulted outsiders.

"Monsieur Leon," said the chemist, "with whom I was talking about it the other day, wonders you do not chose Madeleine. It is very much in fashion just now."

But Madame Bovary, senior, cried out loudly against this name of a sinner. As to Monsieur Homais, he had a preference for all those that recalled some great man, an illustrious fact, or a generous idea, and it was on this system that he had baptized his four children. Thus Napoleon represented glory and Franklin liberty; Irma was perhaps a concession to romanticism, but Athalie was a homage to the greatest masterpiece of the French stage. For his philosophical convictions did not interfere with his artistic tastes; in him the thinker did not stifle the man of sentiment; he could make distinctions, make allowances for imagination and fanaticism. In this tragedy, for example, he found fault with the ideas, but admired the style; he detested the conception, but applauded all the details, and loathed the characters while he grew enthusiastic over their dialogue. When he read the fine passages he was transported, but when he thought that mummers would get something out of them for their show, he was disconsolate; and in this confusion

son chapeau retenu par un cordon, palpite à tous les vents; il y a toujours quelque désir qui entraîne, quelque convenance qui retient.

Elle accoucha un dimanche, vers six heures, au soleil levant.

— C'est une fille! dit Charles.

Elle tourna la tête et s'évanouit,

Presque aussitôt, madame Homais accourut et l'embrassa, ainsi que la mère Lefrançois, du Lion d'or. Le pharmacien, en homme discret, lui adressa seulement quelques félicitations provisoires, par la porte entrebâillée. Il voulut voir l'enfant, et le trouva bien conformé.

Pendant sa convalescence, elle s'occupa beaucoup à chercher un nom pour sa fille. D'abord, elle passa en revue tous ceux qui avaient des terminaisons italiennes, tels que Clara, Louisa, Amanda, Atala; elle aimait assez Galsuinde, plus encore Yseult ou Léocadie. Charles désirait qu'on appelât l'enfant comme sa mère; Emma s'y opposait. On parcourut le calendrier d'un bout à l'autre, et l'on consulta les étrangers.

— M. Léon; disait le pharmacien, avec qui j'en causais l'autre jour, s'étonne que vous ne choisissiez point Madeleine, qui est excessivement à la mode maintenant.

Mais la mère Bovary se récria bien fort sur ce nom de pécheresse. M. Homais, quant à lui, avait en prédilection tous ceux qui rappelaient un grand homme, un fait illustre ou une conception généreuse, et c'est dans ce système-là qu'il avait baptisé ses quatre enfants. Ainsi, Napoléon représentait la gloire et Franklin la liberté; Irma, peut-être, était une concession au romantisme; mais Athalie, un hommage au plus immortel chef-d'oeuvre de la scène française. Car ses convictions philosophiques n'empêchaient pas ses admirations artistiques, le penseur chez lui n'étouffait point l'homme sensible; il savait établir des différences, faire la part de l'imagination et celle du fanatisme. De cette tragédie, par exemple, il blâmait les idées, mais il admirait le style; il maudissait la conception, mais il applaudissait à tous les détails, et s'exaspérait contre les personnages, en s'enthousiasmant de leurs discours. Lorsqu'il lisait les grands morceaux, il était transporté; mais, quand il songeait que les calotins en tiraient avantage pour leur boutique, il était désolé, et dans

of sentiments in which he was involved he would have liked at once to crown Racine with both his hands and discuss with him for a good quarter of an hour.

At last Emma remembered that at the chateau of Vaubyessard she had heard the Marchioness call a young lady Berthe; from that moment this name was chosen; and as old Rouault could not come, Monsieur Homais was requested to stand godfather. His gifts were all products from his establishment, to wit: six boxes of jujubes, a whole jar of racahout, three cakes of marshmallow paste, and six sticks of sugar-candy into the bargain that he had come across in a cupboard. On the evening of the ceremony there was a grand dinner; the cure was present; there was much excitement. Monsieur Homais towards liqueur-time began singing "Le Dieu des bonnes gens." Monsieur Leon sang a barcarolle, and Madame Bovary, senior, who was godmother, a romance of the time of the Empire; finally, M. Bovary, senior, insisted on having the child brought down, and began baptizing it with a glass of champagne that he poured over its head. This mockery of the first of the sacraments made the Abbe Bournisien angry; old Bovary replied by a quotation from *La Guerre des Dieux*; the cure wanted to leave; the ladies implored, Homais interfered; and they succeeded in making the priest sit down again, and he quietly went on with the half-finished coffee in his saucer.

Monsieur Bovary, senior, stayed at Yonville a month, dazzling the natives by a superb policeman's cap with silver tassels that he wore in the morning when he smoked his pipe in the square. Being also in the habit of drinking a good deal of brandy, he often sent the servant to the Lion d'Or to buy him a bottle, which was put down to his son's account, and to perfume his handkerchiefs he used up his daughter-in-law's whole supply of eau-de-cologne.

The latter did not at all dislike his company. He had knocked about the world, he talked about Berlin, Vienna, and Strasbourg, of his soldier times, of the mistresses he had had, the grand luncheons of which he had partaken; then he was amiable, and sometimes even, either on the stairs, or in the garden, would seize hold of her waist, crying:

"Charles, look out for yourself."

cette confusion de sentiments où il s'embarrassait, il aurait voulu tout à la fois pouvoir couronner Racine de ses deux mains et discuter avec lui pendant un bon quart d'heure.

Enfin, Emma se souvint qu'au château de la Vaubyessard elle avait entendu la marquise appeler Berthe une jeune femme; dès lors ce nom-là fut choisi, et, comme le père Rouault ne pouvait venir, on pria M. Homais d'être parrain. Il donna pour cadeaux tous produits de son établissement, à savoir: six boîtes de jujubes, un bocal entier de racahout, trois coffins de pâte à la guimauve, et, de plus, six bâtons de sucre candi qu'il avait retrouvés dans un placard. Le soir de la cérémonie, il y eut un grand dîner; le curé s'y trouvait; on s'échauffa. M. Homais, vers les liqueurs, entonna le Dieu des bonnes gens. M. Léon chanta une barcarolle, et madame Bovary mère, qui était la marraine, une romance du temps de l'Empire; enfin M. Bovary père exigea que l'on descendît l'enfant, et se mit à le baptiser avec un verre de champagne qu'il lui versait de haut sur la tête. Cette dérision du premier des sacrements indigna l'abbé Bournisien; le père Bovary répondit par une citation de la *Guerre des dieux*, le curé voulut partir; les dames suppliaient; Homais s'interposa; et l'on parvint à faire rasseoir l'ecclésiastique, qui reprit tranquillement, dans sa soucoupe, sa demi-tasse de café à moitié bue.

M. Bovary père resta encore un mois à Yonville, dont il éblouit les habitants par un superbe bonnet de police à galons d'argent, qu'il portait le matin, pour fumer sa pipe sur la place. Ayant aussi l'habitude de boire beaucoup d'eau-de-vie, souvent il envoyait la servante au Lion d'or lui en acheter une bouteille, que l'on inscrivait au compte de son fils; et il usa, pour parfumer ses foulards, toute la provision d'eau de Cologne qu'avait sa bru.

Celle-ci ne se déplaisait point dans sa compagnie. Il avait couru le monde: il parlait de Berlin, de Vienne, de Strasbourg, de son temps d'officier, des maîtresses qu'il avait eues, des grands déjeuners qu'il avait faits; puis il se montrait aimable, et parfois même, soit dans l'escalier ou au jardin, il lui saisissait la taille en s'écriant:

— Charles, prends garde à toi!

Then Madame Bovary, senior, became alarmed for her son's happiness, and fearing that her husband might in the long-run have an immoral influence upon the ideas of the young woman, took care to hurry their departure. Perhaps she had more serious reasons for uneasiness. Monsieur Bovary was not the man to respect anything.

One day Emma was suddenly seized with the desire to see her little girl, who had been put to nurse with the carpenter's wife, and, without looking at the calendar to see whether the six weeks of the Virgin were yet passed, she set out for the Rollets' house, situated at the extreme end of the village, between the highroad and the fields.

It was mid-day, the shutters of the houses were closed and the slate roofs that glittered beneath the fierce light of the blue sky seemed to strike sparks from the crest of the gables. A heavy wind was blowing; Emma felt weak as she walked; the stones of the pavement hurt her; she was doubtful whether she would not go home again, or go in somewhere to rest.

At this moment Monsieur Leon came out from a neighbouring door with a bundle of papers under his arm. He came to greet her, and stood in the shade in front of the Lheureux's shop under the projecting grey awning.

Madame Bovary said she was going to see her baby, but that she was beginning to grow tired.

"If—" said Leon, not daring to go on.

"Have you any business to attend to?" she asked.

And on the clerk's answer, she begged him to accompany her. That same evening this was known in Yonville, and Madame Tuvache, the mayor's wife, declared in the presence of her servant that "Madame Bovary was compromising herself."

To get to the nurse's it was necessary to turn to the left on leaving the street, as if making for the cemetery, and to follow between little houses and yards a small path bordered with privet hedges. They were in bloom, and so were the speedwells, eglantines, thistles, and the sweetbriar that sprang up from the thickets. Through openings in the hedges one could see into the huts, some pigs on a dung-heap, or tethered cows

Alors la mère Bovary s'effraya pour le bonheur de son fils, et, craignant que son époux, à la longue, n'eût une influence immorale sur les idées de la jeune femme, elle se hâta de presser le départ. Peut-être avait-elle des inquiétudes plus sérieuses. M. Bovary était homme à ne rien respecter.

Un jour, Emma fut prise tout à coup du besoin de voir sa petite fille, qui avait été mise en nourrice chez la femme du menuisier; et, sans regarder à l'almanach si les six semaines de la Vierge duraient encore, elle s'achemina vers la demeure de Rolet, qui se trouvait à l'extrémité du village, au bas de la côte, entre la grande route et les prairies.

Il était midi; les maisons avaient leurs volets fermés, et les toits d'ardoises, qui reluisaient sous la lumière âpre du ciel bleu, semblaient à la crête de leurs pignons faire pétiller des étincelles. Un vent lourd soufflait. Emma se sentait faible en marchant; les cailloux du trottoir la blessaient; elle hésita si elle ne s'en retournerait pas chez elle, ou entrerait quelque part pour s'asseoir.

À ce moment, M. Léon sortit d'une porte voisine avec une liasse de papiers sous son bras. Il vint la saluer et se mit à l'ombre devant la boutique de Lheureux, sous la tente grise qui avançait.

Madame Bovary dit qu'elle allait voir son enfant, mais qu'elle commençait à être lasse.

— Si..., reprit Léon, n'osant poursuivre.

— Avez-vous affaire quelque part? demanda-t-elle.

Et, sur la réponse du clerc, elle le pria de l'accompagner. Dès le soir, cela fut connu dans Yonville, et madame Tuvache, la femme du maire, déclara devant sa servante que madame Bovary se compromettait.

Pour arriver chez la nourrice il fallait, après la rue, tourner à gauche, comme pour gagner le cimetière, et suivre, entre des maisonnettes et des cours, un petit sentier que bordaient des troènes. Ils étaient en fleur et les véroniques aussi, les églantiers, les orties, et les ronces légères qui s'élançaient des buissons. Par le trou des haies, on apercevait, dans les masures, quelque pourceau sur un fumier, ou des vaches embricolées,

rubbing their horns against the trunk of trees. The two, side by side walked slowly, she leaning upon him, and he restraining his pace, which he regulated by hers; in front of them a swarm of midges fluttered, buzzing in the warm air.

They recognized the house by an old walnut-tree which shaded it. Low and covered with brown tiles, there hung outside it, beneath the dormer-window of the garret, a string of onions. Faggots upright against a thorn fence surrounded a bed of lettuce, a few square feet of lavender, and sweet peas strung on sticks. Dirty water was running here and there on the grass, and all round were several indefinite rags, knitted stockings, a red calico jacket, and a large sheet of coarse linen spread over the hedge. At the noise of the gate the nurse appeared with a baby she was suckling on one arm. With her other hand she was pulling along a poor puny little fellow, his face covered with scrofula, the son of a Rouen hosier, whom his parents, too taken up with their business, left in the country.

"Go in," she said; "your little one is there asleep."

The room on the ground-floor, the only one in the dwelling, had at its farther end, against the wall, a large bed without curtains, while a kneading-trough took up the side by the window, one pane of which was mended with a piece of blue paper. In the corner behind the door, shining hob-nailed shoes stood in a row under the slab of the wash-stand, near a bottle of oil with a feather stuck in its mouth; a Matthieu Laensberg lay on the dusty mantelpiece amid gunflints, candle-ends, and bits of amadou. Finally, the last luxury in the apartment was a "Fame" blowing her trumpets, a picture cut out, no doubt, from some perfumer's prospectus and nailed to the wall with six wooden shoe-pegs.

Emma's child was asleep in a wicker-cradle. She took it up in the wrapping that enveloped it and began singing softly as she rocked herself to and fro.

Leon walked up and down the room; it seemed strange to him to see this beautiful woman in her nankeen dress in the midst of all this poverty. Madam Bovary reddened; he turned away, thinking perhaps there

frottant leurs cornes contre le tronc des arbres. Tous les deux, côte à côte, ils marchaient doucement, elle s'appuyant sur lui et lui retenant son pas qu'il mesurait sur les siens; devant eux, un essaim de mouches voltigeait, en bourdonnant dans l'air chaud.

Ils reconnurent la maison à un vieux noyer qui l'ombrageait. Basse et couverte de tuiles brunes, elle avait en dehors, sous la lucarne de son grenier, un chapelet d'oignons suspendu. Des bourrées, debout contre la clôture d'épines, entouraient un carré de laitues, quelques pieds de lavande et des pots à fleurs montés sur des rames. De l'eau sale coulait en s'éparpillant sur l'herbe, et il y avait tout autour plusieurs guenilles indistinctes, des bas de tricot, une camisole d'indienne rouge, et un grand drap de toile épaisse étalé en long sur la haie. Au bruit de la barrière, la nourrice parut, tenant sur son bras un enfant qui tétait. Elle tirait de l'autre main un pauvre marmot chétif, couvert de scrofules au visage, le fils d'un bonnetier de Rouen, que ses parents trop occupés de leur négoce laissaient à la campagne.

— Entrez, dit-elle; votre petite est là qui dort.

La chambre, au rez-de-chaussée, la seule du logis, avait au fond contre la muraille un large lit sans rideaux, tandis que le pétrin occupait le côté de la fenêtre, dont une vitre était raccommodée avec un soleil de papier bleu. Dans l'angle, derrière la porte, des brodequins à clous luisants étaient rangés sous la dalle du lavoir, près d'une bouteille pleine d'huile qui portait une plume à son goulot; un Mathieu Laensberg traînait sur la cheminée poudreuse, parmi des pierres à fusil, des bouts de chandelle et des morceaux d'amadou. Enfin la dernière superfluité de cet appartement était une Renommée soufflant dans des trompettes, image découpée sans doute à même quelque prospectus de parfumerie, et que six pointes à sabot clouaient au mur.

L'enfant d'Emma dormait à terre, dans un berceau d'osier. Elle la prit avec la couverture qui l'enveloppait, et se mit à chanter doucement en se dandinant.

Léon se promenait dans la chambre; il lui semblait étrange de voir cette belle dame en robe de nankin, tout au milieu de cette misère. Madame Bovary devint rouge; il se détourna, croyant que ses yeux

had been an impertinent look in his eyes. Then she put back the little girl, who had just been sick over her collar. The nurse at once came to dry her, protesting that it wouldn't show.

"She gives me other doses," she said: "I am always a-washing of her. If you would have the goodness to order Camus, the grocer, to let me have a little soap, it would really be more convenient for you, as I needn't trouble you then."

"Very well! very well!" said Emma. "Good morning, Madame Rollet."

And she went out, wiping her shoes at the door.

The good woman accompanied her to the end of the garden, talking all the time of the trouble she had getting up of nights.

"I'm that worn out sometimes as I drop asleep on my chair. I'm sure you might at least give me just a pound of ground coffee; that'd last me a month, and I'd take it of a morning with some milk."

After having submitted to her thanks, Madam Bovary left. She had gone a little way down the path when, at the sound of wooden shoes, she turned round. It was the nurse.

"What is it?"

Then the peasant woman, taking her aside behind an elm tree, began talking to her of her husband, who with his trade and six francs a year that the captain—

"Oh, be quick!" said Emma.

"Well," the nurse went on, heaving sighs between each word, "I'm afraid he'll be put out seeing me have coffee alone, you know men—"

"But you are to have some," Emma repeated; "I will give you some. You bother me!"

"Oh, dear! my poor, dear lady! you see in consequence of his wounds he has terrible cramps in the chest. He even says that cider weakens him."

"Do make haste, Mere Rollet!"

"Well," the latter continued, making a curtsey, "if it weren't asking too much," and she curtsied once more, "if you would"—and her eyes

peut-être avaient eu quelque impertinence. Puis elle recoucha la petite, qui venait de vomir sur sa collerette. La nourrice aussitôt vint l'essuyer, protestant qu'il n'y paraîtrait pas.

— Elle m'en fait bien d'autres, disait-elle, et je ne suis occupée qu'à la rincer continuellement! Si vous aviez donc la complaisance de commander à Camus l'épicier, qu'il me laisse prendre un peu de savon lorsqu'il m'en faut? ce serait même plus commode pour vous, que je ne dérangerais pas.

— C'est bien, c'est bien! dit Emma. Au revoir, mère Rolet!

Et elle sortit, en essuyant ses pieds sur le seuil.

La bonne femme l'accompagna jusqu'au bout de la cour, tout en parlant du mal qu'elle avait à se relever la nuit.

— J'en suis si rompue quelquefois, que je m'endors sur ma chaise; aussi, vous devriez pour le moins me donner une petite livre de café moulu qui me ferait un mois et que je prendrais le matin avec du lait.

Après avoir subi ses remerciements, madame Bovary s'en alla; et elle était quelque peu avancée dans le sentier, lorsqu'à un bruit de sabots elle tourna la tête: c'était la nourrice!

— Qu'y a-t-il?

Alors la paysanne, la tirant à l'écart, derrière un orme, se mit à lui parler de son mari, qui, avec son métier et six francs par an que le capitaine…

— Achevez plus vite, dit Emma.

— Eh bien, reprit la nourrice poussant des soupirs entre chaque mot, j'ai peur qu'il ne se fasse une tristesse de me voir prendre du café toute seule; vous savez, les hommes…

— Puisque vous en aurez, répétait Emma, je vous en donnerai!… Vous m'ennuyez!

— Hélas! ma pauvre chère dame, c'est qu'il a, par suite de ses blessures, des crampes terribles à la poitrine. Il dit même que le cidre l'affaiblit.

— Mais dépêchez-vous, mère Rolet!

— Donc, reprit celle-ci faisant une révérence, si ce n'était pas trop vous demander…, — elle salua encore une fois, — quand vous voudrez,

begged—"a jar of brandy," she said at last, "and I'd rub your little one's feet with it; they're as tender as one's tongue."

Once rid of the nurse, Emma again took Monsieur Leon's arm. She walked fast for some time, then more slowly, and looking straight in front of her, her eyes rested on the shoulder of the young man, whose frock-coat had a black-velvety collar. His brown hair fell over it, straight and carefully arranged. She noticed his nails which were longer than one wore them at Yonville. It was one of the clerk's chief occupations to trim them, and for this purpose he kept a special knife in his writing desk. They returned to Yonville by the water-side. In the warm season the bank, wider than at other times, showed to their foot the garden walls whence a few steps led to the river. It flowed noiselessly, swift, and cold to the eye; long, thin grasses huddled together in it as the current drove them, and spread themselves upon the limpid water like streaming hair; sometimes at the tip of the reeds or on the leaf of a water-lily an insect with fine legs crawled or rested. The sun pierced with a ray the small blue bubbles of the waves that, breaking, followed each other; branchless old willows mirrored their grey backs in the water; beyond, all around, the meadows seemed empty. It was the dinner-hour at the farms, and the young woman and her companion heard nothing as they walked but the fall of their steps on the earth of the path, the words they spoke, and the sound of Emma's dress rustling round her.

The walls of the gardens with pieces of bottle on their coping were hot as the glass windows of a conservatory. Wallflowers had sprung up between the bricks, and with the tip of her open sunshade Madame Bovary, as she passed, made some of their faded flowers crumble into a yellow dust, or a spray of overhanging honeysuckle and clematis caught in its fringe and dangled for a moment over the silk.

They were talking of a troupe of Spanish dancers who were expected shortly at the Rouen theatre.

"Are you going?" she asked.

— et son regard suppliait, — un cruchon d'eau-de- vie, dit-elle enfin, et j'en frotterai les pieds de votre petite, qui les a tendres comme la langue.

Débarrassée de la nourrice, Emma reprit le bras de M. Léon. Elle marcha rapidement pendant quelque temps; puis elle se ralentit, et son regard qu'elle promenait devant elle rencontra l'épaule du jeune homme, dont la redingote avait un collet de velours noir. Ses cheveux châtains tombaient dessus, plats et bien peignés. Elle remarqua ses ongles, qui étaient plus longs qu'on ne les portait à Yonville. C'était une des grandes occupations du clerc que de les entretenir; et il gardait, à cet usage, un canif tout particulier dans son écritoire. Ils s'en revinrent à Yonville en suivant le bord de l'eau. Dans la saison chaude, la berge plus élargie découvrait jusqu'à leur base les murs des jardins, qui avaient un escalier de quelques marches descendant à la rivière. Elle coulait sans bruit, rapide et froide à l'oeil; de grandes herbes minces s'y courbaient ensemble, selon le courant qui les poussait, et comme des chevelures vertes abandonnées s'étalaient dans sa limpidité. Quelquefois, à la pointe des joncs ou sur la feuille des nénuphars, un insecte à pattes fines marchait ou se posait. Le soleil traversait d'un rayon les petits globules bleus des ondes qui se succédaient en se crevant; les vieux saules ébranchés miraient dans l'eau leur écorce grise; au delà, tout alentour, la prairie semblait vide. C'était l'heure du dîner dans les fermes, et la jeune femme et son compagnon n'entendaient en marchant que la cadence de leurs pas sur la terre du sentier, les paroles qu'ils se disaient, et le frôlement de la robe d'Emma qui bruissait tout autour d'elle.

Les murs des jardins, garnis à leur chaperon de morceaux de bouteilles, étaient chauds comme le vitrage d'une serre. Dans les briques, des ravenelles avaient poussé; et, du bord de son ombrelle déployée, madame Bovary, tout en passant, faisait s'égrener en poussière jaune un peu de leurs fleurs flétries, ou bien quelque branche des chèvrefeuilles et des clématites qui pendaient en dehors traînait un moment sur la soie, en s'accrochant aux effilés.

Ils causaient d'une troupe de danseurs espagnols, que l'on attendait bientôt sur le théâtre de Rouen.

— Vous irez? demanda-t-elle.

"If I can," he answered.

Had they nothing else to say to one another? Yet their eyes were full of more serious speech, and while they forced themselves to find trivial phrases, they felt the same languor stealing over them both. It was the whisper of the soul, deep, continuous, dominating that of their voices. Surprised with wonder at this strange sweetness, they did not think of speaking of the sensation or of seeking its cause. Coming joys, like tropical shores, throw over the immensity before them their inborn softness, an odorous wind, and we are lulled by this intoxication without a thought of the horizon that we do not even know.

In one place the ground had been trodden down by the cattle; they had to step on large green stones put here and there in the mud. She often stopped a moment to look where to place her foot, and tottering on a stone that shook, her arms outspread, her form bent forward with a look of indecision, she would laugh, afraid of falling into the puddles of water.

When they arrived in front of her garden, Madame Bovary opened the little gate, ran up the steps and disappeared.

Leon returned to his office. His chief was away; he just glanced at the briefs, then cut himself a pen, and at last took up his hat and went out.

He went to La Pature at the top of the Argueil hills at the beginning of the forest; he threw himself upon the ground under the pines and watched the sky through his fingers.

"How bored I am!" he said to himself, "how bored I am!"

He thought he was to be pitied for living in this village, with Homais for a friend and Monsieru Guillaumin for master.

The latter, entirely absorbed by his business, wearing gold-rimmed spectacles and red whiskers over a white cravat, understood nothing of mental refinements, although he affected a stiff English manner, which in the beginning had impressed the clerk. As to the chemist's spouse, she was the best wife in Normandy, gentle as a sheep, loving her children, her father, her mother, her cousins, weeping for other's woes, let-

— Si je le peux, répondit-il.

N'avaient-ils rien autre chose à se dire? Leurs yeux pourtant étaient pleins d'une causerie plus sérieuse; et, tandis qu'ils s'efforçaient à trouver des phrases banales, ils sentaient une même langueur les envahir tous les deux; c'était comme un murmure de l'âme, profond, continu, qui dominait celui des voix. Surpris d'étonnement à cette suavité nouvelle, ils ne songeaient pas à s'en raconter la sensation ou à en découvrir la cause. Les bonheurs futurs, comme les rivages des tropiques, projettent sur l'immensité qui les précède leurs mollesses natales, une brise parfumée, et l'on s'assoupit dans cet enivrement sans même s'inquiéter de l'horizon que l'on n'aperçoit pas.

La terre, à un endroit, se trouvait effondrée par le pas des bestiaux, il fallut marcher sur de grosses pierres vertes, espacées dans la boue. Souvent elle s'arrêtait une minute à regarder où poser sa bottine, — et, chancelant sur le caillou qui tremblait, les coudes en l'air, la taille penchée, l'oeil indécis, elle riait alors, de peur de tomber dans les flaques d'eau.

Quand ils furent arrivés devant son jardin madame Bovary poussa la petite barrière, monta les marches en courant et disparut.

Léon rentra à son étude. Le patron était absent; il jeta un coup d'oeil sur les dossiers, puis se tailla une plume, prit enfin son chapeau et s'en alla.

Il alla sur la Pâture, au haut de la côte d'Argueil, à l'entrée de la forêt; il se coucha par terre sous les sapins, et regarda le ciel à travers ses doigts.

— Comme je m'ennuie! se disait-il, comme je m'ennuie!

Il se trouvait à plaindre de vivre dans ce village, avec Homais pour ami et M. Guillaumin pour maître.

Ce dernier, tout occupé d'affaires, portant des lunettes à branches d'or et favoris rouges sur cravate blanche, n'entendait rien aux délicatesses de l'esprit, quoiqu'il affectât un genre raide et anglais qui avait ébloui le clerc dans les premiers temps. Quant à la femme du pharmacien, c'était la meilleure épouse de Normandie, douce comme un mouton, chérissant ses enfants, son père, sa mère, ses cousins, pleurant aux

ting everything go in her household, and detesting corsets; but so slow of movement, such a bore to listen to, so common in appearance, and of such restricted conversation, that although she was thirty, he only twenty, although they slept in rooms next each other and he spoke to her daily, he never thought that she might be a woman for another, or that she possessed anything else of her sex than the gown.

And what else was there? Binet, a few shopkeepers, two or three publicans, the cure, and finally, Monsieur Tuvache, the mayor, with his two sons, rich, crabbed, obtuse persons, who farmed their own lands and had feasts among themselves, bigoted to boot, and quite unbearable companions.

But from the general background of all these human faces Emma's stood out isolated and yet farthest off; for between her and him he seemed to see a vague abyss.

In the beginning he had called on her several times along with the druggist. Charles had not appeared particularly anxious to see him again, and Leon did not know what to do between his fear of being indiscreet and the desire for an intimacy that seemed almost impossible.

maux d'autrui, laissant tout aller dans son ménage, et détestant les corsets; — mais si lente à se mouvoir, si ennuyeuse à écouter, d'un aspect si commun et d'une conversation si restreinte, qu'il n'avait jamais songé, quoiqu'elle eût trente ans, qu'il en eût vingt, qu'ils couchassent porte à porte, et qu'il lui parlât chaque jour, qu'elle pût être une femme pour quelqu'un, ni qu'elle possédât de son sexe autre chose que la robe.

Et ensuite, qu'y avait-il? Binet, quelques marchands, deux ou trois cabaretiers, le curé, et enfin M. Tuvache, le maire, avec ses deux fils, gens cossus, bourrus, obtus, cultivant leurs terres eux-mêmes, faisant des ripailles en famille, dévots d'ailleurs, et d'une société tout à fait insupportable.

Mais, sur le fond commun de tous ces visages humains, la figure d'Emma se détachait isolée et plus lointaine cependant; car il sentait entre elle et lui comme de vagues abîmes.

Au commencement, il était venu chez elle plusieurs fois dans la compagnie du pharmacien, Charles n'avait point paru extrêmement curieux de le recevoir; et Léon ne savait comment s'y prendre entre la peur d'être indiscret et le désir d'une intimité qu'il estimait presque impossible.

# Chapter 4

When the first cold days set in Emma left her bedroom for the sitting-room, a long apartment with a low ceiling, in which there was on the mantelpiece a large bunch of coral spread out against the looking-glass. Seated in her arm chair near the window, she could see the villagers pass along the pavement.

Twice a day Leon went from his office to the Lion d'Or. Emma could hear him coming from afar; she leant forward listening, and the young man glided past the curtain, always dressed in the same way, and without turning his head. But in the twilight, when, her chin resting on her left hand, she let the embroidery she had begun fall on her knees, she often shuddered at the apparition of this shadow suddenly gliding past. She would get up and order the table to be laid.

Monsieur Homais called at dinner-time. Skull-cap in hand, he came in on tiptoe, in order to disturb no one, always repeating the same phrase, "Good evening, everybody." Then, when he had taken his seat at the table between the pair, he asked the doctor about his patients, and the latter consulted his as to the probability of their payment. Next they talked of "what was in the paper." Homais by this hour knew it almost by heart, and he repeated it from end to end, with the reflections of the penny-a-liners, and all the stories of individual catastrophes that had occurred in France or abroad. But the subject becoming exhausted, he was not slow in throwing out some remarks on the dishes before him. Sometimes even, half-rising, he delicately pointed out to madame the tenderest morsel, or turning to the servant, gave her some advice on the manipulation of stews and the hygiene of seasoning. He talked aroma, osmazome, juices, and gelatine in a bewildering manner. Moreover, Homais, with his head fuller of recipes than his shop of jars, excelled in making all kinds of preserves, vinegars, and sweet liqueurs; he knew also all the latest inventions in economic

# Chapitre 4

Dès les premiers froids, Emma quitta sa chambre pour habiter la salle, longue pièce à plafond bas où il y avait, sur la cheminée, un polypier touffu s'étalant contre la glace. Assise dans son fauteuil, près de la fenêtre, elle voyait passer les gens du village sur le trottoir.

Léon, deux fois par jour, allait de son étude au Lion d'or. Emma, de loin, l'entendait venir; elle se penchait en écoutant, et le jeune homme glissait derrière le rideau, toujours vêtu de même façon et sans détourner la tête. Mais au crépuscule, lorsque, le menton dans sa main gauche, elle avait abandonné sur ses genoux sa tapisserie commencée, souvent elle tressaillait à l'apparition de cette ombre glissant tout à coup. Elle se levait et commandait qu'on mît le couvert.

M Homais arrivait pendant le dîner. Bonnet grec à la main, il entrait à pas muets pour ne déranger personne et toujours en répétant la même phrase: «Bonsoir la compagnie!» Puis, quand il s'était posé à sa place, contre la table, entre les deux époux, il demandait au médecin des nouvelles de ses malades, et celui-ci le consultait sur la probabilité des honoraires. Ensuite, on causait de ce qu'il y avait dans le journal. Homais, à cette heure-là, le savait presque par coeur; et il le rapportait intégralement, avec les réflexions du journaliste et toutes les histoires des catastrophes individuelles arrivées en France ou à l'étranger. Mais, le sujet se tarissant, il ne tardait pas à lancer quelques observations sur les mets qu'il voyait. Parfois même, se levant à demi, il indiquait délicatement à Madame le morceau le plus tendre, ou, se tournant vers la bonne, lui adressait des conseils pour la manipulation des ragoûts et l'hygiène des assaisonnements; il parlait arome, osmazôme, sucs et gélatine d'une façon à éblouir. La tête d'ailleurs plus remplie de recettes que sa pharmacie ne l'était de bocaux, Homais excellait à faire quantité de confitures, vinaigres et liqueurs douces, et il connaissait aussi toutes

stoves, together with the art of preserving cheese and of curing sick wines.

At eight o'clock Justin came to fetch him to shut up the shop. Then Monsieur Homais gave him a sly look, especially if Felicite was there, for he half noticed that his apprentice was fond of the doctor's house.

"The young dog," he said, "is beginning to have ideas, and the devil take me if I don't believe he's in love with your servant!"

But a more serious fault with which he reproached Justin was his constantly listening to conversation. On Sunday, for example, one could not get him out of the drawing-room, whither Madame Homais had called him to fetch the children, who were falling asleep in the armchairs, and dragging down with their backs calico chair-covers that were too large.

Not many people came to these soirees at the chemist's, his scandal-mongering and political opinions having successfully alienated various respectable persons from him. The clerk never failed to be there. As soon as he heard the bell he ran to meet Madame Bovary, took her shawl, and put away under the shop-counter the thick list shoes that she wore over her boots when there was snow.

First they played some hands at trente-et-un; next Monsieur Homais played ecarte with Emma; Leon behind her gave her advice. Standing up with his hands on the back of her chair he saw the teeth of her comb that bit into her chignon. With every movement that she made to throw her cards the right side of her dress was drawn up. From her turned-up hair a dark colour fell over her back, and growing gradually paler, lost itself little by little in the shade. Then her dress fell on both sides of her chair, puffing out full of folds, and reached the ground. When Leon occasionally felt the sole of his boot resting on it, he drew back as if he had trodden upon some one.

When the game of cards was over, the druggist and the Doctor played dominoes, and Emma, changing her place, leant her elbow on the table, turning over the leaves of "L'Illustration". She had brought

les inventions nouvelles de caléfacteurs économiques, avec l'art de conserver les fromages et de soigner les vins malades.

À huit heures, Justin venait le chercher pour fermer la pharmacie. Alors M. Homais le regardait d'un oeil narquois, surtout si Félicité se trouvait là, s'étant eperçu que son élève afectionnait la maison du médecin.

— Mon gaillard, disait-il, commence à avoir des idées, et je crois, diable m'emporte, qu'il est amoureux de votre bonne!

Mais un défaut plus grave, et qu'il lui reprochait, c'était d'écouter continuellement les conversations. Le dimanche, par exemple, on ne pouvait le faire sortir du salon, où madame Homais l'avait appelé pour prendre les enfants, qui s'endormaient dans les fauteuils, en tirant avec leurs dos les housses de calicot, trop larges.

Il ne venait pas grand monde à ces soirées du pharmacien, sa médisance et ses opinions politiques ayant écarté de lui successivement différentes personnes respectables. Le clerc ne manquait pas de s'y trouver. Dès qu'il entendait la sonnette, il courait au-devant de madame Bovary, prenait son châle, et posait à l'écart, sous le bureau de la pharmacie, les grosses pantoufles de lisière qu'elle portait sur sa chaussure, quand il y avait de la neige.

On faisait d'abord quelques parties de trente-et-un; ensuite M. Hornais jouait à l'écarté avec Emma; Léon, derrière elle, lui donnait des avis. Debout et les mains sur le dossier de sa chaise, il regardait les dents de son peigne qui mordaient son chignon. À chaque mouvement qu'elle faisait pour jeter les cartes, sa robe du côté droit remontait. De ses cheveux retroussés, il descendait une couleur brune sur son dos, et qui, s'apâlissant graduellement, peu à peu se perdait dans l'ombre. Son vêtement, ensuite, retombait des deux côtés sur le siège, en bouffant, plein de plis, et s'étalait jusqu'à terre. Quand Léon parfois sentait la semelle de sa botte poser dessus, il s'écartait, comme s'il eût marché sur quelqu'un.

Lorsque la partie de cartes était finie, l'apothicaire et le médecin jouaient aux dominos, et Emma changeant de place, s'accoudait sur la table, à feuilleter l'Illustration. Elle avait apporté son journal de

her ladies' journal with her. Leon sat down near her; they looked at the engravings together, and waited for one another at the bottom of the pages. She often begged him to read her the verses; Leon declaimed them in a languid voice, to which he carefully gave a dying fall in the love passages. But the noise of the dominoes annoyed him. Monsieur Homais was strong at the game; he could beat Charles and give him a double-six. Then the three hundred finished, they both stretched themselves out in front of the fire, and were soon asleep. The fire was dying out in the cinders; the teapot was empty, Leon was still reading. Emma listened to him, mechanically turning around the lampshade, on the gauze of which were painted clowns in carriages, and tight-rope dances with their balancing-poles. Leon stopped, pointing with a gesture to his sleeping audience; then they talked in low tones, and their conversation seemed the more sweet to them because it was unheard.

Thus a kind of bond was established between them, a constant commerce of books and of romances. Monsieur Bovary, little given to jealousy, did not trouble himself about it.

On his birthday he received a beautiful phrenological head, all marked with figures to the thorax and painted blue. This was an attention of the clerk's. He showed him many others, even to doing errands for him at Rouen; and the book of a novelist having made the mania for cactuses fashionable, Leon bought some for Madame Bovary, bringing them back on his knees in the "Hirondelle," pricking his fingers on their hard hairs.

She had a board with a balustrade fixed against her window to hold the pots. The clerk, too, had his small hanging garden; they saw each other tending their flowers at their windows.

Of the windows of the village there was one yet more often occupied; for on Sundays from morning to night, and every morning when the weather was bright, one could see at the dormer-window of the garret the profile of Monsieur Binet bending over his lathe, whose monotonous humming could be heard at the Lion d'Or.

One evening on coming home Leon found in his room a rug in velvet and wool with leaves on a pale ground. He called Madame Homais,

modes. Léon se mettait près d'elle; ils regardaient ensemble les gravures et s'attendaient au bas des pages. Souvent elle le priait de lui lire des vers; Léon les déclamait d'une voix traînante et qu'il faisait expirer soigneusement aux passages d'amour. Mais le bruit des dominos le contrariait; M. Homais y était fort, il battait Charles à plein double-six. Puis, les trois centaines terminées, ils s'allongeaient tous deux devant le foyer et ne tardaient pas à s'endormir. Le feu se mourait dans les cendres; la théière était vide; Léon lisait encore. Emma l'écoutait, en faisant tourner machinalement l'abat-jour de la lampe, où étaient peints sur la gaze des pierrots dans des voitures et des danseuses de corde, avec leurs balanciers. Léon s'arrêtait, désignant d'un geste son auditoire endormi, alors ils se parlaient à voix basse, et la conversation qu'ils avaient leur semblait plus douce, parce qu'elle n'était pas entendue.

Ainsi s'établit entre eux une sorte d'association, un commerce continuel de livres et de romances; M. Bovary, peu jaloux, ne s'en étonnait pas.

Il reçut pour sa fête une belle tête phrénologique, toute marquetée de chiffres jusqu'au thorax et peinte en bleu. C'était une attention du clerc. Il en avait bien d'autres, jusqu'à lui faire, à Rouen, ses commissions; et le livre d'un romancier ayant mis à la mode la manie des plantes grasses, Léon en achetait pour Madame, qu'il rapportait sur ses genoux, dans l'Hirondelle, tout en se piquant les doigts à leurs poils durs.

Elle fit ajuster, contre sa croisée, une planchette à balustrade pour tenir ses potiches. Le clerc eut aussi son jardinet suspendu; ils s'apercevaient soignant leurs fleurs à leur fenêtre.

Parmi les fenêtres du village, il y en avait une encore plus souvent occupée; car, le dimanche, depuis le matin jusqu'à la nuit, et chaque après-midi, si le temps était clair, on voyait à la lucarne d'un grenier le profil maigre de M. Binet penché sur son tour, dont le ronflement monotone s'entendait jusqu'au Lion d'or

Un soir, en rentrant, Léon trouva dans sa chambre un tapis de velours et de laine avec des feuillages sur fond pâle, il appela madame Homais,

Monsieur Homais, Justin, the children, the cook; he spoke of it to his chief; every one wanted to see this rug. Why did the doctor's wife give the clerk presents? It looked queer. They decided that she must be his lover.

He made this seem likely, so ceaselessly did he talk of her charms and of her wit; so much so, that Binet once roughly answered him:

"What does it matter to me since I'm not in her set?"

He tortured himself to find out how he could make his declaration to her, and always halting between the fear of displeasing her and the shame of being such a coward, he wept with discouragement and desire. Then he took energetic resolutions, wrote letters that he tore up, put it off to times that he again deferred. Often he set out with the determination to dare all; but this resolution soon deserted him in Emma's presence, and when Charles, dropping in, invited him to jump into his chaise to go with him to see some patient in the neighbourhood, he at once accepted, bowed to madame, and went out. Her husband, was he not something belonging to her?

As to Emma, she did not ask herself whether she loved. Love, she thought, must come suddenly, with great outbursts and lightnings—a hurricane of the skies, which falls upon life, revolutionises it, roots up the will like a leaf, and sweeps the whole heart into the abyss. She did not know that on the terrace of houses it makes lakes when the pipes are choked, and she would thus have remained in her security when she suddenly discovered a rent in the wall of it.

M Homais, Justin, les enfants, la cuisinière, il en parla à son patron; tout le monde désira connaître ce tapis; pourquoi la femme du médecin faisait-elle au clerc des générosités? Cela parut drôle, et l'on pensa définitivement qu'elle devait être sa bonne amie.

Il le donnait à croire, tant il vous entretenait sans cesse de ses charmes et de son esprit, si bien que Binet lui répondit une fois fort brutalement:

— Que m'importe, à moi, puisque je ne suis pas de sa société!

Il se torturait à découvrir par quel moyen lui faire sa déclaration; et, toujours hésitant entre la crainte de lui déplaire et la honte d'être si pusillanime, il en pleurait de découragement et de désirs. Puis il prenait des décisions énergiques; il écrivait des lettres qu'il déchirait, s'ajournait à des époques qu'il reculait. Souvent il se mettait en marche, dans le projet de tout oser; mais cette résolution l'abandonnait bien vite en la présence d'Emma, et, quand Charles, survenant, l'invitait à monter dans son boc pour aller voir ensemble quelque malade aux environs, il acceptait aussitôt, saluait Madame et s'en allait. Son mari, n'était-ce pas quelque chose d'elle?

Quant à Emma, elle ne s'interrogea point pour savoir si elle l'aimait. L'amour, croyait-elle, devait arriver tout à coup, avec de grands éclats et des fulgurations, — ouragan des cieux qui tombe sur la vie, la bouleverse, arrache les volontés comme des feuilles et emporte à l'abîme le coeur entier. Elle ne savait pas que, sur la terrasse des maisons, la pluie fait des lacs quand les gouttières sont bouchées, et elle fût ainsi demeurée en sa sécurité, lorsqu'elle découvrit subitement une lézarde dans le mur.

# Chapter 5

It was a Sunday in February, an afternoon when the snow was falling. They had all, Monsieur and Madame Bovary, Homais, and Monsieur Leon, gone to see a yarn-mill that was being built in the valley a mile and a half from Yonville. The druggist had taken Napoleon and Athalie to give them some exercise, and Justin accompanied them, carrying the umbrellas on his shoulder.

Nothing, however, could be less curious than this curiosity. A great piece of waste ground, on which pell-mell, amid a mass of sand and stones, were a few break-wheels, already rusty, surrounded by a quadrangular building pierced by a number of little windows. The building was unfinished; the sky could be seen through the joists of the roofing. Attached to the stop-plank of the gable a bunch of straw mixed with corn-ears fluttered its tricoloured ribbons in the wind.

Homais was talking. He explained to the company the future importance of this establishment, computed the strength of the floorings, the thickness of the walls, and regretted extremely not having a yard-stick such as Monsieur Binet possessed for his own special use.

Emma, who had taken his arm, bent lightly against his shoulder, and she looked at the sun's disc shedding afar through the mist his pale splendour. She turned. Charles was there. His cap was drawn down over his eyebrows, and his two thick lips were trembling, which added a look of stupidity to his face; his very back, his calm back, was irritating to behold, and she saw written upon his coat all the platitude of the bearer.

While she was considering him thus, tasting in her irritation a sort of depraved pleasure, Leon made a step forward. The cold that made him pale seemed to add a more gentle languor to his face; between his cravat and his neck the somewhat loose collar of his shirt showed the skin; the lobe of his ear looked out from beneath a lock of hair, and his large

# Chapitre 5

Ce fut un dimanche de février, une après-midi qu'il neigeait.

Ils étaient tous, M et madame Bovary, Homais et M. Léon, partis voir, à une demi-lieue d'Yonville, dans la vallée, une filature de lin que l'on établissait. L'apothicaire avait emmené avec lui Napoléon et Athalie, pour leur faire faire de l'exercice, et Justin les accompagnait, portant des parapluies sur son épaule.

Rien pourtant n'était moins curieux que cette curiosité Un grand espace de terrain vide, où se trouvaient pêle-mêle, entre des tas de sable et de cailloux, quelques roues d'engrenage déjà rouillées, entourait un long bâtiment quadrangulaire que perçaient quantité de petites fenêtres. Il n'était pas achevé d'être bâti, et l'on voyait le ciel à travers les lambourdes de la toiture. Attaché à la poutrelle du pignon, un bouquet de paille entremêlé d'épis faisait claquer au vent ses rubans tricolores.

Homais parlait. Il expliquait à la compagnie l'importance future de cet établissement, supputait la force des planchers, l'épaisseur des murailles, et regrettait beaucoup de n'avoir pas de canne métrique, comme M. Binet en possédait une pour son usage particulier.

Emma, qui lui donnait le bras, s'appuyait un peu sur son épaule, et elle regardait le disque du soleil irradiant au loin, dans la brume, sa pâleur éblouissante; mais elle tourna la tête: Charles était là. Il avait sa casquette enfoncée sur ses sourcils, et ses deux grosses lèvres tremblotaient, ce qui ajoutait à son visage quelque chose de stupide; son dos même, son dos tranquille était irritant à voir, et elle y trouvait étalée sur la redingote toute la platitude du personnage.

Pendant qu'elle le considérait, goûtant ainsi dans son irritation une sorte de volupté dépravée, Léon s'avança d'un pas. Le froid qui le pâlissait semblait déposer sur sa figure une langueur plus douce; entre sa cravate et son cou, le col de la chemise, un peu lâche, laissait voir la peau; un bout d'oreille dépassait sous une mèche de cheveux, et son grand oeil

blue eyes, raised to the clouds, seemed to Emma more limpid and more beautiful than those mountain-lakes where the heavens are mirrored.

"Wretched boy!" suddenly cried the chemist.

And he ran to his son, who had just precipitated himself into a heap of lime in order to whiten his boots. At the reproaches with which he was being overwhelmed Napoleon began to roar, while Justin dried his shoes with a wisp of straw. But a knife was wanted; Charles offered his.

"Ah!" she said to herself, "he carried a knife in his pocket like a peasant."

The hoar-frost was falling, and they turned back to Yonville.

In the evening Madame Bovary did not go to her neighbour's, and when Charles had left and she felt herself alone, the comparison re-began with the clearness of a sensation almost actual, and with that lengthening of perspective which memory gives to things. Looking from her bed at the clean fire that was burning, she still saw, as she had down there, Leon standing up with one hand behind his cane, and with the other holding Athalie, who was quietly sucking a piece of ice. She thought him charming; she could not tear herself away from him; she recalled his other attitudes on other days, the words he had spoken, the sound of his voice, his whole person; and she repeated, pouting out her lips as if for a kiss:

"Yes, charming! charming! Is he not in love?" she asked herself; "but with whom? With me?"

All the proofs arose before her at once; her heart leapt. The flame of the fire threw a joyous light upon the ceiling; she turned on her back, stretching out her arms.

Then began the eternal lamentation: "Oh, if Heaven had not willed it! And why not? What prevented it?"

When Charles came home at midnight, she seemed to have just awakened, and as he made a noise undressing, she complained of a headache, then asked carelessly what had happened that evening.

"Monsieur Leon," he said, "went to his room early."

She could not help smiling, and she fell asleep, her soul filled with a new delight.

bleu, levé vers les nuages, parut à Emma plus limpide et plus beau que ces lacs des montagnes où le ciel se mire.

— Malheureux! s'écria tout à coup l'apothicaire.

Et il courut à son fils, qui venait de se précipiter dans un tas de chaux pour peindre ses souliers en blanc. Aux reproches dont on l'accablait, Napoléon se prit à pousser des hurlements, tandis que Justin lui essuyait ses chaussures avec un torchis de paille. Mais il eût fallu un couteau; Charles offrit le sien.

— Ah! se dit-elle, il porte un couteau dans sa poche, comme un paysan!

Le givre tombait; et l'on s'en retourna vers Yonville.

Madame Bovary, le soir, n'alla pas chez ses voisins, et, quand Charles fut parti, lorsqu'elle se sentit seule, le parallèle recommença dans la netteté d'une sensation presque immédiate et avec cet allongement de perspective que le souvenir donne aux objets. Regardant de son lit le feu clair qui brûlait, elle voyait encore, comme là-bas, Léon debout, faisant plier d'une main sa badine et tenant de l'autre Athalie, qui suçait tranquillement un morceau de glace. Elle le trouvait charmant; elle ne pouvait s'en détacher; elle se rappela ses autres attitudes en d'autres jours, des phrases qu'il avait dites, le son de sa voix, toute sa personne; et elle répétait, en avançant ses lèvres comme pour un baiser:

— Oui, charmant! charmant!... N'aime-t-il pas? se demanda-t-elle. Qui donc?... mais c'est moi!

Toutes les preuves à la fois s'en étalèrent, son coeur bondit. La flamme de la cheminée faisait trembler au plafond une clarté joyeuse; elle se tourna sur le dos en s'étirant les bras.

Alors commença l'éternelle lamentation: «Oh! si le ciel l'avait voulu! Pourquoi n'est-ce pas? Qui empêchait donc?...»

Quand Charles, à minuit, rentra, elle eut l'air de s'éveiller, et, comme il fit du bruit en se déshabillant, elle se plaignit de la migraine; puis demanda nonchalamment ce qui s'était passé dans la soirée.

— M. Léon, dit-il, est remonté de bonne heure.

Elle ne put s'empêcher de sourire, et elle s'endormit l'âme remplie d'un enchantement nouveau.

The next day, at dusk, she received a visit from Monsieur Lherueux, the draper. He was a man of ability, was this shopkeeper.

Born a Gascon but bred a Norman, he grafted upon his southern volubility the cunning of the Cauchois. His fat, flabby, beardless face seemed dyed by a decoction of liquorice, and his white hair made even more vivid the keen brilliance of his small black eyes. No one knew what he had been formerly; a pedlar said some, a banker at Routot according to others. What was certain was that he made complex calculations in his head that would have frightened Binet himself. Polite to obsequiousness, he always held himself with his back bent in the position of one who bows or who invites.

After leaving at the door his hat surrounded with crape, he put down a green bandbox on the table, and began by complaining to madame, with many civilities, that he should have remained till that day without gaining her confidence. A poor shop like his was not made to attract a "fashionable lady"; he emphasized the words; yet she had only to command, and he would undertake to provide her with anything she might wish, either in haberdashery or linen, millinery or fancy goods, for he went to town regularly four times a month. He was connected with the best houses. You could speak of him at the "Trois Freres," at the "Barbe d'Or," or at the "Grand Sauvage"; all these gentlemen knew him as well as the insides of their pockets. To-day, then he had come to show madame, in passing, various articles he happened to have, thanks to the most rare opportunity. And he pulled out half-a-dozen embroidered collars from the box.

Madame Bovary examined them.

"I do not require anything," she said.

Then Monsieur Lheureux delicately exhibited three Algerian scarves, several packets of English needles, a pair of straw slippers, and finally, four eggcups in cocoanut wood, carved in open work by convicts. Then, with both hands on the table, his neck stretched out, his figure bent forward, open-mouthed, he watched Emma's look, who was walking up and down undecided amid these goods. From time to time, as if to remove some dust, he filliped with his nail the silk of the scarves spread out at full length, and they rustled with a little noise, making in

Le lendemain, à la nuit tombante, elle reçut la visite du sieur Lheureux, marchand de nouveautés. C'était un homme habile que ce boutiquier,

Né Gascon, mais devenu Normand, il doublait sa faconde méridionale de cautèle cauchoise. Sa figure grasse, molle et sans barbe, semblait teinte par une décoction de réglisse claire, et sa chevelure blanche rendait plus vif encore l'éclat rude de ses petits yeux noirs. On ignorait ce qu'il avait été jadis: porteballe, disaient les uns, banquier à Routot, selon les autres. Ce qu'il y a de sûr, c'est qu'il faisait, de tête, des calculs compliqués, à effrayer Binet lui-même. Poli jusqu'à l'obséquiosité, il se tenait toujours les reins à demi courbés, dans la position de quelqu'un qui salue ou qui invite.

Après avoir laissé à la porte son chapeau garni d'un crêpe, il posa sur la table un carton vert, et commença par se plaindre à Madame, avec force civilités, d'être resté jusqu'à ce jour sans obtenir sa confiance. Une pauvre boutique comme la sienne n'était pas faite pour attirer une élégante; il appuya sur le mot. Elle n'avait pourtant, qu'à commander, et il se chargerait de lui fournir ce qu'elle voudrait, tant en mercerie que lingerie, bonneterie ou nouveautés; car il allait à la ville quatre fois par mois, régulièrement. Il était en relation avec les plus fortes maisons. On pouvait parler de lui aux Trois Frères, à la Barbe d'or ou au Grand Sauvage, tous ces messieurs le connaissaient comme leur poche! Aujourd'hui donc, il venait montrer à Madame, en passant, différents articles qu'il se trouvait avoir, grâce à une occasion des plus rares. Et il retira de la boîte une demi- douzaine de cols brodés.

Madame Bovary les examina.

— Je n'ai besoin de rien, dit-elle.

Alors M. Lheureux exhiba délicatement trois écharpes algériennes, plusieurs paquets d'aiguilles anglaises, une paire de pantoufles en paille, et, enfin, quatre coquetiers en coco, ciselés à jour par des forçats. Puis, les deux mains sur la table, le cou tendu, la taille penchée; il suivait, bouche béante, le regard d'Emma, qui se promenait indécis parmi ces marchandises. De temps à autre comme pour en chasser la poussière, il donnait un coup d'ongle sur la soie des écharpes, dépliées, dans toute leur longueur; et elles frémissaient avec un bruit léger, en faisant, à la

the green twilight the gold spangles of their tissue scintillate like little stars.

"How much are they?"

"A mere nothing," he replied, "a mere nothing. But there's no hurry; whenever it's convenient. We are not Jews."

She reflected for a few moments, and ended by again declining Monsieur Lheureux's offer. He replied quite unconcernedly—

"Very well. We shall understand one another by and by. I have always got on with ladies—if I didn't with my own!"

Emma smiled.

"I wanted to tell you," he went on good-naturedly, after his joke, "that it isn't the money I should trouble about. Why, I could give you some, if need be."

She made a gesture of surprise.

"Ah!" said he quickly and in a low voice, "I shouldn't have to go far to find you some, rely on that."

And he began asking after Pere Tellier, the proprietor of the "Cafe Francais," whom Monsieur Bovary was then attending.

"What's the matter with Pere Tellier? He coughs so that he shakes his whole house, and I'm afraid he'll soon want a deal covering rather than a flannel vest. He was such a rake as a young man! Those sort of people, madame, have not the least regularity; he's burnt up with brandy. Still it's sad, all the same, to see an acquaintance go off."

And while he fastened up his box he discoursed about the doctor's patients.

"It's the weather, no doubt," he said, looking frowningly at the floor, "that causes these illnesses. I, too, don't feel the thing. One of these days I shall even have to consult the doctor for a pain I have in my back. Well, good-bye, Madame Bovary. At your service; your very humble servant."

And he closed the door gently.

Emma had her dinner served in her bedroom on a tray by the fire-side; she was a long time over it; everything was well with her.

lumière verdâtre du crépuscule, scintiller, comme de petites étoiles, les paillettes d'or de leur tissu.

— Combien coûtent-elles?

—Une misère, répondit-il, une, misère; mais rien ne presse; quand vous voudrez; nous ne sommes pas des juifs!

Elle réfléchit quelques instants, et finit encore, par remercier M. Lheureux, qui répliqua sans s'émouvoir.

— Eh bien; nous nous entendrons plus tard; avec les dames je me suis toujours arrangé, si ce n'est avec la mienne, cependant!

Emma sourit.

— C'était pour vous dire, reprit-il d'un air bonhomme après sa plaisanterie, que ce n'est pas l'argent qui m'inquiète... Je vous en donnerais, s'il le fallait.

Elle eut un geste de surprise.

— Ah! fit-il vivement et à voix basse, je n'aurais pas besoin d'aller loin pour vous en trouver; comptez-y!

Et il se mit à demander des nouvelles du père Tellier, le maître du Café Français, que M. Bovary soignait alors.

— Qu'est-ce qu'il a donc, le père Tellier?... Il tousse qu'il en secoue toute sa maison, et j'ai bien peur que prochainement il ne lui faille plutôt un paletot de sapin qu'une camisole de flanelle? Il a fait tant de bamboches quand il était jeune! Ces gens-là, madame, n'avaient pas le moindre ordre! il s'est calciné avec l'eau-de-vie! Mais c'est fâcheux tout de même de voir une connaissance s'en aller.

Et, tandis qu'il rebouclait son carton, il discourait ainsi sur la clientèle du médecin.

— C'est le temps, sans doute, dit-il en regardant les carreaux avec une figure rechignée, qui est la cause de ces maladies-là! Moi aussi, je ne me sens pas en mon assiette; il faudra même un de ces jours que je vienne consulter Monsieur, pour une douleur que j'ai dans le dos. Enfin, au revoir, madame Bovary; à votre disposition; serviteur très humble!

Et il referma la porte doucement

Emma se fit servir à dîner dans sa chambre, au coin du feu, sur un plateau; elle fut longue à manger; tout lui sembla bon.

"How good I was!" she said to herself, thinking of the scarves.

She heard some steps on the stairs. It was Leon. She got up and took from the chest of drawers the first pile of dusters to be hemmed. When he came in she seemed very busy.

The conversation languished; Madame Bovary gave it up every few minutes, whilst he himself seemed quite embarrassed. Seated on a low chair near the fire, he turned round in his fingers the ivory thimble-case. She stitched on, or from time to time turned down the hem of the cloth with her nail. She did not speak; he was silent, captivated by her silence, as he would have been by her speech.

"Poor fellow!" she thought.

"How have I displeased her?" he asked himself.

At last, however, Leon said that he should have, one of these days, to go to Rouen on some office business.

"Your music subscription is out; am I to renew it?"

"No," she replied.

"Why?"

"Because—"

And pursing her lips she slowly drew a long stitch of grey thread.

This work irritated Leon. It seemed to roughen the ends of her fingers. A gallant phrase came into his head, but he did not risk it.

"Then you are giving it up?" he went on.

"What?" she asked hurriedly. "Music? Ah! yes! Have I not my house to look after, my husband to attend to, a thousand things, in fact, many duties that must be considered first?"

She looked at the clock. Charles was late. Then, she affected anxiety. Two or three times she even repeated:

"He is so good!"

The clerk was fond of Monsieur Bovary. But this tenderness on his behalf astonished him unpleasantly; nevertheless he took up on his praises, which he said everyone was singing, especially the chemist.

"Ah! he is a good fellow," continued Emma.

— Comme j'ai été sage! se disait-elle en songeant aux écharpes.

Elle entendit des pas dans l'escalier: c'était Léon. Elle se leva, et prit sur la commode; parmi des torchons à ourler, le premier de la pile. Elle semblait fort occupée quand il parut.

La conversation fut languissante, madame Bovary l'abandonnant à chaque minute, tandis qu'il demeurait lui-même comme tout embarrassé. Assis sur une chaise basse, près de la cheminée, il faisait tourner dans ses doigts l'étui d'ivoire; elle poussait son aiguille, ou, de temps à autre, avec son ongle, fronçait les plis de la toile. Elle ne parlait pas; il se taisait, captivé par son silence, comme il l'eût été par ses paroles.

— Pauvre garçon! pensait-elle.

— En quoi lui déplais-je? se demandait-il.

Léon, cependant, finit par dire qu'il devait, un de ces jours, aller à Rouen, pour une affaire de son étude...

— Votre abonnement de musique est terminé, dois-je le reprendre?

— Non, répondit-elle.

— Pourquoi?

— Parce que...

Et, pinçant ses lèvres, elle tira lentement une longue aiguillée de fil gris.

Cet ouvrage irritait Léon. Les doigts d'Emma semblaient s'y écorcher par le bout; il lui vint en tête une phrase galante, mais qu'il ne risqua pas.

— Vous l'abandonnez donc? reprit-il.

— Quoi? dit-elle vivement; la musique? Ah! mon Dieu, oui! n'ai-je pas ma maison à tenir, mon mari à soigner, mille choses enfin, bien des devoirs qui passent auparavant!

Elle regarda la pendule. Charles était en retard. Alors elle fit la soucieuse. Deux ou trois fois même elle répéta:

— Il est si bon!

Le clerc affectionnait M. Bovary. Mais cette tendresse à son endroit l'étonna d'une façon désagréable; néanmoins il continua son éloge, qu'il entendait faire à chacun, disait-il, et surtout au pharmacien.

— Ah! c'est un brave homme, reprit Emma.

"Certainly," replied the clerk.

And he began talking of Madame Homais, whose very untidy appearance generally made them laugh.

"What does it matter?" interrupted Emma. "A good housewife does not trouble about her appearance."

Then she relapsed into silence.

It was the same on the following days; her talks, her manners, everything changed. She took interest in the housework, went to church regularly, and looked after her servant with more severity.

She took Berthe from nurse. When visitors called, Felicite brought her in, and Madame Bovary undressed her to show off her limbs. She declared she adored children; this was her consolation, her joy, her passion, and she accompanied her caresses with lyrical outburst which would have reminded anyone but the Yonville people of Sachette in "Notre Dame de Paris."

When Charles came home he found his slippers put to warm near the fire. His waistcoat now never wanted lining, nor his shirt buttons, and it was quite a pleasure to see in the cupboard the night-caps arranged in piles of the same height. She no longer grumbled as formerly at taking a turn in the garden; what he proposed was always done, although she did not understand the wishes to which she submitted without a murmur; and when Leon saw him by his fireside after dinner, his two hands on his stomach, his two feet on the fender, his two cheeks red with feeding, his eyes moist with happiness, the child crawling along the carpet, and this woman with the slender waist who came behind his arm-chair to kiss his forehead:

"What madness!" he said to himself. "And how to reach her!"

And thus she seemed so virtuous and inaccessible to him that he lost all hope, even the faintest.

But by this renunciation he placed her on an extraordinary pinnacle. To him she stood outside those fleshly attributes from which he had nothing to obtain, and in his heart she rose ever, and became farther removed from him after the magnificent manner of an apotheosis that is taking wing. It was one of those pure feelings that do not interfere

— Certes, reprit le clerc:

Et il se mit à parler de madame Homais, dont la tenue fort négligée leur apprêtait à rire ordinairement.

— Qu'est-ce que cela fait? interrompit Emma. Une bonne mère de famille ne s'inquiète pas de sa toilette.

Puis elle retomba dans son silence.

Il en fut de même les jours suivants; ses discours, ses manières, tout changea. On la vit prendre à coeur son ménage, retourner à l'église régulièrement et tenir sa servante avec plus de sévérité.

Elle retira Berthe de nourrice. Félicité l'amenait quand il venait des visites, et madame Bovary la déshabillait afin de faire voir ses membres. Elle déclarait adorer les enfants; c'était sa consolation, sa joie, sa folie, et elle accompagnait ses caresses d'expansions lyriques, qui, à d'autres qu'à des Yonvillais, eussent rappelé la Sachette de Notre-Dame de Paris.

Quand Charles rentrait, il trouvait auprès des cendres ses pantoufles à chauffer. Ses gilets maintenant ne manquaient plus de doublure, ni ses chemises de boutons, et même il y avait plaisir à considérer dans l'armoire tous les bonnets de coton rangés par piles égales. Elle ne rechignait plus, comme autrefois, à faire des tours dans le jardin; ce qu'il proposait était toujours consenti, bien qu'elle ne devinât pas les volontés auxquelles elle se soumettait sans un murmure; — et lorsque Léon le voyait au coin du feu, après le dîner, les deux mains sur son ventre, les deux pieds sur les chenets, la joue rougie par la digestion, les yeux humides de bonheur, avec l'enfant qui se traînait sur le tapis, et cette femme à taille mince qui par-dessus le dossier du fauteuil venait le baiser au front:

— Quelle folie! se disait-il, et comment arriver jusqu'à elle?

Elle lui parut donc si vertueuse et inaccessible, que toute espérance, même la plus vague, l'abandonna.

Mais, par ce renoncement, il la plaçait en des conditions extraordinaires. Elle se dégagea, pour lui, des qualités charnelles dont il n'avait rien à obtenir; et elle alla, dans son coeur, montant toujours et s'en détachant, à la manière magnifique d'une apothéose qui s'envole. C'était un de ces sentiments purs qui n'embarrassent pas l'exercice de

with life, that are cultivated because they are rare, and whose loss would afflict more than their passion rejoices.

Emma grew thinner, her cheeks paler, her face longer. With her black hair, her large eyes, her aquiline nose, her birdlike walk, and always silent now, did she not seem to be passing through life scarcely touching it, and to bear on her brow the vague impress of some divine destiny? She was so sad and so calm, at once so gentle and so reserved, that near her one felt oneself seized by an icy charm, as we shudder in churches at the perfume of the flowers mingling with the cold of the marble. The others even did not escape from this seduction. The chemist said:

"She is a woman of great parts, who wouldn't be misplaced in a subprefecture."

The housewives admired her economy, the patients her politeness, the poor her charity.

But she was eaten up with desires, with rage, with hate. That dress with the narrow folds hid a distracted fear, of whose torment those chaste lips said nothing. She was in love with Leon, and sought solitude that she might with the more ease delight in his image. The sight of his form troubled the voluptuousness of this mediation. Emma thrilled at the sound of his step; then in his presence the emotion subsided, and afterwards there remained to her only an immense astonishment that ended in sorrow.

Leon did not know that when he left her in despair she rose after he had gone to see him in the street. She concerned herself about his comings and goings; she watched his face; she invented quite a history to find an excuse for going to his room. The chemist's wife seemed happy to her to sleep under the same roof, and her thoughts constantly centered upon this house, like the "Lion d'Or" pigeons, who came there to dip their red feet and white wings in its gutters. But the more Emma recognised her love, the more she crushed it down, that it might not be evident, that she might make it less. She would have liked Leon to guess it, and she imagined chances, catastrophes that should facilitate this. What restrained her was, no doubt, idleness and fear, and a sense of shame also. She

la vie, que l'on cultive parce qu'ils sont rares; et dont la perte affligerait plus que la possession n'est réjouissante.

Emma maigrit, ses joues pâlirent, sa figure s'allongea. Avec ses bandeaux noirs, ses grands yeux, son nez droit, sa démarche d'oiseau, et toujours silencieuse maintenant, ne semblait-elle pas traverser l'existence en y touchant à peine, et porter au front la vague empreinte de quelque prédestination sublime? Elle était si triste et si calme, si douce à la fois et si réservée, que l'on se sentait près d'elle pris par un charme glacial, comme l'on frissonne dans les églises sous le parfum des fleurs mêlé au froid des marbres. Les autres même n'échappaient point à cette séduction. Le pharmacien disait:

— C'est une femme de grands moyens et qui ne serait pas déplacée dans une sous-préfecture.

Les bourgeoises admiraient son économie, les clients sa politesse, les pauvres sa charité.

Mais elle était pleine de convoitises, de rage, de haine. Cette robe aux plis droits cachait un coeur bouleversé, et ces lèvres si pudiques n'en racontaient pas la tourmente. Elle était amoureuse de Léon, et elle recherchait la solitude, afin de pouvoir plus à l'aise se délecter en son image. La vue de sa personne troublait la volupté de cette méditation. Emma palpitait au bruit de ses pas; puis, en sa présence, l'émotion tombait, et il ne lui restait ensuite qu'un immense étonnement qui se finissait en tristesse.

Léon ne savait pas, lorsqu'il sortait de chez elle désespéré, qu'elle se levait derrière lui afin de le voir dans la rue. Elle s'inquiétait de ses démarches, elle épiait son visage; elle inventa toute une histoire pour trouver prétexte à visiter sa chambre. La femme du pharmacien lui semblait bien heureuse de dormir sous le même toit; et ses pensées continuellement s'abattaient sur cette maison, comme les pigeons du Lion d'or qui venaient tremper là, dans les gouttières, leurs pattes roses et leurs ailes blanches. Mais plus Emma s'apercevait de son amour, plus elle le refoulait, afin qu'il ne parût pas, et pour le diminuer. Elle aurait voulu que Léon s'en doutât; et elle imaginait des hasards, des catastrophes qui l'eussent facilité. Ce qui la retenait, sans doute, c'était la paresse ou

thought she had repulsed him too much, that the time was past, that all was lost. Then, pride, and joy of being able to say to herself, "I am virtuous," and to look at herself in the glass taking resigned poses, consoled her a little for the sacrifice she believed she was making.

Then the lusts of the flesh, the longing for money, and the melancholy of passion all blended themselves into one suffering, and instead of turning her thoughts from it, she clave to it the more, urging herself to pain, and seeking everywhere occasion for it. She was irritated by an ill-served dish or by a half-open door; bewailed the velvets she had not, the happiness she had missed, her too exalted dreams, her narrow home.

What exasperated her was that Charles did not seem to notice her anguish. His conviction that he was making her happy seemed to her an imbecile insult, and his sureness on this point ingratitude. For whose sake, then was she virtuous? Was it not for him, the obstacle to all felicity, the cause of all misery, and, as it were, the sharp clasp of that complex strap that bucked her in on all sides.

On him alone, then, she concentrated all the various hatreds that resulted from her boredom, and every effort to diminish only augmented it; for this useless trouble was added to the other reasons for despair, and contributed still more to the separation between them. Her own gentleness to herself made her rebel against him. Domestic mediocrity drove her to lewd fancies, marriage tenderness to adulterous desires. She would have liked Charles to beat her, that she might have a better right to hate him, to revenge herself upon him. She was surprised sometimes at the atrocious conjectures that came into her thoughts, and she had to go on smiling, to hear repeated to her at all hours that she was happy, to pretend to be happy, to let it be believed.

Yet she had loathing of this hypocrisy. She was seized with the temptation to flee somewhere with Leon to try a new life; but at once a vague chasm full of darkness opened within her soul.

"Besides, he no longer loves me," she thought. "What is to become of me? What help is to be hoped for, what consolation, what solace?"

l'épouvante, et la pudeur aussi. Elle songeait qu'elle l'avait repoussé trop loin, qu'il n'était plus temps, que tout était perdu. Puis l'orgueil, la joie de se dire: «je suis vertueuse», et de se regarder dans la glace en prenant des poses résignées, la consolait un peu du sacrifice qu'elle croyait faire.

Alors, les appétits de la chair, les convoitises d'argent et les mélancolies de la passion, tout se confondit dans une même souffrance; — et, au lieu d'en détourner sa pensée; elle l'y attachait davantage, s'excitant à la douleur et en cherchant partout les occasions. Elle s'irritait d'un plat mal servi ou d'une porte entrebâillée, gémissait du velours qu'elle n'avait pas, du bonheur qui lui manquait, de ses rêves trop hauts, de sa maison trop étroite.

Ce qui l'exaspérait, c'est que Charles n'avait pas l'air de se douter de son supplice. La conviction où il était de la rendre heureuse lui semblait une insulte imbécile, et sa sécurité, là- dessus, de l'ingratitude. Pour qui donc était-elle sage? N'était- il pas, lui, obstacle à toute félicité, la cause de toute misère, et comme l'ardillon pointu de cette courroie complexe qui la bouclait de tous côtés?

Donc, elle reporta sur lui seul la haine nombreuse qui résultait de ses ennuis, et chaque effort pour l'amoindrir ne servait qu'à l'augmenter; car cette peine inutile s'ajoutait aux autres motifs de désespoir et contribuait encore plus à l'écartement. Sa propre douceur à elle-même lui donnait des rébellions. La médiocrité domestique la poussait à des fantaisies luxueuses, la tendresse matrimoniale en des désirs adultères. Elle aurait voulu que Charles la battît, pour pouvoir plus justement le détester, s'en venger. Elle s'étonnait parfois des conjectures atroces qui lui arrivaient à la pensée; et il fallait continuer à sourire, s'entendre répéter qu'elle était heureuse, faire semblant de l'être, le laisser croire!

Elle avait des dégoûts, cependant, de cette hypocrisie. Des tentations la prenaient de s'enfuir avec Léon, quelque part, bien loin, pour essayer une destinée nouvelle; mais aussitôt il s'ouvrait dans son âme un gouffre vague, plein d'obscurité.

— D'ailleurs, il ne m'aime plus, pensait-elle; que devenir? quel secours attendre, quelle consolation, quel allégement?

She was left broken, breathless, inert, sobbing in a low voice, with flowing tears.

"Why don't you tell master?" the servant asked her when she came in during these crises.

"It is the nerves," said Emma. "Do not speak to him of it; it would worry him."

"Ah! yes," Felicite went on, "you are just like La Guerine, Pere Guerin's daughter, the fisherman at Pollet, that I used to know at Dieppe before I came to you. She was so sad, so sad, to see her standing upright on the threshold of her house, she seemed to you like a winding-sheet spread out before the door. Her illness, it appears, was a kind of fog that she had in her head, and the doctors could not do anything, nor the priest either. When she was taken too bad she went off quite alone to the sea-shore, so that the customs officer, going his rounds, often found her lying flat on her face, crying on the shingle. Then, after her marriage, it went off, they say."

"But with me," replied Emma, "it was after marriage that it began."

Elle restait brisée, haletante, inerte, sanglotant à voix basse et avec des larmes qui coulaient.

— Pourquoi ne point le dire à Monsieur? lui demandait la domestique, lorsqu'elle entrait pendant ces crises.

— Ce sont les nerfs, répondait Emma; ne lui en parle pas, tu l'affligerais.

— Ah! oui, reprenait Félicité, vous êtes justement comme la Guérine, la fille au père Guérin, le pêcheur du Pollet, que j'ai connue à Dieppe, avant de venir chez vous. Elle était si triste, si triste, qu'à la voir debout sur le seuil de sa maison, elle vous faisait l'effet d'un drap d'enterrement tendu devant la porte. Son mal, à ce qu'il paraît, était une manière de brouillard qu'elle avait dans la tête, et les médecins n'y pouvaient rien, ni le curé non plus. Quand ça la prenait trop fort, elle s'en allait toute seule sur le bord de la mer, si bien que le lieutenant de la douane, en faisant sa tournée, souvent la trouvait étendue à plat ventre et pleurant sur les galets. Puis, après son mariage, ça lui a passé, dit-on.

— Mais, moi, reprenait Emma, c'est après le mariage que ça m'est venu.

# Chapter 6

One evening when the window was open, and she, sitting by it, had been watching Lestiboudois, the beadle, trimming the box, she suddenly heard the Angelus ringing.

It was the beginning of April, when the primroses are in bloom, and a warm wind blows over the flower-beds newly turned, and the gardens, like women, seem to be getting ready for the summer fetes. Through the bars of the arbour and away beyond the river seen in the fields, meandering through the grass in wandering curves. The evening vapours rose between the leafless poplars, touching their outlines with a violet tint, paler and more transparent than a subtle gauze caught athwart their branches. In the distance cattle moved about; neither their steps nor their lowing could be heard; and the bell, still ringing through the air, kept up its peaceful lamentation.

With this repeated tinkling the thoughts of the young woman lost themselves in old memories of her youth and school-days. She remembered the great candlesticks that rose above the vases full of flowers on the altar, and the tabernacle with its small columns. She would have liked to be once more lost in the long line of white veils, marked off here and there by the stuff black hoods of the good sisters bending over their prie-Dieu. At mass on Sundays, when she looked up, she saw the gentle face of the Virgin amid the blue smoke of the rising incense. Then she was moved; she felt herself weak and quite deserted, like the down of a bird whirled by the tempest, and it was unconsciously that she went towards the church, included to no matter what devotions, so that her soul was absorbed and all existence lost in it.

On the Place she met Lestivoudois on his way back, for, in order not to shorten his day's labour, he preferred interrupting his work, then beginning it again, so that he rang the Angelus to suit his own con-

# Chapitre 6

Un soir que la fenêtre était ouverte, et que, assise au bord, elle venait de regarder Lestiboudois, le bedeau, qui taillait le buis, elle entendit tout à coup sonner l'Angelus.

On était au commencement d'avril, quand les primevères sont écloses; un vent tiède se roule sur les plates-bandes labourées, et les jardins, comme des femmes, semblent faire leur toilette pour les fêtes de l'été. Par les barreaux de la tonnelle et au delà tout alentour, on voyait la rivière dans la prairie, où elle dessinait sur l'herbe des sinuosités vagabondes. La vapeur du soir passait entre les peupliers sans feuilles, estompant leurs contours d'une teinte violette, plus pâle et plus transparente qu'une gaze subtile arrêtée sur leurs branchages. Au loin, des bestiaux marchaient; on n'entendait ni leurs pas, ni leurs mugissements; et la cloche, sonnant toujours, continuait dans les airs sa lamentation pacifique.

À ce tintement répété, la pensée de la jeune femme s'égarait dans ses vieux souvenirs de jeunesse et de pension. Elle se rappela les grands chandeliers, qui dépassaient sur l'autel les vases pleins de fleurs et le tabernacle à colonnettes. Elle aurait voulu, comme autrefois, être encore confondue dans la longue ligne des voiles blancs, que marquaient de noir çà et là les capuchons raides des bonnes soeurs inclinées sur leur prie-Dieu; le dimanche, à la messe, quand elle relevait sa tête, elle apercevait le doux visage de la Vierge parmi les tourbillons bleuâtres de l'encens qui montait. Alors un attendrissement la saisit; elle se sentit molle et tout abandonnée, comme un duvet d'oiseau qui tournoie dans la tempête; et ce fut sans en avoir conscience qu'elle s'achemina vers l'église, disposée à n'importe quelle dévotion, pourvu qu'elle y absorbât son âme et que l'existence entière y disparût.

Elle rencontra, sur la place, Lestiboudois, qui s'en revenait; car, pour ne pas rogner la journée, il préférait interrompre sa besogne puis la reprendre, si bien qu'il tintait l'Angelus selon sa commodité. D'ailleurs,

venience. Besides, the ringing over a little earlier warned the lads of catechism hour.

Already a few who had arrived were playing marbles on the stones of the cemetery. Others, astride the wall, swung their legs, kicking with their clogs the large nettles growing between the little enclosure and the newest graves. This was the only green spot. All the rest was but stones, always covered with a fine powder, despite the vestry-broom.

The children in list shoes ran about there as if it were an enclosure made for them. The shouts of their voices could be heard through the humming of the bell. This grew less and less with the swinging of the great rope that, hanging from the top of the belfry, dragged its end on the ground. Swallows flitted to and fro uttering little cries, cut the air with the edge of their wings, and swiftly returned to their yellow nests under the tiles of the coping. At the end of the church a lamp was burning, the wick of a night-light in a glass hung up. Its light from a distance looked like a white stain trembling in the oil. A long ray of the sun fell across the nave and seemed to darken the lower sides and the corners.

"Where is the cure?" asked Madame Bovary of one of the lads, who was amusing himself by shaking a swivel in a hole too large for it.

"He is just coming," he answered.

And in fact the door of the presbytery grated; Abbe Bournisien appeared; the children, pell-mell, fled into the church.

"These young scamps!" murmured the priest, "always the same!"

Then, picking up a catechism all in rags that he had struck with is foot:

"They respect nothing!"

But as soon as he caught sight of Madame Bovary:

"Excuse me," he said; "I did not recognise you."

He thrust the catechism into his pocket, and stopped short, balancing the heavy vestry key between his two fingers.

The light of the setting sun that fell full upon his face paled the lasting of his cassock, shiny at the elbows, unravelled at the hem. Grease

la sonnerie, faite plus tôt, avertissait les gamins de l'heure du catéchisme.

Déjà quelques-uns, qui se trouvaient arrivés, jouaient aux billes sur les dalles du cimetière. D'autres, à califourchon sur le mur, agitaient leurs jambes, en fauchant avec leurs sabots les grandes orties poussées entre la petite enceinte et les dernières tombes. C'était la seule place qui fût verte; tout le reste n'était que pierres, et couvert continuellement d'une poudre fine, malgré le balai de la sacristie.

Les enfants en chaussons couraient là comme sur un parquet fait pour eux, et on entendait les éclats de leurs voix à travers le bourdonnement de la cloche. Il diminuait avec les oscillations de la grosse corde qui, tombant des hauteurs du clocher, traînait à terre par le bout. Des hirondelles passaient en poussant de petits cris, coupaient l'air au tranchant de leur vol, et rentraient vite dans leurs nids jaunes, sous les tuiles du larmier. Au fond de l'église, une lampe brûlait, c'est-à-dire une mèche de veilleuse dans un verre suspendu. Sa lumière, de loin, semblait une tache blanchâtre qui tremblait sur l'huile. Un long rayon de soleil traversait toute la nef et rendait plus sombres encore les bas- côtés et les angles.

— Où est le curé? demanda madame Bovary à un jeune garçon qui s'amusait à secouer le tourniquet dans son trou trop lâche.

— Il va venir, répondit-il.

En effet, la porte du presbytère grinça, l'abbé Bournisien parut; les enfants, pêle-mêle, s'enfuirent dans l'église.

— Ces polissons-là! murmura l'ecclésiastique, toujours les mêmes!

Et, ramassant un catéchisme en lambeaux qu'il venait de heurter avec son pied:

— Ça ne respecte rien!

Mais, dès qu'il aperçut madame Bovary:

— Excusez-moi, dit-il, je ne vous remettais pas.

Il fourra le catéchisme dans sa poche et s'arrêta, continuant à balancer entre deux doigts la lourde clef de la sacristie.

La lueur du soleil couchant qui frappait, en plein son visage pâlissait le lasting de sa soutane, luisante sous les coudes, effiloquée par le bas.

and tobacco stains followed along his broad chest the lines of the buttons, and grew more numerous the farther they were from his neckcloth, in which the massive folds of his red chin rested; this was dotted with yellow spots, that disappeared beneath the coarse hair of his greyish beard. He had just dined and was breathing noisily.

"How are you?" he added.

"Not well," replied Emma; "I am ill."

"Well, and so am I," answered the priest. "These first warm days weaken one most remarkably, don't they? But, after all, we are born to suffer, as St. Paul says. But what does Monsieur Bovary think of it?"

"He!" she said with a gesture of contempt.

"What!" replied the good fellow, quite astonished, "doesn't he prescribe something for you?"

"Ah!" said Emma, "it is no earthly remedy I need."

But the cure from time to time looked into the church, where the kneeling boys were shouldering one another, and tumbling over like packs of cards.

"I should like to know—" she went on.

"You look out, Riboudet," cried the priest in an angry voice; "I'll warm your ears, you imp!"

Then turning to Emma:

"He's Boudet the carpenter's son; his parents are well off, and let him do just as he pleases. Yet he could learn quickly if he would, for he is very sharp. And so sometimes for a joke I call him Riboudet (like the road one takes to go to Maromme) and I even say 'Mon Riboudet.' Ha! Ha! 'Mont Riboudet.' The other day I repeated that just to Monsignor, and he laughed at it; he condescended to laugh at it. And how is Monsieur Bovary?"

She seemed not to hear him. And he went on:

"Always very busy, no doubt; for he and I are certainly the busiest people in the parish. But he is doctor of the body," he added with a thick laugh, "and I of the soul."

Des taches de graisse et de tabac suivaient sur sa poitrine large la ligne des petits boutons, et elles devenaient plus nombreuses en s'écartant de son rabat, où reposaient les plis abondants de sa peau rouge; elle était semée de macules jaunes qui disparaissaient dans les poils rudes de sa barbe grisonnante. Il venait de dîner et respirait bruyamment.

— Comment vous portez-vous? ajouta-t-il.

— Mal, répondit Emma; je souffre.

— Eh bien, moi aussi, reprit l'ecclésiastique. Ces premières chaleurs, n'est-ce pas, vous amollissent étonnamment? Enfin, que voulez-vous! nous sommes nés pour souffrir, comme dit saint Paul. Mais, M. Bovary, qu'est-ce qu'il en pense?

— Lui! fit-elle avec un geste de dédain.

— Quoi! répliqua le bonhomme tout étonné, il ne vous ordonne pas quelque chose?

— Ah! dit Emma, ce ne sont pas les remèdes de la terre qu'il me faudrait.

Mais le curé, de temps à autre, regardait dans l'église, où tous les gamins agenouillés se poussaient de l'épaule, et tombaient comme des capucins de cartes.

— Je voudrais savoir…, reprit-elle.

— Attends, attends, Riboudet, cria l'ecclésiastique d'une voix colère, je m'en vas aller te chauffer les oreilles, mauvais galopin!

Puis, se tournant vers Emma:

— C'est le fils de Boudet le charpentier; ses parents sont à leur aise et lui laissent faire ses fantaisies. Pourtant il apprendrait vite, s'il le voulait, car il est plein d'esprit. Et moi quelquefois, par plaisanterie, je l'appelle donc Riboudet (comme la côte que l'on prend pour aller à Maromme), et je dis même: mon Riboudet. Ah! ah! Mont-Riboudet! L'autre jour, j'ai rapporté ce mot-là à Monseigneur, qui en a ri… il a daigné en rire. — Et M. Bovary, comment va-t-il?

Elle semblait ne pas entendre. Il continua:

— Toujours fort occupé, sans doute? car nous sommes certainement, lui et moi, les deux personnes de la paroisse qui avons le plus à faire. Mais lui, il est le médecin des corps, ajouta-t-il avec un rire épais, et moi, je le suis des âmes!

She fixed her pleading eyes upon the priest.

"Yes," she said, "you solace all sorrows."

"Ah! don't talk to me of it, Madame Bovary. This morning I had to go to Bas-Diauville for a cow that was ill; they thought it was under a spell. All their cows, I don't know how it is—But pardon me! Longuemarre and Boudet! Bless me! Will you leave off?"

And with a bound he ran into the church.

The boys were just then clustering round the large desk, climbing over the precentor's footstool, opening the missal; and others on tiptoe were just about to venture into the confessional. But the priest suddenly distributed a shower of cuffs among them. Seizing them by the collars of their coats, he lifted them from the ground, and deposited them on their knees on the stones of the choir, firmly, as if he meant planting them there.

"Yes," said he, when he returned to Emma, unfolding his large cotton handkerchief, one corner of which he put between his teeth, "farmers are much to be pitied."

"Others, too," she replied.

"Assuredly. Town-labourers, for example."

"It is not they—"

"Pardon! I've there known poor mothers of families, virtuous women, I assure you, real saints, who wanted even bread."

"But those," replied Emma, and the corners of her mouth twitched as she spoke, "those, Monsieur le Cure, who have bread and have no—"

"Fire in the winter," said the priest.

"Oh, what does that matter?"

"What! What does it matter? It seems to me that when one has firing and food—for, after all—"

"My God! my God!" she sighed.

"It is indigestion, no doubt? You must get home, Madame Bovary; drink a little tea, that will strengthen you, or else a glass of fresh water with a little moist sugar."

Elle fixa sur le prêtre des yeux suppliants.

— Oui..., dit-elle, vous soulagez toutes les misères.

— Ah! ne m'en parlez pas, madame Bovary! Ce matin même, il a fallu que j'aille dans le Bas-Diauville pour une vache qui avait l'enfle; ils croyaient que c'était un sort. Toutes leurs vaches, je ne sais comment... Mais, pardon! Longuermarre et Boudet! sac à papier! voulez-vous bien finir!

Et, d'un bond, il s'élança dans l'église.

Les gamins, alors, se pressaient autour du grand pupitre, grimpaient sur le tabouret du chantre, ouvraient le missel; et d'autres, à pas de loup, allaient se hasarder bientôt jusque dans le confessionnal. Mais le curé, soudain, distribua sur tous une grêle de soufflets. Les prenant par le collet de la veste, il les enlevait de terre et les reposait à deux genoux sur les pavés du choeur, fortement, comme s'il eût voulu les y planter.

— Allez, dit-il quand il fut revenu près d'Emma, et en déployant son large mouchoir d'indienne, dont il mit un angle entre ses dents, les cultivateurs sont bien à plaindre!

— Il y en a d'autres, répondit-elle.

— Assurément! les ouvriers des villes, par exemple.

— Ce ne sont pas eux...

— Pardonnez-moi! j'ai connu là de pauvres mères de famille, des femmes vertueuses, je vous assure, de véritables saintes, qui manquaient même de pain.

— Mais celles, reprit Emma (et les coins de sa bouche se tordaient en parlant), celles, monsieur le curé, qui ont du pain, et qui n'ont pas...

— De feu l'hiver, dit le prêtre.

— Eh! qu'importe?

— Comment! qu'importe? Il me semble, à moi, que lorsqu'on est bien chauffé, bien nourri..., car enfin...

— Mon Dieu! mon Dieu! soupirait-elle.

— Vous vous trouvez gênée? fit-il, en s'avançant d'un air inquiet; c'est la digestion, sans doute? Il faut rentrer chez vous, madame Bovary, boire un peu de thé; ça vous fortifiera, ou bien un verre d'eau fraîche avec de la cassonade.

"Why?"

And she looked like one awaking from a dream.

"Well, you see, you were putting your hand to your forehead. I thought you felt faint."

Then, bethinking himself:

"But you were asking me something? What was it? I really don't remember."

"I? Nothing! nothing!" repeated Emma.

And the glance she cast round her slowly fell upon the old man in the cassock. They looked at one another face to face without speaking.

"Then, Madame Bovary," he said at last, "excuse me, but duty first, you know; I must look after my good-for-nothings. The first communion will soon be upon us, and I fear we shall be behind after all. So after Ascension Day I keep them recta an extra hour every Wednesday. Poor children! One cannot lead them too soon into the path of the Lord, as, moreover, he has himself recommended us to do by the mouth of his Divine Son. Good health to you, madame; my respects to your husband."

And he went into the church making a genuflexion as soon as he reached the door.

Emma saw him disappear between the double row of forms, walking with a heavy tread, his head a little bent over his shoulder, and with his two hands half-open behind him.

Then she turned on her heel all of one piece, like a statue on a pivot, and went homewards. But the loud voice of the priest, the clear voices of the boys still reached her ears, and went on behind her.

"Are you a Christian?"

"Yes, I am a Christian."

"What is a Christian?"

"He who, being baptized-baptized-baptized—"

She went up the steps of the staircase holding on to the banisters, and when she was in her room threw herself into an arm-chair.

— Pourquoi?

Et elle avait l'air de quelqu'un qui se réveille d'un songe.

— C'est que vous passiez la main sur votre front. J'ai cru qu'un étourdissement vous prenait.

Puis, se ravisant:

— Mais vous me demandiez quelque chose? Qu'est-ce donc? Je ne sais plus.

— Moi? Rien..., rien..., répétait Emma.

Et son regard, qu'elle promenait autour d'elle, s'abaissa lentement sur le vieillard à soutane. Ils se considéraient tous les deux, face à face, sans parler.

— Alors, madame Bovary, dit-il enfin, faites excuse, mais le devoir avant tout, vous savez; il faut que j'expédie mes garnements. Voilà les premières communions qui vont venir. Nous serons encore surpris, j'en ai peur! Aussi, à partir de l'Ascension, je les tiens recta tous les mercredis une heure de plus. Ces pauvres enfants! on ne saurait les diriger trop tôt dans la voie du Seigneur, comme, du reste, il nous l'a recommandé lui- même par la bouche de son divin Fils... Bonne santé, madame; mes respects à monsieur votre mari!

Et il entra dans l'église, en faisant dès la porte une génuflexion.

Emma le vit qui disparaissait entre la double ligne des bancs, marchant à pas lourds, la tête un peu penchée sur l'épaule, et avec ses deux mains entrouvertes, qu'il portait en dehors.

Puis elle tourna sur ses talons, tout d'un bloc comme une statue sur un pivot, et prit le chemin de sa maison. Mais la grosse voix du curé, la voix claire des gamins arrivaient encore à son oreille et continuaient derrière elle:

— Êtes-vous chrétien?

— Oui, je suis chrétien.

— Qu'est-ce qu'un chrétien?

— C'est celui qui, étant baptisé..., baptisé..., baptisé.

Elle monta les marches de son escalier en se tenant à la rampe, et, quand elle fut dans sa chambre, se laissa tomber dans un fauteuil.

The whitish light of the window-panes fell with soft undulations. The furniture in its place seemed to have become more immobile, and to lose itself in the shadow as in an ocean of darkness. The fire was out, the clock went on ticking, and Emma vaguely marvelled at this calm of all things while within herself was such tumult. But little Berthe was there, between the window and the work-table, tottering on her knitted shoes, and trying to come to her mother to catch hold of the ends of her apron-strings.

"Leave me alone," said the latter, putting her from her with her hand.

The little girl soon came up closer against her knees, and leaning on them with her arms, she looked up with her large blue eyes, while a small thread of pure saliva dribbled from her lips on to the silk apron.

"Leave me alone," repeated the young woman quite irritably.

Her face frightened the child, who began to scream.

"Will you leave me alone?" she said, pushing her with her elbow.

Berthe fell at the foot of the drawers against the brass handle, cutting her cheek, which began to bleed, against it. Madame Bovary sprang to lift her up, broke the bell-rope, called for the servant with all her might, and she was just going to curse herself when Charles appeared. It was the dinner-hour; he had come home.

"Look, dear!" said Emma, in a calm voice, "the little one fell down while she was playing, and has hurt herself."

Charles reassured her; the case was not a serious one, and he went for some sticking plaster.

Madame Bovary did not go downstairs to the dining-room; she wished to remain alone to look after the child. Then watching her sleep, the little anxiety she felt gradually wore off, and she seemed very stupid to herself, and very good to have been so worried just now at so little. Berthe, in fact, no longer sobbed. Her breathing now imperceptibly raised the cotton covering. Big tears lay in the corner of the half-closed eyelids, through whose lashes one could see two pale sunken pupils; the plaster stuck on her cheek drew the skin obliquely.

"It is very strange," thought Emma, "how ugly this child is!"

Le jour blanchâtre des carreaux s'abaissait doucement avec des ondulations. Les meubles à leur place semblaient devenus plus immobiles et se perdre dans l'ombre comme dans un océan ténébreux. La cheminée était éteinte, la pendule battait toujours, et Emma vaguement s'ébahissait à ce calme des choses, tandis qu'il y avait en elle-même tant de bouleversements. Mais, entre la fenêtre et la table à ouvrage, la petite Berthe était là, qui chancelait sur ses bottines de tricot, et essayait de se rapprocher de sa mère, pour lui saisir, par le bout, les rubans de son tablier.

— Laisse-moi! dit celle-ci en l'écartant avec la main.

La petite fille bientôt revint plus près encore contre ses genoux; et, s'y appuyant des bras, elle levait vers elle son gros oeil bleu, pendant qu'un filet de salive pure découlait de sa lèvre sur la soie du tablier.

— Laisse-moi! répéta la jeune femme tout irritée.

Sa figure épouvanta l'enfant, qui se mit à crier.

— Eh! laisse-moi donc! fit-elle en la repoussant du coude.

Berthe alla tomber au pied de la commode, contre la patère de cuivre; elle s'y coupa la joue, le sang sortit. Madame Bovary se précipita pour la relever, cassa le cordon de la sonnette, appela la servante de toutes ses forces, et elle allait commencer à se maudire, lorsque Charles parut. C'était l'heure du dîner, il rentrait.

— Regarde donc, cher ami, lui dit Emma d'une voix tranquille: voilà la petite qui, en jouant, vient de se blesser par terre.

Charles la rassura, le cas n'était point grave, et il alla chercher du diachylum.

Madame Bovary ne descendit, pas dans la salle; elle voulut demeurer seule à garder son enfant. Alors, en la contemplant dormir, ce qu'elle conservait d'inquiétude se dissipa par degrés, et elle se parut à elle-même bien sotte et bien bonne de s'être troublée tout à l'heure pour si peu de chose. Berthe, en effet, ne sanglotait plus. Sa respiration, maintenant, soulevait insensiblement la couverture de coton. De grosses larmes s'arrêtaient au coin de ses paupières à demi closes, qui laissaient voir entre les cils deux prunelles pâles, enfoncées; le sparadrap, collé sur sa joue, en tirait obliquement la peau tendue.

— C'est une chose étrange, pensait Emma, comme cette enfant est laide!

When at eleven o'clock Charles came back from the chemist's shop, whither he had gone after dinner to return the remainder of the sticking-plaster, he found his wife standing by the cradle.

"I assure you it's nothing." he said, kissing her on the forehead. "Don't worry, my poor darling; you will make yourself ill."

He had stayed a long time at the chemist's. Although he had not seemed much moved, Homais, nevertheless, had exerted himself to buoy him up, to "keep up his spirits."

Then they had talked of the various dangers that threaten childhood, of the carelessness of servants. Madame Homais knew something of it, having still upon her chest the marks left by a basin full of soup that a cook had formerly dropped on her pinafore, and her good parents took no end of trouble for her. The knives were not sharpened, nor the floors waxed; there were iron gratings to the windows and strong bars across the fireplace; the little Homais, in spite of their spirit, could not stir without someone watching them; at the slightest cold their father stuffed them with pectorals; and until they were turned four they all, without pity, had to wear wadded head-protectors. This, it is true, was a fancy of Madame Homais'; her husband was inwardly afflicted at it. Fearing the possible consequences of such compression to the intellectual organs. He even went so far as to say to her:

"Do you want to make Caribs or Botocudos of them?"

Charles, however, had several times tried to interrupt the conversation.

"I should like to speak to you," he had whispered in the clerk's ear, who went upstairs in front of him.

"Can he suspect anything?" Leon asked himself. His heart beat, and he racked his brain with surmises.

At last, Charles, having shut the door, asked him to see himself what would be the price at Rouen of a fine daguerreotypes. It was a sentimental surprise he intended for his wife, a delicate attention—his portrait in a frock-coat. But he wanted first to know "how much it would be." The inquiries would not put Monsieur Leon out, since he went to town almost every week.

Quand Charles, à onze heures du soir, revint de la pharmacie (où il avait été remettre, après le dîner, ce qui lui restait du diachylum), il trouva sa femme debout auprès du berceau.

— Puisque je t'assure que ce ne sera rien, dit-il en la baisant au front; ne te tourmente pas, pauvre chérie, tu te rendras malade!

Il était resté longtemps chez l'apothicaire. Bien qu'il ne s'y fût pas montré fort ému, M. Homais, néanmoins, s'était efforcé de le raffermir, de lui remonter le moral.

Alors on avait causé des dangers divers qui menaçaient l'enfance et de l'étourderie des domestiques. Madame Homais en savait quelque chose, ayant encore sur la poitrine les marques d'une écuellée de braise qu'une cuisinière, autrefois, avait laissée tomber dans son sarrau. Aussi ces bons parents prenaient-ils quantité de précautions. Les couteaux jamais n'étaient affilés, ni les appartements cirés. Il y avait aux fenêtres des grilles en fer et aux chambranles de fortes barres. Les petits Homais, malgré leur indépendance, ne pouvaient remuer sans un surveillant derrière eux; au moindre rhume, leur père les bourrait de pectoraux, et jusqu'à plus de quatre ans ils portaient tous, impitoyablement, des bourrelets matelassés. C'était, il est vrai, une manie de madame Homais; son époux en était intérieurement affligé, redoutant pour les organes de l'intellect les résultats possibles d'une pareille compression, et il s'échappait jusqu'à lui dire:

—Tu prétends donc en faire des Caraïbes ou des Botocudos?

Charles, cependant, avait essayé plusieurs fois d'interrompre la conversation.

— J'aurais à vous entretenir, avait-il soufflé bas à l'oreille du clerc, qui se mit à marcher devant lui dans l'escalier.

— Se douterait-il de quelque chose? se demandait Léon. Il avait des battements de coeur et se perdait en conjectures.

Enfin Charles, ayant fermé la porte, le pria de voir lui-même à Rouen quels pouvaient être les prix d'un beau daguerréotype; c'était une surprise sentimentale qu'il réservait à sa femme, une attention fine, son portrait en habit noir. Mais il voulait auparavant savoir à quoi s'en tenir; ces démarches ne devaient pas embarrasser M. Léon, puisqu'il allait à la ville toutes les semaines, à peu près.

Why? Monsieur Homais suspected some "young man's affair" at the bottom of it, an intrigue. But he was mistaken. Leon was after no love-making. He was sadder than ever, as Madame Lefrancois saw from the amount of food he left on his plate. To find out more about it she questioned the tax-collector. Binet answered roughly that he "wasn't paid by the police."

All the same, his companion seemed very strange to him, for Leon often threw himself back in his chair, and stretching out his arms, complained vaguely of life.

"It's because you don't take enough recreation," said the collector.

"What recreation?"

"If I were you I'd have a lathe."

"But I don't know how to turn," answered the clerk.

"Ah! that's true," said the other, rubbing his chin with an air of mingled contempt and satisfaction.

Leon was weary of loving without any result; moreover he was beginning to feel that depression caused by the repetition of the same kind of life, when no interest inspires and no hope sustains it. He was so bored with Yonville and its inhabitants, that the sight of certain persons, of certain houses, irritated him beyond endurance; and the chemist, good fellow though he was, was becoming absolutely unbearable to him. Yet the prospect of a new condition of life frightened as much as it seduced him.

This apprehension soon changed into impatience, and then Paris from afar sounded its fanfare of masked balls with the laugh of grisettes. As he was to finish reading there, why not set out at once? What prevented him? And he began making home-preparations; he arranged his occupations beforehand. He furnished in his head an apartment. He would lead an artist's life there! He would take lessons on the guitar! He would have a dressing-gown, a Basque cap, blue velvet slippers! He even already was admiring two crossed foils over his chimney-piece, with a death's head on the guitar above them.

The difficulty was the consent of his mother; nothing, however, seemed more reasonable. Even his employer advised him to go to some

Dans quel but? Homais soupçonnait là-dessous quelque histoire de jeune homme, une intrigue. Mais il se trompait; Léon ne poursuivait aucune amourette. Plus que jamais il était triste, et madame Lefrançois s'en apercevait bien à la quantité de nourriture qu'il laissait maintenant sur son assiette. Pour en savoir plus long, elle interrogea le percepteur; Binet répliqua, d'un ton rogue, qu'il n'était point payé par la police.

Son camarade, toutefois, lui paraissait fort singulier; car souvent Léon se renversait sur sa chaise en écartant les bras, et se plaignait vaguement de l'existence.

— C'est que vous ne prenez point assez de distractions, disait le percepteur.

— Lesquelles?

— Moi, à votre place, j'aurais un tour!

— Mais je ne sais pas tourner, répondait le clerc.

— Oh! c'est vrai! faisait l'autre en caressant sa mâchoire, avec un air de dédain mêlé de satisfaction.

Léon était las d'aimer sans résultat; puis il commençait à sentir cet accablement que vous cause la répétition de la même vie, lorsque aucun intérêt ne la dirige et qu'aucune espérance ne la soutient. Il était si ennuyé d'Yonville et des Yonvillais, que la vue de certaines gens, de certaines maisons l'irritait à n'y pouvoir tenir; et le pharmacien, tout bonhomme qu'il était, lui devenait complètement insupportable. Cependant, la perspective d'une situation nouvelle l'effrayait autant qu'elle le séduisait.

Cette appréhension se tourna vite en impatience, et Paris alors agita pour lui, dans le lointain, la fanfare de ses bals masqués avec le rire de ses grisettes. Puisqu'il devait y terminer son droit, pourquoi ne partait-il pas? qui l'empêchait? Et il se mit à faire des préparatifs intérieurs: il arrangea d'avance ses occupations. Il se meubla, dans sa tête, un appartement. Il y mènerait une vie d'artiste! Il y prendrait des leçons de guitare! Il aurait une robe de chambre, un béret basque, des pantoufles de velours bleu! Et même il admirait déjà sur sa cheminée deux fleurets en sautoir, avec une tête de mort et la guitare au- dessus.

La chose difficile était le consentement de sa mère; rien pourtant ne paraissait plus raisonnable. Son patron même l'engageait à visiter

other chambers where he could advance more rapidly. Taking a middle course, then, Leon looked for some place as second clerk at Rouen; found none, and at last wrote his mother a long letter full of details, in which he set forth the reasons for going to live at Paris immediately. She consented.

He did not hurry. Every day for a month Hivert carried boxes, valises, parcels for him from Yonville to Rouen and from Rouen to Yonville; and when Leon had packed up his wardrobe, had his three arm-chairs restuffed, bought a stock of neckties, in a word, had made more preparations than for a voyage around the world, he put it off from week to week, until he received a second letter from his mother urging him to leave, since he wanted to pass his examination before the vacation.

When the moment for the farewells had come, Madame Homais wept, Justin sobbed; Homais, as a man of nerve, concealed his emotion; he wished to carry his friend's overcoat himself as far as the gate of the notary, who was taking Leon to Rouen in his carriage. The latter had just time to bid farewell to Monsieur Bovary.

When he reached the head of the stairs, he stopped, he was so out of breath. As he came in, Madame Bovary arose hurriedly.

"It is I again!" said Leon.

"I was sure of it!"

She bit her lips, and a rush of blood flowing under her skin made her red from the roots of her hair to the top of her collar. She remained standing, leaning with her shoulder against the wainscot.

"The doctor is not here?" he went on.

"He is out."

She repeated:

"He is out."

Then there was silence. They looked at one another and their thoughts, confounded in the same agony, clung close together like two throbbing breasts.

"I should like to kiss Berthe," said Leon.

Emma went down a few steps and called Felicite.

une autre étude, où il pût se développer davantage. Prenant donc un parti moyen, Léon chercha quelque place de second clerc à Rouen, n'en trouva pas, et écrivit enfin à sa mère une longue lettre détaillée, où il exposait les raisons d'aller habiter Paris immédiatement. Elle y consentit.

Il ne se hâta point. Chaque jour, durant tout un mois, Hivert transporta pour lui d'Yonville à Rouen, de Rouen à Yonville, des coffres, des valises, des paquets; et, quand Léon eut remonté sa garde-robe, fait rembourrer ses trois fauteuils, acheté une provision de foulards, pris en un mot plus de dispositions que pour un voyage autour du monde, il s'ajourna de semaine en semaine, jusqu'à ce qu'il reçût une seconde lettre maternelle où on le pressait de partir, puisqu'il désirait, avant les vacances, passer son examen.

Lorsque le moment fut venu des embrassades, madame Homais pleura; Justin sanglotait; Homais, en homme fort, dissimula son émotion; il voulut lui-même porter le paletot de son ami jusqu'à la grille du notaire, qui emmenait Léon à Rouen dans sa voiture. Ce dernier avait juste le temps de faire ses adieux à M. Bovary.

Quand il fut au haut de l'escalier, il s'arrêta, tant il se sentait hors d'haleine. À son entrée, madame Bovary se leva vivement.

— C'est encore moi! dit Léon.

— J'en étais sûre!

Elle se mordit les lèvres, et un flot de sang lui courut sous la peau, qui se colora tout en rose, depuis la racine des cheveux jusqu'au bord de sa collerette. Elle restait debout, s'appuyant de l'épaule contre la boiserie.

— Monsieur n'est donc pas là? reprit-il.

— Il est absent.

Elle répéta:

— Il est absent.

Alors il y eut un silence. Ils se regardèrent; et leurs pensées, confondues dans la même angoisse, s'étreignaient étroitement, comme deux poitrines palpitantes.

— Je voudrais bien embrasser Berthe, dit Léon.

Emma descendit quelques marches, et elle appela Félicité.

He threw one long look around him that took in the walls, the decorations, the fireplace, as if to penetrate everything, carry away everything.

But she returned, and the servant brought Berthe, who was swinging a windmill roof downwards at the end of a string.

Leon kissed her several times on the neck.

"Good-bye, poor child! good-bye, dear little one! good-bye!" And he gave her back to her mother.

"Take her away," she said.

They remained alone.

Madame Bovary, her back turned, her face pressed against a window-pane; Leon held his cap in his hand, knocking it softly against his thigh.

"It is going to rain," said Emma.

"I have a cloak," he answered.

"Ah!"

She turned around, her chin lowered, her forehead bent forward. The light fell on it as on a piece of marble, to the curve of the eyebrows, without one's being able to guess what Emma was seeing on the horizon or what she was thinking within herself.

"Well, good-bye," he sighed.

She raised her head with a quick movement.

"Yes, good-bye—go!"

They advanced towards each other; he held out his hand; she hesitated.

"In the English fashion, then," she said, giving her own hand wholly to him, and forcing a laugh.

Leon felt it between his fingers, and the very essence of all his being seemed to pass down into that moist palm.

Then he opened his hand; their eyes met again, and he disappeared.

When he reached the market-place, he stopped and hid behind a pillar to look for the last time at this white house with the four green blinds. He thought he saw a shadow behind the window in the room;

Il jeta vite autour de lui un large coup d'oeil qui s'étala sur les murs, les étagères, la cheminée, comme pour pénétrer tout, emporter tout.

Mais elle rentra, et la servante amena Berthe, qui secouait au bout d'une ficelle un moulin à vent la tête en bas.

Léon la baisa sur le cou à plusieurs reprises.

— Adieu, pauvre enfant! adieu, chère petite, adieu! Et il la remit à sa mère.

— Emmenez-la, dit celle-ci.

Ils restèrent seuls.

Madame Bovary, le dos tourné, avait la figure posée contre un carreau; Léon tenait sa casquette à la main et la battait doucement le long de sa cuisse.

— Il va pleuvoir, dit Emma.

— J'ai un manteau, répondit-il.

— Ah!

Elle se détourna, le menton baissé et le front en avant. La lumière y glissait comme sur un marbre, jusqu'à la courbe des sourcils, sans que l'on pût savoir ce qu'Emma regardait à l'horizon ni ce qu'elle pensait au fond d'elle-même.

— Allons, adieu! soupira-t-il.

Elle releva sa tête d'un mouvement brusque:

— Oui, adieu..., partez!

Ils s'avancèrent l'un vers l'autre; il tendit la main, elle hésita.

— À l'anglaise donc, fit-elle abandonnant la sienne tout en s'efforçant de rire.

Léon la sentit entre ses doigts, et la substance même de tout son être lui semblait descendre dans cette paume humide.

Puis il ouvrit la main; leurs yeux se rencontrèrent encore, et il disparut.

Quand il fut sous les halles, il s'arrêta, et il se cacha derrière un pilier, afin de contempler une dernière fois cette maison blanche avec ses quatre jalousies vertes. Il crut voir une ombre derrière la fenêtre, dans la

but the curtain, sliding along the pole as though no one were touching it, slowly opened its long oblique folds that spread out with a single movement, and thus hung straight and motionless as a plaster wall. Leon set off running.

From afar he saw his employer's gig in the road, and by it a man in a coarse apron holding the horse. Homais and Monsieur Guillaumin were talking. They were waiting for him.

"Embrace me," said the druggist with tears in his eyes. "Here is your coat, my good friend. Mind the cold; take care of yourself; look after yourself."

"Come, Leon, jump in," said the notary.

Homais bent over the splash-board, and in a voice broken by sobs uttered these three sad words:

"A pleasant journey!"

"Good-night," said Monsieur Guillaumin. "Give him his head." They set out, and Homais went back.

Madame Bovary had opened her window overlooking the garden and watched the clouds.

They gathered around the sunset on the side of Rouen and then swiftly rolled back their black columns, behind which the great rays of the sun looked out like the golden arrows of a suspended trophy, while the rest of the empty heavens was white as porcelain. But a gust of wind bowed the poplars, and suddenly the rain fell; it pattered against the green leaves. Then the sun reappeared, the hens clucked, sparrows shook their wings in the damp thickets, and the pools of water on the gravel as they flowed away carried off the pink flowers of an acacia.

"Ah! how far off he must be already!" she thought.

Monsieur Homais, as usual, came at half-past six during dinner.

"Well," said he, "so we've sent off our young friend!"

"So it seems," replied the doctor.

Then turning on his chair:

"Any news at home?"

chambre; mais le rideau, se décrochant de la patère comme si personne n'y touchait, remua lentement ses longs plis obliques, qui d'un seul bond s'étalèrent tous, et il resta droit, plus immobile qu'un mur de plâtre. Léon se mit à courir.

Il aperçut de loin, sur la route, le cabriolet de son patron, et à côté un homme en serpillière qui tenait le cheval. Homais et M. Guillaumin causaient ensemble. On l'attendait.

— Embrassez-moi, dit l'apothicaire les larmes aux yeux. Voilà votre paletot, mon bon ami; prenez garde au froid! Soignez-vous! ménagez-vous!

— Allons, Léon, en voiture! dit le notaire.

Homais se pencha sur le garde-crotte, et d'une voix entrecoupée par les sanglots, laissa tomber ces deux mots tristes:

— Bon voyage!

— Bonsoir, répondit M. Guillaumin. Lâchez tout! Ils partirent, et Homais s'en retourna.

Madame Bovary avait ouvert sa fenêtre sur le jardin, et elle regardait les nuages.

Ils s'amoncelaient au couchant du côté de Rouen, et roulaient vite leurs volutes noires, d'où dépassaient par derrière les grandes lignes du soleil, comme les flèches d'or d'un trophée suspendu, tandis que le reste du ciel vide avait la blancheur d'une porcelaine. Mais une rafale de vent fit se courber les peupliers, et tout à coup la pluie tomba; elle crépitait sur les feuilles vertes. Puis le soleil reparut, les poules chantèrent, des moineaux battaient des ailes dans les buissons humides, et les flaques d'eau sur le sable emportaient en s'écoulant les fleurs roses d'un acacia.

— Ah! qu'il doit être loin déjà! pensa-t-elle.

M. Homais, comme de coutume, vint à six heures et demie, pendant le dîner.

— Eh bien, dit-il en s'asseyant, nous avons donc tantôt embarqué notre jeune homme?

— Il paraît! répondit le médecin.

Puis, se tournant sur sa chaise:

— Et quoi de neuf chez vous?

"Nothing much. Only my wife was a little moved this afternoon. You know women—a nothing upsets them, especially my wife. And we should be wrong to object to that, since their nervous organization is much more malleable than ours."

"Poor Leon!" said Charles. "How will he live at Paris? Will he get used to it?"

Madame Bovary sighed.

"Get along!" said the chemist, smacking his lips. "The outings at restaurants, the masked balls, the champagne—all that'll be jolly enough, I assure you."

"I don't think he'll go wrong," objected Bovary.

"Nor do I," said Monsieur Homais quickly; "although he'll have to do like the rest for fear of passing for a Jesuit. And you don't know what a life those dogs lead in the Latin quarter with actresses. Besides, students are thought a great deal of in Paris. Provided they have a few accomplishments, they are received in the best society; there are even ladies of the Faubourg Saint-Germain who fall in love with them, which subsequently furnishes them opportunities for making very good matches."

"But," said the doctor, "I fear for him that down there—"

"You are right," interrupted the chemist; "that is the reverse of the medal. And one is constantly obliged to keep one's hand in one's pocket there. Thus, we will suppose you are in a public garden. An individual presents himself, well dressed, even wearing an order, and whom one would take for a diplomatist. He approaches you, he insinuates himself; offers you a pinch of snuff, or picks up your hat. Then you become more intimate; he takes you to a cafe, invites you to his country-house, introduces you, between two drinks, to all sorts of people; and three-fourths of the time it's only to plunder your watch or lead you into some pernicious step.

"That is true," said Charles; "but I was thinking especially of illnesses—of typhoid fever, for example, that attacks students from the provinces."

Emma shuddered.

— Pas grand-chose. Ma femme, seulement, a été, cette après-midi, un peu émue. Vous savez, les femmes, un rien les trouble! la mienne surtout! Et l'on aurait tort de se révolter là contre, puisque leur organisation nerveuse est beaucoup plus malléable que la nôtre.

— Ce pauvre Léon! disait Charles, comment va-t-il vivre à Paris?... S'y accoutumera-t-il?

Madame Bovary soupira.

— Allons donc! dit le pharmacien en claquant de la langue, les parties fines chez le traiteur! les bals masqués! le champagne! tout cela va rouler, je vous assure.

— Je ne crois pas qu'il se dérange, objecta Bovary.

— Ni moi! reprit vivement M. Homais, quoiqu'il lui faudra pourtant suivre les autres, au risque de passer pour un jésuite. Et vous ne savez pas la vie que mènent ces farceurs-là, dans le quartier Latin, avec les actrices! Du reste, les étudiants sont fort bien vus à Paris. Pour peu qu'ils aient quelque talent d'agrément, on les reçoit dans les meilleures sociétés, et il y a même des dames du faubourg Saint-Germain qui en deviennent amoureuses, ce qui leur fournit, par la suite, les occasions de faire de très beaux mariages.

— Mais, dit le médecin, j'ai peur pour lui que... là-bas...

— Vous avez raison, interrompit l'apothicaire, c'est le revers de la médaille! et l'on y est obligé continuellement d'avoir la main posée sur son gousset. Ainsi, vous êtes dans un jardin public, je suppose; un quidam se présente, bien mis, décoré même, et qu'on prendrait pour un diplomate; il vous aborde; vous causez; il s'insinue, vous offre une prise ou vous ramasse votre chapeau. Puis on se lie davantage; il vous mène au café, vous invite à venir dans sa maison de campagne, vous fait faire, entre deux vins, toutes sortes de connaissances, et, les trois quarts du temps ce n'est que pour flibuster votre bourse ou vous entraîner en des démarches pernicieuses.

— C'est vrai, répondit Charles; mais je pensais surtout aux maladies, à la fièvre typhoïde, par exemple, qui attaque les étudiants de la province.

Emma tressaillit.

"Because of the change of regimen," continued the chemist, "and of the perturbation that results therefrom in the whole system. And then the water at Paris, don't you know! The dishes at restaurants, all the spiced food, end by heating the blood, and are not worth, whatever people may say of them, a good soup. For my own part, I have always preferred plain living; it is more healthy. So when I was studying pharmacy at Rouen, I boarded in a boarding house; I dined with the professors."

And thus he went on, expounding his opinions generally and his personal likings, until Justin came to fetch him for a mulled egg that was wanted.

"Not a moment's peace!" he cried; "always at it! I can't go out for a minute! Like a plough-horse, I have always to be moiling and toiling. What drudgery!"

Then, when he was at the door:

"By the way, do you know the news?"

"What news?"

"That it is very likely," Homais went on, raising his eyebrows and assuming one of his most serious expression, "that the agricultural meeting of the Seine-Inferieure will be held this year at Yonville-l'Abbaye. The rumour, at all events, is going the round. This morning the paper alluded to it. It would be of the utmost importance for our district. But we'll talk it over later on. I can see, thank you; Justin has the lantern."

— À cause du changement de régime, continua le pharmacien, et de la perturbation qui en résulte dans l'économie générale. Et puis, l'eau de Paris, voyez-vous! les mets de restaurateurs, toutes ces nourritures épicées finissent par vous échauffer le sang et ne valent pas, quoi qu'on en dise, un bon pot-au-feu. J'ai toujours, quant à moi, préféré la cuisine bourgeoise: c'est plus sain! Aussi, lorsque j'étudiais à Rouen la pharmacie, je m'étais mis en pension dans une pension; je mangeais avec les professeurs.

Et il continua donc à exposer ses opinions générales et ses sympathies personnelles, jusqu'au moment où Justin vint le chercher pour un lait de poule qu'il fallait faire.

— Pas un instant de répit! s'écria-t-il, toujours à la chaîne! Je ne peux sortir une minute! Il faut, comme un cheval de labour, être à suer sang et eau! Quel collier de misère!

Puis, quand il fut sur la porte:

— À propos, dit-il, savez-vous la nouvelle?

— Quoi donc?

— C'est qu'il est fort probable, reprit Homais en dressant ses sourcils et en prenant une figure des plus sérieuses, que les comices agricoles de la Seine-Inférieure se tiendront cette année à Yonville-l'Abbaye. Le bruit, du moins, en circule. Ce matin, le journal en touchait quelque chose. Ce serait pour notre arrondissement de la dernière importance! Mais nous en causerons plus tard. J'y vois, je vous remercie; Justin a la lanterne.

# Chapter 7

The next day was a dreary one for Emma. Everything seemed to her enveloped in a black atmosphere floating confusedly over the exterior of things, and sorrow was engulfed within her soul with soft shrieks such as the winter wind makes in ruined castles. It was that reverie which we give to things that will not return, the lassitude that seizes you after everything was done; that pain, in fine, that the interruption of every wonted movement, the sudden cessation of any prolonged vibration, brings on.

As on the return from Vaubyessard, when the quadrilles were running in her head, she was full of a gloomy melancholy, of a numb despair. Leon reappeared, taller, handsomer, more charming, more vague. Though separated from her, he had not left her; he was there, and the walls of the house seemed to hold his shadow. She could not detach her eyes from the carpet where he had walked, from those empty chairs where he had sat. The river still flowed on, and slowly drove its ripples along the slippery banks. They had often walked there to the murmur of the waves over the moss-covered pebbles. How bright the sun had been! What happy afternoons they had seen alone in the shade at the end of the garden! He read aloud, bareheaded, sitting on a footstool of dry sticks; the fresh wind of the meadow set trembling the leaves of the book and the nasturtiums of the arbour. Ah! he was gone, the only charm of her life, the only possible hope of joy. Why had she not seized this happiness when it came to her? Why not have kept hold of it with both hands, with both knees, when it was about to flee from her? And she cursed herself for not having loved Leon. She thirsted for his lips. The wish took possession of her to run after and rejoin him, throw herself into his arms and say to him, "It is I; I am yours." But Emma recoiled beforehand at the difficulties of the enterprise, and her desires, increased by regret, became only the more acute.

# Chapitre 7

Le lendemain fut, pour Emma, une journée funèbre. Tout lui parut enveloppé par une atmosphère noire qui flottait confusément sur l'extérieur des choses, et le chagrin s'engouffrait dans son âme avec des hurlements doux, comme fait le vent d'hiver dans les châteaux abandonnés. C'était cette rêverie que l'on a sur ce qui ne reviendra plus, la lassitude qui vous prend après chaque fait accompli, cette douleur enfin que vous apportent l'interruption de tout mouvement accoutumé, la cessation brusque d'une vibration prolongée.

Comme au retour de la Vaubyessard, quand les quadrilles tourbillonnaient dans sa tête, elle avait une mélancolie morne, un désespoir engourdi. Léon réapparaissait plus grand, plus beau, plus suave, plus vague; quoiqu'il fût séparé d'elle, il ne l'avait pas quittée, il était là, et les murailles de la maison semblaient garder son ombre. Elle ne pouvait détacher sa vue de ce tapis où il avait marché, de ces meubles vides où il s'était assis. La rivière coulait toujours, et poussait lentement ses petits flots le long de la berge glissante. Ils s'y étaient promenés bien des fois, à ce même murmure des ondes, sur les cailloux couverts de mousse. Quels bons soleils ils avaient eus! quelles bonnes après- midi, seuls, à l'ombre, dans le fond du jardin! Il lisait tout haut, tête nue, posé sur un tabouret de bâtons secs; le vent frais de la prairie faisait trembler les pages du livre et les capucines de la tonnelle… Ah! il était parti, le seul charme de sa vie, le seul espoir possible d'une félicité! Comment n'avait-elle pas saisi ce bonheur-là, quand il se présentait! Pourquoi ne l'avoir pas retenu à deux mains, à deux genoux, quand il voulait s'enfuir? Et elle se maudit de n'avoir pas aimé Léon; elle eut soif de ses lèvres. L'envie la prit de courir le rejoindre, de se jeter dans ses bras, de lui dire: «C'est moi, je suis à toi!» Mais Emma s'embarrassait d'avance aux difficultés de l'entreprise, et ses désirs, s'augmentant d'un regret, n'en devenaient que plus actifs.

Henceforth the memory of Leon was the centre of her boredom; it burnt there more brightly than the fire travellers have left on the snow of a Russian steppe. She sprang towards him, she pressed against him, she stirred carefully the dying embers, sought all around her anything that could revive it; and the most distant reminiscences, like the most immediate occasions, what she experienced as well as what she imagined, her voluptuous desires that were unsatisfied, her projects of happiness that crackled in the wind like dead boughs, her sterile virtue, her lost hopes, the domestic tete-a-tete—she gathered it all up, took everything, and made it all serve as fuel for her melancholy.

The flames, however, subsided, either because the supply had exhausted itself, or because it had been piled up too much. Love, little by little, was quelled by absence; regret stifled beneath habit; and this incendiary light that had empurpled her pale sky was overspread and faded by degrees. In the supineness of her conscience she even took her repugnance towards her husband for aspirations towards her lover, the burning of hate for the warmth of tenderness; but as the tempest still raged, and as passion burnt itself down to the very cinders, and no help came, no sun rose, there was night on all sides, and she was lost in the terrible cold that pierced her.

Then the evil days of Tostes began again. She thought herself now far more unhappy; for she had the experience of grief, with the certainty that it would not end.

A woman who had laid on herself such sacrifices could well allow herself certain whims. She bought a Gothic prie-dieu, and in a month spent fourteen francs on lemons for polishing her nails; she wrote to Rouen for a blue cashmere gown; she chose one of Lheureux's finest scarves, and wore it knotted around her waist over her dressing-gown; and, with closed blinds and a book in her hand, she lay stretched out on a couch in this garb.

She often changed her coiffure; she did her hair a la Chinoise, in flowing curls, in plaited coils; she parted in on one side and rolled it under like a man's.

Dès lors, ce souvenir de Léon fut comme le centre de son ennui; il y pétillait plus fort que, dans un steppe de Russie, un feu de voyageurs abandonné sur la neige. Elle se précipitait vers lui, elle se blottissait contre, elle remuait délicatement ce foyer près de s'éteindre, elle allait cherchant tout autour d'elle ce qui pouvait l'aviver davantage; et les réminiscences les plus lointaines comme les plus immédiates occasions, ce qu'elle éprouvait avec ce qu'elle imaginait, ses envies de volupté qui se dispersaient, ses projets de bonheur qui craquaient au vent comme des branchages morts, sa vertu stérile, ses espérances tombées, la litière domestique, elle ramassait tout, prenait tout, et faisait servir tout à réchauffer sa tristesse.

Cependant les flammes s'apaisèrent, soit que la provision d'elle- même s'épuisât, ou que l'entassement fût trop considérable. L'amour, peu à peu, s'éteignit par l'absence, le regret s'étouffa sous l'habitude; et cette lueur d'incendie qui empourprait son ciel pâle se couvrit de plus d'ombre et s'effaça par degrés. Dans l'assoupissement de sa conscience, elle prit même les répugnances du mari pour des aspirations vers l'amant, les brûlures de la haine pour des réchauffements de la tendresse; mais, comme l'ouragan soufflait toujours, et que la passion se consuma jusqu'aux cendres, et qu'aucun secours ne vint, qu'aucun soleil ne parut, il fut de tous côtés nuit complète, et elle demeura perdue dans un froid horrible qui la traversait.

Alors les mauvais jours de Tostes recommencèrent. Elle s'estimait à présent beaucoup plus malheureuse: car elle avait l'expérience du chagrin, avec la certitude qu'il ne finirait pas.

Une femme qui s'était imposé de si grands sacrifices pouvait bien se passer des fantaisies. Elle s'acheta un prie-Dieu gothique, et elle dépensa en un mois pour quatorze francs de citrons à se nettoyer les ongles; elle écrivit à Rouen, afin d'avoir une robe en cachemire bleu; elle choisit chez Lheureux la plus belle de ses écharpes; elle se la nouait à la taille par-dessus sa robe de chambre; et, les volets fermés, avec un livre à la main, elle restait étendue sur un canapé dans cet accoutrement.

Souvent, elle variait sa coiffure: elle se mettait à la chinoise, en boucles molles, en nattes tressées; elle se fit une raie sur le côté de la tête et roula ses cheveux en dessous, comme un homme.

She wanted to learn Italian; she bought dictionaries, a grammar, and a supply of white paper. She tried serious reading, history, and philosophy. Sometimes in the night Charles woke up with a start, thinking he was being called to a patient.

"I'm coming," he stammered.

And it was the noise of a match Emma had struck to relight the lamp. But her reading fared like her piece of embroidery, all of which, only just begun, filled her cupboard; she took it up, left it, passed on to other books.

She had attacks in which she could easily have been driven to commit any folly. She maintained one day, in opposition to her husband, that she could drink off a large glass of brandy, and, as Charles was stupid enough to dare her to, she swallowed the brandy to the last drop.

In spite of her vapourish airs (as the housewives of Yonville called them), Emma, all the same, never seemed gay, and usually she had at the corners of her mouth that immobile contraction that puckers the faces of old maids, and those of men whose ambition has failed. She was pale all over, white as a sheet; the skin of her nose was drawn at the nostrils, her eyes looked at you vaguely. After discovering three grey hairs on her temples, she talked much of her old age.

She often fainted. One day she even spat blood, and, as Charles fussed around her showing his anxiety:

"Bah!" she answered, "what does it matter?"

Charles fled to his study and wept there, both his elbows on the table, sitting in an arm-chair at his bureau under the phrenological head.

Then he wrote to his mother begging her to come, and they had many long consultations together on the subject of Emma.

What should they decide? What was to be done since she rejected all medical treatment?

"Do you know what your wife wants?" replied Madame Bovary senior. "She wants to be forced to occupy herself with some manual work. If she were obliged, like so many others, to earn her living, she

Elle voulut apprendre l'italien: elle acheta des dictionnaires, une grammaire, une provision de papier blanc. Elle essaya des lectures sérieuses, de l'histoire et de la philosophie. La nuit, quelquefois, Charles se réveillait en sursaut, croyant qu'on venait le chercher pour un malade:

— J'y vais, balbutiait-il.

Et c'était le bruit d'une allumette qu'Emma frottait afin de rallumer la lampe. Mais il en était de ses lectures comme de ses tapisseries, qui, toutes commencées encombraient son armoire; elle les prenait, les quittait, passait à d'autres.

Elle avait des accès, où on l'eût poussée facilement à des extravagances. Elle soutint un jour, contre son mari, qu'elle boirait bien un grand demi-verre d'eau-de-vie, et, comme Charles eut la bêtise de l'en défier, elle avala l'eau-de-vie jusqu'au bout.

Malgré ses airs évaporés (c'était le mot des bourgeoises d'Yonville), Emma pourtant ne paraissait pas joyeuse, et, d'habitude, elle gardait aux coins de la bouche cette immobile contraction qui plisse la figure des vieilles filles et celle des ambitieux déchus. Elle était pâle partout, blanche comme du linge; la peau du nez se tirait vers les narines, ses yeux vous regardaient d'une manière vague. Pour s'être découvert trois cheveux gris sur les tempes, elle parla beaucoup de sa vieillesse.

Souvent des défaillances la prenaient. Un jour même, elle eut un crachement de sang, et, comme Charles s'empressait, laissant apercevoir son inquiétude:

— Ah bah! répondit-elle, qu'est-ce que cela fait?

Charles s'alla réfugier dans son cabinet; et il pleura, les deux coudes sur la table, assis dans son fauteuil de bureau, sous la tête phrénologique.

Alors il écrivit à sa mère pour la prier de venir, et ils eurent ensemble de longues conférences au sujet d'Emma.

À quoi se résoudre? que faire, puisqu'elle se refusait à tout traitement?

— Sais-tu ce qu'il faudrait à ta femme? reprenait la mère Bovary. Ce seraient des occupations forcées, des ouvrages manuels! Si elle était comme tant d'autres, contrainte à gagner son pain, elle n'aurait pas ces

wouldn't have these vapours, that come to her from a lot of ideas she stuffs into her head, and from the idleness in which she lives."

"Yet she is always busy," said Charles.

"Ah! always busy at what? Reading novels, bad books, works against religion, and in which they mock at priests in speeches taken from Voltaire. But all that leads you far astray, my poor child. Anyone who has no religion always ends by turning out badly."

So it was decided to stop Emma reading novels. The enterprise did not seem easy. The good lady undertook it. She was, when she passed through Rouen, to go herself to the lending-library and represent that Emma had discontinued her subscription. Would they not have a right to apply to the police if the librarian persisted all the same in his poisonous trade?

The farewells of mother and daughter-in-law were cold. During the three weeks that they had been together they had not exchanged half-a-dozen words apart from the inquiries and phrases when they met at table and in the evening before going to bed.

Madame Bovary left on a Wednesday, the market-day at Yonville.

The Place since morning had been blocked by a row of carts, which, on end and their shafts in the air, spread all along the line of houses from the church to the inn. On the other side there were canvas booths, where cotton checks, blankets, and woollen stockings were sold, together with harness for horses, and packets of blue ribbon, whose ends fluttered in the wind. The coarse hardware was spread out on the ground between pyramids of eggs and hampers of cheeses, from which sticky straw stuck out. Near the corn-machines clucking hens passed their necks through the bars of flat cages. The people, crowding in the same place and unwilling to move thence, sometimes threatened to smash the shop front of the chemist. On Wednesdays his shop was never empty, and the people pushed in less to buy drugs than for consultations. So great was Homais' reputation in the neighbouring villages. His robust aplomb had fascinated the rustics. They considered him a greater doctor than

vapeurs-là, qui lui viennent d'un tas d'idées qu'elle se fourre dans la tête, et du désoeuvrement où elle vit.

— Pourtant elle s'occupe, disait Charles.

— Ah! elle s'occupe! À quoi donc? À lire des romans, de mauvais livres, des ouvrages qui sont contre la religion et dans lesquels on se moque des prêtres par des discours tirés de Voltaire. Mais tout cela va loin, mon pauvre enfant, et quelqu'un qui n'a pas de religion finit toujours par tourner mal.

Donc, il fut résolu que l'on empêcherait Emma de lire des romans. L'entreprise ne semblait point facile. La bonne dame s'en chargea: elle devait quand elle passerait par Rouen, aller en personne chez le loueur de livres et lui représenter qu'Emma cessait ses abonnements. N'aurait-on pas le droit d'avertir la police, si le libraire persistait quand même dans son métier d'empoisonneur?

Les adieux de la belle-mère et de la bru furent secs. Pendant les trois semaines qu'elles étaient restées ensemble, elles n'avaient pas échangé quatre paroles, à part les informations et compliments quand elles se rencontraient à table, et le soir avant de se mettre au lit.

Madame Bovary mère partit un mercredi, qui était jour de marché à Yonville.

La Place, dès le matin, était encombrée par une file de charrettes qui, toutes à cul et les brancards en l'air, s'étendaient le long des maisons depuis l'église, jusqu'à l'auberge. De l'autre côté, il y avait des baraques de toile où l'on vendait des cotonnades, des couvertures et des bas de laine, avec des licous pour les chevaux et des paquets de rubans bleus, qui par le bout s'envolaient au vent. De la grosse quincaillerie s'étalait par terre, entre les pyramides d'oeufs et les bannettes de fromages, d'où sortaient des pailles gluantes; près des machines à blé, des poules qui gloussaient dans des cages plates passaient leurs cous par les barreaux. La foule, s'encombrant au même endroit sans en vouloir bouger, menaçait quelquefois de rompre la devanture de la pharmacie. Les mercredis, elle ne désemplissait pas et l'on s'y poussait, moins pour acheter des médicaments que pour prendre des consultations, tant était fameuse la réputation du sieur Homais dans les villages circonvoisins. Son robuste

all the doctors.

Emma was leaning out at the window; she was often there. The window in the provinces replaces the theatre and the promenade, she was amusing herself with watching the crowd of boors when she saw a gentleman in a green velvet coat. He had on yellow gloves, although he wore heavy gaiters; he was coming towards the doctor's house, followed by a peasant walking with a bent head and quite a thoughtful air.

"Can I see the doctor?" he asked Justin, who was talking on the doorsteps with Felicite.

And, taking him for a servant of the house:

"Tell him that Monsieur Rodolphe Boulanger of La Huchette is here."

It was not from territorial vanity that the new arrival added "of La Huchette" to his name, but to make himself the better known. La Huchette, in fact, was an estate near Yonville, where he had just bought the chateau and two farms that he cultivated himself, without, however, troubling very much about them. He lived as a bachelor, and was supposed to have "at least fifteen thousand francs a year."

Charles came into the room. Monsieur Boulanger introduced his man, who wanted to be bled because he felt "a tingling all over."

"That'll purge me," he urged as an objection to all reasoning.

So Bovary ordered a bandage and a basin, and asked Justin to hold it. Then addressing the peasant, who was already pale:

"Don't be afraid, my lad."

"No, no, sir," said the other; "get on."

And with an air of bravado he held out his great arm. At the prick of the lancet the blood spurted out, splashing against the looking-glass.

"Hold the basin nearer," exclaimed Charles.

"Lor!" said the peasant, "one would swear it was a little fountain flowing. How red my blood is! That's a good sign, isn't it?"

"Sometimes," answered the doctor, "one feels nothing at first, and then syncope sets in, and more especially with people of strong constitution like this man."

At these words the rustic let go the lancet-case he was twisting

aplomb avait fasciné les campagnards. Ils le regardaient comme un plus grand médecin que tous les médecins.

Emma était accoudée à sa fenêtre (elle s'y mettait souvent: la fenêtre, en province, remplace les théâtres et la promenade), et elle s'amusait à considérer la cohue des rustres, lorsqu'elle aperçut un monsieur vêtu d'une redingote de velours vert. Il était ganté de gants jaunes, quoiqu'il fût chaussé de fortes guêtres; et il se dirigeait vers la maison du médecin, suivi d'un paysan marchant la tête basse d'un air tout réfléchi.

— Puis-je voir Monsieur? demanda-t-il à Justin, qui causait sur le seuil avec Félicité.

Et, le prenant pour le domestique de la maison:

— Dites-lui que M. Rodolphe Boulanger de la Huchette est là.

Ce n'était point par vanité territoriale que le nouvel arrivant avait ajouté à son nom la particule, mais afin de se faire mieux connaître. La Huchette, en effet, était un domaine près d'Yonville, dont il venait d'acquérir le château, avec deux fermes qu'il cultivait lui-même, sans trop se gêner cependant. Il vivait, en garçon, et passait pour avoir au moins quinze mille livres de rentes!

Charles entra dans la salle. M. Boulanger lui présenta son homme, qui voulait être saigné parce qu'il éprouvait des fourmis le long du corps.

— Ça me purgera, objectait-il à tous les raisonnements.

Bovary commanda donc d'apporter une bande et une cuvette, et pria Justin de la soutenir. Puis, s'adressant au villageois déjà blême:

— N'ayez point peur, mon brave.

— Non, non, répondit l'autre, marchez toujours!

Et, d'un air fanfaron, il tendit son gros bras. Sous la piqûre de la lancette, le sang jaillit et alla s'éclabousser contre la glace.

— Approche le vase! exclama Charles.

— Guête! disait le paysan, on jurerait une petite fontaine qui coule! Comme j'ai le sang rouge! ce doit être bon signe, n'est-ce pas?

— Quelquefois, reprit l'officier de santé, l'on n'éprouve rien au commencement, puis la syncope se déclare, et plus particulièrement chez les gens bien constitués, comme celui-ci.

Le campagnard, à ces mots, lâcha l'étui qu'il tournait entre ses

between his fingers. A shudder of his shoulders made the chair-back creak. His hat fell off.

"I thought as much," said Bovary, pressing his finger on the vein.

The basin was beginning to tremble in Justin's hands; his knees shook, he turned pale.

"Emma! Emma!" called Charles.

With one bound she came down the staircase.

"Some vinegar," he cried. "O dear! two at once!"

And in his emotion he could hardly put on the compress.

"It is nothing," said Monsieur Boulanger quietly, taking Justin in his arms.

He seated him on the table with his back resting against the wall.

Madame Bovary began taking off his cravat. The strings of his shirt had got into a knot, and she was for some minutes moving her light fingers about the young fellow's neck. Then she poured some vinegar on her cambric handkerchief; she moistened his temples with little dabs, and then blew upon them softly.

The ploughman revived, but Justin's syncope still lasted, and his eyeballs disappeared in the pale sclerotics like blue flowers in milk.

"We must hide this from him," said Charles.

Madame Bovary took the basin to put it under the table. With the movement she made in bending down, her dress (it was a summer dress with four flounces, yellow, long in the waist and wide in the skirt) spread out around her on the flags of the room; and as Emma stooping, staggered a little as she stretched out her arms. The stuff here and there gave with the inflections of her bust. Then she went to fetch a bottle of water, and she was melting some pieces of sugar when the chemist arrived. The servant had been to fetch him in the tumult. Seeing his pupil's eyes staring he drew a long breath; then going around him he looked at him from head to foot.

"Fool!" he said, "really a little fool! A fool in four letters! A phlebotomy's a big affair, isn't it! And a fellow who isn't afraid of anything; a kind of squirrel, just as he is who climbs to vertiginous heights to

doigts. Une saccade de ses épaules fit craquer le dossier de la chaise. Son chapeau tomba.

— Je m'en doutais, dit Bovary en appliquant son doigt sur la veine.

La cuvette commençait à trembler aux mains de Justin; ses genoux chancelèrent, il devint pâle.

— Ma femme! ma femme! appela Charles.

D'un bond, elle descendit l'escalier.

— Du vinaigre! cria-t-il. Ah! mon Dieu, deux à la fois!

Et, dans son émotion, il avait peine à poser la compresse.

— Ce n'est rien, disait tout tranquillement M. Boulanger, tandis qu'il prenait Justin entre ses bras.

Et il l'assit sur la table, lui appuyant le dos contre la muraille.

Madame Bovary se mit à lui retirer sa cravate. Il y avait un noeud aux cordons de la chemise; elle resta quelques minutes à remuer ses doigts légers dans le cou du jeune garçon; ensuite elle versa du vinaigre sur son mouchoir de batiste; elle lui en mouillait les tempes à petits coups et elle soufflait dessus, délicatement.

Le charretier se réveilla; mais la syncope de Justin durait encore, et ses prunelles disparaissaient dans leur sclérotique pâle, comme des fleurs bleues dans du lait.

— Il faudrait, dit Charles, lui cacher cela.

Madame Bovary prit la cuvette. Pour la mettre sous la table, dans le mouvement qu'elle fit en s'inclinant, sa robe (c'était une robe d'été à quatre volants, de couleur jaune, longue de taille, large de jupe), sa robe s'évasa autour d'elle sur les carreaux de la salle; — et, comme Emma, baissée; chancelait un peu en écartant les bras, le gonflement de l'étoffe se crevait de place en place, selon les inflexions de son corsage. Ensuite elle alla prendre une carafe d'eau, et elle faisait fondre des morceaux de sucre lorsque le pharmacien arriva. La servante l'avait été chercher dans l'algarade; en apercevant son élève les yeux ouverts, il reprit haleine. Puis, tournant autour de lui, il le regardait de haut en bas.

— Sot! disait-il; petit sot, vraiment! sot en trois lettres! Grand-chose, après tout, qu'une phlébotomie! et un gaillard qui n'a peur de rien! une espèce d'écureuil, tel que vous le voyez, qui monte locher des

shake down nuts. Oh, yes! you just talk to me, boast about yourself! Here's a fine fitness for practising pharmacy later on; for under serious circumstances you may be called before the tribunals in order to enlighten the minds of the magistrates, and you would have to keep your head then, to reason, show yourself a man, or else pass for an imbecile."

Justin did not answer. The chemist went on:

"Who asked you to come? You are always pestering the doctor and madame. On Wednesday, moreover, your presence is indispensable to me. There are now twenty people in the shop. I left everything because of the interest I take in you. Come, get along! Sharp! Wait for me, and keep an eye on the jars."

When Justin, who was rearranging his dress, had gone, they talked for a little while about fainting-fits. Madame Bovary had never fainted.

"That is extraordinary for a lady," said Monsieur Boulanger; "but some people are very susceptible. Thus in a duel, I have seen a second lose consciousness at the mere sound of the loading of pistols."

"For my part," said the chemist, "the sight of other people's blood doesn't affect me at all, but the mere thought of my own flowing would make me faint if I reflected upon it too much."

Monsieur Boulanger, however, dismissed his servant, advising him to calm himself, since his fancy was over.

"It procured me the advantage of making your acquaintance," he added.

And he looked at Emma as he said this.

Then he put three francs on the corner of the table, bowed negligently, and went out.

He was soon on the other side of the river (this was his way back to La Huchette), and Emma saw him in the meadow, walking under the poplars, slackening his pace now and then as one who reflects.

"She is very pretty," he said to himself; "she is very pretty, this doctor's wife. Fine teeth, black eyes, a dainty foot, a figure like a Parisienne's. Where the devil does she come from? Wherever did that fat fellow pick her up?"

noix à des hauteurs vertigineuses. Ah! oui, parle, vante-toi! voilà de belles dispositions à exercer plus tard la pharmacie; car tu peux te trouver appelé en des circonstances graves, par-devant les tribunaux, afin d'y éclairer la conscience des magistrats; et il faudra pourtant garder son sang-froid, raisonner, se montrer homme, ou bien passer pour un imbécile!

Justin ne répondait pas. L'apothicaire continuait:

— Qui t'a prié de venir? Tu importunes toujours monsieur et madame! Les mercredis, d'ailleurs, ta présence m'est plus indispensable. Il y a maintenant vingt personnes à la maison. J'ai tout quitté à cause de l'intérêt que je te porte. Allons, va-t'en! cours! attends-moi, et surveille les bocaux!

Quand Justin, qui se rhabillait, fut parti, l'on causa quelque peu des évanouissements. Madame Bovary n'en avait jamais eu.

— C'est extraordinaire pour une dame! dit M. Boulanger. Du reste, il y a des gens bien délicats. Ainsi j'ai vu, dans une rencontre, un témoin perdre connaissance rien qu'au bruit des pistolets que l'on chargeait.

— Moi, dit l'apothicaire, la vue du sang des autres ne me fait rien du tout; mais l'idée seulement du mien qui coule suffirait à me causer des défaillances, si j'y réfléchissais trop.

Cependant M. Boulanger congédia son domestique, en l'engageant à se tranquilliser l'esprit, puisque sa fantaisie était passée.

— Elle m'a procuré l'avantage de votre connaissance, ajouta-t-il.

Et il regardait Emma durant cette phrase.

Puis il déposa trois francs sur le coin de la table, salua négligemment et s'en alla.

Il fut bientôt de l'autre côté de la rivière (c'était son chemin pour s'en retourner à la Huchette); et Emma l'aperçut dans la prairie, qui marchait sous les peupliers, se ralentissant de temps à autre, comme quelqu'un qui réfléchit.

— Elle est fort gentille! se disait-il; elle est fort gentille, cette femme du médecin! De belles dents, les yeux noirs, le pied coquet, et de la tournure comme une Parisienne. D'où diable sort- elle? Où donc l'a-t-il trouvée, ce gros garçon-là?

Monsieur Rodolphe Boulanger was thirty-four; he was of brutal temperament and intelligent perspicacity, having, moreover, had much to do with women, and knowing them well. This one had seemed pretty to him; so he was thinking about her and her husband.

"I think he is very stupid. She is tired of him, no doubt. He has dirty nails, and hasn't shaved for three days. While he is trotting after his patients, she sits there botching socks. And she gets bored! She would like to live in town and dance polkas every evening. Poor little woman! She is gaping after love like a carp after water on a kitchen-table. With three words of gallantry she'd adore one, I'm sure of it. She'd be tender, charming. Yes; but how to get rid of her afterwards?"

Then the difficulties of love-making seen in the distance made him by contrast think of his mistress. She was an actress at Rouen, whom he kept; and when he had pondered over this image, with which, even in remembrance, he was satiated:

"Ah! Madame Bovary," he thought, "is much prettier, especially fresher. Virginie is decidedly beginning to grow fat. She is so finiky about her pleasures; and, besides, she has a mania for prawns."

The fields were empty, and around him Rodolphe only heard the regular beating of the grass striking against his boots, with a cry of the grasshopper hidden at a distance among the oats. He again saw Emma in her room, dressed as he had seen her, and he undressed her.

"Oh, I will have her," he cried, striking a blow with his stick at a clod in front of him.

And he at once began to consider the political part of the enterprise. He asked himself:

"Where shall we meet? By what means? We shall always be having the brat on our hands, and the servant, the neighbours, and husband, all sorts of worries. Pshaw! one would lose too much time over it."

Then he resumed:

"She really has eyes that pierce one's heart like a gimlet. And that pale complexion! I adore pale women!"

When he reached the top of the Arguiel hills he had made up his mind.

M. Rodolphe Boulanger avait trente-quatre ans; il était de tempérament brutal et d'intelligence perspicace, ayant d'ailleurs beaucoup fréquenté les femmes, et s'y connaissant bien. Celle-là lui avait paru jolie; il y rêvait donc, et à son mari.

— Je le crois très bête. Elle en est fatiguée sans doute. Il porte des ongles sales et une barbe de trois jours. Tandis qu'il trottine à ses malades, elle reste à ravauder des chaussettes. Et on s'ennuie! on voudrait habiter la ville, danser la polka tous les soirs! Pauvre petite femme! Ça bâille après l'amour, comme une carpe après l'eau sur une table de cuisine. Avec trois mots de galanterie, cela vous adorerait; j'en suis sûr! ce serait tendre! charmant!... Oui, mais comment s'en débarrasser ensuite?

Alors les encombrements du plaisir, entrevus en perspective, le firent, par contraste, songer à sa maîtresse. C'était une comédienne de Rouen, qu'il entretenait; et, quand il se fut arrêté sur cette image, dont il avait, en souvenir même, des rassasiements:

— Ah! madame Bovary, pensa-t-il, est bien plus jolie qu'elle, plus fraîche surtout. Virginie, décidément, commence à devenir trop grosse. Elle est si fastidieuse avec ses joies. Et, d'ailleurs, quelle manie de salicoques!

La campagne était déserte, et Rodolphe n'entendait autour de lui que le battement régulier des herbes qui fouettaient sa chaussure, avec le cri des grillons tapis au loin sous les avoines; il revoyait Emma dans la salle, habillée comme il l'avait vue, et il la déshabillait.

— Oh! je l'aurai! s'écria-t-il en écrasant, d'un coup de bâton, une motte de terre devant lui.

Et aussitôt il examina la partie politique de l'entreprise. Il se demandait:

— Où se rencontrer? par quel moyen? On aura continuellement le marmot sur les épaules, et la bonne, les voisins, le mari, toute sorte de tracasseries considérables. Ah bah! dit-il, on y perd trop de temps!

Puis il recommença:

— C'est qu'elle a des yeux qui vous entrent au coeur comme des vrilles. Et ce teint pâle!... Moi, qui adore les femmes pâles!

Au haut de la côte d'Argueil, sa résolution était prise.

"It's only finding the opportunities. Well, I will call in now and then. I'll send them venison, poultry; I'll have myself bled, if need be. We shall become friends; I'll invite them to my place. By Jove!" added he, "there's the agricultural show coming on. She'll be there. I shall see her. We'll begin boldly, for that's the surest way."

— Il n'y a plus qu'à chercher les occasions. Eh bien, j'y passerai quelquefois, je leur enverrai du gibier, de la volaille; je me ferai saigner, s'il le faut; nous deviendrons amis, je les inviterai chez moi… Ah! parbleu! ajouta-t-il, voilà les comices bientôt; elle y sera, je la verrai. Nous commencerons, et hardiment, car c'est le plus sûr.

# Chapter 8

At last it came, the famous agricultural show. On the morning of the solemnity all the inhabitants at their doors were chatting over the preparations. The pediment of the town hall had been hung with garlands of ivy; a tent had been erected in a meadow for the banquet; and in the middle of the Place, in front of the church, a kind of bombarde was to announce the arrival of the prefect and the names of the successful farmers who had obtained prizes. The National Guard of Buchy (there was none at Yonville) had come to join the corps of firemen, of whom Binet was captain. On that day he wore a collar even higher than usual; and, tightly buttoned in his tunic, his figure was so stiff and motionless that the whole vital portion of his person seemed to have descended into his legs, which rose in a cadence of set steps with a single movement. As there was some rivalry between the tax-collector and the colonel, both, to show off their talents, drilled their men separately. One saw the red epaulettes and the black breastplates pass and re-pass alternately; there was no end to it, and it constantly began again. There had never been such a display of pomp. Several citizens had scoured their houses the evening before; tri-coloured flags hung from half-open windows; all the public-houses were full; and in the lovely weather the starched caps, the golden crosses, and the coloured neckerchiefs seemed whiter than snow, shone in the sun, and relieved with the motley colours the sombre monotony of the frock-coats and blue smocks. The neighbouring farmers' wives, when they got off their horses, pulled out the long pins that fastened around them their dresses, turned up for fear of mud; and the husbands, for their part, in order to save their hats, kept their handkerchiefs around them, holding one corner between their teeth.

The crowd came into the main street from both ends of the village. People poured in from the lanes, the alleys, the houses; and from time to time one heard knockers banging against doors closing behind women

# Chapitre 8

Ils arrivèrent, en effet, ces fameux Comices! Dès le matin de la solennité, tous les habitants, sur leurs portes, s'entretenaient des préparatifs; on avait enguirlandé de lierres le fronton de la mairie; une tente dans un pré était dressée pour le festin, et, au milieu de la Place, devant l'église, une espèce de bombarde devait signaler l'arrivée de M. le préfet et le nom des cultivateurs lauréats. La garde nationale de Buchy (il n'y en avait point à Yonville) était venue s'adjoindre au corps des pompiers, dont Binet était le capitaine. Il portait ce jour-là un col encore plus haut que de coutume; et, sanglé dans sa tunique, il avait le buste si roide et immobile, que toute la partie vitale de sa personne semblait être descendue dans ses deux jambes, qui se levaient en cadence, à pas marqués, d'un seul mouvement. Comme une rivalité subsistait entre le percepteur et le colonel, l'un et l'autre, pour montrer leurs talents, faisaient à part manoeuvrer leurs hommes. On voyait alternativement passer et repasser les épaulettes rouges et les plastrons noirs. Cela ne finissait pas et toujours recommençait! Jamais il n'y avait eu pareil déploiement de pompe! Plusieurs bourgeois, dès la veille, avaient lavé leurs maisons; des drapeaux tricolores pendaient aux fenêtres entrouvertes; tous les cabarets étaient pleins; et, par le beau temps qu'il faisait, les bonnets empesés, les croix d'or et les fichus de couleur paraissaient plus blancs que neige, miroitaient au soleil clair, et relevaient de leur bigarrure éparpillée la sombre monotonie des redingotes et des bourgerons bleus. Les fermières des environs retiraient, en descendant de cheval, la grosse épingle qui leur serrait autour du corps leur robe retroussée de peur des taches; et les maris, au contraire, afin de ménager leurs chapeaux, gardaient par-dessus des mouchoirs de poche, dont ils tenaient un angle entre les dents.

La foule arrivait dans la grande rue par les deux bouts du village. Il s'en dégorgeait des ruelles, des allées, des maisons, et l'on entendait de temps à autre retomber le marteau des portes, derrière les bourgeoises

with their gloves, who were going out to see the fete. What was most admired were two long lamp-stands covered with lanterns, that flanked a platform on which the authorities were to sit. Besides this there were against the four columns of the town hall four kinds of poles, each bearing a small standard of greenish cloth, embellished with inscriptions in gold letters. On one was written, "To Commerce"; on the other, "To Agriculture"; on the third, "To Industry"; and on the fourth, "To the Fine Arts."

But the jubilation that brightened all faces seemed to darken that of Madame Lefrancois, the innkeeper. Standing on her kitchen-steps she muttered to herself:

"What rubbish! what rubbish! With their canvas booth! Do they think the prefect will be glad to dine down there under a tent like a gipsy? They call all this fussing doing good to the place! Then it wasn't worth while sending to Neufchatel for the keeper of a cookshop! And for whom? For cowherds! tatterdemalions!"

The druggist was passing. He had on a frock-coat, nankeen trousers, beaver shoes, and, for a wonder, a hat with a low crown.

"Your servant! Excuse me, I am in a hurry."

And as the fat widow asked where he was going:

"It seems odd to you, doesn't it, I who am always more cooped up in my laboratory than the man's rat in his cheese."

"What cheese?" asked the landlady.

"Oh, nothing! nothing!" Homais continued. "I merely wished to convey to you, Madame Lefrancois, that I usually live at home like a recluse. To-day, however, considering the circumstances, it is necessary—"

"Oh, you're going down there!" she said contemptuously.

"Yes, I am going," replied the druggist, astonished. "Am I not a member of the consulting commission?"

Mere Lefrancois looked at him for a few moments, and ended by saying with a smile—

"That's another pair of shoes! But what does agriculture matter to you? Do you understand anything about it?"

en gants de fil, qui sortaient pour aller voir la fête. Ce que l'on admirait surtout, c'étaient deux longs ifs couverts de lampions qui flanquaient une estrade où s'allaient tenir les autorités; et il y avait de plus, contre les quatre colonnes de la mairie, quatre manières de gaules, portant chacune un petit étendard de toile verdâtre, enrichi d'inscriptions en lettres d'or. On lisait sur l'un: «Au Commerce»; sur l'autre: «À l'Agriculture»; sur le troisième: «À l'Industrie»; et sur le quatrième: «Aux Beaux-Arts».

Mais la jubilation qui épanouissait tous les visages paraissait assombrir madame Lefrançois, l'aubergiste. Debout sur les marches de sa cuisine, elle murmurait dans son menton:

— Quelle bêtise! quelle bêtise avec leur baraque de toile! Croient-ils que le préfet sera bien aise de dîner là-bas, sous une tente, comme un saltimbanque? Ils appellent ces embarras-là, faire le bien du pays! Ce n'était pas la peine, alors, d'aller chercher un gargotier à Neufchâtel! Et pour qui? pour des vachers! des va- nu-pieds!...

L'apothicaire passa. Il portait un habit noir, un pantalon de nankin, des souliers de castor, et par extraordinaire un chapeau, — un chapeau bas de forme.

— Serviteur! dit-il; excusez-moi, je suis pressé.

Et comme la grosse veuve lui demanda où il allait:

— Cela vous semble drôle, n'est-ce pas? moi qui reste toujours plus confiné dans mon laboratoire que le rat du bonhomme dans son fromage.

— Quel fromage? fit l'aubergiste.

— Non, rien! ce n'est rien! reprit Homais. Je voulais vous exprimer seulement, madame Lefrançois, que je demeure d'habitude tout reclus chez moi. Aujourd'hui cependant, vu la circonstance, il faut bien que...

— Ah! vous allez là-bas? dit-elle avec un air de dédain.

— Oui, j'y vais, répliqua l'apothicaire étonné; ne fais-je point partie de la commission consultative?

La mère Lefrançois le considéra quelques minutes, et finit par répondre en souriant:

— C'est autre chose! Mais qu'est-ce que la culture vous regarde? vous vous y entendez donc?

"Certainly I understand it, since I am a druggist—that is to say, a chemist. And the object of chemistry, Madame Lefrancois, being the knowledge of the reciprocal and molecular action of all natural bodies, it follows that agriculture is comprised within its domain. And, in fact, the composition of the manure, the fermentation of liquids, the analyses of gases, and the influence of miasmata, what, I ask you, is all this, if it isn't chemistry, pure and simple?"

The landlady did not answer. Homais went on:

"Do you think that to be an agriculturist it is necessary to have tilled the earth or fattened fowls oneself? It is necessary rather to know the composition of the substances in question—the geological strata, the atmospheric actions, the quality of the soil, the minerals, the waters, the density of the different bodies, their capillarity, and what not. And one must be master of all the principles of hygiene in order to direct, criticize the construction of buildings, the feeding of animals, the diet of domestics. And, moreover, Madame Lefrancois, one must know botany, be able to distinguish between plants, you understand, which are the wholesome and those that are deleterious, which are unproductive and which nutritive, if it is well to pull them up here and re-sow them there, to propagate some, destroy others; in brief, one must keep pace with science by means of pamphlets and public papers, be always on the alert to find out improvements."

The landlady never took her eyes off the "Cafe Francois" and the chemist went on:

"Would to God our agriculturists were chemists, or that at least they would pay more attention to the counsels of science. Thus lately I myself wrote a considerable tract, a memoir of over seventy-two pages, entitled, 'Cider, its Manufacture and its Effects, together with some New Reflections on the Subject,' that I sent to the Agricultural Society of Rouen, and which even procured me the honour of being received among its members—Section, Agriculture; Class, Pomological. Well, if my work had been given to the public—"

But the druggist stopped, Madame Lefrancois seemed so preoccupied.

— Certainement, je m'y entends, puisque je suis pharmacien, c'est-à-dire chimiste! et la chimie, madame Lefrançois, ayant pour objet la connaissance de l'action réciproque et moléculaire de tous les corps de la nature, il s'ensuit que l'agriculture se trouve comprise dans son domaine! Et, en effet, composition des engrais, fermentation des liquides, analyse des gaz et influence des miasmes, qu'est-ce que tout cela, je vous le demande, si ce n'est de la chimie pure et simple?

L'aubergiste ne répondit rien. Homais continua:

— Croyez-vous qu'il faille, pour être agronome, avoir soi-même labouré la terre ou engraissé des volailles? Mais il faut connaître plutôt la constitution des substances dont il s'agit, les gisements géologiques, les actions atmosphériques, la qualité des terrains, des minéraux, des eaux, la densité des différents corps et leur capillarité! que sais-je? Et il faut posséder à fond tous ses principes d'hygiène, pour diriger, critiquer la construction des bâtiments, le régime des animaux, l'alimentation des domestiques! il faut encore, madame Lefrançois, posséder la botanique; pouvoir discerner les plantes, entendez-vous, quelles sont les salutaires d'avec les délétères, quelles les improductives et quelles les nutritives, s'il est bon de les arracher par-ci et de les ressemer par-là, de propager les unes, de détruire les autres; bref, il faut se tenir au courant de la science par les brochures et papiers publics, être toujours en haleine, afin d'indiquer les améliorations…

L'aubergiste ne quittait point des yeux la porte du café Français, et le pharmacien poursuivit:

— Plût à Dieu que nos agriculteurs fussent des chimistes, ou que du moins ils écoutassent davantage les conseils de la science! Ainsi, moi, j'ai dernièrement écrit un fort opuscule, un mémoire de plus de soixante et douze pages, intitulé: Du cidre, de sa fabrication et de ses effets; suivi de quelques réflexions nouvelles à ce sujet, que j'ai envoyé à la Société agronomique de Rouen; ce qui m'a même valu l'honneur d'être reçu parmi ses membres, section d'agriculture, classe de pomologie; eh bien, si mon ouvrage avait été livré à la publicité…

Mais l'apothicaire s'arrêta, tant madame Lefrançois paraissait préoccupée.

"Just look at them!" she said. "It's past comprehension! Such a cook-shop as that!"

And with a shrug of the shoulders that stretched out over her breast the stitches of her knitted bodice, she pointed with both hands at her rival's inn, whence songs were heard issuing.

"Well, it won't last long," she added. "It'll be over before a week."

Homais drew back with stupefaction. She came down three steps and whispered in his ear:

"What! you didn't know it? There is to be an execution in next week. It's Lheureux who is selling him out; he has killed him with bills."

"What a terrible catastrophe!" cried the druggist, who always found expressions in harmony with all imaginable circumstances.

Then the landlady began telling him the story that she had heard from Theodore, Monsieur Guillaumin's servant, and although she detested Tellier, she blamed Lheureux. He was "a wheedler, a sneak."

"There!" she said. "Look at him! he is in the market; he is bowing to Madame Bovary, who's got on a green bonnet. Why, she's taking Monsieur Boulanger's arm."

"Madame Bovary!" exclaimed Homais. "I must go at once and pay her my respects. Perhaps she'll be very glad to have a seat in the enclosure under the peristyle."

And, without heeding Madame Lefrancois, who was calling him back to tell him more about it, the druggist walked off rapidly with a smile on his lips, with straight knees, bowing copiously to right and left, and taking up much room with the large tails of his frock-coat that fluttered behind him in the wind.

Rodolphe, having caught sight of him from afar, hurried on, but Madame Bovary lost her breath; so he walked more slowly, and, smiling at her, said in a rough tone:

"It's only to get away from that fat fellow, you know, the druggist."

She pressed his elbow.

"What's the meaning of that?" he asked himself.

And he looked at her out of the corner of his eyes.

— Voyez-les donc! disait-elle, on n'y comprend rien! une gargote semblable!

Et, avec des haussements d'épaules qui tiraient sur sa poitrine les mailles de son tricot, elle montrait des deux mains le cabaret de son rival, d'où sortaient alors des chansons.

— Du reste, il n'en a pas pour longtemps, ajouta-t-elle; avant huit jours, tout est fini.

Homais se recula de stupéfaction. Elle descendit ses trois marches, et, lui parlant à l'oreille:

— Comment! vous ne savez pas cela? On va le saisir cette semaine. C'est Lheureux qui le fait vendre. Il l'a assassiné de billets.

— Quelle épouvantable catastrophe! s'écria l'apothicaire, qui avait toujours des expressions congruentes à toutes les circonstances imaginables.

L'hôtesse donc se mit à lui raconter cette histoire, qu'elle savait par Théodore, le domestique de M. Guillaumin, et, bien qu'elle exécrât Tellier, elle blâmait Lheureux. C'était un enjôleur, un rampant…

— Ah! tenez, dit-elle, le voilà sous les halles; il salue madame Bovary, qui a un chapeau vert. Elle est même au bras de M. Boulanger.

— Madame Bovary! fit Homais. Je m'empresse d'aller lui offrir mes hommages. Peut-être qu'elle sera bien aise d'avoir une place dans l'enceinte, sous le péristyle.

Et, sans écouter la mère Lefrançois, qui le rappelait pour lui en conter plus long, le pharmacien s'éloigna d'un pas rapide, sourire aux lèvres et jarret tendu, distribuant de droite et de gauche quantité de salutations et emplissant beaucoup d'espace avec les grandes basques de son habit noir, qui flottaient au vent derrière lui.

Rodolphe, l'ayant aperçu de loin, avait pris un train rapide; mais madame Bovary s'essouffla; il se ralentit donc et lui dit en souriant, d'un ton brutal:

— C'est pour éviter ce gros homme: vous savez, l'apothicaire.

Elle lui donna un coup de coude.

— Qu'est-ce que cela signifie? se demanda-t-il.

Et il la considéra du coin de l'oeil, tout en continuant à marcher.

Her profile was so calm that one could guess nothing from it. It stood out in the light from the oval of her bonnet, with pale ribbons on it like the leaves of weeds. Her eyes with their long curved lashes looked straight before her, and though wide open, they seemed slightly puckered by the cheek-bones, because of the blood pulsing gently under the delicate skin. A pink line ran along the partition between her nostrils. Her head was bent upon her shoulder, and the pearl tips of her white teeth were seen between her lips.

"Is she making fun of me?" thought Rodolphe.

Emma's gesture, however, had only been meant for a warning; for Monsieur Lheureux was accompanying them, and spoke now and again as if to enter into the conversation.

"What a superb day! Everybody is out! The wind is east!"

And neither Madame Bovary nor Rodolphe answered him, whilst at the slightest movement made by them he drew near, saying, "I beg your pardon!" and raised his hat.

When they reached the farrier's house, instead of following the road up to the fence, Rodolphe suddenly turned down a path, drawing with him Madame Bovary. He called out:

"Good evening, Monsieur Lheureux! See you again presently."

"How you got rid of him!" she said, laughing.

"Why," he went on, "allow oneself to be intruded upon by others? And as to-day I have the happiness of being with you—"

Emma blushed. He did not finish his sentence. Then he talked of the fine weather and of the pleasure of walking on the grass. A few daisies had sprung up again.

"Here are some pretty Easter daisies," he said, "and enough of them to furnish oracles to all the amorous maids in the place."

He added:

"Shall I pick some? What do you think?"

"Are you in love?" she asked, coughing a little.

"H'm, h'm! who knows?" answered Rodolphe.

The meadow began to fill, and the housewives hustled you with their

Son profil était si calme, que l'on n'y devinait rien. Il se détachait en pleine lumière, dans l'ovale de sa capote qui avait des rubans pâles ressemblant à des feuilles de roseau. Ses yeux aux longs cils courbes regardaient devant elle, et, quoique bien ouverts, ils semblaient un peu bridés par les pommettes, à cause du sang, qui battait doucement sous sa peau fine. Une couleur rose traversait la cloison de son nez. Elle inclinait la tête sur l'épaule, et l'on voyait entre ses lèvres le bout nacré de ses dents blanches.

— Se moque-t-elle de moi? songeait Rodolphe.

Ce geste d'Emma pourtant n'avait été qu'un avertissement; car M. Lheureux les accompagnait, et il leur parlait de temps à autre, comme pour entrer en conversation:

— Voici une journée superbe! tout le monde est dehors! les vents sont à l'est.

Et madame Bovary, non plus que Rodolphe, ne lui répondait guère, tandis qu'au moindre mouvement qu'ils faisaient, il se rapprochait en disant: «Plaît-il?» et portait la main à son chapeau.

Quand ils furent devant la maison du maréchal, au lieu de suivre la route jusqu'à la barrière, Rodolphe, brusquement, prit un sentier, entraînant madame Bovary; il cria:

— Bonsoir, M. Lheureux! au plaisir!

— Comme vous l'avez congédié! dit-elle en riant.

— Pourquoi, reprit-il, se laisser envahir par les autres? et, puisque, aujourd'hui, j'ai le bonheur d'être avec vous…

Emma rougit. Il n'acheva point sa phrase. Alors il parla du beau temps et du plaisir de marcher sur l'herbe. Quelques marguerites étaient repoussées.

— Voici de gentilles pâquerettes, dit-il, et de quoi fournir bien des oracles à toutes les amoureuses du pays.

Il ajouta:

— Si j'en cueillais. Qu'en pensez-vous?

— Est-ce que vous êtes amoureux? fit-elle en toussant un peu.

— Eh! eh! qui sait? répondit Rodolphe.

Le pré commençait à se remplir, et les ménagères vous heurtaient avec

great umbrellas, their baskets, and their babies. One had often to get out of the way of a long file of country folk, servant-maids with blue stockings, flat shoes, silver rings, and who smelt of milk, when one passed close to them. They walked along holding one another by the hand, and thus they spread over the whole field from the row of open trees to the banquet tent. But this was the examination time, and the farmers one after the other entered a kind of enclosure formed by a long cord supported on sticks.

The beasts were there, their noses towards the cord, and making a confused line with their unequal rumps. Drowsy pigs were burrowing in the earth with their snouts, calves were bleating, lambs baaing; the cows, on knees folded in, were stretching their bellies on the grass, slowly chewing the cud, and blinking their heavy eyelids at the gnats that buzzed round them. Plough-men with bare arms were holding by the halter prancing stallions that neighed with dilated nostrils looking towards the mares. These stood quietly, stretching out their heads and flowing manes, while their foals rested in their shadow, or now and then came and sucked them. And above the long undulation of these crowded animals one saw some white mane rising in the wind like a wave, or some sharp horns sticking out, and the heads of men running about. Apart, outside the enclosure, a hundred paces off, was a large black bull, muzzled, with an iron ring in its nostrils, and who moved no more than if he had been in bronze. A child in rags was holding him by a rope.

Between the two lines the committee-men were walking with heavy steps, examining each animal, then consulting one another in a low voice. One who seemed of more importance now and then took notes in a book as he walked along. This was the president of the jury, Monsieur Derozerays de la Panville. As soon as he recognised Rodolphe he came forward quickly, and smiling amiably, said:

"What! Monsieur Boulanger, you are deserting us?"

Rodolphe protested that he was just coming. But when the president had disappeared:

"Ma foi!" said he, "I shall not go. Your company is better than his."

leurs grands parapluies, leurs paniers et leurs bambins. Souvent il fallait se déranger devant une longue file de campagnardes, servantes en bas-bleus, à souliers plats, à bagues d'argent, et qui sentaient le lait, quand on passait près d'elles. Elles marchaient en se tenant par la main, et se répandaient ainsi sur toute la longueur de la prairie, depuis la ligne des trembles jusqu'à la tente du banquet. Mais c'était le moment de l'examen, et les cultivateurs, les uns après les autres, entraient dans une manière d'hippodrome que formait une longue corde portée sur des bâtons.

Les bêtes étaient là, le nez tourné vers la ficelle, et alignant confusément leurs croupes inégales. Des porcs assoupis enfonçaient en terre leur groin; des veaux beuglaient; des brebis bêlaient; les vaches, un jarret replié, étalaient leur ventre sur le gazon, et, ruminant lentement, clignaient leurs paupières lourdes, sous les moucherons qui bourdonnaient autour d'elles. Des charretiers, les bras nus, retenaient par le licou des étalons cabrés, qui hennissaient à pleins naseaux du côté des juments. Elles restaient paisibles, allongeant la tête et la crinière pendante, tandis que leurs poulains se reposaient à leur ombre, ou venaient les téter quelquefois; et, sur la longue ondulation de tous ces corps tassés, on voyait se lever au vent, comme un flot, quelque crinière blanche, ou bien saillir des cornes aiguës, et des têtes d'hommes qui couraient. À l'écart, en dehors des lices, cent pas plus loin, il y avait un grand taureau noir muselé, portant un cercle de fer à la narine, et qui ne bougeait pas plus qu'une bête de bronze. Un enfant en haillons le tenait par une corde.

Cependant, entre les deux rangées, des messieurs s'avançaient d'un pas lourd, examinant chaque animal, puis se consultaient à voix basse. L'un d'eux, qui semblait plus considérable, prenait, tout en marchant, quelques notes sur un album. C'était le président du jury: M. Derozerays de la Panville. Sitôt qu'il reconnut Rodolphe, il s'avança vivement, et lui dit en souriant d'un air aimable:

— Comment, monsieur Boulanger, vous nous abandonnez?

Rodolphe protesta qu'il allait venir, mais quand le président eut disparu:

— Ma foi, non, reprit-il, je n'irai pas; votre compagnie vaut bien la sienne.

And while poking fun at the show, Rodolphe, to move about more easily, showed the gendarme his blue card, and even stopped now and then in front of some fine beast, which Madame Bovary did not at all admire. He noticed this, and began jeering at the Yonville ladies and their dresses; then he apologised for the negligence of his own. He had that incongruity of common and elegant in which the habitually vulgar think they see the revelation of an eccentric existence, of the perturbations of sentiment, the tyrannies of art, and always a certain contempt for social conventions, that seduces or exasperates them. Thus his cambric shirt with plaited cuffs was blown out by the wind in the opening of his waistcoat of grey ticking, and his broad-striped trousers disclosed at the ankle nankeen boots with patent leather gaiters. These were so polished that they reflected the grass. He trampled on horses's dung with them, one hand in the pocket of his jacket and his straw hat on one side.

"Besides," added he, "when one lives in the country—"

"It's waste of time," said Emma.

"That is true," replied Rodolphe. "To think that not one of these people is capable of understanding even the cut of a coat!"

Then they talked about provincial mediocrity, of the lives it crushed, the illusions lost there.

"And I too," said Rodolphe, "am drifting into depression."

"You!" she said in astonishment; "I thought you very light-hearted."

"Ah! yes. I seem so, because in the midst of the world I know how to wear the mask of a scoffer upon my face; and yet, how many a time at the sight of a cemetery by moonlight have I not asked myself whether it were not better to join those sleeping there!"

"Oh! and your friends?" she said. "You do not think of them."

"My friends! What friends? Have I any? Who cares for me?"

And he accompanied the last words with a kind of whistling of the lips.

But they were obliged to separate from each other because of a great pile of chairs that a man was carrying behind them. He was so overladen with them that one could only see the tips of his wooden shoes and the

Et, tout en se moquant des comices, Rodolphe, pour circuler plus à l'aise, montrait au gendarme sa pancarte bleue, et même il s'arrêtait parfois devant quelque beau sujet, que madame Bovary n'admirait guère. Il s'en aperçut, et alors se mit à faire des plaisanteries sur les dames d'Yonville, à propos de leur toilette; puis il s'excusa lui-même du négligé de la sienne. Elle avait cette incohérence de choses communes et recherchées, où le vulgaire, d'habitude, croit entrevoir la révélation d'une existence excentrique, les désordres du sentiment, les tyrannies de l'art, et toujours un certain mépris des conventions sociales, ce qui le séduit ou l'exaspère. Ainsi sa chemise de batiste à manchettes plissées bouffait au hasard du vent, dans l'ouverture de son gilet, qui était de coutil gris, et son pantalon à larges raies découvrait aux chevilles ses bottines de nankin, claquées de cuir verni. Elles étaient si vernies, que l'herbe s'y reflétait. Il foulait avec elles les crottins de cheval, une main dans la poche de sa veste et son chapeau de paille mis de côté.

— D'ailleurs, ajouta-t-il, quand on habite la campagne...

— Tout est peine perdue, dit Emma.

— C'est vrai! répliqua Rodolphe. Songer que pas un seul de ces braves gens n'est capable de comprendre même la tournure d'un habit!

Alors ils parlèrent de la médiocrité provinciale, des existences qu'elle étouffait, des illusions qui s'y perdaient.

— Aussi, disait Rodolphe, je m'enfonce dans une tristesse...

— Vous! fit-elle avec étonnement. Mais je vous croyais très gai?

— Ah! oui, d'apparence, parce qu'au milieu du monde je sais mettre sur mon visage un masque railleur; et cependant que de fois, à la vue d'un cimetière, au clair de lune, je me suis demandé si je ne ferais pas mieux d'aller rejoindre ceux qui sont à dormir...

— Oh! Et vos amis? dit-elle. Vous n'y pensez pas.

— Mes amis? lesquels donc? en ai-je? Qui s'inquiète de moi?

Et il accompagna ces derniers mots d'une sorte de sifflement entre ses lèvres.

Mais ils furent obligés de s'écarter l'un de l'autre, à cause d'un grand échafaudage de chaises qu'un homme portait derrière eux. Il en était si surchargé, que l'on apercevait seulement la pointe de ses sabots, avec le

ends of his two outstretched arms. It was Lestiboudois, the gravedigger, who was carrying the church chairs about amongst the people. Alive to all that concerned his interests, he had hit upon this means of turning the show to account; and his idea was succeeding, for he no longer knew which way to turn. In fact, the villagers, who were hot, quarreled for these seats, whose straw smelt of incense, and they leant against the thick backs, stained with the wax of candles, with a certain veneration.

Madame Bovary again took Rodolphe's arm; he went on as if speaking to himself:

"Yes, I have missed so many things. Always alone! Ah! if I had some aim in life, if I had met some love, if I had found someone! Oh, how I would have spent all the energy of which I am capable, surmounted everything, overcome everything!"

"Yet it seems to me," said Emma, "that you are not to be pitied."

"Ah! you think so?" said Rodolphe.

"For, after all," she went on, "you are free—"

She hesitated:

"Rich—"

"Do not mock me," he replied.

And she protested that she was not mocking him, when the report of a cannon resounded. Immediately all began hustling one another pell-mell towards the village.

It was a false alarm. The prefect seemed not to be coming, and the members of the jury felt much embarrassed, not knowing if they ought to begin the meeting or still wait.

At last at the end of the Place a large hired landau appeared, drawn by two thin horses, which a coachman in a white hat was whipping lustily. Binet had only just time to shout, "Present arms!" and the colonel to imitate him. All ran towards the enclosure; everyone pushed forward. A few even forgot their collars; but the equipage of the prefect seemed to anticipate the crowd, and the two yoked jades, trapesing in their harness, came up at a little trot in front of the peristyle of the town hall at the very moment when the National Guard and firemen deployed, beating drums and marking time.

bout de ses deux bras, écartés droit. C'était Lestiboudois, le fossoyeur, qui charriait dans la multitude les chaises de l'église. Plein d'imagination pour tout ce qui concernait ses intérêts, il avait découvert ce moyen de tirer parti des comices; et son idée lui réussissait, car il ne savait plus auquel, entendre. En effet, les villageois, qui avaient chaud, se disputaient ces sièges dont la paille sentait l'encens, et s'appuyaient contre leurs gros dossiers salis par la cire des cierges, avec une certaine vénération.

Madame Bovary reprit le bras de Rodolphe; il continua comme se parlant à lui-même:

— Oui! tant de choses m'ont manqué! toujours seul! Ah! si j'avais eu un but dans la vie, si j'eusse rencontré une affection, si j'avais trouvé quelqu'un... Oh! comme j'aurais dépensé toute l'énergie dont je suis capable, j'aurais surmonté tout, brisé tout!

— Il me semble pourtant, dit Emma, que vous n'êtes guère à plaindre.

— Ah! vous trouvez? fit Rodolphe.

— Car enfin..., reprit-elle, vous êtes libre.

Elle hésita:

— Riche.

— Ne vous moquez pas de moi, répondit-il.

Et elle jurait qu'elle ne se moquait pas, quand un coup de canon retentit; aussitôt, on se poussa, pêle-mêle, vers le village.

C'était une fausse alerte. M. le préfet n'arrivait pas; et les membres du jury se trouvaient fort embarrassés, ne sachant s'il fallait commencer la séance ou bien attendre encore.

Enfin, au fond de la Place, parut un grand landau de louage, traîné par deux chevaux maigres, que fouettait à tour de bras un cocher en chapeau blanc. Binet n'eut que le temps de crier: «Aux armes!» et le colonel de l'imiter. On courut vers les faisceaux. On se précipita. Quelques-uns même oublièrent leur col. Mais l'équipage préfectoral sembla deviner cet embarras, et les deux rosses accouplées, se dandinant sur leur chaînette, arrivèrent au petit trot devant le péristyle de la mairie, juste au moment où la garde nationale et les pompiers s'y déployaient, tambour battant, et marquant le pas.

"Present!" shouted Binet.

"Halt!" shouted the colonel. "Left about, march."

And after presenting arms, during which the clang of the band, letting loose, rang out like a brass kettle rolling downstairs, all the guns were lowered.

Then was seen stepping down from the carriage a gentleman in a short coat with silver braiding, with bald brow, and wearing a tuft of hair at the back of his head, of a sallow complexion and the most benign appearance. His eyes, very large and covered by heavy lids, were half-closed to look at the crowd, while at the same time he raised his sharp nose, and forced a smile upon his sunken mouth. He recognised the mayor by his scarf, and explained to him that the prefect was not able to come. He himself was a councillor at the prefecture; then he added a few apologies. Monsieur Tuvache answered them with compliments; the other confessed himself nervous; and they remained thus, face to face, their foreheads almost touching, with the members of the jury all round, the municipal council, the notable personages, the National Guard and the crowd. The councillor pressing his little cocked hat to his breast repeated his bows, while Tuvache, bent like a bow, also smiled, stammered, tried to say something, protested his devotion to the monarchy and the honour that was being done to Yonville.

Hippolyte, the groom from the inn, took the head of the horses from the coachman, and, limping along with his club-foot, led them to the door of the "Lion d'Or", where a number of peasants collected to look at the carriage. The drum beat, the howitzer thundered, and the gentlemen one by one mounted the platform, where they sat down in red utrecht velvet arm-chairs that had been lent by Madame Tuvache.

All these people looked alike. Their fair flabby faces, somewhat tanned by the sun, were the colour of sweet cider, and their puffy whiskers emerged from stiff collars, kept up by white cravats with broad bows. All the waist-coats were of velvet, double-breasted; all the watches had, at the end of a long ribbon, an oval cornelian seal; everyone rested his two hands on his thighs, carefully stretching the stride of their trou-

— Balancez! cria Binet.

— Halte! cria le colonel. Par file à gauche!

Et, après, un port d'armes où le cliquetis des capucines, se déroulant, sonna comme un chaudron de cuivre qui dégringole les escaliers, tous les fusils retombèrent.

Alors on vit descendre du carrosse un monsieur vêtu d'un habit court à broderie d'argent, chauve sur le front, portant toupet à l'occiput, ayant le teint blafard et l'apparence des plus bénignes. Ses deux yeux, fort gros et couverts de paupières épaisses, se fermaient à demi pour considérer la multitude, en même temps qu'il levait son nez pointu et faisait sourire sa bouche rentrée. Il reconnut le maire à son écharpe, et lui exposa que M. le préfet n'avait pu venir. Il était, lui, un conseiller de préfecture; puis il ajouta quelques excuses. Tuvache y répondit par des civilités, l'autre s'avoua confus; et ils restaient ainsi, face à face, et leurs fronts se touchant presque, avec les membres du jury tout alentour, le conseil municipal, les notables, la garde nationale et la foule. M. le conseiller, appuyant contre sa poitrine son petit tricorne noir, réitérait ses salutations, tandis que Tuvache, courbé comme un arc, souriait aussi, bégayait, cherchait ses phrases, protestait de son dévouement à la monarchie, et de l'honneur que l'on faisait à Yonville.

Hippolyte, le garçon de l'auberge, vint prendre par la bride les chevaux du cocher, et tout en boitant de son pied bot, il les conduisit sous le porche du Lion d'or, où beaucoup de paysans s'amassèrent à regarder la voiture. Le tambour battit, l'obusier tonna, et les messieurs à la file montèrent s'asseoir sur l'estrade, dans les fauteuils en utrecht rouge qu'avait prêtés madame Tuvache.

Tous ces gens-là se ressemblaient. Leurs molles figures blondes, un peu hâlées par le soleil, avaient la couleur du cidre doux, et leurs favoris bouffants s'échappaient de grands cols roides, que maintenaient des cravates blanches à rosette bien étalée. Tous les gilets étaient de velours, à châle; toutes les montres portaient au bout d'un long ruban quelque cachet ovale en cornaline; et l'on appuyait ses deux mains sur ses deux

sers, whose unsponged glossy cloth shone more brilliantly than the leather of their heavy boots.

The ladies of the company stood at the back under the vestibule between the pillars while the common herd was opposite, standing up or sitting on chairs. As a matter of fact, Lestiboudois had brought thither all those that he had moved from the field, and he even kept running back every minute to fetch others from the church. He caused such confusion with this piece of business that one had great difficulty in getting to the small steps of the platform.

"I think," said Monsieur Lheureux to the chemist, who was passing to his place, "that they ought to have put up two Venetian masts with something rather severe and rich for ornaments; it would have been a very pretty effect."

"To be sure," replied Homais; "but what can you expect? The mayor took everything on his own shoulders. He hasn't much taste. Poor Tuvache! and he is even completely destitute of what is called the genius of art."

Rodolphe, meanwhile, with Madame Bovary, had gone up to the first floor of the town hall, to the "council-room," and, as it was empty, he declared that they could enjoy the sight there more comfortably. He fetched three stools from the round table under the bust of the monarch, and having carried them to one of the windows, they sat down by each other.

There was commotion on the platform, long whisperings, much parleying. At last the councillor got up. They knew now that his name was Lieuvain, and in the crowd the name was passed from one to the other. After he had collated a few pages, and bent over them to see better, he began:

"Gentlemen!

"May I be permitted first of all (before addressing you on the object of our meeting to-day, and this sentiment will, I am sure, be shared by you all), may I be permitted, I say, to pay a tribute to the higher administration, to the government to the monarch, gentle men, our sovereign, to that beloved king, to whom no branch of public or private prosperity is a matter of indifference, and who directs with a hand at once so firm

cuisses, en écartant avec soin la fourche du pantalon, dont le drap non décati reluisait plus brillamment que le cuir des fortes bottes.

Les dames de la société se tenaient derrière, sous le vestibule, entre les colonnes, tandis que le commun de la foule était en face, debout, ou bien assis sur des chaises. En effet, Lestiboudois avait apporté là toutes celles qu'il avait déménagées de la prairie, et même il courait à chaque minute en chercher d'autres dans l'église, et causait un tel encombrement par son commerce, que l'on avait grand-peine à parvenir jusqu'au petit escalier de l'estrade.

— Moi, je trouve, dit M. Lheureux (s'adressant au pharmacien, qui passait pour gagner sa place), que l'on aurait dû planter là deux mâts vénitiens: avec quelque chose d'un peu sévère et de riche comme nouveautés, c'eût été d'un fort joli coup d'oeil.

— Certes, répondit Homais. Mais, que voulez-vous! c'est le maire qui a tout pris sous son bonnet. Il n'a pas grand goût, ce pauvre Tuvache, et il est même complètement dénué de ce qui s'appelle le génie des arts.

Cependant Rodolphe, avec madame Bovary, était monté au premier étage de la mairie, dans la salle des délibérations, et, comme elle était vide, il avait déclaré que l'on y serait bien pour jouir du spectacle plus à son aise. Il prit trois tabourets autour de la table ovale, sous le buste du monarque, et, les ayant approchés de l'une des fenêtres, ils s'assirent l'un près de l'autre.

Il y eut une agitation sur l'estrade, de longs chuchotements, des pourparlers. Enfin, M. le Conseiller se leva. On savait maintenant qu'il s'appelait Lieuvain, et l'on se répétait son nom de l'un à l'autre, dans la foule. Quand il eut donc collationné quelques feuilles et appliqué dessus son oeil pour y mieux voir, il commença:

«Messieurs,

Qu'il me soit permis d'abord (avant de vous entretenir de l'objet de cette réunion d'aujourd'hui, et ce sentiment, j'en suis sûr, sera partagé par vous tous), qu'il me soit permis, dis-je de rendre justice à l'administration supérieure, au gouvernement, au monarque, messieurs, à notre souverain, à ce roi bien-aimé à qui aucune branche de la prospérité publique ou particulière n'est indifférente, et qui dirige à la fois

and wise the chariot of the state amid the incessant perils of a stormy sea, knowing, moreover, how to make peace respected as well as war, industry, commerce, agriculture, and the fine arts?"

"I ought," said Rodolphe, "to get back a little further."

"Why?" said Emma.

But at this moment the voice of the councillor rose to an extraordinary pitch. He declaimed:

"This is no longer the time, gentlemen, when civil discord ensanguined our public places, when the landlord, the business-man, the working-man himself, falling asleep at night, lying down to peaceful sleep, trembled lest he should be awakened suddenly by the noise of incendiary tocsins, when the most subversive doctrines audaciously sapped foundations."

"Well, someone down there might see me," Rodolphe resumed, "then I should have to invent excuses for a fortnight; and with my bad reputation—"

"Oh, you are slandering yourself," said Emma.

"No! It is dreadful, I assure you."

"But, gentlemen," continued the councillor, "if, banishing from my memory the remembrance of these sad pictures, I carry my eyes back to the actual situation of our dear country, what do I see there? Everywhere commerce and the arts are flourishing; everywhere new means of communication, like so many new arteries in the body of the state, establish within it new relations. Our great industrial centres have recovered all their activity; religion, more consolidated, smiles in all hearts; our ports are full, confidence is born again, and France breathes once more!"

"Besides," added Rodolphe, "perhaps from the world's point of view they are right."

"How so?" she asked.

"What!" said he. "Do you not know that there are souls constantly tormented? They need by turns to dream and to act, the purest passions and the most turbulent joys, and thus they fling themselves into all sorts of fantasies, of follies."

Then she looked at him as one looks at a traveller who has voyaged over strange lands, and went on:

d'une main si ferme et si sage le char de l'État parmi les périls incessants d'une mer orageuse, sachant d'ailleurs faire respecter la paix comme la guerre, l'industrie, le commerce, l'agriculture et les beaux- arts.»

— Je devrais, dit Rodolphe, me reculer un peu.

— Pourquoi? dit Emma.

Mais, à ce moment, la voix du Conseiller s'éleva d'un ton extraordinaire. Il déclamait:

«Le temps n'est plus, messieurs, où la discorde civile ensanglantait nos places publiques, où le propriétaire, le négociant, l'ouvrier luimême, en s'endormant le soir d'un sommeil paisible, tremblaient de se voir réveillés tout à coup au bruit des tocsins incendiaires, où les maximes les plus subversives sapaient audacieusement les bases...»

— C'est qu'on pourrait, reprit Rodolphe, m'apercevoir d'en bas; puis j'en aurais pour quinze jours à donner des excuses, et, avec ma mauvaise réputation...

— Oh! vous vous calomniez, dit Emma.

— Non, non, elle est exécrable, je vous jure.

«Mais messieurs, poursuivait le Conseiller, que si, écartant de mon souvenir ces sombres tableaux, je reporte mes yeux sur la situation actuelle de notre belle patrie: qu'y vois-je? Partout fleurissent le commerce et les arts; partout des voies nouvelles de communication, comme autant d'artères nouvelles dans le corps de l'État, y établissent des rapports nouveaux; nos grands centres manufacturiers ont repris leur activité; la religion, plus affermie, sourit à tous les coeurs; nos ports sont pleins, la confiance renaît, et enfin la France respire!...»

— Du reste, ajouta Rodolphe, peut-être, au point de vue du monde, a-t-on raison?

— Comment cela? fit-elle.

— Eh quoi! dit-il, ne savez-vous pas qu'il y a des âmes sans cesse tourmentées? Il leur faut tour à tour le rêve et l'action, les passions les plus pures, les jouissances les plus furieuses, et l'on se jette ainsi dans toutes sortes de fantaisies, de folies.

Alors elle le regarda comme on contemple un voyageur qui a passé par des pays extraordinaires, et elle reprit:

"We have not even this distraction, we poor women!"

"A sad distraction, for happiness isn't found in it."

"But is it ever found?" she asked.

"Yes; one day it comes," he answered.

"And this is what you have understood," said the councillor. "You, farmers, agricultural labourers! you pacific pioneers of a work that belongs wholly to civilization! you, men of progress and morality, you have understood, I say, that political storms are even more redoubtable than atmospheric disturbances!"

"It comes one day," repeated Rodolphe, "one day suddenly, and when one is despairing of it. Then the horizon expands; it is as if a voice cried, 'It is here!' You feel the need of confiding the whole of your life, of giving everything, sacrificing everything to this being. There is no need for explanations; they understand one another. They have seen each other in dreams!" (And he looked at her.) "In fine, here it is, this treasure so sought after, here before you. It glitters, it flashes; yet one still doubts, one does not believe it; one remains dazzled, as if one went out from darkness into light."

And as he ended Rodolphe suited the action to the word. He passed his hand over his face, like a man seized with giddiness. Then he let it fall on Emma's. She took hers away.

"And who would be surprised at it, gentlemen? He only who is so blind, so plunged (I do not fear to say it), so plunged in the prejudices of another age as still to misunderstand the spirit of agricultural populations. Where, indeed, is to be found more patriotism than in the country, greater devotion to the public welfare, more intelligence, in a word? And, gentlemen, I do not mean that superficial intelligence, vain ornament of idle minds, but rather that profound and balanced intelligence that applies itself above all else to useful objects, thus contributing to the good of all, to the common amelioration and to the support of the state, born of respect for law and the practice of duty—"

— Nous n'avons pas même cette distraction, nous autres pauvres femmes!

— Triste distraction car on n'y trouve pas le bonheur.

— Mais le trouve-t-on jamais? demanda-t-elle.

— Oui, il se rencontre un jour, répondit-il.

«Et c'est là ce que vous avez compris, disait le Conseiller. Vous, agriculteurs et ouvriers des campagnes; vous, pionniers pacifiques d'une oeuvre toute de civilisation! vous, hommes de progrès et de moralité! vous avez compris, dis-je, que les orages politiques sont encore plus redoutables vraiment que les désordres de l'atmosphère...»

— Il se rencontre un jour, répéta Rodolphe, un jour, tout à coup, et quand on en désespérait. Alors des horizons s'entrouvrent, c'est comme une voix qui crie: «Le voilà!» Vous sentez le besoin de faire à cette personne la confidence de votre vie; de lui donner tout, de lui sacrifier tout! On ne s'explique pas, on se devine. On s'est entrevu dans ses rêves. (Et il la regardait.) Enfin, il est là, ce trésor que l'on a tant cherché, là, devant vous; il brille, il étincelle. Cependant on en doute encore, on n'ose y croire; on en reste ébloui, comme si l'on sortait des ténèbres à la lumière.

Et, en achevant ces mots; Rodolphe ajouta la pantomime à sa phrase. Il se passa la main sur le visage, tel qu'un homme pris d'étourdissement; puis il la laissa retomber sur celle d'Emma. Elle retira la sienne. Mais le Conseiller lisait toujours:

«Et qui s'en étonnerait, messieurs? Celui-là seul qui serait assez aveugle, assez plongé (je ne crains pas de le dire), assez plongé dans les préjugés d'un autre âge pour méconnaître encore l'esprit des populations agricoles. Où trouver, en effet, plus de patriotisme que dans les campagnes, plus de dévouement à la cause publique, plus d'intelligence en un mot? Et je n'entends pas, messieurs, cette intelligence superficielle, vain ornement des esprits oisifs, mais plus de cette intelligence profonde et modérée, qui s'applique par-dessus toute chose à poursuivre des buts utiles, contribuant ainsi au bien de chacun, à l'amélioration commune et au soutien des États, fruit du respect des lois et de la pratique des devoirs...»

"Ah! again!" said Rodolphe. "Always 'duty.' I am sick of the word. They are a lot of old blockheads in flannel vests and of old women with foot-warmers and rosaries who constantly drone into our ears 'Duty, duty!' Ah! by Jove! one's duty is to feel what is great, cherish the beautiful, and not accept all the conventions of society with the ignominy that it imposes upon us."

"Yet—yet—" objected Madame Bovary.

"No, no! Why cry out against the passions? Are they not the one beautiful thing on the earth, the source of heroism, of enthusiasm, of poetry, music, the arts, of everything, in a word?"

"But one must," said Emma, "to some extent bow to the opinion of the world and accept its moral code."

"Ah! but there are two," he replied. "The small, the conventional, that of men, that which constantly changes, that brays out so loudly, that makes such a commotion here below, of the earth earthly, like the mass of imbeciles you see down there. But the other, the eternal, that is about us and above, like the landscape that surrounds us, and the blue heavens that give us light."

Monsieur Lieuvain had just wiped his mouth with a pocket-handkerchief. He continued:

"And what should I do here gentlemen, pointing out to you the uses of agriculture? Who supplies our wants? Who provides our means of subsistence? Is it not the agriculturist? The agriculturist, gentlemen, who, sowing with laborious hand the fertile furrows of the country, brings forth the corn, which, being ground, is made into a powder by means of ingenious machinery, comes out thence under the name of flour, and from there, transported to our cities, is soon delivered at the baker's, who makes it into food for poor and rich alike. Again, is it not the agriculturist who fattens, for our clothes, his abundant flocks in the pastures? For how should we clothe ourselves, how nourish ourselves, without the agriculturist? And, gentlemen, is it even necessary to go so far for examples? Who has not frequently reflected on all the momentous things that we get out of that modest animal, the ornament of poultry-yards, that provides us at once with a soft pillow for our bed, with

— Ah! encore, dit Rodolphe. Toujours les devoirs, je suis assommé de ces mots-là. Ils sont un tas de vieilles ganaches en gilet de flanelle, et de bigotes à chaufferette et à chapelet, qui continuellement nous chantent aux oreilles: «Le devoir! le devoir!» Eh! parbleu! le devoir, c'est de sentir ce qui est grand, de chérir ce qui est beau, et non pas d'accepter toutes les conventions de la société, avec les ignominies qu'elle nous impose.

— Cependant..., cependant..., objectait madame Bovary.

— Eh non! pourquoi déclamer contre les passions? Ne sont-elles pas la seule belle chose qu'il y ait sur la terre, la source de l'héroïsme, de l'enthousiasme, de la poésie, de la musique, des arts, de tout enfin?

— Mais il faut bien, dit Emma, suivre un peu l'opinion du monde et obéir à sa morale.

— Ah! c'est qu'il y en a deux, répliqua-t-il. La petite, la convenue, celle des hommes, celle qui varie sans cesse et qui braille si fort, s'agite en bas, terre à terre, comme ce rassemblement d'imbéciles que vous voyez. Mais l'autre, l'éternelle, elle est tout autour et au-dessus, comme le paysage qui nous environne et le ciel bleu qui nous éclaire.

M. Lieuvain venait de s'essuyer la bouche avec son mouchoir de poche. Il reprit:

«Et qu'aurais-je à faire, messieurs, de vous démontrer ici l'utilité de l'agriculture? Qui donc pourvoit à nos besoins? qui donc fournit à notre subsistance? N'est-ce pas l'agriculteur? L'agriculteur, messieurs, qui, ensemençant d'une main laborieuse les sillons féconds des campagnes, fait naître le blé, lequel broyé est mis en poudre au moyen d'ingénieux appareils, en sort sous le nom de farine, et, de là, transporté dans les cités, est bientôt rendu chez le boulanger, qui en confectionne un aliment pour le pauvre comme pour le riche. N'est-ce pas l'agriculteur encore qui engraisse, pour nos vêtements, ses abondants troupeaux dans les pâturages? Car comment nous vêtirions-nous, car comment nous nourririons-nous sans l'agriculteur? Et même, messieurs, est- il besoin d'aller si loin chercher des exemples? Qui n'a souvent réfléchi à toute l'importance que l'on retire de ce modeste animal, ornement de nos basses-cours, qui fournit à la fois un oreiller moelleux pour nos

succulent flesh for our tables, and eggs? But I should never end if I were to enumerate one after the other all the different products which the earth, well cultivated, like a generous mother, lavishes upon her children. Here it is the vine, elsewhere the apple tree for cider, there colza, farther on cheeses and flax. Gentlemen, let us not forget flax, which has made such great strides of late years, and to which I will more particularly call your attention."

He had no need to call it, for all the mouths of the multitude were wide open, as if to drink in his words. Tuvache by his side listened to him with staring eyes. Monsieur Derozerays from time to time softly closed his eyelids, and farther on the chemist, with his son Napoleon between his knees, put his hand behind his ear in order not to lose a syllable. The chins of the other members of the jury went slowly up and down in their waistcoats in sign of approval. The firemen at the foot of the platform rested on their bayonets; and Binet, motionless, stood with out-turned elbows, the point of his sabre in the air. Perhaps he could hear, but certainly he could see nothing, because of the visor of his helmet, that fell down on his nose. His lieutenant, the youngest son of Monsieur Tuvache, had a bigger one, for his was enormous, and shook on his head, and from it an end of his cotton scarf peeped out. He smiled beneath it with a perfectly infantine sweetness, and his pale little face, whence drops were running, wore an expression of enjoyment and sleepiness.

The square as far as the houses was crowded with people. One saw folk leaning on their elbows at all the windows, others standing at doors, and Justin, in front of the chemist's shop, seemed quite transfixed by the sight of what he was looking at. In spite of the silence Monsieur Lieuvain's voice was lost in the air. It reached you in fragments of phrases, and interrupted here and there by the creaking of chairs in the crowd; then you suddenly heard the long bellowing of an ox, or else the bleating of the lambs, who answered one another at street corners. In fact, the cowherds and shepherds had driven their beasts thus far, and these lowed from time to time, while with their tongues they tore down some scrap of foliage that hung above their mouths.

couches, sa chair succulente pour nos tables, et des oeufs? Mais je n'en finirais pas, s'il fallait énumérer les uns après les autres les différents produits que la terre bien cultivée, telle qu'une mère généreuse, prodigue à ses enfants. Ici, c'est la vigne; ailleurs, ce sont les pommiers à cidre; là, le colza; plus loin, les fromages; et le lin; messieurs, n'oublions pas le lin! qui a pris dans ces dernières années un accroissement considérable et sur lequel j'appellerai plus particulièrement votre attention.»

Il n'avait pas besoin de l'appeler: car toutes les bouches de la multitude se tenaient ouvertes, comme pour boire ses paroles. Tuvache, à côté de lui, l'écoutait en écarquillant les yeux; M. Derozerays, de temps à autre, fermait doucement les paupières; et, plus loin, le pharmacien, avec son fils Napoléon entre ses jambes, bombait sa main contre son oreille pour ne pas perdre une seule syllabe. Les autres membres du jury balançaient lentement leur menton dans leur gilet, en signe d'approbation. Les pompiers, au bas de l'estrade, se reposaient sur leurs baïonnettes; et Binet, immobile, restait le coude en dehors, avec la pointe du sabre en l'air. Il entendait peut-être, mais il ne devait rien apercevoir, à cause de la visière de son casque qui lui descendait sur le nez. Son lieutenant, le fils cadet du sieur Tuvache, avait encore exagéré le sien; car il en portait un énorme et qui lui vacillait sur la tête, en laissant dépasser un bout de son foulard d'indienne. Il souriait là-dessous avec une douceur tout enfantine, et sa petite figure pâle, où des gouttes ruisselaient, avait une expression de jouissance, d'accablement et de sommeil

La place jusqu'aux maisons était comble de monde. On voyait des gens accoudés à toutes les fenêtres, d'autres debout sur toutes les portes, et Justin, devant la devanture de la pharmacie, paraissait tout fixé dans la contemplation de ce qu'il regardait. Malgré le silence, la voix de M. Lieuvain se perdait dans l'air. Elle vous arrivait par lambeaux de phrases, qu'interrompait, çà et là le bruit des chaises dans la foule; puis on entendait, tout à coup, partir derrière soi un long mugissement de boeuf, ou bien les bêlements des agneaux qui se répondaient au coin des rues. En effet, les vachers et les bergers avaient poussé leurs bêtes jusque-là, et elles beuglaient de temps à autre, tout en arrachant avec leur langue quelque bribe de feuillage qui leur pendait sur le museau.

Rodolphe had drawn nearer to Emma, and said to her in a low voice, speaking rapidly:

"Does not this conspiracy of the world revolt you? Is there a single sentiment it does not condemn? The noblest instincts, the purest sympathies are persecuted, slandered; and if at length two poor souls do meet, all is so organised that they cannot blend together. Yet they will make the attempt; they will flutter their wings; they will call upon each other. Oh! no matter. Sooner or later, in six months, ten years, they will come together, will love; for fate has decreed it, and they are born one for the other."

His arms were folded across his knees, and thus lifting his face towards Emma, close by her, he looked fixedly at her. She noticed in his eyes small golden lines radiating from black pupils; she even smelt the perfume of the pomade that made his hair glossy. Then a faintness came over her; she recalled the Viscount who had waltzed with her at Vaubyessard, and his beard exhaled like this air an odour of vanilla and citron, and mechanically she half-closed her eyes the better to breathe it in. But in making this movement, as she leant back in her chair, she saw in the distance, right on the line of the horizon, the old diligence, the "Hirondelle," that was slowly descending the hill of Leux, dragging after it a long trail of dust. It was in this yellow carriage that Leon had so often come back to her, and by this route down there that he had gone for ever. She fancied she saw him opposite at his windows; then all grew confused; clouds gathered; it seemed to her that she was again turning in the waltz under the light of the lustres on the arm of the Viscount, and that Leon was not far away, that he was coming; and yet all the time she was conscious of the scent of Rodolphe's head by her side. This sweetness of sensation pierced through her old desires, and these, like grains of sand under a gust of wind, eddied to and fro in the subtle breath of the perfume which suffused her soul. She opened wide her nostrils several times to drink in the freshness of the ivy round the capitals. She took off her gloves, she wiped her hands, then fanned her face with her handkerchief, while athwart the throbbing of her temples she heard the murmur of the crowd and the voice of the councillor intoning his phrases

Rodolphe s'était rapproché d'Emma, et il disait d'une voix basse, en parlant vite:

— Est-ce que cette conjuration du monde ne vous révolte pas? Est- il un seul sentiment qu'il ne condamne? Les instincts les plus nobles, les sympathies les plus pures sont persécutés, calomniés, et, s'il se rencontre enfin deux pauvres âmes, tout est organisé pour qu'elles ne puissent se joindre. Elles essayeront cependant, elles battront des ailes, elles s'appelleront. Oh! n'importe, tôt ou tard, dans six mois, dix ans, elles se réuniront, s'aimeront, parce que la fatalité l'exige et qu'elles sont nées l'une pour l'autre.

Il se tenait les bras croisés sur ses genoux, et, ainsi levant la figure vers Emma, il la regardait de près, fixement. Elle distinguait dans ses yeux des petits rayons d'or s'irradiant tout autour de ses pupilles noires, et même elle sentait le parfum de la pommade qui lustrait sa chevelure. Alors une mollesse la saisit, elle se rappela ce vicomte qui l'avait fait valser à la Vaubyessard, et dont la barbe exhalait, comme ces cheveux-là, cette odeur de vanille et de citron; et, machinalement, elle entreferma les paupières pour la mieux respirer: Mais, dans ce geste qu'elle fit en se cambrant sur sa chaise, elle aperçut au loin, tout au fond de l'horizon, la vieille diligence l'Hirondelle, qui descendait lentement la côte des Leux, en traînant après soi un long panache de poussière. C'était dans cette voiture jaune que Léon, si souvent, était revenu vers elle; et par cette route là-bas qu'il était parti pour toujours! Elle crut le voir en face, à sa fenêtre; puis tout se confondit, des nuages passèrent; il lui sembla qu'elle tournait encore dans la valse, sous le feu des lustres, au bras du vicomte, et que Léon n'était pas loin, qui allait venir ... et cependant elle sentait toujours la tête de Rodolphe à côté d'elle. La douceur de cette sensation pénétrait ainsi ses désirs d'autrefois, et comme des grains de sable sous un coup de vent, ils tourbillonnaient dans la bouffée subtile du parfum qui se répandait sur son âme. Elle ouvrit les narines à plusieurs reprises, fortement, pour aspirer la fraîcheur des lierres autour des chapiteaux. Elle retira ses gants, elle s'essuya les mains; puis, avec son mouchoir, elle s'éventait la figure, tandis qu'à travers le battement de ses tempes elle entendait la rumeur de la foule et la voix du Conseiller qui psalmodiait ses phrases.

He said:

"Continue, persevere; listen neither to the suggestions of routine, nor to the over-hasty councils of a rash empiricism. Apply yourselves, above all, to the amelioration of the soil, to good manures, to the development of the equine, bovine, ovine, and porcine races. Let these shows be to you pacific arenas, where the victor in leaving it will hold forth a hand to the vanquished, and will fraternise with him in the hope of better success. And you, aged servants, humble domestics, whose hard labour no Government up to this day has taken into consideration, come hither to receive the reward of your silent virtues, and be assured that the state henceforward has its eye upon you; that it encourages you, protects you; that it will accede to your just demands, and alleviate as much as in it lies the burden of your painful sacrifices."

Monsieur Lieuvain then sat down; Monsieur Derozerays got up, beginning another speech. His was not perhaps so florid as that of the councillor, but it recommended itself by a more direct style, that is to say, by more special knowledge and more elevated considerations. Thus the praise of the Government took up less space in it; religion and agriculture more. He showed in it the relations of these two, and how they had always contributed to civilisation. Rodolphe with Madame Bovary was talking dreams, presentiments, magnetism. Going back to the cradle of society, the orator painted those fierce times when men lived on acorns in the heart of woods. Then they had left off the skins of beasts, had put on cloth, tilled the soil, planted the vine. Was this a good, and in this discovery was there not more of injury than of gain? Monsieur Derozerays set himself this problem. From magnetism little by little Rodolphe had come to affinities, and while the president was citing Cincinnatus and his plough, Diocletian, planting his cabbages, and the Emperors of China inaugurating the year by the sowing of seed, the young man was explaining to the young woman that these irresistible attractions find their cause in some previous state of existence.

"Thus we," he said, "why did we come to know one another? What chance willed it? It was because across the infinite, like two streams that

Il disait:

«Continuez! persévérez! n'écoutez ni les suggestions de la routine, ni les conseils trop hâtifs d'un empirisme téméraire! Appliquez-vous surtout à l'amélioration du sol, aux bons engrais, au développement des races chevalines, bovines, ovines et porcines! Que ces comices soient pour vous comme des arènes pacifiques où le vainqueur, en en sortant, tendra la main au vaincu et fraternisera avec lui, dans l'espoir d'un succès meilleur! Et vous, vénérables serviteurs! humbles domestiques, dont aucun gouvernement jusqu'à ce jour n'avait pris en considération les pénibles labeurs, venez recevoir la récompense de vos vertus silencieuses, et soyez convaincus que l'état, désormais, a les yeux fixés sur vous, qu'il vous encourage, qu'il vous protège, qu'il fera droit à vos justes réclamations et allégera, autant qu'il est en lui, le fardeau de vos pénibles sacrifices!».

M. Lieuvain se rassit alors; M. Derozerays se leva, commençant un autre discours. Le sien peut-être, ne fut point aussi fleuri que celui du Conseiller; mais il se recommandait par un caractère de style plus positif, c'est-à-dire par des connaissances plus spéciales et des considérations plus relevées. Ainsi, l'éloge du gouvernement y tenait moins de place; la religion et l'agriculture en occupaient davantage. On y voyait le rapport de l'une et de l'autre, et comment elles avaient concouru toujours à la civilisation. Rodolphe, avec madame Bovary, causait rêves, pressentiments, magnétisme. Remontant au berceau des sociétés, l'orateur vous dépeignait ces temps farouches où les hommes vivaient de glands, au fond des bois. Puis ils avaient quitté la dépouille des bêtes; endossé le drap, creusé des sillons, planté la vigne. Était-ce un bien, et n'y avait-il pas dans cette découverte plus d'inconvénients que d'avantages? M. Derozerays se posait ce problème. Du magnétisme, peu à peu, Rodolphe en était venu aux affinités, et, tandis que M. le président citait Cincinnatus à sa charrue, Dioclétien plantant ses choux, et les empereurs de la Chine inaugurant l'année par des semailles, le jeune homme expliquait à la jeune femme que ces attractions irrésistibles tiraient leur cause de quelque existence antérieure.

— Ainsi, nous, disait-il, pourquoi nous sommes-nous connus? quel hasard l'a voulu? C'est qu'à travers l'éloignement, sans doute, comme

flow but to unite; our special bents of mind had driven us towards each other."

And he seized her hand; she did not withdraw it.

"For good farming generally!" cried the president.

"Just now, for example, when I went to your house."

"To Monsieur Bizat of Quincampoix."

"Did I know I should accompany you?"

"Seventy francs."

"A hundred times I wished to go; and I followed you—I remained."

"Manures!"

"And I shall remain to-night, to-morrow, all other days, all my life!"

"To Monsieur Caron of Argueil, a gold medal!"

"For I have never in the society of any other person found so complete a charm."

"To Monsieur Bain of Givry-Saint-Martin."

"And I shall carry away with me the remembrance of you."

"For a merino ram!"

"But you will forget me; I shall pass away like a shadow."

"To Monsieur Belot of Notre-Dame."

"Oh, no! I shall be something in your thought, in your life, shall I not?"

"Porcine race; prizes—equal, to Messrs. Leherisse and Cullembourg, sixty francs!"

Rodolphe was pressing her hand, and he felt it all warm and quivering like a captive dove that wants to fly away; but, whether she was trying to take it away or whether she was answering his pressure; she made a movement with her fingers. He exclaimed:

"Oh, I thank you! You do not repulse me! You are good! You understand that I am yours! Let me look at you; let me contemplate you!"

A gust of wind that blew in at the window ruffled the cloth on the table, and in the square below all the great caps of the peasant women were uplifted by it like the wings of white butterflies fluttering.

"Use of oil-cakes," continued the president.

He was hurrying on:

deux fleuves qui coulent pour se rejoindre, nos pentes particulières nous avaient poussés l'un vers l'autre.

Et il saisit sa main; elle ne la retira pas.

«Ensemble de bonnes cultures!» cria le président.

— Tantôt, par exemple, quand je suis venu chez vous...

«À M. Bizet, de Quincampoix.»

— Savais-je que je vous accompagnerais?

«Soixante et dix francs!»

— Cent fois même j'ai voulu partir, et je vous ai suivie, je suis resté.

«Fumiers.»

— Comme je resterais ce soir, demain, les autres jours, toute ma vie!

«À M. Caron, d'Argueil, une médaille d'or!»

— Car jamais je n'ai trouvé dans la société de personne un charme aussi complet.

«À M. Bain, de Givry-Saint-Martin!»

— Aussi, moi, j'emporterai votre souvenir.

«Pour un bélier mérinos...»

— Mais vous m'oublierez, j'aurai passé comme une ombre.

«À M. Belot, de Notre-Dame...»

— Oh! non, n'est-ce pas, je serai quelque chose dans votre pensée, dans votre vie?

«Race porcine, prix ex aequo: à MM. Lehérissé et Cullembourg; soixante francs!»

Rodolphe lui serrait la main, et il la sentait toute chaude et frémissante comme une tourterelle captive qui veut reprendre sa volée; mais, soit qu'elle essayât de la dégager ou bien qu'elle répondît à cette pression, elle fit un mouvement des doigts; il s'écria:

— Oh! merci! Vous ne me repoussez pas! Vous êtes bonne! vous comprenez que je suis à vous! Laissez que je vous voie, que je vous contemple!

Un coup de vent qui arriva par les fenêtres fronça le tapis de la table, et, sur la Place, en bas, tous les grands bonnets des paysannes se soulevèrent, comme des ailes de papillons blancs qui s'agitent.

«Emploi de tourteaux de graines oléagineuses», continua le président.

Il se hâtait:

"Flemish manure-flax-growing-drainage-long leases-domestic service."

Rodolphe was no longer speaking. They looked at one another. A supreme desire made their dry lips tremble, and wearily, without an effort, their fingers intertwined.

"Catherine Nicaise Elizabeth Leroux, of Sassetot-la-Guerriere, for fifty-four years of service at the same farm, a silver medal—value, twenty-five francs!"

"Where is Catherine Leroux?" repeated the councillor.

She did not present herself, and one could hear voices whispering:

"Go up!"

"No."

"Don't be afraid!"

"Oh, how stupid she is!"

"Well, is she there?" cried Tuvache.

"Yes; here she is."

"Then let her come up!"

Then there came forward on the platform a little old woman with timid bearing, who seemed to shrink within her poor clothes. On her feet she wore heavy wooden clogs, and from her hips hung a large blue apron. Her pale face framed in a borderless cap was more wrinkled than a withered russet apple. And from the sleeves of her red jacket looked out two large hands with knotty joints, the dust of barns, the potash of washing the grease of wools had so encrusted, roughened, hardened these that they seemed dirty, although they had been rinsed in clear water; and by dint of long service they remained half open, as if to bear humble witness for themselves of so much suffering endured. Something of monastic rigidity dignified her face. Nothing of sadness or of emotion weakened that pale look. In her constant living with animals she had caught their dumbness and their calm. It was the first time that she found herself in the midst of so large a company, and inwardly scared by the flags, the drums, the gentlemen in frock-coats, and the order of the councillor, she stood motionless, not knowing whether to

«Engrais flamand, — culture du lin, — drainage, — baux à longs termes, — services de domestiques.»

Rodolphe ne parlait plus. Ils se regardaient. Un désir suprême faisait frissonner leurs lèvres sèches; et mollement, sans effort, leurs doigts se confondirent.

«Catherine-Nicaise-Élisabeth Leroux, de Sassetot-la-Guerrière, pour cinquante-quatre ans de service dans la même ferme, une médaille d'argent — du prix de vingt-cinq francs!»

«Où est-elle, Catherine Leroux?» répéta le Conseiller.

Elle ne se présentait pas, et l'on entendait des voix qui chuchotaient:

— Vas-y!

— Non.

— À gauche!

— N'aie pas peur!

— Ah! qu'elle est bête!

— Enfin y est-elle? s'écria Tuvache.

— Oui!... la voilà!

— Qu'elle approche donc!

Alors on vit s'avancer sur l'estrade une petite vieille femme de maintien craintif, et qui paraissait se ratatiner dans ses pauvres vêtements. Elle avait aux pieds de grosses galoches de bois, et, le long des hanches, un grand tablier bleu. Son visage maigre, entouré d'un béguin sans bordure, était plus plissé de rides qu'une pomme de reinette flétrie, et des manches de sa camisole rouge dépassaient deux longues mains, à articulations noueuses. La poussière des granges, la potasse des lessives et le suint des laines les avaient si bien encroûtées, éraillées, durcies, qu'elles semblaient sales quoiqu'elles fussent rincées d'eau claire; et, à force d'avoir servi, elles restaient entrouvertes, comme pour présenter d'elles-mêmes l'humble témoignage de tant de souffrances subies. Quelque chose d'une rigidité monacale relevait l'expression de sa figure. Rien de triste ou d'attendri n'amollissait ce regard pâle. Dans la fréquentation des animaux, elle avait pris leur mutisme et leur placidité. C'était la première fois qu'elle se voyait au milieu d'une compagnie si nombreuse; et, intérieurement effarouchée par les drapeaux, par les tambours, par les messieurs en

advance or run away, nor why the crowd was pushing her and the jury were smiling at her. Thus stood before these radiant bourgeois this half-century of servitude.

"Approach, venerable Catherine Nicaise Elizabeth Leroux!" said the councillor, who had taken the list of prize-winners from the president.

And, looking at the piece of paper and the old woman by turns, he repeated in a fatherly tone:

"Approach! approach!"

"Are you deaf?" said Tuvache, fidgeting in his armchair.

And he began shouting in her ear:

"Fifty-four years of service. A silver medal! Twenty-five francs! For you!"

Then, when she had her medal, she looked at it, and a smile of beatitude spread over her face; and as she walked away they could hear her muttering:

"I'll give it to our cure up home, to say some masses for me!"

"What fanaticism!" exclaimed the chemist, leaning across to the notary.

The meeting was over, the crowd dispersed, and now that the speeches had been read, each one fell back into his place again, and everything into the old grooves; the masters bullied the servants, and these struck the animals, indolent victors, going back to the stalls, a green-crown on their horns.

The National Guards, however, had gone up to the first floor of the town hall with buns spitted on their bayonets, and the drummer of the battalion carried a basket with bottles. Madame Bovary took Rodolphe's arm; he saw her home; they separated at her door; then he walked about alone in the meadow while he waited for the time of the banquet.

The feast was long, noisy, ill served; the guests were so crowded that they could hardly move their elbows; and the narrow planks used for forms almost broke down under their weight. They ate hugely. Each one stuffed himself on his own account. Sweat stood on every brow,

habit noir et par la croix d'honneur du Conseiller, elle demeurait tout immobile, ne sachant s'il fallait s'avancer ou s'enfuir, ni pourquoi la foule la poussait et pourquoi les examinateurs lui souriaient. Ainsi se tenait, devant ces bourgeois épanouis, ce demi-siècle de servitude.

— Approchez, vénérable Catherine-Nicaise-Élisabeth Leroux! dit M. le Conseiller, qui avait pris des mains du président la liste des lauréats.

Et tour à tour examinant la feuille de papier, puis la vieille femme, il répétait d'un ton paternel:

— Approchez, approchez!

— Êtes-vous sourde? dit Tuvache, en bondissant sur son fauteuil.

Et il se mit là lui crier dans l'oreille:

— Cinquante-quatre ans de service! Une médaille d'argent! Vingt-cinq francs! C'est pour vous.

Puis, quand elle eut sa médaille, elle la considéra. Alors un sourire de béatitude se répandit sur sa figure, et on l'entendit qui marmottait en s'en allant:

— Je la donnerai au curé de chez nous, pour qu'il me dise des messes.

— Quel fanatisme! exclama le pharmacien, en se penchant vers le notaire.

La séance était finie; la foule se dispersa; et, maintenant que les discours étaient lus, chacun reprenait son rang et tout rentrait dans la coutume: les maîtres rudoyaient les domestiques, et ceux-ci frappaient les animaux, triomphateurs indolents qui s'en retournaient à l'étable, une couronne verte entre les cornes.

Cependant les gardes nationaux étaient montés au premier étage de la mairie, avec des brioches embrochées à leurs baïonnettes, et le tambour du bataillon qui portait un panier de bouteilles. Madame Bovary prit le bras de Rodolphe; il la reconduisit chez elle; ils se séparèrent devant sa porte; puis il se promena seul dans la prairie, tout en attendant l'heure du banquet.

Le festin fut long, bruyant, mal servi; l'on était si tassé, que l'on avait peine à remuer les coudes, et les planches étroites qui servaient de bancs faillirent se rompre sous le poids des convives. Ils mangeaient abondamment. Chacun s'en donnait pour sa quote-part. La sueur cou-

and a whitish steam, like the vapour of a stream on an autumn morning, floated above the table between the hanging lamps. Rodolphe, leaning against the calico of the tent was thinking so earnestly of Emma that he heard nothing. Behind him on the grass the servants were piling up the dirty plates, his neighbours were talking; he did not answer them; they filled his glass, and there was silence in his thoughts in spite of the growing noise. He was dreaming of what she had said, of the line of her lips; her face, as in a magic mirror, shone on the plates of the shakos, the folds of her gown fell along the walls, and days of love unrolled to all infinity before him in the vistas of the future.

He saw her again in the evening during the fireworks, but she was with her husband, Madame Homais, and the druggist, who was worrying about the danger of stray rockets, and every moment he left the company to go and give some advice to Binet.

The pyrotechnic pieces sent to Monsieur Tuvache had, through an excess of caution, been shut up in his cellar, and so the damp powder would not light, and the principal set piece, that was to represent a dragon biting his tail, failed completely. Now and then a meagre Roman-candle went off; then the gaping crowd sent up a shout that mingled with the cry of the women, whose waists were being squeezed in the darkness. Emma silently nestled against Charles's shoulder; then, raising her chin, she watched the luminous rays of the rockets against the dark sky. Rodolphe gazed at her in the light of the burning lanterns.

They went out one by one. The stars shone out. A few crops of rain began to fall. She knotted her fichu round her bare head.

At this moment the councillor's carriage came out from the inn. His coachman, who was drunk, suddenly dozed off, and one could see from the distance, above the hood, between the two lanterns, the mass of his body, that swayed from right to left with the giving of the traces.

"Truly," said the druggist, "one ought to proceed most rigorously against drunkenness! I should like to see written up weekly at the door of the town hall on a board ad hoc the names of all those who during the

lait sur tous les fronts; et une vapeur blanchâtre, comme la buée d'un fleuve par un matin d'automne, flottait au-dessus de la table, entre les quinquets suspendus. Rodolphe, le dos appuyé contre le calicot de la tente, pensait si fort à Emma, qu'il n'entendait rien. Derrière lui, sur le gazon, des domestiques empilaient des assiettes sales; ses voisins parlaient, il ne leur répondait pas; on lui emplissait son verre, et un silence s'établissait dans sa pensée, malgré les accroissements de la rumeur. Il rêvait à ce qu'elle avait dit et à la forme de ses lèvres; sa figure, comme en un miroir magique, brillait sur la plaque des shakos; les plis de sa robe descendaient le long des murs, et des journées d'amour se déroulaient à l'infini dans les perspectives de l'avenir.

Il la revit le soir, pendant le feu d'artifice; mais elle était avec son mari, madame Homais et le pharmacien, lequel se tourmentait beaucoup sur le danger des fusées perdues; et, à chaque moment, il quittait la compagnie pour aller faire à Binet des recommandations.

Les pièces pyrotechniques envoyées à l'adresse du sieur Tuvache avaient, par excès de précaution, été enfermées dans sa cave; aussi la poudre humide ne s'enflammait guère, et le morceau principal, qui devait figurer un dragon se mordant la queue, rata complètement. De temps à autre, il partait une pauvre chandelle romaine; alors la foule béante poussait une clameur où se mêlait le cri des femmes à qui l'on chatouillait la taille pendant l'obscurité. Emma, silencieuse, se blottissait doucement contre l'épaule de Charles; puis, le menton levé, elle suivait dans le ciel noir le jet lumineux des fusées. Rodolphe la contemplait à la lueur des lampions qui brûlaient.

Ils s'éteignirent peu à peu. Les étoiles s'allumèrent. Quelques gouttes de pluie vinrent à tomber. Elle noua son fichu sur sa tête nue.

À ce moment, le fiacre du Conseiller sortit de l'auberge. Son cocher, qui était ivre, s'assoupit tout à coup; et l'on apercevait de loin, par-dessus la capote, entre les deux lanternes, la masse de son corps qui se balançait de droite et de gauche selon le tangage des soupentes.

— En vérité, dit l'apothicaire, on devrait bien sévir contre l'ivresse! Je voudrais que l'on inscrivît, hebdomadairement, à la porte de la mairie, sur un tableau ad hoc, les noms de tous ceux qui, durant la semaine,

week got intoxicated on alcohol. Besides, with regard to statistics, one would thus have, as it were, public records that one could refer to in case of need. But excuse me!"

And he once more ran off to the captain.

The latter was going back to see his lathe again.

"Perhaps you would not do ill," Homais said to him, "to send one of your men, or to go yourself—"

"Leave me alone!" answered the tax-collector. "It's all right!"

"Do not be uneasy," said the druggist, when he returned to his friends. "Monsieur Binet has assured me that all precautions have been taken. No sparks have fallen; the pumps are full. Let us go to rest."

"Ma foi! I want it," said Madame Homais, yawning at large. "But never mind; we've had a beautiful day for our fete."

Rodolphe repeated in a low voice, and with a tender look:

"Oh, yes! very beautiful!"

And having bowed to one another, they separated.

Two days later, in the "Final de Rouen," there was a long article on the show. Homais had composed it with verve the very next morning.

"Why these festoons, these flowers, these garlands? Whither hurries this crowd like the waves of a furious sea under the torrents of a tropical sun pouring its heat upon our heads?"

Then he spoke of the condition of the peasants. Certainly the Government was doing much, but not enough. "Courage!" he cried to it; "a thousand reforms are indispensable; let us accomplish them!" Then touching on the entry of the councillor, he did not forget "the martial air of our militia;" nor "our most merry village maidens;" nor the "bald-headed old men like patriarchs who were there, and of whom some, the remnants of our phalanxes, still felt their hearts beat at the manly sound of the drums." He cited himself among the first of the members of the jury, and he even called attention in a note to the fact that Monsieur Homais, chemist, had sent a memoir on cider to the agricultural society. When he came to the distribution of the prizes, he painted the joy of the

se seraient intoxiqués avec des alcools. D'ailleurs, sous le rapport de la statistique, on aurait là comme des annales patentes qu'on irait au besoin... Mais excusez.

Et il courut encore vers le capitaine.

Celui-ci rentrait à sa maison. Il allait revoir son tour.

— Peut-être ne feriez-vous pas mal, lui dit Homais, d'envoyer un de vos hommes ou d'aller vous-même...

— Laissez-moi donc tranquille, répondit le percepteur, puisqu'il n'y a rien!

— Rassurez-vous, dit l'apothicaire, quand il fut revenu près de ses amis. M. Binet m'a certifié que les mesures étaient prises. Nulle flammèche ne sera tombée. Les pompes sont pleines. Allons dormir.

— Ma foi! j'en ai besoin, fit madame Homais qui bâillait considérablement; mais, n'importe, nous avons eu pour notre fête une bien belle journée.

Rodolphe répéta d'une voix basse et avec un regard tendre:

— Oh! oui, bien belle!

Et, s'étant salués, on se tourna le dos.

Deux jours après, dans le Fanal de Rouen il y avait un grand article sur les comices. Homais l'avait composé, de verve, dès le lendemain:

«Pourquoi ces festons, ces fleurs, ces guirlandes? Où courait cette foule comme les flots d'une mer en furie, sous les torrents d'un soleil tropical qui répandait sa chaleur sur nos guérets?»

Ensuite, il parlait de la condition des paysans. Certes, le gouvernement faisait beaucoup, mais, pas assez! «Du courage! lui criait-il; mille réformes sont indispensables, accomplissons-les.» Puis, abordant l'entrée du Conseiller, il n'oubliait point «l'air martial de notre milice», ni «nos plus sémillantes villageoises», ni «les vieillards à tête chauve, sorte de patriarches qui étaient là, et dont quelques-uns, débris de nos immortelles phalanges, sentaient encore battre leurs coeurs au son mâle des tambours.» Il se citait des premiers parmi les membres du jury, et même il rappelait, dans une note, que M. Homais, pharmacien, avait envoyé un mémoire sur le cidre à la Société d'agriculture. Quand il arrivait à la distribution des récompenses, il dépeignait la joie des lauré-

prize-winners in dithyrambic strophes. "The father embraced the son, the brother the brother, the husband his consort. More than one showed his humble medal with pride; and no doubt when he got home to his good housewife, he hung it up weeping on the modest walls of his cot.

"About six o'clock a banquet prepared in the meadow of Monsieur Leigeard brought together the principal personages of the fete. The greatest cordiality reigned here. Divers toasts were proposed: Monsieur Lieuvain, the King; Monsieur Tuvache, the Prefect; Monsieur Derozerays, Agriculture; Monsieur Homais, Industry and the Fine Arts, those twin sisters; Monsieur Leplichey, Progress. In the evening some brilliant fireworks on a sudden illumined the air. One would have called it a veritable kaleidoscope, a real operatic scene; and for a moment our little locality might have thought itself transported into the midst of a dream of the 'Thousand and One Nights.'

"Let us state that no untoward event disturbed this family meeting."

And he added: "Only the absence of the clergy was remarked. No doubt the priests understand progress in another fashion. Just as you please, messieurs the followers of Loyola!"

ats en traits dithyrambiques. Le père embrassait son fils, le frère le frère, l'époux l'épouse. Plus d'un montrait avec orgueil son humble médaille, et sans doute, revenu chez lui, près de sa bonne ménagère, il l'aura suspendue en pleurant aux murs discrets de sa chaumine.

«Vers six heures, un banquet, dressé dans l'herbage de M. Liégeard, a réuni les principaux assistants de la fête. La plus grande cordialité n'a cessé d'y régner. Divers toasts ont été portés: M. Lieuvain, au monarque! M. Tuvache, au préfet! M. Derozerays, à l'agriculture! M. Homais, à l'industrie et aux beaux-arts, ces deux soeurs! M. Leplichey, aux améliorations! Le soir, un brillant feu d'artifice a tout à coup illuminé les airs. On eût dit un véritable kaléidoscope, un vrai décor d'Opéra, et un moment notre petite localité, a pu se croire transportée au milieu d'un rêve des Mille et une Nuits.

«Constatons qu'aucun événement fâcheux n'est venu troubler cette réunion de famille.»

Et il ajoutait: «On y a seulement remarqué l'absence du clergé. Sans doute les sacristies entendent le progrès d'une autre manière. Libre à vous, messieurs de Loyola!»

# Chapter 9

Six weeks passed. Rodolphe did not come again. At last one evening he appeared.

The day after the show he had said to himself:

"We mustn't go back too soon; that would be a mistake."

And at the end of a week he had gone off hunting. After the hunting he had thought it was too late, and then he reasoned thus—

"If from the first day she loved me, she must from impatience to see me again love me more. Let's go on with it!"

And he knew that his calculation had been right when, on entering the room, he saw Emma turn pale.

She was alone. The day was drawing in. The small muslin curtain along the windows deepened the twilight, and the gilding of the barometer, on which the rays of the sun fell, shone in the looking-glass between the meshes of the coral.

Rodolphe remained standing, and Emma hardly answered his first conventional phrases.

"I," he said, "have been busy. I have been ill."

"Seriously?" she cried.

"Well," said Rodolphe, sitting down at her side on a footstool, "no; it was because I did not want to come back."

"Why?"

"Can you not guess?"

He looked at her again, but so hard that she lowered her head, blushing. He went on:

"Emma!"

"Sir," she said, drawing back a little.

"Ah! you see," replied he in a melancholy voice, "that I was right not to come back; for this name, this name that fills my whole soul, and that escaped me, you forbid me to use! Madame Bovary! why all

# Chapitre 9

Six semaines s'écoulèrent. Rodolphe ne revint pas. Un soir, enfin, il parut.

Il s'était dit, le lendemain des comices:

— N'y retournons pas de sitôt, ce serait une faute.

Et, au bout de la semaine, il était parti pour la chasse. Après la chasse, il avait songé qu'il était trop tard, puis il fit ce raisonnement:

— Mais, si du premier jour elle m'a aimé, elle doit, par l'impatience de me revoir, m'aimer davantage. Continuons donc!

Et il comprit que son calcul avait été bon lorsque, en entrant dans la salle, il aperçut Emma pâlir.

Elle était seule. Le jour tombait. Les petits rideaux de mousseline, le long des vitres, épaississaient le crépuscule, et la dorure du baromètre, sur qui frappait un rayon de soleil, étalait des feux dans la glace, entre les découpures du polypier.

Rodolphe resta debout; et à peine si Emma répondit à ses premières phrases de politesse.

— Moi, dit-il, j'ai eu des affaires. J'ai été malade.

— Gravement? s'écria-t-elle.

— Eh bien, fit Rodolphe en s'asseyant à ses côtés sur un tabouret, non!... C'est que je n'ai pas voulu revenir.

— Pourquoi?

— Vous ne devinez pas?

Il la regarda encore une fois, mais d'une façon si violente qu'elle baissa la tête en rougissant. Il reprit:

— Emma...

— Monsieur! fit-elle en s'écartant un peu.

— Ah! vous voyez bien, répliqua-t-il d'une voix mélancolique, que j'avais raison de vouloir ne pas revenir; car ce nom, ce nom qui remplit mon âme et qui m'est échappé, vous me l'interdisez! Madame Bovary!...

the world calls you thus! Besides, it is not your name; it is the name of another!"

He repeated:

"Of another!"

And he hid his face in his hands.

"Yes, I think of you constantly. The memory of you drives me to despair. Ah! forgive me! I will leave you! Farewell! I will go far away, so far that you will never hear of me again; and yet—to-day—I know not what force impelled me towards you. For one does not struggle against Heaven; one cannot resist the smile of angels; one is carried away by that which is beautiful, charming, adorable."

It was the first time that Emma had heard such words spoken to herself, and her pride, like one who reposes bathed in warmth, expanded softly and fully at this glowing language.

"But if I did not come," he continued, "if I could not see you, at least I have gazed long on all that surrounds you. At night-every night-I arose; I came hither; I watched your house, its glimmering in the moon, the trees in the garden swaying before your window, and the little lamp, a gleam shining through the window-panes in the darkness. Ah! you never knew that there, so near you, so far from you, was a poor wretch!"

She turned towards him with a sob.

"Oh, you are good!" she said.

"No, I love you, that is all! You do not doubt that! Tell me—one word—only one word!"

And Rodolphe imperceptibly glided from the footstool to the ground; but a sound of wooden shoes was heard in the kitchen, and he noticed the door of the room was not closed.

"How kind it would be of you," he went on, rising, "if you would humour a whim of mine."

It was to go over her house; he wanted to know it; and Madame Bovary seeing no objection to this, they both rose, when Charles came in.

"Good morning, doctor," Rodolphe said to him.

Eh! tout le monde vous appelle comme cela!... Ce n'est pas votre nom, d'ailleurs; c'est le nom d'un autre!

Il répéta:

— D'un autre!

Et il se cacha la figure entre les mains.

— Oui, je pense à vous continuellement!... Votre souvenir me désespère! Ah! pardon!... Je vous quitte... Adieu!... J'irai loin..., si loin, que vous n'entendrez plus parler de moi!... Et cependant..., aujourd'hui..., je ne sais quelle force encore m'a poussé vers vous! Car on ne lutte pas contre le ciel, on ne résiste point au sourire des anges! On se laisse entraîner par ce qui est beau, charmant, adorable!

C'était la première fois qu'Emma s'entendait dire ces choses; et son orgueil, comme quelqu'un qui se délasse dans une étuve, s'étirait mollement et tout entier à la chaleur de ce langage.

— Mais, si je ne suis pas venu, continua-t-il, si je n'ai pu vous voir, ah! du moins j'ai bien contemplé ce qui vous entoure. La nuit, toutes les nuits, je me relevais, j'arrivais jusqu'ici, je regardais votre maison, le toit qui brillait sous la lune, les arbres du jardin qui se balançaient à votre fenêtre, et une petite lampe, une lueur, qui brillait à travers les carreaux, dans l'ombre. Ah! vous ne saviez guère qu'il y avait là, si près et si loin, un pauvre misérable...

Elle se tourna vers lui avec un sanglot.

— Oh! vous êtes bon! dit-elle.

— Non, je vous aime, voilà tout! Vous n'en doutez pas! Dites-le- moi; un mot! un seul mot!

Et Rodolphe, insensiblement, se laissa glisser du tabouret jusqu'à terre; mais on entendit un bruit de sabots dans la cuisine, et la porte de la salle, il s'en aperçut, n'était pas fermée.

— Que vous seriez charitable, poursuivit-il en se relevant, de satisfaire une fantaisie!

C'était de visiter sa maison; il désirait la connaître; et, madame Bovary n'y voyant point d'inconvénient, ils se levaient tous les deux, quand Charles entra.

— Bonjour, docteur, lui dit Rodolphe.

The doctor, flattered at this unexpected title, launched out into obsequious phrases. Of this the other took advantage to pull himself together a little.

"Madame was speaking to me," he then said, "about her health."

Charles interrupted him; he had indeed a thousand anxieties; his wife's palpitations of the heart were beginning again. Then Rodolphe asked if riding would not be good.

"Certainly! excellent! just the thing! There's an idea! You ought to follow it up."

And as she objected that she had no horse, Monsieur Rodolphe offered one. She refused his offer; he did not insist. Then to explain his visit he said that his ploughman, the man of the blood-letting, still suffered from giddiness.

"I'll call around," said Bovary.

"No, no! I'll send him to you; we'll come; that will be more convenient for you."

"Ah! very good! I thank you."

And as soon as they were alone:

"Why don't you accept Monsieur Boulanger's kind offer?"

She assumed a sulky air, invented a thousand excuses, and finally declared that perhaps it would look odd.

"Well, what the deuce do I care for that?" said Charles, making a pirouette. "Health before everything! You are wrong."

"And how do you think I can ride when I haven't got a habit?"

"You must order one," he answered.

The riding-habit decided her.

When the habit was ready, Charles wrote to Monsieur Boulanger that his wife was at his command, and that they counted on his good-nature.

The next day at noon Rodolphe appeared at Charles's door with two saddle-horses. One had pink rosettes at his ears and a deerskin side-saddle.

Le médecin, flatté de ce titre inattendu, se répandit en obséquiosités, et l'autre en profita pour se remettre un peu.

— Madame m'entretenait, fit-il donc, de sa santé…

Charles l'interrompit: il avait mille inquiétudes, en effet; les oppressions de sa femme recommençaient. Alors Rodolphe demanda si l'exercice du cheval ne serait pas bon.

— Certes! excellent, parfait!… Voilà une idée! Tu devrais la suivre.

Et, comme elle objectait qu'elle n'avait point de cheval, M. Rodolphe en offrit un; elle refusa ses offres; il n'insista pas; puis, afin de motiver sa visite, il conta que son charretier, l'homme à la saignée, éprouvait toujours des étourdissements.

— J'y passerai, dit Bovary.

— Non, non, je vous l'enverrai; nous viendrons, ce sera plus commode pour vous.

— Ah! fort bien. Je vous remercie.

Et, dès qu'ils furent seuls:

— Pourquoi n'acceptes-tu pas les propositions de M. Boulanger, qui sont si gracieuses?

Elle prit un air boudeur, chercha mille excuses, et déclara finalement que cela peut-être semblerait drôle.

— Ah! je m'en moque pas mal! dit Charles en faisant une pirouette. La santé avant tout! Tu as tort!

— Eh! comment veux-tu que je monte à cheval, puisque je n'ai pas d'amazone?

— Il faut t'en commander une! répondit-il.

L'amazone la décida.

Quand le costume fut prêt, Charles écrivit à M. Boulanger que sa femme était à sa disposition, et qu'ils comptaient sur sa complaisance.

Le lendemain, à midi, Rodolphe arriva devant la porte de Charles avec deux chevaux de maître. L'un portait des pompons roses aux oreilles et une selle de femme en peau de daim.

Rodolphe had put on high soft boots, saying to himself that no doubt she had never seen anything like them. In fact, Emma was charmed with his appearance as he stood on the landing in his great velvet coat and white corduroy breeches. She was ready; she was waiting for him.

Justin escaped from the chemist's to see her start, and the chemist also came out. He was giving Monsieur Boulanger a little good advice.

"An accident happens so easily. Be careful! Your horses perhaps are mettlesome."

She heard a noise above her; it was Felicite drumming on the windowpanes to amuse little Berthe. The child blew her a kiss; her mother answered with a wave of her whip.

"A pleasant ride!" cried Monsieur Homais. "Prudence! above all, prudence!"

And he flourished his newspaper as he saw them disappear.

As soon as he felt the ground, Emma's horse set off at a gallop. Rodolphe galloped by her side. Now and then they exchanged a word. Her figure slightly bent, her hand well up, and her right arm stretched out, she gave herself up to the cadence of the movement that rocked her in her saddle.

At the bottom of the hill Rodolphe gave his horse its head; they started together at a bound, then at the top suddenly the horses stopped, and her large blue veil fell about her.

It was early in October. There was fog over the land. Hazy clouds hovered on the horizon between the outlines of the hills; others, rent asunder, floated up and disappeared. Sometimes through a rift in the clouds, beneath a ray of sunshine, gleamed from afar the roots of Yonville, with the gardens at the water's edge, the yards, the walls and the church steeple. Emma half closed her eyes to pick out her house, and never had this poor village where she lived appeared so small. From the height on which they were the whole valley seemed an immense pale lake sending off its vapour into the air. Clumps of trees here and there stood out like black rocks, and the tall lines of the poplars that rose above the mist were like a beach stirred by the wind.

Rodolphe avait mis de longues bottes molles, se disant que sans doute elle n'en avait jamais vu de pareilles; en effet, Emma fut charmée, de sa tournure, lorsqu'il apparut sur le palier avec son grand habit de velours et sa culotte de tricot blanc. Elle était prête, elle l'attendait.

Justin s'échappa de la pharmacie pour la voir, et l'apothicaire aussi se dérangea. Il faisait à M. Boulanger des recommandations:

— Un malheur arrive si vite! Prenez garde! Vos chevaux peut-être sont fougueux!

Elle entendit du bruit au-dessus de sa tête: c'était Félicité qui tambourinait contre les carreaux pour divertir la petite Berthe. L'enfant envoya de loin un baiser; sa mère lui répondit d'un signe avec le pommeau de sa cravache.

— Bonne promenade! cria M. Homais. De la prudence, surtout! de la prudence!

Et il agita son journal en les regardant s'éloigner.

Dès qu'il sentit la terre, le cheval d'Emma prit le galop. Rodolphe galopait à côté d'elle. Par moments ils échangeaient une parole. La figure un peu baissée, la main haute et le bras droit déployé, elle s'abandonnait à la cadence du mouvement qui la berçait sur la selle.

Au bas de la côte, Rodolphe lâcha les rênes; ils partirent ensemble, d'un seul bond; puis, en haut, tout à coup, les chevaux s'arrêtèrent, et son grand voile bleu retomba.

On était aux premiers jours d'octobre. Il y avait du brouillard sur la campagne. Des vapeurs s'allongeaient à l'horizon, entre le contour des collines; et d'autres, se déchirant, montaient, se perdaient. Quelquefois, dans un écartement des nuées, sous un rayon de soleil, on apercevait au loin les toits d'Yonville, avec les jardins au bord de l'eau, les cours, les murs, et le clocher de l'église. Emma fermait à demi les paupières pour reconnaître sa maison, et jamais ce pauvre village où elle vivait ne lui avait semblé si petit. De la hauteur où ils étaient, toute la vallée paraissait un immense lac pâle, s'évaporant à l'air. Les massifs d'arbres, de place en place, saillissaient comme des rochers noirs; et les hautes lignes des peupliers, qui dépassaient la brume, figuraient des grèves que le vent remuait.

By the side, on the turf between the pines, a brown light shimmered in the warm atmosphere. The earth, ruddy like the powder of tobacco, deadened the noise of their steps, and with the edge of their shoes the horses as they walked kicked the fallen fir cones in front of them.

Rodolphe and Emma thus went along the skirt of the wood. She turned away from time to time to avoid his look, and then she saw only the pine trunks in lines, whose monotonous succession made her a little giddy. The horses were panting; the leather of the saddles creaked.

Just as they were entering the forest the sun shone out.

"God protects us!" said Rodolphe.

"Do you think so?" she said.

"Forward! forward!" he continued.

He "tchk'd" with his tongue. The two beasts set off at a trot.

Long ferns by the roadside caught in Emma's stirrup. Rodolphe leant forward and removed them as they rode along. At other times, to turn aside the branches, he passed close to her, and Emma felt his knee brushing against her leg. The sky was now blue, the leaves no longer stirred. There were spaces full of heather in flower, and plots of violets alternated with the confused patches of the trees that were grey, fawn, or golden coloured, according to the nature of their leaves. Often in the thicket was heard the fluttering of wings, or else the hoarse, soft cry of the ravens flying off amidst the oaks.

They dismounted. Rodolphe fastened up the horses. She walked on in front on the moss between the paths.

But her long habit got in her way, although she held it up by the skirt; and Rodolphe, walking behind her, saw between the black cloth and the black shoe the fineness of her white stocking, that seemed to him as if it were a part of her nakedness.

She stopped.

"I am tired," she said.

"Come, try again," he went on. "Courage!"

Then some hundred paces farther on she again stopped, and through her veil, that fell sideways from her man's hat over her hips, her face

À côté, sur la pelouse, entre les sapins, une lumière brune circulait dans l'atmosphère tiède. La terre, roussâtre comme de la poudre de tabac, amortissait le bruit des pas; et, du bout de leurs fers, en marchant, les chevaux poussaient devant eux des pommes de pin tombées.

Rodolphe et Emma suivirent ainsi la lisière du bois. Elle se détournait de temps à autre afin d'éviter son regard, et alors elle ne voyait que les troncs des sapins alignés, dont la succession continue l'étourdissait un peu. Les chevaux soufflaient. Le cuir des selles craquait.

Au moment où ils entrèrent dans la forêt, le soleil parut.

— Dieu nous protège! dit Rodolphe.

— Vous croyez? fit-elle.

— Avançons! avançons! reprit-il.

Il claqua de la langue. Les deux bêtes couraient.

De longues fougères, au bord du chemin, se prenaient dans l'étrier d'Emma. Rodolphe, tout en allant, se penchait et il les retirait à mesure. D'autres fois, pour écarter les branches, il passait près d'elle, et Emma sentait son genou lui frôler la jambe. Le ciel était devenu bleu. Les feuilles ne remuaient pas. Il y avait de grands espaces pleins de bruyères tout en fleurs; et des nappes de violettes s'alternaient avec le fouillis des arbres, qui étaient gris, fauves ou dorés, selon la diversité des feuillages. Souvent on entendait, sous les buissons, glisser un petit battement d'ailes, ou bien le cri rauque et doux des corbeaux, qui s'envolaient dans les chênes.

Ils descendirent. Rodolphe attacha les chevaux. Elle allait devant, sur la mousse, entre les ornières.

Mais sa robe trop longue l'embarrassait, bien qu'elle la portât relevée par la queue, et Rodolphe, marchant derrière elle, contemplait entre ce drap noir et la bottine noire, la délicatesse de son bas blanc, qui lui semblait quelque chose de sa nudité.

Elle s'arrêta.

— Je suis fatiguée, dit-elle.

— Allons, essayez encore! reprit-il. Du courage!

Puis, cent pas plus loin, elle s'arrêta de nouveau; et, à travers son voile, qui de son chapeau d'homme descendait obliquement sur ses hanches,

appeared in a bluish transparency as if she were floating under azure waves.

"But where are we going?"

He did not answer. She was breathing irregularly. Rodolphe looked round him biting his moustache.

They came to a larger space where the coppice had been cut. They sat down on the trunk of a fallen tree, and Rodolphe began speaking to her of his love.

He did not begin by frightening her with compliments. He was calm, serious, melancholy.

Emma listened to him with bowed head, and stirred the bits of wood on the ground with the tip of her foot.

But at the words:

"Are not our destinies now one?"

"Oh, no!" she replied. "You know that well. It is impossible!" She rose to go. He seized her by the wrist. She stopped. Then, having gazed at him for a few moments with an amorous and humid look, she said hurriedly:

"Ah! do not speak of it again! Where are the horses? Let us go back."

He made a gesture of anger and annoyance. She repeated:

"Where are the horses? Where are the horses?"

Then smiling a strange smile, his pupil fixed, his teeth set, he advanced with outstretched arms. She recoiled trembling. She stammered:

"Oh, you frighten me! You hurt me! Let me go!"

"If it must be," he went on, his face changing.

And he again became respectful, caressing, timid. She gave him her arm. They went back. He said:

"What was the matter with you? Why? I do not understand. You were mistaken, no doubt. In my soul you are as a Madonna on a pedestal, in a place lofty, secure, immaculate. But I need you to live! I must have your eyes, your voice, your thought! Be my friend, my sister, my angel!"

And he put out his arm round her waist. She feebly tried to disengage herself. He supported her thus as they walked along.

on distinguait son visage dans une transparence bleuâtre, comme si elle eût nagé sous des flots d'azur.

— Où allons-nous donc?

Il ne répondit rien. Elle respirait d'une façon saccadée. Rodolphe jetait les yeux autour de lui et il se mordait la moustache.

Ils arrivèrent à un endroit plus large, où l'on avait abattu des baliveaux. Ils s'assirent sur un tronc d'arbre renversé, et Rodolphe se mit à lui parler de son amour.

Il ne l'effraya point d'abord par des compliments. Il fut calme, sérieux, mélancolique.

Emma l'écoutait la tête basse, et tout en remuant, avec la pointe de son pied, des copeaux par terre.

Mais, à cette phrase:

— Est-ce que nos destinées maintenant ne sont pas communes.

— Eh non! répondit-elle. Vous le savez bien. C'est impossible.

Elle se leva pour partir. Il la saisit au poignet. Elle s'arrêta. Puis, l'ayant considéré quelques minutes d'un oeil amoureux et tout humide, elle dit vivement:

— Ah! tenez, n'en parlons plus... Où sont les chevaux? Retournons.

Il eut un geste de colère et d'ennui. Elle répéta:

— Où sont les chevaux? où sont les chevaux?

Alors, souriant d'un sourire étrange et la prunelle fixe, les dents serrées, il s'avança en écartant les bras. Elle se recula tremblante. Elle balbutiait:

— Oh! vous me faites peur! vous me faites mal! Partons.

— Puisqu'il le faut, reprit-il en changeant de visage.

Et il redevint aussitôt respectueux, caressant, timide. Elle lui donna son bras. Ils s'en retournèrent. Il disait:

— Qu'aviez-vous donc? Pourquoi? Je n'ai pas compris! Vous vous méprenez, sans doute? Vous êtes dans mon âme comme une madone sur un piédestal, à une place haute, solide et immaculée. Mais j'ai besoin de vous pour vivre! J'ai besoin de vos yeux, de votre voix, de votre pensée. Soyez mon amie, ma soeur, mon ange!

Et il allongeait son bras et lui en entourait la taille. Elle tâchait de se dégager mollement. Il la soutenait ainsi, en marchant.

But they heard the two horses browsing on the leaves.

"Oh! one moment!" said Rodolphe. "Do not let us go! Stay!"

He drew her farther on to a small pool where duckweeds made a greenness on the water. Faded water lilies lay motionless between the reeds. At the noise of their steps in the grass, frogs jumped away to hide themselves.

"I am wrong! I am wrong!" she said. "I am mad to listen to you!"

"Why? Emma! Emma!"

"Oh, Rodolphe!" said the young woman slowly, leaning on his shoulder.

The cloth of her habit caught against the velvet of his coat. She threw back her white neck, swelling with a sigh, and faltering, in tears, with a long shudder and hiding her face, she gave herself up to him.

The shades of night were falling; the horizontal sun passing between the branches dazzled the eyes. Here and there around her, in the leaves or on the ground, trembled luminous patches, as it hummingbirds flying about had scattered their feathers. Silence was everywhere; something sweet seemed to come forth from the trees; she felt her heart, whose beating had begun again, and the blood coursing through her flesh like a stream of milk. Then far away, beyond the wood, on the other hills, she heard a vague prolonged cry, a voice which lingered, and in silence she heard it mingling like music with the last pulsations of her throbbing nerves. Rodolphe, a cigar between his lips, was mending with his penknife one of the two broken bridles.

They returned to Yonville by the same road. On the mud they saw again the traces of their horses side by side, the same thickets, the same stones to the grass; nothing around them seemed changed; and yet for her something had happened more stupendous than if the mountains had moved in their places. Rodolphe now and again bent forward and took her hand to kiss it.

She was charming on horseback—upright, with her slender waist, her knee bent on the mane of her horse, her face somewhat flushed by the fresh air in the red of the evening.

Mais ils entendirent les deux chevaux qui broutaient le feuillage.

— Oh! encore, dit Rodolphe. Ne partons pas! Restez!

Il l'entraîna plus loin, autour d'un petit étang, où des lentilles d'eau faisaient une verdure sur les ondes. Des nénuphars flétris se tenaient immobiles entre les joncs. Au bruit de leurs pas dans l'herbe, des grenouilles sautaient pour se cacher.

— J'ai tort, j'ai tort, disait-elle. Je suis folle de vous entendre.

— Pourquoi?... Emma! Emma!

— Oh! Rodolphe!... fit lentement la jeune femme en se penchant sur son épaule.

Le drap de sa robe s'accrochait au velours de l'habit. Elle renversa son cou blanc, qui se gonflait d'un soupir; et, défaillante, tout en pleurs, avec un long frémissement et se cachant la figure, elle s'abandonna.

Les ombres du soir descendaient; le soleil horizontal, passant entre les branches, lui éblouissait les yeux. Çà et là, tout autour d'elle, dans les feuilles ou par terre, des taches lumineuses tremblaient, comme si des colibris, en volant, eussent éparpillé leurs plumes. Le silence était partout; quelque chose de doux semblait sortir des arbres; elle sentait son coeur, dont les battements recommençaient, et le sang circuler dans sa chair comme un fleuve de lait. Alors, elle entendit tout au loin, au delà du bois, sur les autres collines, un cri vague et prolongé, une voix qui se traînait, et elle l'écoutait silencieusement, se mêlant comme une musique aux dernières vibrations de ses nerfs émus. Rodolphe, le cigare aux dents, raccommodait avec son canif une des deux brides cassée.

Ils s'en revinrent à Yonville, par le même chemin. Ils revirent sur la boue les traces de leurs chevaux, côte à côte, et les mêmes buissons, les mêmes cailloux dans l'herbe. Rien autour d'eux n'avait changé; et pour elle, cependant, quelque chose était survenu de plus considérable que si les montagnes se fussent déplacées. Rodolphe, de temps à autre, se penchait et lui prenait sa main pour la baiser.

Elle était charmante, à cheval! Droite, avec sa taille mince, le genou plié sur la crinière de sa bête et un peu colorée par le grand air, dans la rougeur du soir.

On entering Yonville she made her horse prance in the road. People looked at her from the windows.

At dinner her husband thought she looked well, but she pretended not to hear him when he inquired about her ride, and she remained sitting there with her elbow at the side of her plate between the two lighted candles.

"Emma!" he said.

"What?"

"Well, I spent the afternoon at Monsieur Alexandre's. He has an old cob, still very fine, only a little broken-kneed, and that could be bought; I am sure, for a hundred crowns."

He added:

"And thinking it might please you, I have bespoken it—bought it. Have I done right? Do tell me?"

She nodded her head in assent; then a quarter of an hour later:

"Are you going out to-night?" she asked.

"Yes. Why?"

"Oh, nothing, nothing, my dear!"

And as soon as she had got rid of Charles she went and shut herself up in her room.

At first she felt stunned; she saw the trees, the paths, the ditches, Rodolphe, and she again felt the pressure of his arm, while the leaves rustled and the reeds whistled.

But when she saw herself in the glass she wondered at her face. Never had her eyes been so large, so black, of so profound a depth. Something subtle about her being transfigured her.

She repeated, "I have a lover! a lover!" delighting at the idea as if a second puberty had come to her. So at last she was to know those joys of love, that fever of happiness of which she had despaired! She was entering upon marvels where all would be passion, ecstasy, delirium. An azure infinity encompassed her, the heights of sentiment sparkled under her thought, and ordinary existence appeared only afar off, down below in the shade, through the interspaces of these heights.

En entrant dans Yonville, elle caracola sur les pavés. On la regardait des fenêtres.

Son mari, au dîner, lui trouva bonne mine; mais elle eut l'air de ne pas l'entendre lorsqu'il s'informa de sa promenade; et elle restait le coude au bord de son assiette, entre les deux bougies qui brûlaient.

— Emma! dit-il.

— Quoi?

— Eh bien, j'ai passé cette après-midi chez M. Alexandre; il a une ancienne pouliche encore fort belle, un peu couronnée seulement, et qu'on aurait, je suis sûr, pour une centaine d'écus…

Il ajouta:

— Pensant même que cela te serait agréable, je l'ai retenue…, je l'ai achetée… Ai-je bien fait? Dis-moi donc.

Elle remua la tête en signe d'assentiment; puis, un quart d'heure après:

— Sors-tu ce soir? demanda-t-elle.

— Oui. Pourquoi?

— Oh! rien, rien, mon ami.

Et, dès qu'elle fut débarrassée de Charles, elle monta s'enfermer dans sa chambre.

D'abord, ce fut comme un étourdissement; elle voyait les arbres, les chemins, les fossés, Rodolphe, et elle sentait encore l'étreinte de ses bras, tandis que le feuillage frémissait et que les joncs sifflaient.

Mais, en s'apercevant dans la glace, elle s'étonna de son visage. Jamais elle n'avait eu les yeux si grands, si noirs, ni d'une telle profondeur. Quelque chose de subtil épandu sur sa personne la transfigurait.

Elle se répétait: «J'ai un amant! un amant!» se délectant à cette idée comme à celle d'une autre puberté qui lui serait survenue. Elle allait donc posséder enfin ces joies de l'amour, cette fièvre du bonheur dont elle avait désespéré. Elle entrait dans quelque chose de merveilleux où tout serait passion, extase, délire; une immensité bleuâtre l'entourait, les sommets du sentiment étincelaient sous sa pensée, et l'existence ordinaire n'apparaissait qu'au loin, tout en bas, dans l'ombre, entre les intervalles de ces hauteurs.

Then she recalled the heroines of the books that she had read, and the lyric legion of these adulterous women began to sing in her memory with the voice of sisters that charmed her. She became herself, as it were, an actual part of these imaginings, and realised the love-dream of her youth as she saw herself in this type of amorous women whom she had so envied. Besides, Emma felt a satisfaction of revenge. Had she not suffered enough? But now she triumphed, and the love so long pent up burst forth in full joyous bubblings. She tasted it without remorse, without anxiety, without trouble.

The day following passed with a new sweetness. They made vows to one another She told him of her sorrows. Rodolphe interrupted her with kisses; and she looking at him through half-closed eyes, asked him to call her again by her name—to say that he loved her They were in the forest, as yesterday, in the shed of some woodenshoe maker. The walls were of straw, and the roof so low they had to stoop. They were seated side by side on a bed of dry leaves.

From that day forth they wrote to one another regularly every evening. Emma placed her letter at the end of the garden, by the river, in a fissure of the wall. Rodolphe came to fetch it, and put another there, that she always found fault with as too short.

One morning, when Charles had gone out before day break, she was seized with the fancy to see Rodolphe at once. She would go quickly to La Huchette, stay there an hour, and be back again at Yonville while everyone was still asleep. This idea made her pant with desire, and she soon found herself in the middle of the field, walking with rapid steps, without looking behind her.

Day was just breaking. Emma from afar recognised her lover's house. Its two dove-tailed weathercocks stood out black against the pale dawn.

Beyond the farmyard there was a detached building that she thought must be the chateau She entered—it was if the doors at her approach had opened wide of their own accord. A large straight staircase led up to the corridor. Emma raised the latch of a door, and suddenly at the end of the room she saw a man sleeping. It was Rodolphe. She uttered a cry.

Alors elle se rappela les héroïnes des livres qu'elle avait lus, et la légion lyrique de ces femmes adultères se mit à chanter dans sa mémoire avec des voix de soeurs qui la charmaient. Elle devenait elle-même comme une partie véritable de ces imaginations et réalisait la longue rêverie de sa jeunesse, en se considérant dans ce type d'amoureuse qu'elle avait tant envié. D'ailleurs, Emma éprouvait une satisfaction de vengeance. N'avait-elle pas assez souffert! Mais elle triomphait maintenant, et l'amour, si longtemps contenu, jaillissait tout entier avec des bouillonnements joyeux. Elle le savourait sans remords, sans inquiétude, sans trouble.

La journée du lendemain se passa dans une douceur nouvelle. Ils se firent des serments. Elle lui raconta ses tristesses. Rodolphe l'interrompait par ses baisers; et elle lui demandait, en le contemplant les paupières à demi closes, de l'appeler encore par son nom et de répéter qu'il l'aimait. C'était dans la forêt, comme la veille, sous une hutte de sabotiers. Les murs en étaient de paille et le toit descendait si bas, qu'il fallait se tenir courbé. Ils étaient assis l'un contre l'autre, sur un lit de feuilles sèches.

À partir de ce jour-là, ils s'écrivirent régulièrement tous les soirs. Emma portait sa lettre au bout du jardin, près de la rivière, dans une fissure de la terrasse. Rodolphe venait l'y chercher et en plaçait une autre, qu'elle accusait toujours d'être trop courte.

Un matin, que Charles était sorti dès avant l'aube, elle fut prise par la fantaisie de voir Rodolphe à l'instant. On pouvait arriver promptement à la Huchette, y rester une heure et être rentré dans Yonville que tout le monde encore serait endormi. Cette idée la fit haleter de convoitise, et elle se trouva bientôt au milieu de la prairie, où elle marchait à pas rapides, sans regarder derrière elle.

Le jour commençait à paraître. Emma, de loin, reconnut la maison de son amant, dont les deux girouettes à queue-d'aronde se découpaient en noir sur le crépuscule pâle.

Après la cour de la ferme, il y avait un corps de logis qui devait être le château. Elle y entra, comme si les murs, à son approche, se fussent écartés d'eux-mêmes. Un grand escalier droit montait vers un corridor. Emma tourna la clenche d'une porte, et tout à coup, au fond de la chambre, elle aperçut un homme qui dormait. C'était Rodolphe. Elle poussa un cri.

"You here? You here?" he repeated. "How did you manage to come? Ah! your dress is damp."

"I love you," she answered, throwing her arms about his neck.

This first piece of daring successful, now every time Charles went out early Emma dressed quickly and slipped on tiptoe down the steps that led to the waterside.

But when the plank for the cows was taken up, she had to go by the walls alongside of the river; the bank was slippery; in order not to fall she caught hold of the tufts of faded wallflowers. Then she went across ploughed fields, in which she sank, stumbling; and clogging her thin shoes. Her scarf, knotted round her head, fluttered to the wind in the meadows. She was afraid of the oxen; she began to run; she arrived out of breath, with rosy cheeks, and breathing out from her whole person a fresh perfume of sap, of verdure, of the open air. At this hour Rodolphe still slept. It was like a spring morning coming into his room.

The yellow curtains along the windows let a heavy, whitish light enter softly. Emma felt about, opening and closing her eyes, while the drops of dew hanging from her hair formed, as it were, a topaz aureole around her face. Rodolphe, laughing, drew her to him, and pressed her to his breast.

Then she examined the apartment, opened the drawers of the tables, combed her hair with his comb, and looked at herself in his shaving-glass. Often she even put between her teeth the big pipe that lay on the table by the bed, amongst lemons and pieces of sugar near a bottle of water.

It took them a good quarter of an hour to say goodbye. Then Emma cried. She would have wished never to leave Rodolphe. Something stronger than herself forced her to him; so much so, that one day, seeing her come unexpectedly, he frowned as one put out.

"What is the matter with you?" she said. "Are you ill? Tell me!"

At last he declared with a serious air that her visits were becoming imprudent—that she was compromising herself.

— Te voilà! te voilà! répétait-il. Comment as-tu fait pour venir?… Ah! ta robe est mouillée!

— Je t'aime! répondit-elle en lui passant les bras autour du cou.

Cette première audace lui ayant réussi, chaque fois maintenant que Charles sortait de bonne heure, Emma s'habillait vite et descendait à pas de loup le perron qui conduisait au bord de l'eau.

Mais, quand la planche aux vaches était levée, il fallait suivre les murs qui longeaient la rivière; la berge était glissante; elle s'accrochait de la main, pour ne pas tomber, aux bouquets de ravenelles flétries. Puis elle prenait à travers des champs en labour, où elle enfonçait, trébuchait et empêtrait ses bottines minces. Son foulard, noué sur sa tête, s'agitait au vent dans les herbages; elle avait peur des boeufs, elle se mettait à courir; elle arrivait essoufflée, les joues roses, et exhalant de toute sa personne un frais parfum de sève, de verdure et de grand air. Rodolphe, à cette heure-là, dormait encore. C'était comme une matinée de printemps qui entrait dans sa chambre.

Les rideaux jaunes, le long des fenêtres laissaient passer doucement une lourde lumière blonde. Emma tâtonnait en clignant des yeux, tandis que les gouttes de rosée suspendues à ses bandeaux faisaient comme une auréole de topazes tout autour de sa figure. Rodolphe, en riant, l'attirait à lui et il la prenait sur son coeur.

Ensuite, elle examinait l'appartement, elle ouvrait les tiroirs des meubles, elle se peignait avec son peigne et se regardait dans le miroir à barbe. Souvent même, elle mettait entre ses dents le tuyau d'une grosse pipe qui était sur la table de nuit, parmi des citrons et des morceaux de sucre, près d'une carafe d'eau.

Il leur fallait un bon quart d'heure pour les adieux. Alors Emma pleurait; elle aurait voulu ne jamais abandonner Rodolphe. Quelque chose de plus fort qu'elle la poussait vers lui, si bien qu'un jour, la voyant survenir à l'improviste, il fronça le visage comme quelqu'un de contrarié.

— Qu'as-tu donc? dit-elle. Souffres-tu? Parle-moi!

Enfin il déclara, d'un air sérieux, que ses visites devenaient imprudentes et qu'elle se compromettait.

# Chapter 10

Gradually Rodolphe's fears took possession of her. At first, love had intoxicated her; and she had thought of nothing beyond. But now that he was indispensable to her life, she feared to lose anything of this, or even that it should be disturbed. When she came back from his house she looked all about her, anxiously watching every form that passed in the horizon, and every village window from which she could be seen. She listened for steps, cries, the noise of the ploughs, and she stopped short, white, and trembling more than the aspen leaves swaying overhead.

One morning as she was thus returning, she suddenly thought she saw the long barrel of a carbine that seemed to be aimed at her. It stuck out sideways from the end of a small tub half-buried in the grass on the edge of a ditch. Emma, half-fainting with terror, nevertheless walked on, and a man stepped out of the tub like a Jack-in-the-box. He had gaiters buckled up to the knees, his cap pulled down over his eyes, trembling lips, and a red nose. It was Captain Binet lying in ambush for wild ducks.

"You ought to have called out long ago!" he exclaimed; "When one sees a gun, one should always give warning."

The tax-collector was thus trying to hide the fright he had had, for a prefectorial order having prohibited duckhunting except in boats, Monsieur Binet, despite his respect for the laws, was infringing them, and so he every moment expected to see the rural guard turn up. But this anxiety whetted his pleasure, and, all alone in his tub, he congratulated himself on his luck and on his cuteness.

At sight of Emma he seemed relieved from a great weight, and at once entered upon a conversation.

"It isn't warm; it's nipping."

Emma answered nothing. He went on:

# Chapitre 10

Peu à peu, ces craintes de Rodolphe la gagnèrent. L'amour l'avait enivrée d'abord, et elle n'avait songé à rien au delà. Mais, à présent qu'il était indispensable à sa vie, elle craignait d'en perdre quelque chose, ou même qu'il ne fût troublé. Quand elle s'en revenait de chez lui, elle jetait tout alentour des regards inquiets, épiant chaque forme qui passait à l'horizon et chaque lucarne du village d'où l'on pouvait l'apercevoir. Elle écoutait les pas, les cris, le bruit des charrues; et elle s'arrêtait plus blême et plus tremblante que les feuilles des peupliers qui se balançaient sur sa tête.

Un matin, qu'elle s'en retournait ainsi, elle crut distinguer tout à coup le long canon d'une carabine qui semblait la tenir en joue. Il dépassait obliquement le bord d'un petit tonneau, à demi enfoui entre les herbes, sur la marge d'un fossé. Emma, prête à défaillir de terreur, avança cependant, et un homme sortit du tonneau, comme ces diables à boudin qui se dressent du fond des boîtes. Il avait des guêtres bouclées jusqu'aux genoux, sa casquette enfoncée jusqu'aux yeux, les lèvres grelottantes et le nez rouge. C'était le capitaine Binet, à l'affût des canards sauvages.

— Vous auriez dû parler de loin! s'écria-t-il. Quand on aperçoit un fusil, il faut toujours avertir.

Le percepteur, par là, tâchait de dissimuler la crainte qu'il venait d'avoir; car, un arrêté préfectoral ayant interdit la chasse aux canards autrement qu'en bateau, M. Binet, malgré son respect pour les lois, se trouvait en contravention. Aussi croyait-il à chaque minute entendre arriver le garde champêtre. Mais cette inquiétude irritait son plaisir, et, tout seul dans son tonneau, il s'applaudissait de son bonheur et de sa malice.

À la vue d'Emma, il parut soulagé d'un grand poids, et aussitôt, entamant la conversation:

— Il ne fait pas chaud, ça pique!

Emma ne répondit rien. Il poursuivit:

"And you're out so early?"

"Yes," she said stammering; "I am just coming from the nurse where my child is."

"Ah! very good! very good! For myself, I am here, just as you see me, since break of day; but the weather is so muggy, that unless one had the bird at the mouth of the gun—"

"Good evening, Monsieur Binet," she interrupted him, turning on her heel.

"Your servant, madame," he replied drily.

And he went back into his tub.

Emma regretted having left the tax-collector so abruptly. No doubt he would form unfavourable conjectures. The story about the nurse was the worst possible excuse, everyone at Yonville knowing that the little Bovary had been at home with her parents for a year. Besides, no one was living in this direction; this path led only to La Huchette. Binet, then, would guess whence she came, and he would not keep silence; he would talk, that was certain. She remained until evening racking her brain with every conceivable lying project, and had constantly before her eyes that imbecile with the game-bag.

Charles after dinner, seeing her gloomy, proposed, by way of distraction, to take her to the chemist's, and the first person she caught sight of in the shop was the taxcollector again. He was standing in front of the counter, lit up by the gleams of the red bottle, and was saying—

"Please give me half an ounce of vitriol."

"Justin," cried the druggist, "bring us the sulphuric acid."

Then to Emma, who was going up to Madame Homais' room:

"No, stay here; it isn't worth while going up; she is just coming down. Warm yourself at the stove in the meantime. Excuse me. Good-day, doctor," (for the chemist much enjoyed pronouncing the word "doctor," as if addressing another by it reflected on himself some of the grandeur that he found in it). "Now, take care not to upset the mortars! You'd better fetch some chairs from the little room; you know very well that the arm-chairs are not to be taken out of the drawing-room."

— Et vous voilà sortie de bien bonne heure?

— Oui, dit-elle en balbutiant; je viens de chez la nourrice où est mon enfant.

— Ah! fort bien! fort bien! Quant à moi, tel que vous me voyez, dès la pointe du jour je suis là; mais le temps est si crassineux, qu'à moins d'avoir la plume juste au bout…

— Bonsoir, monsieur Binet, interrompit-elle en lui tournant les talons.

— Serviteur, madame, reprit-il d'un ton sec.

Et il rentra dans son tonneau.

Emma se repentit d'avoir quitté si brusquement le percepteur. Sans doute, il allait faire des conjectures défavorables. L'histoire de la nourrice était la pire excuse, tout le monde sachant bien à Yonville que la petite Bovary, depuis un an, était revenue chez ses parents. D'ailleurs, personne n'habitait aux environs; ce chemin ne conduisait qu'à la Huchette; Binet donc avait deviné d'où elle venait, et il ne se tairait pas, il bavarderait, c'était certain! Elle resta jusqu'au soir à se torturer l'esprit dans tous les projets de mensonges imaginables, et ayant sans cesse devant les yeux cet imbécile à carnassière.

Charles, après le dîner, la voyant soucieuse, voulut, par distraction, la conduire chez le pharmacien; et la première personne qu'elle aperçut dans la pharmacie, ce fut encore lui, le percepteur! Il était debout devant le comptoir, éclairé par la lumière du bocal rouge, et il disait:

— Donnez-moi, je vous prie, une demi-once de vitriol.

— Justin, cria l'apothicaire, apporte-nous l'acide sulfurique.

Puis, à Emma, qui voulait monter dans l'appartement de madame Homais:

— Non, restez, ce n'est pas la peine, elle va descendre. Chauffez-vous au poêle en attendant… Excusez-moi… Bonjour, docteur (car le pharmacien se plaisait beaucoup a prononcer ce mot docteur, comme si en l'adressant à un autre, il eût fait rejaillir sur lui-même quelque chose de la pompe qu'il y trouvait)… Mais prends garde de renverser les mortiers! va plutôt chercher les chaises de la petite salle; tu sais bien qu'on ne dérange pas les fauteuils du salon.

And to put his arm-chair back in its place he was darting away from the counter, when Binet asked him for half an ounce of sugar acid.

"Sugar acid!" said the chemist contemptuously, "don't know it; I'm ignorant of it! But perhaps you want oxalic acid. It is oxalic acid, isn't it?"

Binet explained that he wanted a corrosive to make himself some copperwater with which to remove rust from his hunting things. Emma shuddered. The chemist began saying:

"Indeed the weather is not propitious on account of the damp."

"Nevertheless," replied the tax-collector, with a sly look, "there are people who like it."

She was stifling.

"And give me—"

"Will he never go?" thought she.

"Half an ounce of resin and turpentine, four ounces of yellow wax, and three half ounces of animal charcoal, if you please, to clean the varnished leather of my togs."

The druggist was beginning to cut the wax when Madame Homais appeared, Irma in her arms, Napoleon by her side, and Athalie following. She sat down on the velvet seat by the window, and the lad squatted down on a footstool, while his eldest sister hovered round the jujube box near her papa. The latter was filling funnels and corking phials, sticking on labels, making up parcels. Around him all were silent; only from time to time, were heard the weights jingling in the balance, and a few low words from the chemist giving directions to his pupil.

"And how's the little woman?" suddenly asked Madame Homais.

"Silence!" exclaimed her husband, who was writing down some figures in his waste-book.

"Why didn't you bring her?" she went on in a low voice.

"Hush! hush!" said Emma, pointing with her finger to the druggist.

But Binet, quite absorbed in looking over his bill, had probably heard nothing. At last he went out. Then Emma, relieved, uttered a deep sigh.

Et, pour remettre en place son fauteuil, Homais se précipitait hors du comptoir, quand Binet lui demanda une demi-once d'acide de sucre.

— Acide de sucre? fit le pharmacien dédaigneusement. Je ne connais pas, j'ignore! Vous voulez peut-être de l'acide oxalique? C'est oxalique, n'est-il pas vrai?

Binet expliqua qu'il avait besoin d'un mordant pour composer lui-même une eau de cuivre avec quoi dérouiller diverses garnitures de chasse. Emma tressaillit. Le pharmacien se mit à dire:

— En effet, le temps n'est pas propice, à cause de l'humidité.

— Cependant, reprit le percepteur d'un air finaud, il y a des personnes qui s'en arrangent.

Elle étouffait.

— Donnez-moi encore…

— Il ne s'en ira donc jamais! pensait-elle.

— Une demi-once d'arcanson et de térébenthine, quatre onces de cire jaune, et trois demi-onces de noir animal, s'il vous plaît, pour nettoyer les cuirs vernis de mon équipement.

L'apothicaire commençait à tailler de la cire, quand madame Homais parut avec Irma dans ses bras, Napoléon à ses côtés et Athalie qui la suivait. Elle alla s'asseoir sur le banc de velours contre la fenêtre, et le gamin s'accroupit sur un tabouret, tandis que sa soeur aînée rôdait autour de la boîte à jujube, près de son petit papa. Celui-ci emplissait des entonnoirs et bouchait des flacons, il collait des étiquettes, il confectionnait des paquets. On se taisait autour de lui; et l'on entendait seulement de temps à autre tinter les poids dans les balances, avec quelques paroles basses du pharmacien donnant des conseils à son élève.

— Comment va votre jeune personne? demanda tout à coup madame Homais.

— Silence! exclama son mari, qui écrivait des chiffres sur le cahier de brouillons.

— Pourquoi ne l'avez-vous pas amenée? reprit-elle à demi-voix.

— Chut! chut! fit Emma en désignant du doigt l'apothicaire.

Mais Binet, tout entier à la lecture de l'addition, n'avait rien entendu probablement. Enfin il sortit. Alors Emma, débarrassée, poussa un grand soupir.

"How hard you are breathing!" said Madame Homais.

"Well, you see, it's rather warm," she replied.

So the next day they talked over how to arrange their rendezvous. Emma wanted to bribe her servant with a present, but it would be better to find some safe house at Yonville. Rodolphe promised to look for one.

All through the winter, three or four times a week, in the dead of night he came to the garden. Emma had on purpose taken away the key of the gate, which Charles thought lost.

To call her, Rodolphe threw a sprinkle of sand at the shutters. She jumped up with a start; but sometimes he had to wait, for Charles had a mania for chatting by the fireside, and he would not stop. She was wild with impatience; if her eyes could have done it, she would have hurled him out at the window. At last she would begin to undress, then take up a book, and go on reading very quietly as if the book amused her. But Charles, who was in bed, called to her to come too.

"Come, now, Emma," he said, "it is time."

"Yes, I am coming," she answered.

Then, as the candles dazzled him; he turned to the wall and fell asleep. She escaped, smiling, palpitating, undressed.

Rodolphe had a large cloak; he wrapped her in it, and putting his arm round her waist, he drew her without a word to the end of the garden.

It was in the arbour, on the same seat of old sticks where formerly Leon had looked at her so amorously on the summer evenings. She never thought of him now.

The stars shone through the leafless jasmine branches. Behind them they heard the river flowing, and now and again on the bank the rustling of the dry reeds. Masses of shadow here and there loomed out in the darkness, and sometimes, vibrating with one movement, they rose up and swayed like immense black waves pressing forward to engulf them. The cold of the nights made them clasp closer; the sighs of their lips seemed to them deeper; their eyes that they could hardly see, larger;

— Comme vous respirez fort! dit madame Homais.

— Ah! c'est qu'il fait un peu chaud, répondit-elle.

Ils avisèrent donc, le lendemain, à organiser leurs rendez-vous; Emma voulait corrompre sa servante par un cadeau; mais il eût mieux valu découvrir à Yonville quelque maison discrète. Rodolphe promit d'en chercher une.

Pendant tout l'hiver, trois ou quatre fois la semaine, à la nuit noire, il arrivait dans le jardin. Emma, tout exprès, avait retiré la clef de la barrière, que Charles crut perdue.

Pour l'avertir, Rodolphe jetait contre les persiennes une poignée de sable. Elle se levait en sursaut; mais quelquefois il lui fallait attendre, car Charles avait la manie de bavarder au coin du feu, et il n'en finissait pas. Elle se dévorait d'impatience; si ses yeux l'avaient pu, ils l'eussent fait sauter par les fenêtres. Enfin, elle commençait sa toilette de nuit; puis, elle prenait un livre et continuait à lire fort tranquillement, comme si la lecture l'eût amusée. Mais Charles, qui était au lit, l'appelait pour se coucher.

— Viens donc, Emma, disait-il, il est temps.

— Oui, j'y vais! répondait-elle.

Cependant, comme les bougies l'éblouissaient, il se tournait vers le mur et s'endormait. Elle s'échappait en retenant son haleine, souriante, palpitante, déshabillée.

Rodolphe avait un grand manteau; il l'en enveloppait tout entière, et, passant le bras autour de sa taille, il l'entraînait sans parler jusqu'au fond du jardin.

C'était sous la tonnelle, sur ce même banc de bâtons pourris où autrefois Léon la regardait si amoureusement, durant les soirs d'été. Elle ne pensait guère à lui maintenant.

Les étoiles brillaient à travers les branches du jasmin sans feuilles. Ils entendaient derrière eux la rivière qui coulait, et, de temps à autre, sur la berge, le claquement des roseaux secs. Des massifs d'ombre, çà et là, se bombaient dans l'obscurité, et parfois, frissonnant tous d'un seul mouvement, ils se dressaient et se penchaient comme d'immenses vagues noires qui se fussent avancées pour les recouvrir. Le froid de la nuit les faisait s'étreindre davantage; les soupirs de leurs lèvres leur semblaient

and in the midst of the silence low words were spoken that fell on their souls sonorous, crystalline, and that reverberated in multiplied vibrations.

When the night was rainy, they took refuge in the consulting-room between the cart-shed and the stable. She lighted one of the kitchen candles that she had hidden behind the books. Rodolphe settled down there as if at home. The sight of the library, of the bureau, of the whole apartment, in fine, excited his merriment, and he could not refrain from making jokes about Charles, which rather embarrassed Emma. She would have liked to see him more serious, and even on occasions more dramatic; as, for example, when she thought she heard a noise of approaching steps in the alley.

"Someone is coming!" she said.

He blew out the light.

"Have you your pistols?"

"Why?"

"Why, to defend yourself," replied Emma.

"From your husband? Oh, poor devil!"

And Rodolphe finished his sentence with a gesture that said, "I could crush him with a flip of my finger."

She was wonder-stricken at his bravery, although she felt in it a sort of indecency and a naive coarseness that scandalised her.

Rodolphe reflected a good deal on the affair of the pistols. If she had spoken seriously, it was very ridiculous, he thought, even odious; for he had no reason to hate the good Charles, not being what is called devoured by jealousy; and on this subject Emma had taken a great vow that he did not think in the best of taste.

Besides, she was growing very sentimental. She had insisted on exchanging miniatures; they had cut off handfuls of hair, and now she was asking for a ring—a real wedding-ring, in sign of an eternal union. She often spoke to him of the evening chimes, of the voices of nature. Then she talked to him of her mother—hers! and of his mother—his! Rodolphe had lost his twenty years ago. Emma none the less consoled

plus forts; leurs yeux, qu'ils entrevoyaient à peine, leur paraissaient plus grands, et, au milieu du silence, il y avait des paroles dites tout bas qui tombaient sur leur âme avec une sonorité cristalline et qui s'y répercutaient en vibrations multipliées.

Lorsque la nuit était pluvieuse, ils s'allaient réfugier dans le cabinet aux consultations, entre le hangar et l'écurie. Elle allumait un des flambeaux de la cuisine, qu'elle avait caché derrière les livres. Rodolphe s'installait là comme chez lui. La vue de la bibliothèque et du bureau, de tout l'appartement enfin, excitait sa gaieté; et il ne pouvait se retenir de faire sur Charles quantité de plaisanteries qui embarrassaient Emma. Elle eût désiré le voir plus sérieux, et même plus dramatique à l'occasion, comme cette fois où elle crut entendre dans l'allée un bruit de pas qui s'approchaient.

— On vient! dit-elle.

Il souffla la lumière.

— As-tu tes pistolets?

— Pourquoi?

— Mais... pour te défendre, reprit Emma.

— Est-ce de ton mari? Ah! le pauvre garçon!

Et Rodolphe acheva sa phrase avec un geste qui signifiait: «Je l'écraserais d'une chiquenaude.»

Elle fut ébahie de sa bravoure, bien qu'elle y sentît une sorte d'indélicatesse et de grossièreté naïve qui la scandalisa.

Rodolphe réfléchit beaucoup à cette histoire de pistolets. Si elle avait parlé sérieusement, cela était fort ridicule, pensait-il, odieux même, car il n'avait, lui, aucune raison de haïr ce bon Charles, n'étant pas ce qui s'appelle dévoré de jalousie; — et, à ce propos, Emma lui avait fait un grand serment qu'il ne trouvait pas non plus du meilleur goût.

D'ailleurs, elle devenait bien sentimentale. Il avait fallu échanger des miniatures, on s'était coupé des poignées de cheveux, et elle demandait à présent une bague, un véritable anneau de mariage, en signe d'alliance éternelle. Souvent elle lui parlait des cloches du soir ou des voix de la nature; puis elle l'entretenait de sa mère, à elle, et de sa mère, à lui. Rodolphe l'avait perdue depuis vingt ans. Emma, néanmoins, l'en con-

him with caressing words as one would have done a lost child, and she sometimes even said to him, gazing at the moon:

"I am sure that above there together they approve of our love."

But she was so pretty. He had possessed so few women of such ingenuousness. This love without debauchery was a new experience for him, and, drawing him out of his lazy habits, caressed at once his pride and his sensuality. Emma's enthusiasm, which his bourgeois good sense disdained, seemed to him in his heart of hearts charming, since it was lavished on him. Then, sure of being loved, he no longer kept up appearances, and insensibly his ways changed.

He had no longer, as formerly, words so gentle that they made her cry, nor passionate caresses that made her mad, so that their great love, which engrossed her life, seemed to lessen beneath her like the water of a stream absorbed into its channel, and she could see the bed of it. She would not believe it; she redoubled in tenderness, and Rodolphe concealed his indifference less and less.

She did not know if she regretted having yielded to him, or whether she did not wish, on the contrary, to enjoy him the more. The humiliation of feeling herself weak was turning to rancour, tempered by their voluptuous pleasures. It was not affection; it was like a continual seduction. He subjugated her; she almost feared him.

Appearances, nevertheless, were calmer than ever, Rodolphe having succeeded in carrying out the adultery after his own fancy; and at the end of six months, when the spring-time came, they were to one another like a married couple, tranquilly keeping up a domestic flame.

It was the time of year when old Rouault sent his turkey in remembrance of the setting of his leg. The present always arrived with a letter. Emma cut the string that tied it to the basket, and read the following lines:

"My Dear Children,

"I hope this will find you well, and that this one will be as good as the others. For it seems to me a little more tender, if I may venture to say so, and heavier. But next time, for a change, I'll give you a turkeycock, unless you have a preference for some dabs; and send me back the ham-

solait avec des mièvreries de langage, comme on eût fait à un marmot abandonné, et même lui disait quelquefois, en regardant la lune:

— Je suis sûre que là-haut, ensemble, elles approuvent notre amour.

Mais elle était si jolie! il en avait possédé si peu d'une candeur pareille! Cet amour sans libertinage était pour lui quelque chose de nouveau, et qui, le sortant de ses habitudes faciles, caressait à la fois son orgueil et sa sensualité. L'exaltation d'Emma, que son bon sens bourgeois dédaignait, lui semblait au fond du coeur charmante, puisqu'elle s'adressait à sa personne. Alors, sûr d'être aimé, il ne se gêna pas, et insensiblement ses façons changèrent.

Il n'avait plus, comme autrefois, de ces mots si doux qui la faisaient pleurer, ni de ces véhémentes caresses qui la rendaient folle; si bien que leur grand amour, où elle vivait plongée, parut se diminuer sous elle, comme l'eau d'un fleuve qui s'absorberait dans son lit, et elle aperçut la vase. Elle n'y voulut pas croire; elle redoubla de tendresse; et Rodolphe, de moins en moins, cacha son indifférence.

Elle ne savait pas si elle regrettait de lui avoir cédé, ou si elle ne souhaitait point, au contraire, le chérir davantage. L'humiliation de se sentir faible se tournait en une rancune que les voluptés tempéraient. Ce n'était pas de l'attachement, c'était comme une séduction permanente. Il la subjuguait. Elle en avait presque peur.

Les apparences, néanmoins, étaient plus calmes que jamais, Rodolphe ayant réussi à conduire l'adultère selon sa fantaisie; et, au bout de six mois, quand le printemps arriva, ils se trouvaient, l'un vis-à-vis de l'autre, comme deux mariés qui entretiennent tranquillement une flamme domestique.

C'était l'époque où le père Rouault envoyait son dinde, en souvenir de sa jambe remise. Le cadeau arrivait toujours avec une lettre. Emma coupa la corde qui la retenait au panier, et lut les lignes suivantes:

«Mes chers enfants,

«J'espère que la présente vous trouvera en bonne santé et que celui-là vaudra bien les autres; car il me semble un peu plus mollet, si j'ose dire, et plus massif. Mais, la prochaine fois, par changement, je vous donnerai un coq, à moins que vous ne teniez de préférence aux picots;

per, if you please, with the two old ones. I have had an accident with my cart-sheds, whose covering flew off one windy night among the trees. The harvest has not been overgood either. Finally, I don't know when I shall come to see you. It is so difficult now to leave the house since I am alone, my poor Emma."

Here there was a break in the lines, as if the old fellow had dropped his pen to dream a little while.

"For myself, I am very well, except for a cold I caught the other day at the fair at Yvetot, where I had gone to hire a shepherd, having turned away mine because he was too dainty. How we are to be pitied with such a lot of thieves! Besides, he was also rude.

"I heard from a pedlar, who, travelling through your part of the country this winter, had a tooth drawn, that Bovary was as usual working hard. That doesn't surprise me; and he showed me his tooth; we had some coffee together. I asked him if he had seen you, and he said not, but that he had seen two horses in the stables, from which I conclude that business is looking up. So much the better, my dear children, and may God send you every imaginable happiness!

"It grieves me not yet to have seen my dear little grand-daughter, Berthe Bovary. I have planted an Orleans plum-tree for her in the garden under your room, and I won't have it touched unless it is to have jam made for her by and bye, that I will keep in the cupboard for her when she comes.

"Good-bye, my dear children. I kiss you, my girl, you too, my son-in-law, and the little one on both cheeks.

"I am, with best compliments,

"Your loving father,

"Theodore Rouault."

She held the coarse paper in her fingers for some minutes. The spelling mistakes were interwoven one with the other, and Emma followed the kindly thought that cackled right through it like a hen half hidden in the hedge of thorns. The writing had been dried with

et renvoyez-moi la bourriche, s'il vous plaît, avec les deux anciennes. J'ai eu un malheur à ma charreterie, dont la couverture, une nuit qu'il ventait fort, s'est envolée dans les arbres. La récolte non plus n'a pas été trop fameuse. Enfin, je ne sais pas quand j'irai vous voir. Ça m'est tellement difficile de quitter maintenant la maison, depuis que je suis seul, ma pauvre Emma!

«Et il y avait ici un intervalle entre les lignes, comme si le bonhomme eût laissé tomber sa plume pour rêver quelque temps.

«Quant à moi, je vais bien, sauf un rhume que j'ai attrapé l'autre jour à la foire d'Yvetot, où j'étais parti pour retenir un berger, ayant mis le mien dehors, par suite de sa trop grande délicatesse de bouche. Comme on est à plaindre avec tous ces brigands-là! Du reste, c'était aussi un malhonnête.

«J'ai appris d'un colporteur qui, voyageant cet hiver par votre pays, s'est fait arracher une dent, que Bovary travaillait toujours dur. Ça ne m'étonne pas, et il m'a montré sa dent; nous avons pris un café ensemble. Je lui ai demandé s'il t'avait vue, il m'a dit que non, mais qu'il avait vu dans l'écurie deux animaux, d'où je conclus que le métier roule. Tant mieux, mes chers enfants, et que le bon Dieu vous envoie tout le bonheur imaginable.

«Il me fait deuil de ne pas connaître encore ma bien-aimée petite-fille Berthe Bovary. J'ai planté pour elle, dans le jardin, sous ta chambre, un prunier de prunes d'avoine, et je ne veux pas qu'on y touche, si ce n'est pour lui faire plus tard des compotes, que je garderai dans l'armoire, à son intention, quand elle viendra.

«Adieu, mes chers enfants. Je t'embrasse, ma fille; vous aussi, mon gendre, et la petite, sur les deux joues.

«Je suis, avec bien des compliments,

«Votre tendre père,

**«THEODORE ROUAULT.»**

Elle resta quelques minutes à tenir entre ses doigts ce gros papier. Les fautes d'orthographe s'y enlaçaient les unes aux autres, et Emma poursuivait la pensée douce qui caquetait tout au travers comme une poule à demi cachée dans une haie d'épines. On avait séché l'écriture

ashes from the hearth, for a little grey powder slipped from the letter on to her dress, and she almost thought she saw her father bending over the hearth to take up the tongs. How long since she had been with him, sitting on the footstool in the chimney-corner, where she used to burn the end of a bit of wood in the great flame of the sea-sedges!

She remembered the summer evenings all full of sunshine. The colts neighed when anyone passed by, and galloped, galloped. Under her window there was a beehive, and sometimes the bees wheeling round in the light struck against her window like rebounding balls of gold. What happiness there had been at that time, what freedom, what hope! What an abundance of illusions! Nothing was left of them now. She had got rid of them all in her soul's life, in all her successive conditions of life, maidenhood, her marriage, and her love—thus constantly losing them all her life through, like a traveller who leaves something of his wealth at every inn along his road.

But what then, made her so unhappy? What was the extraordinary catastrophe that had transformed her? And she raised her head, looking round as if to seek the cause of that which made her suffer.

An April ray was dancing on the china of the whatnot; the fire burned; beneath her slippers she felt the softness of the carpet; the day was bright, the air warm, and she heard her child shouting with laughter.

In fact, the little girl was just then rolling on the lawn in the midst of the grass that was being turned. She was lying flat on her stomach at the top of a rick. The servant was holding her by her skirt. Lestiboudois was raking by her side, and every time he came near she lent forward, beating the air with both her arms.

"Bring her to me," said her mother, rushing to embrace her. "How I love you, my poor child! How I love you!"

Then noticing that the tips of her ears were rather dirty, she rang at once for warm water, and washed her, changed her linen, her stockings, her shoes, asked a thousand questions about her health, as if on the return from a long journey, and finally, kissing her again and crying a

avec les cendres du foyer, car un peu de poussière grise glissa de la lettre sur sa robe, et elle crut presque apercevoir son père se courbant vers l'âtre pour saisir les pincettes. Comme il y avait longtemps qu'elle n'était plus auprès de lui, sur l'escabeau, dans la cheminée, quand elle faisait brûler le bout d'un bâton à la grande flamme des joncs marins qui pétillaient!...

Elle se rappela des soirs d'été tout pleins de soleil. Les poulains hennissaient quand on passait, et galopaient, galopaient... Il y avait sous sa fenêtre une ruche à miel, et quelquefois les abeilles, tournoyant dans la lumière, frappaient contre les carreaux comme des balles d'or rebondissantes. Quel bonheur dans ce temps-là! quelle liberté! quel espoir! quelle abondance d'illusions! Il n'en restait plus maintenant! Elle en avait dépensé à toutes les aventures de son âme, par toutes les conditions successives, dans la virginité, dans le mariage et dans l'amour; — les perdant ainsi continuellement le long de sa vie, comme un voyageur qui laisse quelque chose de sa richesse à toutes les auberges de la route.

Mais qui donc la rendait si malheureuse? où était la catastrophe extraordinaire qui l'avait bouleversée? Et elle releva la tête, regardant autour d'elle, comme pour chercher la cause de ce qui la faisait souffrir.

Un rayon d'avril chatoyait sur les porcelaines de l'étagère; le feu brûlait; elle sentait sous ses pantoufles la douceur du tapis; le jour était blanc, l'atmosphère tiède, et elle entendit son enfant qui poussait des éclats de rire.

En effet, la petite fille se roulait alors sur le gazon, au milieu de l'herbe qu'on fanait. Elle était couchée à plat ventre, au haut d'une meule. Sa bonne la retenait par la jupe. Lestiboudois ratissait à côté, et, chaque fois qu'il s'approchait, elle se penchait en battant l'air de ses deux bras.

— Amenez-la-moi! dit sa mère se précipitant pour l'embrasser. Comme je t'aime, ma pauvre enfant! comme je t'aime!

Puis, s'apercevant qu'elle avait le bout des oreilles un peu sale, elle sonna vite pour avoir de l'eau chaude, et la nettoya, la changea de linge, de bas, de souliers, fit mille questions sur sa santé, comme au retour d'un voyage, et enfin, la baisant encore et pleurant un peu, elle la remit

little, she gave her back to the servant, who stood quite thunderstricken at this excess of tenderness.

That evening Rodolphe found her more serious than usual.

"That will pass over," he concluded; "it's a whim:"

And he missed three rendezvous running. When he did come, she showed herself cold and almost contemptuous.

"Ah! you're losing your time, my lady!"

And he pretended not to notice her melancholy sighs, nor the handkerchief she took out.

Then Emma repented.

She even asked herself why she detested Charles; if it had not been better to have been able to love him? But he gave her no opportunities for such a revival of sentiment, so that she was much embarrassed by her desire for sacrifice, when the druggist came just in time to provide her with an opportunity.

aux mains de la domestique, qui restait fort ébahie devant cet excès de tendresse.

Rodolphe, le soir, la trouva plus sérieuse que d'habitude.

— Cela se passera, jugea-t-il, c'est un caprice.

Et il manqua consécutivement à trois rendez-vous. Quand il revint, elle se montra froide et presque dédaigneuse.

— Ah! tu perds ton temps, ma mignonne...

Et il eut l'air de ne point remarquer ses soupirs mélancoliques, ni le mouchoir qu'elle tirait.

C'est alors qu'Emma se repentit!

Elle se demanda même pourquoi donc elle exécrait Charles, et s'il n'eût pas été meilleur de le pouvoir aimer. Mais il n'offrait pas grande prise à ces retours du sentiment, si bien qu'elle demeurait fort embarrassée dans sa velléité de sacrifice, lorsque l'apothicaire vint à propos lui fournir une occasion.

# Chapter 11

He had recently read a eulogy on a new method for curing club-foot, and as he was a partisan of progress, he conceived the patriotic idea that Yonville, in order to keep to the fore, ought to have some operations for strephopody or club-foot.

"For," said he to Emma, "what risk is there? See—" (and he enumerated on his fingers the advantages of the attempt), "success, almost certain relief and beautifying of the patient, celebrity acquired by the operator. Why, for example, should not your husband relieve poor Hippolyte of the 'Lion d'Or'? Note that he would not fail to tell about his cure to all the travellers, and then" (Homais lowered his voice and looked round him) "who is to prevent me from sending a short paragraph on the subject to the paper? Eh! goodness me! an article gets about; it is talked of; it ends by making a snowball! And who knows? who knows?"

In fact, Bovary might succeed. Nothing proved to Emma that he was not clever; and what a satisfaction for her to have urged him to a step by which his reputation and fortune would be increased! She only wished to lean on something more solid than love.

Charles, urged by the druggist and by her, allowed himself to be persuaded. He sent to Rouen for Dr. Duval's volume, and every evening, holding his head between both hands, plunged into the reading of it.

While he was studying equinus, varus, and valgus, that is to say, katastrephopody, endostrephopody, and exostrephopody (or better, the various turnings of the foot downwards, inwards, and outwards, with the hypostrephopody and anastrephopody), otherwise torsion downwards and upwards, Monsier Homais, with all sorts of arguments, was exhorting the lad at the inn to submit to the operation.

"You will scarcely feel, probably, a slight pain; it is a simple prick, like a little blood-letting, less than the extraction of certain corns."

Hippolyte, reflecting, rolled his stupid eyes.

# Chapitre 11

Il avait lu dernièrement l'éloge d'une nouvelle méthode pour la cure des pieds-bots; et comme il était partisan du progrès, il conçut cette idée patriotique que Yonville, pour se mettre au niveau, devait avoir des opérations de stréphopodie.

— Car, disait-il à Emma, que risque-t-on? Examinez (et il énumérait, sur ses doigts, les avantages de la tentative); succès presque certain, soulagement et embellissement du malade, célébrité vite acquise à l'opérateur. Pourquoi votre mari, par exemple, ne voudrait-il pas débarrasser ce pauvre Hippolyte, du Lion d'or? Notez qu'il ne manquerait pas de raconter sa guérison à tous les voyageurs, et puis (Homais baissait la voix et regardait autour de lui) qui donc m'empêcherait d'envoyer au journal une petite note là-dessus? Eh! mon Dieu! un article circule…, on en parle…, cela finit par faire la boule de neige! Et qui sait? qui sait?

En effet, Bovary pouvait réussir; rien n'affirmait à Emma qu'il ne fût pas habile, et quelle satisfaction pour elle que de l'avoir engagé à une démarche d'où sa réputation et sa fortune se trouveraient accrues? Elle ne demandait qu'à s'appuyer sur quelque chose de plus solide que l'amour.

Charles, sollicité par l'apothicaire et par elle, se laissa convaincre. Il fit venir de Rouen le volume du docteur Duval, et, tous les soirs, se prenant la tête entre les mains, il s'enfonçait dans cette lecture.

Tandis qu'il étudiait les équins, les varus et les valgus, c'est- à-dire la stréphocatopodie, la stréphendopodie et la stréphexopodie (ou, pour parler mieux, les différentes déviations du pied, soit en bas, en dedans ou en dehors), avec la stréphypopodie et la stréphanopodie (autrement dit torsion en dessous et redressement en haut), M. Homais par toute sorte de raisonnements, exhortait le garçon d'auberge à se faire opérer.

— À peine sentiras-tu, peut-être, une légère douleur; c'est une simple piqûre comme une petite saignée, moins que l'extirpation de certains cors.

Hippolyte, réfléchissant, roulait des yeux stupides.

"However," continued the chemist, "it doesn't concern me. It's for your sake, for pure humanity! I should like to see you, my friend, rid of your hideous caudication, together with that waddling of the lumbar regions which, whatever you say, must considerably interfere with you in the exercise of your calling."

Then Homais represented to him how much jollier and brisker he would feel afterwards, and even gave him to understand that he would be more likely to please the women; and the stable-boy began to smile heavily. Then he attacked him through his vanity:

"Aren't you a man? Hang it! what would you have done if you had had to go into the army, to go and fight beneath the standard? Ah! Hippolyte!"

And Homais retired, declaring that he could not understand this obstinacy, this blindness in refusing the benefactions of science.

The poor fellow gave way, for it was like a conspiracy. Binet, who never interfered with other people's business, Madame Lefrancois, Artemise, the neighbours, even the mayor, Monsieur Tuvache—everyone persuaded him, lectured him, shamed him; but what finally decided him was that it would cost him nothing. Bovary even undertook to provide the machine for the operation. This generosity was an idea of Emma's, and Charles consented to it, thinking in his heart of hearts that his wife was an angel.

So by the advice of the chemist, and after three fresh starts, he had a kind of box made by the carpenter, with the aid of the locksmith, that weighed about eight pounds, and in which iron, wood, sheer-iron, leather, screws, and nuts had not been spared.

But to know which of Hippolyte's tendons to cut, it was necessary first of all to find out what kind of club-foot he had.

He had a foot forming almost a straight line with the leg, which, however, did not prevent it from being turned in, so that it was an equinus together with something of a varus, or else a slight varus with a strong tendency to equinus. But with this equinus, wide in foot like a horse's hoof, with rugose skin, dry tendons, and large toes, on which the black nails looked as if made of iron, the clubfoot ran about like a

— Du reste, reprenait le pharmacien, ça ne me regarde pas! c'est pour toi! par humanité pure! Je voudrais te voir, mon ami, débarrassé de ta hideuse claudication, avec ce balancement de la région lombaire, qui, bien que tu prétendes le contraire, doit te nuire considérablement dans l'exercice de ton métier.

Alors Homais lui représentait combien il se sentirait ensuite plus gaillard et plus ingambe, et même lui donnait à entendre qu'il s'en trouverait mieux pour plaire aux femmes; et le valet d'écurie se prenait à sourire lourdement. Puis il l'attaquait par la vanité:

— N'es-tu pas un homme, saprelotte? Que serait-ce donc, s'il t'avait fallu servir, aller combattre sous les drapeaux?... Ah! Hippolyte!

Et Homais s'éloignait, déclarant qu'il ne comprenait pas cet entêtement, cet aveuglement à se refuser aux bienfaits de la science.

Le malheureux céda, car ce fut comme une conjuration. Binet, qui ne se mêlait jamais des affaires d'autrui, madame Lefrançois, Artémise, les voisins, et jusqu'au maire, M. Tuvache, tout le monde l'engagea, le sermonna, lui faisait honte; mais ce qui acheva de le décider, c'est que ça ne lui coûterait rien. Bovary se chargeait même de fournir la machine pour l'opération. Emma avait eu l'idée de cette générosité; et Charles y consentit, se disant au fond du coeur que sa femme était un ange.

Avec les conseils du pharmacien, et en recommençant trois fois, il fit donc construire par le menuisier, aidé du serrurier, une manière de boîte pesant huit livres environ, et où le fer, le bois, la tôle, le cuir, les vis et les écrous ne se trouvaient point épargnés.

Cependant, pour savoir quel tendon couper à Hippolyte, il fallait connaître d'abord quelle espèce de pied-bot il avait.

Il avait un pied faisant avec la jambe une ligne presque droite, ce qui ne l'empêchait pas d'être tourné en dedans, de sorte que c'était un équin mêlé d'un peu de varus, ou bien un léger varus fortement accusé d'équin. Mais, avec cet équin, large en effet comme un pied de cheval, à peau rugueuse, à tendons secs, à gros orteils, et où les ongles noirs figuraient les clous d'un fer, le stréphopode, depuis le matin jusqu'à la

deer from morn till night. He was constantly to be seen on the Place, jumping round the carts, thrusting his limping foot forwards. He seemed even stronger on that leg than the other. By dint of hard service it had acquired, as it were, moral qualities of patience and energy; and when he was given some heavy work, he stood on it in preference to its fellow.

Now, as it was an equinus, it was necessary to cut the tendon of Achilles, and, if need were, the anterior tibial muscle could be seen to afterwards for getting rid of the varus; for the doctor did not dare to risk both operations at once; he was even trembling already for fear of injuring some important region that he did not know.

Neither Ambrose Pare, applying for the first time since Celsus, after an interval of fifteen centuries, a ligature to an artery, nor Dupuytren, about to open an abscess in the brain, nor Gensoul when he first took away the superior maxilla, had hearts that trembled, hands that shook, minds so strained as Monsieur Bovary when he approached Hippolyte, his tenotome between his fingers. And as at hospitals, near by on a table lay a heap of lint, with waxed thread, many bandages—a pyramid of bandages—every bandage to be found at the druggist's. It was Monsieur Homais who since morning had been organising all these preparations, as much to dazzle the multitude as to keep up his illusions. Charles pierced the skin; a dry crackling was heard. The tendon was cut, the operation over. Hippolyte could not get over his surprise, but bent over Bovary's hands to cover them with kisses.

"Come, be calm," said the druggist; "later on you will show your gratitude to your benefactor."

And he went down to tell the result to five or six inquirers who were waiting in the yard, and who fancied that Hippolyte would reappear walking properly. Then Charles, having buckled his patient into the machine, went home, where Emma, all anxiety, awaited him at the door. She threw herself on his neck; they sat down to table; he ate much, and at dessert he even wanted to take a cup of coffee, a luxury he only permitted himself on Sundays when there was company.

nuit, galopait comme un cerf. On le voyait continuellement sur la place, sautiller tout autour des charrettes, en jetant en avant son support inégal. Il semblait même plus vigoureux de cette jambe-là que de l'autre. À force d'avoir servi, elle avait contracté comme des qualités morales de patience et d'énergie, et quand on lui donnait quelque gros ouvrage, il s'écorait dessus, préférablement.

Or, puisque c'était un équin, il fallait couper le tendon d'Achille, quitte à s'en prendre plus tard au muscle tibial antérieur pour se débarrasser du varus; car le médecin n'osait d'un seul coup risquer deux opérations, et même il tremblait déjà, dans la peur d'attaquer quelque région importante qu'il ne connaissait pas.

Ni Ambroise Paré, appliquant pour la première fois depuis Celse, après quinze siècles d'intervalle, la ligature immédiate d'une artère; ni Dupuytren allant ouvrir un abcès à travers une couche épaisse d'encéphale; ni Gensoul, quand il fit la première ablation de maxillaire supérieur, n'avaient certes le coeur si palpitant, la main si frémissante, l'intellect aussi tendu que M. Bovary quand il approcha d'Hippolyte, son ténotome entre les doigts. Et, comme dans les hôpitaux, on voyait à côté, sur une table, un tas de charpie, des fils cirés, beaucoup de bandes, une pyramide de bandes, tout ce qu'il y avait de bandes chez l'apothicaire. C'était M. Homais qui avait organisé dès le matin tous ces préparatifs, autant pour éblouir la multitude que pour s'illusionner lui-même. Charles piqua la peau; on entendit un craquement sec. Le tendon était coupé, l'opération était finie. Hippolyte n'en revenait pas de surprise; il se penchait sur les mains de Bovary pour les couvrir de baisers.

— Allons, calme-toi, disait l'apothicaire, tu témoigneras plus tard ta reconnaissance envers ton bienfaiteur!

Et il descendit conter le résultat à cinq ou six curieux qui stationnaient dans la cour, et qui s'imaginaient qu'Hippolyte allait reparaître marchant droit. Puis Charles, ayant bouclé son malade dans le moteur mécanique, s'en retourna chez lui, où Emma, tout anxieuse, l'attendait sur la porte. Elle lui sauta au cou; ils se mirent à table; il mangea beaucoup, et même il voulut, au dessert, prendre une tasse de café, débauche qu'il ne se permettait que le dimanche lorsqu'il y avait du monde.

The evening was charming, full of prattle, of dreams together. They talked about their future fortune, of the improvements to be made in their house; he saw people's estimation of him growing, his comforts increasing, his wife always loving him; and she was happy to refresh herself with a new sentiment, healthier, better, to feel at last some tenderness for this poor fellow who adored her. The thought of Rodolphe for one moment passed through her mind, but her eyes turned again to Charles; she even noticed with surprise that he had not bad teeth.

They were in bed when Monsieur Homais, in spite of the servant, suddenly entered the room, holding in his hand a sheet of paper just written. It was the paragraph he intended for the "Fanal de Rouen." He brought it for them to read.

"Read it yourself," said Bovary.

He read:

"'Despite the prejudices that still invest a part of the face of Europe like a net, the light nevertheless begins to penetrate our country places. Thus on Tuesday our little town of Yonville found itself the scene of a surgical operation which is at the same time an act of loftiest philanthropy. Monsieur Bovary, one of our most distinguished practitioners—'"

"Oh, that is too much! too much!" said Charles, choking with emotion.

"No, no! not at all! What next! '—Performed an operation on a club-footed man.' I have not used the scientific term, because you know in a newspaper everyone would not perhaps understand. The masses must—'"

"No doubt," said Bovary; "go on!"

"I proceed," said the chemist. "'Monsieur Bovary, one of our most distinguished practitioners, performed an operation on a club-footed man called Hippolyte Tautain, stableman for the last twenty-five years at the hotel of the "Lion d'Or," kept by Widow Lefrancois, at the Place d'Armes. The novelty of the attempt, and the interest incident to the subject, had attracted such a concourse of persons that there was a veritable obstruction on the threshold of the establishment. The operation,

La soirée fut charmante, pleine de causeries, de rêves en commun. Ils parlèrent de leur fortune future, d'améliorations à introduire dans leur ménage, il voyait sa considération s'étendant, son bien- être s'augmentant, sa femme l'aimant toujours; et elle se trouvait heureuse de se rafraîchir dans un sentiment nouveau, plus sain, meilleur, enfin d'éprouver quelque tendresse pour ce pauvre garçon qui la chérissait. L'idée de Rodolphe, un moment, lui passa par la tête; mais ses yeux se reportèrent sur Charles: elle remarqua même avec surprise qu'il n'avait point les dents vilaines.

Ils étaient au lit lorsque M. Homais, malgré la cuisinière, entra tout à coup dans la chambre, en tenant à la main une feuille de papier fraîche écrite. C'était la réclame qu'il destinait au Fanal de Rouen. Il la leur apportait à lire.

— Lisez vous-même, dit Bovary.

Il lut:

— «Malgré les préjugés qui recouvrent encore une partie de la face de l'Europe comme un réseau, la lumière cependant commence à pénétrer dans nos campagnes. C'est ainsi que, mardi, notre petite cité d'Yonville s'est vue le théâtre d'une expérience chirurgicale qui est en même temps un acte de haute philanthropie. M. Bovary, un de nos praticiens les plus distingués...»

— Ah! c'est trop! c'est trop! disait Charles, que l'émotion suffoquait.

— Mais non, pas du tout! comment donc!... «A opéré d'un pied-bot...» Je n'ai pas mis le terme scientifique, parce que, vous savez, dans un journal..., tout le monde peut-être ne comprendrait pas; il faut que les masses...

— En effet, dit Bovary. Continuez.

— Je reprends, dit le pharmacien. «M. Bovary, un de nos praticiens les plus distingués, a opéré d'un pied-bot le nommé Hippolyte Tautain, garçon d'écurie depuis vingt-cinq ans à l'hôtel du Lion d'or, tenu par madame veuve Lefrançois, sur la place d'Armes. La nouveauté de la tentative et l'intérêt qui s'attachait au sujet avaient attiré un tel concours de population, qu'il y avait véritablement encombrement au seuil de l'établissement. L'opération, du reste, s'est pratiquée comme par

moreover, was performed as if by magic, and barely a few drops of blood appeared on the skin, as though to say that the rebellious tendon had at last given way beneath the efforts of art. The patient, strangely enough—we affirm it as an eye-witness—complained of no pain. His condition up to the present time leaves nothing to be desired. Everything tends to show that his convelescence will be brief; and who knows even if at our next village festivity we shall not see our good Hippolyte figuring in the bacchic dance in the midst of a chorus of joyous boon-companions, and thus proving to all eyes by his verve and his capers his complete cure? Honour, then, to the generous savants! Honour to those indefatigable spirits who consecrate their vigils to the amelioration or to the alleviation of their kind! Honour, thrice honour! Is it not time to cry that the blind shall see, the deaf hear, the lame walk? But that which fanaticism formerly promised to its elect, science now accomplishes for all men. We shall keep our readers informed as to the successive phases of this remarkable cure.'"

This did not prevent Mere Lefrancois, from coming five days after, scared, and crying out:

"Help! he is dying! I am going crazy!"

Charles rushed to the "Lion d'Or," and the chemist, who caught sight of him passing along the Place hatless, abandoned his shop. He appeared himself breathless, red, anxious, and asking everyone who was going up the stairs:

"Why, what's the matter with our interesting strephopode?"

The strephopode was writhing in hideous convulsions, so that the machine in which his leg was enclosed was knocked against the wall enough to break it.

With many precautions, in order not to disturb the position of the limb, the box was removed, and an awful sight presented itself. The outlines of the foot disappeared in such a swelling that the entire skin seemed about to burst, and it was covered with ecchymosis, caused by the famous machine. Hippolyte had already complained of suffering from it. No attention had been paid to him; they had to acknowledge that he had not been altogether wrong, and he was

enchantement, et à peine si quelques gouttes de sang sont venues sur la peau, comme pour dire que le tendon rebelle venait enfin de céder sous les efforts de l'art. Le malade, chose étrange (nous l'affirmons de visu) n'accusa point de douleur. Son état, jusqu'à présent, ne laisse rien à désirer. Tout porte à croire que la convalescence sera courte; et qui sait même si, à la prochaine fête villageoise, nous ne verrons pas notre brave Hippolyte figurer dans des danses bachiques, au milieu d'un choeur de joyeux drilles, et ainsi prouver à tous les yeux, par sa verve et ses entrechats, sa complète guérison? Honneur donc aux savants généreux! honneur à ces esprits infatigables qui consacrent leurs veilles à l'amélioration ou bien au soulagement de leur espèce! Honneur! trois fois honneur! N'est-ce pas le cas de s'écrier que les aveugles verront, les sourds entendront et les boiteux marcheront! Mais ce que le fanatisme autrefois promettait à ses élus, la science maintenant l'accomplit pour tous les hommes! Nous tiendrons nos lecteurs au courant des phases successives de cette cure si remarquable.»

Ce qui n'empêcha pas que, cinq jours après, la mère Lefrançois n'arrivât tout effarée en s'écriant:

— Au secours! il se meurt!... J'en perds la tête!

Charles se précipita vers le Lion d'or, et le pharmacien qui l'aperçut passant sur la place, sans chapeau, abandonna la pharmacie. Il parut lui-même, haletant, rouge, inquiet, et demandant à tous ceux qui montaient l'escalier:

— Qu'a donc notre intéressant stréphopode?

Il se tordait, le stréphopode, dans des convulsions atroces, si bien que le moteur mécanique où était enfermée sa jambe frappait contre la muraille à la défoncer.

Avec beaucoup de précautions, pour ne pas déranger la position du membre, on retira donc la boîte, et l'on vit un spectacle affreux. Les formes du pied disparaissaient dans une telle bouffissure, que la peau tout entière semblait près de se rompre, et elle était couverte d'ecchymoses occasionnées par la fameuse machine. Hippolyte déjà s'était plaint d'en souffrir; on n'y avait pris garde; il fallut reconnaître qu'il n'avait pas eu tort complètement; et on le laissa libre quelques heu-

freed for a few hours. But, hardly had the oedema gone down to some extent, than the two savants thought fit to put back the limb in the apparatus, strapping it tighter to hasten matters. At last, three days after, Hippolyte being unable to endure it any longer, they once more removed the machine, and were much surprised at the result they saw. The livid tumefaction spread over the leg, with blisters here and there, whence there oozed a black liquid. Matters were taking a serious turn. Hippolyte began to worry himself, and Mere Lefrancois, had him installed in the little room near the kitchen, so that he might at least have some distraction.

But the tax-collector, who dined there every day, complained bitterly of such companionship. Then Hippolyte was removed to the billiard-room.

He lay there moaning under his heavy coverings, pale with long beard, sunken eyes, and from time to time turning his perspiring head on the dirty pillow, where the flies alighted. Madame Bovary went to see him. She brought him linen for his poultices; she comforted, and encouraged him. Besides, he did not want for company, especially on market-days, when the peasants were knocking about the billiard-balls round him, fenced with the cues, smoked, drank, sang, and brawled.

"How are you?" they said, clapping him on the shoulder. "Ah! you're not up to much, it seems, but it's your own fault. You should do this! do that!"

And then they told him stories of people who had all been cured by other remedies than his. Then by way of consolation they added:

"You give way too much! Get up! You coddle yourself like a king! All the same, old chap, you don't smell nice!"

Gangrene, in fact, was spreading more and more. Bovary himself turned sick at it. He came every hour, every moment. Hippolyte looked at him with eyes full of terror, sobbing:

"When shall I get well? Oh, save me! How unfortunate I am! How unfortunate I am!"

res. Mais à peine l'oedème eut-il un peu disparu, que les deux savants jugèrent à propos de rétablir le membre dans l'appareil, et en l'y serrant davantage, pour accélérer les choses. Enfin, trois jours après, Hippolyte n'y pouvant plus tenir, ils retirèrent encore une fois la mécanique, tout en s'étonnant beaucoup du résultat qu'ils aperçurent. Une tuméfaction livide s'étendait sur la jambe, et avec des phlyctènes de place en place, par où suintait un liquide noir. Cela prenait une tournure sérieuse. Hippolyte commençait à s'ennuyer, et la mère Lefrançois l'installa dans la petite salle, près de la cuisine, pour qu'il eût au moins quelque distraction.

Mais le percepteur, qui tous les jours y dînait, se plaignit avec amertume d'un tel voisinage. Alors on transporta Hippolyte dans la salle de billard.

Il était là, geignant sous ses grosses couvertures, pâle, la barbe longue, les yeux caves, et, de temps à autre, tournant sa tête en sueur sur le sale oreiller où s'abattaient les mouches. Madame Bovary le venait voir. Elle lui apportait des linges pour ses cataplasmes, et le consolait, l'encourageait. Du reste, il ne manquait pas de compagnie, les jours de marché surtout, lorsque les paysans autour de lui poussaient les billes du billard, escrimaient avec les queues, fumaient, buvaient, chantaient, braillaient.

— Comment vas-tu? disaient-ils en lui frappant sur l'épaule. Ah! tu n'es pas fier, à ce qu'il paraît! mais c'est ta faute. Il faudrait faire ceci, faire cela.

Et on lui racontait des histoires de gens qui avaient tous été guéris par d'autres remèdes que les siens; puis, en manière de consolation, ils ajoutaient:

— C'est que tu t'écoutes trop! lève-toi donc! tu te dorlotes comme un roi! Ah! n'importe, vieux farceur! tu ne sens pas bon!

La gangrène, en effet, montait de plus en plus. Bovary en était malade lui-même. Il venait à chaque heure, à tout moment. Hippolyte le regardait avec des yeux pleins d'épouvante et balbutiait en sanglotant:

— Quand est-ce que je serai guéri?... Ah! sauvez-moi!... Que je suis malheureux! que je suis malheureux!

And the doctor left, always recommending him to diet himself.

"Don't listen to him, my lad," said Mere Lefrancois, "Haven't they tortured you enough already? You'll grow still weaker. Here! swallow this."

And she gave him some good beef-tea, a slice of mutton, a piece of bacon, and sometimes small glasses of brandy, that he had not the strength to put to his lips.

Abbe Bournisien, hearing that he was growing worse, asked to see him. He began by pitying his sufferings, declaring at the same time that he ought to rejoice at them since it was the will of the Lord, and take advantage of the occasion to reconcile himself to Heaven.

"For," said the ecclesiastic in a paternal tone, "you rather neglected your duties; you were rarely seen at divine worship. How many years is it since you approached the holy table? I understand that your work, that the whirl of the world may have kept you from care for your salvation. But now is the time to reflect. Yet don't despair. I have known great sinners, who, about to appear before God (you are not yet at this point I know), had implored His mercy, and who certainly died in the best frame of mind. Let us hope that, like them, you will set us a good example. Thus, as a precaution, what is to prevent you from saying morning and evening a 'Hail Mary, full of grace,' and 'Our Father which art in heaven'? Yes, do that, for my sake, to oblige me. That won't cost you anything. Will you promise me?"

The poor devil promised. The cure came back day after day. He chatted with the landlady; and even told anecdotes interspersed with jokes and puns that Hippolyte did not understand. Then, as soon as he could, he fell back upon matters of religion, putting on an appropriate expression of face.

His zeal seemed successful, for the club-foot soon manifested a desire to go on a pilgrimage to Bon-Secours if he were cured; to which Monsieur Bournisien replied that he saw no objection; two precautions were better than one; it was no risk anyhow.

The druggist was indignant at what he called the manoeuvres of the priest; they were prejudicial, he said, to Hippolyte's convalescence, and he kept repeating to Madame Lefrancois:

Et le médecin s'en allait, toujours en lui recommandant la diète.

— Ne l'écoute point, mon garçon, reprenait la mère Lefrançois; ils t'ont déjà bien assez martyrisé? tu vas t'affaiblir encore. Tiens, avale!

Et elle lui présentait quelque bon bouillon, quelque tranche de gigot, quelque morceau de lard, et parfois des petits verres d'eau-de-vie qu'il n'avait pas le courage de porter à ses lèvres.

L'abbé Bournisien, apprenant qu'il empirait, fit demander à le voir. Il commença par le plaindre de son mal, tout en déclarant qu'il fallait s'en réjouit, puisque c'était la volonté du Seigneur, et profiter vite de l'occasion pour se réconcilier avec le ciel.

— Car, disait l'ecclésiastique d'un ton paterne, tu négligeais un peu tes devoirs; on te voyait rarement à l'office divin; combien y a-t-il d'années que tu ne t'es approché de la sainte table? Je comprends que tes occupations, que le tourbillon du monde aient pu t'écarter du soin de ton salut. Mais à présent, c'est l'heure d'y réfléchir. Ne désespère pas cependant; j'ai connu de grands coupables qui, près de comparaître devant Dieu (tu n'en es point encore là, je le sais bien), avaient imploré sa miséricorde, et qui certainement sont morts dans les meilleures dispositions. Espérons que, tout comme eux, tu nous donneras de bons exemples! Ainsi, par précaution, qui donc t'empêcherait de réciter matin et soir un «Je vous salue, Marie, pleine de grâce», et un «Notre Père, qui êtes aux cieux»? Oui fais cela! pour moi, pour m'obliger. Qu'est-ce que ça coûte?... Me le promets-tu?

Le pauvre diable promit. Le curé revint les jours suivants. Il causait avec l'aubergiste et même racontait des anecdotes entremêlées de plaisanteries, de calembours qu'Hippolyte ne comprenait pas. Puis, dès que la circonstance le permettait, il retombait sur les matières de religion, en prenant une figure convenable.

Son zèle parut réussir; car bientôt le stréphopode témoigna l'envie d'aller en pèlerinage à Bon-Secours, s'il se guérissait: à quoi M. Bournisien répondit qu'il ne voyait pas d'inconvénient; deux précautions valaient mieux qu'une. On ne risquait rien.

L'apothicaire s'indigna contre ce qu'il appelait les manoeuvres du prêtre; elles nuisaient, prétendait-il, à la convalescence d'Hippolyte, et il répétait à madame Lefrançois:

"Leave him alone! leave him alone! You perturb his morals with your mysticism."

But the good woman would no longer listen to him; he was the cause of it all. From a spirit of contradiction she hung up near the bedside of the patient a basin filled with holy-water and a branch of box.

Religion, however, seemed no more able to succour him than surgery, and the invincible gangrene still spread from the extremities towards the stomach. It was all very well to vary the potions and change the poultices; the muscles each day rotted more and more; and at last Charles replied by an affirmative nod of the head when Mere Lefrancois, asked him if she could not, as a forlorn hope, send for Monsieur Canivet of Neufchatel, who was a celebrity.

A doctor of medicine, fifty years of age, enjoying a good position and self-possessed, Charles's colleague did not refrain from laughing disdainfully when he had uncovered the leg, mortified to the knee. Then having flatly declared that it must be amputated, he went off to the chemist's to rail at the asses who could have reduced a poor man to such a state. Shaking Monsieur Homais by the button of his coat, he shouted out in the shop:

"These are the inventions of Paris! These are the ideas of those gentry of the capital! It is like strabismus, chloroform, lithotrity, a heap of monstrosities that the Government ought to prohibit. But they want to do the clever, and they cram you with remedies without, troubling about the consequences. We are not so clever, not we! We are not savants, coxcombs, fops! We are practitioners; we cure people, and we should not dream of operating on anyone who is in perfect health. Straighten club-feet! As if one could straighten club-feet! It is as if one wished, for example, to make a hunchback straight!"

Homais suffered as he listened to this discourse, and he concealed his discomfort beneath a courtier's smile; for he needed to humour Monsier Canivet, whose prescriptions sometimes came as far as Yonville. So he did not take up the defence of Bovary; he did not even make a single remark, and, renouncing his principles, he sacrificed his dignity to the more serious interests of his business.

— Laissez-le! Laissez-le! vous lui perturbez le moral avec votre mysticisme!

Mais la bonne femme ne voulait plus l'entendre. Il était la cause de tout. Par esprit de contradiction, elle accrocha même au chevet du malade un bénitier tout plein, avec une branche de buis.

Cependant la religion pas plus que la chirurgie ne paraissait le secourir, et l'invincible pourriture allait montant toujours des extrémités vers le ventre. On avait beau varier les potions et changer les cataplasmes, les muscles chaque jour se décollaient davantage, et enfin Charles répondit par un signe de tête affirmatif quand la mère Lefrançois lui demanda si elle ne pourrait point, en désespoir de cause, faire venir M. Canivet, de Neufchâtel, qui était une célébrité.

Docteur en médecine, âgé de cinquante ans, jouissant d'une bonne position et sûr de lui-même, le confrère ne se gêna pas pour rire dédaigneusement lorsqu'il découvrit cette jambe gangrenée jusqu'au genou. Puis, ayant déclaré net qu'il la fallait amputer, il s'en alla chez le pharmacien déblatérer contre les ânes qui avaient pu réduire un malheureux homme en un tel état. Secouant M. Homais par le bouton de sa redingote, il vociférait dans la pharmacie:

— Ce sont là des inventions de Paris! Voilà les idées de ces messieurs de la Capitale! c'est comme le strabisme, le chloroforme et la lithotritie, un tas de monstruosités que le gouvernement devrait défendre! Mais on veut faire le malin, et l'on vous fourre des remèdes sans s'inquiéter des conséquences. Nous ne sommes pas si forts que cela, nous autres; nous ne sommes pas des savants, des mirliflores, des jolis coeurs; nous sommes des praticiens, des guérisseurs, et nous n'imaginerions pas d'opérer quelqu'un qui se porte à merveille! Redresser des pieds-bots! est-ce qu'on peut redresser les pieds-bots? c'est comme si l'on voulait, par exemple, rendre droit un bossu!

Homais souffrait en écoutant ce discours, et il dissimulait son malaise sous un sourire de courtisan, ayant besoin de ménager M. Canivet, dont les ordonnances quelquefois arrivaient jusqu'à Yonville; aussi ne prit-il pas la défense de Bovary, ne fit-il même aucune observation, et, abandonnant ses principes, il sacrifia sa dignité aux intérêts plus sérieux de sort négoce.

This amputation of the thigh by Doctor Canivet was a great event in the village. On that day all the inhabitants got up earlier, and the Grande Rue, although full of people, had something lugubrious about it, as if an execution had been expected. At the grocer's they discussed Hippolyte's illness; the shops did no business, and Madame Tuvache, the mayor's wife, did not stir from her window, such was her impatience to see the operator arrive.

He came in his gig, which he drove himself. But the springs of the right side having at length given way beneath the weight of his corpulence, it happened that the carriage as it rolled along leaned over a little, and on the other cushion near him could be seen a large box covered in red sheep-leather, whose three brass clasps shone grandly.

After he had entered like a whirlwind the porch of the "Lion d'Or," the doctor, shouting very loud, ordered them to unharness his horse. Then he went into the stable to see that she was eating her oats all right; for on arriving at a patient's he first of all looked after his mare and his gig. People even said about this: "Ah! Monsieur Canivet's a character!" And he was the more esteemed for this imperturbable coolness. The universe to the last man might have died, and he would not have missed the smallest of his habits.

Homais presented himself.

"I count on you," said the doctor. "Are we ready? Come along!"

But the druggist, turning red, confessed that he was too sensitive to assist at such an operation.

"When one is a simple spectator," he said, "the imagination, you know, is impressed. And then I have such a nervous system!"

"Pshaw!" interrupted Canivet; "on the contrary, you seem to me inclined to apoplexy. Besides, that doesn't astonish me, for you chemist fellows are always poking about your kitchens, which must end by spoiling your constitutions. Now just look at me. I get up every day at four o'clock; I shave with cold water (and am never cold). I don't wear flannels, and I never catch cold; my carcass is good enough! I live now in one way, now in another, like a philosopher, taking pot-luck; that is why I am not squeamish like you, and it is as indifferent to me to carve

Ce fut dans le village un événement considérable que cette amputation de cuisse par le docteur Canivet! Tous les habitants, ce jour-là, s'étaient levés de meilleure heure, et la Grande-Rue, bien que pleine de monde, avait quelque chose de lugubre comme s'il se fût agi d'une exécution capitale. On discutait chez l'épicier sur la maladie d'Hippolyte; les boutiques ne vendaient rien, et madame Tuvache, la femme du maire, ne bougeait pas de sa fenêtre, par l'impatience où elle était de voir venir l'opérateur.

Il arriva dans son cabriolet, qu'il conduisait lui-même. Mais, le ressort du coté droit s'étant à la longue affaissé sous le poids de sa corpulence, il se faisait que la voiture penchait un peu tout en allant, et l'on apercevait sur l'autre coussin près de lui une vaste boîte, recouverte de basane rouge, dont les trois fermoirs de cuivre brillaient magistralement.

Quand il fut entré comme un tourbillon sous le porche du Lion d'or, le docteur, criant très haut, ordonna de dételer son cheval, puis il alla dans l'écurie voir s'il mangeait bien l'avoine; car, en arrivant chez ses malades, il s'occupait d'abord de sa jument et de son cabriolet. On disait même à ce propos: «Ah! M. Canivet, c'est un original!» Et on l'estimait davantage pour cet inébranlable aplomb. L'univers aurait pu crever jusqu'au dernier homme, qu'il n'eût pas failli à la moindre de ses habitudes.

Homais se présenta.

— Je compte sur vous, fit le docteur. Sommes-nous prêts? En marche!

Mais l'apothicaire, en rougissant, avoua qu'il était trop sensible pour assister à une pareille opération.

— Quand on est simple spectateur, disait-il, l'imagination, vous savez, se frappe! Et puis j'ai le système nerveux tellement…

— Ah bah! interrompit Canivet, vous me paraissez, au contraire, porté à l'apoplexie. Et, d'ailleurs, cela ne m'étonne pas; car, vous autres, messieurs les pharmaciens, vous êtes continuellement fourrés dans votre cuisine, ce qui doit finir par altérer votre tempérament. Regardez-moi, plutôt: tous les jours, je me lève à quatre heures, je fais ma barbe à l'eau froide (je n'ai jamais froid), et je ne porte pas de flanelle, je n'attrape aucun rhume, le coffre est bon! Je vis tantôt d'une manière, tantôt d'une autre, en philosophe, au hasard de la fourchette. C'est pourquoi je ne suis point délicat comme

a Christian as the first fowl that turns up. Then, perhaps, you will say, habit! habit!"

Then, without any consideration for Hippolyte, who was sweating with agony between his sheets, these gentlemen entered into a conversation, in which the druggist compared the coolness of a surgeon to that of a general; and this comparison was pleasing to Canivet, who launched out on the exigencies of his art. He looked upon, it as a sacred office, although the ordinary practitioners dishonoured it. At last, coming back to the patient, he examined the bandages brought by Homais, the same that had appeared for the club-foot, and asked for someone to hold the limb for him. Lestiboudois was sent for, and Monsieur Canivet having turned up his sleeves, passed into the billiard-room, while the druggist stayed with Artemise and the landlady, both whiter than their aprons, and with ears strained towards the door.

Bovary during this time did not dare to stir from his house. He kept downstairs in the sitting-room by the side of the fireless chimney, his chin on his breast, his hands clasped, his eyes staring. "What a mishap!" he thought, "what a mishap!" Perhaps, after all, he had made some slip. He thought it over, but could hit upon nothing. But the most famous surgeons also made mistakes; and that is what no one would ever believe! People, on the contrary, would laugh, jeer! It would spread as far as Forges, as Neufchatel, as Rouen, everywhere! Who could say if his colleagues would not write against him. Polemics would ensue; he would have to answer in the papers. Hippolyte might even prosecute him. He saw himself dishonoured, ruined, lost; and his imagination, assailed by a world of hypotheses, tossed amongst them like an empty cask borne by the sea and floating upon the waves.

Emma, opposite, watched him; she did not share his humiliation; she felt another—that of having supposed such a man was worth anything. As if twenty times already she had not sufficiently perceived his mediocrity.

vous, et il m'est aussi parfaitement égal de découper un chrétien que la première volaille venue. Après ça, direz-vous, l'habitude..., l'habitude!...

Alors, sans aucun égard pour Hippolyte, qui suait d'angoisse entre ses draps, ces messieurs engagèrent une conversation où l'apothicaire compara le sang-froid d'un chirurgien à celui d'un général; et ce rapprochement fut agréable à Canivet, qui se répandit en paroles sur les exigences de son art. Il le considérait comme un sacerdoce, bien que les officiers de santé le déshonorassent. Enfin, revenant au malade, il examina les bandes apportées par Homais, les mêmes qui avaient comparu lors du pied- bot, et demanda quelqu'un pour lui tenir le membre. On envoya chercher Lestiboudois, et M. Canivet, ayant retroussé ses manches, passa dans la salle de billard, tandis que l'apothicaire restait avec Artémise et l'aubergiste, plus pâles toutes les deux que leur tablier, et l'oreille tendue contre la porte.

Bovary, pendant ce temps-là, n'osait bouger de sa maison. Il se tenait en bas, dans la salle, assis au coin de la cheminée sans feu, le menton sur sa poitrine, les mains jointes, les yeux fixes. Quelle mésaventure! pensait-il, quel désappointement! Il avait pris pourtant toutes les précautions imaginables. La fatalité s'en était mêlée. N'importe! si Hippolyte plus tard venait à mourir, c'est lui qui l'aurait assassiné. Et puis, quelle raison donnerait-il dans les visites, quand on l'interrogerait? Peut- être, cependant, s'était-il trompé en quelque chose? Il cherchait, ne trouvait pas. Mais les plus fameux chirurgiens se trompaient bien. Voilà ce qu'on ne voudrait jamais croire! on allait rire, au contraire, clabauder! Cela se répandrait jusqu'à Forges! jusqu'à Neufchâtel! jusqu'à Rouen! partout! Qui sait si des confrères n'écriraient pas contre lui? Une polémique s'ensuivrait, il faudrait répondre dans les journaux. Hippolyte même pouvait lui faire un procès. Il se voyait déshonoré, ruiné, perdu! Et son imagination, assaillie par une multitude d'hypothèses, ballottait au milieu d'elles comme un tonneau vide emporté à la mer et qui roule sur les flots.

Emma, en face de lui, le regardait; elle ne partageait pas son humiliation, elle en éprouvait une autre: c'était de s'être imaginé qu'un pareil homme pût valoir quelque chose, comme si vingt fois déjà elle n'avait pas suffisamment aperçu sa médiocrité.

Charles was walking up and down the room; his boots creaked on the floor.

"Sit down," she said; "you fidget me."

He sat down again.

How was it that she—she, who was so intelligent—could have allowed herself to be deceived again? and through what deplorable madness had she thus ruined her life by continual sacrifices? She recalled all her instincts of luxury, all the privations of her soul, the sordidness of marriage, of the household, her dream sinking into the mire like wounded swallows; all that she had longed for, all that she had denied herself, all that she might have had! And for what? for what?

In the midst of the silence that hung over the village a heart-rending cry rose on the air. Bovary turned white to fainting. She knit her brows with a nervous gesture, then went on. And it was for him, for this creature, for this man, who understood nothing, who felt nothing! For he was there quite quiet, not even suspecting that the ridicule of his name would henceforth sully hers as well as his. She had made efforts to love him, and she had repented with tears for having yielded to another!

"But it was perhaps a valgus!" suddenly exclaimed Bovary, who was meditating.

At the unexpected shock of this phrase falling on her thought like a leaden bullet on a silver plate, Emma, shuddering, raised her head in order to find out what he meant to say; and they looked at the other in silence, almost amazed to see each other, so far sundered were they by their inner thoughts. Charles gazed at her with the dull look of a drunken man, while he listened motionless to the last cries of the sufferer, that followed each other in long-drawn modulations, broken by sharp spasms like the far-off howling of some beast being slaughtered. Emma bit her wan lips, and rolling between her fingers a piece of coral that she had broken, fixed on Charles the burning glance of her eyes like two arrows of fire about to dart forth. Everything in him irritated her now; his face, his dress, what he did not say, his whole person, his existence, in fine. She repented of her past virtue as of a crime, and what still remained of it rumbled away beneath the furious blows of her

Charles se promenait de long en large, dans la chambre. Ses bottes craquaient sur le parquet.

— Assieds-toi, dit-elle, tu m'agaces!

Il se rassit.

Comment donc avait-elle fait (elle qui était si intelligente!) pour se méprendre encore une fois? Du reste, par quelle déplorable manie avoir ainsi abîmé son existence en sacrifices continuels? Elle se rappela tous ses instincts de luxe, toutes les privations de son âme, les bassesses du mariage, du ménage, ses rêves tombant dans la boue comme des hirondelles blessées, tout ce qu'elle avait désiré, tout ce qu'elle s'était refusé, tout ce qu'elle aurait pu avoir! et pourquoi? pourquoi?

Au milieu du silence qui emplissait le village, un cri déchirant traversa l'air. Bovary devint pâle à s'évanouir. Elle fronça les sourcils d'un geste nerveux, puis continua. C'était pour lui cependant, pour cet être, pour cet homme qui ne comprenait rien, qui ne sentait rien! car il était là, tout tranquillement, et sans même se douter que le ridicule de son nom allait désormais la salir comme lui. Elle avait fait des efforts pour l'aimer, et elle s'était repentie en pleurant d'avoir cédé à un autre.

— Mais c'était peut-être un valgus! exclama soudain Bovary, qui méditait.

Au choc imprévu de cette phrase tombant sur sa pensée comme une balle de plomb clins un plat d'argent, Emma tressaillant leva la tête pour deviner ce qu'il voulait dire; et ils se regardèrent silencieusement, presque ébahis de se voir, tant ils étaient par leur conscience éloignés l'un de l'autre. Charles la considérait avec le regard trouble d'un homme ivre, tout en écoutant, immobile, les derniers cris de l'amputé qui se suivaient en modulations traînantes, coupées de saccades aiguës, comme le hurlement lointain de quelque bête qu'on égorge. Emma mordait ses lèvres blêmes, et, roulant entre ses doigts un des brins du polypier qu'elle avait cassé, elle fixait sur Charles la pointe ardente de ses prunelles, comme deux flèches de feu prêtes à partir. Tout en lui l'irritait maintenant, sa figure, son costume, ce qu'il ne disait pas, sa personne entière, son existence enfin. Elle se repentait, comme d'un crime, de sa vertu passée, et ce qui en restait encore s'écroulait sous les

pride. She revelled in all the evil ironies of triumphant adultery. The memory of her lover came back to her with dazzling attractions; she threw her whole soul into it, borne away towards this image with a fresh enthusiasm; and Charles seemed to her as much removed from her life, as absent forever, as impossible and annihilated, as if he had been about to die and were passing under her eyes.

There was a sound of steps on the pavement. Charles looked up, and through the lowered blinds he saw at the corner of the market in the broad sunshine Dr. Canivet, who was wiping his brow with his handkerchief. Homais, behind him, was carrying a large red box in his hand, and both were going towards the chemist's.

Then with a feeling of sudden tenderness and discouragement Charles turned to his wife saying to her:

"Oh, kiss me, my own!"

"Leave me!" she said, red with anger.

"What is the matter?" he asked, stupefied. "Be calm; compose yourself. You know well enough that I love you. Come!"

"Enough!" she cried with a terrible look.

And escaping from the room, Emma closed the door so violently that the barometer fell from the wall and smashed on the floor.

Charles sank back into his arm-chair overwhelmed, trying to discover what could be wrong with her, fancying some nervous illness, weeping, and vaguely feeling something fatal and incomprehensible whirling round him.

When Rodolphe came to the garden that evening, he found his mistress waiting for him at the foot of the steps on the lowest stair. They threw their arms round one another, and all their rancour melted like snow beneath the warmth of that kiss.

coups furieux de son orgueil. Elle se délectait dans toutes les ironies mauvaises de l'adultère triomphant. Le souvenir de son amant revenait à elle avec des attractions vertigineuses: elle y jetait son âme, emportée vers cette image par un enthousiasme nouveau; et Charles lui semblait aussi détaché de sa vie, aussi absent pour toujours, aussi impossible et anéanti, que s'il allait mourir et qu'il eût agonisé sous ses yeux.

Il se fit un bruit de pas sur le trottoir. Charles regarda; et, à travers la jalousie baissée, il aperçut au bord des halles, en plein soleil, le docteur Canivet qui s'essuyait le front avec son foulard. Homais, derrière lui, portait à la main une grande boîte rouge, et ils se dirigeaient tous les deux du côté de la pharmacie.

Alors, par tendresse subite et découragement, Charles se tourna vers sa femme en lui disant:

— Embrasse-moi donc, ma bonne!

— Laisse-moi! fit-elle, toute rouge de colère.

— Qu'as-tu? qu'as-tu? répétait-il stupéfait. Calme-toi! reprends-toi!... Tu sais bien que je t'aime! ... viens!

— Assez! s'écria-t-elle d'un air terrible.

Et s'échappant de la salle, Emma ferma la porte si fort, que le baromètre bondit de la muraille et s'écrasa par terre.

Charles s'affaissa dans son fauteuil, bouleversé, cherchant ce qu'elle pouvait avoir, imaginant une maladie nerveuse, pleurant, et sentant vaguement circuler autour de lui quelque chose de funeste et d'incompréhensible.

Quand Rodolphe, le soir, arriva dans le jardin, il trouva sa maîtresse qui l'attendait au bas du perron, sur la première marche. Ils s'étreignirent, et toute leur rancune se fondit comme une neige sous la chaleur de ce baiser.

# Chapter 12

They began to love one another again. Often, even in the middle of the day, Emma suddenly wrote to him, then from the window made a sign to Justin, who, taking his apron off, quickly ran to La Huchette. Rodolphe would come; she had sent for him to tell him that she was bored, that her husband was odious, her life frightful.

"But what can I do?" he cried one day impatiently.

"Ah! if you would—"

She was sitting on the floor between his knees, her hair loose, her look lost.

"Why, what?" said Rodolphe.

She sighed.

"We would go and live elsewhere—somewhere!"

"You are really mad!" he said laughing. "How could that be possible?"

She returned to the subject; he pretended not to understand, and turned the conversation.

What he did not understand was all this worry about so simple an affair as love. She had a motive, a reason, and, as it were, a pendant to her affection.

Her tenderness, in fact, grew each day with her repulsion to her husband. The more she gave up herself to the one, the more she loathed the other. Never had Charles seemed to her so disagreeable, to have such stodgy fingers, such vulgar ways, to be so dull as when they found themselves together after her meeting with Rodolphe. Then, while playing the spouse and virtue, she was burning at the thought of that head whose black hair fell in a curl over the sunburnt brow, of that form at once so strong and elegant, of that man, in a word, who had such experience in his reasoning, such passion in his desires. It was for him that she filed her nails with the care of a chaser, and that there was never enough cold-cream for her skin, nor of patchouli for her handkerchiefs.

# Chapitre 12

Ils recommencèrent à s'aimer. Souvent même, au milieu de la journée, Emma lui écrivait tout à coup; puis, à travers les carreaux, faisait un signe à Justin, qui, dénouant vite sa serpillière, s'envolait à la Huchette. Rodolphe arrivait; c'était pour lui dire qu'elle s'ennuyait, que son mari était odieux et son existence affreuse!

— Est-ce que j'y peux quelque chose? s'écria-t-il un jour, impatienté.

— Ah! si tu voulais! ...

Elle était assise par terre, entre ses genoux, les bandeaux dénoués, le regard perdu.

— Quoi donc? fit Rodolphe.

Elle soupira.

— Nous irions vivre ailleurs..., quelque part...

— Tu es folle, vraiment! dit-il en riant. Est-ce possible?

Elle revint là-dessus; il eut l'air de ne pas comprendre et détourna la conversation.

Ce qu'il ne comprenait pas, c'était tout ce trouble dans une chose aussi simple que l'amour. Elle avait un motif, une raison, et comme un auxiliaire à son attachement.

Cette tendresse, en effet, chaque jour s'accroissait davantage sous la répulsion du mari. Plus elle se livrait à l'un, plus elle exécrait l'autre; jamais Charles ne lui paraissait aussi désagréable, avoir les doigts aussi carrés, l'esprit aussi lourd, les façons si communes qu'après ses rendez-vous avec Rodolphe, quand ils se trouvaient ensemble. Alors, tout en faisant l'épouse et la vertueuse, elle s'enflammait à l'idée de cette tête dont les cheveux noirs se tournaient en une boucle vers le front hâlé, de cette taille à la fois si robuste et si élégante, de cet homme enfin qui possédait tant d'expérience dans la raison, tant d'emportement dans le désir! C'était pour lui qu'elle se limait les ongles avec un soin de ciseleur, et qu'il n'y avait jamais assez de cold-cream sur sa peau, ni de patchouli dans ses

She loaded herself with bracelets, rings, and necklaces. When he was coming she filled the two large blue glass vases with roses, and prepared her room and her person like a courtesan expecting a prince. The servant had to be constantly washing linen, and all day Felicite did not stir from the kitchen, where little Justin, who often kept her company, watched her at work.

With his elbows on the long board on which she was ironing, he greedily watched all these women's clothes spread about him, the dimity petticoats, the fichus, the collars, and the drawers with running strings, wide at the hips and growing narrower below.

"What is that for?" asked the young fellow, passing his hand over the crinoline or the hooks and eyes.

"Why, haven't you ever seen anything?" Felicite answered laughing. "As if your mistress, Madame Homais, didn't wear the same."

"Oh, I daresay! Madame Homais!"

And he added with a meditative air:

"As if she were a lady like madame!"

But Felicite grew impatient of seeing him hanging round her. She was six years older than he, and Theodore, Monsieur Guillaumin's servant, was beginning to pay court to her.

"Let me alone," she said, moving her pot of starch. "You'd better be off and pound almonds; you are always dangling about women. Before you meddle with such things, bad boy, wait till you've got a beard to your chin."

"Oh, don't be cross! I'll go and clean her boots."

And he at once took down from the shelf Emma's boots, all coated with mud, the mud of the rendezvous, that crumbled into powder beneath his fingers, and that he watched as it gently rose in a ray of sunlight.

"How afraid you are of spoiling them!" said the servant, who wasn't so particular when she cleaned them herself, because as soon as the stuff of the boots was no longer fresh madame handed them over to her.

Emma had a number in her cupboard that she squandered one after the other, without Charles allowing himself the slightest observation.

mouchoirs. Elle se chargeait de bracelets, de bagues, de colliers. Quand il devait venir, elle emplissait de roses ses deux grands vases de verre bleu, et disposait son appartement et sa personne comme une courtisane qui attend un prince. Il fallait que la domestique fût sans cesse à blanchir du linge; et, de toute la journée, Félicité ne bougeait de la cuisine, où le petit Justin, qui souvent lui tenait compagnie, la regardait travailler.

Le coude sur la longue planche où elle repassait, il considérait avidement toutes ces affaires de femmes étalées autour de lui: les jupons de basin, les fichus, les collerettes, et les pantalons à coulisse, vastes de hanches et qui se rétrécissaient par le bas.

— À quoi cela sert-il? demandait le jeune garçon en passant sa main sur la crinoline ou les agrafes.

— Tu n'as donc jamais rien vu? répondait en riant Félicité; comme si ta patronne, madame Homais, n'en portait pas de pareils.

— Ah bien oui! madame Homais!

Et il ajoutait d'un ton méditatif:

— Est-ce que c'est une dame comme Madame?

Mais Félicité s'impatientait de le voir tourner ainsi tout autour d'elle. Elle avait six ans de plus, et Théodore, le domestique de M. Guillaumin, commençait à lui faire la cour.

— Laisse-moi tranquille! disait-elle en déplaçant son pot d'empois. Va-t'en plutôt piler des amandes; tu es toujours à fourrager du côté des femmes; attends pour te mêler de ça, méchant mioche, que tu aies de la barbe au menton.

— Allons, ne vous fâchez pas, je m'en vais vous faire ses bottines.

Et aussitôt, il atteignait sur le chambranle les chaussures d'Emma, tout empâtées de crotte — la crotte des rendez-vous — qui se détachait en poudre sous ses doigts, et qu'il regardait monter doucement dans un rayon de soleil.

— Comme tu as peur de les abîmer! disait la cuisinière, qui n'y mettait pas tant de façons quand elle les nettoyait elle-même, parce que Madame, dès que l'étoffe n'était plus fraîche, les lui abandonnait.

Emma en avait une quantité dans son armoire, et qu'elle gaspillait à mesure, sans que jamais Charles se permît la moindre observation.

So also he disbursed three hundred francs for a wooden leg that she thought proper to make a present of to Hippolyte. Its top was covered with cork, and it had spring joints, a complicated mechanism, covered over by black trousers ending in a patent-leather boot. But Hippolyte, not daring to use such a handsome leg every day, begged Madame Bovary to get him another more convenient one. The doctor, of course, had again to defray the expense of this purchase.

So little by little the stable-man took up his work again. One saw him running about the village as before, and when Charles heard from afar the sharp noise of the wooden leg, he at once went in another direction.

It was Monsieur Lheureux, the shopkeeper, who had undertaken the order; this provided him with an excuse for visiting Emma. He chatted with her about the new goods from Paris, about a thousand feminine trifles, made himself very obliging, and never asked for his money. Emma yielded to this lazy mode of satisfying all her caprices. Thus she wanted to have a very handsome ridding-whip that was at an umbrella-maker's at Rouen to give to Rodolphe. The week after Monsieur Lheureux placed it on her table.

But the next day he called on her with a bill for two hundred and seventy francs, not counting the centimes. Emma was much embarrassed; all the drawers of the writing-table were empty; they owed over a fortnight's wages to Lestiboudois, two quarters to the servant, for any quantity of other things, and Bovary was impatiently expecting Monsieur Derozeray's account, which he was in the habit of paying every year about Midsummer.

She succeeded at first in putting off Lheureux. At last he lost patience; he was being sued; his capital was out, and unless he got some in he should be forced to take back all the goods she had received.

"Oh, very well, take them!" said Emma.

"I was only joking," he replied; "the only thing I regret is the whip. My word! I'll ask monsieur to return it to me."

"No, no!" she said.

C'est ainsi qu'il déboursa trois cents francs pour une jambe de bois dont elle jugea convenable de faire cadeau à Hippolyte. Le pilon en était garni de liège, et il y avait des articulations à ressort, une mécanique compliquée recouverte d'un pantalon noir, que terminait une botte vernie. Mais Hippolyte, n'osant à tous les jours se servir d'une si belle jambe, supplia madame Bovary de lui en procurer une autre plus commode. Le médecin, bien entendu, fit encore les frais de cette acquisition.

Donc, le garçon d'écurie peu à peu recommença son métier. On le voyait comme autrefois parcourir le village, et quand Charles entendait de loin, sur les pavés, le bruit sec de son bâton, il prenait bien vite une autre route.

C'était M. Lheureux, le marchand, qui s'était chargé de la commande; cela lui fournit l'occasion de fréquenter Emma. Il causait avec elle des nouveaux déballages de paris, de mille curiosités féminines, se montrait fort complaisant, et jamais ne réclamait d'argent. Emma s'abandonnait à cette facilité de satisfaire tous ses caprices. Ainsi, elle voulut avoir, pour la donner à Rodolphe, une fort belle cravache qui se trouvait à Rouen dans un magasin de parapluies. M. Lheureux, la semaine d'après, la lui posa sur sa table.

Mais le lendemain il se présenta chez elle avec une facture de deux cent soixante et dix francs, sans compter les centimes. Emma fut très embarrassée: tous les tiroirs du secrétaire étaient vides; on devait plus de quinze jours à Lestiboudois, deux trimestres à la servante, quantité d'autres choses encore, et Bovary attendait impatiemment l'envoi de M. Derozerays, qui avait coutume, chaque année, de le payer vers la Saint-Pierre.

Elle réussit d'abord à éconduire Lheureux; enfin il perdit patience; on le poursuivait, ses capitaux étaient absents, et, s'il ne rentrait dans quelques-uns, il serait forcé de lui reprendre toutes les marchandises qu'elle avait.

— Eh! reprenez-les! dit Emma.

— Oh! c'est pour rire! répliqua-t-il. Seulement, je ne regrette que la cravache. Ma foi! je la redemanderai à Monsieur.

— Non! non! fit-elle.

"Ah! I've got you!" thought Lheureux.

And, certain of his discovery, he went out repeating to himself in an undertone, and with his usual low whistle—

"Good! we shall see! we shall see!"

She was thinking how to get out of this when the servant coming in put on the mantelpiece a small roll of blue paper "from Monsieur Derozeray's." Emma pounced upon and opened it. It contained fifteen napoleons; it was the account. She heard Charles on the stairs; threw the gold to the back of her drawer, and took out the key.

Three days after Lheureux reappeared.

"I have an arrangement to suggest to you," he said. "If, instead of the sum agreed on, you would take—"

"Here it is," she said placing fourteen napoleons in his hand.

The tradesman was dumfounded. Then, to conceal his disappointment, he was profuse in apologies and proffers of service, all of which Emma declined; then she remained a few moments fingering in the pocket of her apron the two five-franc pieces that he had given her in change. She promised herself she would economise in order to pay back later on.

"Pshaw!" she thought, "he won't think about it again."

Besides the riding-whip with its silver-gilt handle, Rodolphe had received a seal with the motto *Amor nel cor* furthermore, a scarf for a muffler, and, finally, a cigar-case exactly like the Viscount's, that Charles had formerly picked up in the road, and that Emma had kept. These presents, however, humiliated him; he refused several; she insisted, and he ended by obeying, thinking her tyrannical and overexacting.

Then she had strange ideas.

"When midnight strikes," she said, "you must think of me."

And if he confessed that he had not thought of her, there were floods of reproaches that always ended with the eternal question:

"Do you love me?"

"Why, of course I love you," he answered.

"A great deal?"

"Certainly!"

"You haven't loved any others?"

— Ah! je te tiens! pensa Lheureux.

Et, sûr de sa découverte, il sortit en répétant à demi-voix et avec son petit sifflement habituel:

— Soit! nous verrons! nous verrons!

Elle rêvait comment se tirer de là, quand la cuisinière entrant, déposa sur la cheminée un petit rouleau de papier bleu, de la part de M. Derozerays. Emma sauta dessus, l'ouvrit. Il y avait quinze napoléons. C'était le compte. Elle entendit Charles dans l'escalier; elle jeta l'or au fond de son tiroir et prit la clef.

Trois jours après, Lheureux reparut.

— J'ai un arrangement à vous proposer, dit-il; si, au lieu de la somme convenue, vous vouliez prendre…

— La voilà, fit-elle en lui plaçant dans la main quatorze napoléons.

Le marchand fut stupéfait. Alors, pour dissimuler son désappointement, il se répandit en excuses et en offres de service qu'Emma refusa toutes; puis elle resta quelques minutes palpant dans la poche de son tablier les deux pièces de cent sous qu'il lui avait rendues. Elle se promettait d'économiser, afin de rendre plus tard…

— Ah bah! songea-t-elle, il n'y pensera plus.

Outre la cravache à pommeau de vermeil, Rodolphe avait reçu un cachet avec cette devise: *Amor nel cor*; de plus, une écharpe pour se faire un cache-nez, et enfin un porte-cigares tout pareil à celui du Vicomte, que Charles avait autrefois ramassé sur la route et qu'Emma conservait. Cependant ces cadeaux l'humiliaient. Il en refusa plusieurs; elle insista, et Rodolphe finit par obéir, la trouvant tyrannique et trop envahissante.

Puis elle avait d'étranges idées:

— Quand minuit sonnera, disait-elle, tu penseras à moi!

Et, s'il avouait n'y avoir point songé, c'étaient des reproches en abondance, et qui se terminaient toujours par l'éternel mot:

— M'aimes-tu?

— Mais oui, je t'aime! répondait-il.

— Beaucoup?

— Certainement!

— Tu n'en as pas aimé d'autres, hein?

"Did you think you'd got a virgin?" he exclaimed laughing.

Emma cried, and he tried to console her, adorning his protestations with puns.

"Oh," she went on, "I love you! I love you so that I could not live without you, do you see? There are times when I long to see you again, when I am torn by all the anger of love. I ask myself, Where is he? Perhaps he is talking to other women. They smile upon him; he approaches. Oh no; no one else pleases you. There are some more beautiful, but I love you best. I know how to love best. I am your servant, your concubine! You are my king, my idol! You are good, you are beautiful, you are clever, you are strong!"

He had so often heard these things said that they did not strike him as original. Emma was like all his mistresses; and the charm of novelty, gradually falling away like a garment, laid bare the eternal monotony of passion, that has always the same forms and the same language. He did not distinguish, this man of so much experience, the difference of sentiment beneath the sameness of expression. Because lips libertine and venal had murmured such words to him, he believed but little in the candour of hers; exaggerated speeches hiding mediocre affections must be discounted; as if the fullness of the soul did not sometimes overflow in the emptiest metaphors, since no one can ever give the exact measure of his needs, nor of his conceptions, nor of his sorrows; and since human speech is like a cracked tin kettle, on which we hammer out tunes to make bears dance when we long to move the stars.

But with that superior critical judgment that belongs to him who, in no matter what circumstance, holds back, Rodolphe saw other delights to be got out of this love. He thought all modesty in the way. He treated her quite off-handedly. He made of her something supple and corrupt. Hers was an idiotic sort of attachment, full of admiration for him, of voluptuousness for her, a beatitude that benumbed her; her soul sank into this drunkenness, shrivelled up, drowned in it, like Clarence in his butt of Malmsey.

— Crois-tu m'avoir pris vierge? exclamait-il en riant.

Emma pleurait, et il s'efforçait de la consoler, enjolivant de calembours ses protestations.

— Oh! c'est que je t'aime! reprenait-elle, je t'aime à ne pouvoir me passer de toi, sais-tu bien? J'ai quelquefois des envies de te revoir où toutes les colères de l'amour me déchirent. Je me demande: «Où est-il? Peut-être il parle à d'autres femmes? Elles lui sourient, il s'approche...» Oh! non, n'est-ce pas, aucune ne te plaît? Il y en a de plus belles; mais, moi, je sais mieux aimer! Je suis ta servante et ta concubine! Tu es mon roi, mon idole! tu es bon! tu es beau! tu es intelligent! tu es fort!

Il s'était tant de fois entendu dire ces choses, qu'elles n'avaient pour lui rien d'original. Emma ressemblait à toutes les maîtresses; et le charme de la nouveauté, peu à peu tombant comme un vêtement, laissait voir à nu l'éternelle monotonie de la passion, qui a toujours les mêmes formes et le même langage. Il ne distinguait pas, cet homme si plein de pratique, la dissemblance des sentiments sous la parité des expressions. Parce que des lèvres libertines ou vénales lui avaient murmuré des phrases pareilles, il ne croyait que faiblement à la candeur de celles-là; on en devait rabattre, pensait-il, les discours exagérés cachant les affections médiocres; comme si la plénitude de l'âme ne débordait pas quelquefois par les métaphores les plus vides, puisque personne, jamais, ne peut donner l'exacte mesure de ses besoins, ni de ses conceptions, ni de ses douleurs, et que la parole humaine est comme un chaudron fêlé où nous battons des mélodies à faire danser les ours, quand on voudrait attendrir les étoiles.

Mais, avec cette supériorité de critique appartenant à celui qui, dans n'importe quel engagement, se tient en arrière, Rodolphe aperçut en cet amour d'autres jouissances à exploiter. Il jugea toute pudeur incommode. Il la traita sans façon. Il en fit quelque chose de souple et de corrompu. C'était une sorte d'attachement idiot plein d'admiration pour lui, de voluptés pour elle, une béatitude qui l'engourdissait; et son âme s'enfonçait en cette ivresse et s'y noyait, ratatinée, comme le duc de Clarence dans son tonneau de malvoisie.

By the mere effect of her love Madame Bovary's manners changed. Her looks grew bolder, her speech more free; she even committed the impropriety of walking out with Monsieur Rodolphe, a cigarette in her mouth, "as if to defy the people." At last, those who still doubted doubted no longer when one day they saw her getting out of the "Hirondelle," her waist squeezed into a waistcoat like a man; and Madame Bovary senior, who, after a fearful scene with her husband, had taken refuge at her son's, was not the least scandalised of the women-folk. Many other things displeased her. First, Charles had not attended to her advice about the forbidding of novels; then the "ways of the house" annoyed her; she allowed herself to make some remarks, and there were quarrels, especially one on account of Felicite.

Madame Bovary senior, the evening before, passing along the passage, had surprised her in company of a man—a man with a brown collar, about forty years old, who, at the sound of her step, had quickly escaped through the kitchen. Then Emma began to laugh, but the good lady grew angry, declaring that unless morals were to be laughed at one ought to look after those of one's servants.

"Where were you brought up?" asked the daughter-in-law, with so impertinent a look that Madame Bovary asked her if she were not perhaps defending her own case.

"Leave the room!" said the young woman, springing up with a bound.

"Emma! Mamma!" cried Charles, trying to reconcile them.

But both had fled in their exasperation. Emma was stamping her feet as she repeated:

"Oh! what manners! What a peasant!"

He ran to his mother; she was beside herself. She stammered

"She is an insolent, giddy-headed thing, or perhaps worse!"

And she was for leaving at once if the other did not apologise. So Charles went back again to his wife and implored her to give way; he knelt to her; she ended by saying:

"Very well! I'll go to her."

And in fact she held out her hand to her mother-in-law with the dignity of a marchioness as she said:

Par l'effet seul de ses habitudes amoureuses, madame Bovary changea d'allures. Ses regards devinrent plus hardis, ses discours plus libres; elle eut même l'inconvenance de se promener avec M. Rodolphe, une cigarette à la bouche, comme pour narguer le monde; enfin, ceux qui doutaient encore ne doutèrent plus quand on la vit, un jour, descendre de l'Hirondelle, la taille serrée dans un gilet, à la façon d'un homme; et madame Bovary mère, qui, après une épouvantable scène avec son mari, était venue se réfugier chez son fils, ne fut pas la bourgeoise la moins scandalisée. Bien d'autres choses lui déplurent: d'abord Charles n'avait point écouté ses conseils pour l'interdiction des romans; puis, le genre de la maison lui déplaisait; elle se permit des observations, et l'on se fâcha, une fois surtout, à propos de Félicité.

Madame Bovary mère, la veille au soir, en traversant le corridor, l'avait surprise dans la compagnie d'un homme, un homme à collier brun, d'environ quarante ans, et qui, au bruit de ses pas, s'était vite échappé de la cuisine. Alors Emma se prit à rire; mais la bonne dame s'emporta, déclarant qu'à moins de se moquer des moeurs, on devait surveiller celles des domestiques.

— De quel monde êtes-vous? dit la bru, avec un regard tellement impertinent que madame Bovary lui demanda si elle ne défendait point sa propre cause.

— Sortez! fit la jeune femme se levant d'un bond.

— Emma!... maman!... s'écriait Charles pour les rapatrier.

Mais elles s'étaient enfuies toutes les deux dans leur exaspération. Emma trépignait en répétant:

— Ah! quel savoir-vivre! quelle paysanne!

Il courut à sa mère; elle était hors des gonds, elle balbutiait:

— C'est une insolente! une évaporée! pire, peut-être!

Et elle voulait partir immédiatement, si l'autre ne venait lui faire des excuses. Charles retourna donc vers sa femme et la conjura de céder; il se mit à genoux; elle finit par répondre:

— Soit! j'y vais.

En effet, elle tendit la main à sa belle-mère avec une dignité de marquise, en lui disant:

"Excuse me, madame."

Then, having gone up again to her room, she threw herself flat on her bed and cried there like a child, her face buried in the pillow.

She and Rodolphe had agreed that in the event of anything extraordinary occurring, she should fasten a small piece of white paper to the blind, so that if by chance he happened to be in Yonville, he could hurry to the lane behind the house. Emma made the signal; she had been waiting three-quarters of an hour when she suddenly caught sight of Rodolphe at the corner of the market. She felt tempted to open the window and call him, but he had already disappeared. She fell back in despair.

Soon, however, it seemed to her that someone was walking on the pavement. It was he, no doubt. She went downstairs, crossed the yard. He was there outside. She threw herself into his arms.

"Do take care!" he said.

"Ah! if you knew!" she replied.

And she began telling him everything, hurriedly, disjointedly, exaggerating the facts, inventing many, and so prodigal of parentheses that he understood nothing of it.

"Come, my poor angel, courage! Be comforted! be patient!"

"But I have been patient; I have suffered for four years. A love like ours ought to show itself in the face of heaven. They torture me! I can bear it no longer! Save me!"

She clung to Rodolphe. Her eyes, full of tears, flashed like flames beneath a wave; her breast heaved; he had never loved her so much, so that he lost his head and said:

"What is, it? What do you wish?"

"Take me away," she cried, "carry me off! Oh, I pray you!"

And she threw herself upon his mouth, as if to seize there the unexpected consent if breathed forth in a kiss.

"But—" Rodolphe resumed.

"What?"

"Your little girl!"

She reflected a few moments, then replied:

"We will take her! It can't be helped!"

— Excusez-moi, madame.

Puis, remontée chez elle, Emma se jeta tout à plat ventre sur son lit, et elle y pleura comme un enfant, la tête enfoncée dans l'oreiller.

Ils étaient convenus, elle et Rodolphe, qu'en cas d'événement extraordinaire, elle attacherait à la persienne un petit chiffon de papier blanc, afin que, si par hasard il se trouvait à Yonville, il accourût dans la ruelle, derrière la maison. Emma fit le signal; elle attendait depuis trois quarts d'heure, quand tout à coup elle aperçut Rodolphe au coin des halles. Elle fut tentée d'ouvrir la fenêtre, de l'appeler; mais déjà il avait disparu. Elle retomba désespérée.

Bientôt pourtant il lui sembla que l'on marchait sur le trottoir. C'était lui, sans doute; elle descendit l'escalier, traversa la cour. Il était là, dehors. Elle se jeta dans ses bras.

— Prends donc garde, dit-il.

— Ah! si tu savais! reprit-elle.

Et elle se mit à lui raconter tout, à la hâte, sans suite, exagérant les faits, en inventant plusieurs, et prodiguant les parenthèses si abondamment qu'il n'y comprenait rien.

— Allons, mon pauvre ange, du courage, console-toi, patience!

— Mais voilà quatre ans que je patiente et que je souffre!... Un amour comme le nôtre devrait s'avouer à la face du ciel! Ils sont à me torturer. Je n'y tiens plus! Sauve-moi!

Elle se serrait contre Rodolphe. Ses yeux, pleins de larmes, étincelaient comme des flammes sous l'onde; sa gorge haletait à coups rapides; jamais il ne l'avait tant aimée; si bien qu'il en perdit la tête et qu'il lui dit:

— Que faut-il faire? que veux-tu?

— Emmène-moi! s'écria-t-elle. Enlève-moi!... Oh! je t'en supplie!

Et elle se précipita sur sa bouche, comme pour y saisir le consentement inattendu qui s'en exhalait dans un baiser.

— Mais... reprit Rodolphe.

— Quoi donc?

— Et ta fille?

Elle réfléchit quelques minutes, puis répondit:

— Nous la prendrons, tant pis!

"What a woman!" he said to himself, watching her as she went.

For she had run into the garden. Someone was calling her.

On the following days Madame Bovary senior was much surprised at the change in her daughter-in-law. Emma, in fact, was showing herself more docile, and even carried her deference so far as to ask for a recipe for pickling gherkins.

Was it the better to deceive them both? Or did she wish by a sort of voluptuous stoicism to feel the more profoundly the bitterness of the things she was about to leave? But she paid no heed to them; on the contrary, she lived as lost in the anticipated delight of her coming happiness. It was an eternal subject for conversation with Rodolphe. She leant on his shoulder murmuring:

"Ah! when we are in the mail-coach! Do you think about it? Can it be? It seems to me that the moment I feel the carriage start, it will be as if we were rising in a balloon, as if we were setting out for the clouds. Do you know that I count the hours? And you?"

Never had Madame Bovary been so beautiful as at this period; she had that indefinable beauty that results from joy, from enthusiasm, from success, and that is only the harmony of temperament with circumstances. Her desires, her sorrows, the experience of pleasure, and her ever-young illusions, that had, as soil and rain and winds and the sun make flowers grow, gradually developed her, and she at length blossomed forth in all the plenitude of her nature. Her eyelids seemed chiselled expressly for her long amorous looks in which the pupil disappeared, while a strong inspiration expanded her delicate nostrils and raised the fleshy corner of her lips, shaded in the light by a little black down. One would have thought that an artist apt in conception had arranged the curls of hair upon her neck; they fell in a thick mass, negligently, and with the changing chances of their adultery, that unbound them every day. Her voice now took more mellow infections, her figure also; something subtle and penetrating escaped even from the folds of her gown and from the line of her foot. Charles, as when they were first married, thought her delicious and quite irresistible.

— Quelle femme! se dit-il en la regardant s'éloigner.

Car elle venait de s'échapper dans le jardin. On l'appelait.

La mère Bovary, les jours suivants, fut très étonnée de la métamorphose de sa bru. En effet, Emma se montra plus docile, et même poussa la déférence jusqu'à lui demander une recette pour faire mariner des cornichons.

Était-ce afin de les mieux duper l'un et l'autre? ou bien voulait-elle, par une sorte de stoïcisme voluptueux, sentir plus profondément l'amertume des choses qu'elle allait abandonner? Mais elle n'y prenait garde, au contraire; elle vivait comme perdue dans la dégustation anticipée de son bonheur prochain. C'était avec Rodolphe un éternel sujet de causeries. Elle s'appuyait sur son épaule, elle murmurait:

— Hein! quand nous serons dans la malle-poste!... Y songes-tu? Est-ce possible? Il me semble qu'au moment où je sentirai la voiture s'élancer, ce sera comme si nous montions en ballon, comme si nous partions vers les nuages. Sais-tu que je compte les jours?... Et toi?

Jamais madame Bovary ne fut aussi belle qu'à cette époque; elle avait cette indéfinissable beauté qui résulte de la joie, de l'enthousiasme, du succès, et qui n'est que l'harmonie du tempérament avec les circonstances. Ses convoitises, ses chagrins, l'expérience du plaisir et ses illusions toujours jeunes, comme font aux fleurs le fumier, la pluie, les vents et le soleil, l'avaient par gradations développée, et elle s'épanouissait enfin dans la plénitude de sa nature. Ses paupières semblaient taillées tout exprès pour ses longs regards amoureux où la prunelle se perdait, tandis qu'un souffle fort écartait ses narines minces et relevait le coin charnu de ses lèvres, qu'ombrageait à la lumière un peu de duvet noir. On eût dit qu'un artiste habile en corruptions avait disposé sur sa nuque la torsade de ses cheveux: ils s'enroulaient en une masse lourde, négligemment, et selon les hasards de l'adultère, qui les dénouait tous les jours. Sa voix maintenant prenait des inflexions plus molles, sa taille aussi; quelque chose de subtil qui vous pénétrait se dégageait même des draperies de sa robe et de la cambrure de son pied. Charles, comme aux premiers temps de son mariage, la trouvait délicieuse et tout irrésistible.

When he came home in the middle of the night, he did not dare to wake her. The porcelain night-light threw a round trembling gleam upon the ceiling, and the drawn curtains of the little cot formed as it were a white hut standing out in the shade, and by the bedside Charles looked at them. He seemed to hear the light breathing of his child. She would grow big now; every season would bring rapid progress. He already saw her coming from school as the day drew in, laughing, with ink-stains on her jacket, and carrying her basket on her arm. Then she would have to be sent to the boarding-school; that would cost much; how was it to be done? Then he reflected. He thought of hiring a small farm in the neighbourhood, that he would superintend every morning on his way to his patients. He would save up what he brought in; he would put it in the savings-bank. Then he would buy shares somewhere, no matter where; besides, his practice would increase; he counted upon that, for he wanted Berthe to be well-educated, to be accomplished, to learn to play the piano. Ah! how pretty she would be later on when she was fifteen, when, resembling her mother, she would, like her, wear large straw hats in the summer-time; from a distance they would be taken for two sisters. He pictured her to himself working in the evening by their side beneath the light of the lamp; she would embroider him slippers; she would look after the house; she would fill all the home with her charm and her gaiety. At last, they would think of her marriage; they would find her some good young fellow with a steady business; he would make her happy; this would last for ever.

Emma was not asleep; she pretended to be; and while he dozed off by her side she awakened to other dreams.

To the gallop of four horses she was carried away for a week towards a new land, whence they would return no more. They went on and on, their arms entwined, without a word. Often from the top of a mountain there suddenly glimpsed some splendid city with domes, and bridges, and ships, forests of citron trees, and cathedrals of white marble, on whose pointed steeples were storks' nests. They went at a walking-pace because of the great flag-stones, and on the ground there were bouquets of flowers, offered you by women dressed in red bodices. They heard the

Quand il rentrait au milieu de la nuit, il n'osait pas la réveiller. La veilleuse de porcelaine arrondissait au plafond une clarté tremblante, et les rideaux fermés du petit berceau faisaient comme une hutte blanche qui se bombait dans l'ombre, au bord du lit. Charles les regardait. Il croyait entendre l'haleine légère de son enfant. Elle allait grandir maintenant; chaque saison, vite, amènerait un progrès. Il la voyait déjà revenant de l'école à la tombée du jour, toute rieuse, avec sa brassière tachée d'encre, et portant au bras son panier; puis il faudrait la mettre en pension, cela coûterait beaucoup; comment faire? Alors il réfléchissait. Il pensait à louer une petite ferme aux environs, et qu'il surveillerait lui-même, tous les matins, en allant voir ses malades. Il en économiserait le revenu, il le placerait à la caisse d'épargne; ensuite il achèterait des actions, quelque part, n'importe où; d'ailleurs, la clientèle augmenterait; il y comptait, car il voulait que Berthe fût bien élevée, qu'elle eût des talents, qu'elle apprît le piano. Ah! qu'elle serait jolie, plus tard, à quinze ans, quand, ressemblant à sa mère, elle porterait comme elle, dans l'été, de grands chapeaux de paille! On les prendrait de loin pour les deux soeurs. Il se la figurait travaillant le soir auprès d'eux, sous la lumière de la lampe; elle lui broderait des pantoufles; elle s'occuperait du ménage; elle emplirait toute la maison de sa gentillesse et de sa gaieté. Enfin, ils songeraient à son établissement: on lui trouverait quelque brave garçon ayant un état solide; il la rendrait heureuse; cela durerait toujours.

Emma ne dormait pas, elle faisait semblant d'être endormie; et, tandis qu'il s'assoupissait à ses côtés, elle se réveillait en d'autres rêves.

Au galop de quatre chevaux, elle était emportée depuis huit jours vers un pays nouveau, d'où ils ne reviendraient plus. Ils allaient, ils allaient, les bras enlacés, sans parler. Souvent, du haut d'une montagne, ils apercevaient tout à coup quelque cité splendide avec des dômes, des ponts, des navires, des forêts de citronniers et des cathédrales de marbre blanc, dont les clochers aigus portaient des nids de cigogne. On marchait au pas, à cause des grandes dalles, et il y avait par terre des bouquets de fleurs que vous offraient des femmes habillées en corset rouge. On enten-

chiming of bells, the neighing of mules, together with the murmur of guitars and the noise of fountains, whose rising spray refreshed heaps of fruit arranged like a pyramid at the foot of pale statues that smiled beneath playing waters. And then, one night they came to a fishing village, where brown nets were drying in the wind along the cliffs and in front of the huts. It was there that they would stay; they would live in a low, flat-roofed house, shaded by a palm-tree, in the heart of a gulf, by the sea. They would row in gondolas, swing in hammocks, and their existence would be easy and large as their silk gowns, warm and star-spangled as the nights they would contemplate. However, in the immensity of this future that she conjured up, nothing special stood forth; the days, all magnificent, resembled each other like waves; and it swayed in the horizon, infinite, harmonised, azure, and bathed in sunshine. But the child began to cough in her cot or Bovary snored more loudly, and Emma did not fall asleep till morning, when the dawn whitened the windows, and when little Justin was already in the square taking down the shutters of the chemist's shop.

She had sent for Monsieur Lheureux, and had said to him:

"I want a cloak—a large lined cloak with a deep collar."

"You are going on a journey?" he asked.

"No; but—never mind. I may count on you, may I not, and quickly?"

He bowed.

"Besides, I shall want," she went on, "a trunk—not too heavy—handy."

"Yes, yes, I understand. About three feet by a foot and a half, as they are being made just now."

"And a travelling bag."

"Decidedly," thought Lheureux, "there's a row on here."

"And," said Madame Bovary, taking her watch from her belt, "take this; you can pay yourself out of it."

But the tradesman cried out that she was wrong; they knew one another; did he doubt her? What childishness! She insisted, however,

dait sonner des cloches, hennir les mulets, avec le murmure des guitares et le bruit des fontaines, dont la vapeur s'envolant rafraîchissait des tas de fruits, disposés en pyramide au pied des statues pâles, qui souriaient sous les jets d'eau. Et puis ils arrivaient, un soir, dans un village de pêcheurs, où des filets bruns séchaient au vent, le long de la falaise et des cabanes. C'est là qu'ils s'arrêteraient pour vivre; ils habiteraient une maison basse, à toit plat, ombragée d'un palmier, au fond d'un golfe, au bord de la mer. Ils se promèneraient en gondole, ils se balanceraient en hamac; et leur existence serait facile et large comme leurs vêtements de soie, toute chaude et étoilée comme les nuits douces qu'ils contempleraient. Cependant, sur l'immensité de cet avenir qu'elle se faisait apparaître, rien de particulier ne surgissait; les jours, tous magnifiques, se ressemblaient comme des flots; et cela se balançait à l'horizon, infini, harmonieux, bleuâtre et couvert de soleil. Mais l'enfant se mettait à tousser dans son berceau, ou bien Bovary ronflait plus fort, et Emma ne s'endormait que le matin, quand l'aube blanchissait les carreaux et que déjà le petit Justin, sur la place, ouvrait les auvents de la pharmacie.

Elle avait fait venir M. Lheureux et lui avait dit:

— J'aurais besoin d'un manteau, un grand manteau, à long collet, doublé.

— Vous partez en voyage? demanda-t-il.

— Non! mais..., n'importe, je compte sur vous, n'est-ce pas? et vivement!

Il s'inclina.

— Il me faudrait encore, reprit-elle, une caisse..., pas trop lourde..., commode.

— Oui, oui, j'entends, de quatre-vingt-douze centimètres environ sur cinquante, comme on les fait à présent.

— Avec un sac de nuit.

— Décidément, pensa Lheureux, il y a du grabuge là-dessous.

— Et tenez, dit madame Bovary en tirant sa montre de sa ceinture, prenez cela; vous vous payerez dessus.

Mais le marchand s'écria qu'elle avait tort; ils se connaissaient; est-ce qu'il doutait d'elle? Quel enfantillage! Elle insista cependant pour qu'il

on his taking at least the chain, and Lheureux had already put it in his pocket and was going, when she called him back.

"You will leave everything at your place. As to the cloak"—she seemed to be reflecting—"do not bring it either; you can give me the maker's address, and tell him to have it ready for me."

It was the next month that they were to run away. She was to leave Yonville as if she was going on some business to Rouen. Rodolphe would have booked the seats, procured the passports, and even have written to Paris in order to have the whole mail-coach reserved for them as far as Marseilles, where they would buy a carriage, and go on thence without stopping to Genoa. She would take care to send her luggage to Lheureux whence it would be taken direct to the "Hirondelle," so that no one would have any suspicion. And in all this there never was any allusion to the child. Rodolphe avoided speaking of her; perhaps he no longer thought about it.

He wished to have two more weeks before him to arrange some affairs; then at the end of a week he wanted two more; then he said he was ill; next he went on a journey. The month of August passed, and, after all these delays, they decided that it was to be irrevocably fixed for the 4th September—a Monday.

At length the Saturday before arrived.

Rodolphe came in the evening earlier than usual.

"Everything is ready?" she asked him.

"Yes."

Then they walked round a garden-bed, and went to sit down near the terrace on the kerb-stone of the wall.

"You are sad," said Emma.

"No; why?"

And yet he looked at her strangely in a tender fashion.

"It is because you are going away?" she went on; "because you are leaving what is dear to you—your life? Ah! I understand. I have nothing in the world! you are all to me; so shall I be to you. I will be your people, your country; I will tend, I will love you!"

"How sweet you are!" he said, seizing her in his arms.

prît au moins la chaîne, et déjà Lheureux l'avait mise dans sa poche et s'en allait, quand elle le rappela.

— Vous laisserez tout chez vous. Quant au manteau, — elle eut l'air de réfléchir, — ne l'apportez pas non plus; seulement, vous me donnerez l'adresse de l'ouvrier et avertirez qu'on le tienne à ma disposition.

C'était le mois prochain qu'ils devaient s'enfuir. Elle partirait d'Yonville comme pour aller faire des commissions à Rouen. Rodolphe aurait retenu les places, pris des passeports, et même écrit à Paris, afin d'avoir la malle entière jusqu'à Marseille, où ils achèteraient une calèche et, de là, continueraient sans s'arrêter, par la route de Gênes. Elle aurait eu soin d'envoyer chez Lheureux son bagage, qui serait directement porté à l'Hirondelle, de manière que personne ainsi n'aurait de soupçons; et, dans tout cela, jamais il n'était question de son enfant. Rodolphe évitait d'en parler; peut-être qu'elle n'y pensait pas.

Il voulut avoir encore deux semaines devant lui, pour terminer quelques dispositions; puis, au bout de huit jours, il en demanda quinze autres; puis il se dit malade; ensuite il fit un voyage; le mois d'août se passa, et, après tous ces retards, ils arrêtèrent que ce serait irrévocablement pour le 4 septembre, un lundi.

Enfin le samedi, l'avant-veille, arriva.

Rodolphe vint le soir, plus tôt que de coutume.

— Tout est-il prêt? lui demanda-t-elle.

— Oui.

Alors ils firent le tour d'une plate-bande, et allèrent s'asseoir près de la terrasse, sur la margelle du mur.

— Tu es triste, dit Emma.

— Non, pourquoi?

Et cependant il la regardait singulièrement, d'une façon tendre.

— Est-ce de t'en aller? reprit-elle, de quitter tes affections, ta vie? Ah! je comprends… Mais, moi, je n'ai rien au monde! tu es tout pour moi. Aussi je serai tout pour toi, je te serai une famille, une patrie; je te soignerai, je t'aimerai.

— Que tu es charmante! dit-il en la saisissant dans ses bras.

"Really!" she said with a voluptuous laugh. "Do you love me? Swear it then!"

"Do I love you—love you? I adore you, my love."

The moon, full and purple-coloured, was rising right out of the earth at the end of the meadow. She rose quickly between the branches of the poplars, that hid her here and there like a black curtain pierced with holes. Then she appeared dazzling with whiteness in the empty heavens that she lit up, and now sailing more slowly along, let fall upon the river a great stain that broke up into an infinity of stars; and the silver sheen seemed to writhe through the very depths like a heedless serpent covered with luminous scales; it also resembled some monster candelabra all along which sparkled drops of diamonds running together. The soft night was about them; masses of shadow filled the branches. Emma, her eyes half closed, breathed in with deep sighs the fresh wind that was blowing. They did not speak, lost as they were in the rush of their reverie. The tenderness of the old days came back to their hearts, full and silent as the flowing river, with the softness of the perfume of the syringas, and threw across their memories shadows more immense and more sombre than those of the still willows that lengthened out over the grass. Often some night-animal, hedgehog or weasel, setting out on the hunt, disturbed the lovers, or sometimes they heard a ripe peach falling all alone from the espalier.

"Ah! what a lovely night!" said Rodolphe.

"We shall have others," replied Emma.

And, as if speaking to herself:

"Yet, it will be good to travel. And yet, why should my heart be so heavy? Is it dread of the unknown? The effect of habits left? Or rather—? No; it is the excess of happiness. How weak I am, am I not? Forgive me!"

"There is still time!" he cried. "Reflect! perhaps you may repent!"

"Never!" she cried impetuously.

And coming closer to him:

— Vrai? fit-elle avec un rire de volupté. M'aimes-tu? Jure-le donc!

— Si je t'aime! si je t'aime! mais je t'adore, mon amour!

La lune, toute ronde et couleur de pourpre, se levait à ras de terre, au fond de la prairie. Elle montait vite entre les branches des peupliers, qui la cachaient de place en place, comme un rideau noir, troué. Puis elle parut, éclatante de blancheur, dans le ciel vide qu'elle éclairait; et alors, se ralentissant, elle laissa tomber sur la rivière une grande tache, qui faisait une infinité d'étoiles; et cette lueur d'argent semblait s'y tordre jusqu'au fond, à la manière d'un serpent sans tête couvert d'écailles lumineuses. Cela ressemblait aussi à quelque monstrueux candélabre, d'où ruisselaient, tout du long, des gouttes de diamant en fusion. La nuit douce s'étalait autour d'eux; des nappes d'ombre emplissaient les feuillages. Emma, les yeux à demi clos, aspirait avec de grands soupirs le vent frais qui soufflait. Ils ne se parlaient pas, trop perdus qu'ils étaient dans l'envahissement de leur rêverie. La tendresse des anciens jours leur revenait au coeur, abondante et silencieuse comme la rivière qui coulait, avec autant de mollesse qu'en apportait le parfum des seringas, et projetait dans leur souvenir des ombres plus démesurées et plus mélancoliques que celles des saules immobiles qui s'allongeaient sur l'herbe. Souvent quelque bête nocturne, hérisson ou belette, se mettant en chasse, dérangeait les feuilles, ou bien on entendait par moments une pêche mûre qui tombait toute seule de l'espalier.

— Ah! la belle nuit! dit Rodolphe.

— Nous en aurons d'autres! reprit Emma.

Et, comme se parlant à elle-même:

— Oui, il fera bon voyager... Pourquoi ai-je le coeur triste, cependant? Est-ce l'appréhension de l'inconnu..., l'effet des habitudes quittées..., ou plutôt...? Non, c'est l'excès du bonheur! Que je suis faible, n'est-ce pas? Pardonne-moi!

— Il est encore temps! s'écria-t-il. Réfléchis, tu t'en repentiras peut-être.

— Jamais! fit-elle impétueusement.

Et, en se rapprochant de lui:

"What ill could come to me? There is no desert, no precipice, no ocean I would not traverse with you. The longer we live together the more it will be like an embrace, every day closer, more heart to heart. There will be nothing to trouble us, no cares, no obstacle. We shall be alone, all to ourselves eternally. Oh, speak! Answer me!"

At regular intervals he answered, "Yes—Yes—" She had passed her hands through his hair, and she repeated in a childlike voice, despite the big tears which were falling:

"Rodolphe! Rodolphe! Ah! Rodolphe! dear little Rodolphe!"

Midnight struck.

"Midnight!" said she. "Come, it is to-morrow. One day more!"

He rose to go; and as if the movement he made had been the signal for their flight, Emma said, suddenly assuming a gay air:

"You have the passports?"

"Yes."

"You are forgetting nothing?"

"No."

"Are you sure?"

"Certainly."

"It is at the Hotel de Provence, is it not, that you will wait for me at midday?"

He nodded.

"Till to-morrow then!" said Emma in a last caress.

And she watched him go.

He did not turn round. She ran after him, and, leaning over the water's edge between the bulrushes:

"To-morrow!" she cried.

He was already on the other side of the river and walking fast across the meadow.

After a few moments Rodolphe stopped; and when he saw her with her white gown gradually fade away in the shade like a ghost, he was seized with such a beating of the heart that he leant against a tree lest he should fall.

— Quel malheur donc peut-il me survenir? Il n'y a pas de désert, pas de précipice ni d'océan que je ne traverserais avec toi. À mesure que nous vivrons ensemble, ce sera comme une étreinte chaque jour plus serrée, plus complète! Nous n'aurons rien qui nous trouble, pas de soucis, nul obstacle! Nous serons seuls, tout à nous, éternellement… Parle donc, réponds-moi.

Il répondait à intervalles réguliers: «Oui… oui!…» Elle lui avait passé les mains dans ses cheveux, et elle répétait d'une voix enfantine, malgré de grosses larmes qui coulaient:

— Rodolphe! Rodolphe!… Ah! Rodolphe, cher petit Rodolphe!

Minuit sonna.

— Minuit! dit-elle. Allons, c'est demain! encore un jour!

Il se leva pour partir; et, comme si ce geste qu'il faisait eût été le signal de leur fuite, Emma, tout à coup, prenant un air gai:

— Tu as les passeports?

— Oui.

— Tu n'oublies rien?

— Non.

— Tu en es sûr?

— Certainement.

— C'est à l'hôtel de Provence, n'est-ce pas, que tu m'attendras?… à midi?

Il fit un signe de tête.

— À demain, donc! dit Emma dans une dernière caresse.

Et elle le regarda s'éloigner.

Il ne se détournait pas. Elle courut après lui, et, se penchant au bord de l'eau entre des broussailles:

— À demain! s'écria-t-elle.

Il était déjà de l'autre côté de la rivière et marchait vite dans la prairie.

Au bout de quelques minutes, Rodolphe s'arrêta; et, quand il la vit avec son vêtement blanc peu à peu s'évanouir dans l'ombre comme un fantôme, il fut pris d'un tel battement de coeur, qu'il s'appuya contre un arbre pour ne pas tomber.

"What an imbecile I am!" he said with a fearful oath. "No matter! She was a pretty mistress!"

And immediately Emma's beauty, with all the pleasures of their love, came back to him. For a moment he softened; then he rebelled against her.

"For, after all," he exclaimed, gesticulating, "I can't exile myself—have a child on my hands."

He was saying these things to give himself firmness.

"And besides, the worry, the expense! Ah! no, no, no, no! a thousand times no! That would be too stupid."

— Quel imbécile je suis! fit-il en jurant épouvantablement. N'importe, c'était une jolie maîtresse!

Et, aussitôt, la beauté d'Emma, avec tous les plaisirs de cet amour, lui réapparurent. D'abord il s'attendrit, puis il se révolta contre elle.

— Car enfin, exclamait-il en gesticulant, je ne peux pas m'expatrier, avoir la charge d'une enfant.

Il se disait ces choses pour s'affermir davantage.

— Et, d'ailleurs, les embarras, la dépense… Ah! non, non, mille fois non! cela eût été trop bête!

# Chapter 13

No sooner was Rodolphe at home than he sat down quickly at his bureau under the stag's head that hung as a trophy on the wall. But when he had the pen between his fingers, he could think of nothing, so that, resting on his elbows, he began to reflect. Emma seemed to him to have receded into a far-off past, as if the resolution he had taken had suddenly placed a distance between them.

To get back something of her, he fetched from the cupboard at the bedside an old Rheims biscuit-box, in which he usually kept his letters from women, and from it came an odour of dry dust and withered roses. First he saw a handkerchief with pale little spots. It was a handkerchief of hers. Once when they were walking her nose had bled; he had forgotten it. Near it, chipped at all the corners, was a miniature given him by Emma: her toilette seemed to him pretentious, and her languishing look in the worst possible taste. Then, from looking at this image and recalling the memory of its original, Emma's features little by little grew confused in his remembrance, as if the living and the painted face, rubbing one against the other, had effaced each other. Finally, he read some of her letters; they were full of explanations relating to their journey, short, technical, and urgent, like business notes. He wanted to see the long ones again, those of old times. In order to find them at the bottom of the box, Rodolphe disturbed all the others, and mechanically began rummaging amidst this mass of papers and things, finding pell-mell bouquets, garters, a black mask, pins, and hair—hair! dark and fair, some even, catching in the hinges of the box, broke when it was opened.

Thus dallying with his souvenirs, he examined the writing and the style of the letters, as varied as their orthography. They were tender or jovial, facetious, melancholy; there were some that asked for love, others that asked for money. A word recalled faces to him, certain gestures,

# Chapitre 13

À peine arrivé chez lui, Rodolphe s'assit brusquement à son bureau, sous la tête de cerf faisant trophée contre la muraille. Mais, quand il eut la plume entre les doigts, il ne sut rien trouver, si bien que, s'appuyant sur les deux coudes, il se mit à réfléchir. Emma lui semblait être reculée dans un passé lointain, comme si la résolution qu'il avait prise venait de placer entre eux, tout à coup, un immense intervalle.

Afin de ressaisir quelque chose d'elle, il alla chercher dans l'armoire, au chevet de son lit, une vieille boîte à biscuits de Reims où il enfermait d'habitude ses lettres de femmes, et il s'en échappa une odeur de poussière humide et de roses flétries. D'abord il aperçut un mouchoir de poche, couvert de gouttelettes pâles. C'était un mouchoir à elle, une fois qu'elle avait saigné du nez, en promenade; il ne s'en souvenait plus. Il y avait auprès, se cognant à tous les angles, la miniature donnée par Emma; sa toilette lui parut prétentieuse et son regard en coulisse du plus pitoyable effet; puis, à force de considérer cette image et d'évoquer le souvenir du modèle, les traits d'Emma peu à peu se confondirent en sa mémoire, comme si la figure vivante et la figure peinte, se frottant l'une contre l'autre, se fussent réciproquement effacées. Enfin il lut de ses lettres; elles étaient pleines d'explications relatives à leur voyage, courtes, techniques et pressantes comme des billets d'affaires. Il voulut revoir les longues, celles d'autrefois; pour les trouver au fond de la boîte, Rodolphe dérangea toutes les autres; et machinalement il se mit à fouiller dans ce tas de papiers et de choses, y retrouvant pêle-mêle des bouquets, une jarretière, un masque noir, des épingles et des cheveux — des cheveux! de bruns, de blonds; quelques-uns même, s'accrochant à la ferrure de la boîte, se cassaient quand on l'ouvrait.

Ainsi flânant parmi ses souvenirs, il examinait les écritures et le style des lettres, aussi variés que leurs orthographes. Elles étaient tendres ou joviales, facétieuses, mélancoliques; il y en avait qui demandaient de l'amour et d'autres qui demandaient de l'argent. À propos d'un mot, il

the sound of a voice; sometimes, however, he remembered nothing at all.

In fact, these women, rushing at once into his thoughts, cramped each other and lessened, as reduced to a uniform level of love that equalised them all. So taking handfuls of the mixed-up letters, he amused himself for some moments with letting them fall in cascades from his right into his left hand. At last, bored and weary, Rodolphe took back the box to the cupboard, saying to himself:

"What a lot of rubbish!"

Which summed up his opinion; for pleasures, like schoolboys in a school courtyard, had so trampled upon his heart that no green thing grew there, and that which passed through it, more heedless than children, did not even, like them, leave a name carved upon the wall.

"Come," said he, "let's begin."

He wrote:

"Courage, Emma! courage! I would not bring misery into your life."

"After all, that's true," thought Rodolphe. "I am acting in her interest; I am honest."

"Have you carefully weighed your resolution? Do you know to what an abyss I was dragging you, poor angel? No, you do not, do you? You were coming confident and fearless, believing in happiness in the future. Ah! unhappy that we are—insensate!"

Rodolphe stopped here to think of some good excuse.

"If I told her all my fortune is lost? No! Besides, that would stop nothing. It would all have to be begun over again later on. As if one could make women like that listen to reason!"

He reflected, then went on:

"I shall not forget you, oh believe it; and I shall ever have a profound devotion for you; but some day, sooner or later, this ardour (such is the fate of human things) would have grown less, no doubt. Lassitude would have come to us, and who knows if I should not even have had the atrocious pain of witnessing your remorse, of sharing it myself, since I should have been its cause? The mere idea of the grief that would

se rappelait des visages, de certains gestes, un son de voix; quelquefois pourtant il ne se rappelait rien.

En effet, ces femmes, accourant à la fois dans sa pensée, s'y gênaient les unes les autres et s'y rapetissaient, comme sous un même niveau d'amour qui les égalisait. Prenant donc à poignée les lettres confondues, il s'amusa pendant quelques minutes à les faire tomber en cascades, de sa main droite dans sa main gauche. Enfin, ennuyé, assoupi, Rodolphe alla reporter la boîte dans l'armoire en se disant:

— Quel tas de blagues!...

Ce qui résumait son opinion; car les plaisirs, comme des écoliers dans la cour d'un collège, avaient tellement piétiné sur son coeur, que rien de vert n'y poussait, et ce qui passait par là, plus étourdi que les enfants, n'y laissait pas même, comme eux, son nom gravé sur la muraille.

— Allons, se dit-il, commençons!

Il écrivit:

«Du courage, Emma! du courage! Je ne veux pas faire le malheur de votre existence...»

— Après tout, c'est vrai, pensa Rodolphe; j'agis dans son intérêt; je suis honnête.

«Avez-vous mûrement pesé votre détermination? Savez-vous l'abîme où je vous entraînais, pauvre ange? Non, n'est-ce pas? Vous alliez confiante et folle, croyant au bonheur, à l'avenir... Ah! malheureux que nous sommes! insensés!»

Rodolphe s'arrêta pour trouver ici quelque bonne excuse.

— Si je lui disais que toute ma fortune est perdue?... Ah! non, et d'ailleurs, cela n'empêcherait rien. Ce serait à recommencer plus tard. Est-ce qu'on peut faire entendre raison à des femmes pareilles!

Il réfléchit, puis ajouta:

«Je ne vous oublierai pas, croyez-le bien, et j'aurai continuellement pour vous un dévouement profond; mais, un jour, tôt ou tard, cette ardeur (c'est là le sort des choses humaines) se fût diminuée, sans doute! Il nous serait venu des lassitudes, et qui sait même si je n'aurais pas eu l'atroce douleur d'assister à vos remords et d'y participer moi-même, puisque je les aurais causés. L'idée seule des chagrins qui vous arrivent

come to you tortures me, Emma. Forget me! Why did I ever know you? Why were you so beautiful? Is it my fault? O my God! No, no! Accuse only fate."

"That's a word that always tells," he said to himself.

"Ah, if you had been one of those frivolous women that one sees, certainly I might, through egotism, have tried an experiment, in that case without danger for you. But that delicious exaltation, at once your charm and your torment, has prevented you from understanding, adorable woman that you are, the falseness of our future position. Nor had I reflected upon this at first, and I rested in the shade of that ideal happiness as beneath that of the manchineel tree, without foreseeing the consequences."

"Perhaps she'll think I'm giving it up from avarice. Ah, well! so much the worse; it must be stopped!"

"The world is cruel, Emma. Wherever we might have gone, it would have persecuted us. You would have had to put up with indiscreet questions, calumny, contempt, insult perhaps. Insult to you! Oh! And I, who would place you on a throne! I who bear with me your memory as a talisman! For I am going to punish myself by exile for all the ill I have done you. I am going away. Whither I know not. I am mad. Adieu! Be good always. Preserve the memory of the unfortunate who has lost you. Teach my name to your child; let her repeat it in her prayers."

The wicks of the candles flickered. Rodolphe got up to, shut the window, and when he had sat down again:

"I think it's all right. Ah! and this for fear she should come and hunt me up."

"I shall be far away when you read these sad lines, for I have wished to flee as quickly as possible to shun the temptation of seeing you again. No weakness! I shall return, and perhaps later on we shall talk together very coldly of our old love. Adieu!"

And there was a last "adieu" divided into two words! "A Dieu!" which he thought in very excellent taste.

"Now how am I to sign?" he said to himself. "'Yours devotedly?' No! 'Your friend?' Yes, that's it."

"Your friend."

me torture, Emma! Oubliez-moi! Pourquoi faut-il que je vous aie connue? Pourquoi étiez-vous si belle? Est-ce ma faute? O mon Dieu! non, non, n'en accusez que la fatalité!»

— Voilà un mot qui fait toujours de l'effet, se dit-il.

«Ah! si vous eussiez été une de ces femmes au coeur frivole comme on en voit, certes, j'aurais pu, par égoïsme, tenter une expérience alors sans danger pour vous. Mais cette exaltation délicieuse, qui fait à la fois votre charme et votre tourment, vous a empêchée de comprendre, adorable femme que vous êtes, la fausseté de notre position future. Moi non plus, je n'y avais pas réfléchi d'abord, et je me reposais à l'ombre de ce bonheur idéal, comme à celle du mancenillier, sans prévoir les conséquences.»

— Elle va peut-être croire que c'est par avarice que j'y renonce... Ah! n'importe! tant pis, il faut en finir!

«Le monde est cruel, Emma. Partout où nous eussions été, il nous aurait poursuivis. Il vous aurait fallu subir les questions indiscrètes, la calomnie, le dédain, l'outrage peut-être. L'outrage à vous! Oh!... Et moi qui voudrais vous faire asseoir sur un trône! moi qui emporte votre pensée comme un talisman! Car je me punis par l'exil de tout le mal que je vous ai fait. Je pars. Où? Je n'en sais rien, je suis fou! Adieu! Soyez toujours bonne! Conservez le souvenir du malheureux qui vous a perdue. Apprenez mon nom à votre enfant, qu'il le redise dans ses prières.»

La mèche des deux bougies tremblait. Rodolphe se leva pour aller fermer la fenêtre, et, quand il se fut rassis:

— Il me semble que c'est tout. Ah! encore ceci, de peur qu'elle ne vienne à me relancer:

«Je serai loin quand vous lirez ces tristes lignes; car j'ai voulu m'enfuir au plus vite afin d'éviter la tentation de vous revoir. Pas de faiblesse! Je reviendrai; et peut-être que, plus tard, nous causerons ensemble très froidement de nos anciennes amours. Adieu!»

Et il y avait un dernier adieu, séparé en deux mots: À Dieu! ce qu'il jugeait d'un excellent goût.

— Comment vais-je signer, maintenant? se dit-il. Votre tout dévoué?... Non. Votre ami?... Oui, c'est cela.

«Votre ami.»

He re-read his letter. He considered it very good.

"Poor little woman!" he thought with emotion. "She'll think me harder than a rock. There ought to have been some tears on this; but I can't cry; it isn't my fault." Then, having emptied some water into a glass, Rodolphe dipped his finger into it, and let a big drop fall on the paper, that made a pale stain on the ink. Then looking for a seal, he came upon the one *Amor nel cor.*

"That doesn't at all fit in with the circumstances. Pshaw! never mind!"

After which he smoked three pipes and went to bed.

The next day when he was up (at about two o'clock—he had slept late), Rodolphe had a basket of apricots picked. He put his letter at the bottom under some vine leaves, and at once ordered Girard, his ploughman, to take it with care to Madame Bovary. He made use of this means for corresponding with her, sending according to the season fruits or game.

"If she asks after me," he said, "you will tell her that I have gone on a journey. You must give the basket to her herself, into her own hands. Get along and take care!"

Girard put on his new blouse, knotted his handkerchief round the apricots, and walking with great heavy steps in his thick iron-bound galoshes, made his way to Yonville.

Madame Bovary, when he got to her house, was arranging a bundle of linen on the kitchen-table with Felicite.

"Here," said the ploughboy, "is something for you—from the master."

She was seized with apprehension, and as she sought in her pocket for some coppers, she looked at the peasant with haggard eyes, while he himself looked at her with amazement, not understanding how such a present could so move anyone. At last he went out. Felicite remained. She could bear it no longer; she ran into the sitting room as if to take the apricots there, overturned the basket, tore away the leaves, found the letter, opened it, and, as if some fearful fire were behind her, Emma flew to her room terrified.

Charles was there; she saw him; he spoke to her; she heard nothing, and she went on quickly up the stairs, breathless, distraught, dumb, and

Il relut sa lettre. Elle lui parut bonne.

— Pauvre petite femme! pensa-t-il avec attendrissement. Elle va me croire plus insensible qu'un roc; il eût fallu quelques larmes là-dessus; mais, moi, je ne peux pas pleurer; ce n'est pas ma faute. Alors, s'étant versé de l'eau dans un verre, Rodolphe y trempa son doigt et il laissa tomber de haut une grosse goutte, qui fit une tache pâle sur l'encre; puis, cherchant à cacheter la lettre, le cachet *Amor nel cor* se rencontra.

— Cela ne va guère à la circonstance… Ah bah! n'importe!

Après quoi, il fuma trois pipes et s'alla coucher.

Le lendemain, quand il fut debout (vers deux heures environ, il avait dormi tard), Rodolphe se fit cueillir une corbeille d'abricots. Il disposa la lettre dans le fond, sous des feuilles de vigne, et ordonna tout de suite à Girard, son valet de charrue, de porter cela délicatement chez madame Bovary. Il se servait de ce moyen pour correspondre avec elle, lui envoyant, selon la saison, des fruits ou du gibier.

— Si elle te demande de mes nouvelles, dit-il, tu répondras que je suis parti en voyage. Il faut remettre le panier à elle-même, en mains propres… Va, et prends garde!

Girard passa sa blouse neuve, noua son mouchoir autour des abricots, et marchant à grands pas lourds dans ses grosses galoches ferrées, prit tranquillement le chemin d'Yonville.

Madame Bovary, quand il arriva chez elle, arrangeait avec Félicité, sur la table de la cuisine, un paquet de linge.

— Voilà, dit le valet, ce que notre maître vous envoie.

Elle fut saisie d'une appréhension, et, tout en cherchant quelque monnaie dans sa poche, elle considérait le paysan d'un oeil hagard, tandis qu'il la regardait lui-même avec ébahissement, ne comprenant pas qu'un pareil cadeau pût tant émouvoir quelqu'un. Enfin il sortit. Félicité restait. Elle n'y tenait plus, elle courut dans la salle comme pour y porter les abricots, renversa le panier, arracha les feuilles, trouva la lettre, l'ouvrit, et, comme s'il y avait eu derrière elle un effroyable incendie, Emma se mit à fuir vers sa chambre, tout épouvantée.

Charles y était, elle l'aperçut; il lui parla, elle n'entendit rien, et elle continua vivement à monter les marches; haletante, éperdue, ivre, et

ever holding this horrible piece of paper, that crackled between her fingers like a plate of sheet-iron. On the second floor she stopped before the attic door, which was closed.

Then she tried to calm herself; she recalled the letter; she must finish it; she did not dare to. And where? How? She would be seen!

"Ah, no! here," she thought, "I shall be all right."

Emma pushed open the door and went in.

The slates threw straight down a heavy heat that gripped her temples, stifled her; she dragged herself to the closed garret-window. She drew back the bolt, and the dazzling light burst in with a leap.

Opposite, beyond the roofs, stretched the open country till it was lost to sight. Down below, underneath her, the village square was empty; the stones of the pavement glittered, the weathercocks on the houses were motionless. At the corner of the street, from a lower storey, rose a kind of humming with strident modulations. It was Binet turning.

She leant against the embrasure of the window, and reread the letter with angry sneers. But the more she fixed her attention upon it, the more confused were her ideas. She saw him again, heard him, encircled him with her arms, and throbs of her heart, that beat against her breast like blows of a sledge-hammer, grew faster and faster, with uneven intervals. She looked about her with the wish that the earth might crumble into pieces. Why not end it all? What restrained her? She was free. She advanced, looking at the paving-stones, saying to herself:

"Come! come!"

The luminous ray that came straight up from below drew the weight of her body towards the abyss. It seemed to her that the ground of the oscillating square went up the walls and that the floor dipped on end like a tossing boat. She was right at the edge, almost hanging, surrounded by vast space. The blue of the heavens suffused her, the air was whirling in her hollow head; she had but to yield, to let herself be taken; and the humming of the lathe never ceased, like an angry voice calling her.

"Emma! Emma!" cried Charles.

She stopped.

toujours tenant cette horrible feuille de papier, qui lui claquait dans les doigts comme une plaque de tôle. Au second étage, elle s'arrêta devant la porte du grenier, qui était fermée.

Alors elle voulut se calmer; elle se rappela la lettre; il fallait la finir, elle n'osait pas. D'ailleurs, où? comment? on la verrait.

— Ah! non, ici, pensa-t-elle, je serai bien.

Emma poussa la porte et entra.

Les ardoises laissaient tomber d'aplomb une chaleur lourde, qui lui serrait les tempes et l'étouffait; elle se traîna jusqu'à la mansarde close, dont elle tira le verrou, et la lumière éblouissante jaillit d'un bond.

En face, par-dessus les toits, la pleine campagne s'étalait à perte de vue. En bas, sous elle, la place du village était vide; les cailloux du trottoir scintillaient, les girouettes des maisons se tenaient immobiles; au coin de la rue, il partit d'un étage inférieur une sorte de ronflement à modulations stridentes. C'était Binet qui tournait.

Elle s'était appuyée contre l'embrasure de la mansarde, et elle relisait la lettre avec des ricanements de colère. Mais plus elle y fixait d'attention, plus ses idées se confondaient. Elle le revoyait, elle l'entendait, elle l'entourait de ses deux bras; et des battements de cœur, qui la frappaient sous la poitrine comme à grands coups de bélier, s'accéléraient l'un après l'autre, à intermittences inégales. Elle jetait les yeux tout autour d'elle avec l'envie que la terre croulât. Pourquoi n'en pas finir? Qui la retenait donc? Elle était libre. Et elle s'avança, elle regarda les pavés en se disant:

— Allons! allons!

Le rayon lumineux qui montait d'en bas directement tirait vers l'abîme le poids de son corps. Il lui semblait que le sol de la place oscillant s'élevait le long des murs, et que le plancher s'inclinait par le bout, à la manière d'un vaisseau qui tangue. Elle se tenait tout au bord, presque suspendue, entourée d'un grand espace. Le bleu du ciel l'envahissait, l'air circulait dans sa tête creuse, elle n'avait qu'à céder, qu'à se laisser prendre; et le ronflement du tour ne discontinuait pas, comme une voix furieuse qui l'appelait.

— Ma femme! ma femme! cria Charles.

Elle s'arrêta.

"Wherever are you? Come!"

The thought that she had just escaped from death almost made her faint with terror. She closed her eyes; then she shivered at the touch of a hand on her sleeve; it was Felicite.

"Master is waiting for you, madame; the soup is on the table."

And she had to go down to sit at table.

She tried to eat. The food choked her. Then she unfolded her napkin as if to examine the darns, and she really thought of applying herself to this work, counting the threads in the linen. Suddenly the remembrance of the letter returned to her. How had she lost it? Where could she find it? But she felt such weariness of spirit that she could not even invent a pretext for leaving the table. Then she became a coward; she was afraid of Charles; he knew all, that was certain! Indeed he pronounced these words in a strange manner:

"We are not likely to see Monsieur Rodolphe soon again, it seems."

"Who told you?" she said, shuddering.

"Who told me!" he replied, rather astonished at her abrupt tone. "Why, Girard, whom I met just now at the door of the Cafe Francais. He has gone on a journey, or is to go."

She gave a sob.

"What surprises you in that? He absents himself like that from time to time for a change, and, ma foi, I think he's right, when one has a fortune and is a bachelor. Besides, he has jolly times, has our friend. He's a bit of a rake. Monsieur Langlois told me—"

He stopped for propriety's sake because the servant came in.

She put back into the basket the apricots scattered on the sideboard. Charles, without noticing his wife's colour, had them brought to him, took one, and bit into it.

"Ah! perfect!" said he; "just taste!"

And he handed her the basket, which she put away from her gently.

"Do just smell! What an odour!" he remarked, passing it under her nose several times.

"I am choking," she cried, leaping up.

But by an effort of will the spasm passed; then:

— Où es-tu donc? Arrive!

L'idée qu'elle venait d'échapper à la mort faillit la faire s'évanouir de terreur; elle ferma les yeux; puis elle tressaillit au contact d'une main sur sa manche: c'était Félicité.

— Monsieur vous attend, Madame; la soupe est servie.

Et il fallut descendre! il fallut se mettre à table!

Elle essaya de manger. Les morceaux l'étouffaient. Alors elle déplia sa serviette comme pour en examiner les reprises et voulut réellement s'appliquer à ce travail, compter les fils de la toile. Tout à coup, le souvenir de la lettre lui revint. L'avait-elle donc perdue? Où la retrouver? Mais elle éprouvait une telle lassitude dans l'esprit, que jamais elle ne put inventer un prétexte à sortir de table. Puis elle était devenue lâche; elle avait peur de Charles; il savait tout, c'était sûr! En effet, il prononça ces mots, singulièrement:

— Nous ne sommes pas près, à ce qu'il paraît, de voir M. Rodolphe.

— Qui te l'a dit? fit-elle en tressaillant.

— Qui me l'a dit? répliqua-t-il un peu surpris de ce ton brusque; c'est Girard, que j'ai rencontré tout à l'heure à la porte du café Français. Il est parti en voyage, ou il doit partir.

Elle eut un sanglot.

— Quoi donc t'étonne? Il s'absente ainsi de temps à autre pour se distraire, et, ma foi! je l'approuve. Quand on a de la fortune et que l'on est garçon!... Du reste, il s'amuse joliment, notre ami! c'est un farceur. M. Langlois m'a conté...

Il se tut par convenance, à cause de la domestique qui entrait.

Celle-ci replaça dans la corbeille les abricots répandus sur l'étagère; Charles, sans remarquer la rougeur de sa femme, se les fit apporter, en prit un et mordit à même.

— Oh! parfait! disait-il. Tiens, goûte.

Et il tendit la corbeille, qu'elle repoussa doucement.

— Sens donc: quelle odeur! fit-il en la lui passant sous le nez à plusieurs reprises.

— J'étouffe! s'écria-t-elle en se levant d'un bond.

Mais, par un effort de volonté, ce spasme disparut; puis:

"It is nothing," she said, "it is nothing! It is nervousness. Sit down and go on eating."

For she dreaded lest he should begin questioning her, attending to her, that she should not be left alone.

Charles, to obey her, sat down again, and he spat the stones of the apricots into his hands, afterwards putting them on his plate.

Suddenly a blue tilbury passed across the square at a rapid trot. Emma uttered a cry and fell back rigid to the ground.

In fact, Rodolphe, after many reflections, had decided to set out for Rouen. Now, as from La Huchette to Buchy there is no other way than by Yonville, he had to go through the village, and Emma had recognised him by the rays of the lanterns, which like lightning flashed through the twilight.

The chemist, at the tumult which broke out in the house ran thither. The table with all the plates was upset; sauce, meat, knives, the salt, and cruet-stand were strewn over the room; Charles was calling for help; Berthe, scared, was crying; and Felicite, whose hands trembled, was unlacing her mistress, whose whole body shivered convulsively.

"I'll run to my laboratory for some aromatic vinegar," said the druggist.

Then as she opened her eyes on smelling the bottle:

"I was sure of it," he remarked; "that would wake any dead person for you!"

"Speak to us," said Charles; "collect yourself; it is your Charles, who loves you. Do you know me? See! here is your little girl! Oh, kiss her!"

The child stretched out her arms to her mother to cling to her neck. But turning away her head, Emma said in a broken voice:

"No, no! no one!"

She fainted again. They carried her to her bed.

She lay there stretched at full length, her lips apart, her eyelids closed, her hands open, motionless, and white as a waxen image. Two streams of tears flowed from her eyes and fell slowly upon the pillow.

— Ce n'est rien! dit-elle, ce n'est rien! c'est nerveux! Assieds-toi, mange!

Car elle redoutait qu'on ne fût à la questionner, à la soigner, qu'on ne la quittât plus.

Charles, pour obéir, s'était rassis, et il crachait dans sa main les noyaux des abricots, qu'il déposait ensuite dans son assiette.

Tout à coup, un tilbury bleu passa au grand trot sur la place. Emma poussa un cri et tomba roide par terre, à la renverse.

En effet, Rodolphe, après bien des réflexions, s'était décidé à partir pour Rouen. Or, comme il n'y a, de la Huchette à Buchy, pas d'autre chemin que celui d'Yonville, il lui avait fallu traverser le village, et Emma l'avait reconnu à la lueur des lanternes qui coupaient comme un éclair le crépuscule.

Le pharmacien, au tumulte qui se faisait dans la maison, s'y précipita. La table, avec toutes les assiettes, était renversée; de la sauce, de la viande, les couteaux, la salière et l'huilier jonchaient l'appartement; Charles appelait au secours; Berthe, effarée, criait; et Félicité, dont les mains tremblaient, délaçait Madame, qui avait le long du corps des mouvements convulsifs.

— Je cours, dit l'apothicaire, chercher dans mon laboratoire, un peu de vinaigre aromatique.

Puis, comme elle rouvrait les yeux en respirant le flacon:

— J'en étais sûr, fit-il; cela vous réveillerait un mort.

— Parle-nous! disait Charles, parle-nous! Remets-toi! C'est moi, ton Charles qui t'aime! Me reconnais-tu? Tiens, voilà ta petite fille: embrasse-la donc!

L'enfant avançait les bras vers sa mère pour se pendre à son cou. Mais, détournant la tête, Emma dit d'une voix saccadée:

— Non, non… personne!

Elle s'évanouit encore. On la porta sur son lit.

Elle restait étendue, la bouche ouverte, les paupières fermées, les mains à plat, immobile, et blanche comme une statue de cire. Il sortait de ses yeux deux ruisseaux de larmes qui coulaient lentement sur l'oreiller.

Charles, standing up, was at the back of the alcove, and the chemist, near him, maintained that meditative silence that is becoming on the serious occasions of life.

"Do not be uneasy," he said, touching his elbow; "I think the paroxysm is past."

"Yes, she is resting a little now," answered Charles, watching her sleep. "Poor girl! poor girl! She had gone off now!"

Then Homais asked how the accident had come about. Charles answered that she had been taken ill suddenly while she was eating some apricots.

"Extraordinary!" continued the chemist. "But it might be that the apricots had brought on the syncope. Some natures are so sensitive to certain smells; and it would even be a very fine question to study both in its pathological and physiological relation. The priests know the importance of it, they who have introduced aromatics into all their ceremonies. It is to stupefy the senses and to bring on ecstasies—a thing, moreover, very easy in persons of the weaker sex, who are more delicate than the other. Some are cited who faint at the smell of burnt hartshorn, of new bread—"

"Take care; you'll wake her!" said Bovary in a low voice.

"And not only," the druggist went on, "are human beings subject to such anomalies, but animals also. Thus you are not ignorant of the singularly aphrodisiac effect produced by the Nepeta cataria, vulgarly called catmint, on the feline race; and, on the other hand, to quote an example whose authenticity I can answer for. Bridaux (one of my old comrades, at present established in the Rue Malpalu) possesses a dog that falls into convulsions as soon as you hold out a snuff-box to him. He often even makes the experiment before his friends at his summer-house at Guillaume Wood. Would anyone believe that a simple sternutation could produce such ravages on a quadrupedal organism? It is extremely curious, is it not?"

"Yes," said Charles, who was not listening to him.

"This shows us," went on the other, smiling with benign self-sufficiency, "the innumerable irregularities of the nervous system. With

Charles, debout, se tenait au fond de l'alcôve, et le pharmacien, près de lui, gardait ce silence méditatif qu'il est convenable d'avoir dans les occasions sérieuses de la vie.

— Rassurez-vous, dit-il en lui poussant le coude, je crois que le paroxysme est passé.

— Oui, elle repose un peu maintenant! répondit Charles, qui la regardait dormir. Pauvre femme!... pauvre femme!... la voilà retombée!

Alors Homais demanda comment cet accident était survenu. Charles répondit que cela l'avait saisie tout à coup, pendant qu'elle mangeait des abricots.

— Extraordinaire!... reprit le pharmacien. Mais il se pourrait que les abricots eussent occasionné la syncope! Il y a des natures si impressionnables à l'encontre de certaines odeurs! et ce serait même une belle question à étudier, tant sous le rapport pathologique que sous le rapport physiologique. Les prêtres en connaissaient l'importance, eux qui ont toujours mêlé des aromates à leurs cérémonies. C'est pour vous stupéfier l'entendement et provoquer des extases, chose d'ailleurs facile à obtenir chez les personnes du sexe, qui sont plus délicates que les autres. On en cite qui s'évanouissent à l'odeur de la corne brûlée, du pain tendre...

— Prenez garde de l'éveiller! dit à voix basse Bovary.

— Et non seulement, continua l'apothicaire, les humains sont en butte à ces anomalies, mais encore les animaux. Ainsi, vous n'êtes pas sans savoir l'effet singulièrement aphrodisiaque que produit le nepeta cataria, vulgairement appelé herbe-au-chat, sur la gent féline; et d'autre part, pour citer un exemple que je garantis authentique, Bridoux (un de mes anciens camarades, actuellement établi rue Malpalu) possède un chien qui tombe en convulsions dès qu'on lui présente une tabatière. Souvent même il en fait l'expérience devant ses amis, à son pavillon du bois Guillaume. Croirait-on qu'un simple sternutatoire pût exercer de tels ravages dans l'organisme d'un quadrupède? C'est extrêmement curieux, n'est-il pas vrai?

— Oui, dit Charles, qui n'écoutait pas.

— Cela nous prouve, reprit l'autre en souriant avec un air de suffisance bénigne, les irrégularités sans nombre du système nerveux. Pour

regard to madame, she has always seemed to me, I confess, very susceptible. And so I should by no means recommend to you, my dear friend, any of those so-called remedies that, under the pretence of attacking the symptoms, attack the constitution. No; no useless physicking! Diet, that is all; sedatives, emollients, dulcification. Then, don't you think that perhaps her imagination should be worked upon?"

"In what way? How?" said Bovary.

"Ah! that is it. Such is indeed the question. *That is the question*, as I lately read in a newspaper."

But Emma, awaking, cried out:

"The letter! the letter!"

They thought she was delirious; and she was by midnight. Brain-fever had set in.

For forty-three days Charles did not leave her. He gave up all his patients; he no longer went to bed; he was constantly feeling her pulse, putting on sinapisms and cold-water compresses. He sent Justin as far as Neufchatel for ice; the ice melted on the way; he sent him back again. He called Monsieur Canivet into consultation; he sent for Dr. Lariviere, his old master, from Rouen; he was in despair. What alarmed him most was Emma's prostration, for she did not speak, did not listen, did not even seem to suffer, as if her body and soul were both resting together after all their troubles.

About the middle of October she could sit up in bed supported by pillows. Charles wept when he saw her eat her first bread-and-jelly. Her strength returned to her; she got up for a few hours of an afternoon, and one day, when she felt better, he tried to take her, leaning on his arm, for a walk round the garden. The sand of the paths was disappearing beneath the dead leaves; she walked slowly, dragging along her slippers, and leaning against Charles's shoulder. She smiled all the time.

They went thus to the bottom of the garden near the terrace. She drew herself up slowly, shading her eyes with her hand to look. She looked far off, as far as she could, but on the horizon were only great bonfires of grass smoking on the hills.

ce qui est de Madame, elle m'a toujours paru, je l'avoue, une vraie sensitive. Aussi ne vous conseillerai-je point, mon bon ami, aucun de ces prétendus remèdes qui, sous prétexte d'attaquer les symptômes, attaquent le tempérament. Non, pas de médicamentation oiseuse! du régime, voilà tout! des sédatifs, des émollients, des dulcifiants. Puis, ne pensez-vous pas qu'il faudrait peut-être frapper l'imagination?

— En quoi? comment? dit Bovary.

— Ah! c'est là la question! Telle est effectivement la question: *That is the question!* comme je lisais dernièrement dans le journal.

Mais Emma, se réveillant, s'écria:

— Et la lettre? et la lettre?

On crut qu'elle avait le délire; elle l'eut à partir de minuit: une fièvre cérébrale s'était déclarée.

Pendant quarante-trois jours, Charles ne la quitta pas. Il abandonna tous ses malades; il ne se couchait plus, il était continuellement à lui tâter le pouls, à lui poser des sinapismes, des compresses d'eau froide. Il envoyait Justin jusqu'à Neufchâtel chercher de la glace; la glace se fondait en route; il le renvoyait. Il appela M. Canivet en consultation; il fit venir de Rouen le docteur Larivière, son ancien maître; il était désespéré. Ce qui l'effrayait le plus, c'était l'abattement d'Emma; car elle ne parlait pas, n'entendait rien et même semblait ne point souffrir, — comme si son corps et son âme se fussent ensemble reposés de toutes leurs agitations.

Vers le milieu d'octobre, elle put se tenir assise dans son lit, avec des oreillers derrière elle. Charles pleura quand il la vit manger sa première tartine de confitures. Les forces lui revinrent; elle se levait quelques heures pendant l'après-midi, et, un jour qu'elle se sentait mieux, il essaya de lui faire faire, à son bras, un tour de promenade dans le jardin. Le sable des allées disparaissait sous les feuilles mortes; elle marchait pas à pas, en traînant ses pantoufles, et, s'appuyant de l'épaule contre Charles, elle continuait à sourire.

Ils allèrent ainsi jusqu'au fond, près de la terrasse. Elle se redressa lentement, se mit la main devant ses yeux, pour regarder; elle regarda au loin, tout au loin; mais il n'y avait à l'horizon que de grands feux d'herbe, qui fumaient sur les collines.

"You will tire yourself, my darling!" said Bovary.

And, pushing her gently to make her go into the arbour:

"Sit down on this seat; you'll be comfortable."

"Oh! no; not there!" she said in a faltering voice.

She was seized with giddiness, and from that evening her illness recommenced, with a more uncertain character, it is true, and more complex symptoms. Now she suffered in her heart, then in the chest, the head, the limbs; she had vomitings, in which Charles thought he saw the first signs of cancer.

And besides this, the poor fellow was worried about money matters.

— Tu vas te fatiguer, ma chérie, dit Bovary.

Et, la poussant doucement pour la faire entrer sous la tonnelle:

— Assieds-toi donc sur ce banc: tu seras bien.

— Oh! non, pas là, pas là! fit-elle d'une voix défaillante.

Elle eut un étourdissement, et dès le soir, sa maladie recommença, avec une allure plus incertaine, il est vrai, et des caractères plus complexes. Tantôt elle souffrait au coeur, puis dans la poitrine, dans le cerveau, dans les membres; il lui survint des vomissements où Charles crut apercevoir les premiers symptômes d'un cancer.

Et le pauvre garçon, par là-dessus, avait des inquiétudes d'argent!

# Chapter 14

To begin with, he did not know how he could pay Monsieur Homais for all the physic supplied by him, and though, as a medical man, he was not obliged to pay for it, he nevertheless blushed a little at such an obligation. Then the expenses of the household, now that the servant was mistress, became terrible. Bills rained in upon the house; the tradesmen grumbled; Monsieur Lheureux especially harassed him. In fact, at the height of Emma's illness, the latter, taking advantage of the circumstances to make his bill larger, had hurriedly brought the cloak, the travelling-bag, two trunks instead of one, and a number of other things. It was very well for Charles to say he did not want them. The tradesman answered arrogantly that these articles had been ordered, and that he would not take them back; besides, it would vex madame in her convalescence; the doctor had better think it over; in short, he was resolved to sue him rather than give up his rights and take back his goods. Charles subsequently ordered them to be sent back to the shop. Felicite forgot; he had other things to attend to; then thought no more about them. Monsieur Lheureux returned to the charge, and, by turns threatening and whining, so managed that Bovary ended by signing a bill at six months. But hardly had he signed this bill than a bold idea occurred to him: it was to borrow a thousand francs from Lheureux. So, with an embarrassed air, he asked if it were possible to get them, adding that it would be for a year, at any interest he wished. Lheureux ran off to his shop, brought back the money, and dictated another bill, by which Bovary undertook to pay to his order on the 1st of September next the sum of one thousand and seventy francs, which, with the hundred and eighty already agreed to, made just twelve hundred and fifty, thus lending at six per cent in addition to one-fourth for commission: and the things bringing him in a good third at the least, this ought in twelve months to give him a profit of a hundred and thirty francs. He

# Chapitre 14

D'abord, il ne savait comment faire pour dédommager M. Homais de tous les médicaments pris chez lui; et, quoiqu'il eût pu, comme médecin, ne pas les payer, néanmoins il rougissait un peu de cette obligation. Puis la dépense du ménage, à présent que la cuisinière était maîtresse, devenait effrayante; les notes pleuvaient dans la maison; les fournisseurs murmuraient; M. Lheureux, surtout, le harcelait. En effet, au plus fort de la maladie d'Emma, celui-ci, profitant de la circonstance pour exagérer sa facture, avait vite apporté le manteau, le sac de nuit, deux caisses au lieu d'une, quantité d'autres choses encore. Charles eut beau dire qu'il n'en avait pas besoin, le marchand répondit arrogamment qu'on lui avait commandé tous ces articles et qu'il ne les reprendrait pas; d'ailleurs, ce serait contrarier Madame dans sa convalescence; Monsieur réfléchirait; bref, il était résolu à le poursuivre en justice plutôt que d'abandonner ses droits et que d'emporter ses marchandises. Charles ordonna par la suite de les renvoyer à son magasin; Félicité oublia; il avait d'autres soucis; on n'y pensa plus; M. Lheureux revint à la charge, et, tour à tour menaçant et gémissant, manoeuvra de telle façon, que Bovary finit par souscrire un billet à six mois d'échéance. Mais à peine eut-il signé ce billet, qu'une idée audacieuse lui surgit: c'était d'emprunter mille francs à M. Lheureux. Donc, il demanda, d'un air embarrassé, s'il n'y avait pas moyen de les avoir, ajoutant que ce serait pour un an et au taux que l'on voudrait. Lheureux courut à sa boutique, en rapporta les écus et dicta un autre billet, par lequel Bovary déclarait devoir payer à son ordre, le Ier septembre prochain, la somme de mille soixante et dix francs; ce qui, avec les cent quatre-vingts déjà stipulés, faisait juste douze cent cinquante. Ainsi, prêtant à six pour cent, augmenté d'un quart de commission, et les fournitures lui rapportant un bon tiers pour le moins, cela devait, en douze mois, donner cent trente francs de bénéfice; et il espérait que l'affaire ne s'arrêterait pas là, qu'on

hoped that the business would not stop there; that the bills would not be paid; that they would be renewed; and that his poor little money, having thriven at the doctor's as at a hospital, would come back to him one day considerably more plump, and fat enough to burst his bag.

Everything, moreover, succeeded with him. He was adjudicator for a supply of cider to the hospital at Neufchatel; Monsieur Guillaumin promised him some shares in the turf-pits of Gaumesnil, and he dreamt of establishing a new diligence service between Arcueil and Rouen, which no doubt would not be long in ruining the ramshackle van of the "Lion d'Or," and that, travelling faster, at a cheaper rate, and carrying more luggage, would thus put into his hands the whole commerce of Yonville.

Charles several times asked himself by what means he should next year be able to pay back so much money. He reflected, imagined expedients, such as applying to his father or selling something. But his father would be deaf, and he—he had nothing to sell. Then he foresaw such worries that he quickly dismissed so disagreeable a subject of meditation from his mind. He reproached himself with forgetting Emma, as if, all his thoughts belonging to this woman, it was robbing her of something not to be constantly thinking of her.

The winter was severe, Madame Bovary's convalescence slow. When it was fine they wheeled her arm-chair to the window that overlooked the square, for she now had an antipathy to the garden, and the blinds on that side were always down. She wished the horse to be sold; what she formerly liked now displeased her. All her ideas seemed to be limited to the care of herself. She stayed in bed taking little meals, rang for the servant to inquire about her gruel or to chat with her. The snow on the market-roof threw a white, still light into the room; then the rain began to fall; and Emma waited daily with a mind full of eagerness for the inevitable return of some trifling events which nevertheless had no relation to her. The most important was the arrival of the "Hirondelle" in the evening. Then the landlady shouted out, and other voices answered, while Hippolyte's lantern, as he fetched the boxes from the boot, was like a star in the darkness. At mid-day Charles came in; then he went out again; next she took some beef-

ne pourrait payer les billets, qu'on les renouvellerait, et que son pauvre argent, s'étant nourri chez le médecin comme dans une maison de santé, lui reviendrait, un jour, considérablement plus dodu, et gros à faire craquer le sac.

Tout, d'ailleurs, lui réussissait. Il était adjudicataire d'une fourniture de cidre pour l'hôpital de Neufchâtel; M. Guillaumin lui promettait des actions dans les tourbières de Grumesnil, et il rêvait d'établir un nouveau service de diligences entre Argueil et Rouen, qui ne tarderait pas, sans doute, à ruiner la guimbarde du Lion d'or, et qui, marchant plus vite, étant à prix plus bas et portant plus de bagages, lui mettrait ainsi dans les mains tout le commerce d'Yonville.

Charles se demanda plusieurs fois par quel moyen, l'année prochaine, pouvoir rembourser tant d'argent; et il cherchait, imaginait des expédients, comme de recourir à son père ou de vendre quelque chose. Mais son père serait sourd, et il n'avait, lui, rien à vendre. Alors il découvrait de tels embarras, qu'il écartait vite de sa conscience un sujet de méditation aussi désagréable. Il se reprochait d'en oublier Emma; comme si, toutes ses pensées appartenant à cette femme, c'eût été lui dérober quelque chose que de n'y pas continuellement réfléchir.

L'hiver fut rude. La convalescence de Madame fut longue. Quand il faisait beau, on la poussait dans son fauteuil auprès de la fenêtre, celle qui regardait la Place; car elle avait maintenant le jardin en antipathie, et la persienne de ce côté restait constamment fermée. Elle voulut que l'on vendît le cheval; ce qu'elle aimait autrefois, à présent lui déplaisait. Toutes ses idées paraissaient se borner au soin d'elle-même. Elle restait dans son lit à faire de petites collations, sonnait sa domestique pour s'informer de ses tisanes ou pour causer avec elle. Cependant la neige sur le toit des halles jetait dans la chambre un reflet blanc, immobile; ensuite ce fut la pluie qui tombait. Et Emma quotidiennement attendait, avec une sorte d'anxiété, l'infaillible retour d'événements minimes, qui pourtant ne lui importaient guère. Le plus considérable était, le soir, l'arrivée de l'Hirondelle. Alors l'aubergiste criait et d'autres voix répondaient, tandis que le falot d'Hippolyte, qui cherchait des coffres sur la bâche, faisait comme une étoile dans l'obscurité. À midi, Charles rent-

tea, and towards five o'clock, as the day drew in, the children coming back from school, dragging their wooden shoes along the pavement, knocked the clapper of the shutters with their rulers one after the other.

It was at this hour that Monsieur Bournisien came to see her. He inquired after her health, gave her news, exhorted her to religion, in a coaxing little prattle that was not without its charm. The mere thought of his cassock comforted her.

One day, when at the height of her illness, she had thought herself dying, and had asked for the communion; and, while they were making the preparations in her room for the sacrament, while they were turning the night table covered with syrups into an altar, and while Felicite was strewing dahlia flowers on the floor, Emma felt some power passing over her that freed her from her pains, from all perception, from all feeling. Her body, relieved, no longer thought; another life was beginning; it seemed to her that her being, mounting toward God, would be annihilated in that love like a burning incense that melts into vapour. The bed-clothes were sprinkled with holy water, the priest drew from the holy pyx the white wafer; and it was fainting with a celestial joy that she put out her lips to accept the body of the Saviour presented to her. The curtains of the alcove floated gently round her like clouds, and the rays of the two tapers burning on the night-table seemed to shine like dazzling halos. Then she let her head fall back, fancying she heard in space the music of seraphic harps, and perceived in an azure sky, on a golden throne in the midst of saints holding green palms, God the Father, resplendent with majesty, who with a sign sent to earth angels with wings of fire to carry her away in their arms.

This splendid vision dwelt in her memory as the most beautiful thing that it was possible to dream, so that now she strove to recall her sensation. That still lasted, however, but in a less exclusive fashion and with a deeper sweetness. Her soul, tortured by pride, at length found rest in Christian humility, and, tasting the joy of weakness, she saw within herself the destruction of her will, that must have left a wide entrance for the inroads of heavenly grace. There existed, then, in the place of

rait; ensuite il sortait; puis elle prenait un bouillon, et, vers cinq heures, à la tombée du jour, les enfants qui s'en revenaient de la classe, traînant leurs sabots sur le trottoir, frappaient tous avec leurs règles la cliquette des auvents, les uns après les autres.

C'était à cette heure-là que M. Bournisien venait la voir. Il s'enquérait de sa santé, lui apportait des nouvelles et l'exhortait à la religion dans un petit bavardage câlin qui ne manquait pas d'agrément. La vue seule de sa soutane la réconfortait.

Un jour qu'au plus fort de sa maladie elle s'était crue agonisante, elle avait demandé la communion; et, à mesure que l'on faisait dans sa chambre les préparatifs pour le sacrement, que l'on disposait en autel la commode encombrée de sirops et que Félicité semait par terre des fleurs de dahlia, Emma sentait quelque chose de fort passant sur elle, qui la débarrassait de ses douleurs, de toute perception, de tout sentiment. Sa chair allégée ne pesait plus, une autre vie commençait; il lui sembla que son être, montant vers Dieu, allait s'anéantir dans cet amour comme un encens allumé qui se dissipe en vapeur. On aspergea d'eau bénite les draps du lit; le prêtre retira du saint ciboire la blanche hostie; et ce fut en défaillant d'une joie céleste qu'elle avança les lèvres pour accepter le corps du Sauveur qui se présentait. Les rideaux de son alcôve se gonflaient mollement, autour d'elle, en façon de nuées, et les rayons des deux cierges brûlant sur la commode lui parurent être des gloires éblouissantes. Alors elle laissa retomber sa tête, croyant entendre dans les espaces le chant des harpes séraphiques et apercevoir en un ciel d'azur, sur un trône d'or, au milieu des saints tenant des palmes vertes, Dieu le Père tout éclatant de majesté, et qui d'un signe faisait descendre vers la terre des anges aux ailes de flamme pour l'emporter dans leurs bras.

Cette vision splendide demeura dans sa mémoire comme la chose la plus belle qu'il fût possible de rêver; si bien qu'à présent elle s'efforçait d'en ressaisir la sensation, qui continuait cependant, mais d'une manière moins exclusive et avec une douceur aussi profonde. Son âme, courbatue d'orgueil, se reposait enfin dans l'humilité chrétienne; et, savourant le plaisir d'être faible, Emma contemplait en elle-même la destruction de sa volonté, qui devait faire aux envahissements de la

happiness, still greater joys—another love beyond all loves, without pause and without end, one that would grow eternally! She saw amid the illusions of her hope a state of purity floating above the earth mingling with heaven, to which she aspired. She wanted to become a saint. She bought chaplets and wore amulets; she wished to have in her room, by the side of her bed, a reliquary set in emeralds that she might kiss it every evening.

The cure marvelled at this humour, although Emma's religion, he thought, might, from its fervour, end by touching on heresy, extravagance. But not being much versed in these matters, as soon as they went beyond a certain limit he wrote to Monsieur Boulard, bookseller to Monsignor, to send him "something good for a lady who was very clever." The bookseller, with as much indifference as if he had been sending off hardware to niggers, packed up, pellmell, everything that was then the fashion in the pious book trade. There were little manuals in questions and answers, pamphlets of aggressive tone after the manner of Monsieur de Maistre, and certain novels in rose-coloured bindings and with a honied style, manufactured by troubadour seminarists or penitent blue-stockings. There were the *Think of it; the Man of the World at Mary's Feet*, by Monsieur de ***, decorated with many Orders; *The Errors of Voltaire, for the Use of the Young*, etc.

Madame Bovary's mind was not yet sufficiently clear to apply herself seriously to anything; moreover, she began this reading in too much hurry. She grew provoked at the doctrines of religion; the arrogance of the polemic writings displeased her by their inveteracy in attacking people she did not know; and the secular stories, relieved with religion, seemed to her written in such ignorance of the world, that they insensibly estranged her from the truths for whose proof she was looking. Nevertheless, she persevered; and when the volume slipped from her hands, she fancied herself seized with the finest Catholic melancholy that an ethereal soul could conceive.

As for the memory of Rodolphe, she had thrust it back to the bottom of her heart, and it remained there more solemn and more motion-

grâce une large entrée. Il existait donc à la place du bonheur des félicités plus grandes, un autre amour au-dessus de tous les amours, sans intermittence ni fin, et qui s'accroîtrait éternellement! Elle entrevit, parmi les illusions de son espoir, un état de pureté flottant au-dessus de la terre, se confondant avec le ciel, et où elle aspira d'être. Elle voulut devenir une sainte. Elle acheta des chapelets, elle porta des amulettes; elle souhaitait avoir dans sa chambre, au chevet de sa couche, un reliquaire enchâssé d'émeraudes, pour le baiser tous les soirs.

Le Curé s'émerveillait de ces dispositions, bien que la religion d'Emma, trouvait-il, pût, à force de ferveur, finir par friser l'hérésie et même l'extravagance. Mais, n'étant pas très versé dans ces matières sitôt qu'elles dépassaient une certaine mesure, il écrivit à M. Boulard, libraire de Monseigneur, de lui envoyer quelque chose de fameux pour une personne du sexe, qui était pleine d'esprit. Le libraire, avec autant d'indifférence que s'il eût expédié de la quincaillerie à des nègres, vous emballa pêle- mêle tout ce qui avait cours pour lors dans le négoce des livres pieux. C'étaient de petits manuels par demandes et par réponses, des pamphlets d'un ton rogue dans la manière de M. de Maistre, et des espèces de romans à cartonnage rose et à style douceâtre, fabriqués par des séminaristes troubadours ou des bas bleus repenties. Il y avait le *Pensez-y bien*; *l'Homme du monde aux pieds de Marie*, par M. de, décoré de plusieurs ordres; *des Erreurs de Voltaire, à l'usage des jeunes gens*, etc.

Madame Bovary n'avait pas encore l'intelligence assez nette pour s'appliquer sérieusement à n'importe quoi; d'ailleurs, elle entreprit ces lectures avec trop de précipitation. Elle s'irrita contre les prescriptions du culte; l'arrogance des écrits polémiques lui déplut par leur acharnement à poursuivre des gens qu'elle ne connaissait pas; et les contes profanes relevés de religion lui parurent écrits dans une telle ignorance du monde, qu'ils l'écartèrent insensiblement des vérités dont elle attendait la preuve. Elle persista pourtant, et, lorsque le volume lui tombait des mains, elle se croyait prise par la plus fine mélancolie catholique qu'une âme éthérée pût concevoir.

Quant au souvenir de Rodolphe, elle l'avait descendu tout au fond de son coeur; et il restait là, plus solennel et plus immobile qu'une momie

less than a king's mummy in a catacomb. An exhalation escaped from this embalmed love, that, penetrating through everything, perfumed with tenderness the immaculate atmosphere in which she longed to live. When she knelt on her Gothic prie-Dieu, she addressed to the Lord the same suave words that she had murmured formerly to her lover in the outpourings of adultery. It was to make faith come; but no delights descended from the heavens, and she arose with tired limbs and with a vague feeling of a gigantic dupery. This searching after faith, she thought, was only one merit the more, and in the pride of her devoutness Emma compared herself to those grand ladies of long ago whose glory she had dreamed of over a portrait of La Valliere, and who, trailing with so much majesty the lace-trimmed trains of their long gowns, retired into solitudes to shed at the feet of Christ all the tears of hearts that life had wounded.

Then she gave herself up to excessive charity. She sewed clothes for the poor, she sent wood to women in childbed; and Charles one day, on coming home, found three good-for-nothings in the kitchen seated at the table eating soup. She had her little girl, whom during her illness her husband had sent back to the nurse, brought home. She wanted to teach her to read; even when Berthe cried, she was not vexed. She had made up her mind to resignation, to universal indulgence. Her language about everything was full of ideal expressions. She said to her child:

"Is your stomach-ache better, my angel?"

Madame Bovary senior found nothing to censure except perhaps this mania of knitting jackets for orphans instead of mending her own house-linen; but, harassed with domestic quarrels, the good woman took pleasure in this quiet house, and she even stayed there till after Easter, to escape the sarcasms of old Bovary, who never failed on Good Friday to order chitterlings.

Besides the companionship of her mother-in-law, who strengthened her a little by the rectitude of her judgment and her grave ways, Emma almost every day had other visitors. These were Madame Langlois, Madame Caron, Madame Dubreuil, Madame Tuvache, and regularly

de roi dans un souterrain. Une exhalaison s'échappait de ce grand amour embaumé et qui, passant à travers tout, parfumait de tendresse l'atmosphère d'immaculation où elle voulait vivre. Quand elle se mettait à genoux sur son prie-Dieu gothique, elle adressait au Seigneur les mêmes paroles de suavité qu'elle murmurait jadis à son amant, dans les épanchements de l'adultère. C'était pour faire venir la croyance; mais aucune délectation ne descendait des cieux, et elle se relevait, les membres fatigués, avec le sentiment vague d'une immense duperie. Cette recherche, pensait-elle, n'était qu'un mérite de plus; et dans l'orgueil de sa dévotion, Emma se comparait à ces grandes dames d'autrefois, dont elle avait rêvé la gloire sur un portrait de la Vallière, et qui, traînant avec tant de majesté la queue chamarrée de leurs longues robes, se retiraient en des solitudes pour y répandre aux pieds du Christ toutes les larmes d'un coeur que l'existence blessait.

Alors, elle se livra à des charités excessives. Elle cousait des habits pour les pauvres; elle envoyait du bois aux femmes en couches; et Charles, un jour en rentrant, trouva dans la cuisine trois vauriens attablés qui mangeaient un potage. Elle fit revenir à la maison sa petite fille, que son mari, durant sa maladie, avait renvoyée chez la nourrice. Elle voulut lui apprendre à lire; Berthe avait beau pleurer, elle ne s'irritait plus. C'était un parti pris de résignation, une indulgence universelle. Son langage, à propos de tout, était plein d'expressions idéales. Elle disait à son enfant:

— Ta colique est-elle passée, mon ange?

Madame Bovary mère ne trouvait rien à blâmer, sauf peut-être cette manie de tricoter des camisoles pour les orphelins, au lieu de raccommoder ses torchons. Mais, harassée de querelles domestiques, la bonne femme se plaisait en cette maison tranquille, et même elle y demeura jusques après Pâques, afin d'éviter les sarcasmes du père Bovary, qui ne manquait pas, tous les vendredis saints, de se commander une andouille.

Outre la compagnie de sa belle-mère, qui la raffermissait un peu par sa rectitude de jugement et ses façons graves, Emma, presque tous les jours, avait encore d'autres sociétés. C'était madame Langlois, madame Caron, madame Dubreuil, madame Tuvache et, régulièrement, de deux à

from two to five o'clock the excellent Madame Homais, who, for her part, had never believed any of the tittle-tattle about her neighbour. The little Homais also came to see her; Justin accompanied them. He went up with them to her bedroom, and remained standing near the door, motionless and mute. Often even Madame Bovary; taking no heed of him, began her toilette. She began by taking out her comb, shaking her head with a quick movement, and when he for the first time saw all this mass of hair that fell to her knees unrolling in black ringlets, it was to him, poor child! like a sudden entrance into something new and strange, whose splendour terrified him.

Emma, no doubt, did not notice his silent attentions or his timidity. She had no suspicion that the love vanished from her life was there, palpitating by her side, beneath that coarse holland shirt, in that youthful heart open to the emanations of her beauty. Besides, she now enveloped all things with such indifference, she had words so affectionate with looks so haughty, such contradictory ways, that one could no longer distinguish egotism from charity, or corruption from virtue. One evening, for example, she was angry with the servant, who had asked to go out, and stammered as she tried to find some pretext. Then suddenly:

"So you love him?" she said.

And without waiting for any answer from Felicite, who was blushing, she added:

"There! run along; enjoy yourself!"

In the beginning of spring she had the garden turned up from end to end, despite Bovary's remonstrances. However, he was glad to see her at last manifest a wish of any kind. As she grew stronger she displayed more wilfulness. First, she found occasion to expel Mere Rollet, the nurse, who during her convalescence had contracted the habit of coming too often to the kitchen with her two nurslings and her boarder, better off for teeth than a cannibal. Then she got rid of the Homais family, successively dismissed all the other visitors, and even frequented church less assiduously, to the great approval of the druggist, who said to her in a friendly way:

"You were going in a bit for the cassock!"

cinq heures, l'excellente madame Homais, qui n'avait jamais voulu croire, celle-là, à aucun des cancans que l'on débitait sur sa voisine. Les petits Homais aussi venaient la voir; Justin les accompagnait. Il montait avec eux dans la chambre, et il restait debout près de la porte, immobile, sans parler. Souvent même, madame Bovary, n'y prenant garde, se mettait à sa toilette. Elle commençait par retirer son peigne, en secouant sa tête d'un mouvement brusque; et, quand il aperçut la première fois cette chevelure entière qui descendait jusqu'aux jarrets en déroulant ses anneaux noirs, ce fut pour lui, le pauvre enfant, comme l'entrée subite dans quelque chose d'extraordinaire et de nouveau dont la splendeur l'effraya.

Emma, sans doute, ne remarquait pas ses empressements silencieux ni ses timidités. Elle ne se doutait point que l'amour, disparu de sa vie, palpitait là, près d'elle, sous cette chemise de grosse toile, dans ce coeur d'adolescent ouvert aux émanations de sa beauté. Du reste, elle enveloppait tout maintenant d'une telle indifférence, elle avait des paroles si affectueuses et des regards si hautains, des façons si diverses, que l'on ne distinguait plus l'égoïsme de la charité, ni la corruption de la vertu. Un soir, par exemple, elle s'emporta contre sa domestique, qui lui demandait à sortir et balbutiait en cherchant un prétexte; puis tout à coup:

— Tu l'aimes donc? dit-elle.

Et, sans attendre la réponse de Félicité, qui rougissait elle ajouta d'un air triste:

— Allons, cours-y! amuse-toi!

Elle fit, au commencement du printemps, bouleverser le jardin d'un bout à l'autre, malgré les observations de Bovary; il fut heureux, cependant de lui voir enfin manifester une volonté quelconque. Elle en témoigna davantage à mesure qu'elle se rétablissait. D'abord, elle trouva moyen d'expulser la mère Rolet, la nourrice, qui avait pris l'habitude, pendant sa convalescence, de venir trop souvent à la cuisine avec ses deux nourrissons et son pensionnaire, plus endenté qu'un cannibale. Puis elle se dégagea de la famille Homais, congédia successivement toutes les autres visites et même fréquenta l'église avec moins d'assiduité, à la grande approbation de l'apothicaire, qui lui dit alors amicalement:

— Vous donniez un peu dans la calotte!

As formerly, Monsieur Bournisien dropped in every day when he came out after catechism class. He preferred staying out of doors to taking the air "in the grove," as he called the arbour. This was the time when Charles came home. They were hot; some sweet cider was brought out, and they drank together to madame's complete restoration.

Binet was there; that is to say, a little lower down against the terrace wall, fishing for crayfish. Bovary invited him to have a drink, and he thoroughly understood the uncorking of the stone bottles.

"You must," he said, throwing a satisfied glance all round him, even to the very extremity of the landscape, "hold the bottle perpendicularly on the table, and after the strings are cut, press up the cork with little thrusts, gently, gently, as indeed they do seltzer-water at restaurants."

But during his demonstration the cider often spurted right into their faces, and then the ecclesiastic, with a thick laugh, never missed this joke:

"Its goodness strikes the eye!"

He was, in fact, a good fellow and one day he was not even scandalised at the chemist, who advised Charles to give madame some distraction by taking her to the theatre at Rouen to hear the illustrious tenor, Lagardy. Homais, surprised at this silence, wanted to know his opinion, and the priest declared that he considered music less dangerous for morals than literature.

But the chemist took up the defence of letters. The theatre, he contended, served for railing at prejudices, and, beneath a mask of pleasure, taught virtue.

"*Castigat ridendo mores*, Monsieur Bournisien! Thus consider the greater part of Voltaire's tragedies; they are cleverly strewn with philosophical reflections, that made them a vast school of morals and diplomacy for the people."

"I," said Binet, "once saw a piece called the *Gamin de Paris*, in which there was the character of an old general that is really hit off to a T. He sets down a young swell who had seduced a working girl, who at the ending—"

M. Bournisien, comme autrefois, survenait tous les jours, en sortant du catéchisme. Il préférait rester dehors, à prendre l'air au milieu du bocage, il appelait ainsi la tonnelle. C'était l'heure où Charles rentrait. Ils avaient chaud; on apportait du cidre doux, et ils buvaient ensemble au complet rétablissement de Madame.

Binet se trouvait là, c'est-à-dire un peu plus bas, contre le mur de la terrasse, à pêcher des écrevisses. Bovary l'invitait à se rafraîchir, et il s'entendait parfaitement à déboucher les cruchons.

— Il faut, disait-il en promenant autour de lui et jusqu'aux extrémités du paysage un regard satisfait, tenir ainsi la bouteille d'aplomb sur la table, et, après que les ficelles sont coupées, pousser le liège à petits coups, doucement, doucement, comme on fait, d'ailleurs, à l'eau de Seltz, dans les restaurants.

Mais le cidre, pendant sa démonstration, souvent leur jaillissait en plein visage, et alors l'ecclésiastique, avec un rire opaque, ne manquait jamais cette plaisanterie:

— Sa bonté saute aux yeux!

Il était brave homme, en effet, et même, un jour, ne fut point scandalisé du pharmacien, qui conseillait à Charles, pour distraire Madame, de la mener au théâtre de Rouen voir l'illustre ténor Lagardy. Homais s'étonnant de ce silence, voulut savoir son opinion, et le prêtre déclara qu'il regardait la musique comme moins dangereuse pour les moeurs que la littérature.

Mais le pharmacien prit la défense des lettres. Le théâtre, prétendait-il, servait à fronder les préjugés, et, sous le masque du plaisir, enseignait la vertu.

— *Castigat ridendo mores*, monsieur Bournisien! Ainsi, regardez la plupart des tragédies de Voltaire; elles sont semées habilement de réflexions philosophiques qui en font pour le peuple une véritable école de morale et de diplomatie.

— Moi, dit Binet, j'ai vu autrefois une pièce intitulée le *Gamin de Paris*, où l'on remarque le caractère d'un vieux général qui est vraiment tapé! Il rembarre un fils de famille qui avait séduit une ouvrière, qui à la fin…

"Certainly," continued Homais, "there is bad literature as there is bad pharmacy, but to condemn in a lump the most important of the fine arts seems to me a stupidity, a Gothic idea, worthy of the abominable times that imprisoned Galileo."

"I know very well," objected the cure, "that there are good works, good authors. However, if it were only those persons of different sexes united in a bewitching apartment, decorated rouge, those lights, those effeminate voices, all this must, in the long-run, engender a certain mental libertinage, give rise to immodest thoughts and impure temptations. Such, at any rate, is the opinion of all the Fathers. Finally," he added, suddenly assuming a mystic tone of voice while he rolled a pinch of snuff between his fingers, "if the Church has condemned the theatre, she must be right; we must submit to her decrees."

"Why," asked the druggist, "should she excommunicate actors? For formerly they openly took part in religious ceremonies. Yes, in the middle of the chancel they acted; they performed a kind of farce called 'Mysteries,' which often offended against the laws of decency."

The ecclesiastic contented himself with uttering a groan, and the chemist went on:

"It's like it is in the Bible; there there are, you know, more than one piquant detail, matters really libidinous!"

And on a gesture of irritation from Monsieur Bournisien:

"Ah! you'll admit that it is not a book to place in the hands of a young girl, and I should be sorry if Athalie—"

"But it is the Protestants, and not we," cried the other impatiently, "who recommend the Bible."

"No matter," said Homais. "I am surprised that in our days, in this century of enlightenment, anyone should still persist in proscribing an intellectual relaxation that is inoffensive, moralising, and sometimes even hygienic; is it not, doctor?"

"No doubt," replied the doctor carelessly, either because, sharing the same ideas, he wished to offend no one, or else because he had not any ideas.

— Certainement! continuait Homais, il y a la mauvaise littérature comme il y a la mauvaise pharmacie, mais condamner en bloc le plus important des beaux arts me paraît une balourdise, une idée gothique, digne de ces temps abominables où l'on enfermait Galilée.

— Je sais bien, objecta le Curé, qu'il existe de bons ouvrages, de bons auteurs; cependant, ne serait-ce que ces personnes de sexe différent réunies dans un appartement enchanteur, orné de pompes mondaines, et puis ces déguisements païens, ce fard, ces flambeaux, ces voix efféminées, tout cela doit finir par engendrer un certain libertinage d'esprit et vous donner des pensées déshonnêtes, des tentations impures. Telle est du moins l'opinion de tous les Pères. Enfin, ajouta-t-il en prenant subitement un ton de voix mystique, tandis qu'il roulait sur son pouce une prise de tabac, si l'Église a condamné les spectacles, c'est qu'elle avait raison; il faut nous soumettre à ses décrets.

— Pourquoi, demanda l'apothicaire, excommunie-t-elle les comédiens? car, autrefois, ils concouraient ouvertement aux cérémonies du culte. Oui, on jouait, on représentait au milieu du choeur des espèces de farces appelées mystères, dans lesquelles les lois de la décence souvent se trouvaient offensées.

L'ecclésiastique se contenta de pousser un gémissement, et le pharmacien poursuivit:

— C'est comme dans la Bible; il y a... savez-vous..., plus d'un détail... piquant, des choses... vraiment... gaillardes!

Et, sur un geste d'irritation que faisait M. Bournisien:

— Ah! vous conviendrez que ce n'est pas un livre à mettre entre les mains d'une jeune personne, et je serais fâché qu'Athalie...

— Mais ce sont les protestants, et non pas nous, s'écria l'autre impatienté, qui recommandent la Bible!

— N'importe! dit Homais, je m'étonne que, de nos jours, en un siècle de lumières, on s'obstine encore à proscrire un délassement intellectuel qui est inoffensif, moralisant et même hygiénique quelquefois, n'est-ce pas, docteur?

— Sans doute, répondit le médecin nonchalamment, soit que, ayant les mêmes idées, il voulût n'offenser personne, ou bien qu'il n'eût pas d'idées.

The conversation seemed at an end when the chemist thought fit to shoot a Parthian arrow.

"I've known priests who put on ordinary clothes to go and see dancers kicking about."

"Come, come!" said the cure.

"Ah! I've known some!"

And separating the words of his sentence, Homais repeated:

"I—have—known—some!"

"Well, they were wrong," said Bournisien, resigned to anything.

"By Jove! they go in for more than that," exclaimed the druggist.

"Sir!" replied the ecclesiastic, with such angry eyes that the druggist was intimidated by them.

"I only mean to say," he replied in less brutal a tone, "that toleration is the surest way to draw people to religion."

"That is true! that is true!" agreed the good fellow, sitting down again on his chair.

But he stayed only a few moments. Then, as soon as he had gone, Monsieur Homais said to the doctor:

"That's what I call a cock-fight. I beat him, did you see, in a way!—Now take my advice. Take madame to the theatre, if it were only for once in your life, to enrage one of these ravens, hang it! If anyone could take my place, I would accompany you myself. Be quick about it. Lagardy is only going to give one performance; he's engaged to go to England at a high salary. From what I hear, he's a regular dog; he's rolling in money; he's taking three mistresses and a cook along with him. All these great artists burn the candle at both ends; they require a dissolute life, that suits the imagination to some extent. But they die at the hospital, because they haven't the sense when young to lay by. Well, a pleasant dinner! Goodbye till to-morrow."

The idea of the theatre quickly germinated in Bovary's head, for he at once communicated it to his wife, who at first refused, alleging the fatigue, the worry, the expense; but, for a wonder, Charles did not give in, so sure was he that this recreation would be good for her. He saw nothing to prevent it: his mother had sent them three hundred francs

La conversation semblait finie, quand le pharmacien jugea convenable de pousser une dernière botte.

— J'en ai connu, des prêtres, qui s'habillaient en bourgeois pour aller voir gigoter des danseuses.

— Allons donc! fit le curé.

— Ah! j'en ai connu!

Et, séparant les syllabes de sa phrase, Homais répéta:

— J'en — ai — connu.

— Eh bien! ils avaient tort, dit Bournisien résigné à tout entendre.

— Parbleu! ils en font bien d'autres! exclama l'apothicaire.

— Monsieur!... reprit l'ecclésiastique avec des yeux si farouches, que le pharmacien en fut intimidé.

— Je veux seulement dire, répliqua-t-il alors d'un ton moins brutal, que la tolérance est le plus sûr moyen d'attirer les âmes à la religion.

— C'est vrai! c'est vrai! concéda le bonhomme en se rasseyant sur sa chaise.

Mais il n'y resta que deux minutes. Puis, dès qu'il fut parti, M. Homais dit au médecin:

— Voilà ce qui s'appelle une prise de bec! Je l'ai roulé, vous avez vu, d'une manière!... Enfin, croyez-moi, conduisez Madame au spectacle, ne serait-ce que pour faire une fois dans votre vie enrager un de ces corbeaux-là, saprelotte! Si quelqu'un pouvait me remplacer, je vous accompagnerais moi-même. Dépêchez-vous! Lagardy ne donnera qu'une seule représentation; il est engagé en Angleterre à des appointements considérables. C'est, à ce qu'on assure, un fameux lapin! il roule sur l'or! il mène avec lui trois maîtresses et son cuisinier! Tous ces grands artistes brûlent la chandelle par les deux bouts; il leur faut une existence dévergondée qui excite un peu l'imagination. Mais ils meurent à l'hôpital, parce qu'ils n'ont pas eu l'esprit, étant jeunes, de faire des économies. Allons, bon appétit; à demain!

Cette idée de spectacle germa vite dans la tête de Bovary; car aussitôt il en fit part à sa femme, qui refusa tout d'abord, alléguant la fatigue, le dérangement, la dépense; mais, par extraordinaire, Charles ne céda pas, tant il jugeait cette récréation lui devoir être profitable. Il n'y voyait aucun empêchement; sa mère leur avait expédié trois cents

which he had no longer expected; the current debts were not very large, and the falling in of Lheureux's bills was still so far off that there was no need to think about them. Besides, imagining that she was refusing from delicacy, he insisted the more; so that by dint of worrying her she at last made up her mind, and the next day at eight o'clock they set out in the "Hirondelle."

The druggist, whom nothing whatever kept at Yonville, but who thought himself bound not to budge from it, sighed as he saw them go.

"Well, a pleasant journey!" he said to them; "happy mortals that you are!"

Then addressing himself to Emma, who was wearing a blue silk gown with four flounces:

"You are as lovely as a Venus. You'll cut a figure at Rouen."

The diligence stopped at the "Croix-Rouge" in the Place Beauvoisine. It was the inn that is in every provincial faubourg, with large stables and small bedrooms, where one sees in the middle of the court chickens pilfering the oats under the muddy gigs of the commercial travellers—a good old house, with worm-eaten balconies that creak in the wind on winter nights, always full of people, noise, and feeding, whose black tables are sticky with coffee and brandy, the thick windows made yellow by the flies, the damp napkins stained with cheap wine, and that always smells of the village, like ploughboys dressed in Sundayclothes, has a cafe on the street, and towards the countryside a kitchen-garden. Charles at once set out. He muddled up the stage-boxes with the gallery, the pit with the boxes; asked for explanations, did not understand them; was sent from the box-office to the acting-manager; came back to the inn, returned to the theatre, and thus several times traversed the whole length of the town from the theatre to the boulevard.

Madame Bovary bought a bonnet, gloves, and a bouquet. The doctor was much afraid of missing the beginning, and, without having had time to swallow a plate of soup, they presented themselves at the doors of the theatre, which were still closed.

francs sur lesquels il ne comptait plus, les dettes courantes n'avaient rien d'énorme, et l'échéance des billets à payer au sieur Lheureux était encore si longue, qu'il n'y fallait pas songer. D'ailleurs, imaginant qu'elle y mettait de la délicatesse, Charles insista davantage; si bien qu'elle finit, à force d'obsessions, par se décider. Et, le lendemain, à huit heures, ils s'emballèrent dans l'hirondelle.

L'apothicaire, que rien ne retenait à Yonville, mais qui se croyait contraint de n'en pas bouger, soupira en les voyant partir.

— Allons, bon voyage! leur dit-il, heureux mortels que vous êtes!

Puis, s'adressant à Emma, qui portait une robe de soie bleue à quatre falbalas:

— Je vous trouve jolie comme un Amour! Vous allez faire florès à Rouen.

La diligence descendait à l'hôtel de la Croix rouge, sur la place Beauvoisine. C'était une de ces auberges comme il y en a dans tous les faubourgs de province, avec de grandes écuries et de petites chambres à coucher, où l'on voit au milieu de la cour des poules picorant l'avoine sous les cabriolets crottés des commis voyageurs; — bons vieux gîtes à balcon de bois vermoulu qui craquent au vent dans les nuits d'hiver, continuellement pleins de monde, de vacarme et de mangeaille, dont les tables noires sont poissées par les glorias, les vitres épaisses jaunies par les mouches, les serviettes humides tachées par le vin bleu; et qui, sentant toujours le village, comme des valets de ferme habillés en bourgeois, ont un café sur la rue, et du côté de la campagne un jardin à légumes. Charles immédiatement se mit en courses. Il confondit l'avant-scène avec les galeries, le parquet avec les loges, demanda des explications, ne les comprit pas, fut renvoyé du contrôleur au directeur, revint à l'auberge, retourna au bureau, et, plusieurs fois ainsi, arpenta toute la longueur de la ville, depuis le théâtre jusqu'au boulevard.

Madame s'acheta un chapeau, des gants, un bouquet. Monsieur craignait beaucoup de manquer le commencement; et, sans avoir eu le temps d'avaler un bouillon, ils se présentèrent devant les portes du théâtre, qui étaient encore fermées.

# Chapter 15

The crowd was waiting against the wall, symmetrically enclosed between the balustrades. At the corner of the neighbouring streets huge bills repeated in quaint letters "*Lucie de Lammermoor*-Lagardy-Opera-etc." The weather was fine, the people were hot, perspiration trickled amid the curls, and handkerchiefs taken from pockets were mopping red foreheads; and now and then a warm wind that blew from the river gently stirred the border of the tick awnings hanging from the doors of the public-houses. A little lower down, however, one was refreshed by a current of icy air that smelt of tallow, leather, and oil. This was an exhalation from the Rue des Charrettes, full of large black warehouses where they made casks.

For fear of seeming ridiculous, Emma before going in wished to have a little stroll in the harbour, and Bovary prudently kept his tickets in his hand, in the pocket of his trousers, which he pressed against his stomach.

Her heart began to beat as soon as she reached the vestibule. She involuntarily smiled with vanity on seeing the crowd rushing to the right by the other corridor while she went up the staircase to the reserved seats. She was as pleased as a child to push with her finger the large tapestried door. She breathed in with all her might the dusty smell of the lobbies, and when she was seated in her box she bent forward with the air of a duchess.

The theatre was beginning to fill; opera-glasses were taken from their cases, and the subscribers, catching sight of one another, were bowing. They came to seek relaxation in the fine arts after the anxieties of business; but "business" was not forgotten; they still talked cottons, spirits of wine, or indigo. The heads of old men were to be seen, inexpressive and peaceful, with their hair and complexions looking like silver medals tarnished by steam of lead. The young beaux were strutting about in the

# Chapitre 15

La foule stationnait contre le mur, parquée symétriquement entre des balustrades. À l'angle des rues voisines, de gigantesques affiches répétaient en caractères baroques: «*Lucie de Lamermoor*... Lagardy... Opéra..., etc.» Il faisait beau; on avait chaud; la sueur coulait dans les frisures, tous les mouchoirs tirés épongeaient les fronts rouges; et parfois un vent tiède, qui soufflait de la rivière, agitait mollement la bordure des tentes en coutil suspendues à la porte des estaminets. Un peu plus bas, cependant, on était rafraîchi par un courant d'air glacial qui sentait le suif, le cuir et l'huile. C'était l'exhalaison de la rue des Charrettes, pleine de grands magasins noirs où l'on roule des barriques.

De peur de paraître ridicule, Emma voulut, avant d'entrer, faire un tour de promenade sur le port, et Bovary, par prudence, garda les billets à sa main, dans la poche de son pantalon, qu'il appuyait contre son ventre.

Un battement de coeur la prit dès le vestibule. Elle sourit involontairement de vanité, en voyant la foule qui se précipitait à droite par l'autre corridor, tandis qu'elle montait l'escalier des premières. Elle eut plaisir, comme un enfant, à pousser de son doigt les larges portes tapissées; elle aspira de toute sa poitrine l'odeur poussiéreuse des couloirs, et, quand elle fut assise dans sa loge, elle se cambra la taille avec une désinvolture de duchesse.

La salle commençait à se remplir, on tirait les lorgnettes de leurs étuis, et les abonnés, s'apercevant de loin, se faisaient des salutations. Ils venaient se délasser dans les beaux-arts des inquiétudes de la vente; mais, n'oubliant point les affaires, ils causaient encore cotons, trois-six ou indigo. On voyait là des têtes de vieux, inexpressives et pacifiques, et qui, blanchâtres de chevelure et de teint, ressemblaient à des médailles d'argent ternies par une vapeur de plomb. Les jeunes beaux se pavana-

pit, showing in the opening of their waistcoats their pink or applegreen cravats, and Madame Bovary from above admired them leaning on their canes with golden knobs in the open palm of their yellow gloves.

Now the lights of the orchestra were lit, the lustre, let down from the ceiling, throwing by the glimmering of its facets a sudden gaiety over the theatre; then the musicians came in one after the other; and first there was the protracted hubbub of the basses grumbling, violins squeaking, cornets trumpeting, flutes and flageolets fifing. But three knocks were heard on the stage, a rolling of drums began, the brass instruments played some chords, and the curtain rising, discovered a country-scene.

It was the cross-roads of a wood, with a fountain shaded by an oak to the left. Peasants and lords with plaids on their shoulders were singing a hunting-song together; then a captain suddenly came on, who evoked the spirit of evil by lifting both his arms to heaven. Another appeared; they went away, and the hunters started afresh.

She felt herself transported to the reading of her youth, into the midst of Walter Scott. She seemed to hear through the mist the sound of the Scotch bagpipes re-echoing over the heather. Then her remembrance of the novel helping her to understand the libretto, she followed the story phrase by phrase, while vague thoughts that came back to her dispersed at once again with the bursts of music. She gave herself up to the lullaby of the melodies, and felt all her being vibrate as if the violin bows were drawn over her nerves. She had not eyes enough to look at the costumes, the scenery, the actors, the painted trees that shook when anyone walked, and the velvet caps, cloaks, swords—all those imaginary things that floated amid the harmony as in the atmosphere of another world. But a young woman stepped forward, throwing a purse to a squire in green. She was left alone, and the flute was heard like the murmur of a fountain or the warbling of birds. Lucie attacked her cavatina in G major bravely. She plained of love; she longed for wings. Emma, too, fleeing from life, would have liked to fly away in an embrace. Suddenly Edgar-Lagardy appeared.

ient au parquet, étalant, dans l'ouverture de leur gilet, leur cravate rose ou vert pomme; et madame Bovary les admirait d'en haut, appuyant sur des badines à pomme d'or la paume tendue de leurs gants jaunes.

Cependant, les bougies de l'orchestre s'allumèrent; le lustre descendit du plafond, versant, avec le rayonnement de ses facettes, une gaieté subite dans la salle; puis les musiciens entrèrent les uns après les autres, et ce fut d'abord un long charivari de basses ronflant, de violons grinçant, de pistons trompettant, de flûtes et de flageolets qui piaulaient. Mais on entendit trois coups sur la scène; un roulement de timbales commença, les instruments de cuivre plaquèrent des accords, et le rideau, se levant, découvrit un paysage.

C'était le carrefour d'un bois, avec une fontaine, à gauche, ombragée par un chêne. Des paysans et des seigneurs, le plaid sur l'épaule, chantaient tous ensemble une chanson de chasse; puis il survint un capitaine qui invoquait l'ange du mal en levant au ciel ses deux bras; un autre parut; ils s'en allèrent, et les chasseurs reprirent.

Elle se retrouvait dans les lectures de sa jeunesse, en plein Walter Scott. Il lui semblait entendre, à travers le brouillard, le son des cornemuses écossaises se répéter sur les bruyères. D'ailleurs, le souvenir du roman facilitant l'intelligence du libretto, elle suivait l'intrigue phrase à phrase, tandis que d'insaisissables pensées qui lui revenaient, se dispersaient, aussitôt, sous les rafales de la musique. Elle se laissait aller au bercement des mélodies et se sentait elle-même vibrer de tout son être comme si les archets des violons se fussent promenés sur ses nerfs. Elle n'avait pas assez d'yeux pour contempler les costumes, les décors, les personnages, les arbres peints qui tremblaient quand on marchait, et les toques de velours, les manteaux, les épées, toutes ces imaginations qui s'agitaient dans l'harmonie comme dans l'atmosphère d'un autre monde. Mais une jeune femme s'avança en jetant une bourse à un écuyer vert. Elle resta seule, et alors on entendit une flûte qui faisait comme un murmure de fontaine ou comme des gazouillements d'oiseau. Lucie entama d'un air brave sa cavatine en sol majeur; elle se plaignait d'amour, elle demandait des ailes. Emma, de même, aurait voulu, fuyant la vie, s'envoler dans une étreinte. Tout à coup, Edgar- Lagardy parut.

He had that splendid pallor that gives something of the majesty of marble to the ardent races of the South. His vigorous form was tightly clad in a brown-coloured doublet; a small chiselled poniard hung against his left thigh, and he cast round laughing looks showing his white teeth. They said that a Polish princess having heard him sing one night on the beach at Biarritz, where he mended boats, had fallen in love with him. She had ruined herself for him. He had deserted her for other women, and this sentimental celebrity did not fail to enhance his artistic reputation. The diplomatic mummer took care always to slip into his advertisements some poetic phrase on the fascination of his person and the susceptibility of his soul. A fine organ, imperturbable coolness, more temperament than intelligence, more power of emphasis than of real singing, made up the charm of this admirable charlatan nature, in which there was something of the hairdresser and the toreador.

From the first scene he evoked enthusiasm. He pressed Lucy in his arms, he left her, he came back, he seemed desperate; he had outbursts of rage, then elegiac gurglings of infinite sweetness, and the notes escaped from his bare neck full of sobs and kisses. Emma leant forward to see him, clutching the velvet of the box with her nails. She was filling her heart with these melodious lamentations that were drawn out to the accompaniment of the double-basses, like the cries of the drowning in the tumult of a tempest. She recognised all the intoxication and the anguish that had almost killed her. The voice of a prima donna seemed to her to be but echoes of her conscience, and this illusion that charmed her as some very thing of her own life. But no one on earth had loved her with such love. He had not wept like Edgar that last moonlit night when they said, "To-morrow! to-morrow!" The theatre rang with cheers; they recommenced the entire movement; the lovers spoke of the flowers on their tomb, of vows, exile, fate, hopes; and when they uttered the final adieu, Emma gave a sharp cry that mingled with the vibrations of the last chords.

"But why," asked Bovary, "does that gentleman persecute her?"

"No, no!" she answered; "he is her lover!"

Il avait une de ces pâleurs splendides qui donnent quelque chose de la majesté des marbres aux races ardentes du Midi. Sa taille vigoureuse était prise dans un pourpoint de couleur brune; un petit poignard ciselé lui battait sur la cuisse gauche, et il roulait des regards langoureusement en découvrant ses dents blanches. On disait qu'une princesse polonaise, l'écoutant un soir chanter sur la plage de Biarritz, où il radoubait des chaloupes, en était devenue amoureuse. Elle s'était ruinée à cause de lui. Il l'avait plantée là pour d'autres femmes, et cette célébrité sentimentale ne laissait pas que de servir à sa réputation artistique. Le cabotin diplomate avait même soin de faire toujours glisser dans les réclames une phrase poétique sur la fascination de sa personne et la sensibilité de son âme. Un bel organe, un imperturbable aplomb, plus de tempérament que d'intelligence et plus d'emphase que de lyrisme, achevaient de rehausser cette admirable nature de charlatan, où il y avait du coiffeur et du toréador.

Dès la première scène, il enthousiasma. Il pressait Lucie dans ses bras, il la quittait, il revenait, il semblait désespéré: il avait des éclats de colère, puis des râles élégiaques d'une douceur infinie, et les notes s'échappaient de son cou nu, pleines de sanglots et de baisers. Emma se penchait pour le voir, égratignant avec ses ongles le velours de sa loge. Elle s'emplissait le coeur de ces lamentations mélodieuses qui se traînaient à l'accompagnement des contrebasses, comme des cris de naufragés dans le tumulte d'une tempête. Elle reconnaissait tous les enivrements et les angoisses dont elle avait manqué mourir. La voix de la chanteuse ne lui semblait être que le retentissement de sa conscience, et cette illusion qui la charmait quelque chose même de sa vie. Mais personne sur la terre ne l'avait aimée d'un pareil amour. Il ne pleurait pas comme Edgar, le dernier soir, au clair de lune, lorsqu'ils se disaient: «À demain; à demain!...» La salle craquait sous les bravos; on recommença la strette entière; les amoureux parlaient des fleurs de leur tombe, de serments, d'exil, de fatalité, d'espérances, et quand ils poussèrent l'adieu final, Emma jeta un cri aigu, qui se confondit avec la vibration des derniers accords.

— Pourquoi donc, demanda Bovary, ce seigneur est-il à la persécuter?

— Mais non, répondit-elle; c'est son amant.

"Yet he vows vengeance on her family, while the other one who came on before said:

"'I love Lucie and she loves me!' Besides, he went off with her father arm in arm. For he certainly is her father, isn't he—the ugly little man with a cock's feather in his hat?"

Despite Emma's explanations, as soon as the recitative duet began in which Gilbert lays bare his abominable machinations to his master Ashton, Charles, seeing the false troth-ring that is to deceive Lucie, thought it was a love-gift sent by Edgar. He confessed, moreover, that he did not understand the story because of the music, which interfered very much with the words.

"What does it matter?" said Emma. "Do be quiet!"

"Yes, but you know," he went on, leaning against her shoulder, "I like to understand things."

"Be quiet! be quiet!" she cried impatiently.

Lucie advanced, half supported by her women, a wreath of orange blossoms in her hair, and paler than the white satin of her gown. Emma dreamed of her marriage day; she saw herself at home again amid the corn in the little path as they walked to the church. Oh, why had not she, like this woman, resisted, implored? She, on the contrary, had been joyous, without seeing the abyss into which she was throwing herself. Ah! if in the freshness of her beauty, before the soiling of marriage and the disillusions of adultery, she could have anchored her life upon some great, strong heart, then virtue, tenderness, voluptuousness, and duty blending, she would never have fallen from so high a happiness. But that happiness, no doubt, was a lie invented for the despair of all desire. She now knew the smallness of the passions that art exaggerated. So, striving to divert her thoughts, Emma determined now to see in this reproduction of her sorrows only a plastic fantasy, well enough to please the eye, and she even smiled internally with disdainful pity when at the back of the stage under the velvet hangings a man appeared in a black cloak.

His large Spanish hat fell at a gesture he made, and immediately the instruments and the singers began the sextet. Edgar, flashing with

— Pourtant il jure de se venger sur sa famille, tandis que l'autre, celui qui est venu tout à l'heure, disait:

«J'aime Lucie et je m'en crois aimé.» D'ailleurs, il est parti avec son père, bras dessus, bras dessous. Car c'est bien son père, n'est-ce pas, le petit laid qui porte une plume de coq à son chapeau?

Malgré les explications d'Emma, dès le duo récitatif où Gilbert expose à son maître Ashton ses abominables manoeuvres, Charles, en voyant le faux anneau de fiançailles qui doit abuser Lucie, crut que c'était un souvenir d'amour envoyé par Edgar. Il avouait, du reste, ne pas comprendre l'histoire, — à cause de la musique — qui nuisait beaucoup aux paroles.

— Qu'importe? dit Emma; tais-toi!

— C'est que j'aime, reprit-il en se penchant sur son épaule, à me rendre compte, tu sais bien.

— Tais-toi! tais-toi! fit-elle impatientée.

Lucie s'avançait, à demi soutenue par ses femmes, une couronne d'oranger dans les cheveux, et plus pâle que le satin blanc de sa robe. Emma rêvait au jour de son mariage; et elle se revoyait là- bas, au milieu des blés, sur le petit sentier, quand on marchait vers l'église. Pourquoi donc n'avait-elle pas, comme celle-là, résisté, supplié? Elle était joyeuse, au contraire, sans s'apercevoir de l'abîme où elle se précipitait... Ah! si, dans la fraîcheur de sa beauté, avant les souillures du mariage et la désillusion de l'adultère, elle avait pu placer sa vie sur quelque grand coeur solide, alors la vertu, la tendresse, les voluptés et le devoir se confondant, jamais elle ne serait descendue d'une félicité si haute. Mais ce bonheur-là, sans doute, était un mensonge imaginé pour le désespoir de tout désir. Elle connaissait à présent la petitesse des passions que l'art exagérait. S'efforçant donc d'en détourner sa pensée, Emma voulait ne plus voir dans cette reproduction de ses douleurs qu'une fantaisie plastique bonne à amuser les yeux, et même elle souriait intérieurement d'une pitié dédaigneuse, quand au fond du théâtre, sous la portière de velours, un homme apparut en manteau noir.

Son grand chapeau à l'espagnole tomba dans un geste qu'il fit; et aussitôt les instruments et les chanteurs entonnèrent le sextuor. Edgar,

fury, dominated all the others with his clearer voice; Ashton hurled homicidal provocations at him in deep notes; Lucie uttered her shrill plaint, Arthur at one side, his modulated tones in the middle register, and the bass of the minister pealed forth like an organ, while the voices of the women repeating his words took them up in chorus delightfully. They were all in a row gesticulating, and anger, vengeance, jealousy, terror, and stupefaction breathed forth at once from their half-opened mouths. The outraged lover brandished his naked sword; his guipure ruffle rose with jerks to the movements of his chest, and he walked from right to left with long strides, clanking against the boards the silver-gilt spurs of his soft boots, widening out at the ankles. He, she thought must have an inexhaustible love to lavish it upon the crowd with such effusion. All her small fault-findings faded before the poetry of the part that absorbed her; and, drawn towards this man by the illusion of the character, she tried to imagine to herself his life—that life resonant, extraordinary, splendid, and that might have been hers if fate had willed it. They would have known one another, loved one another. With him, through all the kingdoms of Europe she would have travelled from capital to capital, sharing his fatigues and his pride, picking up the flowers thrown to him, herself embroidering his costumes. Then each evening, at the back of a box, behind the golden trellis-work she would have drunk in eagerly the expansions of this soul that would have sung for her alone; from the stage, even as he acted, he would have looked at her. But the mad idea seized her that he was looking at her; it was certain. She longed to run to his arms, to take refuge in his strength, as in the incarnation of love itself, and to say to him, to cry out, "Take me away! carry me with you! let us go! Thine, thine! all my ardour and all my dreams!"

The curtain fell.

The smell of the gas mingled with that of the breaths, the waving of the fans, made the air more suffocating. Emma wanted to go out; the crowd filled the corridors, and she fell back in her arm-chair with palpitations that choked her. Charles, fearing that she would faint, ran to the refreshment-room to get a glass of barley-water.

étincelant de furie, dominait tous les autres de sa voix plus claire. Ashton lui lançait en notes graves des provocations homicides, Lucie poussait sa plainte aiguë, Arthur modulait à l'écart des sons moyens, et la basse-taille du ministre ronflait comme un orgue, tandis que les voix de femmes, répétant ses paroles, reprenaient en choeur, délicieusement. Ils étaient tous sur la même ligne à gesticuler; et la colère, la vengeance, la jalousie, la terreur, la miséricorde et la stupéfaction s'exhalaient à la fois de leurs bouches entrouvertes. L'amoureux outragé brandissait son épée nue; sa collerette de guipure se levait par saccades, selon les mouvements de sa poitrine, et il allait de droite et de gauche, à grands pas, faisant sonner contre les planches les éperons vermeils de ses bottes molles, qui s'évasaient à la cheville. Il devait avoir, pensait-elle, un intarissable amour, pour en déverser sur la foule à si larges effluves. Toutes ses velléités de dénigrement s'évanouissaient sous la poésie du rôle qui l'envahissait, et, entraînée vers l'homme par l'illusion du personnage, elle tâcha de se figurer sa vie, cette vie retentissante, extraordinaire, splendide, et qu'elle aurait pu mener cependant, si le hasard l'avait voulu. Ils se seraient connus, ils se seraient aimés! Avec lui, par tous les royaumes de l'Europe, elle aurait voyagé de capitale en capitale, partageant ses fatigues et son orgueil, ramassant les fleurs qu'on lui jetait, brodant elle-même ses costumes; puis, chaque soir, au fond d'une loge, derrière la grille à treillis d'or, elle eût recueilli, béante, les expansions de cette âme qui n'aurait chanté que pour elle seule; de la scène, tout en jouant, il l'aurait regardée. Mais une folie la saisit: il la regardait, c'est sûr! Elle eut envie de courir dans ses bras pour se réfugier en sa force, comme dans l'incarnation de l'amour même, et de lui dire, de s'écrier: «Enlève-moi, emmène-moi, partons! À toi, à toi! toutes mes ardeurs et tous mes rêves!»

Le rideau se baissa.

L'odeur du gaz se mêlait aux haleines; le vent des éventails rendait l'atmosphère plus étouffante. Emma voulut sortir; la foule encombrait les corridors, et elle retomba dans son fauteuil avec des palpitations qui la suffoquaient. Charles, ayant peur de la voir s'évanouir, courut à la buvette lui chercher un verre d'orgeat.

He had great difficulty in getting back to his seat, for his elbows were jerked at every step because of the glass he held in his hands, and he even spilt three-fourths on the shoulders of a Rouen lady in short sleeves, who feeling the cold liquid running down to her loins, uttered cries like a peacock, as if she were being assassinated. Her husband, who was a millowner, railed at the clumsy fellow, and while she was with her handkerchief wiping up the stains from her handsome cherry-coloured taffeta gown, he angrily muttered about indemnity, costs, reimbursement. At last Charles reached his wife, saying to her, quite out of breath:

"Ma foi! I thought I should have had to stay there. There is such a crowd—SUCH a crowd!"

He added:

"Just guess whom I met up there! Monsieur Leon!"

"Leon?"

"Himself! He's coming along to pay his respects."

And as he finished these words the ex-clerk of Yonville entered the box.

He held out his hand with the ease of a gentleman; and Madame Bovary extended hers, without doubt obeying the attraction of a stronger will. She had not felt it since that spring evening when the rain fell upon the green leaves, and they had said good-bye standing at the window. But soon recalling herself to the necessities of the situation, with an effort she shook off the torpor of her memories, and began stammering a few hurried words.

"Ah, good-day! What! you here?"

"Silence!" cried a voice from the pit, for the third act was beginning.

"So you are at Rouen?"

"Yes."

"And since when?"

"Turn them out! turn them out!"

People were looking at them. They were silent.

But from that moment she listened no more; and the chorus of the guests, the scene between Ashton and his servant, the grand duet in D major, all were for her as far off as if the instruments had grown less

Il eut grand-peine à regagner sa place, car on lui heurtait les coudes à tous les pas, à cause du verre qu'il tenait entre ses mains, et même il en versa les trois quarts sur les épaules d'une Rouennaise en manches courtes, qui, sentant le liquide froid lui couler dans les reins, jeta des cris de paon, comme si on l'eût assassinée. Son mari, qui était un filateur, s'emporta contre le maladroit; et, tandis qu'avec son mouchoir elle épongeait les taches sur sa belle robe de taffetas cerise, il murmurait d'un ton bourru les mots d'indemnité, de frais, de remboursement. Enfin, Charles arriva près de sa femme, en lui disant tout essoufflé:

— J'ai cru, ma foi, que j'y resterais! Il y a un monde!... un monde!...

Il ajouta:

— Devine un peu qui j'ai rencontré là-haut? M. Léon!

— Léon?

— Lui-même! Il va venir te présenter ses civilités.

Et, comme il achevait ces mots, l'ancien clerc d'Yonville entra dans la loge.

Il tendit sa main avec un sans-façon de gentilhomme: et madame Bovary machinalement avança la sienne, sans doute obéissant à l'attraction d'une volonté plus forte. Elle ne l'avait pas sentie depuis ce soir de printemps où il pleuvait sur les feuilles vertes, quand ils se dirent adieu, debout au bord de la fenêtre. Mais, vite, se rappelant à la convenance de la situation, elle secoua dans un effort cette torpeur de ses souvenirs et se mit à balbutier des phrases rapides.

— Ah! bonjour... Comment! vous voilà?

— Silence! cria une voix du parterre, car le troisième acte commençait.

— Vous êtes donc à Rouen?

— Oui.

— Et depuis quand?

— À la porte! à la porte!

On se tournait vers eux; ils se turent.

Mais, à partir de ce moment, elle n'écouta plus; et le choeur des conviés, la scène d'Ashton et de son valet, le grand duo en ré majeur, tout passa pour elle dans l'éloignement, comme si les instruments fus-

sonorous and the characters more remote. She remembered the games at cards at the druggist's, and the walk to the nurse's, the reading in the arbour, the tete-a-tete by the fireside—all that poor love, so calm and so protracted, so discreet, so tender, and that she had nevertheless forgotten. And why had he come back? What combination of circumstances had brought him back into her life? He was standing behind her, leaning with his shoulder against the wall of the box; now and again she felt herself shuddering beneath the hot breath from his nostrils falling upon her hair.

"Does this amuse you?" said he, bending over her so closely that the end of his moustache brushed her cheek.

She replied carelessly:

"Oh, dear me, no, not much."

Then he proposed that they should leave the theatre and go and take an ice somewhere.

"Oh, not yet; let us stay," said Bovary. "Her hair's undone; this is going to be tragic."

But the mad scene did not at all interest Emma, and the acting of the singer seemed to her exaggerated.

"She screams too loud," said she, turning to Charles, who was listening.

"Yes—a little," he replied, undecided between the frankness of his pleasure and his respect for his wife's opinion.

Then with a sigh Leon said:

"The heat is—"

"Unbearable! Yes!"

"Do you feel unwell?" asked Bovary.

"Yes, I am stifling; let us go."

Monsieur Leon put her long lace shawl carefully about her shoulders, and all three went off to sit down in the harbour, in the open air, outside the windows of a cafe.

First they spoke of her illness, although Emma interrupted Charles from time to time, for fear, she said, of boring Monsieur Leon; and the latter told them that he had come to spend two years at Rouen in a large office, in order to get practice in his profession, which was different in

sent devenus moins sonores et les personnages plus reculés; elle se rappelait les parties de cartes chez le pharmacien, et la promenade chez la nourrice, les lectures sous la tonnelle, les tête-à-tête au coin du feu, tout ce pauvre amour si calme et si long, si discret, si tendre, et qu'elle avait oublié cependant. Pourquoi donc revenait-il? quelle combinaison d'aventures le replaçait dans sa vie? Il se tenait derrière elle, s'appuyant de l'épaule contre la cloison; et, de temps à autre, elle se sentait frissonner sous le souffle tiède de ses narines qui lui descendait dans la chevelure.

— Est-ce que cela vous amuse? dit-il en se penchant sur elle de si près, que la pointe de sa moustache lui effleura la joue.

Elle répondit nonchalamment:

— Oh! mon Dieu, non! pas beaucoup.

Alors il fit la proposition de sortir du théâtre, pour aller prendre des glaces quelque part.

— Ah! pas encore! restons! dit Bovary. Elle a les cheveux dénoués: cela promet d'être tragique.

Mais la scène de la folie n'intéressait point Emma, et le jeu de la chanteuse lui parut exagéré.

— Elle crie trop fort, dit-elle en se tournant vers Charles, qui écoutait.

— Oui… peut-être… un peu, répliqua-t-il, indécis entre la franchise de son plaisir et le respect qu'il portait aux opinions de sa femme.

Puis Léon dit en soupirant

— Il fait une chaleur…

— Insupportable! c'est vrai.

— Es-tu gênée? demanda Bovary.

— Oui, j'étouffe; partons.

M. Léon posa délicatement sur ses épaules son long châle de dentelle, et ils allèrent tous les trois s'asseoir sur le port, en plein air, devant le vitrage d'un café.

Il fut d'abord question de sa maladie, bien qu'Emma interrompît Charles de temps à autre, par crainte, disait-elle, d'ennuyer M. Léon; et celui-ci leur raconta qu'il venait à Rouen passer deux ans dans une forte étude, afin de se rompre aux affaires, qui étaient différentes en

Normandy and Paris. Then he inquired after Berthe, the Homais, Mere Lefrancois, and as they had, in the husband's presence, nothing more to say to one another, the conversation soon came to an end.

People coming out of the theatre passed along the pavement, humming or shouting at the top of their voices, "Oh beautiful angel, my Lucie!" Then Leon, playing the dilettante, began to talk music. He had seen Tambourini, Rubini, Persiani, Grisi, and, compared with them, Lagardy, despite his grand outbursts, was nowhere.

"Yet," interrupted Charles, who was slowly sipping his rum-sherbet, "they say that he is quite admirable in the last act. I regret leaving before the end, because it was beginning to amuse me."

"Why," said the clerk, "he will soon give another performance."

But Charles replied that they were going back next day.

"Unless," he added, turning to his wife, "you would like to stay alone, kitten?"

And changing his tactics at this unexpected opportunity that presented itself to his hopes, the young man sang the praises of Lagardy in the last number. It was really superb, sublime. Then Charles insisted:

"You would get back on Sunday. Come, make up your mind. You are wrong if you feel that this is doing you the least good."

The tables round them, however, were emptying; a waiter came and stood discreetly near them. Charles, who understood, took out his purse; the clerk held back his arm, and did not forget to leave two more pieces of silver that he made chink on the marble.

"I am really sorry," said Bovary, "about the money which you are—"

The other made a careless gesture full of cordiality, and taking his hat said:

"It is settled, isn't it? To-morrow at six o'clock?"

Charles explained once more that he could not absent himself longer, but that nothing prevented Emma—

"But," she stammered, with a strange smile, "I am not sure—"

"Well, you must think it over. We'll see. Night brings counsel."

Normandie de celles que l'on traitait à Paris. Puis il s'informa de Berthe, de la famille Homais, de la mère Lefrançois; et, comme ils n'avaient, en présence du mari, rien de plus à se dire, bientôt la conversation s'arrêta.

Des gens qui sortaient du spectacle passèrent sur le trottoir, tout fredonnant ou braillant à plein gosier: O bel ange, ma Lucie! Alors Léon, pour faire le dilettante, se mit à parler musique. Il avait vu Tamburini, Rubini, Persiani, Grisi; et à côté d'eux, Lagardy, malgré ses grands éclats, ne valait rien.

— Pourtant, interrompit Charles qui mordait à petits coups son sorbet au rhum, on prétend qu'au dernier acte il est admirable tout à fait; je regrette d'être parti avant la fin, car ça commençait à m'amuser.

— Au reste, reprit le clerc, il donnera bientôt une autre représentation.

Mais Charles répondit qu'ils s'en allaient dès le lendemain.

— À moins, ajouta-t-il en se tournant vers sa femme, que tu ne veuilles rester seule, mon petit chat?

Et, changeant de manoeuvre devant cette occasion inattendue qui s'offrait à son espoir, le jeune homme entama l'éloge de Lagardy dans le morceau final. C'était quelque chose de superbe, de sublime! Alors Charles insista:

— Tu reviendrais dimanche. Voyons, décide-toi! tu as tort, si tu sens le moins du monde que cela te fait du bien.

Cependant les tables, alentour, se dégarnissaient; un garçon vint discrètement se poster près d'eux; Charles qui comprit, tira sa bourse; le clerc le retint par le bras, et même n'oublia point de laisser, en plus, deux pièces blanches, qu'il fit sonner contre le marbre.

— Je suis fâché, vraiment, murmura Bovary, de l'argent que vous…

L'autre eut un geste dédaigneux plein de cordialité, et, prenant son chapeau:

— C'est convenu, n'est-ce pas, demain, à six heures?

Charles se récria encore une fois qu'il ne pouvait s'absenter plus longtemps; mais rien n'empêchait Emma…

— C'est que…, balbutia-t-elle avec un singulier sourire, je ne sais pas trop…

— Eh bien! tu réfléchiras, nous verrons, la nuit porte conseil…

Then to Leon, who was walking along with them:

"Now that you are in our part of the world, I hope you'll come and ask us for some dinner now and then."

The clerk declared he would not fail to do so, being obliged, moreover, to go to Yonville on some business for his office. And they parted before the Saint-Herbland Passage just as the clock in the cathedral struck half-past eleven.

Puis à Léon, qui les accompagnait:

— Maintenant que vous voilà dans nos contrées, vous viendrez, j'espère de temps à autre, nous demander à dîner?

Le clerc affirma qu'il n'y manquerait pas, ayant d'ailleurs besoin de se rendre à Yonville pour une affaire de son étude. Et l'on se sépara devant le passage Saint-Herbland, au moment où onze heures et demie sonnaient à la cathédrale.

# Part III

# Troisième Partie

# Chapter 1

Monsieur Leon, while studying law, had gone pretty often to the dancing-rooms, where he was even a great success amongst the grisettes, who thought he had a distinguished air. He was the best-mannered of the students; he wore his hair neither too long nor too short, didn't spend all his quarter's money on the first day of the month, and kept on good terms with his professors. As for excesses, he had always abstained from them, as much from cowardice as from refinement.

Often when he stayed in his room to read, or else when sitting of an evening under the lime-trees of the Luxembourg, he let his Code fall to the ground, and the memory of Emma came back to him. But gradually this feeling grew weaker, and other desires gathered over it, although it still persisted through them all. For Leon did not lose all hope; there was for him, as it were, a vague promise floating in the future, like a golden fruit suspended from some fantastic tree.

Then, seeing her again after three years of absence his passion reawakened. He must, he thought, at last make up his mind to possess her. Moreover, his timidity had worn off by contact with his gay companions, and he returned to the provinces despising everyone who had not with varnished shoes trodden the asphalt of the boulevards. By the side of a Parisienne in her laces, in the drawing-room of some illustrious physician, a person driving his carriage and wearing many orders, the poor clerk would no doubt have trembled like a child; but here, at Rouen, on the harbour, with the wife of this small doctor he felt at his ease, sure beforehand he would shine. Self-possession depends on its environment. We don't speak on the first floor as on the fourth; and the wealthy woman seems to have, about her, to guard her virtue, all her banknotes, like a cuirass in the lining of her corset.

On leaving the Bovarys the night before, Leon had followed them through the streets at a distance; then having seen them stop at the

# Chapitre 1

M. Léon, tout en étudiant son droit, avait passablement fréquenté la Chaumière, où il obtint même de fort jolis succès près des grisettes, qui lui trouvaient l'air distingué. C'était le plus convenable des étudiants: il ne portait les cheveux ni trop longs ni trop courts, ne mangeait pas le 1er du mois l'argent de son trimestre, et se maintenait en de bons termes avec ses professeurs. Quant à faire des excès, il s'en était toujours abstenu, autant par pusillanimité que par délicatesse.

Souvent, lorsqu'il restait à lire dans sa chambre, ou bien assis le soir sous les tilleuls du Luxembourg, il laissait tomber son Code par terre, et le souvenir d'Emma lui revenait. Mais peu à peu ce sentiment s'affaiblit, et d'autres convoitises s'accumulèrent par-dessus, bien qu'il persistât cependant à travers elles; car Léon ne perdait pas toute espérance, et il y avait pour lui comme une promesse incertaine qui se balançait dans l'avenir, tel qu'un fruit d'or suspendu à quelque feuillage fantastique.

Puis, en la revoyant après trois années d'absence, sa passion se réveilla. Il fallait, pensa-t-il, se résoudre enfin à la vouloir posséder. D'ailleurs, sa timidité s'était usée au contact des compagnies folâtres, et il revenait en province, méprisant tout ce qui ne foulait pas d'un pied verni l'asphalte du boulevard. Auprès d'une Parisienne en dentelles, dans le salon de quelque docteur illustre, personnage à décorations et à voiture, le pauvre clerc, sans doute, eût tremblé comme un enfant; mais ici, à Rouen, sur le port, devant la femme de ce petit médecin, il se sentait à l'aise, sûr d'avance qu'il éblouirait. L'aplomb dépend des milieux où il se pose: on ne parle pas à l'entresol comme au quatrième étage, et la femme riche semble avoir autour d'elle, pour garder sa vertu, tous ses billets de banque, comme une cuirasse, dans la doublure de son corset.

En quittant la veille au soir M. et madame Bovary, Léon, de loin, les avait suivis dans la rue; puis les ayant vus s'arrêter à la Croix rouge, il

"Croix-Rouge," he turned on his heel, and spent the night meditating a plan.

So the next day about five o'clock he walked into the kitchen of the inn, with a choking sensation in his throat, pale cheeks, and that resolution of cowards that stops at nothing.

"The gentleman isn't in," answered a servant.

This seemed to him a good omen. He went upstairs.

She was not disturbed at his approach; on the contrary, she apologised for having neglected to tell him where they were staying.

"Oh, I divined it!" said Leon.

"How?"

He pretended he had been guided towards her by chance, by, instinct. She began to smile; and at once, to repair his folly, Leon told her that he had spent his morning in looking for her in all the hotels in the town one after the other.

"So you have made up your mind to stay?" he added.

"Yes," she said, "and I am wrong. One ought not to accustom oneself to impossible pleasures when there are a thousand demands upon one."

"Oh, I can imagine!"

"Ah! no; for you, you are a man!"

But men too had had their trials, and the conversation went off into certain philosophical reflections. Emma expatiated much on the misery of earthly affections, and the eternal isolation in which the heart remains entombed.

To show off, or from a naive imitation of this melancholy which called forth his, the young man declared that he had been awfully bored during the whole course of his studies. The law irritated him, other vocations attracted him, and his mother never ceased worrying him in every one of her letters. As they talked they explained more and more fully the motives of their sadness, working themselves up in their progressive confidence. But they sometimes stopped short of the complete exposition of their thought, and then sought to invent a phrase that might express it all the same. She did not confess her passion for another; he did not say that he had forgotten her.

avait tourné les talons et passé toute la nuit à méditer un plan.

Le lendemain donc, vers cinq heures, il entra dans la cuisine de l'auberge, la gorge serrée, les joues pâles, et avec cette résolution des poltrons que rien n'arrête.

— Monsieur n'y est point, répondit un domestique.

Cela lui parut de bon augure. Il monta.

Elle ne fut pas troublée à son abord; elle lui fit, au contraire, des excuses pour avoir oublié de lui dire où ils étaient descendus.

— Oh! je l'ai deviné, reprit Léon.

— Comment?

Il prétendit avoir été guidé vers elle, au hasard, par un instinct. Elle se mit à sourire, et aussitôt, pour réparer sa sottise, Léon raconta qu'il avait passé sa matinée à la chercher successivement dans tous les hôtels de la ville.

— Vous vous êtes donc décidée à rester? ajouta-t-il.

— Oui, dit-elle, et j'ai eu tort. Il ne faut pas s'accoutumer à des plaisirs impraticables, quand on a autour de soi mille exigences...

— Oh! je m'imagine...

— Eh! non, car vous n'êtes pas une femme, vous.

Mais les hommes avaient aussi leurs chagrins, et la conversation s'engagea par quelques réflexions philosophiques. Emma s'étendit beaucoup sur la misère des affections terrestres et l'éternel isolement où le coeur reste enseveli.

Pour se faire valoir, ou par une imitation naïve de cette mélancolie qui provoquait la sienne, le jeune homme déclara s'être ennuyé prodigieusement tout le temps de ses études. La procédure l'irritait, d'autres vocations l'attiraient, et sa mère ne cessait, dans chaque lettre, de le tourmenter. Car ils précisaient de plus en plus les motifs de leur douleur, chacun, à mesure qu'il parlait, s'exaltant un peu dans cette confidence progressive. Mais ils s'arrêtaient quelquefois devant l'exposition complète de leur idée, et cherchaient alors à imaginer une phrase qui pût la traduire cependant. Elle ne confessa point sa passion pour un autre; il ne dit pas qu'il l'avait oubliée.

Perhaps he no longer remembered his suppers with girls after masked balls; and no doubt she did not recollect the rendezvous of old when she ran across the fields in the morning to her lover's house. The noises of the town hardly reached them, and the room seemed small, as if on purpose to hem in their solitude more closely. Emma, in a dimity dressing-gown, leant her head against the back of the old arm-chair; the yellow wall-paper formed, as it were, a golden background behind her, and her bare head was mirrored in the glass with the white parting in the middle, and the tip of her ears peeping out from the folds of her hair.

"But pardon me!" she said. "It is wrong of me. I weary you with my eternal complaints."

"No, never, never!"

"If you knew," she went on, raising to the ceiling her beautiful eyes, in which a tear was trembling, "all that I had dreamed!"

"And I! Oh, I too have suffered! Often I went out; I went away. I dragged myself along the quays, seeking distraction amid the din of the crowd without being able to banish the heaviness that weighed upon me. In an engraver's shop on the boulevard there is an Italian print of one of the Muses. She is draped in a tunic, and she is looking at the moon, with forget-me-nots in her flowing hair. Something drove me there continually; I stayed there hours together."

Then in a trembling voice:

"She resembled you a little."

Madame Bovary turned away her head that he might not see the irrepressible smile she felt rising to her lips.

"Often," he went on, "I wrote you letters that I tore up."

She did not answer. He continued:

"I sometimes fancied that some chance would bring you. I thought I recognised you at street-corners, and I ran after all the carriages through whose windows I saw a shawl fluttering, a veil like yours."

She seemed resolved to let him go on speaking without interruption. Crossing her arms and bending down her face, she looked at the

Peut-être ne se rappelait-il plus ses soupers après le bal, avec des débardeuses; et elle ne se souvenait pas sans doute, des rendez-vous d'autrefois, quand elle courait le matin dans les herbes, vers le château de son amant. Les bruits de la ville arrivaient à peine jusqu'à eux; et la chambre semblait petite, tout exprès pour resserrer davantage leur solitude. Emma, vêtue d'un peignoir en basin, appuyait son chignon contre le dossier du vieux fauteuil; le papier jaune de la muraille faisait comme un fond d'or derrière elle; et sa tête nue se répétait dans la glace avec la raie blanche au milieu, et le bout de ses oreilles dépassant sous ses bandeaux.

— Mais pardon, dit-elle, j'ai tort! je vous ennuie avec mes éternelles plaintes!

— Non, jamais! jamais!

— Si vous saviez, reprit-elle, en levant au plafond ses beaux yeux qui roulaient une larme, tout ce que j'avais rêvé!

— Et moi, donc! Oh! j'ai bien souffert! Souvent je sortais, je m'en allais, je me traînais le long des quais, m'étourdissant au bruit de la foule sans pouvoir bannir l'obsession qui me poursuivait. Il y a sur le boulevard, chez un marchand d'estampes, une gravure italienne qui représente une Muse. Elle est drapée d'une tunique et elle regarde la lune, avec des myosotis sur sa chevelure dénouée. Quelque chose incessamment me poussait là; j'y suis resté des heures entières.

Puis, d'une voix tremblante:

— Elle vous ressemblait un peu.

Madame Bovary détourna la tête, pour qu'il ne vît pas sur ses lèvres l'irrésistible sourire qu'elle y sentait monter.

— Souvent, reprit-il, je vous écrivais des lettres qu'ensuite je déchirais.

Elle ne répondait pas. Il continua:

— Je m'imaginais quelquefois qu'un hasard vous amènerait. J'ai cru vous reconnaître au coin des rues; et je courais après tous les fiacres où flottait à la portière un châle, un voile pareil au vôtre...

Elle semblait déterminée à le laisser parler sans l'interrompre. Croisant les bras et baissant la figure, elle considérait la rosette de ses

rosettes on her slippers, and at intervals made little movements inside the satin of them with her toes.

At last she sighed.

"But the most wretched thing, is it not—is to drag out, as I do, a useless existence. If our pains were only of some use to someone, we should find consolation in the thought of the sacrifice."

He started off in praise of virtue, duty, and silent immolation, having himself an incredible longing for self-sacrifice that he could not satisfy.

"I should much like," she said, "to be a nurse at a hospital."

"Alas! men have none of these holy missions, and I see nowhere any calling—unless perhaps that of a doctor."

With a slight shrug of her shoulders, Emma interrupted him to speak of her illness, which had almost killed her. What a pity! She should not be suffering now! Leon at once envied the calm of the tomb, and one evening he had even made his will, asking to be buried in that beautiful rug with velvet stripes he had received from her. For this was how they would have wished to be, each setting up an ideal to which they were now adapting their past life. Besides, speech is a rolling-mill that always thins out the sentiment.

But at this invention of the rug she asked:

"But why?"

"Why?"

He hesitated.

"Because I loved you so!"

And congratulating himself at having surmounted the difficulty, Leon watched her face out of the corner of his eyes.

It was like the sky when a gust of wind drives the clouds across. The mass of sad thoughts that darkened them seemed to be lifted from her blue eyes; her whole face shone.

He waited. At last she replied:

"I always suspected it."

Then they went over all the trifling events of that far-off existence, whose joys and sorrows they had just summed up in one word. They

pantoufles, et elle faisait dans leur satin de petits mouvements, par intervalles, avec les doigts de son pied.

Cependant, elle soupira:

— Ce qu'il y a de plus lamentable, n'est-ce pas, c'est de traîner, comme moi, une existence inutile? Si nos douleurs pouvaient servir à quelqu'un, on se consolerait dans la pensée du sacrifice!

Il se mit à vanter la vertu, le devoir et les immolations silencieuses, ayant lui-même un incroyable besoin de dévouement qu'il ne pouvait assouvir.

— J'aimerais beaucoup, dit-elle, à être une religieuse d'hôpital.

— Hélas! répliqua-t-il, les hommes n'ont point de ces missions saintes, et je ne vois nulle part aucun métier..., à moins peut- être que celui de médecin...

Avec un haussement léger de ses épaules, Emma l'interrompit pour se plaindre de sa maladie où elle avait manqué mourir; quel dommage! elle ne souffrirait plus maintenant. Léon tout de suite envia le calme du tombeau, et même, un soir, il avait écrit son testament en recommandant qu'on l'ensevelît dans ce beau couvre- pied, à bandes de velours, qu'il tenait d'elle; car c'est ainsi qu'ils auraient voulu avoir été, l'un et l'autre se faisant un idéal sur lequel ils ajustaient à présent leur vie passée. D'ailleurs, la parole est un laminoir qui allonge toujours les sentiments.

Mais à cette invention du couvre-pied:

— Pourquoi donc? demanda-t-elle.

— Pourquoi?

Il hésitait.

— Parce que je vous ai bien aimée!

Et, s'applaudissant d'avoir franchi la difficulté, Léon, du coin de l'oeil, épia sa physionomie.

Ce fut comme le ciel, quand un coup de vent chasse les nuages. L'amas des pensées tristes qui les assombrissaient parut se retirer de ses yeux bleus; tout son visage rayonna.

Il attendait. Enfin elle répondit:

— Je m'en étais toujours doutée...

Alors, ils se racontèrent les petits événements de cette existence lointaine, dont ils venaient de résumer, par un seul mot, les plaisirs et les

recalled the arbour with clematis, the dresses she had worn, the furniture of her room, the whole of her house.

"And our poor cactuses, where are they?"

"The cold killed them this winter."

"Ah! how I have thought of them, do you know? I often saw them again as of yore, when on the summer mornings the sun beat down upon your blinds, and I saw your two bare arms passing out amongst the flowers."

"Poor friend!" she said, holding out her hand to him.

Leon swiftly pressed his lips to it. Then, when he had taken a deep breath:

"At that time you were to me I know not what incomprehensible force that took captive my life. Once, for instance, I went to see you; but you, no doubt, do not remember it."

"I do," she said; "go on."

"You were downstairs in the ante-room, ready to go out, standing on the last stair; you were wearing a bonnet with small blue flowers; and without any invitation from you, in spite of myself, I went with you. Every moment, however, I grew more and more conscious of my folly, and I went on walking by you, not daring to follow you completely, and unwilling to leave you. When you went into a shop, I waited in the street, and I watched you through the window taking off your gloves and counting the change on the counter. Then you rang at Madame Tuvache's; you were let in, and I stood like an idiot in front of the great heavy door that had closed after you."

Madame Bovary, as she listened to him, wondered that she was so old. All these things reappearing before her seemed to widen out her life; it was like some sentimental immensity to which she returned; and from time to time she said in a low voice, her eyes half closed:

"Yes, it is true—true—true!"

They heard eight strike on the different clocks of the Beauvoisine quarter, which is full of schools, churches, and large empty hotels. They no longer spoke, but they felt as they looked upon each other a buzzing in their heads, as if something sonorous had escaped from the fixed eyes

mélancolies. Il se rappelait le berceau de clématite, les robes qu'elle avait portées, les meubles de sa chambre, toute sa maison.

— Et nos pauvres cactus, où sont-ils?

— Le froid les a tués cet hiver.

— Ah! que j'ai pensé à eux, savez-vous? Souvent je les revoyais comme autrefois, quand, par les matins d'été, le soleil frappait sur les jalousies… et j'apercevais vos deux bras nus qui passaient entre les fleurs.

— Pauvre ami! fit-elle en lui tendant la main.

Léon, bien vite, y colla ses lèvres. Puis, quand il eut largement respiré:

— Vous étiez, dans ce temps-là, pour moi, je ne sais quelle force incompréhensible qui captivait ma vie. Une fois, par exemple, je suis venu chez vous; mais vous ne vous en souvenez pas, sans doute?

— Si, dit-elle. Continuez.

— Vous étiez en bas, dans l'antichambre, prête à sortir, sur la dernière marche; — vous aviez même un chapeau à petites fleurs bleues; et, sans nulle invitation de votre part, malgré moi, je vous ai accompagnée. À chaque minute, cependant, j'avais de plus en plus conscience de ma sottise, et je continuais à marcher près de vous, n'osant vous suivre tout à fait, et ne voulant pas vous quitter. Quand vous entriez dans une boutique, je restais dans la rue, je vous regardais par le carreau défaire vos gants et compter la monnaie sur le comptoir. Ensuite vous avez sonné chez madame Tuvache, on vous a ouvert, et je suis resté comme un idiot devant la grande porte lourde, qui était retombée sur vous.

Madame Bovary, en l'écoutant, s'étonnait d'être si vieille; toutes ces choses qui réapparaissaient lui semblaient élargir son existence; cela faisait comme des immensités sentimentales où elle se reportait; et elle disait de temps à autre, à voix basse et les paupières à demi fermées:

— Oui, c'est vrai!… c'est vrai!… c'est vrai…

Ils entendirent huit heures sonner aux différentes horloges du quartier Beauvoisine, qui est plein de pensionnats, d'églises et de grands hôtels abandonnés. Ils ne se parlaient plus; mais ils sentaient, en se regardant, un bruissement dans leurs têtes, comme si quelque chose

of each of them. They were hand in hand now, and the past, the future, reminiscences and dreams, all were confounded in the sweetness of this ecstasy. Night was darkening over the walls, on which still shone, half hidden in the shade, the coarse colours of four bills representing four scenes from the "Tour de Nesle," with a motto in Spanish and French at the bottom. Through the sash-window a patch of dark sky was seen between the pointed roofs.

She rose to light two wax-candles on the drawers, then she sat down again.

"Well!" said Leon.

"Well!" she replied.

He was thinking how to resume the interrupted conversation, when she said to him:

"How is it that no one until now has ever expressed such sentiments to me?"

The clerk said that ideal natures were difficult to understand. He from the first moment had loved her, and he despaired when he thought of the happiness that would have been theirs, if thanks to fortune, meeting her earlier, they had been indissolubly bound to one another.

"I have sometimes thought of it," she went on.

"What a dream!" murmured Leon.

And fingering gently the blue binding of her long white sash, he added:

"And who prevents us from beginning now?"

"No, my friend," she replied; "I am too old; you are too young. Forget me! Others will love you; you will love them."

"Not as you!" he cried.

"What a child you are! Come, let us be sensible. I wish it."

She showed him the impossibility of their love, and that they must remain, as formerly, on the simple terms of a fraternal friendship.

Was she speaking thus seriously? No doubt Emma did not herself know, quite absorbed as she was by the charm of the seduction, and

de sonore se fût réciproquement échappé, de leurs prunelles fixes. Ils venaient de se joindre les mains; et le passé, l'avenir, les réminiscences et les rêves, tout se trouvait confondu dans la douceur de cette extase. La nuit s'épaississait sur les murs, où brillaient encore, à demi perdues dans l'ombre, les grosses couleurs de quatre estampes représentant quatre scènes de la Tour de Nesle, avec une légende au bas, en espagnol et en français. Par la fenêtre à guillotine, on voyait un coin de ciel noir entre des toits pointus.

Elle se leva pour allumer deux bougies sur la commode, puis elle vint se rasseoir.

— Eh bien... fit Léon.

— Eh bien? répondit-elle.

Et il cherchait comment renouer le dialogue, interrompu, quand elle lui dit:

— D'où vient que personne, jusqu'à présent, ne m'a jamais exprimé des sentiments pareils?

Le clerc se récria que les natures idéales étaient difficiles à comprendre. Lui, du premier coup d'oeil, il l'avait aimée; et il se désespérait en pensant au bonheur qu'ils auraient eu si, par une grâce du hasard, se rencontrant plus tôt, ils se fussent attachés l'un à l'autre d'une manière indissoluble.

— J'y ai songé quelquefois, reprit-elle.

— Quel rêve! murmura Léon.

Et, maniant délicatement le liséré bleu de sa longue ceinture blanche, il ajouta:

— Qui nous empêche donc de recommencer?

— Non, mon ami, répondit-elle. Je suis trop vieille... vous êtes trop jeune... oubliez-moi! D'autres vous aimeront... vous les aimerez.

— Pas comme vous! s'écria-t-il.

— Enfant que vous êtes! Allons, soyons sage je le veux!

Elle lui représenta les impossibilités de leur amour, et qu'ils devaient se tenir, comme autrefois, dans les simples termes d'une amitié fraternelle.

Était-ce sérieusement qu'elle parlait ainsi? Sans doute qu'Emma n'en savait rien elle-même, tout occupée par le charme de la séduction et la

the necessity of defending herself from it; and contemplating the young man with a moved look, she gently repulsed the timid caresses that his trembling hands attempted.

"Ah! forgive me!" he cried, drawing back.

Emma was seized with a vague fear at this shyness, more dangerous to her than the boldness of Rodolphe when he advanced to her open-armed. No man had ever seemed to her so beautiful. An exquisite candour emanated from his being. He lowered his long fine eyelashes, that curled upwards. His cheek, with the soft skin reddened, she thought, with desire of her person, and Emma felt an invincible longing to press her lips to it. Then, leaning towards the clock as if to see the time:

"Ah! how late it is!" she said; "how we do chatter!"

He understood the hint and took up his hat.

"It has even made me forget the theatre. And poor Bovary has left me here especially for that. Monsieur Lormeaux, of the Rue Grand-Pont, was to take me and his wife."

And the opportunity was lost, as she was to leave the next day.

"Really!" said Leon.

"Yes."

"But I must see you again," he went on. "I wanted to tell you—"

"What?"

"Something—important—serious. Oh, no! Besides, you will not go; it is impossible. If you should—listen to me. Then you have not understood me; you have not guessed—"

"Yet you speak plainly," said Emma.

"Ah! you can jest. Enough! enough! Oh, for pity's sake, let me see you once—only once!"

"Well—"

She stopped; then, as if thinking better of it:

"Oh, not here!"

"Where you will."

"Will you—"

She seemed to reflect; then abruptly:

nécessité de s'en défendre; et, contemplant le jeune homme d'un regard attendri, elle repoussait doucement les timides caresses que ses mains frémissantes essayaient.

— Ah! pardon, dit-il en se reculant.

Et Emma fut prise d'un vague effroi, devant cette timidité, plus dangereuse pour elle que la hardiesse de Rodolphe quand il s'avançait les bras ouverts. Jamais aucun homme ne lui avait paru si beau. Une exquise candeur s'échappait de son maintien. Il baissait ses longs cils fins qui se recourbaient. Sa joue à l'épiderme suave rougissait — pensait-elle: — du désir de sa personne, et Emma sentait une invincible envie d'y porter ses lèvres. Alors, se penchant vers la pendule comme pour regarder l'heure:

— Qu'il est tard, mon Dieu! dit-elle; que nous bavardons!

Il comprit l'allusion et chercha son chapeau.

— J'en ai même oublié le spectacle! Ce pauvre Bovary qui m'avait laissée tout exprès! M Lormeaux, de la rue Grand-Pont, devait m'y conduire avec sa femme.

Et l'occasion était perdue, car elle partait dès le lendemain.

— Vrai? fit Léon.

— Oui.

— Il faut pourtant que je vous voie encore, reprit-il; j'avais à vous dire…

— Quoi?

— Une chose… grave, sérieuse. Eh! non, d'ailleurs, vous ne partirez pas, c'est impossible! Si vous saviez… Écoutez-moi… Vous ne m'avez donc pas compris? vous n'avez pas deviné?…

— Cependant vous parlez bien, dit Emma.

— Ah! des plaisanteries! Assez, assez! Faites, par pitié, que je vous revoie… une fois… une seule.

— Eh bien…

Elle s'arrêta; puis, comme se ravisant:

— Oh! pas ici!

— Où vous voudrez.

— Voulez-vous…

Elle parut réfléchir, et, d'un ton bref:

"To-morrow at eleven o'clock in the cathedral."

"I shall be there," he cried, seizing her hands, which she disengaged.

And as they were both standing up, he behind her, and Emma with her head bent, he stooped over her and pressed long kisses on her neck.

"You are mad! Ah! you are mad!" she said, with sounding little laughs, while the kisses multiplied.

Then bending his head over her shoulder, he seemed to beg the consent of her eyes. They fell upon him full of an icy dignity.

Leon stepped back to go out. He stopped on the threshold; then he whispered with a trembling voice:

"Tomorrow!"

She answered with a nod, and disappeared like a bird into the next room.

In the evening Emma wrote the clerk an interminable letter, in which she cancelled the rendezvous; all was over; they must not, for the sake of their happiness, meet again. But when the letter was finished, as she did not know Leon's address, she was puzzled.

"I'll give it to him myself," she said; "he will come."

The next morning, at the open window, and humming on his balcony, Leon himself varnished his pumps with several coatings. He put on white trousers, fine socks, a green coat, emptied all the scent he had into his handkerchief, then having had his hair curled, he uncurled it again, in order to give it a more natural elegance.

"It is still too early," he thought, looking at the hairdresser's cuckoo-clock, that pointed to the hour of nine.

He read an old fashion journal, went out, smoked a cigar, walked up three streets, thought it was time, and went slowly towards the porch of Notre Dame.

It was a beautiful summer morning. Silver plate sparkled in the jeweller's windows, and the light falling obliquely on the cathedral made mirrors of the corners of the grey stones; a flock of birds fluttered in

— Demain, à onze heures, dans la cathédrale.

— J'y serai! s'écria-t-il en saisissant ses mains, qu'elle dégagea.

Et, comme ils se trouvaient debout tous les deux, lui placé derrière elle et Emma baissant la tête, il se pencha vers son cou et la baisa longuement à la nuque.

— Mais vous êtes fou! ah! vous êtes fou! disait-elle avec de petits rires sonores, tandis que les baisers se multipliaient.

Alors, avançant la tête par-dessus son épaule, il sembla chercher le consentement de ses yeux. Ils tombèrent sur lui, pleins d'une majesté glaciale.

Léon fit trois pas en arrière, pour sortir. Il resta sur le seuil. Puis il chuchota d'une voix tremblante:

— À demain.

Elle répondit par un signe de tête, et disparut comme un oiseau dans la pièce à côté.

Emma, le soir, écrivit au clerc une interminable lettre où elle se dégageait du rendez-vous: tout maintenant était fini, et ils ne devaient plus, pour leur bonheur, se rencontrer. Mais, quand la lettre fut close, comme elle ne savait pas l'adresse de Léon, elle se trouva fort embarrassée.

— Je la lui donnerai moi-même, se dit-elle; il viendra.

Léon, le lendemain, fenêtre ouverte et chantonnant sur son balcon, vernit lui-même ses escarpins, et à plusieurs couches. Il passa un pantalon blanc, des chaussettes fines, un habit vert, répandit dans son mouchoir tout ce qu'il possédait de senteurs, puis, s'étant fait friser, se défrisa, pour donner à sa chevelure plus d'élégance naturelle.

— Il est encore trop tôt! pensa-t-il en regardant le coucou du perruquier, qui marquait neuf heures.

Il lut un vieux journal de modes, sortit, fuma un cigare, remonta trois rues, songea qu'il était temps et se dirigea lestement vers le parvis Notre-Dame.

C'était par un beau matin d'été. Des argenteries reluisaient aux boutiques des orfèvres, et la lumière qui arrivait obliquement sur la cathédrale posait des miroitements à la cassure des pierres grises; une

the grey sky round the trefoil bell-turrets; the square, resounding with cries, was fragrant with the flowers that bordered its pavement, roses, jasmines, pinks, narcissi, and tube-roses, unevenly spaced out between moist grasses, catmint, and chickweed for the birds; the fountains gurgled in the centre, and under large umbrellas, amidst melons, piled up in heaps, flower-women, bare-headed, were twisting paper round bunches of violets.

The young man took one. It was the first time that he had bought flowers for a woman, and his breast, as he smelt them, swelled with pride, as if this homage that he meant for another had recoiled upon himself.

But he was afraid of being seen; he resolutely entered the church.

The beadle, who was just then standing on the threshold in the middle of the left doorway, under the "Dancing Marianne," with feather cap, and rapier dangling against his calves, came in, more majestic than a cardinal, and as shining as a saint on a holy pyx.

He came towards Leon, and, with that smile of wheedling benignity assumed by ecclesiastics when they question children:

"The gentleman, no doubt, does not belong to these parts? The gentleman would like to see the curiosities of the church?"

"No!" said the other.

And he first went round the lower aisles. Then he went out to look at the Place. Emma was not coming yet. He went up again to the choir.

The nave was reflected in the full fonts with the beginning of the arches and some portions of the glass windows. But the reflections of the paintings, broken by the marble rim, were continued farther on upon the flag-stones, like a many-coloured carpet. The broad daylight from without streamed into the church in three enormous rays from the three opened portals. From time to time at the upper end a sacristan passed, making the oblique genuflexion of devout persons in a hurry. The crystal lustres hung motionless. In the choir a silver lamp was burning, and from the side chapels and dark places of the church

compagnie d'oiseaux tourbillonnaient dans le ciel bleu, autour des clochetons à trèfles; la place, retentissante de cris, sentait les fleurs qui bordaient son pavé, roses, jasmins, oeillets, narcisses et tubéreuses, espacés inégalement par des verdures humides, de l'herbe-au-chat et du mouron pour les oiseaux; la fontaine, au milieu, gargouillait, et, sous de larges parapluies, parmi des cantaloups s'étageant en pyramides, des marchandes, nu-tête, tournaient dans du papier des bouquets de violettes.

Le jeune homme en prit un. C'était la première fois qu'il achetait des fleurs pour une femme; et sa poitrine, en les respirant, se gonfla d'orgueil, comme si cet hommage qu'il destinait à une autre se fût retourné vers lui.

Cependant il avait peur d'être aperçu; il entra résolument dans l'église.

Le Suisse, alors, se tenait sur le seuil, au milieu du portail à gauche, au-dessous de la Marianne dansant plumet en tête, rapière au mollet, canne au poing, plus majestueux qu'un cardinal et reluisant comme un saint ciboire.

Il s'avança vers Léon, et, avec ce sourire de bénignité pateline que prennent les ecclésiastiques lorsqu'ils interrogent les enfants:

— Monsieur, sans doute, n'est pas d'ici? Monsieur désire voir les curiosités de l'église?

— Non, dit l'autre.

Et il fit d'abord le tour des bas-côtés. Puis il vint regarder sur la place. Emma n'arrivait pas. Il remonta jusqu'au choeur.

La nef se mirait dans les bénitiers pleins, avec le commencement des ogives et quelques portions de vitrail. Mais le reflet des peintures, se brisant au bord du marbre, continuait plus loin, sur les dalles, comme un tapis bariolé. Le grand jour du dehors s'allongeait dans l'église en trois rayons énormes, par les trois portails ouverts. De temps à autre, au fond, un sacristain passait en faisant devant l'autel l'oblique génuflexion des dévots pressés. Les lustres de cristal pendaient immobiles. Dans le choeur, une lampe d'argent brûlait; et, des chapelles latérales, des parties sombres de l'église, il s'échappait quelquefois comme des exhalais-

sometimes rose sounds like sighs, with the clang of a closing grating, its echo reverberating under the lofty vault.

Leon with solemn steps walked along by the walls. Life had never seemed so good to him. She would come directly, charming, agitated, looking back at the glances that followed her, and with her flounced dress, her gold eyeglass, her thin shoes, with all sorts of elegant trifles that he had never enjoyed, and with the ineffable seduction of yielding virtue. The church like a huge boudoir spread around her; the arches bent down to gather in the shade the confession of her love; the windows shone resplendent to illumine her face, and the censers would burn that she might appear like an angel amid the fumes of the sweet-smelling odours.

But she did not come. He sat down on a chair, and his eyes fell upon a blue stained window representing boatmen carrying baskets. He looked at it long, attentively, and he counted the scales of the fishes and the button-holes of the doublets, while his thoughts wandered off towards Emma.

The beadle, standing aloof, was inwardly angry at this individual who took the liberty of admiring the cathedral by himself. He seemed to him to be conducting himself in a monstrous fashion, to be robbing him in a sort, and almost committing sacrilege.

But a rustle of silk on the flags, the tip of a bonnet, a lined cloak—it was she! Leon rose and ran to meet her.

Emma was pale. She walked fast.

"Read!" she said, holding out a paper to him. "Oh, no!"

And she abruptly withdrew her hand to enter the chapel of the Virgin, where, kneeling on a chair, she began to pray.

The young man was irritated at this bigot fancy; then he nevertheless experienced a certain charm in seeing her, in the middle of a rendezvous, thus lost in her devotions, like an Andalusian marchioness; then he grew bored, for she seemed never coming to an end.

Emma prayed, or rather strove to pray, hoping that some sudden resolution might descend to her from heaven; and to draw down divine aid she filled full her eyes with the splendours of the tabernacle. She

ons de soupirs, avec le son d'une grille qui retombait, en répercutant son écho sous les hautes voûtes.

Léon, à pas sérieux, marchait auprès des murs. Jamais la vie ne lui avait paru si bonne. Elle allait venir tout à l'heure, charmante, agitée, épiant derrière elle les regards qui la suivaient, — et avec sa robe à volants, son lorgnon d'or, ses bottines minces, dans toute sorte d'élégances dont il n'avait pas goûté, et dans l'ineffable séduction de la vertu qui succombe. L'église, comme un boudoir gigantesque, se disposait autour d'elle; les voûtes s'inclinaient pour recueillir dans l'ombre la confession de son amour; les vitraux resplendissaient pour illuminer son visage, et les encensoirs allaient brûler pour qu'elle apparût comme un ange, dans la fumée des parfums.

Cependant elle ne venait pas. Il se plaça sur une chaise et ses yeux rencontrèrent un vitrage bleu où l'on voit des bateliers qui portent des corbeilles. Il le regarda longtemps, attentivement, et il comptait les écailles des poissons et les boutonnières des pourpoints, tandis, que sa pensée vagabondait à la recherche d'Emma.

Le Suisse, à l'écart, s'indignait intérieurement contre cet individu, qui se permettait d'admirer seul la cathédrale. Il lui semblait se conduire d'une façon monstrueuse, le voler en quelque sorte, et presque commettre un sacrilège.

Mais un froufrou de soie sur les dalles, la bordure d'un chapeau, un camail noir... C'était elle! Léon se leva et courut à sa rencontre.

Emma était pâle. Elle marchait vite.

— Lisez! dit-elle en lui tendant un papier... Oh non!

Et brusquement elle retira sa main, pour entrer dans la chapelle de la Vierge, où, s'agenouillant contre une chaise, elle se mit en prière.

Le jeune homme fut irrité de cette fantaisie bigote; puis il éprouva pourtant un certain charme à la voir, au milieu du rendez- vous, ainsi perdue dans les oraisons comme une marquise andalouse; puis il ne tarda pas à s'ennuyer, car elle n'en finissait.

Emma priait, ou plutôt s'efforçait de prier, espérant qu'il allait lui descendre du ciel quelque résolution subite; et, pour attirer le secours divin, elle s'emplissait les yeux des splendeurs du tabernacle, elle aspi-

breathed in the perfumes of the full-blown flowers in the large vases, and listened to the stillness of the church, that only heightened the tumult of her heart.

She rose, and they were about to leave, when the beadle came forward, hurriedly saying:

"Madame, no doubt, does not belong to these parts? Madame would like to see the curiosities of the church?"

"Oh, no!" cried the clerk.

"Why not?" said she.

For she clung with her expiring virtue to the Virgin, the sculptures, the tombs—anything.

Then, in order to proceed "by rule," the beadle conducted them right to the entrance near the square, where, pointing out with his cane a large circle of block-stones without inscription or carving:

"This," he said majestically, "is the circumference of the beautiful bell of Ambroise. It weighed forty thousand pounds. There was not its equal in all Europe. The workman who cast it died of the joy—"

"Let us go on," said Leon.

The old fellow started off again; then, having got back to the chapel of the Virgin, he stretched forth his arm with an all-embracing gesture of demonstration, and, prouder than a country squire showing you his espaliers, went on:

"This simple stone covers Pierre de Breze, lord of Varenne and of Brissac, grand marshal of Poitou, and governor of Normandy, who died at the battle of Montlhery on the 16th of July, 1465."

Leon bit his lips, fuming.

"And on the right, this gentleman all encased in iron, on the prancing horse, is his grandson, Louis de Breze, lord of Breval and of Montchauvet, Count de Maulevrier, Baron de Mauny, chamberlain to the king, Knight of the Order, and also governor of Normandy; died on the 23rd of July, 1531—a Sunday, as the inscription specifies; and below, this figure, about to descend into the tomb, portrays the same person. It is not possible, is it, to see a more perfect representation of annihilation?"

rait le parfum des juliennes blanches épanouies dans les grands vases, et prêtait l'oreille au silence de l'église, qui ne faisait qu'accroître le tumulte de son coeur.

Elle se relevait, et ils allaient partir, quand le Suisse s'approcha vivement, en disant:

— Madame, sans doute, n'est pas d'ici? Madame désire voir les curiosités de l'église?

— Eh non! s'écria le clerc.

— Pourquoi pas? reprit-elle.

Car elle se raccrochait de sa vertu chancelante à la Vierge, aux sculptures, aux tombeaux, à toutes les occasions.

Alors, afin de procéder dans l'ordre, le Suisse les conduisit jusqu'à l'entrée près de la place, où, leur montrant avec sa canne un grand cercle de pavés noirs, sans inscriptions ni ciselures:

— Voilà, fit-il majestueusement, la circonférence de la belle cloche d'Amboise. Elle pesait quarante mille livres. Il n'y avait pas sa pareille dans toute l'Europe. L'ouvrier qui l'a fondue en est mort de joie…

— Partons, dit Léon.

Le bonhomme se remit en marche; puis, revenu à la chapelle de la Vierge, il étendit les bras dans un geste synthétique de démonstration, et, plus orgueilleux qu'un propriétaire campagnard vous montrant ses espaliers:

— Cette simple dalle recouvre Pierre de Brézé, seigneur de la Varenne et de Brissac, grand maréchal de Poitou et gouverneur de Normandie, mort à la bataille de Montlhéry, le 16 juillet 1465.

Léon, se mordant les lèvres, trépignait.

— Et, à droite, ce gentilhomme tout bardé de fer, sur un cheval qui se cabre, est son petit-fils Louis de Brézé, seigneur de Breval et de Montchauvet, comte de Maulevrier, baron de Mauny, chambellan du roi, chevalier de l'Ordre et pareillement gouverneur de Normandie, mort le 23 juillet 1531, un dimanche, comme l'inscription porte; et, au-dessous, cet homme prêt à descendre au tombeau vous figure exactement le même. Il n'est point possible, n'est-ce pas, de voir une plus parfaite représentation du néant?

Madame Bovary put up her eyeglasses. Leon, motionless, looked at her, no longer even attempting to speak a single word, to make a gesture, so discouraged was he at this two-fold obstinacy of gossip and indifference.

The everlasting guide went on:

"Near him, this kneeling woman who weeps is his spouse, Diane de Poitiers, Countess de Breze, Duchess de Valentinois, born in 1499, died in 1566, and to the left, the one with the child is the Holy Virgin. Now turn to this side; here are the tombs of the Ambroise. They were both cardinals and archbishops of Rouen. That one was minister under Louis XII. He did a great deal for the cathedral. In his will he left thirty thousand gold crowns for the poor."

And without stopping, still talking, he pushed them into a chapel full of balustrades, some put away, and disclosed a kind of block that certainly might once have been an ill-made statue.

"Truly," he said with a groan, "it adorned the tomb of Richard Coeur de Lion, King of England and Duke of Normandy. It was the Calvinists, sir, who reduced it to this condition. They had buried it for spite in the earth, under the episcopal seat of Monsignor. See! this is the door by which Monsignor passes to his house. Let us pass on quickly to see the gargoyle windows."

But Leon hastily took some silver from his pocket and seized Emma's arm. The beadle stood dumfounded, not able to understand this untimely munificence when there were still so many things for the stranger to see. So calling him back, he cried:

"Sir! sir! The steeple! the steeple!"

"No, thank you!" said Leon.

"You are wrong, sir! It is four hundred and forty feet high, nine less than the great pyramid of Egypt. It is all cast; it—"

Leon was fleeing, for it seemed to him that his love, that for nearly two hours now had become petrified in the church like the stones, would vanish like a vapour through that sort of truncated funnel, of oblong cage, of open chimney that rises so grotesquely from the cathe-

Madame Bovary prit son lorgnon. Léon, immobile, la regardait, n'essayant même plus de dire un seul mot, de faire un seul geste, tant il se sentait découragé devant ce double parti pris de bavardage et d'indifférence.

L'éternel guide continuait:

— Près de lui, cette femme à genoux qui pleure est son épouse Diane de Poitiers, comtesse de Brézé, duchesse de Valentinois, née en 1499, morte en 1566; et, à gauche, celle qui porte un enfant, la sainte Vierge. Maintenant, tournez-vous de ce côté: voici les tombeaux d'Amboise. Ils ont été tous les deux cardinaux et archevêques de Rouen. Celui-là était ministre du roi Louis XII. Il a fait beaucoup de bien à la Cathédrale. On a trouvé dans son testament trente mille écus d'or pour les pauvres.

Et, sans s'arrêter, tout en parlant, il les poussa dans une chapelle encombrée par des balustrades, en dérangea quelques-unes, et découvrit une sorte de bloc, qui pouvait bien avoir été une statue mal faite.

— Elle décorait autrefois, dit-il avec un long gémissement, la tombe de Richard Coeur de Lion, roi d'Angleterre et duc de Normandie. Ce sont les calvinistes, monsieur, qui vous l'ont réduite en cet état. Ils l'avaient, par méchanceté, ensevelie dans de la terre, sous le siège épiscopal de Monseigneur. Tenez, voici la porte par où il se rend à son habitation, Monseigneur. Passons voir les vitraux de la Gargouille.

Mais Léon tira vivement une pièce blanche de sa poche et saisit Emma par le bras. Le Suisse demeura tout stupéfait, ne comprenant point cette munificence intempestive, lorsqu'il restait encore à l'étranger tant de choses à voir. Aussi, le rappelant:

— Eh! monsieur. La flèche! la flèche!...

— Merci, fit Léon.

— Monsieur a tort! Elle aura quatre cent quarante pieds, neuf de moins que la grande pyramide d'Égypte. Elle est toute en fonte, elle...

Léon fuyait; car il lui semblait que son amour, qui, depuis deux heures bientôt, s'était immobilisé dans l'église comme les pierres, allait maintenant s'évaporer, telle qu'une fumée, par cette espèce de tuyau tronqué, de cage oblongue, de cheminée à jour, qui se hasarde si grotesquement

dral like the extravagant attempt of some fantastic brazier.

"But where are we going?" she said.

Making no answer, he walked on with a rapid step; and Madame Bovary was already, dipping her finger in the holy water when behind them they heard a panting breath interrupted by the regular sound of a cane. Leon turned back.

"Sir!"

"What is it?"

And he recognised the beadle, holding under his arms and balancing against his stomach some twenty large sewn volumes. They were works "which treated of the cathedral."

"Idiot!" growled Leon, rushing out of the church.

A lad was playing about the close.

"Go and get me a cab!"

The child bounded off like a ball by the Rue Quatre-Vents; then they were alone a few minutes, face to face, and a little embarrassed.

"Ah! Leon! Really—I don't know—if I ought."

She whispered. Then with a more serious air:

"Do you know, it is very improper—"

"How so?" replied the clerk. "It is done at Paris."

And that, as an irresistible argument, decided her.

Still the cab did not come. Leon was afraid she might go back into the church. At last the cab appeared.

"At all events, go out by the north porch," cried the beadle, who was left alone on the threshold, "so as to see the Resurrection, the Last Judgment, Paradise, King David, and the Condemned in Hell-flames."

"Where to, sir?" asked the coachman.

"Where you like," said Leon, forcing Emma into the cab.

And the lumbering machine set out.

It went down the Rue Grand-Pont, crossed the Place des Arts, the Quai Napoleon, the Pont Neuf, and stopped short before the statue of Pierre Corneille.

"Go on," cried a voice that came from within.

sur la cathédrale comme la tentative extravagante de quelque chaudronnier fantaisiste.

— Où allons-nous donc? disait-elle.

Sans répondre, il continuait à marcher d'un pas rapide, et déjà madame Bovary trempait son doigt dans l'eau bénite, quand ils entendirent derrière eux un grand souffle haletant, entrecoupé régulièrement par le rebondissement d'une canne. Léon se détourna.

— Monsieur!

— Quoi?

Et il reconnut le Suisse, portant sous son bras et maintenant en équilibre contre son ventre une vingtaine environ de forts volumes brochés. C'étaient les ouvrages qui frottaient de la cathédrale.

— Imbécile! grommela Léon s'élançant hors de l'église.

Un gamin polissonnait sur le parvis:

— Va me chercher un fiacre!

L'enfant partit comme une balle, par la rue des Quatre-Vents; alors ils restèrent seuls quelques minutes, face à face et un peu embarrassés.

— Ah! Léon!... Vraiment..., je ne sais... si je dois...!

Elle minaudait. Puis, d'un air sérieux:

— C'est très inconvenant, savez-vous?

— En quoi? répliqua le clerc. Cela se fait à Paris!

Et cette parole, comme un irrésistible argument, la détermina.

Cependant le fiacre n'arrivait pas. Léon avait peur qu'elle ne rentrât dans l'église. Enfin le fiacre parut.

— Sortez du moins par le portail du nord! leur cria le Suisse, qui était resté sur le seuil, pour voir la Résurrection, le Jugement dernier, le Paradis, le Roi David, et les Réprouvés dans les flammes d'enfer.

— Où Monsieur va-t-il? demanda le cocher.

— Où vous voudrez! dit Léon poussant Emma dans la voiture.

Et la lourde machine se mit en route

Elle descendit la rue Grand-Pont, traversa la place des Arts, le quai Napoléon, le pont Neuf et s'arrêta court devant la statue de Pierre Corneille.

— Continuez! fit une voix qui sortait de l'intérieur.

The cab went on again, and as soon as it reached the Carrefour Lafayette, set off down-hill, and entered the station at a gallop.

"No, straight on!" cried the same voice.

The cab came out by the gate, and soon having reached the Cours, trotted quietly beneath the elm-trees. The coachman wiped his brow, put his leather hat between his knees, and drove his carriage beyond the side alley by the meadow to the margin of the waters.

It went along by the river, along the towing-path paved with sharp pebbles, and for a long while in the direction of Oyssel, beyond the isles.

But suddenly it turned with a dash across Quatremares, Sotteville, La Grande-Chaussee, the Rue d'Elbeuf, and made its third halt in front of the Jardin des Plantes.

"Get on, will you?" cried the voice more furiously.

And at once resuming its course, it passed by Saint-Sever, by the Quai'des Curandiers, the Quai aux Meules, once more over the bridge, by the Place du Champ de Mars, and behind the hospital gardens, where old men in black coats were walking in the sun along the terrace all green with ivy. It went up the Boulevard Bouvreuil, along the Boulevard Cauchoise, then the whole of Mont-Riboudet to the Deville hills.

It came back; and then, without any fixed plan or direction, wandered about at hazard. The cab was seen at Saint-Pol, at Lescure, at Mont Gargan, at La Rougue-Marc and Place du Gaillardbois; in the Rue Maladrerie, Rue Dinanderie, before Saint-Romain, Saint-Vivien, Saint-Maclou, Saint-Nicaise—in front of the Customs, at the "Vieille Tour," the "Trois Pipes," and the Monumental Cemetery. From time to time the coachman, on his box cast despairing eyes at the public-houses. He could not understand what furious desire for locomotion urged these individuals never to wish to stop. He tried to now and then, and at once exclamations of anger burst forth behind him. Then he lashed his perspiring jades afresh, but indifferent to their jolting, running up against things here and there, not caring if he did, demoralised, and almost weeping with thirst, fatigue, and depression.

La voiture repartit, et, se laissant, dès le carrefour La Fayette, emporter par la descente, elle entra au grand galop dans la gare du chemin de fer.

— Non, tout droit! cria la même voix.

Le fiacre sortit des grilles, et bientôt, arrivé sur le Cours, trotta doucement, au milieu des grands ormes. Le cocher s'essuya le front, mit son chapeau de cuir entre ses jambes et poussa la voiture en dehors des contre-allées, au bord de l'eau, près du gazon.

Elle alla le long de la rivière, sur le chemin de halage pavé de cailloux secs, et, longtemps, du côté d'Oyssel, au delà des îles.

Mais tout à coup, elle s'élança d'un bond à travers Quatremares, Sotteville, la Grande-Chaussée, la rue d'Elbeuf, et fit sa troisième halte devant le jardin des plantes.

— Marchez donc! s'écria la voix plus furieusement.

Et aussitôt, reprenant sa course, elle passa par Saint-Sever, par le quai des Curandiers, par le quai aux Meules, encore une fois par le pont, par la place du Champ-de-Mars et derrière les jardins de l'hôpital, où des vieillards en veste noire se promènent au soleil, le long d'une terrasse toute verdie par des lierres. Elle remonta le boulevard Bouvreuil, parcourut le boulevard Cauchoise, puis tout le Mont-Riboudet jusqu'à la côte de Deville.

Elle revint; et alors, sans parti pris ni direction, au hasard, elle vagabonda. On la vit à Saint-Pol, à Lescure, au mont Gargan, à la Rouge-Mare, et place du Gaillard-bois; rue Maladrerie, rue Dinanderie, devant Saint-Romain, Saint-Vivien, Saint-Maclou, Saint-Nicaise, — devant la Douane, — à la basse Vieille-Tour, aux Trois-Pipes et au Cimetière Monumental. De temps à autre, le cocher sur son siège jetait aux cabarets des regards désespérés. Il ne comprenait pas quelle fureur de la locomotion poussait ces individus à ne vouloir point s'arrêter. Il essayait quelquefois, et aussitôt il entendait derrière lui partir des exclamations de colère. Alors il cinglait de plus belle ses deux rosses tout en sueur, mais sans prendre garde aux cahots, accrochant par-ci par- là, ne s'en souciant, démoralisé, et presque pleurant de soif, de fatigue et de tristesse.

And on the harbour, in the midst of the drays and casks, and in the streets, at the corners, the good folk opened large wonder-stricken eyes at this sight, so extraordinary in the provinces, a cab with blinds drawn, and which appeared thus constantly shut more closely than a tomb, and tossing about like a vessel.

Once in the middle of the day, in the open country, just as the sun beat most fiercely against the old plated lanterns, a bared hand passed beneath the small blinds of yellow canvas, and threw out some scraps of paper that scattered in the wind, and farther off lighted like white butterflies on a field of red clover all in bloom.

At about six o'clock the carriage stopped in a back street of the Beauvoisine Quarter, and a woman got out, who walked with her veil down, and without turning her head.

Et sur le port, au milieu des camions et des barriques, et dans les rues, au coin des bornes, les bourgeois ouvraient de grands yeux ébahis devant cette chose si extraordinaire en province, une voiture à stores tendus, et qui apparaissait ainsi continuellement, plus close qu'un tombeau et ballottée comme un navire.

Une fois, au milieu du jour, en pleine campagne, au moment où le soleil dardait le plus fort contre les vieilles lanternes argentées, une main nue passa sous les petits rideaux de toile jaune et jeta des déchirures de papier, qui se dispersèrent au vent et s'abattirent plus loin, comme des papillons blancs, sur un champ de trèfles rouges tout en fleur.

Puis, vers six heures, la voiture s'arrêta dans une ruelle du quartier Beauvoisine, et une femme en descendit qui marchait le voile baissé, sans détourner la tête.

# Chapter 2

On reaching the inn, Madame Bovary was surprised not to see the diligence. Hivert, who had waited for her fifty-three minutes, had at last started.

Yet nothing forced her to go; but she had given her word that she would return that same evening. Moreover, Charles expected her, and in her heart she felt already that cowardly docility that is for some women at once the chastisement and atonement of adultery.

She packed her box quickly, paid her bill, took a cab in the yard, hurrying on the driver, urging him on, every moment inquiring about the time and the miles traversed. He succeeded in catching up the "Hirondelle" as it neared the first houses of Quincampoix.

Hardly was she seated in her corner than she closed her eyes, and opened them at the foot of the hill, when from afar she recognised Felicite, who was on the lookout in front of the farrier's shop. Hivert pulled in his horses and, the servant, climbing up to the window, said mysteriously:

"Madame, you must go at once to Monsieur Homais. It's for something important."

The village was silent as usual. At the corner of the streets were small pink heaps that smoked in the air, for this was the time for jam-making, and everyone at Yonville prepared his supply on the same day. But in front of the chemist's shop one might admire a far larger heap, and that surpassed the others with the superiority that a laboratory must have over ordinary stores, a general need over individual fancy.

She went in. The large arm-chair was upset, and even the "Fanal de Rouen" lay on the ground, outspread between two pestles. She pushed open the lobby door, and in the middle of the kitchen, amid brown jars full of picked currants, of powdered sugar and lump sugar, of the scales

# Chapitre 2

En arrivant à l'auberge, madame Bovary fut étonnée de ne pas apercevoir la diligence. Hivert, qui l'avait attendue cinquante- trois minutes, avait fini par s'en aller.

Rien pourtant ne la forçait à partir; mais elle avait donné sa parole qu'elle reviendrait le soir même. D'ailleurs, Charles l'attendait; et déjà elle se sentait au coeur cette lâche docilité qui est, pour bien des femmes, comme le châtiment tout à la fois et la rançon de l'adultère.

Vivement elle fit sa malle, paya la note, prit dans la cour un cabriolet, et, pressant le palefrenier, l'encourageant, s'informant à toute minute de l'heure et des kilomètres parcourus, parvint à rattraper l'Hirondelle vers les premières maisons de Quincampoix.

À peine assise dans son coin, elle ferma les yeux et les rouvrit au bas de la côte, où elle reconnut de loin Félicité, qui se tenait en vedette devant la maison du maréchal. Hivert retint ses chevaux, et la cuisinière, se haussant jusqu'au vasistas, dit mystérieusement:

— Madame il faut que vous alliez tout de suite chez M. Homais. C'est pour quelque chose de pressé.

Le village était silencieux comme d'habitude. Au coin des rues, il y avait de petits tas roses qui fumaient l'air, c'était le moment des confitures, et tout le monde à Yonville, confectionnait sa provision le même jour. Mais on admirait devant la boutique du pharmacien, un tas beaucoup plus large, et qui dépassait les autres de la supériorité qu'une officine doit avoir sur les fourneaux bourgeois, un besoin général sur des fantaisies individuelles.

Elle entra. Le grand fauteuil était renversé, et même le Fanal de Rouen gisait par terre, étendu entre les deux pilons. Elle poussa la porte du couloir; et, au milieu de la cuisine, parmi les jarres brunes pleines de groseilles égrenées, du sucre râpé, du sucre en morceaux, des balances

on the table, and of the pans on the fire, she saw all the Homais, small and large, with aprons reaching to their chins, and with forks in their hands. Justin was standing up with bowed head, and the chemist was screaming:

"Who told you to go and fetch it in the Capharnaum."

"What is it? What is the matter?"

"What is it?" replied the druggist. "We are making preserves; they are simmering; but they were about to boil over, because there is too much juice, and I ordered another pan. Then he, from indolence, from laziness, went and took, hanging on its nail in my laboratory, the key of the Capharnaum."

It was thus the druggist called a small room under the leads, full of the utensils and the goods of his trade. He often spent long hours there alone, labelling, decanting, and doing up again; and he looked upon it not as a simple store, but as a veritable sanctuary, whence there afterwards issued, elaborated by his hands, all sorts of pills, boluses, infusions, lotions, and potions, that would bear far and wide his celebrity. No one in the world set foot there, and he respected it so, that he swept it himself. Finally, if the pharmacy, open to all comers, was the spot where he displayed his pride, the Capharnaum was the refuge where, egoistically concentrating himself, Homais delighted in the exercise of his predilections, so that Justin's thoughtlessness seemed to him a monstrous piece of irreverence, and, redder than the currants, he repeated:

"Yes, from the Capharnaum! The key that locks up the acids and caustic alkalies! To go and get a spare pan! a pan with a lid! and that I shall perhaps never use! Everything is of importance in the delicate operations of our art! But, devil take it! one must make distinctions, and not employ for almost domestic purposes that which is meant for pharmaceutical! It is as if one were to carve a fowl with a scalpel; as if a magistrate—"

"Now be calm," said Madame Homais.

And Athalie, pulling at his coat, cried:

"Papa! papa!"

sur la table, des bassines sur le feu, elle aperçut tous les Homais, grands et petits, avec des tabliers qui leur montaient jusqu'au menton et tenant des fourchettes à la main. Justin, debout, baissait la tête, et le pharmacien criait:

— Qui t'avait dit de l'aller chercher dans le capharnaüm?

— Qu'est-ce donc? qu'y a-t-il?

— Ce qu'il y a? répondit l'apothicaire. On fait des confitures: elles cuisent; mais elles allaient déborder à cause du bouillon trop fort, et je commande une autre bassine. Alors, lui, par mollesse, par paresse, a été prendre, suspendue à son clou dans mon laboratoire, la clef du capharnaüm!

L'apothicaire appelait ainsi un cabinet, sous les toits, plein des ustensiles et des marchandises de sa profession. Souvent il y passait seul de longues heures à étiqueter, à transvaser, à reficeler; et il le considérait non comme un simple magasin, mais comme un véritable sanctuaire, d'où s'échappaient ensuite, élaborées par ses mains, toutes sortes de pilules, bols, tisanes, lotions et potions, qui allaient répandre aux alentours sa célébrité. Personne au monde n'y mettait les pieds; et il le respectait si fort, qu'il le balayait lui-même. Enfin, si la pharmacie, ouverte à tout venant, était l'endroit où il étalait son orgueil, le capharnaüm était le refuge où, se concentrant égoïstement, Homais se délectait dans l'exercice de ses prédilections; aussi l'étourderie de Justin lui paraissait-elle monstrueuse d'irrévérence; et, plus rubicond que les groseilles, il répétait:

— Oui, du capharnaüm! La clef qui enferme les acides avec les alcalis caustiques! Avoir été prendre une bassine de réserve! une bassine à couvercle! et dont jamais peut-être je ne me servirai! Tout a son importance dans les opérations délicates de notre art! Mais que diable! il faut établir des distinctions et ne pas employer à des usages presque domestiques ce qui est destiné pour les pharmaceutiques! C'est comme si on découpait une poularde avec un scalpel, comme si un magistrat...

— Mais calme-toi! disait madame Homais.

Et Athalie, le tirant par sa redingote:

— Papa! papa!

"No, let me alone," went on the druggist "let me alone, hang it! My word! One might as well set up for a grocer. That's it! go it! respect nothing! break, smash, let loose the leeches, burn the mallow-paste, pickle the gherkins in the window jars, tear up the bandages!"

"I thought you had—" said Emma.

"Presently! Do you know to what you exposed yourself? Didn't you see anything in the corner, on the left, on the third shelf? Speak, answer, articulate something."

"I—don't—know," stammered the young fellow.

"Ah! you don't know! Well, then, I do know! You saw a bottle of blue glass, sealed with yellow wax, that contains a white powder, on which I have even written 'Dangerous!' And do you know what is in it? Arsenic! And you go and touch it! You take a pan that was next to it!"

"Next to it!" cried Madame Homais, clasping her hands. "Arsenic! You might have poisoned us all."

And the children began howling as if they already had frightful pains in their entrails.

"Or poison a patient!" continued the druggist. "Do you want to see me in the prisoner's dock with criminals, in a court of justice? To see me dragged to the scaffold? Don't you know what care I take in managing things, although I am so thoroughly used to it? Often I am horrified myself when I think of my responsibility; for the Government persecutes us, and the absurd legislation that rules us is a veritable Damocles' sword over our heads."

Emma no longer dreamed of asking what they wanted her for, and the druggist went on in breathless phrases:

"That is your return for all the kindness we have shown you! That is how you recompense me for the really paternal care that I lavish on you! For without me where would you be? What would you be doing? Who provides you with food, education, clothes, and all the means of figuring one day with honour in the ranks of society? But you must pull hard at the oar if you're to do that, and get, as, people say, callosities upon your hands. *Fabricando fit faber, age quod agis.*"

— Non, laissez-moi! reprenait l'apothicaire, laissez-moi! fichtre! Autant s'établir, épicier, ma parole d'honneur! Allons, va! ne respecte rien! casse! brise! lâche les sangsues! brûle la guimauve! marine des cornichons dans les bocaux! lacère les bandages!

— Vous aviez pourtant... dit Emma.

— Tout à l'heure! — Sais-tu à quoi tu t'exposais?... N'as-tu rien vu, dans le coin, à gauche, sur la troisième tablette? Parle, réponds, articule quelque chose!

— Je ne... sais pas, balbutia le jeune garçon.

— Ah! tu ne sais pas! Eh bien, je sais, moi! Tu as vu une bouteille, en verre bleu, cachetée avec de la cire jaune, qui contient une poudre blanche, sur laquelle même j'avais écrit: Dangereux! et sais-tu ce qu'il y avait dedans? De l'arsenic! et tu vas toucher à cela! prendre une bassine qui est à côté!

— À côté! s'écria madame Homais en joignant les mains. De l'arsenic? Tu pouvais nous empoisonner tous!

Et les enfants se mirent à pousser des cris, comme s'ils avaient déjà senti dans leurs entrailles d'atroces douleurs.

— Ou bien empoisonner un malade! continuait l'apothicaire. Tu voulais donc que j'allasse sur le banc des criminels, en cour d'assises? me voir traîner à l'échafaud? Ignores-tu le soin que j'observe dans les manutentions, quoique j'en aie cependant une furieuse habitude. Souvent je m'épouvante moi-même, lorsque je pense à ma responsabilité! car le gouvernement nous persécute, et l'absurde législation qui nous régit est comme une véritable épée de Damoclès suspendue sur notre tête!

Emma ne songeait plus à demander ce qu'on lui voulait, et le pharmacien poursuivait en phrases haletantes:

— Voilà comme tu reconnais les bontés qu'on a pour toi! voilà comme tu me récompenses des soins tout paternels que je te prodigue! Car, sans moi, où serais-tu? que ferais-tu? Qui te fournit la nourriture, l'éducation, l'habillement, et tous les moyens de figurer un jour, avec honneur dans les rangs de la société! Mais il faut pour cela suer ferme sur l'aviron, et acquérir, comme on dit, du cal aux mains. *Fabricando fil faber, age quod agis.*

He was so exasperated he quoted Latin. He would have quoted Chinese or Greenlandish had he known those two languages, for he was in one of those crises in which the whole soul shows indistinctly what it contains, like the ocean, which, in the storm, opens itself from the seaweeds on its shores down to the sands of its abysses.

And he went on:

"I am beginning to repent terribly of having taken you up! I should certainly have done better to have left you to rot in your poverty and the dirt in which you were born. Oh, you'll never be fit for anything but to herd animals with horns! You have no aptitude for science! You hardly know how to stick on a label! And there you are, dwelling with me snug as a parson, living in clover, taking your ease!"

But Emma, turning to Madame Homais:

"I was told to come here—"

"Oh, dear me!" interrupted the good woman, with a sad air, "how am I to tell you? It is a misfortune!"

She could not finish, the druggist was thundering:

"Empty it! Clean it! Take it back! Be quick!"

And seizing Justin by the collar of his blouse, he shook a book out of his pocket.

The lad stooped, but Homais was the quicker, and, having picked up the volume, contemplated it with staring eyes and open mouth.

"CONJUGAL—LOVE!" he said, slowly separating the two words. "Ah! very good! very good! very pretty! And illustrations! Oh, this is too much!"

Madame Homais came forward.

"No, do not touch it!"

The children wanted to look at the pictures.

"Leave the room," he said imperiously.

And they went out.

First he walked up and down with the open volume in his hand, rolling his eyes, choking, tumid, apoplectic. Then he came straight to his pupil, and, planting himself in front of him with crossed arms:

Il citait du latin, tant il était exaspéré. Il eût cité du chinois et du groenlandais, s'il eût connu ces deux langues; car il se trouvait dans une de ces crises où l'âme entière montre indistinctement ce qu'elle enferme, comme l'Océan, qui, dans les tempêtes, s'entrouvre depuis les fucus de son rivage jusqu'au sable de ses abîmes.

Et il reprit:

— Je commence à terriblement me repentir de m'être chargé de ta personne! J'aurais certes mieux fait de te laisser autrefois croupir dans ta misère et dans la crasse où tu es né! Tu ne seras jamais bon qu'à être un gardeur de bêtes à cornes! Tu n'as nulle aptitude pour les sciences! à peine si tu sais coller une étiquette! Et tu vis là, chez moi, comme un chanoine, comme un coq en pâte, à te goberger!

Mais Emma, se tournant vers madame Homais:

— On m'avait fait venir…

— Ah! mon Dieu! interrompit d'un air triste la bonne dame, comment vous dirai-je bien?… C'est un malheur!

Elle n'acheva pas. L'apothicaire tonnait:

Vide-la! écure-la! reporte-la! dépêche-toi donc!

Et, secouant Justin par le collet de son bourgeron, il fit tomber un livre de sa poche.

L'enfant se baissa. Homais fut plus prompt, et, ayant ramassé le volume, il le contemplait, les yeux écarquillés, la mâchoire ouverte.

— L'amour… conjugal! dit-il en séparant lentement ces deux mots. Ah! très bien! très bien! très joli! Et des gravures!… Ah! c'est trop fort!

Madame Homais s'avança.

— Non! n'y touche pas!

Les enfants voulurent voir les images.

— Sortez! fit-il impérieusement.

Et ils sortirent.

Il marcha d'abord de long en large, à grands pas, gardant le volume ouvert entre ses doigts, roulant les yeux, suffoqué, tuméfié, apoplectique. Puis il vint droit à son élève, et, se plantant devant lui les bras croisés:

"Have you every vice, then, little wretch? Take care! you are on a downward path. Did not you reflect that this infamous book might fall in the hands of my children, kindle a spark in their minds, tarnish the purity of Athalie, corrupt Napoleon. He is already formed like a man. Are you quite sure, anyhow, that they have not read it? Can you certify to me—"

"But really, sir," said Emma, "you wished to tell me—"

"Ah, yes! madame. Your father-in-law is dead."

In fact, Monsieur Bovary senior had expired the evening before suddenly from an attack of apoplexy as he got up from table, and by way of greater precaution, on account of Emma's sensibility, Charles had begged Homais to break the horrible news to her gradually.

Homais had thought over his speech; he had rounded, polished it, made it rhythmical; it was a masterpiece of prudence and transitions, of subtle turns and delicacy; but anger had got the better of rhetoric.

Emma, giving up all chance of hearing any details, left the pharmacy; for Monsieur Homais had taken up the thread of his vituperations. However, he was growing calmer, and was now grumbling in a paternal tone whilst he fanned himself with his skull-cap.

"It is not that I entirely disapprove of the work. Its author was a doctor! There are certain scientific points in it that it is not ill a man should know, and I would even venture to say that a man must know. But later—later! At any rate, not till you are man yourself and your temperament is formed."

When Emma knocked at the door. Charles, who was waiting for her, came forward with open arms and said to her with tears in his voice:

"Ah! my dear!"

And he bent over her gently to kiss her. But at the contact of his lips the memory of the other seized her, and she passed her hand over her face shuddering.

But she made answer:

"Yes, I know, I know!"

He showed her the letter in which his mother told the event without any sentimental hypocrisy. She only regretted her husband had not

— Mais tu as donc tous les vices, petit malheureux?... Prends garde, tu es sur une pente!... Tu n'as donc pas réfléchi qu'il pouvait, ce livre infâme, tomber entre les mains de mes enfants, mettre l'étincelle dans leur cerveau, ternir la pureté d'Athalie, corrompre Napoléon! Il est déjà formé comme un homme. Es-tu bien sûr, au moins, qu'ils ne l'aient pas lu? peux-tu me certifier...?

— Mais enfin, monsieur, fit Emma, vous aviez à me dire...?

— C'est vrai, madame... Votre beau-père est mort!

En effet, le sieur Bovary père venait de décéder l'avant-veille, tout à coup, d'une attaque d'apoplexie, au sortir de table; et, par excès de précaution pour la sensibilité d'Emma, Charles avait prié M. Homais de lui apprendre avec ménagement cette horrible nouvelle.

Il avait médité sa phrase, il l'avait arrondie, polie, rythmée; c'était un chef-d'oeuvre de prudence et de transitions, de tournures fines et de délicatesse; mais la colère avait emporté la rhétorique.

Emma, renonçant à avoir aucun détail, quitta donc la pharmacie; car M. Homais avait repris le cours de ses vitupérations. Il se calmait cependant, et, à présent, il grommelait d'un ton paterne, tout en s'éventant avec son bonnet grec:

— Ce n'est pas que je désapprouve entièrement l'ouvrage! L'auteur était médecin. Il y a là-dedans certains côtés scientifiques qu'il n'est pas mal à un homme de connaître et, j'oserais dire, qu'il faut qu'un homme connaisse. Mais plus tard, plus tard! Attends du moins que tu sois homme toi-même et que ton tempérament soit fait.

Au coup de marteau d'Emma, Charles, qui l'attendait, s'avança les bras ouverts et lui dit avec des larmes dans la voix:

— Ah! ma chère amie...

Et il s'inclina doucement pour l'embrasser. Mais, au contact de ses lèvres, le souvenir de l'autre la saisit, et elle se passa la main sur son visage en frissonnant.

Cependant elle répondit:

— Oui, je sais..., je sais...

Il lui montra la lettre où sa mère narrait l'événement, sans aucune hypocrisie sentimentale. Seulement, elle regrettait que son mari n'eût

received the consolations of religion, as he had died at Daudeville, in the street, at the door of a cafe after a patriotic dinner with some ex-officers.

Emma gave him back the letter; then at dinner, for appearance's sake, she affected a certain repugnance. But as he urged her to try, she resolutely began eating, while Charles opposite her sat motionless in a dejected attitude.

Now and then he raised his head and gave her a long look full of distress. Once he sighed:

"I should have liked to see him again!"

She was silent. At last, understanding that she must say something:

"How old was your father?" she asked.

"Fifty-eight."

"Ah!"

And that was all.

A quarter of an hour after he added:

"My poor mother! what will become of her now?"

She made a gesture that signified she did not know.

Seeing her so taciturn, Charles imagined her much affected, and forced himself to say nothing, not to reawaken this sorrow which moved him. And, shaking off his own:

"Did you enjoy yourself yesterday?" he asked.

"Yes."

When the cloth was removed, Bovary did not rise, nor did Emma; and as she looked at him, the monotony of the spectacle drove little by little all pity from her heart. He seemed to her paltry, weak, a cipher—in a word, a poor thing in every way. How to get rid of him? What an interminable evening! Something stupefying like the fumes of opium seized her.

They heard in the passage the sharp noise of a wooden leg on the boards. It was Hippolyte bringing back Emma's luggage. In order to put it down he described painfully a quarter of a circle with his stump.

"He doesn't even remember any more about it," she thought, looking at the poor devil, whose coarse red hair was wet with perspiration.

pas reçu les secours de la religion, étant mort à Doudeville, dans la rue, sur le seuil d'un café, après un repas patriotique avec d'anciens officiers.

Emma rendit la lettre; puis, au dîner, par savoir-vivre, elle affecta quelque répugnance. Mais comme il la reforçait, elle se mit résolument à manger, tandis que Charles, en face d'elle, demeurait immobile, dans une posture accablée.

De temps à autre, relevant la tête, il lui envoyait un long regard tout plein de détresse. Une fois il soupira:

— J'aurais voulu le revoir encore!

Elle se taisait. Enfin, comprenant qu'il fallait parler:

— Quel âge avait-il, ton père?

— Cinquante-huit ans!

— Ah!

Et ce fut tout.

Un quart d'heure après, il ajouta:

— Ma pauvre mère?... que va-t-elle devenir, à présent?

Elle fit un geste d'ignorance.

À la voir si taciturne, Charles la supposait affligée et il se contraignait à ne rien dire, pour ne pas aviver cette douleur qui l'attendrissait. Cependant, secouant la sienne:

— T'es-tu bien amusée hier? demanda-t-il.

— Oui.

Quand la nappe fut ôtée, Bovary ne se leva pas, Emma non plus; et, à mesure qu'elle l'envisageait, la monotonie de ce spectacle bannissait peu à peu tout apitoiement de son coeur. Il lui semblait chétif, faible, nul, enfin être un pauvre homme, de toutes les façons. Comment se débarrasser de lui? Quelle interminable soirée! Quelque chose de stupéfiant comme une vapeur d'opium l'engourdissait.

Ils entendirent dans le vestibule le bruit sec d'un bâton sur les planches. C'était Hippolyte qui apportait les bagages de Madame. Pour les déposer, il décrivit péniblement un quart de cercle avec son pilon.

— Il n'y pense même plus! se disait-elle en regardant le pauvre diable, dont la grosse chevelure rouge dégouttait de sueur.

Bovary was searching at the bottom of his purse for a centime, and without appearing to understand all there was of humiliation for him in the mere presence of this man, who stood there like a personified reproach to his incurable incapacity.

"Hallo! you've a pretty bouquet," he said, noticing Leon's violets on the chimney.

"Yes," she replied indifferently; "it's a bouquet I bought just now from a beggar."

Charles picked up the flowers, and freshening his eyes, red with tears, against them, smelt them delicately. She took them quickly from his hand and put them in a glass of water.

The next day Madame Bovary senior arrived. She and her son wept much. Emma, on the pretext of giving orders, disappeared.

The following day they had a talk over the mourning. They went and sat down with their workboxes by the waterside under the arbour.

Charles was thinking of his father, and was surprised to feel so much affection for this man, whom till then he had thought he cared little about. Madame Bovary senior was thinking of her husband. The worst days of the past seemed enviable to her. All was forgotten beneath the instinctive regret of such a long habit, and from time to time whilst she sewed, a big tear rolled along her nose and hung suspended there a moment. Emma was thinking that it was scarcely forty-eight hours since they had been together, far from the world, all in a frenzy of joy, and not having eyes enough to gaze upon each other. She tried to recall the slightest details of that past day. But the presence of her husband and mother-in-law worried her. She would have liked to hear nothing, to see nothing, so as not to disturb the meditation on her love, that, do what she would, became lost in external sensations.

She was unpicking the lining of a dress, and the strips were scattered around her. Madame Bovary senior was plying her scissor without looking up, and Charles, in his list slippers and his old brown surtout that he used as a dressing-gown, sat with both hands in his pockets, and did not speak either; near them Berthe, in a little white pinafore, was raking sand in the walks with her spade.

Bovary cherchait un patard au fond de sa bourse; et, sans paraître comprendre tout ce qu'il y avait pour lui d'humiliation dans la seule présence de cet homme qui se tenait là, comme le reproche personnifié de son incurable ineptie:

— Tiens! tu as un joli bouquet! dit-il en remarquant sur la cheminée les violettes de Léon.

— Oui, fit-elle avec indifférence; c'est un bouquet que j'ai acheté tantôt... à une mendiante.

Charles prit les violettes, et, rafraîchissant dessus ses yeux tout rouges de larmes, il les humait délicatement. Elle les retira vite de sa main, et alla les porter dans un verre d'eau.

Le lendemain, madame Bovary mère arriva. Elle et son fils pleurèrent beaucoup. Emma, sous prétexte d'ordres à donner, disparut.

Le jour d'après, il fallut aviser ensemble aux affaires de deuil. On alla s'asseoir, avec les boîtes à ouvrage, au bord de l'eau, sous la tonnelle.

Charles pensait à son père, et il s'étonnait de sentir tant d'affection pour cet homme qu'il avait cru jusqu'alors n'aimer que très médiocrement. Madame Bovary mère pensait à son mari. Les pires jours d'autrefois lui réapparaissaient enviables. Tout s'effaçait sous le regret instinctif d'une si longue habitude; et, de temps à autre, tandis qu'elle poussait son aiguille, une grosse larme descendait le long de son nez et s'y tenait un moment suspendue. Emma pensait qu'il y avait quarante-huit heures à peine, ils étaient ensemble, loin du monde, tout en ivresse, et n'ayant pas assez d'yeux pour se contempler. Elle tâchait de ressaisir les plus imperceptibles détails de cette journée disparue. Mais la présence de la belle-mère et du mari la gênait. Elle aurait voulu ne rien entendre, ne rien voir, afin de ne pas déranger le recueillement de son amour qui allait se perdant, quoi qu'elle fît, sous les sensations extérieures.

Elle décousait la doublure d'une robe, dont les bribes s'éparpillaient autour d'elle; la mère Bovary, sans lever les yeux, faisait crier ses ciseaux, et Charles, avec ses pantoufles de lisière et sa vieille redingote brune qui lui servait de robe de chambre, restait les deux mains dans ses poches et ne parlait pas non plus; près d'eux, Berthe, en petit tablier blanc, raclait avec sa pelle le sable des allées.

Suddenly she saw Monsieur Lheureux, the linendraper, come in through the gate.

He came to offer his services "under the sad circumstances." Emma answered that she thought she could do without. The shopkeeper was not to be beaten.

"I beg your pardon," he said, "but I should like to have a private talk with you."

Then in a low voice:

"It's about that affair—you know."

Charles crimsoned to his ears.

"Oh, yes! certainly."

And in his confusion, turning to his wife:

"Couldn't you, my darling?"

She seemed to understand him, for she rose; and Charles said to his mother:

"It is nothing particular. No doubt, some household trifle."

He did not want her to know the story of the bill, fearing her reproaches.

As soon as they were alone, Monsieur Lheureux in sufficiently clear terms began to congratulate Emma on the inheritance, then to talk of indifferent matters, of the espaliers, of the harvest, and of his own health, which was always so-so, always having ups and downs. In fact, he had to work devilish hard, although he didn't make enough, in spite of all people said, to find butter for his bread.

Emma let him talk on. She had bored herself so prodigiously the last two days.

"And so you're quite well again?" he went on. "Ma foi! I saw your husband in a sad state. He's a good fellow, though we did have a little misunderstanding."

She asked what misunderstanding, for Charles had said nothing of the dispute about the goods supplied to her.

"Why, you know well enough," cried Lheureux. "It was about your little fancies—the travelling trunks."

He had drawn his hat over his eyes, and, with his hands behind his

Tout à coup, ils virent entrer par la barrière M. Lheureux, le marchand d'étoffes.

Il venait offrir ses services, eu égard à la fatale circonstance. Emma répondit qu'elle croyait pouvoir s'en passer. Le marchand ne se tint pas pour battu.

— Mille excuses, dit-il; je désirerais avoir un entretien particulier.

Puis, d'une voix basse:

— C'est relativement à cette affaire..., vous savez?

Charles devint cramoisi jusqu'aux oreilles.

— Ah! oui..., effectivement.

Et, dans son trouble, se tournant vers sa femme:

— Ne pourrais-tu pas..., ma chérie...?

Elle parut le comprendre, car elle se leva, et Charles dit à sa mère:

— Ce n'est rien! Sans doute quelque bagatelle de ménage.

Il ne voulait point qu'elle connût l'histoire du billet, redoutant ses observations.

Dès qu'ils furent seuls, M. Lheureux se mit, en termes assez nets, à féliciter Emma sur la succession, puis à causer de choses indifférentes, des espaliers, de la récolte et de sa santé à lui, qui allait toujours couci-couci, entre le zist et le zest. En effet, il se donnait un mal de cinq cents diables, bien qu'il ne fît pas, malgré les propos du monde, de quoi avoir seulement du beurre sur son pain.

Emma le laissait parler. Elle s'ennuyait si prodigieusement depuis deux jours!

— Et vous voilà tout à fait rétablie? continuait-il. Ma foi, j'ai vu votre pauvre mari dans de beaux états! C'est un brave garçon, quoique nous ayons eu ensemble des difficultés.

Elle demanda lesquelles, car Charles lui avait caché la contestation des fournitures.

— Mais vous le savez bien! fit Lheureux. C'était pour vos petites fantaisies, les boîtes de voyage.

Il avait baissé son chapeau sur ses yeux, et, les deux mains derrière

back, smiling and whistling, he looked straight at her in an unbearable manner. Did he suspect anything? She was lost in all kinds of apprehensions. At last, however, he went on:

"We made it up, all the same, and I've come again to propose another arrangement."

This was to renew the bill Bovary had signed. The doctor, of course, would do as he pleased; he was not to trouble himself, especially just now, when he would have a lot of worry.

"And he would do better to give it over to someone else—to you, for example. With a power of attorney it could be easily managed, and then we (you and I) would have our little business transactions together."

She did not understand. He was silent. Then, passing to his trade, Lheureux declared that madame must require something. He would send her a black barege, twelve yards, just enough to make a gown.

"The one you've on is good enough for the house, but you want another for calls. I saw that the very moment that I came in. I've the eye of an American!"

He did not send the stuff; he brought it. Then he came again to measure it; he came again on other pretexts, always trying to make himself agreeable, useful, "enfeoffing himself," as Homais would have said, and always dropping some hint to Emma about the power of attorney. He never mentioned the bill; she did not think of it. Charles, at the beginning of her convalescence, had certainly said something about it to her, but so many emotions had passed through her head that she no longer remembered it. Besides, she took care not to talk of any money questions. Madame Bovary seemed surprised at this, and attributed the change in her ways to the religious sentiments she had contracted during her illness.

But as soon as she was gone, Emma greatly astounded Bovary by her practical good sense. It would be necessary to make inquiries, to look into mortgages, and see if there were any occasion for a sale by auction or a liquidation. She quoted technical terms casually, pronounced the grand words of order, the future, foresight, and constantly exaggerated the difficulties of settling his father's affairs so much, that at last one day

le dos, souriant et sifflotant, il la regardait en face, d'une manière insupportable. Soupçonnait-il quelque chose? Elle demeurait perdue dans toutes sortes d'appréhensions. À la fin pourtant, il reprit:

— Nous nous sommes rapatriés, et je venais encore lui proposer un arrangement.

C'était de renouveler le billet signé par Bovary. Monsieur, du reste, agirait à sa guise; il ne devait point se tourmenter, maintenant surtout qu'il allait avoir une foule d'embarras.

— Et même il ferait mieux de s'en décharger sur quelqu'un, sur vous, par exemple; avec une procuration, ce serait commode, et alors nous aurions ensemble de petites affaires…

Elle ne comprenait pas. Il se tut. Ensuite, passant à son négoce, Lheureux déclara que Madame ne pouvait se dispenser de lui prendre quelque chose. Il lui enverrait un barège noir, douze mètres, de quoi faire une robe.

— Celle que vous avez là est bonne pour la maison. Il vous en faut une autre pour les visites. J'ai vu ça, moi, du premier coup en entrant. J'ai l'oeil américain.

Il n'envoya point d'étoffe, il l'apporta. Puis il revint pour l'aunage; il revint sous d'autres prétextes, tâchant chaque fois, de se rendre aimable, serviable, s'inféodant, comme eût dit Homais, et toujours glissant à Emma quelques conseils sur la procuration. Il ne parlait point du billet. Elle n'y songeait pas; Charles, au début de sa convalescence, lui en avait bien conté quelque chose; mais tant d'agitations avaient passé dans sa tête, qu'elle ne s'en souvenait plus. D'ailleurs, elle se garda d'ouvrir aucune discussion d'intérêt; la mère Bovary en fut surprise, et attribua son changement d'humeur aux sentiments religieux qu'elle avait contractés étant malade.

Mais, dès qu'elle fut partie, Emma ne tarda pas à émerveiller Bovary par son bon sens pratique. Il allait falloir prendre des informations, vérifier les hypothèques, voir s'il y avait lieu à une licitation ou à une liquidation. Elle citait des termes techniques, au hasard, prononçait les grands mots d'ordre, d'avenir, de prévoyance, et continuellement exagérait les embarras de la succession; si bien qu'un jour elle lui montra

she showed him the rough draft of a power of attorney to manage and administer his business, arrange all loans, sign and endorse all bills, pay all sums, etc. She had profited by Lheureux's lessons.

Charles naively asked her where this paper came from.

"Monsieur Guillaumin."

And with the utmost coolness she added:

"I don't trust him overmuch. Notaries have such a bad reputation. Perhaps we ought to consult—we only know—no one."

"Unless Leon—" replied Charles, who was reflecting.

But it was difficult to explain matters by letter. Then she offered to make the journey, but he thanked her. She insisted. It was quite a contest of mutual consideration. At last she cried with affected waywardness:

"No, I will go!"

"How good you are!" he said, kissing her forehead.

The next morning she set out in the "Hirondelle" to go to Rouen to consult Monsieur Leon, and she stayed there three days.

le modèle d'une autorisation générale pour «gérer et administrer ses affaires, faire tous emprunts, signer et endosser tous billets, payer toutes sommes, etc.» Elle avait profité des leçons de Lheureux.

Charles, naïvement, lui demanda d'où venait ce papier.

— De M. Guillaumin.

Et, avec le plus grand sang-froid du monde, elle ajouta:

— Je ne m'y fie pas trop. Les notaires ont si mauvaise réputation! Il faudrait peut-être consulter… Nous ne connaissons que… Oh! personne.

— À moins que Léon…, répliqua Charles, qui réfléchissait.

Mais il était difficile de s'entendre par correspondance. Alors elle s'offrit à faire ce voyage. Il la remercia. Elle insista. Ce fut un assaut de prévenances. Enfin, elle s'écria d'un ton de mutinerie factice:

— Non, je t'en prie, j'irai.

— Comme tu es bonne! dit-il en la baisant au front.

Dès le lendemain, elle s'embarqua dans l'Hirondelle pour aller à Rouen consulter M. Léon; et elle y resta trois jours.

# Chapter 3

They were three full, exquisite days—a true honeymoon.

They were at the Hotel-de-Boulogne, on the harbour; and they lived there, with drawn blinds and closed doors, with flowers on the floor, and iced syrups were brought them early in the morning.

Towards evening they took a covered boat and went to dine on one of the islands.

It was the time when one hears by the side of the dockyard the caulking-mallets sounding against the hull of vessels. The smoke of the tar rose up between the trees; there were large fatty drops on the water, undulating in the purple colour of the sun, like floating plaques of Florentine bronze.

They rowed down in the midst of moored boats, whose long oblique cables grazed lightly against the bottom of the boat.

The din of the town gradually grew distant; the rolling of carriages, the tumult of voices, the yelping of dogs on the decks of vessels. She took off her bonnet, and they landed on their island.

They sat down in the low-ceilinged room of a tavern, at whose door hung black nets. They ate fried smelts, cream and cherries. They lay down upon the grass; they kissed behind the poplars; and they would fain, like two Robinsons, have lived for ever in this little place, which seemed to them in their beatitude the most magnificent on earth. It was not the first time that they had seen trees, a blue sky, meadows; that they had heard the water flowing and the wind blowing in the leaves; but, no doubt, they had never admired all this, as if Nature had not existed before, or had only begun to be beautiful since the gratification of their desires.

At night they returned. The boat glided along the shores of the islands. They sat at the bottom, both hidden by the shade, in silence.

# Chapitre 3

Ce furent trois jours pleins, exquis, splendides, une vraie lune de miel.

Ils étaient à l'hôtel de Boulogne, sur le port. Et ils vivaient là, volets fermés, portes closes, avec des fleurs par terre et des sirops à la glace, qu'on leur apportait dès le matin.

Vers le soir, ils prenaient une barque couverte et allaient dîner dans une île.

C'était l'heure où l'on entend, au bord des chantiers, retentir le maillet des calfats contre la coque des vaisseaux. La fumée du goudron s'échappait d'entre les arbres, et l'on voyait sur la rivière de larges gouttes grasses, ondulant inégalement sous la couleur pourpre du soleil, comme des plaques de bronze florentin, qui flottaient.

Ils descendaient au milieu des barques amarrées, dont les longs câbles obliques frôlaient un peu le dessus de la barque.

Les bruits de la ville insensiblement s'éloignaient, le roulement des charrettes, le tumulte des voix, le jappement des chiens sur le pont des navires. Elle dénouait son chapeau et ils abordaient à leur île.

Ils se plaçaient dans la salle basse d'un cabaret, qui avait à sa porte des filets noirs suspendus. Ils mangeaient de la friture d'éperlans, de la crème et des cerises. Ils se couchaient sur l'herbe; ils s'embrassaient à l'écart sous les peupliers; et ils auraient voulu, comme deux Robinsons, vivre perpétuellement dans ce petit endroit, qui leur semblait, en leur béatitude, le plus magnifique de la terre. Ce n'était pas la première fois qu'ils apercevaient des arbres, du ciel bleu, du gazon, qu'ils entendaient l'eau couler et la brise soufflant dans le feuillage; mais ils n'avaient sans doute jamais admiré tout cela, comme si la nature n'existait pas auparavant, ou qu'elle n'eût commencé à être belle que depuis l'assouvissance de leurs désirs.

À la nuit, ils repartaient. La barque suivait le bord des îles. Ils restaient au fond, tous les deux cachés par l'ombre, sans parler. Les avirons carrés

The square oars rang in the iron thwarts, and, in the stillness, seemed to mark time, like the beating of a metronome, while at the stern the rudder that trailed behind never ceased its gentle splash against the water.

Once the moon rose; they did not fail to make fine phrases, finding the orb melancholy and full of poetry. She even began to sing:

"One night, do you remember, we were sailing," etc.

Her musical but weak voice died away along the waves, and the winds carried off the trills that Leon heard pass like the flapping of wings about him.

She was opposite him, leaning against the partition of the shallop, through one of whose raised blinds the moon streamed in. Her black dress, whose drapery spread out like a fan, made her seem more slender, taller. Her head was raised, her hands clasped, her eyes turned towards heaven. At times the shadow of the willows hid her completely; then she reappeared suddenly, like a vision in the moonlight.

Leon, on the floor by her side, found under his hand a ribbon of scarlet silk.

The boatman looked at it, and at last said:

"Perhaps it belongs to the party I took out the other day. A lot of jolly folk, gentlemen and ladies, with cakes, champagne, cornets—everything in style! There was one especially, a tall handsome man with small moustaches, who was that funny! And they all kept saying, 'Now tell us something, Adolphe—Dolpe,' I think."

She shivered.

"You are in pain?" asked Leon, coming closer to her.

"Oh, it's nothing! No doubt, it is only the night air."

"And who doesn't want for women, either," softly added the sailor, thinking he was paying the stranger a compliment.

Then, spitting on his hands, he took the oars again.

Yet they had to part. The adieux were sad. He was to send his letters to Mere Rollet, and she gave him such precise instructions about a double envelope that he admired greatly her amorous astuteness.

sonnaient entre les tolets de fer; et cela marquait dans le silence comme un battement de métronome, tandis qu'à l'arrière la bauce qui traînait ne discontinuait pas son petit clapotement doux dans l'eau.

Une fois, la lune parut; alors ils ne manquèrent pas à faire des phrases, trouvant l'astre mélancolique et plein de poésie; même elle se mit à chanter:

Un soir, t'en souvient-il? nous voguions, etc.

Sa voix harmonieuse et faible se perdait sur les flots; et le vent emportait les roulades que Léon écoutait passer, comme des battements d'ailes, autour de lui.

Elle se tenait en face, appuyée contre la cloison de la chaloupe, où la lune entrait par un des volets ouverts. Sa robe noire, dont les draperies s'élargissaient en éventail, l'amincissait, la rendait plus grande. Elle avait la tête levée, les mains jointes, et les deux yeux vers le ciel. Parfois l'ombre des saules la cachait en entier, puis elle réapparaissait tout à coup, comme une vision, dans la lumière de la lune.

Léon, par terre, à côté d'elle, rencontra sous sa main un ruban de soie ponceau.

Le batelier l'examina et finit par dire:

— Ah! c'est peut-être à une compagnie que j'ai promenée l'autre jour. Ils sont venus un tas de farceurs, messieurs et dames, avec des gâteaux, du champagne, des cornets à pistons, tout le tremblement! Il y en avait un surtout, un grand bel homme, à petites moustaches, qui était joliment amusant! et ils disaient comme ça: «Allons, conte-nous quelque chose..., Adolphe..., Dodolphe..., je crois.»

Elle frissonna.

— Tu souffres? fit Léon en se rapprochant d'elle.

— Oh! ce n'est rien. Sans doute, la fraîcheur de la nuit.

— Et qui ne doit pas manquer de femmes, non plus, ajouta doucement le vieux matelot, croyant dire une politesse à l'étranger.

Puis, crachant dans ses mains, il reprit ses avirons.

Il fallut pourtant se séparer! Les adieux furent tristes. C'était chez la mère Rolet qu'il devait envoyer ses lettres; et elle lui fit des recommandations si précises à propos de la double enveloppe, qu'il admira grandement son astuce amoureuse.

"So you can assure me it is all right?" she said with her last kiss.

"Yes, certainly."

"But why," he thought afterwards as he came back through the streets alone, "is she so very anxious to get this power of attorney?"

— Ainsi, tu m'affirmes que tout est bien? dit-elle dans le dernier baiser.

— Oui certes! — Mais pourquoi donc, songea-t-il après, en s'en revenant seul par les rues, tient-elle si fort à cette procuration?

# Chapter 4

Leon soon put on an air of superiority before his comrades, avoided their company, and completely neglected his work.

He waited for her letters; he re-read them; he wrote to her. He called her to mind with all the strength of his desires and of his memories. Instead of lessening with absence, this longing to see her again grew, so that at last on Saturday morning he escaped from his office.

When, from the summit of the hill, he saw in the valley below the church-spire with its tin flag swinging in the wind, he felt that delight mingled with triumphant vanity and egoistic tenderness that millionaires must experience when they come back to their native village.

He went rambling round her house. A light was burning in the kitchen. He watched for her shadow behind the curtains, but nothing appeared.

Mere Lefrancois, when she saw him, uttered many exclamations. She thought he "had grown and was thinner," while Artemise, on the contrary, thought him stouter and darker.

He dined in the little room as of yore, but alone, without the tax-gatherer; for Binet, tired of waiting for the "Hirondelle," had definitely put forward his meal one hour, and now he dined punctually at five, and yet he declared usually the rickety old concern "was late."

Leon, however, made up his mind, and knocked at the doctor's door. Madame was in her room, and did not come down for a quarter of an hour. The doctor seemed delighted to see him, but he never stirred out that evening, nor all the next day.

He saw her alone in the evening, very late, behind the garden in the lane; in the lane, as she had the other one! It was a stormy night, and they talked under an umbrella by lightning flashes.

Their separation was becoming intolerable.

# Chapitre 4

Léon, bientôt, prit devant ses camarades un air de supériorité, s'abstint de leur compagnie, et négligea complètement les dossiers.

Il attendait ses lettres; il les relisait. Il lui écrivait. Il l'évoquait de toute la force de son désir et de ses souvenirs. Au lieu de diminuer par l'absence, cette envie de la revoir s'accrut, si bien qu'un samedi matin il s'échappa de son étude.

Lorsque, du haut de la côte, il aperçut dans la vallée le clocher de l'église avec son drapeau de fer-blanc qui tournait au vent, il sentit cette délectation mêlée de vanité triomphante et d'attendrissement égoïste que doivent avoir les millionnaires, quand ils reviennent visiter leur village.

Il alla rôder autour de sa maison. Une lumière brillait dans la cuisine. Il guetta son ombre derrière les rideaux. Rien ne parut.

La mère Lefrançois, en le voyant, fit de grandes exclamations, et elle le trouva «grandi et minci», tandis qu'Artémise, au contraire, le trouva «forci et bruni».

Il dîna dans la petite salle, comme autrefois, mais seul, sans le percepteur; car Binet, fatigué d'attendre l'Hirondelle, avait définitivement avancé son repas d'une heure, et, maintenant, il dînait à cinq heures juste, encore prétendait-il le plus souvent que la vieille patraque retardait.

Léon pourtant se décida; il alla frapper à la porte du médecin: Madame était dans sa chambre, d'où elle ne descendit qu'un quart d'heure après. Monsieur parut enchanté de le revoir; mais il ne bougea de la soirée, ni de tout le jour suivant.

Il la vit seule, le soir, très tard, derrière le jardin, dans la ruelle; — dans la ruelle, comme avec l'autre! Il faisait de l'orage, et ils causaient sous un parapluie à la lueur des éclairs.

Leur séparation devenait intolérable.

"I would rather die!" said Emma.

She was writhing in his arms, weeping.

"Adieu! adieu! When shall I see you again?"

They came back again to embrace once more, and it was then that she promised him to find soon, by no matter what means, a regular opportunity for seeing one another in freedom at least once a week. Emma never doubted she should be able to do this. Besides, she was full of hope. Some money was coming to her.

On the strength of it she bought a pair of yellow curtains with large stripes for her room, whose cheapness Monsieur Lheureux had commended; she dreamed of getting a carpet, and Lheureux, declaring that it wasn't "drinking the sea," politely undertook to supply her with one. She could no longer do without his services. Twenty times a day she sent for him, and he at once put by his business without a murmur. People could not understand either why Mere Rollet breakfasted with her every day, and even paid her private visits.

It was about this time, that is to say, the beginning of winter, that she seemed seized with great musical fervour.

One evening when Charles was listening to her, she began the same piece four times over, each time with much vexation, while he, not noticing any difference, cried:

"Bravo! very goodl You are wrong to stop. Go on!"

"Oh, no; it is execrable! My fingers are quite rusty."

The next day he begged her to play him something again.

"Very well; to please you!"

And Charles confessed she had gone off a little. She played wrong notes and blundered; then, stopping short:

"Ah! it is no use. I ought to take some lessons; but—"

She bit her lips and added:

"Twenty francs a lesson, that's too dear!"

"Yes, so it is—rather," said Charles, giggling stupidly. "But it seems to me that one might be able to do it for less; for there are artists of no reputation, and who are often better than the celebrities."

"Find them!" said Emma.

— Plutôt mourir! disait Emma.

Elle se tordait sur son bras, tout en pleurant.

— Adieu!... adieu!... Quand te reverrai-je?

Ils revinrent sur leurs pas pour s'embrasser encore; et ce fut là qu'elle lui fit la promesse de trouver bientôt, par n'importe quel moyen, l'occasion permanente de se voir en liberté, au moins une fois la semaine. Emma n'en doutait pas. Elle était, d'ailleurs, pleine d'espoir. Il allait lui venir de l'argent.

Aussi, elle acheta pour sa chambre une paire de rideaux jaunes à larges raies, dont M. Lheureux lui avait vanté le bon marché; elle rêva un tapis, et Lheureux, affirmant «que ce n'était pas la mer à boire», s'engagea poliment à lui en fournir un. Elle ne pouvait plus se passer de ses services. Vingt fois dans la journée elle l'envoyait chercher, et aussitôt il plantait là ses affaires, sans se permettre un murmure. On ne comprenait point davantage pourquoi la mère Rolet déjeunait chez elle tous les jours, et même lui faisait des visites en particulier.

Ce fut vers cette époque, c'est-à-dire vers le commencement de l'hiver, qu'elle parut prise d'une grande ardeur musicale.

Un soir que Charles l'écoutait, elle recommença quatre fois de suite le même morceau, et toujours en se dépitant, tandis que, sans y remarquer de différence, il s'écriait:

— Bravo!..., très bien!... Tu as tort! va donc!

— Eh non! c'est exécrable! j'ai les doigts rouillés.

Le lendemain, il la pria de lui jouer encore quelque chose.

— Soit, pour te faire plaisir!

Et Charles avoua qu'elle avait un peu perdu. Elle se trompait de portée, barbouillait; puis, s'arrêtant court:

— Ah! c'est fini! il faudrait que je prisse des leçons; mais...

Elle se mordit les lèvres et ajouta:

— Vingt francs par cachet, c'est trop cher!

— Oui, en effet..., un peu..., dit Charles tout en ricanant niaisement. Pourtant, il me semble que l'on pourrait peut-être à moins; car il y a des artistes sans réputation qui souvent valent mieux que les célébrités.

— Cherche-les, dit Emma.

The next day when he came home he looked at her shyly, and at last could no longer keep back the words.

"How obstinate you are sometimes! I went to Barfucheres to-day. Well, Madame Liegard assured me that her three young ladies who are at La Misericorde have lessons at fifty sous apiece, and that from an excellent mistress!"

She shrugged her shoulders and did not open her piano again.

But when she passed by it (if Bovary were there), she sighed:

"Ah! my poor piano!"

And when anyone came to see her, she did not fail to inform them she had given up music, and could not begin again now for important reasons. Then people commiserated her: "What a pity! she had so much talent!" They even spoke to Bovary about it. They put him to shame, and especially the chemist.

"You are wrong. One should never let any of the faculties of nature lie fallow. Besides, just think, my good friend, that by inducing madame to study; you are economising on the subsequent musical education of your child. For my own part, I think that mothers ought themselves to instruct their children. That is an idea of Rousseau's, still rather new perhaps, but that will end by triumphing, I am certain of it, like mothers nursing their own children and vaccination."

So Charles returned once more to this question of the piano. Emma replied bitterly that it would be better to sell it. This poor piano, that had given her vanity so much satisfaction—to see it go was to Bovary like the indefinable suicide of a part of herself.

"If you liked," he said, "a lesson from time to time, that wouldn't after all be very ruinous."

"But lessons," she replied, "are only of use when followed up."

And thus it was she set about obtaining her husband's permission to go to town once a week to see her lover. At the end of a month she was even considered to have made considerable progress.

Le lendemain, en rentrant, il la contempla d'un oeil finaud, et ne put à la fin retenir cette phrase:

— Quel entêtement tu as quelquefois! J'ai été à Barfeuchères aujourd'hui. Eh bien, madame Liégeard m'a certifié que ses trois demoiselles, qui sont à la Miséricorde, prenaient des leçons moyennant cinquante sous la séance, et d'une fameuse maîtresse encore!

Elle haussa les épaules, et ne rouvrit plus son instrument.

Mais, lorsqu'elle passait auprès (si Bovary se trouvait là), elle soupirait:

— Ah! mon pauvre piano!

Et quand on venait la voir, elle ne manquait pas de vous apprendre qu'elle avait abandonné la musique et ne pouvait maintenant s'y remettre, pour des raisons majeures. Alors on la plaignait. C'était dommage! elle qui avait un si beau talent! On en parla même à Bovary. On lui faisait honte, et surtout le pharmacien:

— Vous avez tort! il ne faut jamais laisser en friche les facultés de la nature. D'ailleurs, songez, mon bon ami, qu'en engageant Madame à étudier, vous économisez pour plus tard sur l'éducation musicale de votre enfant! Moi, le trouve que les mères doivent instruire elles-mêmes leurs enfants. C'est une idée de Rousseau, peut-être un peu neuve encore, mais qui finira par triompher, j'en suis sûr, comme l'allaitement maternel et la vaccination.

Charles revint donc encore une fois sur cette question du piano. Emma répondit, avec aigreur qu'il valait mieux le vendre. Ce pauvre piano, qui lui avait causé tant de vaniteuses satisfactions, le voir s'en aller, c'était pour Bovary comme l'indéfinissable suicide d'une partie d'elle-même!

— Si tu voulais..., disait-il, de temps à autre, une leçon, cela ne serait pas, après tout, extrêmement ruineux.

— Mais les leçons, répliquait-elle, ne sont profitables que suivies.

Et voilà comme elle s'y prit pour obtenir de son époux la permission d'aller à la ville, une fois la semaine, voir son amant. On trouva même, au bout d'un mois, qu'elle avait fait des progrès considérables.

# Chapter 5

She went on Thursdays. She got up and dressed silently, in order not to awaken Charles, who would have made remarks about her getting ready too early. Next she walked up and down, went to the windows, and looked out at the Place. The early dawn was broadening between the pillars of the market, and the chemist's shop, with the shutters still up, showed in the pale light of the dawn the large letters of his signboard.

When the clock pointed to a quarter past seven, she went off to the "Lion d'Or," whose door Artemise opened yawning. The girl then made up the coals covered by the cinders, and Emma remained alone in the kitchen. Now and again she went out. Hivert was leisurely harnessing his horses, listening, moreover, to Mere Lefrancois, who, passing her head and nightcap through a grating, was charging him with commissions and giving him explanations that would have confused anyone else. Emma kept beating the soles of her boots against the pavement of the yard.

At last, when he had eaten his soup, put on his cloak, lighted his pipe, and grasped his whip, he calmly installed himself on his seat.

The "Hirondelle" started at a slow trot, and for about a mile stopped here and there to pick up passengers who waited for it, standing at the border of the road, in front of their yard gates. Those who had secured seats the evening before kept it waiting; some even were still in bed in their houses. Hivert called, shouted, swore; then he got down from his seat and went and knocked loudly at the doors. The wind blew through the cracked windows.

The four seats, however, filled up. The carriage rolled off; rows of apple-trees followed one upon another, and the road between its two long ditches, full of yellow water, rose, constantly narrowing towards the horizon.

# Chapitre 5

C'était le jeudi. Elle se levait, et elle s'habillait silencieusement pour ne point éveiller Charles qui lui aurait fait des observations sur ce qu'elle s'apprêtait de trop bonne heure. Ensuite elle marchait de long en large; elle se mettait devant les fenêtres, elle regardait la Place. Le petit jour circulait entre les piliers des halles, et la maison du pharmacien, dont les volets étaient fermés, laissait apercevoir dans la couleur pâle de l'aurore les majuscules de son enseigne.

Quand la pendule marquait sept heures et un quart, elle s'en allait au lion d'or, dont Artémise, en bâillant, venait lui ouvrir la porte. Celle-ci déterrait pour Madame les charbons enfouis sous les cendres. Emma restait seule dans la cuisine. De temps à autre, elle sortait. Hivert attelait sans se dépêcher, et en écoutant d'ailleurs la mère Lefrançois, qui, passant par un guichet sa tête en bonnet de coton, le chargeait de commissions et lui donnait des explications à troubler un tout autre homme. Emma battait la semelle de ses bottines contre les pavés de la cour.

Enfin, lorsqu'il avait mangé sa soupe, endossé sa limousine, allumé sa pipe et empoigné son fouet, il s'installait tranquillement sur le siège.

L'Hirondelle partait au petit trot, et, durant trois quarts de lieue, s'arrêtait de place en place pour prendre des voyageurs, qui la guettaient debout, au bord du chemin, devant la barrière des cours. Ceux qui avaient prévenu la veille se faisaient attendre; quelques-uns même étaient encore au lit dans leur maison; Hivert appelait, — criait, sacrait, puis il descendait de son siège et allait frapper de grands coups contre les portes. Le vent soufflait par les vasistas fêlés.

Cependant les quatre banquettes se garnissaient, la voiture roulait, les pommiers à la file se succédaient; et la route, entre ses deux longs fossés pleins d'eau jaune, allait continuellement se rétrécissant vers l'horizon.

Emma knew it from end to end; she knew that after a meadow there was a sign-post, next an elm, a barn, or the hut of a lime-kiln tender. Sometimes even, in the hope of getting some surprise, she shut her eyes, but she never lost the clear perception of the distance to be traversed.

At last the brick houses began to follow one another more closely, the earth resounded beneath the wheels, the "Hirondelle" glided between the gardens, where through an opening one saw statues, a periwinkle plant, clipped yews, and a swing. Then on a sudden the town appeared.

Sloping down like an amphitheatre, and drowned in the fog, it widened out beyond the bridges confusedly. Then the open country spread away with a monotonous movement till it touched in the distance the vague line of the pale sky. Seen thus from above, the whole landscape looked immovable as a picture; the anchored ships were massed in one corner, the river curved round the foot of the green hills, and the isles, oblique in shape, lay on the water, like large, motionless, black fishes. The factory chimneys belched forth immense brown fumes that were blown away at the top. One heard the rumbling of the foundries, together with the clear chimes of the churches that stood out in the mist. The leafless trees on the boulevards made violet thickets in the midst of the houses, and the roofs, all shining with the rain, threw back unequal reflections, according to the height of the quarters in which they were. Sometimes a gust of wind drove the clouds towards the Saint Catherine hills, like aerial waves that broke silently against a cliff.

A giddiness seemed to her to detach itself from this mass of existence, and her heart swelled as if the hundred and twenty thousand souls that palpitated there had all at once sent into it the vapour of the passions she fancied theirs. Her love grew in the presence of this vastness, and expanded with tumult to the vague murmurings that rose towards her. She poured it out upon the square, on the walks, on the streets, and the old Norman city outspread before her eyes as an enormous capital, as a Babylon into which she was entering. She leant with both hands against the window, drinking in the breeze; the three horses galloped, the stones grated in the mud, the diligence rocked, and Hivert, from

Emma la connaissait d'un bout à l'autre; elle savait qu'après un herbage il y avait un poteau, ensuite un orme, une grange ou une cahute de cantonnier; quelquefois même, afin de se faire des surprises, elle fermait les yeux. Mais elle ne perdait jamais le sentiment net de la distance à parcourir.

Enfin, les maisons de briques se rapprochaient, la terre résonnait sous les roues, l'Hirondelle glissait entre des jardins où l'on apercevait, par une claire-voie, des statues, un vignot, des ifs taillés et une escarpolette. Puis, d'un seul coup d'oeil, la ville apparaissait.

Descendant tout en amphithéâtre et noyée dans le brouillard, elle s'élargissait au delà des ponts, confusément. La pleine campagne remontait ensuite d'un mouvement monotone, jusqu'à toucher au loin la base indécise du ciel pâle. Ainsi vu d'en haut, le paysage tout entier avait l'air immobile comme une peinture; les navires à l'ancre se tassaient dans un coin; le fleuve arrondissait sa courbe au pied des collines vertes, et les îles, de forme oblongue, semblaient sur l'eau de grands poissons noirs arrêtés. Les cheminées des usines poussaient d'immenses panaches bruns qui s'envolaient par le bout. On entendait le ronflement des fonderies avec le carillon clair des églises qui se dressaient dans la brume. Les arbres des boulevards, sans feuilles, faisaient des broussailles violettes au milieu des maisons, et les toits, tout reluisants de pluie, miroitaient inégalement, selon la hauteur des quartiers. Parfois un coup de vent emportait les nuages vers la côte Sainte-Catherine, comme des flots aériens qui se brisaient en silence contre une falaise.

Quelque chose de vertigineux se dégageait pour elle de ces existences amassées, et son coeur s'en gonflait abondamment, comme si les cent vingt mille âmes qui palpitaient là lui eussent envoyé toutes à la fois la vapeur des passions qu'elle leur supposait. Son amour s'agrandissait devant l'espace, et s'emplissait de tumulte aux bourdonnements vagues qui montaient. Elle le reversait au dehors, sur les places, sur les promenades, sur les rues, et la vieille cité normande s'étalait à ses yeux comme une capitale démesurée, comme une Babylone où elle entrait. Elle se penchait des deux mains par le vasistas, en humant la brise; les trois chevaux galopaient, les pierres grinçaient dans la boue, la diligence se

afar, hailed the carts on the road, while the bourgeois who had spent the night at the Guillaume woods came quietly down the hill in their little family carriages.

They stopped at the barrier; Emma undid her overshoes, put on other gloves, rearranged her shawl, and some twenty paces farther she got down from the "Hirondelle."

The town was then awakening. Shop-boys in caps were cleaning up the shop-fronts, and women with baskets against their hips, at intervals uttered sonorous cries at the corners of streets. She walked with downcast eyes, close to the walls, and smiling with pleasure under her lowered black veil.

For fear of being seen, she did not usually take the most direct road. She plunged into dark alleys, and, all perspiring, reached the bottom of the Rue Nationale, near the fountain that stands there. It is the quarter for theatres, public-houses, and whores. Often a cart would pass near her, bearing some shaking scenery. Waiters in aprons were sprinkling sand on the flagstones between green shrubs. It all smelt of absinthe, cigars, and oysters.

She turned down a street; she recognised him by his curling hair that escaped from beneath his hat.

Leon walked along the pavement. She followed him to the hotel. He went up, opened the door, entered—What an embrace!

Then, after the kisses, the words gushed forth. They told each other the sorrows of the week, the presentiments, the anxiety for the letters; but now everything was forgotten; they gazed into each other's faces with voluptuous laughs, and tender names.

The bed was large, of mahogany, in the shape of a boat. The curtains were in red levantine, that hung from the ceiling and bulged out too much towards the bell-shaped bedside; and nothing in the world was so lovely as her brown head and white skin standing out against this purple colour, when, with a movement of shame, she crossed her bare arms, hiding her face in her hands.

The warm room, with its discreet carpet, its gay ornaments, and its calm light, seemed made for the intimacies of passion. The curtain-

balançait, et Hivert, de loin, hélait les carrioles sur la route, tandis que les bourgeois qui avaient passé la nuit au bois Guillaume descendaient la côte tranquillement, dans leur petite voiture de famille.

On s'arrêtait à la barrière; Emma débouclait ses socques, mettait d'autres gants, rajustait son châle, et, vingt pas plus loin, elle sortait de l'hirondelle.

La ville alors s'éveillait. Des commis, en bonnet grec, frottaient la devanture des boutiques, et des femmes qui tenaient des paniers sur la hanche poussaient par intervalles un cri sonore, au coin des rues. Elle marchait les yeux à terre, frôlant les murs, et souriant de plaisir sous son voile noir baissé.

Par peur d'être vue, elle ne prenait pas ordinairement le chemin le plus court. Elle s'engouffrait dans les ruelles sombres, et elle arrivait tout en sueur vers le bas de la rue Nationale, près de la fontaine qui est là. C'est le quartier du théâtre, des estaminets et des filles. Souvent une charrette passait près d'elle, portant quelque décor qui tremblait. Des garçons en tablier versaient du sable sur les dalles, entre des arbustes verts. On sentait l'absinthe, le cigare et les huîtres.

Elle tournait une rue; elle le reconnaissait à sa chevelure frisée qui s'échappait de son chapeau.

Léon, sur le trottoir, continuait à marcher. Elle le suivait jusqu'à l'hôtel; il montait, il ouvrait la porte, il entrait... Quelle étreinte!

Puis les paroles, après les baisers, se précipitaient. On se racontait les chagrins de la semaine, les pressentiments, les inquiétudes pour les lettres; mais à présent tout s'oubliait, et ils se regardaient face à face, avec des rires de volupté et des appellations de tendresse.

Le lit était un grand lit d'acajou en forme de nacelle. Les rideaux de levantine rouge, qui descendaient du plafond, se cintraient trop bas vers le chevet évasé; — et rien au monde n'était beau comme sa tête brune et sa peau blanche se détachant sur cette couleur pourpre, quand, par un geste de pudeur, elle fermait ses deux bras nus, en se cachant la figure dans les mains.

Le tiède appartement, avec son tapis discret, ses ornements folâtres et sa lumière tranquille, semblait tout commode pour les intimités de

rods, ending in arrows, their brass pegs, and the great balls of the fire-dogs shone suddenly when the sun came in. On the chimney between the candelabra there were two of those pink shells in which one hears the murmur of the sea if one holds them to the ear.

How they loved that dear room, so full of gaiety, despite its rather faded splendour! They always found the furniture in the same place, and sometimes hairpins, that she had forgotten the Thursday before, under the pedestal of the clock. They lunched by the fireside on a little round table, inlaid with rosewood. Emma carved, put bits on his plate with all sorts of coquettish ways, and she laughed with a sonorous and libertine laugh when the froth of the champagne ran over from the glass to the rings on her fingers. They were so completely lost in the possession of each other that they thought themselves in their own house, and that they would live there till death, like two spouses eternally young. They said "our room," "our carpet," she even said "my slippers," a gift of Leon's, a whim she had had. They were pink satin, bordered with swansdown. When she sat on his knees, her leg, then too short, hung in the air, and the dainty shoe, that had no back to it, was held only by the toes to her bare foot.

He for the first time enjoyed the inexpressible delicacy of feminine refinements. He had never met this grace of language, this reserve of clothing, these poses of the weary dove. He admired the exaltation of her soul and the lace on her petticoat. Besides, was she not "a lady" and a married woman—a real mistress, in fine?

By the diversity of her humour, in turn mystical or mirthful, talkative, taciturn, passionate, careless, she awakened in him a thousand desires, called up instincts or memories. She was the mistress of all the novels, the heroine of all the dramas, the vague *She* of all the volumes of verse. He found again on her shoulder the amber colouring of the "Odalisque Bathing"; she had the long waist of feudal chatelaines, and she resembled the "Pale Woman of Barcelona." But above all she was the Angel!

la passion. Les bâtons se terminant en flèche, les patères de cuivre et les grosses boules de chenets reluisaient tout à coup, si le soleil entrait. Il y avait sur la cheminée, entre les candélabres, deux de ces grandes coquilles roses où l'on entend le bruit de la mer quand on les applique à son oreille.

Comme ils aimaient cette bonne chambre pleine de gaieté, malgré sa splendeur un peu fanée! Ils retrouvaient toujours les meubles à leur place, et parfois des épingles à cheveux qu'elle avait oubliées, l'autre jeudi, sous le socle de la pendule. Ils déjeunaient au coin du feu, sur un petit guéridon incrusté de palissandre. Emma découpait, lui mettait les morceaux dans son assiette en débitant toutes sortes de chatteries; et elle riait d'un rire sonore et libertin quand la mousse du vin de Champagne débordait du verre léger sur les bagues de ses doigts. Ils étaient si complètement perdus en la possession d'eux-mêmes, qu'ils se croyaient là dans leur maison particulière, et devant y vivre jusqu'à la mort, comme deux éternels jeunes époux. Ils disaient notre chambre, notre tapis, nos fauteuils, même elle disait mes pantoufles, un cadeau de Léon, une fantaisie qu'elle avait eue. C'étaient des pantoufles en satin rose, bordées de cygne. Quand elle s'asseyait sur ses genoux, sa jambe, alors trop courte, pendait en l'air; et la mignarde chaussure, qui n'avait pas de quartier, tenait seulement par les orteils à son pied nu.

Il savourait pour la première fois l'inexprimable délicatesse des élégances féminines. Jamais il n'avait rencontré cette grâce de langage, cette réserve du vêtement, ces poses de colombe assoupie. Il admirait l'exaltation de son âme et les dentelles de sa jupe. D'ailleurs, n'était-ce pas une femme du monde, et une femme mariée! une vraie maîtresse enfin?

Par la diversité de son humeur, tour à tour mystique ou joyeuse, babillarde, taciturne, emportée, nonchalante, elle allait rappelant en lui mille désirs, évoquant des instincts ou des réminiscences. Elle était l'amoureuse de tous les romans, l'héroïne de tous les drames, le vague *Elle* de tous les volumes de vers. Il retrouvait sur ses épaules la couleur ambrée de l'odalisque au bain; elle avait le corsage long des châtelaines féodales; elle ressemblait aussi à la femme pâle de Barcelone, mais elle était par-dessus tout Ange!

Often looking at her, it seemed to him that his soul, escaping towards her, spread like a wave about the outline of her head, and descended drawn down into the whiteness of her breast.

He knelt on the ground before her, and with both elbows on her knees looked at her with a smile, his face upturned.

She bent over him, and murmured, as if choking with intoxication:

"Oh, do not move! do not speak! look at me! Something so sweet comes from your eyes that helps me so much!"

She called him "child."

"Child, do you love me?"

And she did not listen for his answer in the haste of her lips that fastened to his mouth.

On the clock there was a bronze cupid, who smirked as he bent his arm beneath a golden garland. They had laughed at it many a time, but when they had to part everything seemed serious to them.

Motionless in front of each other, they kept repeating:

"Till Thursday, till Thursday."

Suddenly she seized his head between her hands, kissed him hurriedly on the forehead, crying, "Adieu!" and rushed down the stairs.

She went to a hairdresser's in the Rue de la Comedie to have her hair arranged. Night fell; the gas was lighted in the shop.

She heard the bell at the theatre calling the mummers to the performance, and she saw, passing opposite, men with white faces and women in faded gowns going in at the stage-door.

It was hot in the room, small, and too low where the stove was hissing in the midst of wigs and pomades. The smell of the tongs, together with the greasy hands that handled her head, soon stunned her, and she dozed a little in her wrapper. Often, as he did her hair, the man offered her tickets for a masked ball.

Then she went away. She went up the streets; reached the Croix-Rouge, put on her overshoes, that she had hidden in the morning under the seat, and sank into her place among the impatient passengers. Some got out at the foot of the hill. She remained alone in the carriage.

Souvent, en la regardant, il lui semblait que son âme, s'échappant vers elle, se répandait comme une onde sur le contour de sa tête, et descendait entraînée dans la blancheur de sa poitrine.

Il se mettait par terre, devant elle; et, les deux coudes sur ses genoux, il la considérait avec un sourire, et le front tendu.

Elle se penchait vers lui et murmurait, comme suffoquée d'enivrement:

— Oh! ne bouge pas! ne parle pas! regarde-moi! Il sort de tes yeux quelque chose de si doux, qui me fait tant de bien!

Elle l'appelait enfant

— Enfant, m'aimes-tu?

Et elle n'entendait guère sa réponse, dans la précipitation de ses lèvres qui lui, montaient à la bouche.

Il y avait sur la pendule un petit Cupidon de bronze, qui minaudait en arrondissant les bras sous une guirlande dorée. Ils en rirent bien des fois; mais, quand il fallait se séparer, tout leur semblait sérieux.

Immobiles l'un devant l'autre, ils se répétaient

— À jeudi!... à jeudi!

Tout à coup elle lui prenait la tête dans les deux mains, le baisait vite au front en s'écriant: «Adieu!» et s'élançait dans l'escalier.

Elle allait rue de la Comédie, chez un coiffeur, se faire arranger ses bandeaux. La nuit tombait; on allumait le gaz dans la boutique.

Elle entendait la clochette du théâtre qui appelait les cabotins à la représentation; et elle voyait, en face, passer des hommes à figure blanche et des femmes en toilette fanée, qui entraient par la porte des coulisses.

Il faisait chaud dans ce petit appartement trop bas, où le poêle bourdonnait au milieu des perruques et des pommades. L'odeur des fers, avec ces mains grasses qui lui maniaient la tête, ne tardait pas à l'étourdir, et elle s'endormait un peu sous son peignoir. Souvent le garçon, en la coiffant, lui proposait des billets pour le bal masqué.

Puis elle s'en allait! Elle remontait les rues; elle arrivait à la Croix rouge; elle reprenait ses socques, qu'elle avait cachés le matin sous une banquette, et se tassait à sa place parmi les voyageurs impatientés. Quelques-uns descendaient au bas de la côte. Elle restait seule dans la voiture.

At every turning all the lights of the town were seen more and more completely, making a great luminous vapour about the dim houses. Emma knelt on the cushions and her eyes wandered over the dazzling light. She sobbed; called on Leon, sent him tender words and kisses lost in the wind.

On the hillside a poor devil wandered about with his stick in the midst of the diligences. A mass of rags covered his shoulders, and an old staved-in beaver, turned out like a basin, hid his face; but when he took it off he discovered in the place of eyelids empty and bloody orbits. The flesh hung in red shreds, and there flowed from it liquids that congealed into green scale down to the nose, whose black nostrils sniffed convulsively. To speak to you he threw back his head with an idiotic laugh; then his bluish eyeballs, rolling constantly, at the temples beat against the edge of the open wound.

He sang a little song as he followed the carriages:

*Maids in the warmth of a summer day Dream of love, and of love always.*

And all the rest was about birds and sunshine and green leaves.

Sometimes he appeared suddenly behind Emma, bareheaded, and she drew back with a cry. Hivert made fun of him. He would advise him to get a booth at the Saint Romain fair, or else ask him, laughing, how his young woman was.

Often they had started when, with a sudden movement, his hat entered the diligence through the small window, while he clung with his other arm to the footboard, between the wheels splashing mud. His voice, feeble at first and quavering, grew sharp; it resounded in the night like the indistinct moan of a vague distress; and through the ringing of the bells, the murmur of the trees, and the rumbling of the empty vehicle, it had a far-off sound that disturbed Emma. It went to the bottom of her soul, like a whirlwind in an abyss, and carried her away into the distances of a boundless melancholy. But Hivert, noticing a weight behind, gave the blind man sharp cuts with his whip. The thong lashed his wounds, and he fell back into the mud with a yell.

À chaque tournant, on apercevait de plus en plus tous les éclairages de la ville qui faisaient une large vapeur lumineuse au-dessus des maisons confondues. Emma se mettait à genoux sur les coussins, et elle égarait ses yeux dans cet éblouissement. Elle sanglotait, appelait Léon, et lui envoyait des paroles tendres et des baisers qui se perdaient au vent.

Il y avait dans la côte un pauvre diable vagabondant avec son bâton, tout au milieu des diligences. Un amas de guenilles lui recouvrait les épaules, et un vieux castor défoncé, s'arrondissant en cuvette, lui cachait la figure; mais, quand il le retirait, il découvrait, à la place des paupières, deux orbites béantes tout ensanglantées. La chair s'effiloquait par lambeaux rouges; et il en coulait des liquides qui se figeaient en gales vertes jusqu'au nez, dont les narines noires reniflaient convulsivement. Pour vous parier, il se renversait la tête avec un rire idiot; — alors ses prunelles bleuâtres, roulant d'un mouvement continu, allaient se cogner, vers les tempes, sur le bord de la plaie vive.

Il chantait une petite chanson en suivant les voitures:

*Souvent la chaleur d'un beau jour Fait rêver fillette à l'amour.*

Et il y avait dans tout le reste des oiseaux, du soleil et du feuillage.

Quelquefois, il apparaissait tout à coup derrière Emma, tête nue. Elle se retirait avec un cri. Hivert venait le plaisanter. Il l'engageait à prendre une baraque à la foire Saint-Romain, ou bien lui demandait, en riant, comment se portait sa bonne amie.

Souvent, on était en marche, lorsque son chapeau, d'un mouvement brusque entrait dans la diligence par le vasistas 93, tandis qu'il se cramponnait, de l'autre bras, sur le marchepied, entre l'éclaboussure des roues. Sa voix, faible d'abord et vagissante, devenait aiguë. Elle se traînait dans la nuit, comme l'indistincte lamentation d'une vague détresse; et, à travers la sonnerie des grelots, le murmure des arbres et le ronflement de la boîte creuse, elle avait quelque chose de lointain qui bouleversait Emma. Cela lui descendait au fond de l'âme comme un tourbillon dans un abîme, et l'emportait parmi les espaces d'une mélancolie sans bornes. Mais Hivert, qui s'apercevait d'un contrepoids, allongeait à l'aveugle de grands coups avec son fouet. La mèche le cinglait sur ses plaies, et il tombait dans la boue en poussant un hurlement.

Then the passengers in the "Hirondelle" ended by falling asleep, some with open mouths, others with lowered chins, leaning against their neighbour's shoulder, or with their arm passed through the strap, oscillating regularly with the jolting of the carriage; and the reflection of the lantern swinging without, on the crupper of the wheeler; penetrating into the interior through the chocolate calico curtains, threw sanguineous shadows over all these motionless people. Emma, drunk with grief, shivered in her clothes, feeling her feet grow colder and colder, and death in her soul.

Charles at home was waiting for her; the "Hirondelle" was always late on Thursdays. Madame arrived at last, and scarcely kissed the child. The dinner was not ready. No matter! She excused the servant. This girl now seemed allowed to do just as she liked.

Often her husband, noting her pallor, asked if she were unwell.

"No," said Emma.

"But," he replied, "you seem so strange this evening."

"Oh, it's nothing! nothing!"

There were even days when she had no sooner come in than she went up to her room; and Justin, happening to be there, moved about noiselessly, quicker at helping her than the best of maids. He put the matches ready, the candlestick, a book, arranged her nightgown, turned back the bedclothes.

"Come!" said she, "that will do. Now you can go."

For he stood there, his hands hanging down and his eyes wide open, as if enmeshed in the innumerable threads of a sudden reverie.

The following day was frightful, and those that came after still more unbearable, because of her impatience to once again seize her happiness; an ardent lust, inflamed by the images of past experience, and that burst forth freely on the seventh day beneath Leon's caresses. His ardours were hidden beneath outbursts of wonder and gratitude. Emma tasted this love in a discreet, absorbed fashion, maintained it by all the artifices of her tenderness, and trembled a little lest it should be lost later on.

Puis les voyageurs de l'hirondelle finissaient par s'endormir, les uns la bouche ouverte, les autres le menton baissé, s'appuyant sur l'épaule de leur voisin, ou bien le bras passé dans la courroie, tout en oscillant régulièrement au branle de la voiture; et le reflet de la lanterne qui se balançait en dehors, sur la croupe des limoniers, pénétrant dans l'intérieur par les rideaux de calicot chocolat, posait des ombres sanguinolentes sur tous ces individus immobiles. Emma, ivre de tristesse, grelottait sous ses vêtements; et se sentait de plus en plus froid aux pieds, avec la mort dans l'âme.

Charles, à la maison, l'attendait; l'Hirondelle était toujours en retard le jeudi. Madame arrivait enfin! À peine si elle embrassait la petite. Le dîner n'était pas prêt, n'importe! elle excusait la cuisinière. Tout maintenant semblait permis à cette fille.

Souvent son mari, remarquant sa pâleur, lui demandait si elle ne se trouvait point malade.

— Non, disait Emma.

— Mais, répliquait-il, tu es toute drôle ce soir?

— Eh! ce n'est rien! ce n'est rien!

Il y avait même des jours où, à peine rentrée, elle montait dans sa chambre; et Justin, qui se trouvait là, circulait à pas muets, plus ingénieux à la servir qu'une excellente camériste. Il plaçait les allumettes, le bougeoir, un livre, disposait sa camisole, ouvrait les draps.

— Allons, disait-elle, c'est bien, va-t'en!

Car il restait debout, les mains pendantes et les yeux ouverts, comme enlacé dans les fils innombrables d'une rêverie soudaine.

La journée du lendemain était affreuse, et les suivantes étaient plus intolérables encore par l'impatience qu'avait Emma de ressaisir son bonheur, — convoitise âpre, enflammée d'images connues, et qui, le septième jour, éclatait tout à l'aise dans les caresses de Léon. Ses ardeurs, à lui, se cachaient sous des expansions d'émerveillement et de reconnaissance. Emma goûtait cet amour d'une façon discrète et absorbée, l'entretenait par tous les artifices de sa tendresse, et tremblait un peu qu'il ne se perdît plus tard.

She often said to him, with her sweet, melancholy voice—

"Ah! you too, you will leave me! You will marry! You will be like all the others."

He asked:

"What others?"

"Why, like all men," she replied.

Then added, repulsing him with a languid movement:

"You are all evil!"

One day, as they were talking philosophically of earthly disillusions, to experiment on his jealousy, or yielding, perhaps, to an over-strong need to pour out her heart, she told him that formerly, before him, she had loved someone. "Not like you," she went on quickly, protesting by the head of her child that "nothing had passed between them."

The young man believed her, but none the less questioned her to find out what he was.

"He was a ship's captain, my dear."

Was this not preventing any inquiry, and, at the same time, assuming a higher ground through this pretended fascination exercised over a man who must have been of warlike nature and accustomed to receive homage?

The clerk then felt the lowliness of his position; he longed for epaulettes, crosses, titles. All that would please her—he gathered that from her spendthrift habits.

Emma nevertheless concealed many of these extravagant fancies, such as her wish to have a blue tilbury to drive into Rouen, drawn by an English horse and driven by a groom in top-boots. It was Justin who had inspired her with this whim, by begging her to take him into her service as valet-de-chambre, and if the privation of it did not lessen the pleasure of her arrival at each rendezvous, it certainly augmented the bitterness of the return.

Often, when they talked together of Paris, she ended by murmuring:

"Ah! how happy we should be there!"

"Are we not happy?" gently answered the young man passing his hands over her hair.

Souvent elle lui disait, avec des douceurs de voix mélancolique:

— Ah! tu me quitteras, toi... tu te marieras!... tu seras comme les autres.

Il demandait:

— Quels autres?

— Mais les hommes, enfin, répondait-elle.

Puis, elle ajoutait en le repoussant d'un geste langoureux:

— Vous êtes tous des infâmes!

Un jour qu'ils causaient philosophiquement des désillusions terrestres, elle vint à dire (pour expérimenter sa jalousie ou cédant peut-être à un besoin d'épanchement trop fort) qu'autrefois, avant lui, elle avait aimé quelqu'un, «pas comme toi!» reprit-elle vite, protestant sur la tête de sa fille qu'il ne s'était rien passé.

Le jeune homme la crut, et néanmoins la questionna pour savoir ce qu'il faisait.

— Il était capitaine de vaisseau, mon ami.

N'était-ce pas prévenir toute recherche, et en même temps se poser très haut, par cette prétendue fascination exercée sur un homme qui devait être de nature belliqueuse et accoutumé, à des hommages?

Le clerc sentit alors l'infimité de sa position; il envia des épaulettes, des croix, des titres. Tout cela devait lui plaire: il s'en doutait à ses habitudes dispendieuses.

Cependant Emma taisait quantité de ses extravagances, telle que l'envie d'avoir, pour l'amener à Rouen, un tilbury bleu, attelé d'un cheval anglais, et conduit par un groom en bottes à revers. C'était Justin qui lui en avait inspiré le caprice, en la suppliant de le prendre chez elle comme valet de chambre; et, si cette privation n'atténuait pas à chaque rendez-vous le plaisir de l'arrivée, elle augmentait certainement l'amertume du retour.

Souvent lorsqu'ils parlaient ensemble de Paris, elle finissait par murmurer:

— Ah! que nous serions bien là pour vivre!

— Ne sommes-nous pas heureux? reprenait doucement le jeune homme, en lui passant la main sur ses bandeaux.

"Yes, that is true," she said. "I am mad. Kiss me!"

To her husband she was more charming than ever. She made him pistachio-creams, and played him waltzes after dinner. So he thought himself the most fortunate of men and Emma was without uneasiness, when, one evening suddenly he said:

"It is Mademoiselle Lempereur, isn't it, who gives you lessons?"

"Yes."

"Well, I saw her just now," Charles went on, "at Madame Liegeard's. I spoke to her about you, and she doesn't know you."

This was like a thunderclap. However, she replied quite naturally:

"Ah! no doubt she forgot my name."

"But perhaps," said the doctor, "there are several Demoiselles Lempereur at Rouen who are music-mistresses."

"Possibly!"

Then quickly:

"But I have my receipts here. See!"

And she went to the writing-table, ransacked all the drawers, rummaged the papers, and at last lost her head so completely that Charles earnestly begged her not to take so much trouble about those wretched receipts.

"Oh, I will find them," she said.

And, in fact, on the following Friday, as Charles was putting on one of his boots in the dark cabinet where his clothes were kept, he felt a piece of paper between the leather and his sock. He took it out and read:

"Received, for three months' lessons and several pieces of music, the sum of sixty-three francs.—Felicie Lempereur, professor of music."

"How the devil did it get into my boots?"

"It must," she replied, "have fallen from the old box of bills that is on the edge of the shelf."

From that moment her existence was but one long tissue of lies, in which she enveloped her love as in veils to hide it.

— Oui, c'est vrai, disait-elle, le suis folle; embrasse-moi!

Elle était pour son mari plus charmante que jamais, lui faisait des crèmes à la pistache et jouait des valses après dîner. Il se trouvait donc le plus fortuné des mortels, et Emma vivait sans inquiétude, lorsqu'un soir, tout à coup:

— C'est mademoiselle Lempereur, n'est-ce pas, qui te donne des leçons?

— Oui.

— Eh bien, je l'ai vue tantôt, reprit Charles, chez madame Liégeard. Je lui ai parlé de toi; elle ne te connaît pas.

Ce fut comme un coup de foudre. Cependant elle répliqua d'un air naturel:

— Ah! sans doute, elle aura oublié mon nom?

— Mais il y a peut-être à Rouen, dit le médecin, plusieurs demoiselles Lempereur qui sont maîtresses de piano?

— C'est possible!

Puis, vivement:

— J'ai pourtant ses reçus, tiens! regarde.

Et elle alla au secrétaire, fouilla tous les tiroirs, confondit les papiers et finit si bien par perdre la tête, que Charles l'engagea fort à ne point se donner tant de mal pour ces misérables quittances.

— Oh! je les trouverai, dit-elle.

En effet, dès le vendredi suivant, Charles, en passant une de ses bottes dans le cabinet noir où l'on serrait ses habits, sentit une feuille de papier entre le cuir et sa chaussette, il la prit et lut:

«Reçu, pour trois mois de leçons, plus diverses fournitures, la somme de soixante-cinq francs. FELICIE LEMPEREUR, professeur de musique.»

— Comment diable est-ce dans mes bottes?

— Ce sera, sans doute, répondit-elle, tombé du vieux carton aux factures, qui est sur le bord de la planche.

À partir de ce moment, son existence ne fut plus qu'un assemblage de mensonges, où elle enveloppait son amour comme dans des voiles, pour le cacher.

It was a want, a mania, a pleasure carried to such an extent that if she said she had the day before walked on the right side of a road, one might know she had taken the left.

One morning, when she had gone, as usual, rather lightly clothed, it suddenly began to snow, and as Charles was watching the weather from the window, he caught sight of Monsieur Bournisien in the chaise of Monsieur Tuvache, who was driving him to Rouen. Then he went down to give the priest a thick shawl that he was to hand over to Emma as soon as he reached the "Croix-Rouge." When he got to the inn, Monsieur Bournisien asked for the wife of the Yonville doctor. The landlady replied that she very rarely came to her establishment. So that evening, when he recognised Madame Bovary in the "Hirondelle," the cure told her his dilemma, without, however, appearing to attach much importance to it, for he began praising a preacher who was doing wonders at the Cathedral, and whom all the ladies were rushing to hear.

Still, if he did not ask for any explanation, others, later on, might prove less discreet. So she thought well to get down each time at the "Croix-Rouge," so that the good folk of her village who saw her on the stairs should suspect nothing.

One day, however, Monsieur Lheureux met her coming out of the Hotel de Boulogne on Leon's arm; and she was frightened, thinking he would gossip. He was not such a fool.

But three days after he came to her room, shut the door, and said:

"I must have some money."

She declared she could not give him any. Lheureux burst into lamentations and reminded her of all the kindnesses he had shown her.

In fact, of the two bills signed by Charles, Emma up to the present had paid only one. As to the second, the shopkeeper, at her request, had consented to replace it by another, which again had been renewed for a long date. Then he drew from his pocket a list of goods not paid for; to wit, the curtains, the carpet, the material for the armchairs, several dresses, and divers articles of dress, the bills for which amounted to about two thousand francs.

She bowed her head. He went on:

C'était un besoin, une manie, un plaisir, au point que, si elle disait avoir passé, hier par le côté droit d'une rue, il fallait croire qu'elle avait pris par le côté gauche.

Un matin qu'elle venait de partir, selon sa coutume, assez légèrement vêtue, il tomba de la neige tout à coup; et comme Charles regardait le temps à la fenêtre, il aperçut M. Bournisien dans le boc du sieur Tuvache qui le conduisait à Rouen. Alors il descendit confier à l'ecclésiastique un gros châle pour qu'il le remît à Madame, sitôt qu'il arriverait à la Croix rouge. À peine fut-il à l'auberge que Bournisien demanda où était la femme du médecin d'Yonville. L'hôtelière répondit qu'elle fréquentait fort peu son établissement. Aussi, le soir, en reconnaissant madame Bovary dans l'Hirondelle, le curé lui conta son embarras, sans paraître, du reste y attacher de l'importance; car il entama l'éloge d'un prédicateur qui pour lors faisait merveilles à la cathédrale, et que toutes les dames couraient entendre.

N'importe s'il n'avait point demandé d'explications, d'autres plus tard pourraient se montrer moins discrets. Aussi jugea-t-elle utile de descendre chaque fois à la Croix rouge, de sorte que les bonnes gens de son village qui la voyaient dans l'escalier ne se doutaient de rien.

Un jour pourtant, M. Lheureux la rencontra qui sortait de l'hôtel de Boulogne au bras de Léon; et elle eut peur, s'imaginant qu'il bavarderait. Il n'était pas si bête.

Mais trois jours après, il entra dans sa chambre, ferma la porte et dit:

— J'aurais besoin d'argent.

Elle déclara ne pouvoir lui en donner. Lheureux se répandit en gémissements, et rappela toutes les complaisances qu'il avait eues.

En effet, des deux billets souscrits par Charles, Emma jusqu'à présent n'en avait payé qu'un seul. Quant au second, le marchand, sur sa prière, avait consenti à le remplacer par deux autres, qui même avaient été renouvelés à une fort longue échéance. Puis il tira de sa poche une liste de fournitures non soldées, à savoir: les rideaux, le tapis, l'étoffe pour les fauteuils, plusieurs robes et divers articles de toilette, dont la valeur se montait à la somme de deux mille francs environ.

Elle baissa la tête; il reprit:

"But if you haven't any ready money, you have an estate."

And he reminded her of a miserable little hovel situated at Barneville, near Aumale, that brought in almost nothing. It had formerly been part of a small farm sold by Monsieur Bovary senior; for Lheureux knew everything, even to the number of acres and the names of the neighbours.

"If I were in your place," he said, "I should clear myself of my debts, and have money left over."

She pointed out the difficulty of getting a purchaser. He held out the hope of finding one; but she asked him how she should manage to sell it.

"Haven't you your power of attorney?" he replied.

The phrase came to her like a breath of fresh air.

"Leave me the bill," said Emma.

"Oh, it isn't worth while," answered Lheureux.

He came back the following week and boasted of having, after much trouble, at last discovered a certain Langlois, who, for a long time, had had an eye on the property, but without mentioning his price.

"Never mind the price!" she cried.

But they would, on the contrary, have to wait, to sound the fellow. The thing was worth a journey, and, as she could not undertake it, he offered to go to the place to have an interview with Langlois. On his return he announced that the purchaser proposed four thousand francs.

Emma was radiant at this news.

"Frankly," he added, "that's a good price."

She drew half the sum at once, and when she was about to pay her account the shopkeeper said:

"It really grieves me, on my word! to see you depriving yourself all at once of such a big sum as that."

Then she looked at the bank-notes, and dreaming of the unlimited number of rendezvous represented by those two thousand francs, she stammered:

"What! what!"

"Oh!" he went on, laughing good-naturedly, "one puts anything one likes on receipts. Don't you think I know what household affairs are?"

— Mais, si vous n'avez pas d'espèces, vous avez du bien.

Et il indiqua une méchante masure sise à Barneville, près d'Aumale, qui ne rapportait pas grand-chose. Cela dépendait autrefois d'une petite ferme vendue par M. Bovary père, car Lheureux savait tout, jusqu'à la contenance d'hectares, avec le nom des voisins.

— Moi, à votre place, disait-il, je me libérerais, et j'aurais encore le surplus de l'argent.

Elle objecta la difficulté d'un acquéreur; il donna l'espoir d'en trouver; mais elle demanda comment faire pour qu'elle pût vendre.

— N'avez-vous pas la procuration? répondit-il.

Ce mot lui arriva comme une bouffée d'air frais.

— Laissez-moi la note, dit Emma.

— Oh! ce n'est pas la peine! reprit Lheureux.

Il revint la semaine suivante, et se vanta d'avoir, après force démarches, fini par découvrir un certain Langlois qui, depuis longtemps, guignait la propriété sans faire connaître son prix.

— N'importe le prix! s'écria-t-elle.

Il fallait attendre, au contraire, tâter ce gaillard-là. La chose valait la peine d'un voyage, et, comme elle ne pouvait faire ce voyage, il offrir de se rendre sur les lieux, pour s'aboucher avec Langlois. Une fois revenu, il annonça que l'acquéreur proposait quatre mille francs.

Emma s'épanouit à cette nouvelle.

— Franchement, ajouta-t-il, c'est bien payé.

Elle toucha la moitié de la somme immédiatement, et, quand elle fut pour solder son mémoire, le marchand lui dit:

— Cela me fait de la peine, parole d'honneur, de vous voir vous dessaisir tout d'un coup d'une somme aussi conséquente que celle- là.

Alors, elle regarda les billets de banque; et, rêvant au nombre illimité de rendez-vous que ces deux mille francs représentaient:

— Comment! comment! balbutia-t-elle.

— Oh! reprit-il en riant d'un air bonhomme, on met tout ce que l'on veut sur les factures. Est-ce que je ne connais pas les ménages?

And he looked at her fixedly, while in his hand he held two long papers that he slid between his nails. At last, opening his pocket-book, he spread out on the table four bills to order, each for a thousand francs.

"Sign these," he said, "and keep it all!"

She cried out, scandalised.

"But if I give you the surplus," replied Monsieur Lheureux impudently, "is that not helping you?"

And taking a pen he wrote at the bottom of the account, "Received of Madame Bovary four thousand francs."

"Now who can trouble you, since in six months you'll draw the arrears for your cottage, and I don't make the last bill due till after you've been paid?"

Emma grew rather confused in her calculations, and her ears tingled as if gold pieces, bursting from their bags, rang all round her on the floor. At last Lheureux explained that he had a very good friend, Vincart, a broker at Rouen, who would discount these four bills. Then he himself would hand over to madame the remainder after the actual debt was paid.

But instead of two thousand francs he brought only eighteen hundred, for the friend Vincart (which was only fair) had deducted two hundred francs for commission and discount.

Then he carelessly asked for a receipt.

"You understand—in business—sometimes. And with the date, if you please, with the date."

A horizon of realisable whims opened out before Emma. She was prudent enough to lay by a thousand crowns, with which the first three bills were paid when they fell due; but the fourth, by chance, came to the house on a Thursday, and Charles, quite upset, patiently awaited his wife's return for an explanation.

If she had not told him about this bill, it was only to spare him such domestic worries; she sat on his knees, caressed him, cooed to him, gave him a long enumeration of all the indispensable things that had been got on credit.

"Really, you must confess, considering the quantity, it isn't too dear."

Et il la considérait fixement, tout en tenant à sa main deux longs papiers qu'il faisait glisser entre ses ongles. Enfin, ouvrant son portefeuille, il étala sur la table quatre billets à ordre, de mille francs chacun.

— Signez-moi cela, dit-il, et gardez tout.

Elle se récria, scandalisée.

— Mais, si je vous donne le surplus, répondit effrontément M. Lheureux, n'est-ce pas vous rendre service, à vous?

Et, prenant une plume, il écrivit au bas du mémoire: «Reçu de madame Bovary quatre mille francs.»

— Qui vous inquiète, puisque vous toucherez dans six mois l'arriéré de votre baraque, et que je vous place l'échéance du dernier billet pour après le payement?

Emma s'embarrassait un peu dans ses calculs, et les oreilles lui tintaient comme si des pièces d'or, s'éventrant de leurs sacs, eussent sonné tout autour d'elle sur le parquet. Enfin Lheureux expliqua qu'il avait un sien ami Vinçart, banquier à Rouen, lequel allait escompter ces quatre billets, puis il remettrait lui-même à Madame le surplus de la dette réelle.

Mais au lieu de deux mille francs, il n'en apporta que dix-huit cents, car l'ami Vinçart (comme de juste) en avait prélevé deux cents, pour frais de commission et d'escompte.

Puis il réclama négligemment une quittance.

— Vous comprenez..., dans le commerce..., quelquefois... Et avec la date, s'il vous plaît, la date.

Un horizon de fantaisies réalisables s'ouvrit alors devant Emma. Elle eut assez de prudence pour mettre en réserve mille écus, avec quoi furent payés, lorsqu'ils échurent, les trois premiers billets; mais le quatrième, par hasard, tomba dans la maison un jeudi, et Charles, bouleversé, attendit patiemment le retour de sa femme pour avoir des explications.

Si elle ne l'avait point instruit de ce billet, c'était afin de lui épargner des tracas domestiques; elle s'assit sur ses genoux, le caressa, roucoula, fit une longue énumération de toutes les choses indispensables prises à crédit.

— Enfin, tu conviendras que, vu la quantité, ce n'est pas trop cher.

Charles, at his wit's end, soon had recourse to the eternal Lheureux, who swore he would arrange matters if the doctor would sign him two bills, one of which was for seven hundred francs, payable in three months. In order to arrange for this he wrote his mother a pathetic letter. Instead of sending a reply she came herself; and when Emma wanted to know whether he had got anything out of her:

"Yes," he replied; "but she wants to see the account."

The next morning at daybreak Emma ran to Lheureux to beg him to make out another account for not more than a thousand francs, for to show the one for four thousand it would be necessary to say that she had paid two-thirds, and confess, consequently, the sale of the estate—a negotiation admirably carried out by the shopkeeper, and which, in fact, was only actually known later on.

Despite the low price of each article, Madame Bovary senior, of course, thought the expenditure extravagant.

"Couldn't you do without a carpet? Why have recovered the arm-chairs? In my time there was a single arm-chair in a house, for elderly persons—at any rate it was so at my mother's, who was a good woman, I can tell you.

"Everybody can't be rich! No fortune can hold out against waste! I should be ashamed to coddle myself as you do! And yet I am old. I need looking after. And there! there! fitting up gowns! fallals! What! silk for lining at two francs, when you can get jaconet for ten sous, or even for eight, that would do well enough!"

Emma, lying on a lounge, replied as quietly as possible:

"Ah! Madame, enough! enough!"

The other went on lecturing her, predicting they would end in the workhouse. But it was Bovary's fault. Luckily he had promised to destroy that power of attorney.

"What?"

"Ah! he swore he would," went on the good woman.

Emma opened the window, called Charles, and the poor fellow was

Charles, à bout d'idées, bientôt eut recours à l'éternel Lheureux, qui jura de calmer les choses, si Monsieur lui signait deux billets, dont l'un de sept cents francs, payable dans trois mois. Pour se mettre en mesure, il écrivit à sa mère une lettre pathétique. Au lieu d'envoyer la réponse, elle vint elle-même; et, quand Emma voulut savoir s'il en avait tiré quelque chose:

— Oui, répondit-il. Mais elle demande à connaître la facture.

Le lendemain, au point du jour, Emma courut chez M. Lheureux le prier de refaire une autre note, qui ne dépassât point mille francs; car pour montrer celle de quatre mille, il eût fallu dire qu'elle en avait payé les deux tiers, avouer conséquemment la vente de l'immeuble, négociation bien conduite par le marchand, et qui ne fut effectivement connue que plus tard.

Malgré le prix très bas de chaque article, madame Bovary mère ne manqua point de trouver la dépense exagérée.

— Ne pouvait-on se passer d'un tapis? Pourquoi avoir renouvelé l'étoffe des fauteuils? De mon temps, on avait dans une maison un seul fauteuil, pour les personnes âgées, — du moins, c'était comme cela chez ma mère, qui était une honnête femme, je vous assure.

— Tout le monde ne peut être riche! Aucune fortune ne tient contre le coulage! Je rougirais de me dorloter comme vous faites! et pourtant, moi, je suis vieille, j'ai besoin de soins... En voilà! en voilà, des ajustements! des flaflas! Comment! de la soie pour doublure, à deux francs!... tandis qu'on trouve du jaconas à dix sous, et même à huit sous qui fait parfaitement l'affaire.

Emma, renversée sur la causeuse, répliquait le plus tranquillement possible:

— Eh! madame, assez! assez!...

L'autre continuait à la sermonner, prédisant qu'ils finiraient à l'hôpital. D'ailleurs, c'était la faute de Bovary. Heureusement qu'il avait promis d'anéantir cette procuration...

— Comment?

— Ah! il me l'a juré, reprit la bonne femme.

Emma ouvrit la fenêtre, appela Charles, et le pauvre garçon fut con-

obliged to confess the promise torn from him by his mother.

Emma disappeared, then came back quickly, and majestically handed her a thick piece of paper.

"Thank you," said the old woman.

And she threw the power of attorney into the fire.

Emma began to laugh, a strident, piercing, continuous laugh; she had an attack of hysterics.

"Oh, my God!" cried Charles. "Ah! you really are wrong! You come here and make scenes with her!"

His mother, shrugging her shoulders, declared it was "all put on."

But Charles, rebelling for the first time, took his wife's part, so that Madame Bovary, senior, said she would leave. She went the very next day, and on the threshold, as he was trying to detain her, she replied:

"No, no! You love her better than me, and you are right. It is natural. For the rest, so much the worse! You will see. Good day—for I am not likely to come soon again, as you say, to make scenes."

Charles nevertheless was very crestfallen before Emma, who did not hide the resentment she still felt at his want of confidence, and it needed many prayers before she would consent to have another power of attorney. He even accompanied her to Monsieur Guillaumin to have a second one, just like the other, drawn up.

"I understand," said the notary; "a man of science can't be worried with the practical details of life."

And Charles felt relieved by this comfortable reflection, which gave his weakness the flattering appearance of higher pre-occupation.

And what an outburst the next Thursday at the hotel in their room with Leon! She laughed, cried, sang, sent for sherbets, wanted to smoke cigarettes, seemed to him wild and extravagant, but adorable, superb.

He did not know what recreation of her whole being drove her more and more to plunge into the pleasures of life. She was becoming irritable, greedy, voluptuous; and she walked about the streets with him carrying her head high, without fear, so she said, of compromising herself. At times, however, Emma shuddered at the sudden thought of meeting

traint d'avouer la parole arrachée par sa mère.

Emma disparut, puis rentra vite en lui tendant majestueusement une grosse feuille de papier.

— Je vous remercie, dit la vieille femme.

Et elle jeta dans le feu la procuration.

Emma se mit à rire d'un rire strident, éclatant, continu: elle avait une attaque de nerfs.

— Ah! mon Dieu! s'écria Charles. Eh! tu as tort aussi toi! tu viens lui faire des scènes!...

Sa mère, en haussant les épaules, prétendait que tout cela c'étaient des gestes.

Mais Charles, pour la première fois se révoltant, prit la défense de sa femme, si bien que madame Bovary mère voulut s'en aller. Elle partit dès le lendemain, et, sur le seuil, comme il essayait à la retenir, elle répliqua:

— Non, non! Tu l'aimes mieux que moi, et tu as raison, c'est dans l'ordre. Au reste, tant pis! tu verras!... Bonne santé!... car je ne suis pas près, comme tu dis, de venir lui faire des scènes.

Charles n'en resta pas moins fort penaud vis-à-vis d'Emma, celle- ci ne cachant point la rancune qu'elle lui gardait pour avoir manqué de confiance; il fallut bien des prières avant qu'elle consentît à reprendre sa procuration, et même il l'accompagna chez M. Guillaumin pour lui en faire faire une seconde, toute pareille.

— Je comprends cela, dit le notaire; un homme de science ne peut s'embarrasser aux détails pratiques de la vie.

Et Charles se sentit soulagé par cette réflexion pateline, qui donnait à sa faiblesse les apparences flatteuses d'une préoccupation supérieure.

Quel débordement, le jeudi d'après, à l'hôtel, dans leur chambre, avec Léon! Elle rit, pleura, chanta, dansa, fit monter des sorbets, voulut fumer des cigarettes, lui parut extravagante, mais adorable, superbe.

Il ne savait pas quelle réaction de tout son être la poussait davantage à se précipiter sur les jouissances de la vie. Elle devenait irritable, gourmande, et voluptueuse; et elle se promenait avec lui dans les rues, tête haute, sans peur, disait- elle, de se compromettre. Parfois, cependant, Emma tressaillait à l'idée soudaine de rencontrer Rodolphe; car il lui

Rodolphe, for it seemed to her that, although they were separated forever, she was not completely free from her subjugation to him.

One night she did not return to Yonville at all. Charles lost his head with anxiety, and little Berthe would not go to bed without her mamma, and sobbed enough to break her heart. Justin had gone out searching the road at random. Monsieur Homais even had left his pharmacy.

At last, at eleven o'clock, able to bear it no longer, Charles harnessed his chaise, jumped in, whipped up his horse, and reached the "Croix-Rouge" about two o'clock in the morning. No one there! He thought that the clerk had perhaps seen her; but where did he live? Happily, Charles remembered his employer's address, and rushed off there.

Day was breaking, and he could distinguish the escutcheons over the door, and knocked. Someone, without opening the door, shouted out the required information, adding a few insults to those who disturb people in the middle of the night.

The house inhabited by the clerk had neither bell, knocker, nor porter. Charles knocked loudly at the shutters with his hands. A policeman happened to pass by. Then he was frightened, and went away.

"I am mad," he said; "no doubt they kept her to dinner at Monsieur Lormeaux'."

But the Lormeaux no longer lived at Rouen.

"She probably stayed to look after Madame Dubreuil. Why, Madame Dubreuil has been dead these ten months!

"Where can she be?"

An idea occurred to him. At a cafe he asked for a Directory, and hurriedly looked for the name of Mademoiselle Lempereur, who lived at No. 74 Rue de la Renelle-des-Maroquiniers.

As he was turning into the street, Emma herself appeared at the other end of it. He threw himself upon her rather than embraced her, crying:

"What kept you yesterday?"

"I was not well."

"What was it? Where? How?"

She passed her hand over her forehead and answered:

"At Mademoiselle Lempereur's."

semblait, bien qu'ils fussent séparés pour toujours, qu'elle n'était pas complètement affranchie de sa dépendance.

Un soir, elle ne rentra point à Yonville. Charles en perdait la tête, et la petite Berthe, ne voulant pas se coucher sans sa maman, sanglotait à se rompre la poitrine. Justin était parti au hasard sur la route. M. Homais en avait quitté sa pharmacie.

Enfin, à onze heures, n'y tenant plus, Charles attela son boc, sauta dedans, fouetta sa bête et arriva vers deux heures du matin à la Croix rouge. Personne. Il pensa que le clerc peut-être l'avait vue; mais où demeurait-il? Charles, heureusement, se rappela l'adresse de son patron. Il y courut.

Le jour commençait à paraître. Il distingua des panonceaux au- dessus d'une porte; il frappa. Quelqu'un, sans ouvrir, lui cria le renseignement demandé, tout en ajoutant force injures contre ceux qui dérangeaient le monde pendant la nuit.

La maison que le clerc habitait n'avait ni sonnette, ni marteau, ni portier. Charles donna de grands coups de poing contre les auvents: Un agent de police vint à passer; alors il eut peur et s'en alla.

— Je suis fou, se disait-il; sans doute, on l'aura retenue à dîner chez M. Lormeaux.

La famille Lormeaux n'habitait plus Rouen.

— Elle sera restée à soigner madame Dubreuil. Eh! madame Dubreuil est morte depuis dix mois!...

Où est-elle donc?

Une idée lui vint. Il demanda, dans un café, l'Annuaire; et chercha vite le nom de mademoiselle Lempereur, qui demeurait rue de la Renelle-des-Maroquiniers, n° 74.

Comme il entrait dans cette rue, Emma parut elle-même à l'autre bout; il se jeta sur elle plutôt qu'il ne l'embrassa, en s'écriant:

— Qui t'a retenue hier?

— J'ai été malade.

— Et de quoi?... Où?... Comment?...

Elle se passa la main sur le front, et répondit:

— Chez mademoiselle Lempereur.

"I was sure of it! I was going there."

"Oh, it isn't worth while," said Emma. "She went out just now; but for the future don't worry. I do not feel free, you see, if I know that the least delay upsets you like this."

This was a sort of permission that she gave herself, so as to get perfect freedom in her escapades. And she profited by it freely, fully. When she was seized with the desire to see Leon, she set out upon any pretext; and as he was not expecting her on that day, she went to fetch him at his office.

It was a great delight at first, but soon he no longer concealed the truth, which was, that his master complained very much about these interruptions.

"Pshaw! come along," she said.

And he slipped out.

She wanted him to dress all in black, and grow a pointed beard, to look like the portraits of Louis XIII. She wanted to see his lodgings; thought them poor. He blushed at them, but she did not notice this, then advised him to buy some curtains like hers, and as he objected to the expense:

"Ah! ah! you care for your money," she said laughing.

Each time Leon had to tell her everything that he had done since their last meeting. She asked him for some verses—some verses "for herself," a "love poem" in honour of her. But he never succeeded in getting a rhyme for the second verse; and at last ended by copying a sonnet in a "Keepsake."

This was less from vanity than from the one desire of pleasing her. He did not question her ideas; he accepted all her tastes; he was rather becoming her mistress than she his. She had tender words and kisses that thrilled his soul. Where could she have learnt this corruption almost incorporeal in the strength of its profanity and dissimulation?

— J'en étais sûr! J'y allais.

— Oh! ce n'est pas la peine, dit Emma. Elle vient de sortit tout à l'heure; mais, à l'avenir, tranquillise-toi. Je ne suis pas libre, tu comprends, si je sais que le moindre retard te bouleverse ainsi.

C'était une manière de permission qu'elle se donnait de ne point se gêner dans ses escapades. Aussi en profita-t-elle tout à son aise, largement. Lorsque l'envie la prenait de voir Léon, elle partait sous n'importe quel prétexte, et, comme il ne l'attendait pas ce jour-là, elle allait le chercher à son étude.

Ce fut un grand bonheur les premières fois; mais bientôt il ne cacha plus la vérité, à savoir: que son patron se plaignait fort de ces dérangements.

— Ah bah! viens donc, disait-elle.

Et il s'esquivait.

Elle voulut qu'il se vêtît tout en noir et se laissât pousser une pointe au menton, pour ressembler aux portraits de Louis XIII. Elle désira connaître son logement, le trouva médiocre; il en rougit, elle n'y prit garde, puis lui conseilla d'acheter des rideaux pareils aux siens, et comme il objectait la dépense:

— Ah! ah! tu tiens à tes petits écus! dit-elle en riant.

Il fallait que Léon, chaque fois, lui racontât toute sa conduite, depuis le dernier rendez-vous. Elle demanda des vers, des vers pour elle, une pièce d'amour en son honneur; jamais il ne put parvenir à trouver la rime du second vers, et il finit par copier un sonnet dans un keepsake.

Ce fut moins par vanité que dans le seul but de lui complaire. Il ne discutait pas ses idées; il acceptait tous ses goûts; il devenait sa maîtresse plutôt qu'elle n'était la sienne. Elle avait des paroles tendres avec des baisers qui lui emportaient l'âme. Où donc avait-elle appris cette corruption, presque immatérielle à force d'être profonde et dissimulée?

# Chapter 6

During the journeys he made to see her, Leon had often dined at the chemist's, and he felt obliged from politeness to invite him in turn.

"With pleasure!" Monsieur Homais replied; "besides, I must invigorate my mind, for I am getting rusty here. We'll go to the theatre, to the restaurant; we'll make a night of it."

"Oh, my dear!" tenderly murmured Madame Homais, alarmed at the vague perils he was preparing to brave.

"Well, what? Do you think I'm not sufficiently ruining my health living here amid the continual emanations of the pharmacy? But there! that is the way with women! They are jealous of science, and then are opposed to our taking the most legitimate distractions. No matter! Count upon me. One of these days I shall turn up at Rouen, and we'll go the pace together."

The druggist would formerly have taken good care not to use such an expression, but he was cultivating a gay Parisian style, which he thought in the best taste; and, like his neighbour, Madame Bovary, he questioned the clerk curiously about the customs of the capital; he even talked slang to dazzle the bourgeois, saying bender, crummy, dandy, macaroni, the cheese, cut my stick and *I'll hook it*, for "I am going."

So one Thursday Emma was surprised to meet Monsieur Homais in the kitchen of the "Lion d'Or," wearing a traveller's costume, that is to say, wrapped in an old cloak which no one knew he had, while he carried a valise in one hand and the foot-warmer of his establishment in the other. He had confided his intentions to no one, for fear of causing the public anxiety by his absence.

The idea of seeing again the place where his youth had been spent no doubt excited him, for during the whole journey he never ceased talking, and as soon as he had arrived, he jumped quickly out of the

# Chapitre 6

Dans les voyages qu'il faisait pour la voir, Léon souvent avait dîné chez le pharmacien, et s'était cru contraint, par politesse, de l'inviter à son tour.

— Volontiers! avait répondu M. Homais; il faut, d'ailleurs, que je me retrempe un peu, car je m'encroûte ici. Nous irons au spectacle, au restaurant, nous ferons des folies!

— Ah! bon ami! murmura tendrement madame Homais, effrayée des périls vagues qu'il se disposait à courir.

— Eh bien, quoi? tu trouves que je ne ruine pas assez ma santé à vivre parmi les émanations continuelles de la pharmacie! Voilà, du reste, le caractère des femmes: elles sont jalouses de la Science, puis s'opposent à ce que l'on prenne les plus légitimes distractions. N'importe, comptez sur moi; un de ces jours, je tombe à Rouen et nous ferons sauter ensemble les monacos.

L'apothicaire, autrefois, se fût bien gardé d'une telle expression; mais il donnait maintenant dans un genre folâtre et parisien qu'il trouvait du meilleur goût; et, comme madame Bovary, sa voisine, il interrogeait le clerc curieusement sur les moeurs de la capitale, même il parlait argot afin d'éblouir... les bourgeois, disant _turne, bazar, chicard, chicandard, Breda-street, _et *Je me la casse*, pour: Je m'en vais.

Donc, un jeudi, Emma fut surprise de rencontrer, dans la cuisine du Lion d'or, M. Homais en costume de voyageur, c'est-à-dire couvert d'un vieux manteau qu'on ne lui connaissait pas, tandis qu'il portait d'une main une valise, et, de l'autre, la chancelière de son établissement. Il n'avait confié son projet à personne, dans la crainte d'inquiéter le public par son absence.

L'idée de revoir les lieux où s'était passée sa jeunesse l'exaltait sans doute, car tout le long du chemin il n'arrêta pas de discourir; puis, à peine arrivé, il sauta vivement de la voiture pour se mettre en quête

diligence to go in search of Leon. In vain the clerk tried to get rid of him. Monsieur Homais dragged him off to the large Cafe de la Normandie, which he entered majestically, not raising his hat, thinking it very provincial to uncover in any public place.

Emma waited for Leon three quarters of an hour. At last she ran to his office; and, lost in all sorts of conjectures, accusing him of indifference, and reproaching herself for her weakness, she spent the afternoon, her face pressed against the window-panes.

At two o'clock they were still at a table opposite each other. The large room was emptying; the stove-pipe, in the shape of a palm-tree, spread its gilt leaves over the white ceiling, and near them, outside the window, in the bright sunshine, a little fountain gurgled in a white basin, where; in the midst of watercress and asparagus, three torpid lobsters stretched across to some quails that lay heaped up in a pile on their sides.

Homais was enjoying himself. Although he was even more intoxicated with the luxury than the rich fare, the Pommard wine all the same rather excited his faculties; and when the omelette au rhum appeared, he began propounding immoral theories about women. What seduced him above all else was chic. He admired an elegant toilette in a well-furnished apartment, and as to bodily qualities, he didn't dislike a young girl.

Leon watched the clock in despair. The druggist went on drinking, eating, and talking.

"You must be very lonely," he said suddenly, "here at Rouen. To be sure your lady-love doesn't live far away."

And the other blushed:

"Come now, be frank. Can you deny that at Yonville—"

The young man stammered something.

"At Madame Bovary's, you're not making love to—"

"To whom?"

"The servant!"

He was not joking; but vanity getting the better of all prudence, Leon, in spite of himself protested. Besides, he only liked dark women.

"I approve of that," said the chemist; "they have more passion."

de Léon; et le clerc eut beau se débattre, M. Homais l'entraîna vers le grand café de Normandie, où il entra majestueusement sans retirer son chapeau, estimant fort provincial de se découvrir dans un endroit public.

Emma attendit Léon trois quarts d'heure. Enfin elle courut à son étude, et, perdue dans toute sorte de conjectures, l'accusant d'indifférence et se reprochant à elle-même sa faiblesse, elle passa l'après-midi le front collé contre les carreaux.

Ils étaient encore à deux heures attablés l'un devant l'autre. La grande salle se vidait; le tuyau du poêle, en forme de palmier, arrondissait au plafond blanc sa gerbe dorée; et près d'eux, derrière le vitrage, en plein soleil, un petit jet d'eau gargouillait dans un bassin de marbre où, parmi du cresson et des asperges, trois homards engourdis s'allongeaient jusqu'à des cailles, toutes couchées en pile, sur le flanc.

Homais se délectait. Quoiqu'il se grisât de luxe encore plus que de bonne chère, le vin de Pomard, cependant, lui excitait un peu les facultés, et, lorsque apparut l'omelette au rhum, il exposa sur les femmes des théories immorales. Ce qui le séduisait par- dessus tout, c'était le chic. Il adorait une toilette élégante dans un appartement bien meublé, et, quant aux qualités corporelles, ne détestait pas le morceau.

Léon contemplait la pendule avec désespoir. L'apothicaire buvait, mangeait, parlait.

— Vous devez être, dit-il tout à coup, bien privé à Rouen. Du reste, vos amours ne logent pas loin.

Et, comme l'autre rougissait:

— Allons, soyez franc! Nierez-vous qu'à Yonville…?

Le jeune homme balbutia.

— Chez madame Bovary, vous ne courtisiez point…?

— Et qui donc?

— La bonne!

Il ne plaisantait pas; mais, la vanité l'emportant sur toute prudence, Léon, malgré lui, se récria. D'ailleurs, il n'aimait que les femmes brunes.

— Je vous approuve, dit le pharmacien; elles ont plus de tempérament.

And whispering into his friend's ear, he pointed out the symptoms by which one could find out if a woman had passion. He even launched into an ethnographic digression: the German was vapourish, the French woman licentious, the Italian passionate.

"And negresses?" asked the clerk.

"They are an artistic taste!" said Homais. "Waiter! two cups of coffee!"

"Are we going?" at last asked Leon impatiently.

"Ja!"

But before leaving he wanted to see the proprietor of the establishment and made him a few compliments.

Then the young man, to be alone, alleged he had some business engagement.

"Ah! I will escort you," said Homais.

And all the while he was walking through the streets with him he talked of his wife, his children; of their future, and of his business; told him in what a decayed condition it had formerly been, and to what a degree of perfection he had raised it.

Arrived in front of the Hotel de Boulogne, Leon left him abruptly, ran up the stairs, and found his mistress in great excitement.

At mention of the chemist she flew into a passion. He, however, piled up good reasons; it wasn't his fault; didn't she know Homais—did she believe that he would prefer his company? But she turned away; he drew her back, and, sinking on his knees, clasped her waist with his arms in a languorous pose, full of concupiscence and supplication.

She was standing up, her large flashing eyes looked at him seriously, almost terribly. Then tears obscured them, her red eyelids were lowered, she gave him her hands, and Leon was pressing them to his lips when a servant appeared to tell the gentleman that he was wanted.

"You will come back?" she said.

"Yes."

"But when?"

"Immediately."

Et se penchant à l'oreille de son ami, il indiqua les symptômes auxquels on reconnaissait qu'une femme avait du tempérament. Il se lança même dans une digression ethnographique: l'Allemande était vaporeuse, la Française libertine, l'Italienne passionnée.

— Et les négresses? demanda le clerc.

— C'est un goût d'artiste, dit Homais. — Garçon! deux demi- tasses!

— Partons-nous? reprit à la fin Léon s'impatientant.

— *Yes.*

Mais il voulut, avant de s'en aller, voir le maître de l'établissement et lui adressa quelques félicitations.

Alors le jeune homme, pour être seul, allégua qu'il avait affaire.

— Ah! je vous escorte! dit Homais.

Et, tout en descendant les rues avec lui, il parlait de sa femme, de ses enfants, de leur avenir et de sa pharmacie, racontait en quelle décadence elle était autrefois, et le point de perfection où il l'avait montée.

Arrivé devant l'hôtel de Boulogne, Léon le quitta brusquement, escalada l'escalier, et trouva sa maîtresse en grand émoi.

Au nom du pharmacien, elle s'emporta. Cependant, il accumulait de bonnes raisons; ce n'était pas sa faute, ne connaissait-elle pas M. Homais? pouvait-elle croire qu'il préférât sa compagnie? Mais elle se détournait; il la retint; et, s'affaissant sur les genoux, il lui entoura la taille de ses deux bras, dans une pose langoureuse toute pleine de concupiscence et de supplication.

Elle était debout; ses grands yeux enflammés le regardaient sérieusement et presque d'une façon terrible. Puis des larmes les obscurcirent, ses paupières roses s'abaissèrent, elle abandonna ses mains, et Léon les portait à sa bouche lorsque parut un domestique, avertissant Monsieur qu'on le demandait.

— Tu vas revenir? dit-elle.

— Oui.

— Mais quand?

— Tout à l'heure.

"It's a trick," said the chemist, when he saw Leon. "I wanted to interrupt this visit, that seemed to me to annoy you. Let's go and have a glass of garus at Bridoux'."

Leon vowed that he must get back to his office. Then the druggist joked him about quill-drivers and the law.

"Leave Cujas and Barthole alone a bit. Who the devil prevents you? Be a man! Let's go to Bridoux'. You'll see his dog. It's very interesting."

And as the clerk still insisted:

"I'll go with you. I'll read a paper while I wait for you, or turn over the leaves of a 'Code.'"

Leon, bewildered by Emma's anger, Monsieur Homais' chatter, and, perhaps, by the heaviness of the luncheon, was undecided, and, as it were, fascinated by the chemist, who kept repeating:

"Let's go to Bridoux'. It's just by here, in the Rue Malpalu."

Then, through cowardice, through stupidity, through that indefinable feeling that drags us into the most distasteful acts, he allowed himself to be led off to Bridoux', whom they found in his small yard, superintending three workmen, who panted as they turned the large wheel of a machine for making seltzer-water. Homais gave them some good advice. He embraced Bridoux; they took some garus. Twenty times Leon tried to escape, but the other seized him by the arm saying:

"Presently! I'm coming! We'll go to the 'Fanal de Rouen' to see the fellows there. I'll introduce you to Thornassin."

At last he managed to get rid of him, and rushed straight to the hotel. Emma was no longer there.

She had just gone in a fit of anger. She detested him now. This failing to keep their rendezvous seemed to her an insult, and she tried to rake up other reasons to separate herself from him. He was incapable of heroism, weak, banal, more spiritless than a woman, avaricious too, and cowardly.

Then, growing calmer, she at length discovered that she had, no doubt, calumniated him. But the disparaging of those we love always alienates us from them to some extent. We must not touch our idols; the gilt sticks to our fingers.

— C'est un truc, dit le pharmacien en apercevant Léon. J'ai voulu interrompre cette visite qui me paraissait vous contrarier. Allons chez Bridoux prendre un verre de garus.

Léon jura qu'il lui fallait retourner à son étude. Alors l'apothicaire fit des plaisanteries sur les paperasses, la procédure.

— Laissez donc un peu Cujas et Bartole, que diable! Qui vous empêche? Soyez un brave! Allons chez Bridoux; vous verrez son chien. C'est très curieux!

Et comme le clerc s'obstinait toujours:

— J'y vais aussi. Je lirai un journal en vous attendant, ou je feuilleterai un Code.

Léon, étourdi par la colère d'Emma, le bavardage de M. Homais et peut-être les pesanteurs du déjeuner, restait indécis et comme sous la fascination du pharmacien qui répétait:

— Allons chez Bridoux! c'est à deux pas, rue Malpalu.

Alors, par lâcheté, par bêtise, par cet inqualifiable sentiment qui nous entraîne aux actions les plus antipathiques, il se laissa conduire chez Bridoux; et ils le trouvèrent dans sa petite cour, surveillant trois garçons qui haletaient à tourner la grande roue d'une machine pour faire de l'eau de Seltz... Homais leur donna des conseils; il embrassa Bridoux; on prit le garus. Vingt fois Léon voulut s'en aller; mais l'autre l'arrêtait par le bras en lui disant:

— Tout à l'heure! je sors. Nous irons au Fanal de Rouen, voir ces messieurs. Je vous présenterai à Thomassin.

Il s'en débarrassa pourtant et courut d'un bond jusqu'à l'hôtel. Emma n'y était plus.

Elle venait de partir, exaspérée. Elle le détestait maintenant. Ce manque de parole au rendez-vous lui semblait un outrage, et elle cherchait encore d'autres raisons pour s'en détacher: il était incapable d'héroïsme, faible, banal, plus mou qu'une femme, avare d'ailleurs et pusillanime.

Puis, se calmant, elle finit par découvrir qu'elle l'avait sans doute calomnié. Mais le dénigrement de ceux que nous aimons toujours nous en détache quelque peu. Il ne faut pas toucher aux idoles: la dorure en reste aux mains.

They gradually came to talking more frequently of matters outside their love, and in the letters that Emma wrote him she spoke of flowers, verses, the moon and the stars, naive resources of a waning passion striving to keep itself alive by all external aids. She was constantly promising herself a profound felicity on her next journey. Then she confessed to herself that she felt nothing extraordinary. This disappointment quickly gave way to a new hope, and Emma returned to him more inflamed, more eager than ever. She undressed brutally, tearing off the thin laces of her corset that nestled around her hips like a gliding snake. She went on tiptoe, barefooted, to see once more that the door was closed, then, pale, serious, and, without speaking, with one movement, she threw herself upon his breast with a long shudder.

Yet there was upon that brow covered with cold drops, on those quivering lips, in those wild eyes, in the strain of those arms, something vague and dreary that seemed to Leon to glide between them subtly as if to separate them.

He did not dare to question her; but, seeing her so skilled, she must have passed, he thought, through every experience of suffering and of pleasure. What had once charmed now frightened him a little. Besides, he rebelled against his absorption, daily more marked, by her personality. He begrudged Emma this constant victory. He even strove not to love her; then, when he heard the creaking of her boots, he turned coward, like drunkards at the sight of strong drinks.

She did not fail, in truth, to lavish all sorts of attentions upon him, from the delicacies of food to the coquettries of dress and languishing looks. She brought roses to her breast from Yonville, which she threw into his face; was anxious about his health, gave him advice as to his conduct; and, in order the more surely to keep her hold on him, hoping perhaps that heaven would take her part, she tied a medal of the Virgin round his neck. She inquired like a virtuous mother about his companions. She said to him:

"Don't see them; don't go out; think only of ourselves; love me!"

Ils en vinrent à parler plus souvent de choses indifférentes à leur amour; et, dans les lettres qu'Emma lui envoyait, il était question de fleurs, de vers, de la lune et des étoiles, ressources naïves d'une passion affaiblie, qui essayait de s'aviver à tous les secours extérieurs. Elle se promettait continuellement, pour son prochain voyage, une félicité profonde; puis elle s'avouait ne rien sentir d'extraordinaire. Cette déception s'effaçait vite sous un espoir nouveau, et Emma revenait à lui plus enflammée, plus avide. Elle se déshabillait brutalement, arrachant le lacet mince de son corset, qui sifflait autour de ses hanches comme une couleuvre qui glisse. Elle allait sur la pointe de ses pieds nus regarder encore une fois si la porte était fermée, puis elle faisait d'un seul geste tomber ensemble tous ses vêtements; — et, pâle, sans parler, sérieuse, elle s'abattait contre sa poitrine, avec un long frisson.

Cependant, il y avait sur ce front couvert de gouttes froides, sur ces lèvres balbutiantes, dans ces prunelles égarées, dans l'étreinte de ces bras, quelque chose d'extrême, de vague et de lugubre, qui semblait à Léon se glisser entre eux, subtilement, comme pour les séparer.

Il n'osait lui faire des questions; mais, la discernant si expérimentée, elle avait dû passer, se disait-il, par toutes les épreuves de la souffrance et du plaisir. Ce qui le charmait autrefois l'effrayait un peu maintenant. D'ailleurs, il se révoltait contre l'absorption, chaque jour plus grande, de sa personnalité. Il en voulait à Emma de cette victoire permanente. Il s'efforçait même à ne pas la chérir; puis, au craquement de ses bottines, il se sentait lâche, comme les ivrognes à la vue des liqueurs fortes.

Elle ne manquait point, il est vrai, de lui prodiguer toute sorte d'attentions, depuis les recherches de table jusqu'aux coquetteries du costume et aux langueurs du regard. Elle apportait d'Yonville des roses dans son sein, qu'elle lui jetait à la figure, montrait des inquiétudes pour sa santé, lui donnait des conseils sur sa conduite; et, afin de le retenir davantage, espérant que le ciel peut-être s'en mêlerait, elle lui passa autour du cou une médaille de la Vierge. Elle s'informait, comme une mère vertueuse, de ses camarades. Elle lui disait:

— Ne les vois pas, ne sors pas, ne pense qu'à nous; aime-moi!

She would have liked to be able to watch over his life; and the idea occurred to her of having him followed in the streets. Near the hotel there was always a kind of loafer who accosted travellers, and who would not refuse. But her pride revolted at this.

"Bah! so much the worse. Let him deceive me! What does it matter to me? As If I cared for him!"

One day, when they had parted early and she was returning alone along the boulevard, she saw the walls of her convent; then she sat down on a form in the shade of the elm-trees. How calm that time had been! How she longed for the ineffable sentiments of love that she had tried to figure to herself out of books!

The first month of her marriage, her rides in the wood, the viscount that waltzed, and Lagardy singing, all repassed before her eyes. And Leon suddenly appeared to her as far off as the others.

"Yet I love him," she said to herself.

No matter! She was not happy—she never had been. Whence came this insufficiency in life—this instantaneous turning to decay of everything on which she leant? But if there were somewhere a being strong and beautiful, a valiant nature, full at once of exaltation and refinement, a poet's heart in an angel's form, a lyre with sounding chords ringing out elegiac epithalamia to heaven, why, perchance, should she not find him? Ah! how impossible! Besides, nothing was worth the trouble of seeking it; everything was a lie. Every smile hid a yawn of boredom, every joy a curse, all pleasure satiety, and the sweetest kisses left upon your lips only the unattainable desire for a greater delight.

A metallic clang droned through the air, and four strokes were heard from the convent-clock. Four o'clock! And it seemed to her that she had been there on that form an eternity. But an infinity of passions may be contained in a minute, like a crowd in a small space.

Emma lived all absorbed in hers, and troubled no more about money matters than an archduchess.

Once, however, a wretched-looking man, rubicund and bald, came to her house, saying he had been sent by Monsieur Vincart of Rouen. He

Elle aurait voulu pouvoir surveiller sa vie, et l'idée lui vint de le faire suivre dans les rues. Il y avait toujours, près de l'hôtel, une sorte de vagabond qui accostait les voyageurs et qui ne refuserait pas... Mais sa fierté se révolta.

— Eh! tant pis! qu'il me trompe, que m'importe! est-ce que j'y tiens?

Un jour qu'ils s'étaient quittés de bonne heure, et qu'elle s'en revenait seule par le boulevard, elle aperçut les murs de son couvent; alors elle s'assit sur un banc, à l'ombre des ormes. Quel calme dans ce temps-là! comme elle enviait les ineffables sentiments d'amour qu'elle tâchait, d'après des livres, de se figurer!

Les premiers mois de son mariage, ses promenades à cheval dans la forêt, le Vicomte qui valsait, et Lagardy chantant, tout repassa devant ses yeux... Et Léon lui parut soudain dans le même éloignement que les autres.

— Je l'aime pourtant! se disait-elle.

N'importe! elle n'était pas heureuse, ne l'avait jamais été. D'où venait donc cette insuffisance de la vie, cette pourriture instantanée des choses où elle s'appuyait?... Mais, s'il y avait quelque part un être fort et beau, une nature valeureuse, pleine à la fois d'exaltation et de raffinements, un coeur de poète sous une forme d'ange, lyre aux cordes d'airain, sonnant vers le ciel des épithalames élégiaques, pourquoi, par hasard, ne le trouverait-elle pas? Oh! quelle impossibilité! Rien, d'ailleurs, ne valait la peine d'une recherche; tout mentait! Chaque sourire cachait un bâillement d'ennui, chaque joie une malédiction, tout plaisir son dégoût, et les meilleurs baisers ne vous laissaient sur la lèvre qu'une irréalisable envie d'une volupté plus haute.

Un râle métallique se traîna dans les airs et, quatre coups se firent entendre à la cloche du couvent. Quatre heures! et il lui semblait qu'elle était là, sur ce banc, depuis l'éternité. Mais un infini de passions peut tenir dans une minute, comme une foule dans un petit espace.

Emma vivait tout occupée des siennes, et ne s'inquiétait pas plus de l'argent qu'une archiduchesse.

Une fois pourtant, un homme d'allure chétive, rubicond et chauve, entra chez elle, se déclarant envoyé par M. Vinçart, de Rouen. Il retira

took out the pins that held together the side-pockets of his long green overcoat, stuck them into his sleeve, and politely handed her a paper.

It was a bill for seven hundred francs, signed by her, and which Lheureux, in spite of all his professions, had paid away to Vincart.

She sent her servant for him. He could not come.

Then the stranger, who had remained standing, casting right and left curious glances, that his thick, fair eyebrows hid, asked with a naive air:

"What answer am I to take Monsieur Vincart?"

"Oh," said Emma, "tell him that I haven't it. I will send next week; he must wait; yes, till next week."

And the fellow went without another word.

But the next day at twelve o'clock she received a summons, and the sight of the stamped paper, on which appeared several times in large letters, "Maitre Hareng, bailiff at Buchy," so frightened her that she rushed in hot haste to the linendraper's.

She found him in his shop, doing up a parcel.

"Your obedient!" he said; "I am at your service."

But Lheureux, all the same, went on with his work, helped by a young girl of about thirteen, somewhat hunch-backed, who was at once his clerk and his servant.

Then, his clogs clattering on the shop-boards, he went up in front of Madame Bovary to the first door, and introduced her into a narrow closet, where, in a large bureau in sapon-wood, lay some ledgers, protected by a horizontal padlocked iron bar. Against the wall, under some remnants of calico, one glimpsed a safe, but of such dimensions that it must contain something besides bills and money. Monsieur Lheureux, in fact, went in for pawnbroking, and it was there that he had put Madame Bovary's gold chain, together with the earrings of poor old Tellier, who, at last forced to sell out, had bought a meagre store of grocery at Quincampoix, where he was dying of catarrh amongst his candles, that were less yellow than his face.

Lheureux sat down in a large cane arm-chair, saying:

"What news?"

les épingles qui fermaient la poche latérale de sa longue redingote verte, les piqua sur sa manche et tendit poliment un papier.

C'était un billet de sept cents francs, souscrit par elle, et que Lheureux, malgré toutes ses protestations, avait passé à l'ordre de Vinçart.

Elle expédia chez lui sa domestique. Il ne pouvait venir.

Alors, l'inconnu, qui était resté debout, lançant de droite et de gauche des regards curieux que dissimulaient ses gros sourcils blonds, demanda d'un air naïf:

— Quelle réponse apporter à M. Vinçart?

— Eh bien, répondit Emma, dites-lui... que je n'en ai pas... Ce sera la semaine prochaine... Qu'il attende... oui, la semaine prochaine.

Et le bonhomme s'en alla sans souffler mot.

Mais, le lendemain, à midi, elle reçut un protêt; et la vue du papier timbré, où s'étalait à plusieurs reprises et en gros caractères: «Maître Hareng, huissier à Buchy», l'effraya si fort, qu'elle courut en toute hâte chez le marchand d'étoffes.

Elle le trouva dans sa boutique, en train de ficeler un paquet.

— Serviteur! dit-il, je suis à vous.

Lheureux n'en continua pas moins sa besogne, aidé par une jeune fille de treize ans environ, un peu bossue, et qui lui servait à la fois de commis et de cuisinière.

Puis, faisant claquer ses sabots sur les planches de la boutique, il monta devant Madame au premier étage, et l'introduisit dans un étroit cabinet, où un gros bureau en bois de sape supportait quelques registres, défendus transversalement par une barre de fer cadenassée. Contre le mur, sous des coupons d'indienne, on entrevoyait un coffre-fort, mais d'une telle dimension, qu'il devait contenir autre chose que des billets et de l'argent. M. Lheureux, en effet, prêtait sur gages, et c'est là qu'il avait mis la chaîne en or de madame Bovary, avec les boucles d'oreilles du pauvre père Tellier, qui, enfin contraint de vendre, avait acheté à Quincampoix un maigre fonds d'épicerie, où il se mourait de son catarrhe, au milieu de ses chandelles moins jaunes que sa figure.

Lheureux s'assit dans son large fauteuil de paille, en disant:

— Quoi de neuf?

"See!"

And she showed him the paper.

"Well how can I help it?"

Then she grew angry, reminding him of the promise he had given not to pay away her bills. He acknowledged it.

"But I was pressed myself; the knife was at my own throat."

"And what will happen now?" she went on.

"Oh, it's very simple; a judgment and then a distraint—that's about it!"

Emma kept down a desire to strike him, and asked gently if there was no way of quieting Monsieur Vincart.

"I dare say! Quiet Vincart! You don't know him; he's more ferocious than an Arab!"

Still Monsieur Lheureux must interfere.

"Well, listen. It seems to me so far I've been very good to you."

And opening one of his ledgers:

"See," he said.

Then running up the page with his finger:

"Let's see! let's see! August 3d, two hundred francs; June 17th, a hundred and fifty; March 23d, forty-six. In April—"

He stopped, as if afraid of making some mistake.

"Not to speak of the bills signed by Monsieur Bovary, one for seven hundred francs, and another for three hundred. As to your little installments, with the interest, why, there's no end to 'em; one gets quite muddled over 'em. I'll have nothing more to do with it."

She wept; she even called him "her good Monsieur Lheureux." But he always fell back upon "that rascal Vincart." Besides, he hadn't a brass farthing; no one was paying him now-a-days; they were eating his coat off his back; a poor shopkeeper like him couldn't advance money.

Emma was silent, and Monsieur Lheureux, who was biting the feathers of a quill, no doubt became uneasy at her silence, for he went on:

"Unless one of these days I have something coming in, I might—"

— Tenez.

Et elle lui montra le papier.

— Eh bien, qu'y puis-je?

Alors, elle s'emporta, rappelant la parole qu'il avait donnée de ne pas faire circuler ses billets; il en convenait.

— Mais j'ai été forcé moi-même, j'avais le couteau sur la gorge.

— Et que va-t-il arriver, maintenant? reprit-elle.

— Oh! c'est bien simple: un jugement du tribunal, et puis la saisie...; bernique!

Emma se retenait pour ne pas le battre. Elle lui demanda doucement s'il n'y avait pas moyen de calmer M. Vinçart.

— Ah bien, oui! calmer Vinçart; vous ne le connaissez guère; il est plus féroce qu'un Arabe.

Pourtant il fallait que M. Lheureux s'en mêlât.

— Écoutez donc! il me semble que, jusqu'à présent, j'ai été assez bon pour vous.

Et, déployant un de ses registres:

— Tenez!

Puis, remontant la page avec son doigt:

— Voyons..., voyons... Le 3 août, deux cents francs... Au 17 juin, cent cinquante... 23 mars, quarante-six... En avril...

Il s'arrêta, comme craignant de faire quelque sottise.

— Et je ne dis rien des billets souscrits par Monsieur, un de sept cents francs, un autre de trois cents! Quant à vos petits acomptes, aux intérêts, ça n'en finit pas, on s'y embrouille. Je ne m'en mêle plus!

Elle pleurait, elle l'appela même «son bon monsieur Lheureux». Mais il se rejetait toujours sur ce «mâtin de Vinçart». D'ailleurs, il n'avait pas un centime, personne à présent ne le payait, on lui mangeait la laine sur le dos, un pauvre boutiquier comme lui ne pouvait faire d'avances.

Emma se taisait; et M. Lheureux, qui mordillonnait les barbes d'une plume, sans doute s'inquiéta de son silence, car il reprit:

— Au moins, si un de ces jours j'avais quelques rentrées... Je pourrais...

"Besides," said she, "as soon as the balance of Barneville—"

"What!"

And on hearing that Langlois had not yet paid he seemed much surprised. Then in a honied voice:

"And we agree, you say?"

"Oh! to anything you like."

On this he closed his eyes to reflect, wrote down a few figures, and declaring it would be very difficult for him, that the affair was shady, and that he was being bled, he wrote out four bills for two hundred and fifty francs each, to fall due month by month.

"Provided that Vincart will listen to me! However, it's settled. I don't play the fool; I'm straight enough."

Next he carelessly showed her several new goods, not one of which, however, was in his opinion worthy of madame.

"When I think that there's a dress at threepence-halfpenny a yard, and warranted fast colours! And yet they actually swallow it! Of course you understand one doesn't tell them what it really is!" He hoped by this confession of dishonesty to others to quite convince her of his probity to her.

Then he called her back to show her three yards of guipure that he had lately picked up "at a sale."

"Isn't it lovely?" said Lheureux. "It is very much used now for the backs of arm-chairs. It's quite the rage."

And, more ready than a juggler, he wrapped up the guipure in some blue paper and put it in Emma's hands.

"But at least let me know—"

"Yes, another time," he replied, turning on his heel.

That same evening she urged Bovary to write to his mother, to ask her to send as quickly as possible the whole of the balance due from the father's estate. The mother-in-law replied that she had nothing more, the winding up was over, and there was due to them besides Barneville an income of six hundred francs, that she would pay them punctually.

Then Madame Bovary sent in accounts to two or three patients, and she made large use of this method, which was very successful. She was

— Du reste, dit-elle, dès que l'arriéré de Barneville…

— Comment?…

Et, en apprenant que Langlois n'avait pas encore payé, il parut fort surpris. Puis, d'une voix mielleuse:

— Et nous convenons, dites-vous…?

— Oh! de ce que vous voudrez!

Alors, il ferma les yeux pour réfléchir, écrivit quelques chiffres, et, déclarant qu'il aurait grand mal, que la chose était scabreuse et qu'il se saignait, il dicta quatre billets de deux cent cinquante francs, chacun, espacés les uns des autres à un mois d'échéance.

— Pourvu que Vinçart veuille m'entendre! Du reste c'est convenu, je ne lanterne pas, je suis rond comme une pomme.

Ensuite il lui montra négligemment plusieurs marchandises nouvelles, mais dont pas une, dans son opinion, n'était digne de Madame.

— Quand je pense que voilà une robe à sept sous le mètre, et certifiée bon teint! Ils gobent cela pourtant! on ne leur conte pas ce qui en est, vous pensez bien, voulant par cet aveu de coquinerie envers les autres la convaincre tout à fait de sa probité.

Puis il la rappela, pour lui montrer trois aunes de guipure qu'il avait trouvées dernièrement «dans une vendue».

— Est-ce beau! disait Lheureux; on s'en sert beaucoup maintenant, comme têtes de fauteuils, c'est le genre.

Et, plus prompt qu'un escamoteur, il enveloppa la guipure de papier bleu et la mit dans les mains d'Emma.

— Au moins, que je sache…?

— Ah! plus tard, reprit-il en lui tournant les talons.

Dès le soir, elle pressa Bovary d'écrire à sa mère pour qu'elle leur envoyât bien vite tout l'arriéré de l'héritage. La belle-mère répondit n'avoir plus rien; la liquidation était close, et il leur restait, outre Barneville, six cents livres de rente, qu'elle leur servirait exactement.

Alors Madame expédia des factures chez deux ou trois clients, et bientôt usa largement de ce moyen, qui lui réussissait. Elle avait tou-

always careful to add a postscript: "Do not mention this to my husband; you know how proud he is. Excuse me. Yours obediently." There were some complaints; she intercepted them.

To get money she began selling her old gloves, her old hats, the old odds and ends, and she bargained rapaciously, her peasant blood standing her in good stead. Then on her journey to town she picked up nicknacks secondhand, that, in default of anyone else, Monsieur Lheureux would certainly take off her hands. She bought ostrich feathers, Chinese porcelain, and trunks; she borrowed from Felicite, from Madame Lefrancois, from the landlady at the Croix-Rouge, from everybody, no matter where. With the money she at last received from Barneville she paid two bills; the other fifteen hundred francs fell due. She renewed the bills, and thus it was continually.

Sometimes, it is true, she tried to make a calculation, but she discovered things so exorbitant that she could not believe them possible. Then she recommenced, soon got confused, gave it all up, and thought no more about it.

The house was very dreary now. Tradesmen were seen leaving it with angry faces. Handkerchiefs were lying about on the stoves, and little Berthe, to the great scandal of Madame Homais, wore stockings with holes in them. If Charles timidly ventured a remark, she answered roughly that it wasn't her fault.

What was the meaning of all these fits of temper? He explained everything through her old nervous illness, and reproaching himself with having taken her infirmities for faults, accused himself of egotism, and longed to go and take her in his arms.

"Ah, no!" he said to himself; "I should worry her."

And he did not stir.

After dinner he walked about alone in the garden; he took little Berthe on his knees, and unfolding his medical journal, tried to teach her to read. But the child, who never had any lessons, soon looked up with large, sad eyes and began to cry. Then he comforted her; went to fetch water in her can to make rivers on the sand path, or broke off branches from the privet hedges to plant trees in the beds. This did not

jours soin d'ajouter en post-scriptum: «N'en parlez pas à mon mari, vous savez comme il est fier... Excusez-moi... Votre servante...» Il y eut quelques réclamations; elle les intercepta.

Pour se faire de l'argent, elle se mit à vendre ses vieux gants, ses vieux chapeaux, la vieille ferraille; et elle marchandait avec rapacité, — son sang de paysanne la poussant au gain. Puis, dans ses voyages à la ville, elle brocanterait des babioles, que M. Lheureux, à défaut d'autres, lui prendrait certainement. Elle s'acheta des plumes d'autruche, de la porcelaine chinoise et des bahuts; elle empruntait à Félicité, à madame Lefrançois, à l'hôtelière de la Croix rouge, à tout le monde, n'importe où. Avec l'argent qu'elle reçut enfin de Barneville, elle paya deux billets; les quinze cents autres francs s'écoulèrent. Elle s'engagea de nouveau, et toujours ainsi!

Parfois, il est vrai, elle tâchait de faire des calculs; mais elle découvrait des choses si exorbitantes, qu'elle n'y pouvait croire. Alors elle recommençait, s'embrouillait vite, plantait tout là et n'y pensait plus.

La maison était bien triste, maintenant! On en voyait sortir les fournisseurs avec des figures furieuses. Il y avait des mouchoirs traînant sur les fourneaux; et la petite Berthe, au grand scandale de madame Homais, portait des bas percés. Si Charles, timidement, hasardait une observation, elle répondait avec brutalité que ce n'était point sa faute!

Pourquoi ces emportements? Il expliquait tout par son ancienne maladie nerveuse; et, se, reprochant d'avoir pris pour des défauts ses infirmités, il s'accusait d'égoïsme, avait envie de courir l'embrasser.

— Oh! non, se disait-il, je l'ennuierais!

Et il restait.

Après le dîner, il se promenait seul dans le jardin; il prenait la petite Berthe sur ses genoux, et, déployant son journal de médecine, essayait de lui apprendre à lire. L'enfant, qui n'étudiait jamais, ne tardait pas à ouvrir de grands yeux tristes et se mettait à pleurer. Alors il la consolait; il allait lui chercher de l'eau dans l'arrosoir pour faire des rivières sur le sable, ou cassait les branches des troènes pour planter des arbres dans

spoil the garden much, all choked now with long weeds. They owed Lestiboudois for so many days. Then the child grew cold and asked for her mother.

"Call the servant," said Charles. "You know, dearie, that mamma does not like to be disturbed."

Autumn was setting in, and the leaves were already falling, as they did two years ago when she was ill. Where would it all end? And he walked up and down, his hands behind his back.

Madame was in her room, which no one entered. She stayed there all day long, torpid, half dressed, and from time to time burning Turkish pastilles which she had bought at Rouen in an Algerian's shop. In order not to have at night this sleeping man stretched at her side, by dint of manoeuvring, she at last succeeded in banishing him to the second floor, while she read till morning extravagant books, full of pictures of orgies and thrilling situations. Often, seized with fear, she cried out, and Charles hurried to her.

"Oh, go away!" she would say.

Or at other times, consumed more ardently than ever by that inner flame to which adultery added fuel, panting, tremulous, all desire, she threw open her window, breathed in the cold air, shook loose in the wind her masses of hair, too heavy, and, gazing upon the stars, longed for some princely love. She thought of him, of Leon. She would then have given anything for a single one of those meetings that surfeited her.

These were her gala days. She wanted them to be sumptuous, and when he alone could not pay the expenses, she made up the deficit liberally, which happened pretty well every time. He tried to make her understand that they would be quite as comfortable somewhere else, in a smaller hotel, but she always found some objection.

One day she drew six small silver-gilt spoons from her bag (they were old Roualt's wedding present), begging him to pawn them at once for her, and Leon obeyed, though the proceeding annoyed him. He was afraid of compromising himself.

Then, on, reflection, he began to think his mistress's ways were grow-

les plates-bandes, ce qui gâtait peu le jardin; tout encombré de longues herbes; on devait tant de journées à Lestiboudois! Puis l'enfant avait froid et demandait sa mère.

— Appelle ta bonne, disait Charles. Tu sais bien, ma petite, que ta maman ne veut pas qu'on la dérange.

L'automne commençait et déjà les feuilles tombaient, — comme il y a deux ans, lorsqu'elle était malade! — Quand donc tout cela finira-t-il!... Et il continuait à marcher, les deux mains derrière le dos.

Madame était dans sa chambre. On n'y montait pas. Elle restait là tout le long du jour, engourdie, à peine vêtue, et, de temps à autre, faisant fumer des pastilles du sérail qu'elle avait achetées à Rouen, dans la boutique d'un Algérien. Pour ne pas avoir la nuit auprès d'elle, cet homme étendu qui dormait, elle finit, à force de grimaces, par le reléguer au second étage; et elle lisait jusqu'au matin des livres extravagants où il y avait des tableaux orgiaques avec des situations sanglantes. Souvent une terreur la prenait, elle poussait un cri, Charles accourait.

— Ah! va-t'en! disait-elle.

Ou, d'autres fois, brûlée plus fort par cette flamme intime que l'adultère avivait, haletante, émue, tout en désir, elle ouvrait sa fenêtre, aspirait l'air froid, éparpillait au vent sa chevelure trop lourde, et, regardant les étoiles, souhaitait des amours de prince. Elle pensait à lui, à Léon. Elle eût alors tout donné pour un seul de ces rendez-vous, qui la rassasiaient.

C'était ses jours de gala. Elle les voulait splendides! et, lorsqu'il ne pouvait payer seul la dépense, elle complétait le surplus libéralement, ce qui arrivait à peu près toutes les fois. Il essaya de lui faire comprendre qu'ils seraient aussi bien ailleurs, dans quelque hôtel plus modeste; mais elle trouva des objections.

Un jour, elle tira de son sac six petites cuillers en vermeil (c'était le cadeau de noces du père Rouault), en le priant d'aller immédiatement porter cela, pour elle, au mont-de-piété; et Léon obéit, bien que cette démarche lui déplût. Il avait peur de se compromettre.

Puis, en y réfléchissant, il trouva que sa maîtresse prenait des allures

ing odd, and that they were perhaps not wrong in wishing to separate him from her.

In fact someone had sent his mother a long anonymous letter to warn her that he was "ruining himself with a married woman," and the good lady at once conjuring up the eternal bugbear of families, the vague pernicious creature, the siren, the monster, who dwells fantastically in depths of love, wrote to Lawyer Dubocage, his employer, who behaved perfectly in the affair. He kept him for three quarters of an hour trying to open his eyes, to warn him of the abyss into which he was falling. Such an intrigue would damage him later on, when he set up for himself. He implored him to break with her, and, if he would not make this sacrifice in his own interest, to do it at least for his, Dubocage's sake.

At last Leon swore he would not see Emma again, and he reproached himself with not having kept his word, considering all the worry and lectures this woman might still draw down upon him, without reckoning the jokes made by his companions as they sat round the stove in the morning. Besides, he was soon to be head clerk; it was time to settle down. So he gave up his flute, exalted sentiments, and poetry; for every bourgeois in the flush of his youth, were it but for a day, a moment, has believed himself capable of immense passions, of lofty enterprises. The most mediocre libertine has dreamed of sultanas; every notary bears within him the debris of a poet.

He was bored now when Emma suddenly began to sob on his breast, and his heart, like the people who can only stand a certain amount of music, dozed to the sound of a love whose delicacies he no longer noted.

They knew one another too well for any of those surprises of possession that increase its joys a hundred-fold. She was as sick of him as he was weary of her. Emma found again in adultery all the platitudes of marriage.

But how to get rid of him? Then, though she might feel humiliated at the baseness of such enjoyment, she clung to it from habit or from corruption, and each day she hungered after them the more, exhausting all felicity in wishing for too much of it. She accused Leon of her

étranges, et qu'on n'avait peut-être pas tort de vouloir l'en détacher.

En effet, quelqu'un avait envoyé à sa mère une longue lettre anonyme, pour la prévenir qu'il se perdait avec une femme mariée; et aussitôt la bonne dame, entrevoyant l'éternel épouvantail des familles, c'est-à-dire la vague créature pernicieuse, la sirène, le monstre, qui habite fantastiquement les profondeurs de l'amour, écrivit à maître Dubocage son patron, lequel fut parfait dans cette affaire. Il le tint durant trois quarts d'heure, voulant lui dessiller les yeux, l'avertir du gouffre. Une telle intrigue nuirait plus tard à son établissement. Il le supplia de rompre, et, s'il ne faisait ce sacrifice dans son propre intérêt, qu'il le fît au moins pour lui, Dubocage!

Léon enfin avait juré de ne plus revoir Emma; et il se reprochait de n'avoir pas tenu sa parole, considérant tout ce que cette femme pourrait encore lui attirer d'embarras et de discours, sans compter les plaisanteries de ses camarades, qui se débitaient le matin, autour du poêle. D'ailleurs, il allait devenir premier clerc: c'était le moment d'être sérieux. Aussi renonçait-il à la flûte, aux sentiments exaltés, à l'imagination; — car tout bourgeois, dans l'échauffement de sa jeunesse, ne fût-ce qu'un jour, une minute, s'est cru capable d'immenses passions, de hautes entreprises. Le plus médiocre libertin a rêvé des sultanes; chaque notaire porte en soi les débris d'un poète.

Il s'ennuyait maintenant lorsque Emma, tout à coup, sanglotait sur sa poitrine; et son coeur, comme les gens qui ne peuvent endurer qu'une certaine dose de musique, s'assoupissait d'indifférence au vacarme d'un amour dont il ne distinguait plus les délicatesses.

Ils se connaissaient trop pour avoir ces ébahissements de la possession qui en centuplent la joie. Elle était aussi dégoûtée de lui qu'il était fatigué d'elle. Emma retrouvait dans l'adultère toutes les platitudes du mariage.

Mais comment pouvoir s'en débarrasser? Puis, elle avait beau se sentir humiliée de la bassesse d'un tel bonheur, elle y tenait par habitude ou par corruption; et, chaque jour, elle s'y acharnait davantage, tarissant toute félicité à la vouloir trop grande. Elle accusait Léon de ses espoirs

baffled hopes, as if he had betrayed her; and she even longed for some catastrophe that would bring about their separation, since she had not the courage to make up her mind to it herself.

She none the less went on writing him love letters, in virtue of the notion that a woman must write to her lover.

But whilst she wrote it was another man she saw, a phantom fashioned out of her most ardent memories, of her finest reading, her strongest lusts, and at last he became so real, so tangible, that she palpitated wondering, without, however, the power to imagine him clearly, so lost was he, like a god, beneath the abundance of his attributes. He dwelt in that azure land where silk ladders hang from balconies under the breath of flowers, in the light of the moon. She felt him near her; he was coming, and would carry her right away in a kiss. Then she fell back exhausted, for these transports of vague love wearied her more than great debauchery.

She now felt constant ache all over her. Often she even received summonses, stamped paper that she barely looked at. She would have liked not to be alive, or to be always asleep.

On Mid-Lent she did not return to Yonville, but in the evening went to a masked ball. She wore velvet breeches, red stockings, a club wig, and three-cornered hat cocked on one side. She danced all night to the wild tones of the trombones; people gathered round her, and in the morning she found herself on the steps of the theatre together with five or six masks, debardeuses and sailors, Leon's comrades, who were talking about having supper.

The neighbouring cafes were full. They caught sight of one on the harbour, a very indifferent restaurant, whose proprietor showed them to a little room on the fourth floor.

The men were whispering in a corner, no doubt consorting about expenses. There were a clerk, two medical students, and a shopman—what company for her! As to the women, Emma soon perceived from the tone of their voices that they must almost belong to the lowest class. Then she was frightened, pushed back her chair, and cast down her eyes.

déçus, comme s'il l'avait trahie; et même elle souhaitait une catastrophe qui amenât leur séparation, puisqu'elle n'avait pas le courage de s'y décider.

Elle n'en continuait pas moins à lui écrire des lettres amoureuses, en vertu de cette idée, qu'une femme doit toujours écrire à son amant.

Mais, en écrivant, elle percevait un autre homme, un fantôme fait de ses plus ardents souvenirs, de ses lectures les plus belles, de ses convoitises les plus fortes; et il devenait à la fin si véritable, et accessible, qu'elle en palpitait émerveillée, sans pouvoir néanmoins le nettement imaginer, tant il se perdait, comme un dieu, sous l'abondance de ses attributs. Il habitait la contrée bleuâtre où les échelles de soie se balancent à des balcons, sous le souffle des fleurs, dans la clarté de la lune. Elle le sentait près d'elle, il allait venir et l'enlèverait tout entière dans un baiser. Ensuite elle retombait à plat, brisée; car ces élans d'amour vague la fatiguaient plus que de grandes débauches.

Elle éprouvait maintenant une courbature incessante et universelle. Souvent même, Emma recevait des assignations, du papier timbré qu'elle regardait à peine. Elle aurait voulu ne plus vivre, ou continuellement dormir.

Le jour de la mi-carême, elle ne rentra pas à Yonville; elle alla le soir au bal masqué. Elle mit un pantalon de velours et des bas rouges, avec une perruque à catogan et un lampion sur l'oreille. Elle sauta toute la nuit au son furieux des trombones; on faisait cercle autour d'elle; et elle se trouva le matin sur le péristyle du théâtre parmi cinq ou six masques, débardeuses et matelots, des camarades de Léon, qui parlaient d'aller souper.

Les cafés d'alentour étaient pleins. Ils avisèrent sur le port un restaurant des plus médiocres, dont le maître leur ouvrit, au quatrième étage, une petite chambre.

Les hommes chuchotèrent dans un coin, sans doute se consultant sur la dépense. Il y avait un clerc, deux carabins et un commis: quelle société pour elle! Quant aux femmes Emma s'aperçut vite, au timbre de leurs voix, qu'elles devaient être, presque toutes, du dernier rang. Elle eut peur alors, recula sa chaise et baissa les yeux.

The others began to eat; she ate nothing. Her head was on fire, her eyes smarted, and her skin was ice-cold. In her head she seemed to feel the floor of the ball-room rebounding again beneath the rhythmical pulsation of the thousands of dancing feet. And now the smell of the punch, the smoke of the cigars, made her giddy. She fainted, and they carried her to the window.

Day was breaking, and a great stain of purple colour broadened out in the pale horizon over the St. Catherine hills. The livid river was shivering in the wind; there was no one on the bridges; the street lamps were going out.

She revived, and began thinking of Berthe asleep yonder in the servant's room. Then a cart filled with long strips of iron passed by, and made a deafening metallic vibration against the walls of the houses.

She slipped away suddenly, threw off her costume, told Leon she must get back, and at last was alone at the Hotel de Boulogne. Everything, even herself, was now unbearable to her. She wished that, taking wing like a bird, she could fly somewhere, far away to regions of purity, and there grow young again.

She went out, crossed the Boulevard, the Place Cauchoise, and the Faubourg, as far as an open street that overlooked some gardens. She walked rapidly; the fresh air calming her; and, little by little, the faces of the crowd, the masks, the quadrilles, the lights, the supper, those women, all disappeared like mists fading away. Then, reaching the "Croix-Rouge," she threw herself on the bed in her little room on the second floor, where there were pictures of the "Tour de Nesle." At four o'clock Hivert awoke her.

When she got home, Felicite showed her behind the clock a grey paper. She read:

"In virtue of the seizure in execution of a judgment."

What judgment? As a matter of fact, the evening before another paper had been brought that she had not yet seen, and she was stunned by these words:

"By order of the king, law, and justice, to Madame Bovary."

Les autres se mirent à manger. Elle ne mangea pas; elle avait le front en feu, des picotements aux paupières et un froid de glace à la peau. Elle sentait dans sa tête le plancher du bal, rebondissant encore sous la pulsation rythmique des mille pieds qui dansaient. Puis, l'odeur du punch avec la fumée des cigares l'étourdit. Elle s'évanouissait; on la porta devant la fenêtre.

Le jour commençait à se lever, et une grande tache de couleur pourpre s'élargissait dans le ciel pâle, du côté de Sainte- Catherine. La rivière livide frissonnait au vent; il n'y avait personne sur les ponts; les réverbères s'éteignaient.

Elle se ranima cependant, et vint à penser à Berthe, qui dormait là-bas, dans la chambre de sa bonne. Mais une charrette pleine de longs rubans de fer passa, en jetant contre le mur des maisons une vibration métallique assourdissante.

Elle s'esquiva brusquement, se débarrassa de son costume, dit à Léon qu'il lui fallait s'en retourner, et enfin resta seule à l'hôtel de Boulogne. Tout et elle-même lui étaient insupportables. Elle aurait voulu, s'échappant comme un oiseau, aller se rajeunir quelque part, bien loin, dans les espaces immaculés.

Elle sortit, elle traversa le boulevard, la place Cauchoise et le faubourg, jusqu'à une rue découverte qui dominait des jardins. Elle marchait vite, le grand air la calmait: et peu à peu les figures de la foule, les masques, les quadrilles, les lustres, le souper, ces femmes, tout disparaissait comme des brumes emportées. Puis, revenue à la Croix rouge, elle se jeta sur son lit, dans la petite chambre du second, où il y avait les images de la Tour de Nesle. À quatre heures du soir, Hivert la réveilla.

En rentrant chez elle, Félicité lui montra derrière la pendule un papier gris. Elle lut:

«En vertu de la grosse, en forme exécutoire d'un jugement...»

Quel jugement? La veille, en effet, on avait apporté un autre papier qu'elle ne connaissait pas; aussi fut-elle stupéfaite de ces mots:

«Commandement de par le roi, la loi et justice, à madame Bovary...»

Then, skipping several lines, she read:

"Within twenty-four hours, without fail—" But what? "To pay the sum of eight thousand francs." And there was even at the bottom, "She will be constrained thereto by every form of law, and notably by a writ of distraint on her furniture and effects."

What was to be done? In twenty-four hours—tomorrow. Lheureux, she thought, wanted to frighten her again; for she saw through all his devices, the object of his kindnesses. What reassured her was the very magnitude of the sum.

However, by dint of buying and not paying, of borrowing, signing bills, and renewing these bills that grew at each new falling-in, she had ended by preparing a capital for Monsieur Lheureux which he was impatiently awaiting for his speculations.

She presented herself at his place with an offhand air.

"You know what has happened to me? No doubt it's a joke!"

"No."

"How so?"

He turned away slowly, and, folding his arms, said to her:

"My good lady, did you think I should go on to all eternity being your purveyor and banker, for the love of God? Now be just. I must get back what I've laid out. Now be just."

She cried out against the debt.

"Ah! so much the worse. The court has admitted it. There's a judgment. It's been notified to you. Besides, it isn't my fault. It's Vincart's."

"Could you not—?"

"Oh, nothing whatever."

"But still, now talk it over."

And she began beating about the bush; she had known nothing about it; it was a surprise.

"Whose fault is that?" said Lheureux, bowing ironically. "While I'm slaving like a nigger, you go gallivanting about."

"Ah! no lecturing."

"It never does any harm," he replied.

Alors, sautant plusieurs lignes, elle aperçut:

«Dans vingt-quatre heures pour tout délai.» — Quoi donc?»Payer la somme totale de huit mille francs.» Et même il y avait plus bas: «Elle y sera contrainte par toute voie de droit, et notamment par la saisie exécutoire de ses meubles et effets.»

Que faire?… C'était dans vingt-quatre heures; demain! Lheureux, pensa-t-elle, voulait sans doute l'effrayer encore; car elle devina du coup toutes ses manoeuvres, le but de ses complaisances. Ce qui la rassurait, c'était l'exagération même de la somme.

Cependant, à force d'acheter, de ne pas payer, d'emprunter, de souscrire des billets, puis de renouveler ces billets, qui s'enflaient à chaque échéance nouvelle, elle avait fini par préparer au sieur Lheureux un capital, qu'il attendait impatiemment pour ses spéculations.

Elle se présenta chez lui d'un air dégagé.

— Vous savez ce qui m'arrive? C'est une plaisanterie sans doute!

— Non.

— Comment cela?

Il se détourna lentement, et lui dit en se croisant les bras:

— Pensiez-vous, ma petite dame, que j'allais, jusqu'à la consommation des siècles, être votre fournisseur et banquier pour l'amour de Dieu? Il faut bien que je rentre dans mes déboursés, soyons justes!

Elle se récria sur la dette.

— Ah! tant pis! le tribunal l'a reconnue! il y a jugement! on vous l'a signifié! D'ailleurs, ce n'est pas moi, c'est Vinçart.

— Est-ce que vous ne pourriez…?

— Oh! rien du tout.

— Mais…, cependant…, raisonnons.

Et elle battit la campagne; elle n'avait rien su… c'était une surprise…

— À qui la faute? dit Lheureux en la saluant ironiquement. Tandis que je suis, moi, à bûcher comme un nègre, vous vous repassez du bon temps.

— Ah! pas de morale!

— Ça ne nuit jamais, répliqua-t-il.

She turned coward; she implored him; she even pressed her pretty white and slender hand against the shopkeeper's knee.

"There, that'll do! Anyone'd think you wanted to seduce me!"

"You are a wretch!" she cried.

"Oh, oh! go it! go it!"

"I will show you up. I shall tell my husband."

"All right! I too. I'll show your husband something."

And Lheureux drew from his strong box the receipt for eighteen hundred francs that she had given him when Vincart had discounted the bills.

"Do you think," he added, "that he'll not understand your little theft, the poor dear man?"

She collapsed, more overcome than if felled by the blow of a pole-axe. He was walking up and down from the window to the bureau, repeating all the while:

"Ah! I'll show him! I'll show him!"

Then he approached her, and in a soft voice said:

"It isn't pleasant, I know; but, after all, no bones are broken, and, since that is the only way that is left for you paying back my money—"

"But where am I to get any?" said Emma, wringing her hands.

"Bah! when one has friends like you!"

And he looked at her in so keen, so terrible a fashion, that she shuddered to her very heart.

"I promise you," she said, "to sign—"

"I've enough of your signatures."

"I will sell something."

"Get along!" he said, shrugging his shoulders; "you've not got anything."

And he called through the peep-hole that looked down into the shop:

"Annette, don't forget the three coupons of No. 14."

The servant appeared. Emma understood, and asked how much money would be wanted to put a stop to the proceedings.

"It is too late."

"But if I brought you several thousand francs—a quarter of the sum—a third—perhaps the whole?"

Elle fut lâche, elle le supplia; et même elle appuya sa jolie main blanche et longue, sur les genoux du marchand.

— Laissez-moi donc! On dirait que vous voulez me séduire!

— Vous êtes un misérable! s'écria-t-elle.

— Oh! oh! comme vous y allez! reprit-il en riant.

— Je ferai savoir qui vous êtes. Je dirai à mon mari…

— Eh bien, moi, je lui montrerai quelque chose, à votre mari!

Et Lheureux tira de son coffre-fort le reçu de dix-huit cents francs, qu'elle lui avait donné lors de l'escompte Vinçart.

— Croyez-vous, ajouta-t-il, qu'il ne comprenne pas votre petit vol, ce pauvre cher homme?

Elle s'affaissa, plus assommée qu'elle n'eût été par un coup de massue. Il se promenait depuis la fenêtre jusqu'au bureau, tout en répétant:

— Ah! je lui montrerai bien… je lui montrerai bien…

Ensuite il se rapprocha d'elle, et, d'une voix douce:

— Ce n'est pas amusant, je le sais; personne, après tout n'en est mort, et, puisque c'est le seul moyen qui vous reste de me rendre mon argent…

— Mais où en trouverai-je? dit Emma en se tordant les bras.

— Ah bah! quand on a comme vous des amis!

Et il la regardait d'une façon si perspicace et si terrible, qu'elle en frissonna jusqu'aux entrailles.

— Je vous promets, dit-elle, je signerai…

— J'en ai assez, de vos signatures!

— Je vendrai encore…

— Allons donc! fit-il en haussant les épaules, vous n'avez plus rien.

Et il cria dans le judas qui s'ouvrait sur la boutique:

— Annette! n'oublie pas les trois coupons du n° 14.

La servante parut; Emma comprit, et demanda «ce qu'il faudrait d'argent pour arrêter toutes les poursuites».

— Il est trop tard!

— Mais, si je vous apportais plusieurs mille francs, le quart de la somme, le tiers, presque tout?

"No; it's no use!"

And he pushed her gently towards the staircase.

"I implore you, Monsieur Lheureux, just a few days more!"

She was sobbing.

"There! tears now!"

"You are driving me to despair!"

"What do I care?" said he, shutting the door.

— Eh! non, c'est inutile!

Il la poussait doucement vers l'escalier.

— Je vous en conjure, monsieur Lheureux, quelques jours encore!

Elle sanglotait.

— Allons, bon! des larmes!

— Vous me désespérez!

— Je m'en moque pas mal! dit-il en refermant la porte.

# Chapter 7

She was stoical the next day when Maitre Hareng, the bailiff, with two assistants, presented himself at her house to draw up the inventory for the distraint.

They began with Bovary's consulting-room, and did not write down the phrenological head, which was considered an "instrument of his profession"; but in the kitchen they counted the plates; the saucepans, the chairs, the candlesticks, and in the bedroom all the nick-nacks on the whatnot. They examined her dresses, the linen, the dressing-room; and her whole existence to its most intimate details, was, like a corpse on whom a post-mortem is made, outspread before the eyes of these three men.

Maitre Hareng, buttoned up in his thin black coat, wearing a white choker and very tight foot-straps, repeated from time to time:

"Allow me, madame. You allow me?"

Often he uttered exclamations:

"Charming! very pretty."

Then he began writing again, dipping his pen into the horn inkstand in his left hand.

When they had done with the rooms they went up to the attic.

She kept a desk there in which Rodolphe's letters were locked. It had to be opened.

"Ah! a correspondence," said Maitre Hareng, with a discreet smile. "But allow me, for I must make sure the box contains nothing else."

And he tipped up the papers lightly, as if to shake out napoleons. Then she grew angered to see this coarse hand, with fingers red and pulpy like slugs, touching these pages against which her heart had beaten.

They went at last. Felicite came back. Emma had sent her out to watch for Bovary in order to keep him off, and they hurriedly installed the man in possession under the roof, where he swore he would remain.

# Chapitre 7

Elle fut stoïque, le lendemain, lorsque maître Hareng, l'huissier, avec deux témoins, se présenta chez elle pour faire le procès- verbal de la saisie.

Ils commencèrent par le cabinet de Bovary et n'inscrivirent point la tête phrénologique, qui fut considérée comme instrument de sa profession; mais ils comptèrent dans la cuisine les plats, les marmites, les chaises, les flambeaux, et, dans sa chambre à coucher, toutes les babioles de l'étagère. Ils examinèrent ses robes, le linge, le cabinet de toilette; et son existence, jusque dans ses recoins les plus intimes, fut, comme un cadavre que l'on autopsie, étalée tout du long aux regards de ces trois hommes.

Maître Hareng, boutonné dans un mince habit noir, en cravate blanche, et portant des sous-pieds fort tendus, répétait de temps à autre:

— Vous permettez; madame? vous permettez?

Souvent il faisait des exclamations:

— Charmant!... fort joli!

Puis il se remettait à écrire, trempant sa plume dans l'encrier de corne qu'il tenait de la main gauche.

Quand ils en eurent fini avec les appartements, ils montèrent au grenier.

Elle y gardait un pupitre où étaient enfermées les lettres de Rodolphe. Il fallut l'ouvrir.

— Ah! une correspondance! dit maître Hareng avec un sourire discret. Mais permettez! car je dois m'assurer si la boîte ne contient pas autre chose.

Et il inclina les papiers, légèrement, comme pour en faire tomber des napoléons. Alors l'indignation la prit, à voir cette grosse main, aux doigts rouges et mous comme des limaces, qui se posait sur ces pages où son coeur avait battu.

Ils partirent enfin! Félicité rentra. Elle l'avait envoyée aux aguets pour détourner Bovary; et elles installèrent vivement sous les toits le gardien de la saisie, qui jura de s'y tenir.

During the evening Charles seemed to her careworn. Emma watched him with a look of anguish, fancying she saw an accusation in every line of his face. Then, when her eyes wandered over the chimney-piece ornamented with Chinese screens, over the large curtains, the armchairs, all those things, in a word, that had, softened the bitterness of her life, remorse seized her or rather an immense regret, that, far from crushing, irritated her passion. Charles placidly poked the fire, both his feet on the fire-dogs.

Once the man, no doubt bored in his hiding-place, made a slight noise.

"Is anyone walking upstairs?" said Charles.

"No," she replied; "it is a window that has been left open, and is rattling in the wind."

The next day, Sunday, she went to Rouen to call on all the brokers whose names she knew. They were at their country-places or on journeys. She was not discouraged; and those whom she did manage to see she asked for money, declaring she must have some, and that she would pay it back. Some laughed in her face; all refused.

At two o'clock she hurried to Leon, and knocked at the door. No one answered. At length he appeared.

"What brings you here?"

"Do I disturb you?"

"No; but—"

And he admitted that his landlord didn't like his having "women" there.

"I must speak to you," she went on.

Then he took down the key, but she stopped him.

"No, no! Down there, in our home!"

And they went to their room at the Hotel de Boulogne.

On arriving she drank off a large glass of water. She was very pale. She said to him:

"Leon, you will do me a service?"

And, shaking him by both hands that she grasped tightly, she added:

Charles, pendant la soirée, lui parut soucieux. Emma l'épiait d'un regard plein d'angoisse, croyant apercevoir dans les rides de son visage des accusations. Puis, quand ses yeux se reportaient sur la cheminée garnie d'écrans chinois, sur les larges rideaux, sur les fauteuils, sur toutes ces choses enfin qui avaient adouci l'amertume de sa vie, un remords la prenait, ou plutôt un regret immense et qui irritait la passion, loin de l'anéantir. Charles tisonnait avec placidité, les deux pieds sur les chenets.

Il y eut un moment où le gardien, sans doute s'ennuyant dans sa cachette, fit un peu de bruit.

— On marche là-haut? dit Charles.

— Non! reprit-elle, c'est une lucarne restée ouverte que le vent remue.

Elle partit pour Rouen, le lendemain dimanche, afin d'aller chez tous les banquiers dont elle connaissait le nom. Ils étaient à la campagne ou en voyage. Elle ne se rebuta pas; et ceux qu'elle put rencontrer, elle leur demandait de l'argent, protestant qu'il lui en fallait, qu'elle le rendrait. Quelques-uns lui rirent au nez; tous la refusèrent.

À deux heures, elle courut chez Léon, frappa contre sa porte. On n'ouvrit pas. Enfin il parut.

— Qui t'amène?

— Cela te dérange?

— Non..., mais...

Et il avoua que le propriétaire n'aimait point que l'on reçût «des femmes».

— J'ai à te parler, reprit-elle.

Alors il atteignit sa clef. Elle l'arrêta.

— Oh! non, là-bas, chez nous.

Et ils allèrent dans leur chambre, à l'hôtel de Boulogne.

Elle but en arrivant un grand verre d'eau. Elle était très pâle. Elle lui dit:

— Léon, tu vas me rendre un service.

Et, le secouant par ses deux mains, qu'elle serrait étroitement, elle ajouta:

"Listen, I want eight thousand francs."

"But you are mad!"

"Not yet."

And thereupon, telling him the story of the distraint, she explained her distress to him; for Charles knew nothing of it; her mother-in-law detested her; old Rouault could do nothing; but he, Leon, he would set about finding this indispensable sum.

"How on earth can I?"

"What a coward you are!" she cried.

Then he said stupidly:

"You are exaggerating the difficulty. Perhaps, with a thousand crowns or so the fellow could be stopped."

All the greater reason to try and do something; it was impossible that they could not find three thousand francs. Besides, Leon, could be security instead of her.

"Go, try, try! I will love you so!"

He went out, and came back at the end of an hour, saying, with solemn face:

"I have been to three people with no success."

Then they remained sitting face to face at the two chimney corners, motionless, in silence. Emma shrugged her shoulders as she stamped her feet. He heard her murmuring:

"If I were in your place I should soon get some."

"But where?"

"At your office."

And she looked at him.

An infernal boldness looked out from her burning eyes, and their lids drew close together with a lascivious and encouraging look, so that the young man felt himself growing weak beneath the mute will of this woman who was urging him to a crime. Then he was afraid, and to avoid any explanation he smote his forehead, crying:

"Morel is to come back to-night; he will not refuse me, I hope" (this was one of his friends, the son of a very rich merchant); "and I will bring it you to-morrow," he added.

— Écoute, j'ai besoin de huit mille francs!

— Mais tu es folle!

— Pas encore!

Et, aussitôt, racontant l'histoire de la saisie, elle lui exposa sa détresse; car Charles ignorait tout, sa belle-mère la détestait, le père Rouault ne pouvait rien; mais lui, Léon, il allait se mettre en course pour trouver cette indispensable somme...

— Comment veux-tu...?

— Quel lâche tu fais! s'écria-t-elle.

Alors il dit bêtement:

— Tu t'exagères le mal. Peut-être qu'avec un millier d'écus ton bonhomme se calmerait.

Raison de plus pour tenter quelque démarche; il n'était pas possible que l'on ne découvrît point trois mille francs. D'ailleurs, Léon pouvait s'engager à sa place.

— Va! essaye! il le faut! cours!... Oh! tâche! tâche! je t'aimerai bien!

Il sortit, revint au bout d'une heure, et dit avec une figure solennelle:

— J'ai été chez trois personnes... inutilement!

Puis ils restèrent assis l'un en face de l'autre, aux deux coins de la cheminée, immobiles, sans parler. Emma haussait les épaules, tout en trépignant. Il l'entendit qui murmurait:

— Si j'étais à ta place, moi, j'en trouverais bien!

— Où donc?

— À ton étude!

Et elle le regarda.

Une hardiesse infernale s'échappait de ses prunelles enflammées, et les paupières se rapprochaient d'une façon lascive et encourageante; — si bien que le jeune homme se sentit faiblir sous la muette volonté de cette femme qui lui conseillait un crime. Alors il eut peur, et pour éviter tout éclaircissement, il se frappa le front en s'écriant:

— Morel doit revenir cette nuit! il ne me refusera pas, j'espère (c'était un de ses amis, le fils d'un négociant fort riche), et je t'apporterai cela demain, ajouta-t-il.

Emma did not seem to welcome this hope with all the joy he had expected. Did she suspect the lie? He went on, blushing—

"However, if you don't see me by three o'clock do not wait for me, my darling. I must be off now; forgive me! Goodbye!"

He pressed her hand, but it felt quite lifeless. Emma had no strength left for any sentiment.

Four o'clock struck, and she rose to return to Yonville, mechanically obeying the force of old habits.

The weather was fine. It was one of those March days, clear and sharp, when the sun shines in a perfectly white sky. The Rouen folk, in Sunday-clothes, were walking about with happy looks. She reached the Place du Parvis. People were coming out after vespers; the crowd flowed out through the three doors like a stream through the three arches of a bridge, and in the middle one, more motionless than a rock, stood the beadle.

Then she remembered the day when, all anxious and full of hope, she had entered beneath this large nave, that had opened out before her, less profound than her love; and she walked on weeping beneath her veil, giddy, staggering, almost fainting.

"Take care!" cried a voice issuing from the gate of a courtyard that was thrown open.

She stopped to let pass a black horse, pawing the ground between the shafts of a tilbury, driven by a gentleman in sable furs. Who was it? She knew him. The carriage darted by and disappeared.

Why, it was he—the Viscount. She turned away; the street was empty. She was so overwhelmed, so sad, that she had to lean against a wall to keep herself from falling.

Then she thought she had been mistaken. Anyhow, she did not know. All within her and around her was abandoning her. She felt lost, sinking at random into indefinable abysses, and it was almost with joy that, on reaching the "Croix-Rouge," she saw the good Homais, who was watching a large box full of pharmaceutical stores being hoisted on to the "Hirondelle." In his hand he held tied in a silk handkerchief six cheminots for his wife.

Emma n'eut point l'air d'accueillir cet espoir avec autant de joie qu'il l'avait imaginé. Soupçonnait-elle le mensonge? Il reprit en rougissant:

— Pourtant, si tu ne me voyais pas à trois heures, ne m'attends plus, ma chérie. Il faut que je m'en aille, excuse-moi. Adieu!

Il serra sa main, mais il la sentit tout inerte. Emma n'avait plus la force d'aucun sentiment.

Quatre heures sonnèrent; et elle se leva pour s'en retourner à Yonville, obéissant comme un automate à l'impulsion des habitudes.

Il faisait beau; c'était un de ces jours du mois de mars clairs et âpres, où le soleil reluit dans un ciel tout blanc. Des Rouennais endimanchés se promenaient d'un air heureux. Elle arriva sur la place du Parvis. On sortait des vêpres; la foule s'écoulait par les trois portails, comme un fleuve par les trois arches d'un pont, et, au milieu, plus immobile qu'un roc, se tenait le suisse.

Alors elle se rappela ce jour où, tout anxieuse et pleine d'espérances, elle était entrée sous cette grande nef qui s'étendait devant elle moins profonde que son amour; et elle continua de marcher, en pleurant sous son voile, étourdie, chancelante, près de défaillir.

— Gare! cria une voix sortant d'une porte cochère qui s'ouvrait.

Elle s'arrêta pour laisser passer un cheval noir, piaffant dans les brancards d'un tilbury que conduisait un gentleman en fourrure de zibeline. Qui était-ce donc? Elle le connaissait… La voiture s'élança et disparut.

Mais c'était lui, le Vicomte! Elle se détourna: la rue était déserte. Et elle fut si accablée, si triste, qu'elle s'appuya contre un mur pour ne pas tomber.

Puis elle pensa qu'elle s'était trompée. Au reste, elle n'en savait rien. Tout, en elle-même et au dehors, l'abandonnait. Elle se sentait perdue, roulant au hasard dans des abîmes indéfinissables; et ce fut presque avec joie qu'elle aperçut, en arrivant à la Croix rouge, ce bon Homais qui regardait charger sur l'Hirondelle une grande boîte pleine de provisions pharmaceutiques. Il tenait à sa main, dans un foulard, six cheminots pour son épouse.

Madame Homais was very fond of these small, heavy turban-shaped loaves, that are eaten in Lent with salt butter; a last vestige of Gothic food that goes back, perhaps, to the time of the Crusades, and with which the robust Normans gorged themselves of yore, fancying they saw on the table, in the light of the yellow torches, between tankards of hippocras and huge boars' heads, the heads of Saracens to be devoured. The druggist's wife crunched them up as they had done—heroically, despite her wretched teeth. And so whenever Homais journeyed to town, he never failed to bring her home some that he bought at the great baker's in the Rue Massacre.

"Charmed to see you," he said, offering Emma a hand to help her into the "Hirondelle."

Then he hung up his cheminots to the cords of the netting, and remained bare-headed in an attitude pensive and Napoleonic.

But when the blind man appeared as usual at the foot of the hill he exclaimed:

"I can't understand why the authorities tolerate such culpable industries. Such unfortunates should be locked up and forced to work. Progress, my word! creeps at a snail's pace. We are floundering about in mere barbarism."

The blind man held out his hat, that flapped about at the door, as if it were a bag in the lining that had come unnailed.

"This," said the chemist, "is a scrofulous affection."

And though he knew the poor devil, he pretended to see him for the first time, murmured something about "cornea," "opaque cornea," "sclerotic," "facies," then asked him in a paternal tone:

"My friend, have you long had this terrible infirmity? Instead of getting drunk at the public, you'd do better to die yourself."

He advised him to take good wine, good beer, and good joints. The blind man went on with his song; he seemed, moreover, almost idiotic. At last Monsieur Homais opened his purse.

"Now there's a sou; give me back two lairds, and don't forget my advice: you'll be the better for it."

Hivert openly cast some doubt on the efficacy of it. But the druggist

Madame Homais aimait beaucoup ces petits pains lourds, en forme de turban, que l'on mange dans le carême avec du beurre salé: dernier échantillon des nourritures gothiques, qui remonte peut-être au siècle des croisades, et dont les robustes Normands s'emplissaient autrefois, croyant voir sur la table, à la lueur des torches jaunes, entre les brocs d'hypocras et les gigantesques charcuteries, des têtes de Sarrasins à dévorer. La femme de l'apothicaire les croquait comme eux, héroïquement, malgré sa détestable dentition; aussi, toutes les fois que M. Homais faisait un voyage à la ville, il ne manquait pas de lui en rapporter, qu'il prenait toujours chez le grand faiseur, rue Massacre.

— Charmé de vous voir! dit-il en offrant la main à Emma pour l'aider à monter dans l'Hirondelle.

Puis il suspendit les cheminots aux lanières du filet, et resta nu-tête et les bras croisés, dans une attitude pensive et napoléonienne.

Mais, quand l'Aveugle, comme d'habitude, apparut au bas de la côte, il s'écria:

— Je ne comprends pas que l'autorité tolère encore de si coupables industries! On devrait enfermer ces malheureux, que l'on forcerait à quelque travail! Le Progrès, ma parole d'honneur, marche à pas de tortue! nous pataugeons en pleine barbarie!

L'Aveugle tendait son chapeau, qui ballottait au bord de la portière, comme une poche de la tapisserie déclouée.

— Voilà, dit le pharmacien, une affection scrofuleuse!

Et, bien qu'il connût ce pauvre diable, il feignit de le voir pour la première fois, murmura les mots de cornée, cornée opaque, sclérotique, faciès, puis lui demanda d'un ton paterne:

— Y a-t-il longtemps, mon ami, que tu as cette épouvantable infirmité? Au lieu de t'enivrer au cabaret, tu ferais mieux de suivre un régime.

Il l'engageait à prendre de bon vin, de bonne bière, de bons rôtis. L'Aveugle continuait sa chanson; il paraissait, d'ailleurs, presque idiot. Enfin, M. Homais ouvrit sa bourse.

— Tiens, voilà un sou, rends-moi deux liards; et n'oublie pas mes recommandations, tu t'en trouveras bien.

Hivert se permit tout haut quelque doute sur leur efficacité. Mais

said that he would cure himself with an antiphlogistic pomade of his own composition, and he gave his address:

"Monsieur Homais, near the market, pretty well known."

"Now," said Hivert, "for all this trouble you'll give us your performance."

The blind man sank down on his haunches, with his head thrown back, whilst he rolled his greenish eyes, lolled out his tongue, and rubbed his stomach with both hands as he uttered a kind of hollow yell like a famished dog. Emma, filled with disgust, threw him over her shoulder a five-franc piece. It was all her fortune. It seemed to her very fine thus to throw it away.

The coach had gone on again when suddenly Monsieur Homais leant out through the window, crying:

"No farinaceous or milk food, wear wool next the skin, and expose the diseased parts to the smoke of juniper berries."

The sight of the well-known objects that defiled before her eyes gradually diverted Emma from her present trouble. An intolerable fatigue overwhelmed her, and she reached her home stupefied, discouraged, almost asleep.

"Come what may come!" she said to herself.

"And then, who knows? Why, at any moment could not some extraordinary event occur? Lheureux even might die!"

At nine o'clock in the morning she was awakened by the sound of voices in the Place. There was a crowd round the market reading a large bill fixed to one of the posts, and she saw Justin, who was climbing on to a stone and tearing down the bill. But at this moment the rural guard seized him by the collar. Monsieur Homais came out of his shop, and Mere Lefrangois, in the midst of the crowd, seemed to be perorating.

"Madame! madame!" cried Felicite, running in, "it's abominable!"

And the poor girl, deeply moved, handed her a yellow paper that she had just torn off the door. Emma read with a glance that all her furniture was for sale.

Then they looked at one another silently. The servant and mistress had no secret one from the other. At last Felicite sighed:

l'apothicaire certifia qu'il le guérirait lui-même, avec une pommade antiphlogistique de sa composition, et il donna son adresse:

— M. Homais, près des halles, suffisamment connu.

— Eh bien, pour la peine, dit Hivert, tu vas nous montrer la comédie.

L'Aveugle s'affaissa sur ses jarrets, et, la tête renversée, tout en roulant ses yeux verdâtres et tirant la langue, il se frottait l'estomac à deux mains, tandis qu'il poussait une sorte de hurlement sourd, comme un chien affamé. Emma, prise de dégoût, lui envoya, par-dessus l'épaule, une pièce de cinq francs. C'était toute sa fortune. Il lui semblait beau de la jeter ainsi.

La voiture était repartie, quand soudain M. Homais se pencha en dehors du vasistas et cria:

— Pas de farineux ni de laitage! Porter de la laine sur la peau et exposer les parties malades à la fumée de baies de genièvre!

Le spectacle des objets connus qui défilaient devant ses yeux peu à peu détournait Emma de sa douleur présente. Une intolérable fatigue l'accablait, et elle arriva chez elle hébétée, découragée, presque endormie.

— Advienne que pourra! se disait-elle.

Et puis, qui sait? pourquoi, d'un moment à l'autre, ne surgirait- il pas un événement extraordinaire? Lheureux même pouvait mourir.

Elle fut, à neuf heures du matin, réveillée par un bruit de voix sur la place. Il y avait un attroupement autour des halles pour lire une grande affiche collée contre un des poteaux, et elle vit Justin qui montait sur une borne et qui déchirait l'affiche. Mais, à ce moment, le garde champêtre lui posa la main sur le collet. M. Homais sortit de la pharmacie, et la mère Lefrançois, au milieu de la foule, avait l'air de pérorer.

— Madame! madame! s'écria Félicité en entrant, c'est une abomination!

Et la pauvre fille, émue, lui tendit un papier jaune qu'elle venait d'arracher à la porte. Emma lut d'un clin d'oeil que tout son mobilier était à vendre.

Alors elles se considérèrent silencieusement. Elles n'avaient, la servante et la maîtresse, aucun secret l'une pour l'autre. Enfin Félicité soupira:

"If I were you, madame, I should go to Monsieur Guillaumin."

"Do you think—"

And this question meant to say:

"You who know the house through the servant, has the master spoken sometimes of me?"

"Yes, you'd do well to go there."

She dressed, put on her black gown, and her hood with jet beads, and that she might not be seen (there was still a crowd on the Place), she took the path by the river, outside the village.

She reached the notary's gate quite breathless. The sky was sombre, and a little snow was falling.

At the sound of the bell, Theodore in a red waistcoat appeared on the steps; he came to open the door almost familiarly, as to an acquaintance, and showed her into the dining-room.

A large porcelain stove crackled beneath a cactus that filled up the niche in the wall, and in black wood frames against the oak-stained paper hung Steuben's "Esmeralda" and Schopin's "Potiphar." The ready-laid table, the two silver chafing-dishes, the crystal door-knobs, the parquet and the furniture, all shone with a scrupulous, English cleanliness; the windows were ornamented at each corner with stained glass.

"Now this," thought Emma, "is the dining-room I ought to have."

The notary came in pressing his palm-leaf dressing-gown to his breast with his left arm, while with the other hand he raised and quickly put on again his brown velvet cap, pretentiously cocked on the right side, whence looked out the ends of three fair curls drawn from the back of the head, following the line of his bald skull.

After he had offered her a seat he sat down to breakfast, apologising profusely for his rudeness.

"I have come," she said, "to beg you, sir—"

"What, madame? I am listening."

And she began explaining her position to him.

Monsieur Guillaumin knew it, being secretly associated with the linendraper, from whom he always got capital for the loans on mortgages that he was asked to make.

— Si j'étais de vous, madame, j'irais chez M. Guillaumin.

— Tu crois?...

Et cette interrogation voulait dire:

— Toi qui connais la maison par le domestique, est-ce que le maître quelquefois aurait parlé de moi?

— Oui, allez-y, vous ferez bien.

Elle s'habilla, mit sa robe noire avec sa capote à grains de jais; et, pour qu'on ne la vît pas (il y avait toujours beaucoup de monde sur la place), elle prit en dehors du village, par le sentier au bord de l'eau.

Elle arriva tout essoufflée devant la grille du notaire; le ciel était sombre et un peu de neige tombait.

Au bruit de la sonnette, Théodore, en gilet rouge, parut sur le perron; il vint lui ouvrir presque familièrement, comme à une connaissance, et l'introduisit dans la salle à manger.

Un large poêle de porcelaine bourdonnait sous un cactus qui emplissait la niche, et, dans des cadres de bois noir, contre la tenture de papier chêne, il y avait la Esméralda de Steuben, avec la Putiphar de Schopin. La table servie, deux réchauds d'argent, le bouton des portes en cristal, le parquet et les meubles, tout reluisait d'une propreté méticuleuse, anglaise; les carreaux étaient décorés, à chaque angle, par des verres de couleur.

— Voilà une salle à manger, pensait Emma, comme il m'en faudrait une.

Le notaire entra, serrant du bras gauche contre son corps sa robe de chambre à palmes, tandis qu'il ôtait et remettait vite de l'autre main sa toque de velours marron, prétentieusement posée sur le côté droit, où retombaient les bouts de trois mèches blondes qui, prises à l'occiput, contournaient son crâne chauve.

Après qu'il eut offert un siège, il s'assit pour déjeuner, tout en s'excusant beaucoup de l'impolitesse.

— Monsieur, dit-elle, je vous prierais...

— De quoi, madame? J'écoute.

Elle se mit à lui exposer sa situation.

Maître Guillaumin la connaissait, étant lié secrètement avec le marchand d'étoffes, chez lequel il trouvait toujours des capitaux pour les prêts hypothécaires qu'on lui demandait à contracter.

So he knew (and better than she herself) the long story of the bills, small at first, bearing different names as endorsers, made out at long dates, and constantly renewed up to the day, when, gathering together all the protested bills, the shopkeeper had bidden his friend Vincart take in his own name all the necessary proceedings, not wishing to pass for a tiger with his fellow-citizens.

She mingled her story with recriminations against Lheureux, to which the notary replied from time to time with some insignificant word. Eating his cutlet and drinking his tea, he buried his chin in his sky-blue cravat, into which were thrust two diamond pins, held together by a small gold chain; and he smiled a singular smile, in a sugary, ambiguous fashion. But noticing that her feet were damp, he said:

"Do get closer to the stove; put your feet up against the porcelain."

She was afraid of dirtying it. The notary replied in a gallant tone:

"Beautiful things spoil nothing."

Then she tried to move him, and, growing moved herself, she began telling him about the poorness of her home, her worries, her wants. He could understand that; an elegant woman! and, without leaving off eating, he had turned completely round towards her, so that his knee brushed against her boot, whose sole curled round as it smoked against the stove.

But when she asked for a thousand sous, he closed his lips, and declared he was very sorry he had not had the management of her fortune before, for there were hundreds of ways very convenient, even for a lady, of turning her money to account. They might, either in the turf-peats of Grumesnil or building-ground at Havre, almost without risk, have ventured on some excellent speculations; and he let her consume herself with rage at the thought of the fabulous sums that she would certainly have made.

"How was it," he went on, "that you didn't come to me?"

"I hardly know," she said.

"Why, hey? Did I frighten you so much? It is I, on the contrary, who ought to complain. We hardly know one another; yet I am very devoted to you. You do not doubt that, I hope?"

Donc, il savait (et mieux qu'elle) la longue histoire de ces billets, minimes d'abord, portant comme endosseurs des noms divers, espacés à de longues échéances et renouvelés continuellement, jusqu'au jour où, ramassant tous les protêts, le marchand avait chargé son ami Vinçart de faire en son nom propre les poursuites qu'il fallait, ne voulant point passer pour un tigre parmi ses concitoyens.

Elle entremêla son récit de récriminations contre Lheureux, récriminations auxquelles le notaire répondait de temps à autre par une parole insignifiante. Mangeant sa côtelette et buvant son thé, il baissait le menton dans sa cravate bleu de ciel, piquée par deux épingles de diamants que rattachait une chaînette d'or; et il souriait d'un singulier sourire, d'une façon douceâtre et ambiguë. Mais, s'apercevant qu'elle avait les pieds humides:

— Approchez-vous donc du poêle... plus haut..., contre la porcelaine.

Elle avait peur de la salir. Le notaire reprit d'un ton galant:

— Les belles choses ne gâtent rien.

Alors elle tâcha de l'émouvoir, et, s'émotionnant elle-même, elle vint à lui conter l'étroitesse de son ménage, ses tiraillements, ses besoins. Il comprenait cela: une femme élégante! et, sans s'interrompre de manger, il s'était tourné vers elle complètement, si bien qu'il frôlait du genou sa bottine, dont la semelle se recourbait tout en fumant contre le poêle.

Mais, lorsqu'elle lui demanda mille écus, il serra les lèvres, puis se déclara très peiné de n'avoir pas eu autrefois la direction de sa fortune, car il y avait cent moyens fort commodes, même pour une dame, de faire valoir son argent. On aurait pu, soit dans les tourbières de Grumesnil ou les terrains du Havre, hasarder presque à coup sûr d'excellentes spéculations; et il la laissa se dévorer de rage à l'idée des sommes fantastiques qu'elle aurait certainement gagnées.

— D'où vient, reprit-il, que vous n'êtes pas venue chez moi?

— Je ne sais trop, dit-elle.

— Pourquoi, hein?... Je vous faisais donc bien peur? C'est moi, au contraire, qui devrais me plaindre! À peine si nous nous connaissons! Je vous suis pourtant très dévoué; vous n'en doutez plus, j'espère?

He held out his hand, took hers, covered it with a greedy kiss, then held it on his knee; and he played delicately with her fingers whilst he murmured a thousand blandishments.

His insipid voice murmured like a running brook; a light shone in his eyes through the glimmering of his spectacles, and his hand was advancing up Emma's sleeve to press her arm. She felt against her cheek his panting breath. This man oppressed her horribly.

She sprang up and said to him:

"Sir, I am waiting."

"For what?" said the notary, who suddenly became very pale.

"This money."

"But—"

Then, yielding to the outburst of too powerful a desire:

"Well, yes!"

He dragged himself towards her on his knees, regardless of his dressing-gown.

"For pity's sake, stay. I love you!"

He seized her by her waist.

Madame Bovary's face flushed purple. She recoiled with a terrible look, crying:

"You are taking a shameless advantage of my distress, sir! I am to be pitied—not to be sold."

And she went out.

The notary remained quite stupefied, his eyes fixed on his fine embroidered slippers. They were a love gift, and the sight of them at last consoled him. Besides, he reflected that such an adventure might have carried him too far.

"What a wretch! what a scoundrel! what an infamy!" she said to herself, as she fled with nervous steps beneath the aspens of the path. The disappointment of her failure increased the indignation of her outraged modesty; it seemed to her that Providence pursued her implacably, and, strengthening herself in her pride, she had never felt so much esteem for herself nor so much contempt for others. A spirit of warfare trans-

Il tendit sa main, prit la sienne, la couvrit d'un baiser vorace, puis la garda sur son genou; et il jouait avec ses doigts délicatement, tout en lui contant mille douceurs.

Sa voix fade susurrait, comme un ruisseau qui coule; une étincelle jaillissait de sa pupille à travers le miroitement de ses lunettes, et ses mains s'avançaient dans la manche d'Emma, pour lui palper le bras. Elle sentait contre sa joue le souffle d'une respiration haletante. Cet homme la gênait horriblement.

Elle se leva d'un bond et lui dit:

— Monsieur, j'attends!

— Quoi donc? fit le notaire, qui devint tout à coup extrêmement pâle.

— Cet argent.

— Mais...

Puis, cédant à l'irruption d'un désir trop fort:

— Eh bien, oui!...

Il se traînait à genoux vers elle, sans égard pour sa robe de chambre.

— De grâce, restez! je vous aime!

Il la saisit par la taille.

Un flot de pourpre monta vite au visage de madame Bovary. Elle se recula d'un air terrible, en s'écriant:

— Vous profitez impudemment de ma détresse, monsieur! Je suis à plaindre, mais pas à vendre!

Et elle sortit.

Le notaire resta fort stupéfait, les yeux fixés sur ses belles pantoufles en tapisserie. C'était un présent de l'amour. Cette vue à la fin le consola. D'ailleurs, il songeait qu'une aventure pareille l'aurait entraîné trop loin.

— Quel misérable! quel goujat!... quelle infamie! se disait-elle, en fuyant d'un pied nerveux sous les trembles de la route. Le désappointement de l'insuccès renforçait l'indignation de sa pudeur outragée; il lui semblait que la Providence s'acharnait à la poursuivre, et, s'en rehaussant d'orgueil, jamais elle n'avait eu tant d'estime pour elle-même ni tant de mépris pour les autres. Quelque chose de belliqueux la transportait. Elle

formed her. She would have liked to strike all men, to spit in their faces, to crush them, and she walked rapidly straight on, pale, quivering, maddened, searching the empty horizon with tear-dimmed eyes, and as it were rejoicing in the hate that was choking her.

When she saw her house a numbness came over her. She could not go on; and yet she must. Besides, whither could she flee?

Felicite was waiting for her at the door.

"Well?"

"No!" said Emma.

And for a quarter of an hour the two of them went over the various persons in Yonville who might perhaps be inclined to help her. But each time that Felicite named someone Emma replied:

"Impossible! they will not!"

"And the master'll soon be in."

"I know that well enough. Leave me alone."

She had tried everything; there was nothing more to be done now; and when Charles came in she would have to say to him:

"Go away! This carpet on which you are walking is no longer ours. In your own house you do not possess a chair, a pin, a straw, and it is I, poor man, who have ruined you."

Then there would be a great sob; next he would weep abundantly, and at last, the surprise past, he would forgive her.

"Yes," she murmured, grinding her teeth, "he will forgive me, he who would give a million if I would forgive him for having known me! Never! never!"

This thought of Bovary's superiority to her exasperated her. Then, whether she confessed or did not confess, presently, immediately, to-morrow, he would know the catastrophe all the same; so she must wait for this horrible scene, and bear the weight of his magnanimity. The desire to return to Lheureux's seized her—what would be the use? To write to her father—it was too late; and perhaps, she began to repent now that she had not yielded to that other, when she heard the trot of a horse in the alley. It was he; he was opening the gate; he was whiter than the plaster wall. Rushing to the stairs, she ran out quickly to the square;

aurait voulu battre les hommes, leur cracher au visage, les broyer tous; et elle continuait à marcher rapidement devant elle, pâle, frémissante, enragée, furetant d'un oeil en pleurs l'horizon vide, et comme se délectant à la haine qui l'étouffait.

Quand elle aperçut sa maison, un engourdissement la saisit. Elle ne pouvait avancer; il le fallait cependant; d'ailleurs, où fuir?

Félicité l'attendait sur la porte.

— Eh bien?

— Non! dit Emma.

Et, pendant un quart d'heure, toutes les deux, elles avisèrent les différentes personnes d'Yonville disposées peut-être à la secourir. Mais, chaque fois que Félicité nommait quelqu'un, Emma répliquait:

— Est-ce possible! Ils ne voudront pas!

— Et monsieur qui va rentrer!

— Je le sais bien... Laisse-moi seule.

Elle avait tout tenté. Il n'y avait plus rien à faire maintenant; et, quand Charles paraîtrait, elle allait donc lui dire:

— Retire-toi. Ce tapis où tu marches n'est plus à nous. De ta maison, tu n'as pas un meuble, une épingle, une paille, et c'est moi qui t'ai ruiné, pauvre homme!

Alors ce serait un grand sanglot, puis il pleurerait abondamment, et enfin, la surprise passée, il pardonnerait.

— Oui, murmurait-elle en grinçant des dents, il me pardonnera, lui qui n'aurait pas assez d'un million à m'offrir pour que je l'excuse de m'avoir connue... Jamais! jamais!

Cette idée de la supériorité de Bovary sur elle l'exaspérait. Puis, qu'elle avouât ou n'avouât pas, tout à l'heure, tantôt, demain, il n'en saurait pas moins la catastrophe; donc, il fallait attendre cette horrible scène et subir le poids de sa magnanimité. L'envie lui vint de retourner chez Lheureux: à quoi bon? d'écrire à son père; il était trop tard; et peut-être qu'elle se repentait maintenant de n'avoir pas cédé à l'autre, lorsqu'elle entendit le trot d'un cheval dans l'allée. C'était lui, il ouvrait la barrière, il était plus blême que le mur de plâtre. Bondissant dans l'escalier, elle s'échappa vivement par la place; et la femme du maire,

and the wife of the mayor, who was talking to Lestiboudois in front of the church, saw her go in to the tax-collector's.

She hurried off to tell Madame Caron, and the two ladies went up to the attic, and, hidden by some linen spread across props, stationed themselves comfortably for overlooking the whole of Binet's room.

He was alone in his garret, busy imitating in wood one of those indescribable bits of ivory, composed of crescents, of spheres hollowed out one within the other, the whole as straight as an obelisk, and of no use whatever; and he was beginning on the last piece—he was nearing his goal. In the twilight of the workshop the white dust was flying from his tools like a shower of sparks under the hoofs of a galloping horse; the two wheels were turning, droning; Binet smiled, his chin lowered, his nostrils distended, and, in a word, seemed lost in one of those complete happinesses that, no doubt, belong only to commonplace occupations, which amuse the mind with facile difficulties, and satisfy by a realisation of that beyond which such minds have not a dream.

"Ah! there she is!" exclaimed Madame Tuvache.

But it was impossible because of the lathe to hear what she was saying.

At last these ladies thought they made out the word "francs," and Madame Tuvache whispered in a low voice:

"She is begging him to give her time for paying her taxes."

"Apparently!" replied the other.

They saw her walking up and down, examining the napkin-rings, the candlesticks, the banister rails against the walls, while Binet stroked his beard with satisfaction.

"Do you think she wants to order something of him?" said Madame Tuvache.

"Why, he doesn't sell anything," objected her neighbour.

The tax-collector seemed to be listening with wide-open eyes, as if he did not understand. She went on in a tender, suppliant manner. She came nearer to him, her breast heaving; they no longer spoke.

"Is she making him advances?" said Madame Tuvache.

Binet was scarlet to his very ears. She took hold of his hands.

qui causait devant l'église avec Lestiboudois, la vit entrer chez le percepteur.

Elle courut le dire à madame Caron. Ces deux dames montèrent dans le grenier; et cachées par du linge étendu sur des perches, se postèrent commodément pour apercevoir tout l'intérieur de Binet.

Il était seul, dans sa mansarde, en train d'imiter, avec du bois, une de ces ivoireries indescriptibles, composées de croissants, de sphères creusées les unes dans les autres, le tout droit comme un obélisque et ne servant à rien; et il entamait la dernière pièce, il touchait au but! Dans le clair-obscur de l'atelier, la poussière blonde s'envolait de son outil, comme une aigrette d'étincelles sous les fers d'un cheval au galop; les deux roues tournaient, ronflaient; Binet souriait, le menton baissé, les narines ouvertes, et semblait enfin perdu dans un de ces bonheurs complets, n'appartenant sans doute qu'aux occupations médiocres, qui amusent l'intelligence par des difficultés faciles, et l'assouvissent en une réalisation au delà de laquelle il n'y a pas à rêver.

— Ah! la voici! fit madame Tuvache.

Mais il n'était guère possible, à cause du tour, d'entendre ce qu'elle disait.

Enfin, ces dames crurent distinguer le mot francs, et la mère Tuvache souffla tout bas:

— Elle le prie, pour obtenir un retard à ses contributions.

— D'apparence! reprit l'autre.

Elles la virent qui marchait de long en large, examinant contre les murs les ronds de serviette, les chandeliers, les pommes de rampe, tandis que Binet se caressait la barbe avec satisfaction.

— Viendrait-elle lui commander quelque chose? dit madame Tuvache.

— Mais il ne vend rien! objecta sa voisine.

Le percepteur avait l'air d'écouter, tout en écarquillant les yeux, comme s'il ne comprenait pas. Elle continuait d'une manière tendre, suppliante. Elle se rapprocha; son sein haletait; ils ne parlaient plus.

— Est-ce qu'elle lui fait des avances? dit madame Tuvache.

Binet était rouge jusqu'aux oreilles. Elle lui prit les mains.

"Oh, it's too much!"

And no doubt she was suggesting something abominable to him; for the tax-collector—yet he was brave, had fought at Bautzen and at Lutzen, had been through the French campaign, and had even been recommended for the cross—suddenly, as at the sight of a serpent, recoiled as far as he could from her, crying:

"Madame! what do you mean?"

"Women like that ought to be whipped," said Madame Tuvache.

"But where is she?" continued Madame Caron.

For she had disappeared whilst they spoke; then catching sight of her going up the Grande Rue, and turning to the right as if making for the cemetery, they were lost in conjectures.

"Nurse Rollet," she said on reaching the nurse's, "I am choking; unlace me!"

She fell on the bed sobbing. Nurse Rollet covered her with a petticoat and remained standing by her side. Then, as she did not answer, the good woman withdrew, took her wheel and began spinning flax.

"Oh, leave off!" she murmured, fancying she heard Binet's lathe.

"What's bothering her?" said the nurse to herself. "Why has she come here?"

She had rushed thither; impelled by a kind of horror that drove her from her home.

Lying on her back, motionless, and with staring eyes, she saw things but vaguely, although she tried to with idiotic persistence. She looked at the scales on the walls, two brands smoking end to end, and a long spider crawling over her head in a rent in the beam. At last she began to collect her thoughts. She remembered—one day—Leon—Oh! how long ago that was—the sun was shining on the river, and the clematis were perfuming the air. Then, carried away as by a rushing torrent, she soon began to recall the day before.

"What time is it?" she asked.

Mere Rollet went out, raised the fingers of her right hand to that side of the sky that was brightest, and came back slowly, saying:

— Ah! c'est trop fort!

Et sans doute qu'elle lui proposait une abomination; car le percepteur, — il était brave pourtant, il avait combattu à Bautzen et à Lutzen, fait la campagne de France, et même été porté pour la croix; — tout à coup, comme à la vue d'un serpent, se recula bien loin en s'écriant:

— Madame! y pensez-vous?...

— On devrait fouetter ces femmes-là! dit madame Tuvache.

— Où est-elle donc? reprit madame Caron.

Car elle avait disparu durant ces mots; puis, l'apercevant qui enfilait la Grande-Rue et tournait à droite comme pour gagner le cimetière, elles se perdirent en conjectures.

— Mère Rolet, dit-elle en arrivant chez la nourrice, j'étouffe!... délacez-moi.

Elle tomba sur le lit; elle sanglotait. La mère Rolet la couvrit d'un jupon et resta debout près d'elle. Puis, comme elle ne répondait pas, la bonne femme s'éloigna, prit son rouet et se mit à filer du lin.

— Oh! finissez! murmura-t-elle, croyant entendre le tour de Binet.

— Qui la gêne? se demandait la nourrice. Pourquoi vient-elle ici?

Elle y était accourue, poussée par une sorte d'épouvante qui la chassait de sa maison.

Couchée sur le dos, immobile et les yeux fixes, elle discernait vaguement les objets, bien qu'elle y appliquât son attention avec une persistance idiote. Elle contemplait les écaillures de la muraille, deux tisons fumant bout à bout, et une longue araignée qui marchait au-dessus de sa tête, dans la fente de la poutrelle. Enfin, elle rassembla ses idées. Elle se souvenait... Un jour, avec Léon... Oh! comme c'était loin... Le soleil brillait sur la rivière et les clématites embaumaient... Alors, emportée dans ses souvenirs comme dans un torrent qui bouillonne, elle arriva bientôt à se rappeler la journée de la veille.

— Quelle heure est-il? demanda-t-elle.

La mère Rolet sortit, leva les doigts de sa main droite du côté que le ciel était le plus clair, et rentra lentement en disant:

"Nearly three."

"Ah! thanks, thanks!"

For he would come; he would have found some money. But he would, perhaps, go down yonder, not guessing she was here, and she told the nurse to run to her house to fetch him.

"Be quick!"

"But, my dear lady, I'm going, I'm going!"

She wondered now that she had not thought of him from the first. Yesterday he had given his word; he would not break it. And she already saw herself at Lheureux's spreading out her three bank-notes on his bureau. Then she would have to invent some story to explain matters to Bovary. What should it be?

The nurse, however, was a long while gone. But, as there was no clock in the cot, Emma feared she was perhaps exaggerating the length of time. She began walking round the garden, step by step; she went into the path by the hedge, and returned quickly, hoping that the woman would have come back by another road. At last, weary of waiting, assailed by fears that she thrust from her, no longer conscious whether she had been here a century or a moment, she sat down in a corner, closed her eyes, and stopped her ears. The gate grated; she sprang up. Before she had spoken Mere Rollet said to her:

"There is no one at your house!"

"What?"

"Oh, no one! And the doctor is crying. He is calling for you; they're looking for you."

Emma answered nothing. She gasped as she turned her eyes about her, while the peasant woman, frightened at her face, drew back instinctively, thinking her mad. Suddenly she struck her brow and uttered a cry; for the thought of Rodolphe, like a flash of lightning in a dark night, had passed into her soul. He was so good, so delicate, so generous! And besides, should he hesitate to do her this service, she would know well enough how to constrain him to it by re-waking, in a single moment, their lost love. So she set out towards La Huchette, not seeing

— Trois heures, bientôt.

— Ah! merci! merci!

Car il allait venir. C'était sûr! Il aurait trouvé de l'argent. Mais il irait peut-être là-bas, sans se douter qu'elle fût là; et elle commanda à la nourrice de courir chez elle pour l'amener.

— Dépêchez-vous!

— Mais, ma chère dame, j'y vais! j'y vais!

Elle s'étonnait, à présent, de n'avoir pas songé à lui tout d'abord; hier, il avait donné sa parole, il n'y manquerait pas; et elle se voyait déjà chez Lheureux, étalant sur son bureau les trois billets de banque. Puis il faudrait inventer une histoire qui expliquât les choses à Bovary. Laquelle?

Cependant la nourrice était bien longue à revenir. Mais, comme il n'y avait point d'horloge dans la chaumière, Emma craignait de s'exagérer peut-être la longueur du temps. Elle se mit à faire des tours de promenade dans le jardin, pas à pas; elle alla dans le sentier le long de la haie, et s'en retourna vivement, espérant que la bonne femme serait rentrée par une autre route. Enfin, lasse d'attendre, assaillie de soupçons qu'elle repoussait, ne sachant plus si elle était là depuis un siècle ou une minute, elle s'assit dans un coin et ferma les yeux, se boucha les oreilles. La barrière grinça: elle fit un bond; avant qu'elle eût parlé, la mère Rolet lui avait dit:

— Il n'y a personne chez vous!

— Comment?

— Oh! personne! Et monsieur pleure. Il vous appelle. On vous cherche.

Emma ne répondit rien. Elle haletait, tout en roulant les yeux autour d'elle, tandis que la paysanne, effrayée de son visage, se reculait instinctivement, la croyant folle. Tout à coup elle se frappa le front, poussa un cri, car le souvenir de Rodolphe, comme un grand éclair dans une nuit sombre, lui avait passé dans l'âme. Il était si bon, si délicat, si généreux! Et, d'ailleurs, s'il hésitait à lui rendre ce service, elle saurait bien l'y contraindre en rappelant d'un seul clin d'oeil leur amour perdu. Elle partit donc vers la Huchette, sans s'apercevoir qu'elle courait s'offrir à ce qui

that she was hastening to offer herself to that which but a while ago had so angered her, not in the least conscious of her prostitution.

l'avait tantôt si fort exaspérée, ni se douter le moins du monde de cette prostitution.

# Chapter 8

She asked herself as she walked along, "What am I going to say? How shall I begin?" And as she went on she recognised the thickets, the trees, the sea-rushes on the hill, the chateau yonder. All the sensations of her first tenderness came back to her, and her poor aching heart opened out amorously. A warm wind blew in her face; the melting snow fell drop by drop from the buds to the grass.

She entered, as she used to, through the small park-gate. She reached the avenue bordered by a double row of dense lime-trees. They were swaying their long whispering branches to and fro. The dogs in their kennels all barked, and the noise of their voices resounded, but brought out no one.

She went up the large straight staircase with wooden balusters that led to the corridor paved with dusty flags, into which several doors in a row opened, as in a monastery or an inn. His was at the top, right at the end, on the left. When she placed her fingers on the lock her strength suddenly deserted her. She was afraid, almost wished he would not be there, though this was her only hope, her last chance of salvation. She collected her thoughts for one moment, and, strengthening herself by the feeling of present necessity, went in.

He was in front of the fire, both his feet on the mantelpiece, smoking a pipe.

"What! it is you!" he said, getting up hurriedly.

"Yes, it is I, Rodolphe. I should like to ask your advice."

And, despite all her efforts, it was impossible for her to open her lips.

"You have not changed; you are charming as ever!"

"Oh," she replied bitterly, "they are poor charms since you disdained them."

# Chapitre 8

Elle se demandait tout en marchant: «Que vais-je dire? Par où commencerai-je?» Et à mesure qu'elle avançait, elle reconnaissait les buissons, les arbres, les joncs marins sur la colline, le château là-bas. Elle se retrouvait dans les sensations de sa première tendresse, et son pauvre coeur comprimé s'y dilatait amoureusement. Un vent tiède lui soufflait au visage; la neige, se fondant, tombait goutte à goutte des bourgeons sur l'herbe.

Elle entra, comme autrefois, par la petite porte du parc, puis arriva à la cour d'honneur, que bordait un double rang de tilleuls touffus. Ils balançaient, en sifflant, leurs longues branches. Les chiens au chenil aboyèrent tous, et l'éclat de leurs voix retentissait sans qu'il parût personne.

Elle monta le large escalier droit, à balustres de bois, qui conduisait au corridor pavé de dalles poudreuses où s'ouvraient plusieurs chambres à la file, comme dans les monastères ou les auberges. La sienne était au bout, tout au fond, à gauche. Quand elle vint à poser les doigts sur la serrure, ses forces subitement l'abandonnèrent. Elle avait peur qu'il ne fût pas là, le souhaitait presque, et c'était pourtant son seul espoir, la dernière chance de salut. Elle se recueillit une minute, et, retrempant son courage au sentiment de la nécessité présente, elle entra.

Il était devant le feu, les deux pieds sur le chambranle, en train de fumer une pipe.

— Tiens! c'est vous! dit-il en se levant brusquement.

— Oui, c'est moi!... je voudrais, Rodolphe, vous demander un conseil.

Et malgré tous ses efforts, il lui était impossible de desserrer la bouche.

— Vous n'avez pas changé, vous êtes toujours charmante!

— Oh! reprit-elle amèrement, ce sont de tristes charmes, mon ami, puisque vous les avez dédaignés.

Then he began a long explanation of his conduct, excusing himself in vague terms, in default of being able to invent better.

She yielded to his words, still more to his voice and the sight of him, so that, she pretended to believe, or perhaps believed; in the pretext he gave for their rupture; this was a secret on which depended the honour, the very life of a third person.

"No matter!" she said, looking at him sadly. "I have suffered much."

He replied philosophically:

"Such is life!"

"Has life," Emma went on, "been good to you at least, since our separation?"

"Oh, neither good nor bad."

"Perhaps it would have been better never to have parted."

"Yes, perhaps."

"You think so?" she said, drawing nearer,.

And she sighed.

"Oh, Rodolphe! if you but knew! I loved you so!"

It was then that she took his hand, and they remained some time, their fingers intertwined, like that first day at the Show. With a gesture of pride he struggled against this emotion. But sinking upon his breast she said to him:

"How did you think I could live without you? One cannot lose the habit of happiness. I was desolate. I thought I should die. I will tell you about all that and you will see. And you—you fled from me!"

For, all the three years, he had carefully avoided her in consequence of that natural cowardice that characterises the stronger sex. Emma went on, with dainty little nods, more coaxing than an amorous kitten:

"You love others, confess it! Oh, I understand them, dear! I excuse them. You probably seduced them as you seduced me. You are indeed a man; you have everything to make one love you. But we'll begin again, won't we? We will love one another. See! I am laughing; I am happy! Oh, speak!"

And she was charming to see, with her eyes, in which trembled a tear, like the rain of a storm in a blue corolla.

Alors il entama une explication de sa conduite, s'excusant en termes vagues, faute de pouvoir inventer mieux.

Elle se laissa prendre à ses paroles, plus encore à sa voix et par le spectacle de sa personne; si bien qu'elle fit semblant de croire, ou crut-elle peut-être, au prétexte de leur rupture; c'était un secret d'où dépendaient l'honneur et même la vie d'une troisième personne.

— N'importe! fit-elle en le regardant tristement, j'ai bien souffert!

Il répondit d'un ton philosophique:

— L'existence est ainsi!

— A-t-elle du moins, reprit Emma, été bonne pour vous depuis notre séparation?

— Oh! ni bonne... ni mauvaise.

— Il aurait peut-être mieux valu ne jamais nous quitter.

— Oui..., peut-être!

— Tu crois? dit-elle en se rapprochant.

Et elle soupira.

— O Rodolphe! si tu savais... Je t'ai bien aimé!

Ce fut alors qu'elle prit sa main, et ils restèrent quelque temps les doigts entrelacés, — comme le premier jour, aux Comices! Par un geste d'orgueil, il se débattait sous l'attendrissement. Mais, s'affaissant contre sa poitrine, elle lui dit:

— Comment voulais-tu que je vécusse sans toi? On ne peut pas se déshabituer du bonheur! J'étais désespérée! j'ai cru mourir! Je te conterai tout cela, tu verras. Et toi... tu m'as fuie!...

Car, depuis trois ans, il l'avait soigneusement évitée par suite de cette lâcheté naturelle qui caractérise le sexe fort; et Emma continuait avec des gestes mignons de tête, plus câline qu'une chatte amoureuse:

— Tu en aimes d'autres, avoue-le. Oh! je les comprends, va! je les excuse; tu les auras séduites, comme tu m'avais séduite. Tu es un homme, toi! tu as tout ce qu'il faut pour te faire chérir. Mais nous recommencerons, n'est-ce pas? nous nous aimerons! Tiens, je ris, je suis heureuse!... parle donc!

Et elle était ravissante à voir, avec son regard où tremblait une larme, comme l'eau d'un orage dans un calice bleu.

He had drawn her upon his knees, and with the back of his hand was caressing her smooth hair, where in the twilight was mirrored like a golden arrow one last ray of the sun. She bent down her brow; at last he kissed her on the eyelids quite gently with the tips of his lips.

"Why, you have been crying! What for?"

She burst into tears. Rodolphe thought this was an outburst of her love. As she did not speak, he took this silence for a last remnant of resistance, and then he cried out:

"Oh, forgive me! You are the only one who pleases me. I was imbecile and cruel. I love you. I will love you always. What is it. Tell me!"

He was kneeling by her.

"Well, I am ruined, Rodolphe! You must lend me three thousand francs."

"But—but—" said he, getting up slowly, while his face assumed a grave expression.

"You know," she went on quickly, "that my husband had placed his whole fortune at a notary's. He ran away. So we borrowed; the patients don't pay us. Moreover, the settling of the estate is not yet done; we shall have the money later on. But to-day, for want of three thousand francs, we are to be sold up. It is to be at once, this very moment, and, counting upon your friendship, I have come to you."

"Ah!" thought Rodolphe, turning very pale, "that was what she came for."

At last he said with a calm air:

"Dear madame, I have not got them."

He did not lie. If he had had them, he would, no doubt, have given them, although it is generally disagreeable to do such fine things: a demand for money being, of all the winds that blow upon love, the coldest and most destructive.

First she looked at him for some moments.

"You have not got them!"

She repeated several times:

"You have not got them! I ought to have spared myself this last shame. You never loved me. You are no better than the others."

Il l'attira sur ses genoux, et il caressait du revers de la main ses bandeaux lisses, où, dans la clarté du crépuscule, miroitait comme une flèche d'or un dernier rayon du soleil. Elle penchait le front; il finit par la baiser sur les paupières, tout doucement, du bout de ses lèvres.

— Mais tu as pleuré! dit-il. Pourquoi?

Elle éclata en sanglots. Rodolphe crut que c'était l'explosion de son amour; comme elle se taisait, il prit ce silence pour une dernière pudeur, et alors il s'écria:

— Ah! pardonne-moi! tu es la seule qui me plaise. J'ai été imbécile et méchant! Je t'aime, je t'aimerai toujours!… Qu'as- tu? dis-le donc!

Il s'agenouillait.

— Eh bien!… je suis ruinée, Rodolphe! Tu vas me prêter trois mille francs!

— Mais…, mais…, dit-il en se relevant peu à peu, tandis que sa physionomie prenait une expression grave.

— Tu sais, continuait-elle vite, que mon mari avait placé toute sa fortune chez un notaire; il s'est enfui. Nous avons emprunté; les clients ne payaient pas. Du reste la liquidation n'est pas finie; nous en aurons plus tard. Mais, aujourd'hui, faute de trois mille francs, on va nous saisir; c'est à présent, à l'instant même; et, comptant sur ton amitié, je suis venue.

— Ah! pensa Rodolphe, qui devint très pâle tout à coup, c'est pour cela qu'elle est venue!

Enfin il dit d'un air calme:

— Je ne les ai pas, chère madame.

Il ne mentait point. Il les eût eus qu'il les aurait donnés, sans doute, bien qu'il soit généralement désagréable de faire de si belles actions: une demande pécuniaire, de toutes les bourrasques qui tombent sur l'amour, étant la plus froide et la plus déracinante.

Elle resta d'abord quelques minutes à le regarder.

— Tu ne les as pas!

Elle répéta plusieurs fois:

— Tu ne les as pas!… J'aurais dû m'épargner cette dernière honte. Tu ne m'as jamais aimée! tu ne vaux pas mieux que les autres!

She was betraying, ruining herself.

Rodolphe interrupted her, declaring he was "hard up" himself.

"Ah! I pity you," said Emma. "Yes—very much."

And fixing her eyes upon an embossed carabine, that shone against its panoply:

"But when one is so poor one doesn't have silver on the butt of one's gun. One doesn't buy a clock inlaid with tortoise shell," she went on, pointing to a buhl timepiece, "nor silver-gilt whistles for one's whips," and she touched them, "nor charms for one's watch. Oh, he wants for nothing! even to a liqueur-stand in his room! For you love yourself; you live well. You have a chateau, farms, woods; you go hunting; you travel to Paris. Why, if it were but that," she cried, taking up two studs from the mantelpiece, "but the least of these trifles, one can get money for them.

"Oh, I do not want them, keep them!"

And she threw the two links away from her, their gold chain breaking as it struck against the wall.

"But I! I would have given you everything. I would have sold all, worked for you with my hands, I would have begged on the highroads for a smile, for a look, to hear you say 'Thanks!' And you sit there quietly in your arm-chair, as if you had not made me suffer enough already! But for you, and you know it, I might have lived happily. What made you do it? Was it a bet? Yet you loved me—you said so. And but a moment since—Ah! it would have been better to have driven me away. My hands are hot with your kisses, and there is the spot on the carpet where at my knees you swore an eternity of love! You made me believe you; for two years you held me in the most magnificent, the sweetest dream! Eh! Our plans for the journey, do you remember? Oh, your letter! your letter! it tore my heart! And then when I come back to him—to him, rich, happy, free—to implore the help the first stranger would give, a suppliant, and bringing back to him all my tenderness, he repulses me because it would cost him three thousand francs!"

"I haven't got them," replied Rodolphe, with that perfect calm with which resigned rage covers itself as with a shield.

Elle se trahissait, elle se perdait.

Rodolphe l'interrompit, affirmant qu'il se trouvait «gêné» lui- même.

— Ah! je te plains! dit Emma. Oui, considérablement!…

Et, arrêtant ses yeux sur une carabine damasquinée qui brillait dans la panoplie:

— Mais, lorsqu'on est si pauvre, on ne met pas d'argent à la crosse de son fusil! On n'achète pas une pendule avec des incrustations d'écaille! continuait-elle en montrant l'horloge de Boulle; ni des sifflets de vermeil pour ses fouets — elle les touchait! — ni des breloques pour sa montre! Oh! rien ne lui manque! Jusqu'à un porte-liqueurs dans sa chambre; car tu t'aimes, tu vis bien, tu as un château, des fermes, des bois; tu chasses à courre, tu voyages à Paris… Eh! quand ce ne serait que cela, s'écria-t-elle en prenant sur la cheminée ses boutons de manchettes, que la moindre de ces niaiseries! on en peut faire de l'argent!…

Oh! je n'en veux pas! garde-les!

Et elle lança bien loin les deux boutons, dont la chaîne d'or se rompit en cognant contre la muraille.

— Mais, moi, je t'aurais tout donné, j'aurais tout vendu, j'aurais travaillé de mes mains, j'aurais mendié sur les routes, pour un sourire, pour un regard, pour t'entendre dire: «Merci!» Et tu restes là tranquillement dans ton fauteuil, comme si déjà tu ne m'avais pas fait assez souffrir? Sans toi, sais-tu bien, j'aurais pu vivre heureuse! Qui t'y forçait? Était-ce une gageure? Tu m'aimais cependant, tu le disais… Et tout à l'heure encore… Ah! il eût mieux valu me chasser! J'ai les mains chaudes de tes baisers, et voilà la place, sur le tapis, où tu jurais à mes genoux une éternité d'amour. Tu m'y as fait croire: tu m'as pendant deux ans, traînée dans le rêve le plus magnifique et le plus suave!… Hein! nos projets de voyage, tu te rappelles? Oh! ta lettre, ta lettre! elle m'a déchiré le coeur!… Et puis, quand je reviens vers lui, vers lui, qui est riche, heureux, libre! pour implorer un secours que le premier venu rendrait, suppliante et lui rapportant toute ma tendresse, il me repousse, parce que ça lui coûterait trois mille francs!

— Je ne les ai pas! répondit Rodolphe avec ce calme parfait dont se recouvrent comme d'un bouclier les colères résignées.

She went out. The walls trembled, the ceiling was crushing her, and she passed back through the long alley, stumbling against the heaps of dead leaves scattered by the wind. At last she reached the ha-ha hedge in front of the gate; she broke her nails against the lock in her haste to open it. Then a hundred steps farther on, breathless, almost falling, she stopped. And now turning round, she once more saw the impassive chateau, with the park, the gardens, the three courts, and all the windows of the facade.

She remained lost in stupor, and having no more consciousness of herself than through the beating of her arteries, that she seemed to hear bursting forth like a deafening music filling all the fields. The earth beneath her feet was more yielding than the sea, and the furrows seemed to her immense brown waves breaking into foam. Everything in her head, of memories, ideas, went off at once like a thousand pieces of fireworks. She saw her father, Lheureux's closet, their room at home, another landscape. Madness was coming upon her; she grew afraid, and managed to recover herself, in a confused way, it is true, for she did not in the least remember the cause of the terrible condition she was in, that is to say, the question of money. She suffered only in her love, and felt her soul passing from her in this memory; as wounded men, dying, feel their life ebb from their bleeding wounds.

Night was falling, crows were flying about.

Suddenly it seemed to her that fiery spheres were exploding in the air like fulminating balls when they strike, and were whirling, whirling, to melt at last upon the snow between the branches of the trees. In the midst of each of them appeared the face of Rodolphe. They multiplied and drew near her, penetrating, her. It all disappeared; she recognised the lights of the houses that shone through the fog.

Now her situation, like an abyss, rose up before her. She was panting as if her heart would burst. Then in an ecstasy of heroism, that made her almost joyous, she ran down the hill, crossed the cow-plank, the foot-path, the alley, the market, and reached the chemist's shop.

Elle sortit. Les murs tremblaient, le plafond l'écrasait; et elle repassa par la longue allée, en trébuchant contre les tas de feuilles mortes que le vent dispersait. Enfin elle arriva au saut- de-loup devant la grille; elle se cassa les ongles contre la serrure, tant elle se dépêchait pour l'ouvrir. Puis, cent pas plus loin, essoufflée, près de tomber, elle s'arrêta. Et alors, se détournant, elle aperçut encore une fois l'impassible château, avec le parc, les jardins, les trois cours, et toutes les fenêtres de la façade.

Elle resta perdue de stupeur, et n'ayant plus conscience d'elle- même que par le battement de ses artères, qu'elle croyait entendre s'échapper comme une assourdissante musique qui emplissait la campagne. Le sol sous ses pieds était plus mou qu'une onde, et les sillons lui parurent d'immenses vagues brunes, qui déferlaient. Tout ce qu'il y avait dans sa tête de réminiscences, d'idées, s'échappait à la fois, d'un seul bond, comme les mille pièces d'un feu d'artifice. Elle vit son père, le cabinet de Lheureux, leur chambre là-bas, un autre paysage. La folie la prenait, elle eut peur, et parvint à se ressaisir, d'une manière confuse, il est vrai; car elle ne se rappelait point la cause de son horrible état, c'est-à-dire la question d'argent. Elle ne souffrait que de son amour, et sentait son âme l'abandonner par ce souvenir, comme les blessés, en agonisant, sentent l'existence qui s'en va par leur plaie qui saigne.

La nuit tombait, des corneilles volaient.

Il lui sembla tout à coup que des globules couleur de feu éclataient dans l'air comme des balles fulminantes en s'aplatissant, et tournaient, tournaient, pour aller se fondre sur la neige, entre les branches des arbres. Au milieu de chacun d'eux, la figure de Rodolphe apparaissait. Ils se multiplièrent, et ils se rapprochaient, la pénétraient; tout disparut. Elle reconnut les lumières des maisons, qui rayonnaient de loin dans le brouillard.

Alors sa situation, telle qu'un abîme, se représenta. Elle haletait à se rompre la poitrine. Puis, dans un transport d'héroïsme qui la rendait presque joyeuse, elle descendit la côte en courant, traversa la planche aux vaches, le sentier, l'allée, les halles, et arriva devant la boutique du pharmacien.

She was about to enter, but at the sound of the bell someone might come, and slipping in by the gate, holding her breath, feeling her way along the walls, she went as far as the door of the kitchen, where a candle stuck on the stove was burning. Justin in his shirt-sleeves was carrying out a dish.

"Ah! they are dining; I will wait."

He returned; she tapped at the window. He went out.

"The key! the one for upstairs where he keeps the—"

"What?"

And he looked at her, astonished at the pallor of her face, that stood out white against the black background of the night. She seemed to him extraordinarily beautiful and majestic as a phantom. Without understanding what she wanted, he had the presentiment of something terrible.

But she went on quickly in a love voice; in a sweet, melting voice:

"I want it; give it to me."

As the partition wall was thin, they could hear the clatter of the forks on the plates in the dining-room.

She pretended that she wanted to kill the rats that kept her from sleeping.

"I must tell master."

"No, stay!"

Then with an indifferent air:

"Oh, it's not worth while; I'll tell him presently. Come, light me upstairs."

She entered the corridor into which the laboratory door opened. Against the wall was a key labelled Capharnaum.

"Justin!" called the druggist impatiently.

"Let us go up."

And he followed her.

The key turned in the lock, and she went straight to the third shelf, so well did her memory guide her, seized the blue jar, tore out the cork, plunged in her hand, and withdrawing it full of a white powder, she began eating it.

"Stop!" he cried, rushing at her.

Il n'y avait personne. Elle allait entrer; mais, au bruit de la sonnette, on pouvait venir; et, se glissant par la barrière, retenant son haleine, tâtant les murs, elle s'avança jusqu'au seuil de la cuisine, où brûlait une chandelle posée sur le fourneau. Justin, en manches de chemise, emportait un plat.

— Ah! ils dînent. Attendons.

Il revint. Elle frappa contre la vitre. Il sortit.

— La clef! celle d'en haut, où sont les...

— Comment?

Et il la regardait, tout étonné par la pâleur de son visage, qui tranchait en blanc sur le fond noir de la nuit. Elle lui apparut extraordinairement belle, et majestueuse comme un fantôme; sans comprendre ce qu'elle voulait, il pressentait quelque chose de terrible.

Mais elle reprit vivement, à voix basse, d'une voix douce, dissolvante:

— Je la veux! donne-la-moi.

Comme la cloison était mince, on entendait le cliquetis des fourchettes sur les assiettes dans la salle à manger.

Elle prétendit avoir besoin de tuer les rats qui l'empêchaient de dormir.

— Il faudrait que j'avertisse monsieur.

— Non! reste!

Puis, d'un air indifférent:

— Eh! ce n'est pas la peine, je lui dirai tantôt. Allons, éclaire-moi!

Elle entra dans le corridor où s'ouvrait la porte du laboratoire. Il y avait contre la muraille une clef étiquetée capharnaüm.

— Justin! cria l'apothicaire, qui s'impatientait.

— Montons!

Et il la suivit.

La clef tourna dans la serrure, et elle alla droit vers la troisième tablette, tant son souvenir la guidait bien, saisit le bocal bleu, en arracha le bouchon, y fourra sa main, et, la retirant pleine d'une poudre blanche, elle se mit à manger à même.

— Arrêtez! s'écria-t-il en se jetant sur elle.

"Hush! someone will come."

He was in despair, was calling out.

"Say nothing, or all the blame will fall on your master."

Then she went home, suddenly calmed, and with something of the serenity of one that had performed a duty.

When Charles, distracted by the news of the distraint, returned home, Emma had just gone out. He cried aloud, wept, fainted, but she did not return. Where could she be? He sent Felicite to Homais, to Monsieur Tuvache, to Lheureux, to the "Lion d'Or," everywhere, and in the intervals of his agony he saw his reputation destroyed, their fortune lost, Berthe's future ruined. By what?—Not a word! He waited till six in the evening. At last, unable to bear it any longer, and fancying she had gone to Rouen, he set out along the highroad, walked a mile, met no one, again waited, and returned home.

She had come back.

"What was the matter? Why? Explain to me."

She sat down at her writing-table and wrote a letter, which she sealed slowly, adding the date and the hour.

Then she said in a solemn tone:

"You are to read it to-morrow; till then, I pray you, do not ask me a single question. No, not one!"

"But—"

"Oh, leave me!"

She lay down full length on her bed.

A bitter taste that she felt in her mouth awakened her. She saw Charles, and again closed her eyes.

She was studying herself curiously, to see if she were not suffering. But no! nothing as yet. She heard the ticking of the clock, the crackling of the fire, and Charles breathing as he stood upright by her bed.

"Ah! it is but a little thing, death!" she thought. "I shall fall asleep and all will be over."

She drank a mouthful of water and turned to the wall.

The frightful taste of ink continued.

"I am thirsty; oh! so thirsty," she sighed.

— Tais-toi! on viendrait…

Il se désespérait, voulait appeler.

— N'en dis rien, tout retomberait sur ton maître!

Puis elle s'en retourna subitement apaisée, et presque dans la sérénité d'un devoir accompli.

Quand Charles, bouleversé par la nouvelle de la saisie, était rentré à la maison, Emma venait d'en sortir. Il cria, pleura, s'évanouit, mais elle ne revint pas. Où pouvait-elle être? Il envoya Félicité chez Homais, chez M. Tuvache, chez Lheureux, au Lion d'or, partout; et, dans les intermittences de son angoisse, il voyait sa considération anéantie, leur fortune perdue, l'avenir de Berthe brisé! Par quelle cause?… pas un mot! Il attendit jusqu'à six heures du soir. Enfin, n'y pouvant plus tenir, et imaginant qu'elle était partie pour Rouen, il alla sur la grande route, fit une demi-lieue, ne rencontra personne, attendit encore et s'en revint.

Elle était rentrée.

— Qu'y avait-il?… Pourquoi?… Explique-moi!…

Elle s'assit à son secrétaire, et écrivit une lettre qu'elle cacheta lentement, ajoutant la date du jour et l'heure.

Puis elle dit d'un ton solennel:

— Tu la liras demain; d'ici là, je t'en prie, ne m'adresse pas une seule question!… Non, pas une!

— Mais…

— Oh! laisse-moi!

Et elle se coucha tout du long sur son lit.

Une saveur âcre qu'elle sentait dans sa bouche la réveilla. Elle entrevit Charles et referma les yeux.

Elle s'épiait curieusement, pour discerner si elle ne souffrait pas. Mais non! rien encore. Elle entendait le battement de la pendule, le bruit du feu, et Charles, debout près de sa couche, qui respirait.

— Ah! c'est bien peu de chose, la mort! Pensait-elle; je vais m'endormir, et tout sera fini!

Elle but une gorgée d'eau et se tourna vers la muraille.

Cet affreux goût d'encre continuait.

— J'ai soif!… oh! j'ai bien soif! soupira-t-elle.

"What is it?" said Charles, who was handing her a glass.

"It is nothing! Open the window; I am choking."

She was seized with a sickness so sudden that she had hardly time to draw out her handkerchief from under the pillow.

"Take it away," she said quickly; "throw it away."

He spoke to her; she did not answer. She lay motionless, afraid that the slightest movement might make her vomit. But she felt an icy cold creeping from her feet to her heart.

"Ah! it is beginning," she murmured.

"What did you say?"

She turned her head from side to side with a gentle movement full of agony, while constantly opening her mouth as if something very heavy were weighing upon her tongue. At eight o'clock the vomiting began again.

Charles noticed that at the bottom of the basin there was a sort of white sediment sticking to the sides of the porcelain.

"This is extraordinary—very singular," he repeated.

But she said in a firm voice:

"No, you are mistaken."

Then gently, and almost as caressing her, he passed his hand over her stomach. She uttered a sharp cry. He fell back terror-stricken.

Then she began to groan, faintly at first. Her shoulders were shaken by a strong shuddering, and she was growing paler than the sheets in which her clenched fingers buried themselves. Her unequal pulse was now almost imperceptible.

Drops of sweat oozed from her bluish face, that seemed as if rigid in the exhalations of a metallic vapour. Her teeth chattered, her dilated eyes looked vaguely about her, and to all questions she replied only with a shake of the head; she even smiled once or twice. Gradually, her moaning grew louder; a hollow shriek burst from her; she pretended she was better and that she would get up presently. But she was seized with convulsions and cried out:

"Ah! my God! It is horrible!"

He threw himself on his knees by her bed.

— Qu'as-tu donc? dit Charles, qui lui tendait un verre.

— Ce n'est rien!... Ouvre la fenêtre..., j'étouffe!

Et elle fut prise d'une nausée si soudaine, qu'elle eut à peine le temps de saisir son mouchoir sous l'oreiller.

— Enlève-le! dit-elle vivement; jette-le!

Il la questionna; elle ne répondit pas. Elle se tenait immobile, de peur que la moindre émotion ne la fît vomir. Cependant, elle sentait un froid de glace qui lui montait des pieds jusqu'au coeur.

— Ah! voilà que ça commence! murmura-t-elle.

— Que dis-tu?

Elle roulait sa tête avec un geste doux plein d'angoisse, et tout en ouvrant continuellement les mâchoires, comme si elle eût porté sur sa langue quelque chose de très lourd. À huit heures, les vomissements reparurent.

Charles observa qu'il y avait au fond de la cuvette une sorte de gravier blanc, attaché aux parois de la porcelaine.

— C'est extraordinaire! c'est singulier! répéta-t-il.

Mais elle dit d'une voix forte:

— Non, tu te trompes!

Alors, délicatement et presque en la caressant, il lui passa la main sur l'estomac. Elle jeta un cri aigu. Il se recula tout effrayé.

Puis elle se mit à geindre, faiblement d'abord. Un grand frisson lui secouait les épaules, et elle devenait plus pâle que le drap où s'enfonçaient ses doigts crispés. Son pouls inégal était presque insensible maintenant.

Des gouttes suintaient sur sa figure bleuâtre, qui semblait comme figée dans l'exhalaison d'une vapeur métallique. Ses dents claquaient, ses yeux agrandis regardaient vaguement autour d'elle, et à toutes les questions elle ne répondait qu'en hochant la tête; même elle sourit deux ou trois fois. Peu à peu, ses gémissements furent plus forts. Un hurlement sourd lui échappa; elle prétendit qu'elle allait mieux et qu'elle se lèverait tout à l'heure. Mais les convulsions la saisirent; elle s'écria:

— Ah! c'est atroce, mon Dieu!

Il se jeta à genoux contre son lit.

"Tell me! what have you eaten? Answer, for heaven's sake!"

And he looked at her with a tenderness in his eyes such as she had never seen.

"Well, there—there!" she said in a faint voice.

He flew to the writing-table, tore open the seal, and read aloud: "Accuse no one." He stopped, passed his hands across his eyes, and read it over again.

"What! help—help!"

He could only keep repeating the word: "Poisoned! poisoned!" Felicite ran to Homais, who proclaimed it in the market-place; Madame Lefrancois heard it at the "Lion d'Or"; some got up to go and tell their neighbours, and all night the village was on the alert.

Distraught, faltering, reeling, Charles wandered about the room. He knocked against the furniture, tore his hair, and the chemist had never believed that there could be so terrible a sight.

He went home to write to Monsieur Canivet and to Doctor Lariviere. He lost his head, and made more than fifteen rough copies. Hippolyte went to Neufchatel, and Justin so spurred Bovary's horse that he left it foundered and three parts dead by the hill at Bois-Guillaume.

Charles tried to look up his medical dictionary, but could not read it; the lines were dancing.

"Be calm," said the druggist; "we have only to administer a powerful antidote. What is the poison?"

Charles showed him the letter. It was arsenic.

"Very well," said Homais, "we must make an analysis."

For he knew that in cases of poisoning an analysis must be made; and the other, who did not understand, answered:

"Oh, do anything! save her!"

Then going back to her, he sank upon the carpet, and lay there with his head leaning against the edge of her bed, sobbing.

"Don't cry," she said to him. "Soon I shall not trouble you any more."

"Why was it? Who drove you to it?"

She replied:

"It had to be, my dear!"

— Parle! qu'as-tu mangé? Réponds, au nom du ciel!

Et il la regardait avec des yeux d'une tendresse comme elle n'en avait jamais vu.

— Eh bien, là..., là!... dit-elle d'une voix défaillante.

Il bondit au secrétaire, brisa le cachet et lut tout haut: Qu'on n'accuse personne... Il s'arrêta, se passa la main sur les yeux, et relut encore.

— Comment!... Au secours! à moi!

Et il ne pouvait que répéter ce mot: «Empoisonnée! empoisonnée!» Félicité courut chez Homais, qui l'exclama sur la place; madame Lefrançois l'entendit au Lion d'or; quelques-uns se levèrent pour l'apprendre à leurs voisins, et toute la nuit le village fut en éveil.

Éperdu, balbutiant, près de tomber, Charles tournait dans la chambre. Il se heurtait aux meubles, s'arrachait les cheveux, et jamais le pharmacien n'avait cru qu'il pût y avoir de si épouvantable spectacle.

Il revint chez lui pour écrire à M. Canivet et au docteur Larivière. Il perdait la tête; il fit plus de quinze brouillons. Hippolyte partit à Neufchâtel, et Justin talonna si fort le cheval de Bovary, qu'il le laissa dans la côte du bois Guillaume, fourbu et aux trois quarts crevé.

Charles voulut feuilleter son dictionnaire de médecine; il n'y voyait pas, les lignes dansaient.

— Du calme! dit l'apothicaire. Il s'agit seulement d'administrer quelque puissant antidote. Quel est le poison?

Charles montra la lettre. C'était de l'arsenic.

— Eh bien, reprit Homais, il faudrait en faire l'analyse.

Car il savait qu'il faut, dans tous les empoisonnements, faire une analyse; et l'autre, qui ne comprenait pas, répondit:

— Ah! faites! faites! sauvez-la...

Puis, revenu près d'elle, il s'affaissa par terre sur le tapis, et il restait la tête appuyée contre le bord de sa couche, à sangloter.

— Ne pleure pas! lui dit-elle. Bientôt je ne te tourmenterai plus!

— Pourquoi? Qui t'a forcée?

Elle répliqua:

— Il le fallait, mon ami.

"Weren't you happy? Is it my fault? I did all I could!"

"Yes, that is true—you are good—you."

And she passed her hand slowly over his hair. The sweetness of this sensation deepened his sadness; he felt his whole being dissolving in despair at the thought that he must lose her, just when she was confessing more love for him than ever. And he could think of nothing; he did not know, he did not dare; the urgent need for some immediate resolution gave the finishing stroke to the turmoil of his mind.

So she had done, she thought, with all the treachery; and meanness, and numberless desires that had tortured her. She hated no one now; a twilight dimness was settling upon her thoughts, and, of all earthly noises, Emma heard none but the intermittent lamentations of this poor heart, sweet and indistinct like the echo of a symphony dying away.

"Bring me the child," she said, raising herself on her elbow.

"You are not worse, are you?" asked Charles.

"No, no!"

The child, serious, and still half-asleep, was carried in on the servant's arm in her long white nightgown, from which her bare feet peeped out. She looked wonderingly at the disordered room, and half-closed her eyes, dazzled by the candles burning on the table. They reminded her, no doubt, of the morning of New Year's day and Mid-Lent, when thus awakened early by candle-light she came to her mother's bed to fetch her presents, for she began saying:

"But where is it, mamma?"

And as everybody was silent:

"But I can't see my little stocking."

Felicite held her over the bed while she still kept looking towards the mantelpiece.

"Has nurse taken it?" she asked.

And at this name, that carried her back to the memory of her adulteries and her calamities, Madame Bovary turned away her head, as

— N'étais-tu pas heureuse? Est-ce ma faute? J'ai fait tout ce que j'ai pu pourtant!

— Oui..., c'est vrai..., tu es bon, toi!

Et elle lui passait la main dans les cheveux, lentement. La douceur de cette sensation surchargeait sa tristesse; il sentait tout son être s'écrouler de désespoir à l'idée qu'il fallait la perdre, quand, au contraire, elle avouait pour lui plus d'amour que jamais; et il ne trouvait rien; il ne savait pas, il n'osait, l'urgence d'une résolution immédiate achevant de le bouleverser.

Elle en avait fini, songeait-elle, avec toutes les trahisons, les bassesses et les innombrables convoitises qui la torturaient. Elle ne haïssait personne, maintenant; une confusion de crépuscule s'abattait en sa pensée, et de tous les bruits de la terre Emma n'entendait plus que l'intermittente lamentation de ce pauvre coeur, douce et indistincte, comme le dernier écho d'une symphonie qui s'éloigne.

— Amenez-moi la petite, dit-elle en se soulevant du coude.

— Tu n'es pas plus mal, n'est-ce pas? demanda Charles.

— Non! non!

L'enfant arriva sur le bras de sa bonne, dans sa longue chemise de nuit, d'où sortaient ses pieds nus, sérieuse et presque rêvant encore. Elle considérait avec étonnement la chambre tout en désordre, et clignait des yeux, éblouie par les flambeaux qui brûlaient sur les meubles. Ils lui rappelaient sans doute les matins du jour de l'an ou de la mi-carême, quand, ainsi réveillée de bonne heure à la clarté des bougies, elle venait dans le lit de sa mère pour y recevoir ses étrennes, car elle se mit à dire:

— Où est-ce donc, maman?

Et comme tout le monde se taisait:

— Mais je ne vois pas mon petit soulier!

Félicité la penchait vers le lit, tandis qu'elle regardait toujours du côté de la cheminée.

— Est-ce nourrice qui l'aurait pris? demanda-t-elle.

Et, à ce nom, qui la reportait dans le souvenir de ses adultères et de ses calamités, madame Bovary détourna sa tête, comme au dégoût d'un

at the loathing of another bitterer poison that rose to her mouth. But Berthe remained perched on the bed.

"Oh, how big your eyes are, mamma! How pale you are! how hot you are!"

Her mother looked at her.

"I am frightened!" cried the child, recoiling.

Emma took her hand to kiss it; the child struggled.

"That will do. Take her away," cried Charles, who was sobbing in the alcove.

Then the symptoms ceased for a moment; she seemed less agitated; and at every insignificant word, at every respiration a little more easy, he regained hope. At last, when Canivet came in, he threw himself into his arms.

"Ah! it is you. Thanks! You are good! But she is better. See! look at her."

His colleague was by no means of this opinion, and, as he said of himself, "never beating about the bush," he prescribed, an emetic in order to empty the stomach completely.

She soon began vomiting blood. Her lips became drawn. Her limbs were convulsed, her whole body covered with brown spots, and her pulse slipped beneath the fingers like a stretched thread, like a harp-string nearly breaking.

After this she began to scream horribly. She cursed the poison, railed at it, and implored it to be quick, and thrust away with her stiffened arms everything that Charles, in more agony than herself, tried to make her drink. He stood up, his handkerchief to his lips, with a rattling sound in his throat, weeping, and choked by sobs that shook his whole body. Felicite was running hither and thither in the room. Homais, motionless, uttered great sighs; and Monsieur Canivet, always retaining his self-command, nevertheless began to feel uneasy.

"The devil! yet she has been purged, and from the moment that the cause ceases—"

"The effect must cease," said Homais, "that is evident."

"Oh, save her!" cried Bovary.

autre poison plus fort qui lui remontait à la bouche. Berthe, cependant, restait posée sur le lit.

— Oh! comme tu as de grands yeux, maman! comme tu es pâle! comme tu sues!...

Sa mère la regardait.

— J'ai peur! dit la petite en se reculant.

Emma prit sa main pour la baiser; elle se débattait.

— Assez! qu'on l'emmène! s'écria Charles, qui sanglotait dans l'alcôve.

Puis les symptômes s'arrêtèrent un moment; elle paraissait moins agitée; et, à chaque parole insignifiante, à chaque souffle de sa poitrine un peu plus calme, il reprenait espoir. Enfin, lorsque Canivet entra, il se jeta dans ses bras en pleurant.

— Ah! c'est vous! merci! vous êtes bon! Mais tout va mieux. Tenez, regardez-la...

Le confrère ne fut nullement de cette opinion, et, n'y allant pas, comme il le disait lui-même, par quatre chemins, il prescrivit de l'émétique, afin de dégager complètement l'estomac.

Elle ne tarda pas à vomir du sang. Ses lèvres se serrèrent davantage. Elle avait les membres crispés, le corps couvert de taches brunes, et son pouls glissait sous les doigts comme un fil tendu, comme une corde de harpe près de se rompre.

Puis elle se mettait à crier, horriblement. Elle maudissait le poison, l'invectivait, le suppliait de se hâter, et repoussait de ses bras roidis tout ce que Charles, plus agonisant qu'elle, s'efforçait de lui faire boire. Il était debout, son mouchoir sur les lèvres, râlant, pleurant, et suffoqué par des sanglots qui le secouaient jusqu'aux talons; Félicité courait çà et là dans la chambre; Homais, immobile, poussait de gros soupirs, et M. Canivet, gardant toujours son aplomb, commençait néanmoins à se sentir troublé.

— Diable!... cependant... elle est purgée, et, du moment que la cause cesse...

— L'effet doit cesser, dit Homais; c'est évident.

— Mais sauvez-la! exclamait Bovary.

And, without listening to the chemist, who was still venturing the hypothesis, "It is perhaps a salutary paroxysm," Canivet was about to administer some theriac, when they heard the cracking of a whip; all the windows rattled, and a post-chaise drawn by three horses abreast, up to their ears in mud, drove at a gallop round the corner of the market. It was Doctor Lariviere.

The apparition of a god would not have caused more commotion. Bovary raised his hands; Canivet stopped short; and Homais pulled off his skull-cap long before the doctor had come in.

He belonged to that great school of surgery begotten of Bichat, to that generation, now extinct, of philosophical practitioners, who, loving their art with a fanatical love, exercised it with enthusiasm and wisdom. Everyone in his hospital trembled when he was angry; and his students so revered him that they tried, as soon as they were themselves in practice, to imitate him as much as possible. So that in all the towns about they were found wearing his long wadded merino overcoat and black frock-coat, whose buttoned cuffs slightly covered his brawny hands—very beautiful hands, and that never knew gloves, as though to be more ready to plunge into suffering. Disdainful of honours, of titles, and of academies, like one of the old Knight-Hospitallers, generous, fatherly to the poor, and practising virtue without believing in it, he would almost have passed for a saint if the keenness of his intellect had not caused him to be feared as a demon. His glance, more penetrating than his bistouries, looked straight into your soul, and dissected every lie athwart all assertions and all reticences. And thus he went along, full of that debonair majesty that is given by the consciousness of great talent, of fortune, and of forty years of a labourious and irreproachable life.

He frowned as soon as he had passed the door when he saw the cadaverous face of Emma stretched out on her back with her mouth open. Then, while apparently listening to Canivet, he rubbed his fingers up and down beneath his nostrils, and repeated:

"Good! good!"

But he made a slow gesture with his shoulders. Bovary watched him; they looked at one another; and this man, accustomed as he was to the

Aussi, sans écouter le pharmacien, qui hasardait encore cette hypothèse: «C'est peut-être un paroxysme salutaire», Canivet allait administrer de la thériaque, lorsqu'on entendit le claquement d'un fouet; toutes les vitres frémirent, et, une berline de poste qu'enlevaient à plein poitrail trois chevaux crottés jusqu'aux oreilles, débusqua d'un bond au coin des halles. C'était le docteur Larivière.

L'apparition d'un dieu n'eût pas causé plus d'émoi. Bovary leva les mains, Canivet s'arrêta court, et Homais retira son bonnet grec bien avant que le docteur fût entré.

Il appartenait à la grande école chirurgicale sortie du tablier de Bichat, à cette génération, maintenant disparue, de praticiens philosophes qui, chérissant leur art d'un amour fanatique, l'exerçaient avec exaltation et sagacité! Tout tremblait dans son hôpital quand il se mettait en colère, et ses élèves le vénéraient si bien, qu'ils s'efforçaient, à peine établis, de l'imiter le plus possible; de sorte que l'on retrouvait sur eux, par les villes d'alentour, sa longue douillette de mérinos et son large habit noir, dont les parements déboutonnés couvraient un peu ses mains charnues, de fort belles mains, et qui n'avaient jamais de gants, comme pour être plus promptes à plonger dans les misères. Dédaigneux des croix, des titres et des académies, hospitalier, libéral, paternel avec les pauvres et pratiquant la vertu sans y croire, il eût presque passé pour un saint si la finesse de son esprit ne l'eût fait craindre comme un démon. Son regard, plus tranchant que ses bistouris, vous descendait droit dans l'âme et désarticulait tout mensonge à travers les allégations et les pudeurs. Et il allait ainsi, plein de cette majesté débonnaire que donnent la conscience d'un grand talent, de la fortune, et quarante ans d'une existence laborieuse et irréprochable.

Il fronça les sourcils dès la porte, en apercevant la face cadavéreuse d'Emma, étendue sur le dos, la bouche ouverte. Puis, tout en ayant l'air d'écouter Canivet, il se passait l'index sous les narines et répétait:

— C'est bien, c'est bien.

Mais il fit un geste lent des épaules. Bovary l'observa: ils se regardèrent; et cet homme, si habitué pourtant à l'aspect des douleurs, ne put retenir

sight of pain, could not keep back a tear that fell on his shirt-frill.

He tried to take Canivet into the next room. Charles followed him.

"She is very ill, isn't she? If we put on sinapisms? Anything! Oh, think of something, you who have saved so many!"

Charles caught him in both his arms, and gazed at him wildly, imploringly, half-fainting against his breast.

"Come, my poor fellow, courage! There is nothing more to be done."

And Doctor Lariviere turned away.

"You are going?"

"I will come back."

He went out only to give an order to the coachman, with Monsieur Canivet, who did not care either to have Emma die under his hands.

The chemist rejoined them on the Place. He could not by temperament keep away from celebrities, so he begged Monsieur Lariviere to do him the signal honour of accepting some breakfast.

He sent quickly to the "Lion d'Or" for some pigeons; to the butcher's for all the cutlets that were to be had; to Tuvache for cream; and to Lestiboudois for eggs; and the druggist himself aided in the preparations, while Madame Homais was saying as she pulled together the strings of her jacket:

"You must excuse us, sir, for in this poor place, when one hasn't been told the night before—"

"Wine glasses!" whispered Homais.

"If only we were in town, we could fall back upon stuffed trotters."

"Be quiet! Sit down, doctor!"

He thought fit, after the first few mouthfuls, to give some details as to the catastrophe.

"We first had a feeling of siccity in the pharynx, then intolerable pains at the epigastrium, super purgation, coma."

"But how did she poison herself?"

"I don't know, doctor, and I don't even know where she can have procured the arsenious acid."

Justin, who was just bringing in a pile of plates, began to tremble.

une larme qui tomba sur son jabot.

Il voulut emmener Canivet dans la pièce voisine. Charles le suivit.

— Elle est bien mal, n'est-ce pas? Si l'on posait des sinapismes? je ne sais quoi! Trouvez donc quelque chose, vous qui en avez tant sauvé!

Charles lui entourait le corps de ses deux bras, et il le contemplait d'une manière effarée, suppliante, à demi pâmé contre sa poitrine.

— Allons, mon pauvre garçon, du courage! Il n'y a plus rien à faire.

Et le docteur Larivière se détourna.

— Vous partez?

— Je vais revenir.

Il sortit comme pour donner un ordre au postillon, avec le sieur Canivet, qui ne se souciait pas non plus de voir Emma mourir entre ses mains.

Le pharmacien les rejoignit sur la place. Il ne pouvait, par tempérament, se séparer des gens célèbres. Aussi conjura-t-il M. Larivière de lui faire cet insigne honneur d'accepter à déjeuner.

On envoya bien vite prendre des pigeons au Lion d'or, tout ce qu'il y avait de côtelettes à la boucherie, de la crème chez Tuvache, des oeufs chez Lestiboudois, et l'apothicaire aidait lui- même aux préparatifs, tandis que madame Homais disait, en tirant les cordons de sa camisole:

— Vous ferez excuse, monsieur; car dans notre malheureux pays, du moment qu'on n'est pas prévenu la veille...

— Les verres à patte!!! souffla Homais.

— Au moins, si nous étions à la ville, nous aurions la ressource des pieds farcis.

— Tais-toi!... À table, docteur!

Il jugea bon, après les premiers morceaux, de fournir quelques détails sur la catastrophe:

— Nous avons eu d'abord un sentiment de siccité au pharynx, puis des douleurs intolérables à l'épigastre, superpurgation, coma.

— Comment s'est-elle donc empoisonnée?

— Je l'ignore, docteur, et même je ne sais pas trop où elle a pu se procurer cet acide arsénieux.

Justin, qui apportait alors une pile d'assiettes, fut saisi d'un tremblement.

"What's the matter?" said the chemist.

At this question the young man dropped the whole lot on the ground with a crash.

"Imbecile!" cried Homais, "awkward lout! block-head! confounded ass!"

But suddenly controlling himself:

"I wished, doctor, to make an analysis, and primo I delicately introduced a tube—"

"You would have done better," said the physician, "to introduce your fingers into her throat."

His colleague was silent, having just before privately received a severe lecture about his emetic, so that this good Canivet, so arrogant and so verbose at the time of the clubfoot, was to-day very modest. He smiled without ceasing in an approving manner.

Homais dilated in Amphytrionic pride, and the affecting thought of Bovary vaguely contributed to his pleasure by a kind of egotistic reflex upon himself. Then the presence of the doctor transported him. He displayed his erudition, cited pell-mell cantharides, upas, the manchineel, vipers.

"I have even read that various persons have found themselves under toxicological symptoms, and, as it were, thunderstricken by black-pudding that had been subjected to a too vehement fumigation. At least, this was stated in a very fine report drawn up by one of our pharmaceutical chiefs, one of our masters, the illustrious Cadet de Gassicourt!"

Madame Homais reappeared, carrying one of those shaky machines that are heated with spirits of wine; for Homais liked to make his coffee at table, having, moreover, torrefied it, pulverised it, and mixed it himself.

"*Saccharum*, doctor?" said he, offering the sugar.

Then he had all his children brought down, anxious to have the physician's opinion on their constitutions.

At last Monsieur Lariviere was about to leave, when Madame Homais asked for a consultation about her husband. He was making his blood too thick by going to sleep every evening after dinner.

— Qu'as-tu? dit le pharmacien.

Le jeune homme, à cette question, laissa tout tomber par terre, avec un grand fracas.

— Imbécile! s'écria Homais, maladroit! lourdaud! fichu âne!

Mais, soudain, se maîtrisant:

— J'ai voulu, docteur, tenter une analyse, et primo, j'ai délicatement introduit dans un tube...

— Il aurait mieux valu, dit le chirurgien, lui introduire vos doigts dans la gorge.

Son confrère se taisait, ayant tout à l'heure reçu confidentiellement une forte semonce à propos de son émétique, de sorte que ce bon Canivet, si arrogant et verbeux lors du pied-bot, était très modeste aujourd'hui; il souriait sans discontinuer, d'une manière approbative.

Homais s'épanouissait dans son orgueil d'amphitryon, et l'affligeante idée de Bovary contribuait vaguement à son plaisir, par un retour égoïste qu'il faisait sur lui-même. Puis la présence du Docteur le transportait. Il étalait son érudition, il citait pêle-mêle les cantharides, l'upas, le mancenillier, la vipère.

— Et même j'ai lu que différentes personnes s'étaient trouvées intoxiquées, docteur, et comme foudroyées par des boudins qui avaient subi une trop véhémente fumigation! Du moins, c'était dans un fort beau rapport, composé par une de nos sommités pharmaceutiques, un de nos maîtres, l'illustre Cadet de Gassicourt!

Madame Homais réapparut, portant une de ces vacillantes machines que l'on chauffe avec de l'esprit-de-vin; car Homais tenait à faire son café sur la table, l'ayant d'ailleurs torréfié lui-même, porphyrisé lui-même, mixtionné lui-même.

— *Saccharum*, docteur, dit-il en offrant du sucre.

Puis il fit descendre tous ses enfants, curieux d'avoir l'avis du chirurgien sur leur constitution.

Enfin, M. Larivière allait partir, quand madame Homais lui demanda une consultation pour son mari. Il s'épaississait le sang à s'endormir chaque soir après le dîner.

"Oh, it isn't his blood that's too thick," said the physician.

And, smiling a little at his unnoticed joke, the doctor opened the door. But the chemist's shop was full of people; he had the greatest difficulty in getting rid of Monsieur Tuvache, who feared his spouse would get inflammation of the lungs, because she was in the habit of spitting on the ashes; then of Monsieur Binet, who sometimes experienced sudden attacks of great hunger; and of Madame Caron, who suffered from tinglings; of Lheureux, who had vertigo; of Lestiboudois, who had rheumatism; and of Madame Lefrancois, who had heartburn. At last the three horses started; and it was the general opinion that he had not shown himself at all obliging.

Public attention was distracted by the appearance of Monsieur Bournisien, who was going across the market with the holy oil.

Homais, as was due to his principles, compared priests to ravens attracted by the odour of death. The sight of an ecclesiastic was personally disagreeable to him, for the cassock made him think of the shroud, and he detested the one from some fear of the other.

Nevertheless, not shrinking from what he called his mission, he returned to Bovary's in company with Canivet whom Monsieur Lariviere, before leaving, had strongly urged to make this visit; and he would, but for his wife's objections, have taken his two sons with him, in order to accustom them to great occasions; that this might be a lesson, an example, a solemn picture, that should remain in their heads later on.

The room when they went in was full of mournful solemnity. On the work-table, covered over with a white cloth, there were five or six small balls of cotton in a silver dish, near a large crucifix between two lighted candles. Emma, her chin sunken upon her breast, had her eyes inordinately wide open, and her poor hands wandered over the sheets with that hideous and soft movement of the dying, that seems as if they wanted already to cover themselves with the shroud. Pale as a statue and with eyes red as fire, Charles, not weeping, stood opposite her at the foot of the bed, while the priest, bending one knee, was muttering words in a low voice.

— Oh! ce n'est pas le sens qui le gêne.

Et, souriant un peu de ce calembour inaperçu, le docteur ouvrit la porte. Mais la pharmacie regorgeait de monde; et il eut grand- peine à pouvoir se débarrasser du sieur Tuvache, qui redoutait pour son épouse une fluxion de poitrine, parce qu'elle avait coutume de cracher dans les cendres; puis de M. Binet, qui éprouvait parfois des fringales, et de madame Caron, qui avait des picotements; de Lheureux, qui avait des vertiges; de Lestiboudois, qui avait un rhumatisme; de madame Lefrançois, qui avait des aigreurs. Enfin les trois chevaux détalèrent, et l'on trouva généralement qu'il n'avait point montré de complaisance.

L'attention publique fut distraite par l'apparition de M. Bournisien, qui passait sous les halles avec les saintes huiles.

Homais, comme il le devait à ses principes, compara les prêtres à des corbeaux qu'attire l'odeur des morts; la vue d'un ecclésiastique lui était personnellement désagréable, car la soutane le faisait rêver au linceul, et il exécrait l'une un peu par épouvante de l'autre.

Néanmoins, ne reculant pas devant ce qu'il appelait sa mission, il retourna chez Bovary en compagnie de Canivet, que M. Larivière, avant de partir, avait engagé fortement à cette démarche; et même, sans les représentations de sa femme, il eût emmené avec lui ses deux fils, afin de les accoutumer aux fortes circonstances, pour que ce fût une leçon, un exemple, un tableau solennel qui leur restât plus tard dans la tête.

La chambre, quand ils entrèrent, était toute pleine d'une solennité lugubre. Il y avait sur la table à ouvrage, recouverte d'une serviette blanche, cinq ou six petites boules de coton dans un plat d'argent, près d'un gros crucifix, entre deux chandeliers qui brûlaient. Emma, le menton contre sa poitrine, ouvrait démesurément les paupières; et ses pauvres mains se traînaient sur les draps, avec ce geste hideux et doux des agonisants qui semblent vouloir déjà se recouvrir du suaire. Pâle comme une statue, et les yeux rouges comme des charbons, Charles, sans pleurer, se tenait en face d'elle, au pied du lit, tandis que le prêtre, appuyé sur un genou, marmottait des paroles basses.

She turned her face slowly, and seemed filled with joy on seeing suddenly the violet stole, no doubt finding again, in the midst of a temporary lull in her pain, the lost voluptuousness of her first mystical transports, with the visions of eternal beatitude that were beginning.

The priest rose to take the crucifix; then she stretched forward her neck as one who is athirst, and glueing her lips to the body of the Man-God, she pressed upon it with all her expiring strength the fullest kiss of love that she had ever given. Then he recited the Misereatur and the Indulgentiam, dipped his right thumb in the oil, and began to give extreme unction. First upon the eyes, that had so coveted all worldly pomp; then upon the nostrils, that had been greedy of the warm breeze and amorous odours; then upon the mouth, that had uttered lies, that had curled with pride and cried out in lewdness; then upon the hands that had delighted in sensual touches; and finally upon the soles of the feet, so swift of yore, when she was running to satisfy her desires, and that would now walk no more.

The cure wiped his fingers, threw the bit of cotton dipped in oil into the fire, and came and sat down by the dying woman, to tell her that she must now blend her sufferings with those of Jesus Christ and abandon herself to the divine mercy.

Finishing his exhortations, he tried to place in her hand a blessed candle, symbol of the celestial glory with which she was soon to be surrounded. Emma, too weak, could not close her fingers, and the taper, but for Monsieur Bournisien would have fallen to the ground.

However, she was not quite so pale, and her face had an expression of serenity as if the sacrament had cured her.

The priest did not fail to point this out; he even explained to Bovary that the Lord sometimes prolonged the life of persons when he thought it meet for their salvation; and Charles remembered the day when, so near death, she had received the communion.

Perhaps there was no need to despair, he thought.

In fact, she looked around her slowly, as one awakening from a dream; then in a distinct voice she asked for her looking-glass, and remained some time bending over it, until the big tears fell from her

Elle tourna sa figure lentement, et parut saisie de joie à voir tout à coup l'étole violette, sans doute retrouvant au milieu d'un apaisement extraordinaire la volupté perdue de ses premiers élancements mystiques, avec des visions de béatitude éternelle qui commençaient.

Le prêtre se releva pour prendre le crucifix; alors elle allongea le cou comme quelqu'un qui a soif, et, collant ses lèvres sur le corps de l'Homme-Dieu, elle y déposa de toute sa force expirante le plus grand baiser d'amour qu'elle eût jamais donné. Ensuite il récita le Misereatur et Undulgentiam, trempa son pouce droit dans l'huile et commença les onctions: d'abord sur les yeux, qui avaient tant convoité toutes les somptuosités terrestres; puis sur les narines, friandes de brises tièdes et de senteurs amoureuses; puis sur la bouche, qui s'était ouverte pour le mensonge, qui avait gémi d'orgueil et crié dans la luxure; puis sur les mains, qui se délectaient aux contacts suaves, et enfin sur la plante des pieds, si rapides autrefois quand elle courait à l'assouvissance de ses désirs, et qui maintenant ne marcheraient plus.

Le curé s'essuya les doigts, jeta dans le feu les brins de coton trempés d'huile, et revint s'asseoir près de la moribonde pour lui dire qu'elle devait à présent joindre ses souffrances à celles de Jésus-Christ et s'abandonner à la miséricorde divine.

En finissant ses exhortations, il essaya de lui mettre dans la main un cierge bénit, symbole des gloires célestes dont elle allait tout à l'heure être environnée. Emma, trop faible, ne put fermer les doigts, et le cierge, sans M. Bournisien, serait tombé à terre.

Cependant elle n'était plus aussi pâle, et son visage avait une expression de sérénité, comme si le sacrement l'eût guérie.

Le prêtre ne manqua point d'en faire l'observation; il expliqua, même à Bovary que le Seigneur, quelquefois, prolongeait l'existence des personnes lorsqu'il le jugeait convenable pour leur salut; et Charles se rappela un jour où, ainsi près de mourir, elle avait reçu la communion.

— Il ne fallait peut-être pas se désespérer, pensa-t-il.

En effet, elle regarda tout autour d'elle, lentement, comme quelqu'un qui se réveille d'un songe; puis, d'une voix distincte, elle demanda son miroir, et elle resta penchée dessus quelque temps, jusqu'au moment où

eyes. Then she turned away her head with a sigh and fell back upon the pillows.

Her chest soon began panting rapidly; the whole of her tongue protruded from her mouth; her eyes, as they rolled, grew paler, like the two globes of a lamp that is going out, so that one might have thought her already dead but for the fearful labouring of her ribs, shaken by violent breathing, as if the soul were struggling to free itself. Felicite knelt down before the crucifix, and the druggist himself slightly bent his knees, while Monsieur Canivet looked out vaguely at the Place. Bournisien had again begun to pray, his face bowed against the edge of the bed, his long black cassock trailing behind him in the room. Charles was on the other side, on his knees, his arms outstretched towards Emma. He had taken her hands and pressed them, shuddering at every beat of her heart, as at the shaking of a falling ruin. As the death-rattle became stronger the priest prayed faster; his prayers mingled with the stifled sobs of Bovary, and sometimes all seemed lost in the muffled murmur of the Latin syllables that tolled like a passing bell.

Suddenly on the pavement was heard a loud noise of clogs and the clattering of a stick; and a voice rose—a raucous voice—that sang:

*Maids in the warmth of a summer day Dream of love and of love always.*

Emma raised herself like a galvanised corpse, her hair undone, her eyes fixed, staring.

*Where the sickle blades have been, Nannette, gathering ears of corn, Passes bending down, my queen, To the earth where they were born.*

"The blind man!" she cried.

And Emma began to laugh, an atrocious, frantic, despairing laugh, thinking she saw the hideous face of the poor wretch that stood out against the eternal night like a menace.

*The wind is strong this summer day, Her petticoat has flown away.*

She fell back upon the mattress in a convulsion. They all drew near. She was dead.

de grosses larmes lui découlèrent des yeux. Alors elle se renversa la tête en poussant un soupir et retomba sur l'oreiller.

Sa poitrine aussitôt se mit à haleter rapidement. La langue tout entière lui sortit hors de la bouche; ses yeux, en roulant, pâlissaient comme deux globes de lampe qui s'éteignent, à la croire déjà morte, sans l'effrayante accélération de ses côtes, secouées par un souffle furieux, comme si l'âme eût fait des bonds pour se détacher. Félicité s'agenouilla devant le crucifix, et le pharmacien lui-même fléchit un peu les jarrets, tandis que M. Canivet regardait vaguement sur la place. Bournisien s'était remis en prière, la figure inclinée contre le bord de la couche, avec sa longue soutane noire qui traînait derrière lui dans l'appartement. Charles était de l'autre côté, à genoux, les bras étendus vers Emma. Il avait pris ses mains et il les serrait, tressaillant à chaque battement de son coeur, comme au contrecoup d'une ruine qui tombe. À mesure que le râle devenait plus fort, l'ecclésiastique précipitait ses oraisons; elles se mêlaient aux sanglots étouffés de Bovary, et quelquefois tout semblait disparaître dans le sourd murmure des syllabes latines, qui tintaient comme un glas de cloche.

Tout à coup, on entendit sur le trottoir un bruit de gros sabots, avec le frôlement d'un bâton; et une voix s'éleva, une voix rauque, qui chantait:

*Souvent la chaleur d'un beau jour Fait rêver fillette à l'amour.*

Emma se releva comme un cadavre que l'on galvanise, les cheveux dénoués, la prunelle fixe, béante.

*Pour amasser diligemment Les épis que la faux moissonne, Ma Nanette va s'inclinant Vers le sillon qui nous les donne.*

— L'Aveugle s'écria-t-elle.

Et Emma se mit à rire, d'un rire atroce, frénétique, désespéré, croyant voir la face hideuse du misérable, qui se dressait dans les ténèbres éternelles comme un épouvantement.

*Il souffla bien fort ce jour-là, Et le jupon court s'envola!*

Une convulsion la rabattit sur le matelas. Tous s'approchèrent. Elle n'existait plus.

# Chapter 9

There is always after the death of anyone a kind of stupefaction; so difficult is it to grasp this advent of nothingness and to resign ourselves to believe in it. But still, when he saw that she did not move, Charles threw himself upon her, crying:

"Farewell! farewell!"

Homais and Canivet dragged him from the room.

"Restrain yourself!"

"Yes." said he, struggling, "I'll be quiet. I'll not do anything. But leave me alone. I want to see her. She is my wife!"

And he wept.

"Cry," said the chemist; "let nature take her course; that will solace you."

Weaker than a child, Charles let himself be led downstairs into the sitting-room, and Monsieur Homais soon went home.

On the Place he was accosted by the blind man, who, having dragged himself as far as Yonville, in the hope of getting the antiphlogistic pomade, was asking every passer-by where the druggist lived.

"There now! as if I hadn't got other fish to fry. Well, so much the worse; you must come later on."

And he entered the shop hurriedly.

He had to write two letters, to prepare a soothing potion for Bovary, to invent some lie that would conceal the poisoning, and work it up into an article for the "Fanal," without counting the people who were waiting to get the news from him; and when the Yonvillers had all heard his story of the arsenic that she had mistaken for sugar in making a vanilla cream. Homais once more returned to Bovary's.

He found him alone (Monsieur Canivet had left), sitting in an armchair near the window, staring with an idiotic look at the flags of the floor.

# Chapitre 9

Il y a toujours après la mort de quelqu'un comme une stupéfaction qui se dégage, tant il est difficile de comprendre cette survenue du néant et de se résigner à y croire. Mais, quand il s'aperçut pourtant de son immobilité, Charles se jeta sur elle en criant:

— Adieu! adieu!

Homais et Canivet l'entraînèrent hors de la chambre.

— Modérez-vous!

— Oui, disait-il en se débattant, je serai raisonnable, je ne ferai pas de mal. Mais laissez-moi! je veux la voir! c'est ma femme!

Et il pleurait.

— Pleurez, reprit le pharmacien, donnez cours à la nature, cela vous soulagera!

Devenu plus faible qu'un enfant, Charles se laissa conduire en bas, dans la salle, et M. Homais bientôt s'en retourna chez lui.

Il fut sur la Place accosté par l'Aveugle, qui, s'étant traîné jusqu'à Yonville dans l'espoir de la pommade antiphlogistique, demandait à chaque passant où demeurait l'apothicaire.

— Allons, bon! comme si je n'avais pas d'autres chiens à fouetter! Ah! tant pis, reviens plus tard!

Et il entra précipitamment dans la pharmacie.

Il avait à écrire deux lettres, à faire une potion calmante pour Bovary, à trouver un mensonge qui pût cacher l'empoisonnement et à le rédiger en article pour le Fanal, sans compter les personnes qui l'attendaient, afin d'avoir des informations; et, quand les Yonvillais eurent tous entendu son histoire d'arsenic qu'elle avait pris pour du sucre, en faisant une crème à la vanille, Homais, encore une fois, retourna chez Bovary.

Il le trouva seul (M. Canivet venait de partir), assis dans le fauteuil, près de la fenêtre, et contemplant d'un regard idiot les pavés de la salle.

"Now," said the chemist, "you ought yourself to fix the hour for the ceremony."

"Why? What ceremony?"

Then, in a stammering, frightened voice:

"Oh, no! not that. No! I want to see her here."

Homais, to keep himself in countenance, took up a water-bottle on the whatnot to water the geraniums.

"Ah! thanks," said Charles; "you are good."

But he did not finish, choking beneath the crowd of memories that this action of the druggist recalled to him.

Then to distract him, Homais thought fit to talk a little horticulture: plants wanted humidity. Charles bowed his head in sign of approbation.

"Besides, the fine days will soon be here again."

"Ah!" said Bovary.

The druggist, at his wit's end, began softly to draw aside the small window-curtain.

"Hallo! there's Monsieur Tuvache passing."

Charles repeated like a machine:

"Monsieur Tuvache passing!"

Homais did not dare to speak to him again about the funeral arrangements; it was the priest who succeeded in reconciling him to them.

He shut himself up in his consulting-room, took a pen, and after sobbing for some time, wrote:

"I wish her to be buried in her wedding-dress, with white shoes, and a wreath. Her hair is to be spread out over her shoulders. Three coffins, one of oak, one of mahogany, one of lead. Let no one say anything to me. I shall have strength. Over all there is to be placed a large piece of green velvet. This is my wish; see that it is done."

The two men were much surprised at Bovary's romantic ideas. The chemist at once went to him and said:

"This velvet seems to me a superfetation. Besides, the expense—"

"What's that to you?" cried Charles. "Leave me! You did not love her. Go!"

— Il faudrait à présent, dit le pharmacien, fixer vous-même l'heure de la cérémonie.

— Pourquoi? quelle cérémonie?

Puis d'une voix balbutiante et effrayée:

— Oh! non, n'est-ce pas? non, je veux la garder.

Homais, par contenance; prit une carafe sur l'étagère pour arroser les géraniums.

— Ah! merci, dit Charles, vous êtes bon!

Et il n'acheva pas, suffoquant sous une abondance de souvenirs que ce geste du pharmacien lui rappelait.

Alors, pour le distraire, Homais jugea convenable de causer un peu horticulture; les plantes avaient besoin d'humidité. Charles baissa la tête en signe d'approbation.

— Du reste, les beaux jours maintenant vont revenir.

— Ah! fit Bovary.

L'apothicaire, à bout d'idées, se mit à écarter doucement les petits rideaux du vitrage.

— Tiens, voilà M. Tuvache qui passe.

Charles répéta comme une machine:

— M. Tuvache qui passe.

Homais n'osa lui reparler des dispositions funèbres; ce fut l'ecclésiastique qui parvint à l'y résoudre.

Il s'enferma dans son cabinet, prit une plume, et, après avoir sangloté quelque temps, il écrivit:

«Je veux qu'on l'enterre dans sa robe de noces, avec des souliers blancs, une couronne. On lui étaiera les cheveux sur les épaules; trois cercueils, un de chêne, un d'acajou, un de plomb. Qu'on ne me dise rien, j'aurai de la force. On lui mettra par-dessus tout une grande pièce de velours vert. Je le veux. Faites-le.»

Ces messieurs s'étonnèrent beaucoup des idées romanesques de Bovary, et aussitôt le pharmacien alla lui dire:

— Ce velours me parait une superfétation. La dépense, d'ailleurs…

— Est-ce que cela vous regarde? s'écria Charles. Laissez-moi! vous ne l'aimiez pas! Allez-vous-en!

The priest took him by the arm for a turn in the garden. He discoursed on the vanity of earthly things. God was very great, was very good: one must submit to his decrees without a murmur; nay, must even thank him.

Charles burst out into blasphemies.

"I hate your God!"

"The spirit of rebellion is still upon you," sighed the ecclesiastic.

Bovary was far away. He was walking with great strides along by the wall, near the espalier, and he ground his teeth; he raised to heaven looks of malediction, but not so much as a leaf stirred.

A fine rain was falling: Charles, whose chest was bare, at last began to shiver; he went in and sat down in the kitchen.

At six o'clock a noise like a clatter of old iron was heard on the Place; it was the "Hirondelle" coming in, and he remained with his forehead against the windowpane, watching all the passengers get out, one after the other. Felicite put down a mattress for him in the drawing-room. He threw himself upon it and fell asleep.

Although a philosopher, Monsieur Homais respected the dead. So bearing no grudge to poor Charles, he came back again in the evening to sit up with the body; bringing with him three volumes and a pocket-book for taking notes.

Monsieur Bournisien was there, and two large candles were burning at the head of the bed, that had been taken out of the alcove.

The druggist, on whom the silence weighed, was not long before he began formulating some regrets about this "unfortunate young woman." and the priest replied that there was nothing to do now but pray for her.

"Yet," Homais went on, "one of two things; either she died in a state of grace (as the Church has it), and then she has no need of our prayers; or else she departed impertinent (that is, I believe, the ecclesiastical expression), and then—"

Bournisien interrupted him, replying testily that it was none the less necessary to pray.

"But," objected the chemist, "since God knows all our needs, what can be the good of prayer?"

L'ecclésiastique le prit par-dessous le bras pour lui faire faire un tour de promenade dans le jardin. Il discourait sur la vanité des choses terrestres. Dieu était bien grand, bien bon; on devait sans murmure se soumettre à ses décrets, même le remercier.

Charles éclata en blasphèmes.

— Je l'exècre, votre Dieu!

— L'esprit de révolte est encore en vous, soupira l'ecclésiastique.

Bovary était loin. Il marchait à grands pas, le long du mur, près de l'espalier, et il grinçait des dents, il levait au ciel des regards de malédiction; mais pas une feuille seulement n'en bougea.

Une petite pluie tombait. Charles, qui avait la poitrine nue, finit par grelotter; il rentra s'asseoir dans la cuisine.

À six heures; on entendit un bruit de ferraille sur la Place: c'était l'Hirondelle qui arrivait; et il resta le front contre les carreaux, à voir descendre les uns après les autres tous les voyageurs. Félicité lui étendit un matelas dans le salon; il se jeta dessus et s'endormit.

Bien que philosophe, M. Homais respectait les morts. Aussi, sans garder rancune au pauvre Charles, il revint le soir pour faire la veillée du cadavre, apportant avec lui trois volumes, et un portefeuille afin de prendre des notes.

M. Bournisien s'y trouvait, et deux grands cierges brûlaient au chevet du lit, que l'on avait tiré hors de l'alcôve.

L'apothicaire, à qui le silence pesait, ne tarda pas à formuler quelques plaintes sur cette «infortunée jeune femme»; et le prêtre répondit qu'il ne restait plus maintenant qu'à prier pour elle.

— Cependant, reprit Homais, de deux choses l'une: ou elle est morte en état de grâce (comme s'exprime l'Église), et alors elle n'a nul besoin de nos prières; ou bien elle est décédée impénitente (c'est, je crois, l'expression ecclésiastique), et alors…

Bournisien l'interrompit, répliquant d'un ton bourru qu'il n'en fallait pas moins prier.

— Mais, objecta le pharmacien, puisque Dieu connaît tous nos besoins, à quoi peut servir la prière?

"What!" cried the ecclesiastic, "prayer! Why, aren't you a Christian?"

"Excuse me," said Homais; "I admire Christianity. To begin with, it enfranchised the slaves, introduced into the world a morality—"

"That isn't the question. All the texts—"

"Oh! oh! As to texts, look at history; it, is known that all the texts have been falsified by the Jesuits."

Charles came in, and advancing towards the bed, slowly drew the curtains.

Emma's head was turned towards her right shoulder, the corner of her mouth, which was open, seemed like a black hole at the lower part of her face; her two thumbs were bent into the palms of her hands; a kind of white dust besprinkled her lashes, and her eyes were beginning to disappear in that viscous pallor that looks like a thin web, as if spiders had spun it over. The sheet sunk in from her breast to her knees, and then rose at the tips of her toes, and it seemed to Charles that infinite masses, an enormous load, were weighing upon her.

The church clock struck two. They could hear the loud murmur of the river flowing in the darkness at the foot of the terrace. Monsieur Bournisien from time to time blew his nose noisily, and Homais' pen was scratching over the paper.

"Come, my good friend," he said, "withdraw; this spectacle is tearing you to pieces."

Charles once gone, the chemist and the cure recommenced their discussions.

"Read Voltaire," said the one, "read D'Holbach, read the 'Encyclopaedia'!"

"Read the 'Letters of some Portuguese Jews,'" said the other; "read 'The Meaning of Christianity,' by Nicolas, formerly a magistrate."

They grew warm, they grew red, they both talked at once without listening to each other. Bournisien was scandalized at such audacity; Homais marvelled at such stupidity; and they were on the point of insulting one another when Charles suddenly reappeared. A fascination drew him. He was continually coming upstairs.

— Comment! fit l'ecclésiastique, la prière! Vous n'êtes donc pas chrétien?

— Pardonnez! dit Homais. J'admire le christianisme. Il a d'abord affranchi les esclaves, introduit dans le monde une morale...

— Il ne s'agit pas de cela! Tous les textes...

— Oh! oh! quant aux textes, ouvrez l'histoire; on sait qu'ils ont été falsifiés par les jésuites.

Charles entra, et, s'avançant vers le lit, il tira lentement les rideaux.

Emma avait la tête penchée sur l'épaule droite. Le coin de sa bouche, qui se tenait ouverte, faisait comme un trou noir au bas de son visage; les deux pouces restaient infléchis dans la paume des mains; une sorte de poussière blanche lui parsemait les cils, et ses yeux commençaient à disparaître dans une pâleur visqueuse qui ressemblait à une toile mince, comme si des araignées avaient filé dessus. Le drap se creusait depuis ses seins jusqu'à ses genoux, se relevant ensuite à la pointe des orteils; et il semblait à Charles que des masses infinies, qu'un poids énorme pesait sur elle.

L'horloge de l'église sonna deux heures. On entendait le gros murmure de la rivière qui coulait dans les ténèbres, au pied de la terrasse. M. Bournisien, de temps à autre, se mouchait bruyamment, et Homais faisait grincer sa plume sur le papier.

— Allons, mon bon ami, dit-il, retirez-vous, ce spectacle vous déchire!

Charles une fois parti, le pharmacien et le curé recommencèrent leurs discussions.

— Lisez Voltaire! disait l'un; lisez d'Holbach, lisez l'Encyclopédie!

— Lisez les Lettres de quelques juifs portugais disait l'autre; lisez la Raison du christianisme, par Nicolas, ancien magistrat!

Ils s'échauffaient, ils étaient rouges, ils parlaient à la fois sans s'écouter; Bournisien se scandalisait d'une telle audace; Homais s'émerveillait d'une telle bêtise; et ils n'étaient pas loin de s'adresser des injures, quand Charles, tout à coup, reparut. Une fascination l'attirait. Il remontait continuellement l'escalier.

He stood opposite her, the better to see her, and he lost himself in a contemplation so deep that it was no longer painful.

He recalled stories of catalepsy, the marvels of magnetism, and he said to himself that by willing it with all his force he might perhaps succeed in reviving her. Once he even bent towards he, and cried in a low voice, "Emma! Emma!" His strong breathing made the flames of the candles tremble against the wall.

At daybreak Madame Bovary senior arrived. Charles as he embraced her burst into another flood of tears. She tried, as the chemist had done, to make some remarks to him on the expenses of the funeral. He became so angry that she was silent, and he even commissioned her to go to town at once and buy what was necessary.

Charles remained alone the whole afternoon; they had taken Berthe to Madame Homais'; Felicite was in the room upstairs with Madame Lefrancois.

In the evening he had some visitors. He rose, pressed their hands, unable to speak. Then they sat down near one another, and formed a large semicircle in front of the fire. With lowered faces, and swinging one leg crossed over the other knee, they uttered deep sighs at intervals; each one was inordinately bored, and yet none would be the first to go.

Homais, when he returned at nine o'clock (for the last two days only Homais seemed to have been on the Place), was laden with a stock of camphor, of benzine, and aromatic herbs. He also carried a large jar full of chlorine water, to keep off all miasmata. Just then the servant, Madame Lefrancois, and Madame Bovary senior were busy about Emma, finishing dressing her, and they were drawing down the long stiff veil that covered her to her satin shoes.

Felicite was sobbing:

"Ah! my poor mistress! my poor mistress!"

"Look at her," said the landlady, sighing; "how pretty she still is! Now, couldn't you swear she was going to get up in a minute?"

Then they bent over her to put on her wreath.

They had to raise the head a little, and a rush of black liquid issued,

Il se posait en face d'elle pour la mieux voir, et il se perdait en cette contemplation, qui n'était plus douloureuse à force d'être profonde.

Il se rappelait des histoires de catalepsie, les miracles du magnétisme; et il se disait qu'en le voulant extrêmement, il parviendrait peut-être à la ressusciter. Une fois même il se pencha vers elle, et il cria tout bas: «Emma! Emma!» Son haleine, fortement poussée, fit trembler la flamme des cierges contre le mur.

Au petit jour, madame Bovary mère arriva; Charles en l'embrassant, eut un nouveau débordement de pleurs. Elle essaya, comme avait tenté le pharmacien, de lui faire quelques observations sur les dépenses de l'enterrement. Il s'emporta si fort qu'elle se tut, et même il la chargea de se rendre immédiatement à la ville pour acheter ce qu'il fallait.

Charles resta seul toute l'après-midi: on avait conduit Berthe chez madame Homais; Félicité se tenait en haut, dans la chambre, avec la mère Lefrançois.

Le soir, il reçut des visites. Il se levait, vous serrait les mains sans pouvoir parler, puis l'on s'asseyait auprès des autres, qui faisaient devant la cheminée un grand demi-cercle. La figure basse et le jarret sur le genou, ils dandinaient leur jambe, tout en poussant par intervalles un gros soupir; et chacun s'ennuyait d'une façon démesurée; c'était pourtant à qui ne partirait pas.

Homais, quand il revint à neuf heures (on ne voyait que lui sur la Place depuis deux jours), était chargé d'une provision de camphre, de benjoin et d'herbes aromatiques. Il portait aussi un vase plein de chlore, pour bannir les miasmes. À ce moment, la domestique, madame Lefrançois et la mère Bovary tournaient autour d'Emma, en achevant de l'habiller; et elles abaissèrent le long voile raide, qui la recouvrit jusqu'à ses souliers de satin.

Félicité sanglotait:

— Ah! ma pauvre maîtresse! ma pauvre maîtresse!

— Regardez-la, disait en soupirant l'aubergiste, comme elle est mignonne encore! Si l'on ne jurerait pas qu'elle va se lever tout à l'heure.

Puis elles se penchèrent, pour lui mettre sa couronne.

Il fallut soulever un peu la tête, et alors un flot de liquides noirs sortit,

as if she were vomiting, from her mouth.

"Oh, goodness! The dress; take care!" cried Madame Lefrancois. "Now, just come and help," she said to the chemist. "Perhaps you're afraid?"

"I afraid?" replied he, shrugging his shoulders. "I dare say! I've seen all sorts of things at the hospital when I was studying pharmacy. We used to make punch in the dissecting room! Nothingness does not terrify a philosopher; and, as I often say, I even intend to leave my body to the hospitals, in order, later on, to serve science."

The cure on his arrival inquired how Monsieur Bovary was, and, on the reply of the druggist, went on:

"The blow, you see, is still too recent."

Then Homais congratulated him on not being exposed, like other people, to the loss of a beloved companion; whence there followed a discussion on the celibacy of priests.

"For," said the chemist, "it is unnatural that a man should do without women! There have been crimes—"

"But, good heaven!" cried the ecclesiastic, "how do you expect an individual who is married to keep the secrets of the confessional, for example?"

Homais fell foul of the confessional. Bournisien defended it; he enlarged on the acts of restitution that it brought about. He cited various anecdotes about thieves who had suddenly become honest. Military men on approaching the tribunal of penitence had felt the scales fall from their eyes. At Fribourg there was a minister—

His companion was asleep. Then he felt somewhat stifled by the overheavy atmosphere of the room; he opened the window; this awoke the chemist.

"Come, take a pinch of snuff," he said to him. "Take it; it'll relieve you."

A continual barking was heard in the distance.

"Do you hear that dog howling?" said the chemist.

"They smell the dead," replied the priest. "It's like bees; they leave their hives on the decease of any person." Homais made no remark upon these prejudices, for he had again dropped asleep.

comme un vomissement, de sa bouche.

— Ah! mon Dieu! la robe, prenez garde! s'écria madame Lefrançois. Aidez-nous donc! disait-elle au pharmacien. Est-ce que vous avez peur, par hasard?

— Moi, peur? répliqua-t-il en haussant les épaules. Ah bien, oui! J'en ai vu d'autres à l'Hôtel-Dieu, quand j'étudiais la pharmacie! Nous faisions du punch dans l'amphithéâtre aux dissections! Le néant n'épouvante pas un philosophe; et même, je le dis souvent, j'ai l'intention de léguer mon corps aux hôpitaux, afin de servir plus tard à la Science.

En arrivant, le Curé demanda comment se portait Monsieur; et, sur la réponse de l'apothicaire, il reprit:

— Le coup, vous comprenez, est encore trop récent!

Alors Homais le félicita de n'être pas exposé, comme tout le monde, à perdre une compagne chérie; d'où s'ensuivit une discussion sur le célibat des prêtres.

— Car, disait le pharmacien, il n'est pas naturel qu'un homme se passe de femmes! On a vu des crimes…

— Mais, sabre de bois! s'écria l'ecclésiastique, comment voulez- vous qu'un individu pris dans le mariage puisse garder, par exemple, le secret de la confession?

Homais attaqua la confession. Bournisien la défendit; il s'étendit sur les restitutions qu'elle faisait opérer. Il cita différentes anecdotes de voleurs devenus honnêtes tout à coup. Des militaires, s'étant approchés du tribunal de la pénitence, avaient senti les écailles leur tomber des yeux. Il y avait à Fribourg un ministre…

Son compagnon dormait. Puis, comme il étouffait un peu dans l'atmosphère trop lourde de la chambre, il ouvrit la fenêtre, ce qui réveilla le pharmacien.

— Allons, une prise! lui dit-il. Acceptez, cela dissipe.

Des aboiements continus se traînaient au loin, quelque part.

— Entendez-vous un chien qui hurle? dit le pharmacien.

— On prétend, qu'ils sentent les morts, répondit l'ecclésiastique. C'est comme les abeilles: elles s'envolent de la ruche au décès des personnes. Homais ne releva pas ces préjugés, car il s'était rendormi.

Monsieur Bournisien, stronger than he, went on moving his lips gently for some time, then insensibly his chin sank down, he let fall his big black boot, and began to snore.

They sat opposite one another, with protruding stomachs, puffed-up faces, and frowning looks, after so much disagreement uniting at last in the same human weakness, and they moved no more than the corpse by their side, that seemed to be sleeping.

Charles coming in did not wake them. It was the last time; he came to bid her farewell.

The aromatic herbs were still smoking, and spirals of bluish vapour blended at the window-sash with the fog that was coming in. There were few stars, and the night was warm.

The wax of the candles fell in great drops upon the sheets of the bed. Charles watched them burn, tiring his eyes against the glare of their yellow flame.

The watering on the satin gown shimmered white as moonlight. Emma was lost beneath it; and it seemed to him that, spreading beyond her own self, she blended confusedly with everything around her—the silence, the night, the passing wind, the damp odours rising from the ground.

Then suddenly he saw her in the garden at Tostes, on a bench against the thorn hedge, or else at Rouen in the streets, on the threshold of their house, in the yard at Bertaux. He again heard the laughter of the happy boys beneath the apple-trees: the room was filled with the perfume of her hair; and her dress rustled in his arms with a noise like electricity. The dress was still the same.

For a long while he thus recalled all his lost joys, her attitudes, her movements, the sound of her voice. Upon one fit of despair followed another, and even others, inexhaustible as the waves of an overflowing sea.

A terrible curiosity seized him. Slowly, with the tips of his fingers, palpitating, he lifted her veil. But he uttered a cry of horror that awoke the other two. They dragged him down into the sitting-room.

Then Felicite came up to say that he wanted some of her hair.

M. Bournisien, plus robuste, continua quelque temps à remuer tout bas les lèvres; puis, insensiblement, il baissa le menton, lâcha son gros livre noir et se mit à ronfler.

Ils étaient en face l'un de l'autre, le ventre en avant, la figure bouffie, l'air renfrogné, après tant de désaccord se rencontrant enfin dans la même faiblesse humaine; et ils ne bougeaient pas plus que le cadavre à côté d'eux, qui avait l'air de dormir.

Charles, en entrant, ne les réveilla point. C'était la dernière fois. Il venait lui faire ses adieux.

Les herbes aromatiques fumaient encore, et des tourbillons de vapeur bleuâtre se confondaient au bord de la croisée avec le brouillard qui entrait. Il y avait quelques étoiles, et la nuit était douce.

La cire des cierges tombait par grosses larmes sur les draps du lit. Charles les regardait brûler, fatiguant ses yeux contre le rayonnement de leur flamme jaune.

Des moires frissonnaient sur la robe de satin, blanche comme un clair de lune. Emma disparaissait dessous; et il lui semblait que, s'épandant au dehors d'elle-même, elle se perdait confusément dans l'entourage des choses, dans le silence, dans la nuit, dans le vent qui passait, dans les senteurs humides qui montaient.

Puis, tout à coup, il la voyait dans le jardin de Tostes, sur le banc, contre la haie d'épines, ou bien à Rouen dans les rues, sur le seuil de leur maison, dans la cour des Bertaux. Il entendait encore le rire des garçons en gaieté qui dansaient sous les pommiers; la chambre était pleine du parfum de sa chevelure, et sa robe lui frissonnait dans les bras avec un bruit d'étincelles. C'était la même, celle-là!

Il fut longtemps à se rappeler ainsi toutes les félicités disparues, ses attitudes, ses gestes, le timbre de sa voix. Après un désespoir, il en venait un autre, et toujours, intarissablement, comme les flots d'une marée qui déborde.

Il eut une curiosité terrible: lentement, du bout des doigts, en palpitant, il releva son voile. Mais il poussa un cri d'horreur qui réveilla les deux autres. Ils l'entraînèrent en bas, dans la salle.

Puis Félicité vint dire qu'il demandait des cheveux.

"Cut some off," replied the druggist.

And as she did not dare to, he himself stepped forward, scissors in hand. He trembled so that he pierced the skin of the temple in several places. At last, stiffening himself against emotion, Homais gave two or three great cuts at random that left white patches amongst that beautiful black hair.

The chemist and the cure plunged anew into their occupations, not without sleeping from time to time, of which they accused each other reciprocally at each fresh awakening. Then Monsieur Bournisien sprinkled the room with holy water and Homais threw a little chlorine water on the floor.

Felicite had taken care to put on the chest of drawers, for each of them, a bottle of brandy, some cheese, and a large roll. And the druggist, who could not hold out any longer, about four in the morning sighed:

"My word! I should like to take some sustenance."

The priest did not need any persuading; he went out to go and say mass, came back, and then they ate and hobnobbed, giggling a little without knowing why, stimulated by that vague gaiety that comes upon us after times of sadness, and at the last glass the priest said to the druggist, as he clapped him on the shoulder:

"We shall end by understanding one another."

In the passage downstairs they met the undertaker's men, who were coming in. Then Charles for two hours had to suffer the torture of hearing the hammer resound against the wood. Next day they lowered her into her oak coffin, that was fitted into the other two; but as the bier was too large, they had to fill up the gaps with the wool of a mattress. At last, when the three lids had been planed down, nailed, soldered, it was placed outside in front of the door; the house was thrown open, and the people of Yonville began to flock round.

Old Rouault arrived, and fainted on the Place when he saw the black cloth!

— Coupez-en! répliqua l'apothicaire.

Et, comme elle n'osait, il s'avança lui-même, les ciseaux à la main. Il tremblait si fort, qu'il piqua la peau des tempes en plusieurs places. Enfin, se raidissant contre l'émotion, Homais donna deux ou trois grands coups au hasard, ce qui fit des marques blanches dans cette belle chevelure noire.

Le pharmacien et le curé se replongèrent dans leurs occupations, non sans dormir de temps à autre, ce dont ils s'accusaient réciproquement à chaque réveil nouveau. Alors M. Bournisien aspergeait la chambre d'eau bénite et Homais jetait un peu de chlore par terre.

Félicité avait eu soin de mettre pour eux, sur la commode, une bouteille d'eau-de-vie, un fromage et une grosse brioche. Aussi l'apothicaire, qui n'en pouvait plus, soupira, vers quatre heures du matin:

— Ma foi, je me sustenterais avec plaisir!

L'ecclésiastique ne se fit point prier; il sortit pour aller dire sa messe, revint; puis ils mangèrent et trinquèrent, tout en ricanant un peu, sans savoir pourquoi, excités par cette gaieté vague qui vous prend après des séances de tristesse; et, au dernier petit verre, le prêtre dit au pharmacien, tout en lui frappant sur l'épaule:

— Nous finirons par nous entendre!

Ils rencontrèrent en bas, dans le vestibule, les ouvriers qui arrivaient. Alors Charles, pendant deux heures, eut à subir le supplice du marteau qui résonnait sur les planches. Puis on la descendit dans son cercueil de chêne, que l'on emboîta dans les deux autres; mais, comme la bière était trop large, il fallut boucher les interstices avec la laine d'un matelas. Enfin, quand les trois couvercles furent rabotés, cloués, soudés, on l'exposa devant la porte; on ouvrit toute grande la maison, et les gens d'Yonville commencèrent à affluer.

Le père Rouault arriva. Il s'évanouit sur la Place en apercevant le drap noir.

# Chapter 10

He had only received the chemist's letter thirty-six hours after the event; and, from consideration for his feelings, Homais had so worded it that it was impossible to make out what it was all about.

First, the old fellow had fallen as if struck by apoplexy. Next, he understood that she was not dead, but she might be. At last, he had put on his blouse, taken his hat, fastened his spurs to his boots, and set out at full speed; and the whole of the way old Rouault, panting, was torn by anguish. Once even he was obliged to dismount. He was dizzy; he heard voices round about him; he felt himself going mad.

Day broke. He saw three black hens asleep in a tree. He shuddered, horrified at this omen. Then he promised the Holy Virgin three chasubles for the church, and that he would go barefooted from the cemetery at Bertaux to the chapel of Vassonville.

He entered Maromme shouting for the people of the inn, burst open the door with a thrust of his shoulder, made for a sack of oats, emptied a bottle of sweet cider into the manger, and again mounted his nag, whose feet struck fire as it dashed along.

He said to himself that no doubt they would save her; the doctors would discover some remedy surely. He remembered all the miraculous cures he had been told about.

Then she appeared to him dead. She was there; before his eyes, lying on her back in the middle of the road. He reined up, and the hallucination disappeared.

At Quincampoix, to give himself heart, he drank three cups of coffee one after the other.

He fancied they had made a mistake in the name in writing. He looked for the letter in his pocket, felt it there, but did not dare to open it.

At last he began to think it was all a joke; someone's spite, the jest of some wag; and besides, if she were dead, one would have known it. But

# Chapitre 10

Il n'avait reçu la lettre du pharmacien que trente-six heures après l'événement; et, par égard pour sa sensibilité, M. Homais l'avait rédigée de telle façon qu'il était impossible de savoir à quoi s'en tenir.

Le bonhomme tomba d'abord comme frappé d'apoplexie. Ensuite il comprit qu'elle n'était pas morte. Mais elle pouvait l'être… Enfin il avait passé sa blouse, pris son chapeau, accroché un éperon à son soulier et était parti ventre à terre; et, tout le long de la route, le père Rouault, haletant, se dévora d'angoisses. Une fois même, il fut obligé de descendre. Il n'y voyait plus, il entendait des voix autour de lui, il se sentait devenir fou.

Le jour se leva. Il aperçut trois poules noires qui dormaient dans un arbre; il tressaillit, épouvanté de ce présage. Alors il promit à la sainte Vierge trois chasubles pour l'église, et qu'il irait pieds nus depuis le cimetière des Bertaux jusqu'à la chapelle de Vassonville.

Il entra dans Maromme en hélant les gens de l'auberge, enfonça la porte d'un coup d'épaule, bondit au sac d'avoine, versa dans la mangeoire une bouteille de cidre doux, et renfourcha son bidet, qui faisait feu des quatre fers.

Il se disait qu'on la sauverait sans doute; les médecins découvriraient un remède, c'était sûr. Il se rappela toutes les guérisons miraculeuses qu'on lui avait contées.

Puis elle lui apparaissait morte. Elle était là, devant lui, étendue sur le dos, au milieu de la route. Il tirait la bride et l'hallucination disparaissait.

À Quincampoix, pour se donner du coeur, il but trois cafés l'un sur l'autre.

Il songea qu'on s'était trompé de nom en écrivant. Il chercha la lettre dans sa poche, l'y sentit, mais il n'osa pas l'ouvrir.

Il en vint à supposer que c'était peut-être une farce, une vengeance de quelqu'un, une fantaisie d'homme en goguette; et, d'ailleurs,

no! There was nothing extraordinary about the country; the sky was blue, the trees swayed; a flock of sheep passed. He saw the village; he was seen coming bending forward upon his horse, belabouring it with great blows, the girths dripping with blood.

When he had recovered consciousness, he fell, weeping, into Bovary's arms:

"My girl! Emma! my child! tell me—"

The other replied, sobbing:

"I don't know! I don't know! It's a curse!"

The druggist separated them.

"These horrible details are useless. I will tell this gentleman all about it. Here are the people coming. Dignity! Come now! Philosophy!"

The poor fellow tried to show himself brave, and repeated several times:

"Yes! courage!"

"Oh," cried the old man, "so I will have, by God! I'll go along o' her to the end!"

The bell began tolling. All was ready; they had to start.

And seated in a stall of the choir, side by side, they saw pass and repass in front of them continually the three chanting choristers. The serpent-player was blowing with all his might. Monsieur Bournisien, in full vestments, was singing in a shrill voice. He bowed before the tabernacle, raising his hands, stretched out his arms. Lestiboudois went about the church with his whalebone stick. The bier stood near the lectern, between four rows of candles. Charles felt inclined to get up and put them out.

Yet he tried to stir himself to a feeling of devotion, to throw himself into the hope of a future life in which he should see her again. He imagined to himself she had gone on a long journey, far away, for a long time. But when he thought of her lying there, and that all was over, that they would lay her in the earth, he was seized with a fierce, gloomy, despairful rage. At times he thought he felt nothing more, and he enjoyed this lull in his pain, whilst at the same time he reproached himself for being a wretch.

si elle était morte, on le saurait? Mais non! la campagne n'avait rien d'extraordinaire: le ciel était bleu, les arbres se balançaient; un troupeau de moutons passa. Il aperçut le village; on le vit accourant tout penché sur son cheval, qu'il bâtonnait à grands coups, et dont les sangles dégouttelaient de sang.

Quand il eut repris connaissance, il tomba tout en pleurs dans les bras de Bovary:

— Ma fille! Emma! mon enfant! expliquez-moi...?

Et l'autre répondait avec des sanglots:

— Je ne sais pas, je ne sais pas! c'est une malédiction!

L'apothicaire les sépara.

— Ces horribles détails sont inutiles. J'en instruirai monsieur. Voici le monde qui vient. De la dignité, fichtre! de la philosophie!

Le pauvre garçon voulut paraître fort, et. il répéta plusieurs fois:

— Oui..., du courage!

— Eh bien, s'écria le bonhomme, j'en aurai, nom d'un tonnerre de Dieu! Je m'en vas la conduire jusqu'au bout.

La cloche tintait. Tout était prêt. Il fallut se mettre en marche.

Et, assis dans une stalle du choeur, l'un près de l'autre, ils virent passer, devant eux et repasser continuellement les trois chantres qui psalmodiaient. Le serpent soufflait à pleine poitrine. M. Bournisien, en grand appareil, chantait d'une voix aiguë; il saluait le tabernacle, élevait les mains, étendait les bras. Lestiboudois circulait dans l'église avec sa latte de baleine; près du lutrin, la bière reposait entre quatre rangs de cierges. Charles avait envie de se lever pour les éteindre.

Il tâchait cependant de s'exciter à la dévotion, de s'élancer dans l'espoir d'une vie future où il la reverrait. Il imaginait qu'elle était partie en voyage, bien loin, depuis longtemps. Mais, quand il pensait qu'elle se trouvait là-dessous, et que tout était fini, qu'on l'emportait dans la terre, il se prenait d'une rage farouche, noire, désespérée. Parfois il croyait ne plus rien sentir; et il savourait cet adoucissement de sa douleur, tout en se reprochant d'être un misérable.

The sharp noise of an iron-ferruled stick was heard on the stones, striking them at irregular intervals. It came from the end of the church, and stopped short at the lower aisles. A man in a coarse brown jacket knelt down painfully. It was Hippolyte, the stable-boy at the "Lion d'Or." He had put on his new leg.

One of the choristers went round the nave making a collection, and the coppers chinked one after the other on the silver plate.

"Oh, make haste! I am in pain!" cried Bovary, angrily throwing him a five-franc piece.

The churchman thanked him with a deep bow.

They sang, they knelt, they stood up; it was endless! He remembered that once, in the early times, they had been to mass together, and they had sat down on the other side, on the right, by the wall. The bell began again. There was a great moving of chairs; the bearers slipped their three staves under the coffin, and everyone left the church.

Then Justin appeared at the door of the shop. He suddenly went in again, pale, staggering.

People were at the windows to see the procession pass. Charles at the head walked erect. He affected a brave air, and saluted with a nod those who, coming out from the lanes or from their doors, stood amidst the crowd.

The six men, three on either side, walked slowly, panting a little. The priests, the choristers, and the two choirboys recited the De profundis, and their voices echoed over the fields, rising and falling with their undulations. Sometimes they disappeared in the windings of the path; but the great silver cross rose always before the trees.

The women followed in black cloaks with turned-down hoods; each of them carried in her hands a large lighted candle, and Charles felt himself growing weaker at this continual repetition of prayers and torches, beneath this oppressive odour of wax and of cassocks. A fresh breeze was blowing; the rye and colza were sprouting, little dewdrops trembled at the roadsides and on the hawthorn hedges. All sorts of joyous sounds filled the air; the jolting of a cart rolling afar off in the

On entendit sur les dalles comme le bruit sec d'un bâton ferré qui les frappait à temps égaux. Cela venait du fond, et s'arrêta court dans les bas-côtés de l'église. Un homme en grosse veste brune s'agenouilla péniblement. C'était Hippolyte, le garçon du Lion d'or. Il avait mis sa jambe neuve.

L'un des chantres vint faire le tour de la nef pour quêter, et les gros sous, les uns après les autres, sonnaient dans le plat d'argent.

— Dépêchez-vous donc! Je souffre, moi! s'écria Bovary tout en lui jetant avec colère une pièce de cinq francs.

L'homme d'église le remercia par une longue révérence.

On chantait, on s'agenouillait, on se relevait, cela n'en finissait pas! Il se rappela qu'une fois, dans les premiers temps, ils avaient ensemble assisté à la messe, et ils s'étaient mis de l'autre côté, à droite, contre le mur. La cloche recommença. Il y eut un grand mouvement de chaises. Les porteurs glissèrent leurs trois bâtons sous la bière, et l'on sortit de l'église.

Justin alors parut sur le seuil de la pharmacie. Il y rentra tout à coup, pâle, chancelant.

On se tenait aux fenêtres pour voir passer le cortège. Charles, en avant, se cambrait la taille. Il affectait un air brave et saluait d'un signe ceux qui, débouchant des ruelles ou des portes, se rangeaient dans la foule.

Les six hommes, trois de chaque côté, marchaient au petit pas et en haletant un peu. Les prêtres, les chantres et les deux enfants de choeur récitaient le De profundis; et leurs voix s'en allaient sur la campagne, montant et s'abaissant avec des ondulations. Parfois ils disparaissaient aux détours du sentier; mais la grande croix d'argent se dressait toujours entre les arbres.

Les femmes suivaient, couvertes de mantes noires à capuchon rabattu; elles portaient à la main un gros cierge qui brûlait, et Charles se sentait défaillir à cette continuelle répétition de prières et de flambeaux, sous ces odeurs affadissantes de cire et de soutane. Une brise fraîche soufflait, les seigles et les colzas verdoyaient, des gouttelettes de rosée tremblaient au bord du chemin, sur les haies d'épines. Toutes sortes de bruits joyeux emplissaient l'horizon: le claquement d'une charrette rou-

ruts, the crowing of a cock, repeated again and again, or the gambling of a foal running away under the apple-trees: The pure sky was fretted with rosy clouds; a bluish haze rested upon the cots covered with iris. Charles as he passed recognised each courtyard. He remembered mornings like this, when, after visiting some patient, he came out from one and returned to her.

The black cloth bestrewn with white beads blew up from time to time, laying bare the coffin. The tired bearers walked more slowly, and it advanced with constant jerks, like a boat that pitches with every wave.

They reached the cemetery.

The men went right down to a place in the grass where a grave was dug.

They ranged themselves all round; and while the priest spoke, the red soil thrown up at the sides kept noiselessly slipping down at the corners.

Then when the four ropes were arranged the coffin was placed upon them. He watched it descend; it seemed descending for ever.

At last a thud was heard; the ropes creaked as they were drawn up. Then Bournisien took the spade handed to him by Lestiboudois; with his left hand all the time sprinkling water, with the right he vigorously threw in a large spadeful; and the wood of the coffin, struck by the pebbles, gave forth that dread sound that seems to us the reverberation of eternity.

The ecclesiastic passed the holy water sprinkler to his neighbour. This was Homais. He swung it gravely, then handed it to Charles, who sank to his knees in the earth and threw in handfuls of it, crying, "Adieu!" He sent her kisses; he dragged himself towards the grave, to engulf himself with her.

They led him away, and he soon grew calmer, feeling perhaps, like the others, a vague satisfaction that it was all over.

Old Rouault on his way back began quietly smoking a pipe, which Homais in his innermost conscience thought not quite the thing. He also noticed that Monsieur Binet had not been present, and that Tuvache had "made off" after mass, and that Theodore, the notary's servant wore

lant au loin dans les ornières, le cri d'un coq qui se répétait ou la galopade d'un poulain que l'on voyait s'enfuir sous les pommiers. Le ciel pur était tacheté de nuages roses; des fumignons bleuâtres se rabattaient sur les chaumières couvertes d'iris; Charles, en passant, reconnaissait les cours. Il se souvenait de matins comme celui-ci, où, après avoir visité quelque malade, il en sortait, et retournait vers elle.

Le drap noir, semé de larmes blanches, se levait de temps à autre en découvrant la bière. Les porteurs fatigués se ralentissaient, et elle avançait par saccades continues, comme une chaloupe qui tangue à chaque flot.

On arriva.

Les hommes continuèrent jusqu'en bas, à une place dans le gazon où la fosse était creusée.

On se rangea tout autour; et, tandis que le prêtre parlait, la terre rouge, rejetée sur les bords, coulait par les coins, sans bruit, continuellement.

Puis, quand les quatre cordes furent disposées, on poussa la bière dessus. Il la regarda descendre. Elle descendait toujours.

Enfin on entendit un choc; les cordes en grinçant remontèrent. Alors Bournisien prit la bêche que lui tendait Lestiboudois; de sa main gauche, tout en aspergeant de la droite, il poussa vigoureusement une large pelletée; et le bois du cercueil, heurté par les cailloux, fit ce bruit formidable qui nous semble être le retentissement de l'éternité.

L'ecclésiastique passa le goupillon à son voisin. C'était M. Homais. Il le secoua gravement, puis le tendit à Charles, qui s'affaissa jusqu'aux genoux dans la terre, et il en jetait à pleines mains tout en criant: «Adieu!» Il lui envoyait des baisers; il se traînait vers la fosse pour s'y engloutir avec elle.

On l'emmena; et il ne tarda pas à s'apaiser, éprouvant peut-être, comme tous les autres, la vague satisfaction d'en avoir fini.

Le père Rouault, en revenant, se mit tranquillement à fumer une pipe; ce que Homais, dans son for intérieur, jugea peu convenable. Il remarqua de même que M. Binet s'était abstenu de paraître, que Tuvache «avait filé» après la messe, et que Théodore, le domestique du notaire,

a blue coat, "as if one could not have got a black coat, since that is the custom, by Jove!" And to share his observations with others he went from group to group. They were deploring Emma's death, especially Lheureux, who had not failed to come to the funeral.

"Poor little woman! What a trouble for her husband!"

The druggist continued:

"Do you know that but for me he would have committed some fatal attempt upon himself?"

"Such a good woman! To think that I saw her only last Saturday in my shop."

"I haven't had leisure," said Homais, "to prepare a few words that I would have cast upon her tomb."

Charles on getting home undressed, and old Rouault put on his blue blouse. It was a new one, and as he had often during the journey wiped his eyes on the sleeves, the dye had stained his face, and the traces of tears made lines in the layer of dust that covered it.

Madame Bovary senior was with them. All three were silent. At last the old fellow sighed:

"Do you remember, my friend, that I went to Tostes once when you had just lost your first deceased? I consoled you at that time. I thought of something to say then, but now—"

Then, with a loud groan that shook his whole chest:

"Ah! this is the end for me, do you see! I saw my wife go, then my son, and now to-day it's my daughter."

He wanted to go back at once to Bertaux, saying that he could not sleep in this house. He even refused to see his granddaughter.

"No, no! It would grieve me too much. Only you'll kiss her many times for me. Good-bye! you're a good fellow! And then I shall never forget that," he said, slapping his thigh. "Never fear, you shall always have your turkey."

But when he reached the top of the hill he turned back, as he had turned once before on the road of Saint-Victor when he had parted from her. The windows of the village were all on fire beneath the slanting rays

portait un habit bleu, «comme si l'on ne pouvait pas trouver un habit noir, puisque c'est l'usage, que diable!» Et pour communiquer ses observations, il allait d'un groupe à l'autre. On y déplorait la mort d'Emma, et surtout Lheureux, qui n'avait point manqué de venir à l'enterrement.

— Cette pauvre petite dame! quelle douleur pour son mari!

L'apothicaire reprenait:

— Sans moi, savez-vous bien, il se serait porté sur lui-même à quelque attentat funeste!

— Une si bonne personne! Dire pourtant que je l'ai encore vue samedi dernier dans ma boutique!

— Je n'ai pas eu le loisir, dit Homais, de préparer quelques paroles que j'aurais jetées sur sa tombe.

En rentrant, Charles se déshabilla, et le père Rouault repassa sa blouse bleue. Elle était neuve, et, comme il s'était, pendant la route, souvent essuyé les yeux avec les manches, elle avait déteint sur sa figure; et la trace des pleurs y faisait des lignes dans la couche de poussière qui la salissait.

Madame Bovary mère était avec eux. Ils se taisaient tous les trois. Enfin le bonhomme soupira:

— Vous rappelez-vous, mon ami, que je suis venu à Tostes une fois, quand vous veniez de perdre votre première défunte. Je vous consolais dans ce temps-là! Je trouvais quoi dire; mais à présent...

Puis, avec un long gémissement qui souleva toute sa poitrine:

— Ah! c'est la fin pour moi, voyez-vous! J'ai vu partir ma femme..., mon fils après..., et voilà ma fille, aujourd'hui!

Il voulut s'en retourner tout de suite aux Bertaux, disant qu'il ne pourrait pas dormir dans cette maison-là. Il refusa même de voir sa petite-fille.

— Non! Non! ça me ferait trop de deuil. Seulement, vous l'embrasserez bien! Adieu!... vous êtes un bon garçon! Et puis, jamais je n'oublierai ça, dit-il en se frappant la cuisse; n'ayez peur! vous recevrez toujours votre dinde.

Mais, quand il fut au haut de la côte, il se détourna, comme autrefois il s'était détourné sur le chemin de Saint-Victor, en se séparant d'elle. Les fenêtres du village étaient tout en feu sous les rayons obliques du

of the sun sinking behind the field. He put his hand over his eyes, and saw in the horizon an enclosure of walls, where trees here and there formed black clusters between white stones; then he went on his way at a gentle trot, for his nag had gone lame.

Despite their fatigue, Charles and his mother stayed very long that evening talking together. They spoke of the days of the past and of the future. She would come to live at Yonville; she would keep house for him; they would never part again. She was ingenious and caressing, rejoicing in her heart at gaining once more an affection that had wandered from her for so many years. Midnight struck. The village as usual was silent, and Charles, awake, thought always of her.

Rodolphe, who, to distract himself, had been rambling about the wood all day, was sleeping quietly in his chateau, and Leon, down yonder, always slept.

There was another who at that hour was not asleep.

On the grave between the pine-trees a child was on his knees weeping, and his heart, rent by sobs, was beating in the shadow beneath the load of an immense regret, sweeter than the moon and fathomless as the night. The gate suddenly grated. It was Lestiboudois; he came to fetch his spade, that he had forgotten. He recognised Justin climbing over the wall, and at last knew who was the culprit who stole his potatoes.

soleil, qui se couchait dans la prairie. Il mit sa main devant ses yeux; et il aperçut à l'horizon un enclos de murs où des arbres, çà et là, faisaient des bouquets noirs entre des pierres blanches, puis il continua sa route, au petit trot, car son bidet boitait.

Charles et sa mère restèrent le soir, malgré leur fatigue, fort longtemps à causer ensemble. Ils parlèrent des jours d'autrefois et de l'avenir. Elle viendrait habiter Yonville, elle tiendrait son ménage, ils ne se quitteraient plus. Elle fut ingénieuse et caressante, se réjouissant intérieurement à ressaisir une affection qui depuis tant d'années lui échappait. Minuit sonna. Le village, comme d'habitude, était silencieux, et Charles, éveillé, pensait toujours à elle.

Rodolphe, qui, pour se distraire, avait battu le bois toute la journée, dormait tranquillement dans son château; et Léon, là-bas, dormait aussi.

Il y en avait un autre qui, à cette heure-là, ne dormait pas.

Sur la fosse, entre les sapins, un enfant pleurait agenouillé, et sa poitrine, brisée par les sanglots, haletait dans l'ombre, sous la pression d'un regret immense plus doux que la lune et plus insondable que la nuit. La grille tout à coup craqua. C'était Lestiboudois; il venait chercher sa bêche qu'il avait oubliée tantôt. Il reconnut Justin escaladant le mur, et sut alors à quoi s'en tenir sur le malfaiteur qui lui dérobait ses pommes de terre.

# Chapter 11

The next day Charles had the child brought back. She asked for her mamma. They told her she was away; that she would bring her back some playthings. Berthe spoke of her again several times, then at last thought no more of her. The child's gaiety broke Bovary's heart, and he had to bear besides the intolerable consolations of the chemist.

Money troubles soon began again, Monsieur Lheureux urging on anew his friend Vincart, and Charles pledged himself for exorbitant sums; for he would never consent to let the smallest of the things that had belonged to HER be sold. His mother was exasperated with him; he grew even more angry than she did. He had altogether changed. She left the house.

Then everyone began "taking advantage" of him. Mademoiselle Lempereur presented a bill for six months' teaching, although Emma had never taken a lesson (despite the receipted bill she had shown Bovary); it was an arrangement between the two women. The man at the circulating library demanded three years' subscriptions; Mere Rollet claimed the postage due for some twenty letters, and when Charles asked for an explanation, she had the delicacy to reply:

"Oh, I don't know. It was for her business affairs."

With every debt he paid Charles thought he had come to the end of them. But others followed ceaselessly.

He sent in accounts for professional attendance. He was shown the letters his wife had written. Then he had to apologise.

Felicite now wore Madame Bovary's gowns; not all, for he had kept some of them, and he went to look at them in her dressing-room, locking himself up there; she was about her height, and often Charles, seeing her from behind, was seized with an illusion, and cried out:

"Oh, stay, stay!"

But at Whitsuntide she ran away from Yonville, carried off by Theodore, stealing all that was left of the wardrobe.

# Chapitre 11

Charles, le lendemain, fit revenir la petite. Elle demanda sa maman. On lui répondit qu'elle était absente, qu'elle lui rapporterait des joujoux. Berthe en reparla plusieurs fois; puis, à la longue, elle n'y pensa plus. La gaieté de cette enfant navrait Bovary, et il avait à subir les intolérables consolations du pharmacien.

Les affaires d'argent bientôt recommencèrent, M. Lheureux excitant de nouveau son ami Vinçart, et Charles s'engagea pour des sommes exorbitantes; car jamais il ne voulut consentir à laisser vendre le moindre des meubles ne lui avaient appartenu. Sa mère en fut exaspérée. Il s'indigna plus fort qu'elle. Il avait changé tout à fait. Elle abandonna la maison.

Alors chacun se mit à profiter. Mademoiselle Lempereur réclama six mois de leçons, bien qu'Emma n'en eût jamais pris une seule (malgré cette facture acquittée qu'elle avait fait voir à Bovary): c'était une convention entre elles deux; le loueur de livres réclama trois ans d'abonnement; la mère Rolet réclama le port d'une vingtaine de lettres; et, comme Charles demandait des explications, elle eut la délicatesse de répondre:

— Ah! je ne sais rien! c'était pour ses affaires.

À chaque dette qu'il payait, Charles croyait en avoir fini. Il en survenait d'autres, continuellement.

Il exigea l'arriéré d'anciennes visites. On lui montra les lettres que sa femme avait envoyées. Alors il fallut faire des excuses.

Félicité portait maintenant les robes de Madame; non pas toutes, car il en avait gardé quelques-unes, et il les allait voir dans son cabinet de toilette, où il s'enfermait; elle était à peu près de sa taille, souvent Charles, en l'apercevant par derrière, était saisi d'une illusion, et s'écriait:

— Oh! reste! reste!

Mais, à la Pentecôte, elle décampa d'Yonville, enlevée par Théodore, et en volant tout ce qui restait de la garde-robe.

It was about this time that the widow Dupuis had the honour to inform him of the "marriage of Monsieur Leon Dupuis her son, notary at Yvetot, to Mademoiselle Leocadie Leboeuf of Bondeville." Charles, among the other congratulations he sent him, wrote this sentence:

"How glad my poor wife would have been!"

One day when, wandering aimlessly about the house, he had gone up to the attic, he felt a pellet of fine paper under his slipper. He opened it and read: "Courage, Emma, courage. I would not bring misery into your life." It was Rodolphe's letter, fallen to the ground between the boxes, where it had remained, and that the wind from the dormer window had just blown towards the door. And Charles stood, motionless and staring, in the very same place where, long ago, Emma, in despair, and paler even than he, had thought of dying. At last he discovered a small R at the bottom of the second page. What did this mean? He remembered Rodolphe's attentions, his sudden, disappearance, his constrained air when they had met two or three times since. But the respectful tone of the letter deceived him.

"Perhaps they loved one another platonically," he said to himself.

Besides, Charles was not of those who go to the bottom of things; he shrank from the proofs, and his vague jealousy was lost in the immensity of his woe.

Everyone, he thought, must have adored her; all men assuredly must have coveted her. She seemed but the more beautiful to him for this; he was seized with a lasting, furious desire for her, that inflamed his despair, and that was boundless, because it was now unrealisable.

To please her, as if she were still living, he adopted her predilections, her ideas; he bought patent leather boots and took to wearing white cravats. He put cosmetics on his moustache, and, like her, signed notes of hand. She corrupted him from beyond the grave.

He was obliged to sell his silver piece by piece; next he sold the drawing-room furniture. All the rooms were stripped; but the bedroom, her own room, remained as before. After his dinner Charles went up there. He pushed the round table in front of the fire, and drew up her arm-

Ce fut vers cette époque que madame veuve Dupuis eut l'honneur de lui faire part du «mariage de M. Léon Dupuis, son fils, notaire à Yvetot, avec mademoiselle Léocadie Leboeuf, de Bondeville». Charles, parmi les félicitations qu'il lui adressa, écrivit cette phrase:

«Comme ma pauvre femme aurait été heureuse!»

Un jour qu'errant sans but dans la maison, il était monté jusqu'au grenier, il sentit sous sa pantoufle une boulette de papier fin. Il l'ouvrit et il lut: «Du courage, Emma! du courage! Je ne veux pas faire le malheur de votre existence.» C'était la lettre de Rodolphe, tombée à terre entre des caisses, qui était restée là, et que le vent de la lucarne venait de pousser vers la porte. Et Charles demeura tout immobile et béant à cette même place où jadis, encore plus pâle que lui, Emma, désespérée, avait voulu mourir. Enfin, il découvrit un petit R au bas de la seconde page. Qu'était-ce? il se rappela les assiduités de Rodolphe, sa disparition soudaine et l'air contraint qu'il avait eu en la rencontrant depuis, deux ou trois fois. Mais le ton respectueux de la lettre l'illusionna.

— Ils se sont peut-être aimés platoniquement, se dit-il.

D'ailleurs, Charles n'était pas de ceux qui descendent au fond des choses: il recula devant les preuves, et sa jalousie incertaine se perdit dans l'immensité de son chagrin.

On avait dû, pensait-il, l'adorer. Tous les hommes, à coup sûr, l'avaient convoitée. Elle lui en parut plus belle; et il en conçut un désir permanent, furieux, qui enflammait son désespoir et qui n'avait pas de limites, parce qu'il était maintenant irréalisable.

Pour lui plaire, comme si elle vivait encore, il adopta ses prédilections, ses idées; il s'acheta des bottes vernies, il prit l'usage des cravates blanches. Il mettait du cosmétique à ses moustaches, il souscrivit comme elle des billets à ordre. Elle le corrompait par delà le tombeau.

Il fut obligé de vendre l'argenterie pièce à pièce, ensuite il vendit les meubles du salon. Tous les appartements se dégarnirent; mais la chambre, sa chambre à elle, était restée comme autrefois. Après son dîner, Charles montait là. Il poussait devant le feu la table ronde, et il

chair. He sat down opposite it. A candle burnt in one of the gilt candlesticks. Berthe by his side was painting prints.

He suffered, poor man, at seeing her so badly dressed, with laceless boots, and the arm-holes of her pinafore torn down to the hips; for the charwoman took no care of her. But she was so sweet, so pretty, and her little head bent forward so gracefully, letting the dear fair hair fall over her rosy cheeks, that an infinite joy came upon him, a happiness mingled with bitterness, like those ill-made wines that taste of resin. He mended her toys, made her puppets from cardboard, or sewed up half-torn dolls. Then, if his eyes fell upon the workbox, a ribbon lying about, or even a pin left in a crack of the table, he began to dream, and looked so sad that she became as sad as he.

No one now came to see them, for Justin had run away to Rouen, where he was a grocer's assistant, and the druggist's children saw less and less of the child, Monsieur Homais not caring, seeing the difference of their social position, to continue the intimacy.

The blind man, whom he had not been able to cure with the pomade, had gone back to the hill of Bois-Guillaume, where he told the travellers of the vain attempt of the druggist, to such an extent, that Homais when he went to town hid himself behind the curtains of the "Hirondelle" to avoid meeting him. He detested him, and wishing, in the interests of his own reputation, to get rid of him at all costs, he directed against him a secret battery, that betrayed the depth of his intellect and the baseness of his vanity. Thus, for six consecutive months, one could read in the "Fanal de Rouen" editorials such as these:

"All who bend their steps towards the fertile plains of Picardy have, no doubt, remarked, by the Bois-Guillaume hill, a wretch suffering from a horrible facial wound. He importunes, persecutes one, and levies a regular tax on all travellers. Are we still living in the monstrous times of the Middle Ages, when vagabonds were permitted to display in our public places leprosy and scrofulas they had brought back from the Crusades?"

Or:

approchait son fauteuil. Il s'asseyait en face. Une chandelle brûlait dans un des flambeaux dorés. Berthe, près de lui, enluminait des estampes.

Il souffrait, le pauvre homme, à la voir si mal vêtue, avec ses brodequins sans lacet et l'emmanchure de ses blouses déchirée jusqu'aux hanches, car la femme de ménage n'en prenait guère de souci. Mais elle était si douce, si gentille, et sa petite tête se penchait si gracieusement en laissant retomber sur ses joues roses sa bonne chevelure blonde, qu'une délectation infinie l'envahissait, plaisir tout mêlé d'amertume comme ces vins mal faits qui sentent la résine. Il raccommodait ses joujoux, lui fabriquait des pantins avec du carton, ou recousait le ventre déchiré de ses poupées. Puis, s'il rencontrait des yeux la boîte à ouvrage, un ruban qui traînait ou même une épingle restée dans une fente de la table, il se prenait à rêver, et il avait l'air si triste, qu'elle devenait triste comme lui.

Personne à présent ne venait les voir; car Justin s'était enfui à Rouen, où il est devenu garçon épicier, et les enfants de l'apothicaire fréquentaient de moins en moins la petite, M. Homais ne se souciant pas, vu la différence de leurs conditions sociales, que l'intimité se prolongeât.

L'Aveugle, qu'il n'avait pu guérir avec sa pommade, était retourné dans la côte du Bois-Guillaume, où il narrait aux voyageurs la vaine tentative du pharmacien, à tel point que Homais, lorsqu'il allait à la ville, se dissimulait derrière les rideaux de l'Hirondelle, afin d'éviter sa rencontre. Il l'exécrait; et, dans l'intérêt de sa propre réputation, voulant s'en débarrasser à toute force, il dressa contre lui une batterie cachée, qui décelait la profondeur de son intelligence et la scélératesse de sa vanité. Durant six mois consécutifs, on put donc lire dans le Fanal de Rouen des entrefilets ainsi conçus:

«Toutes les personnes qui se dirigent vers les fertiles contrées de la Picardie auront remarqué sans doute, dans la côte du Bois- Guillaume, un misérable atteint d'une horrible plaie faciale. Il vous importune, vous persécute et prélève un véritable impôt sur les voyageurs. Sommes-nous encore à ces temps monstrueux du Moyen Age, où il était permis aux vagabonds d'étaler par nos places publiques la lèpre et les scrofules qu'ils avaient rapportées de la croisade?»

Ou bien:

"In spite of the laws against vagabondage, the approaches to our great towns continue to be infected by bands of beggars. Some are seen going about alone, and these are not, perhaps, the least dangerous. What are our ediles about?"

Then Homais invented anecdotes:

"Yesterday, by the Bois-Guillaume hill, a skittish horse—" And then followed the story of an accident caused by the presence of the blind man.

He managed so well that the fellow was locked up. But he was released. He began again, and Homais began again. It was a struggle. Homais won it, for his foe was condemned to life-long confinement in an asylum.

This success emboldened him, and henceforth there was no longer a dog run over, a barn burnt down, a woman beaten in the parish, of which he did not immediately inform the public, guided always by the love of progress and the hate of priests. He instituted comparisons between the elementary and clerical schools to the detriment of the latter; called to mind the massacre of St. Bartholomew a propos of a grant of one hundred francs to the church, and denounced abuses, aired new views. That was his phrase. Homais was digging and delving; he was becoming dangerous.

However, he was stifling in the narrow limits of journalism, and soon a book, a work was necessary to him. Then he composed "General Statistics of the Canton of Yonville, followed by Climatological Remarks." The statistics drove him to philosophy. He busied himself with great questions: the social problem, moralisation of the poorer classes, pisciculture, caoutchouc, railways, etc. He even began to blush at being a bourgeois. He affected the artistic style, he smoked. He bought two chic Pompadour statuettes to adorn his drawing-room.

He by no means gave up his shop. On the contrary, he kept well abreast of new discoveries. He followed the great movement of chocolates; he was the first to introduce "cocoa" and "revalenta" into the Seine-Inferieure. He was enthusiastic about the hydro-electric Pulvermacher chains; he wore one himself, and when at night he took off his flannel vest, Madame Homais stood quite dazzled before the golden spiral

«Malgré les lois contre le vagabondage, les abords de nos grandes villes continuent à être infestés par des bandes de pauvres. On en voit qui circulent isolément, et qui, peut-être, ne sont pas les moins dangereux. À quoi songent nos édiles?»

Puis Homais inventait des anecdotes:

«Hier, dans la côte du Bois-Guillaume, un cheval ombrageux...» Et suivait le récit d'un accident occasionné par la présence de l'Aveugle.

Il fit si bien, qu'on l'incarcéra. Mais on le relâcha. Il recommença, et Homais aussi recommença. C'était une lutte. Il eut la victoire; car son ennemi fut condamné à une réclusion perpétuelle dans un hospice.

Ce succès l'enhardit; et dès lors il n'y eut plus dans l'arrondissement un chien écrasé, une grange incendiée, une femme battue, dont aussitôt il ne fît part au public, toujours guidé par l'amour du progrès et la haine des prêtres. Il établissait des comparaisons entre les écoles primaires et les frères ignorantins, au détriment de ces derniers, rappelait la Saint-Barthélemy à propos d'une allocation de cent francs faite à l'église, et dénonçait des abus, lançait des boutades. C'était son mot. Homais sapait; il devenait dangereux.

Cependant il étouffait dans les limites étroites du journalisme, et bientôt il lui fallut le livre, l'ouvrage! Alors il composa une Statistique générale du canton d'Yonville, suivie d'observations climatologiques, et la statistique le poussa vers la philosophie. Il se préoccupa des grandes questions: problème social, moralisation des classes pauvres, pisciculture, caoutchouc, chemins de fer, etc. Il en vint à rougir d'être un bourgeois. Il affectait le genre artiste, il fumait! Il s'acheta deux statuettes chic Pompadour, pour décorer son salon.

Il n'abandonnait point la pharmacie; au contraire! il se tenait au courant des découvertes. Il suivait le grand mouvement des chocolats. C'est le premier qui ait fait venir dans la Seine- Inférieure du cho-ca et de la revalentia. Il s'éprit d'enthousiasme pour les chaînes hydro-électriques Pulvermacher; il en portait une lui-même; et, le soir, quand il retirait son gilet de flanelle, madame Homais restait tout éblouie devant la spirale

beneath which he was hidden, and felt her ardour redouble for this man more bandaged than a Scythian, and splendid as one of the Magi.

He had fine ideas about Emma's tomb. First he proposed a broken column with some drapery, next a pyramid, then a Temple of Vesta, a sort of rotunda, or else a "mass of ruins." And in all his plans Homais always stuck to the weeping willow, which he looked upon as the indispensable symbol of sorrow.

Charles and he made a journey to Rouen together to look at some tombs at a funeral furnisher's, accompanied by an artist, one Vaufrylard, a friend of Bridoux's, who made puns all the time. At last, after having examined some hundred designs, having ordered an estimate and made another journey to Rouen, Charles decided in favour of a mausoleum, which on the two principal sides was to have a "spirit bearing an extinguished torch."

As to the inscription, Homais could think of nothing so fine as *Sta viator*, and he got no further; he racked his brain, he constantly repeated *Sta viator*. At last he hit upon *Amabilen conjugem calcas*, which was adopted.

A strange thing was that Bovary, while continually thinking of Emma, was forgetting her. He grew desperate as he felt this image fading from his memory in spite of all efforts to retain it. Yet every night he dreamt of her; it was always the same dream. He drew near her, but when he was about to clasp her she fell into decay in his arms.

For a week he was seen going to church in the evening. Monsieur Bournisien even paid him two or three visits, then gave him up. Moreover, the old fellow was growing intolerant, fanatic, said Homais. He thundered against the spirit of the age, and never failed, every other week, in his sermon, to recount the death agony of Voltaire, who died devouring his excrements, as everyone knows.

In spite of the economy with which Bovary lived, he was far from being able to pay off his old debts. Lheureux refused to renew any more bills. A distraint became imminent. Then he appealed to his mother, who consented to let him take a mortgage on her property, but with a

d'or sous laquelle il disparaissait, et sentait redoubler ses ardeurs pour cet homme plus garrotté qu'un Scythe et splendide comme un mage.

Il eut de belles idées à propos du tombeau d'Emma. Il proposa d'abord un tronçon de colonne avec une draperie, ensuite une pyramide, puis un temple de Vesta, une manière de rotonde… ou bien «un amas de ruines». Et, dans tous les plans, Homais ne démordait point du saule pleureur, qu'il considérait comme le symbole obligé de la tristesse.

Charles et lui firent ensemble un voyage à Rouen, pour voir des tombeaux, chez un entrepreneur de sépultures, — accompagnés d'un artiste peintre, un nommé Vaufrylard, ami de Bridoux, et qui, tout le temps, débita des calembours. Enfin, après avoir examiné une centaine de dessins, s'être commandé un devis et avoir fait un second voyage à Rouen, Charles se décida pour un mausolée qui devait porter sur ses deux faces principales «un génie tenant une torche éteinte».

Quant à l'inscription, Homais ne trouvait rien de beau comme: *Sta viator*, et il en restait là; il se creusait l'imagination; il répétait continuellement: *Sta viator*… Enfin, il découvrit: *amabilem conjugem calcas*! qui fut adopté.

Une chose étrange, c'est que Bovary, tout en pensant à Emma continuellement, l'oubliait; et il se désespérait à sentir cette image lui échapper de la mémoire au milieu des efforts qu'il faisait pour la retenir. Chaque nuit pourtant, il la rêvait; c'était toujours le même rêve: il s'approchait d'elle; mais, quand il venait à l'étreindre, elle tombait en pourriture dans ses bras.

On le vit pendant une semaine entrer le soir à l'église. M. Bournisien lui fit même deux ou trois visites, puis l'abandonna. D'ailleurs, le bonhomme tournait à l'intolérance, au fanatisme, disait Homais; il fulminait contre l'esprit du siècle, et ne manquait pas, tous les quinze jours, au sermon, de raconter l'agonie de Voltaire, lequel mourut en dévorant ses excréments, comme chacun sait.

Malgré l'épargne où vivait Bovary, il était loin de pouvoir amortir ses anciennes dettes. Lheureux refusa de renouveler aucun billet. La saisie devint imminente. Alors il eut recours à sa mère, qui consentit à lui laisser prendre une hypothèque sur ses biens, mais en lui envoyant

great many recriminations against Emma; and in return for her sacrifice she asked for a shawl that had escaped the depredations of Felicite. Charles refused to give it her; they quarrelled.

She made the first overtures of reconciliation by offering to have the little girl, who could help her in the house, to live with her. Charles consented to this, but when the time for parting came, all his courage failed him. Then there was a final, complete rupture.

As his affections vanished, he clung more closely to the love of his child. She made him anxious, however, for she coughed sometimes, and had red spots on her cheeks.

Opposite his house, flourishing and merry, was the family of the chemist, with whom everything was prospering. Napoleon helped him in the laboratory, Athalie embroidered him a skullcap, Irma cut out rounds of paper to cover the preserves, and Franklin recited Pythagoras' table in a breath. He was the happiest of fathers, the most fortunate of men.

Not so! A secret ambition devoured him. Homais hankered after the cross of the Legion of Honour. He had plenty of claims to it.

"First, having at the time of the cholera distinguished myself by a boundless devotion; second, by having published, at my expense, various works of public utility, such as" (and he recalled his pamphlet entitled, "Cider, its manufacture and effects," besides observation on the lanigerous plant-louse, sent to the Academy; his volume of statistics, and down to his pharmaceutical thesis); "without counting that I am a member of several learned societies" (he was member of a single one).

"In short!" he cried, making a pirouette, "if it were only for distinguishing myself at fires!"

Then Homais inclined towards the Government. He secretly did the prefect great service during the elections. He sold himself—in a word, prostituted himself. He even addressed a petition to the sovereign in which he implored him to "do him justice"; he called him "our good king," and compared him to Henri IV.

And every morning the druggist rushed for the paper to see if his nomination were in it. It was never there. At last, unable to bear it any

force récriminations contre Emma; et elle demandait, en retour de son sacrifice, un châle, échappé aux ravages de Félicité. Charles le lui refusa. Ils se brouillèrent.

Elle fit les premières ouvertures de raccommodement, en lui proposant de prendre chez elle la petite, qui la soulagerait dans sa maison. Charles y consentit. Mais, au moment du départ, tout courage l'abandonna. Alors, ce fut une rupture définitive, complète.

À mesure que ses affections disparaissaient, il se resserrait plus étroitement à l'amour de son enfant. Elle l'inquiétait cependant; car elle toussait quelquefois, et avait des plaques rouges aux pommettes.

En face de lui s'étalait, florissante et hilare, la famille du pharmacien, que tout au monde contribuait à satisfaire. Napoléon l'aidait au laboratoire, Athalie lui brodait un bonnet grec, Irma découpait des rondelles de papier pour couvrir les confitures, et Franklin récitait tout d'une haleine la table de Pythagore. Il était le plus heureux des pères, le plus fortuné des hommes.

Erreur! une ambition sourde le rongeait: Homais désirait la croix. Les titres ne lui manquaient point:

I° S'être, lors du choléra, signalé par un dévouement sans bornes; 2° avoir publié, et à mes frais, différents ouvrages d'utilité publique, tels que… (et il rappelait son mémoire intitulé: Du cidre, de sa fabrication et de ses effets; plus, des observations sur le puceron laniger, envoyées à l'Académie; son volume de statistique, et jusqu'à sa thèse de pharmacien); sans compter que je suis membre de plusieurs sociétés savantes (il l'était d'une seule).

— Enfin, s'écriait-il, en faisant une pirouette, quand ce ne serait que de me signaler aux incendies!

Alors Homais inclina vers le Pouvoir. Il rendit secrètement à M. le préfet de grands services dans les élections. Il se vendit enfin, il se prostitua. Il adressa même au souverain une pétition où il le suppliait de lui faire justice; il l'appelait notre bon roi et le comparait à Henri IV.

Et chaque matin, l'apothicaire se précipitait sur le journal pour y découvrir sa nomination; elle ne venait pas. Enfin, n'y tenant plus, il fit

longer, he had a grass plot in his garden designed to represent the Star of the Cross of Honour with two little strips of grass running from the top to imitate the ribband. He walked round it with folded arms, meditating on the folly of the Government and the ingratitude of men.

From respect, or from a sort of sensuality that made him carry on his investigations slowly, Charles had not yet opened the secret drawer of a rosewood desk which Emma had generally used. One day, however, he sat down before it, turned the key, and pressed the spring. All Leon's letters were there. There could be no doubt this time. He devoured them to the very last, ransacked every corner, all the furniture, all the drawers, behind the walls, sobbing, crying aloud, distraught, mad. He found a box and broke it open with a kick. Rodolphe's portrait flew full in his face in the midst of the overturned love-letters.

People wondered at his despondency. He never went out, saw no one, refused even to visit his patients. Then they said "he shut himself up to drink."

Sometimes, however, some curious person climbed on to the garden hedge, and saw with amazement this long-bearded, shabbily clothed, wild man, who wept aloud as he walked up and down.

In the evening in summer he took his little girl with him and led her to the cemetery. They came back at nightfall, when the only light left in the Place was that in Binet's window.

The voluptuousness of his grief was, however, incomplete, for he had no one near him to share it, and he paid visits to Madame Lefrancois to be able to speak of her. But the landlady only listened with half an ear, having troubles like himself. For Lheureux had at last established the "Favorites du Commerce," and Hivert, who enjoyed a great reputation for doing errands, insisted on a rise of wages, and was threatening to go over "to the opposition shop."

One day when he had gone to the market at Argueil to sell his horse—his last resource—he met Rodolphe.

They both turned pale when they caught sight of one another. Rodolphe, who had only sent his card, first stammered some apologies,

dessiner dans son jardin un gazon figurant l'étoile de l'honneur, avec deux petits tordillons d'herbe qui partaient du sommet pour imiter le ruban. Il se promenait autour, les bras croisés, en méditant sur l'ineptie du gouvernement et l'ingratitude des hommes.

Par respect, ou par une sorte de sensualité qui lui faisait mettre de la lenteur dans ses investigations, Charles n'avait pas encore ouvert le compartiment secret d'un bureau de palissandre dont Emma se servait habituellement. Un jour, enfin, il s'assit devant, tourna la clef et poussa le ressort. Toutes les lettres de Léon s'y trouvaient. Plus de doute, cette fois! Il dévora jusqu'à la dernière, fouilla dans tous les coins, tous les meubles, tous les tiroirs, derrière les murs, sanglotant, hurlant, éperdu, fou. Il découvrit une boîte, la défonça d'un coup de pied. Le portrait de Rodolphe lui sauta en plein visage, au milieu des billets doux bouleversés.

On s'étonna de son découragement. Il ne sortait plus, ne recevait personne, refusait même d'aller voir ses malades. Alors on prétendit qu'il s'enfermait pour boire.

Quelquefois pourtant, un curieux se haussait par-dessus la haie du jardin, et apercevait avec ébahissement cet homme à barbe longue, couvert d'habits sordides, farouche, et qui pleurait tout haut en marchant.

Le soir, dans l'été, il prenait avec lui sa petite fille et la conduisait au cimetière. Ils s'en revenaient à la nuit close, quand il n'y avait plus d'éclairé sur la Place que la lucarne de Binet.

Cependant la volupté de sa douleur était incomplète, car il n'avait autour de lui personne qui la partageât; et il faisait des visites à la mère Lefrançois afin de pouvoir parler d'elle. Mais l'aubergiste ne l'écoutait que d'une oreille, ayant comme lui des chagrins, car M. Lheureux venait enfin d'établir les Favorites du commerce, et Hivert, qui jouissait d'une grande réputation pour les commissions, exigeait un surcroît d'appointements et menaçait de s'engager «à la Concurrence».

Un jour qu'il était allé au marché d'Argueil pour y vendre son cheval, — dernière ressource, — il rencontra Rodolphe.

Ils pâlirent en s'apercevant. Rodolphe, qui avait seulement envoyé sa carte, balbutia d'abord quelques excuses, puis s'enhardit et même

then grew bolder, and even pushed his assurance (it was in the month of August and very hot) to the length of inviting him to have a bottle of beer at the public-house.

Leaning on the table opposite him, he chewed his cigar as he talked, and Charles was lost in reverie at this face that she had loved. He seemed to see again something of her in it. It was a marvel to him. He would have liked to have been this man.

The other went on talking agriculture, cattle, pasturage, filling out with banal phrases all the gaps where an allusion might slip in. Charles was not listening to him; Rodolphe noticed it, and he followed the succession of memories that crossed his face. This gradually grew redder; the nostrils throbbed fast, the lips quivered. There was at last a moment when Charles, full of a sombre fury, fixed his eyes on Rodolphe, who, in something of fear, stopped talking. But soon the same look of weary lassitude came back to his face.

"I don't blame you," he said.

Rodolphe was dumb. And Charles, his head in his hands, went on in a broken voice, and with the resigned accent of infinite sorrow:

"No, I don't blame you now."

He even added a fine phrase, the only one he ever made:

"It is the fault of fatality!"

Rodolphe, who had managed the fatality, thought the remark very offhand from a man in his position, comic even, and a little mean.

The next day Charles went to sit down on the seat in the arbour. Rays of light were straying through the trellis, the vine leaves threw their shadows on the sand, the jasmines perfumed the air, the heavens were blue, Spanish flies buzzed round the lilies in bloom, and Charles was suffocating like a youth beneath the vague love influences that filled his aching heart.

At seven o'clock little Berthe, who had not seen him all the afternoon, went to fetch him to dinner.

His head was thrown back against the wall, his eyes closed, his mouth open, and in his hand was a long tress of black hair.

"Come along, papa," she said.

poussa l'aplomb (il faisait très chaud, on était au mois d'août), jusqu'à l'inviter à prendre une bouteille de bière au cabaret.

Accoudé en face de lui, il mâchait son cigare tout en causant, et Charles se perdait en rêveries devant cette figure qu'elle avait aimée. Il lui semblait revoir quelque chose d'elle. C'était un émerveillement. Il aurait voulu être cet homme.

L'autre continuait à parler culture, bestiaux, engrais, bouchant avec des phrases banales tous les interstices où pouvait se glisser une allusion. Charles ne l'écoutait pas; Rodolphe s'en apercevait, et il suivait sur la mobilité de sa figure le passage des souvenirs. Elle s'empourprait peu à peu, les narines battaient vite, les lèvres frémissaient; il y eut même un instant où Charles, plein d'une fureur sombre, fixa ses yeux contre Rodolphe qui, dans une sorte d'effroi, s'interrompit. Mais bientôt la même lassitude funèbre réapparut sur son visage.

— Je ne vous en veux pas, dit-il.

Rodolphe était resté muet. Et Charles, la tête dans ses deux mains, reprit d'une voix éteinte et avec l'accent résigné des douleurs infinies:

— Non, je ne vous en veux plus!

Il ajouta même un grand mot, le seul qu'il ait jamais dit:

— C'est la faute de la fatalité!

Rodolphe, qui avait conduit cette fatalité, le trouva bien débonnaire pour un homme dans sa situation, comique même, et un peu vil.

Le lendemain, Charles alla s'asseoir sur le banc, dans la tonnelle. Des jours passaient par le treillis; les feuilles de vigne dessinaient leurs ombres sur le sable, le jasmin embaumait, le ciel était bleu, des cantharides bourdonnaient autour des lis en fleur, et Charles suffoquait comme un adolescent sous les vagues effluves amoureux qui gonflaient son coeur chagrin.

À sept heures, la petite Berthe, qui ne l'avait pas vu de toute l'aprèsmidi, vint le chercher pour dîner.

Il avait la tête renversée contre le mur, les yeux clos, la bouche ouverte, et tenait dans ses mains une longue mèche de cheveux noirs.

— Papa, viens donc! dit-elle.

And thinking he wanted to play; she pushed him gently. He fell to the ground. He was dead.

Thirty-six hours after, at the druggist's request, Monsieur Canivet came thither. He made a post-mortem and found nothing.

When everything had been sold, twelve francs seventy-five centimes remained, that served to pay for Mademoiselle Bovary's going to her grandmother. The good woman died the same year; old Rouault was paralysed, and it was an aunt who took charge of her. She is poor, and sends her to a cotton-factory to earn a living.

Since Bovary's death three doctors have followed one another at Yonville without any success, so severely did Homais attack them. He has an enormous practice; the authorities treat him with consideration, and public opinion protects him.

He has just received the cross of the Legion of Honour.

Et, croyant qu'il voulait jouer, elle le poussa doucement. Il tomba par terre. Il était mort.

Trente-six heures après, sur la demande de l'apothicaire, M. Canivet accourut. Il l'ouvrit et ne trouva rien.

Quand tout fut vendu, il resta douze francs soixante et quinze centimes qui servirent à payer le voyage de mademoiselle Bovary chez sa grand-mère. La bonne femme mourut dans l'année même; le père Rouault étant paralysé, ce fut une tante qui s'en chargea. Elle est pauvre et l'envoie, pour gagner sa vie, dans une filature de coton.

Depuis la mort de Bovary, trois médecins se sont succédé à Yonville sans pouvoir y réussir, tant M. Homais les a tout de suite battus en brèche. Il fait une clientèle d'enfer; l'autorité le ménage et l'opinion publique le protège.

Il vient de recevoir la croix d'honneur.

59767599R10416

Made in the USA
Columbia, SC
07 June 2019